OIL BRAT

JONATHAN BENNETT

Queen's Quay Press
10, Queen's Quay West, PH-6
Toronto, ON, M5J 2R9, Canada

Copyright © 2011 by Jonathan Bennett

Set in Adobe Garamond Pro and CA Traktor

ISBN: 978-0-9877891-0-5

Book design by Edward Kanerva

CONTENTS

ACKNOWLEDGEMENTS

Novels are engraved by the personae of the writer's encounters with the world, so thanks to the many persons who have shared portions of their lives with me. However, once words are on paper, some additional help has to kick in ... for that reason, I'd like to thank Lauren Earle, Michelle Evans, Paola González, Natalie Grimbault, and Katie Todd for their feedback with the manuscript in its various stages of development. I'd also like to single out Lauren Earle and Judith Winter for their copy editing, and Ed Kanerva for managing every step of the production process. Last, a special thanks to Mark Stanski for his strategic advice.

Jonathan Bennett, Toronto, 2011

CHILDHOOD

1. CATHERINE AND INNIS

Catherine does the ironing. Innis does the cooking. Catherine is as tall as Daddy and she walks like a stork. One foot moves at a time, and it carefully follows the other. Mommy tells three-year-old Dylan that Catherine is elegant. You can never hear her coming. She wears white tennis shoes almost always. Innis is very fat and she waddles, rotating her torso as she does. Unlike Catherine, you can always hear Innis coming. She seems to hurry but she never gets anywhere very fast. Her breathing is labored and her wheezing broadcasts her arrival. She wears sandals that make a flip-flap noise as she walks. She also walks in heavy steps so there is a rhythmic thumpety thump that accompanies the flip-flap.

Catherine wears glasses and is more serious. Most of the time, that is. She'd never laugh in the main house. But in the evenings when she's with Innis in the maids' quarters, she sometimes laughs. Mommy and Daddy have never seen Catherine laugh. They never go into the maids' quarters like Dylan does, though they might have heard the laughing. Dylan loves it when Catherine laughs. Catherine only laughs when everything is right in the world. When Catherine laughs, Innis is laughing way ahead of her. Innis has the best laugh. She doubles up laughing, tears roll down her cheeks, and she has to start slapping herself to stop. She slaps herself very hard because Innis obviously believes that laughing as hard as she does is not good for her health. She believes that the pain of the slaps will make her stop laughing. But it seldom does.

Catherine is blacker than Innis. Her skin is so dark that it makes her hair look gray. Maybe it is a little gray, thinks Dylan. Catherine's hair is short and kinky, and quite sharp when you touch it. Innis's hair is kinky too, but softer. Catherine braids Innis's hair at the end of the day when the pair of them is in the maids' rooms. Catherine's hair doesn't need braiding. It's too short. The maids' rooms at night are bright. They are illuminated by light bulbs with no shades. The light from the naked light bulbs is fierce. Catherine and Innis like it like this. They both like a bright room.

Catherine seems to be in charge. She often tells Mommy what to do. When she tells Mommy to go and have an afternoon nap, off Mommy goes. Catherine looks after the babies. When Daniel or Domenic is crying for a bottle, Catherine's the one that takes the baby and feeds it. It's Catherine's job to bathe Dylan, but Innis adores Dylan and stays to play with him, so he gets a double dose of attention.

Catherine looks on over her glasses while sewing something with cotton and thread. Innis plays with Dylan. She plays a game with Dylan in which a wind-up paddle wheel boat and a rubber ducky do battle. Rubber ducky usually wins because it's bigger and has a more powerful paddle action. When rubber ducky lands on top of the paddle wheel boat, the boat submerges under the water and surfaces in quite a different area of the bath. The paddle wheels still turn. The paddle wheel boat doesn't seem to know or mind very much that it has just been bombed by a wind-up rubber ducky.

Catherine watches Innis and Dylan play in the bath. Innis is on her knees leaning over the side of the bathtub. This makes her face level with Dylan's. Innis's face is very fat. It's also very smooth. Little droplets of steam from the bathwater condense on her face. The droplets glisten under the lights in the bathroom. The bathroom is almost as bright as Catherine and Innis's rooms. It's the brightest room in the house.

After Innis and Dylan have played for a while, Catherine puts her sewing aside and informs Innis that bath time is over. Innis puts on a sad face. Dylan mimics it. Catherine gets to her feet. It's Catherine's job to dry Dylan. She stretches toward Dylan with a towel draped over both arms. Bath time is over for this day.

Dylan stands up and holds both arms up in the air. If he doesn't do this quickly enough, his arms will be trapped inside the towel. With his arms thus pinned, Innis would be quick to take advantage and tickle his feet. With his arms free, Dylan can fend her off. Catherine's long arms hoist swaddled Dylan out of the bathtub. He is hoisted so high that if he stretches out his hands, he can touch the ceiling light bulb. For an instant, it takes his breath away. He knows this happens every night when Catherine gets him out of the tub. But even though he knows this, it still both frightens and pleases him. It's very high up and it wouldn't be nice to be dropped. But Catherine would never drop him. Her hands are sure and her arms are strong.

Catherine dries Dylan. She sits Dylan on her lap and loosens the towel so it now sits over his shoulders. Her touch with the towel is soft and tender and detailed. She's even more gentle than Dylan's mom, especially when drying his hair. While Catherine is drying Dylan, Innis sits facing them where Catherine sat to do her sewing. She plays the little piggies game with Dylan's toes. When she gets to the pinkie toe, it goes "wee wee wee," squealing up his legs that are ever so ticklish after his bath. Catherine sometimes gives Innis a cautionary stare when she's playing this game after his bath. It won't do to get Dylan excited before bedtime, she reminds Innis. Dylan assures her he isn't excited. He's just happy.

Catherine puts Dylan into his jammies. Then Innis's strong black hands lift

Dylan up to place him on her hip and take him to his room. Catherine stays behind to clean up the mess in the bathroom. Dylan jumps onto his bed and it's his job to show Innis which book he wants Mommy to read from. Dylan decides and then tells Innis. He has to identify the book by color and size. Innis doesn't read too well. She does not even read as well as Dylan, who knows all his letters and even some words. After he's been handed the book, Innis and Dylan look at the pictures. Catherine enters the bedroom to kiss Dylan goodnight. Her kiss is gentle and her goodnight voice is soft. Innis kisses and hugs him too. Her kiss is smoochy and her hug is so rough that it squeezes the breath out of Dylan's lungs. Then Dylan's mommy is called for. Dylan is ready to be tucked in, they tell her.

Mommy comes in to read the story. She lies down on the bed with Dylan. Mommy reads stories with happy endings. Her voice is soft and soothing. She likes Winnie the Pooh stories and they all have happy endings. Better still, a whole story can be finished in one bedtime. Dylan is not so fond of the stories that are two, three, and even four bedtimes long. He forgets what was told the night before. After Mommy has finished reading, Dylan is sleepy. He gets another kiss and a hug from Mommy. Mommy's kisses and hugs are the best. Without them, Dylan thinks that it would be impossible to sleep.

Innis is going to take Dylan home with her. The visit is planned for Innis's day off. Innis lives in San Fernando. She informs Dylan that San Fernando is the second biggest town in Trinidad. Dylan is going to meet Innis's family in the second biggest town in Trinidad. Innis has been asking Dylan's mom for some time about when she can take Dylan to her home. She will care for him in her home just as she does in Mrs. Douglas's home, she promises. Dylan also asks his mom if he can visit Innis at her home. Finally, Dylan's mom says yes. That's because Dylan has turned four years old and he's now big enough to go visiting. They will travel to San Fernando on a bus. Dylan has never been on a bus before.

Dylan goes to the maids' quarters. There is a laundry, a kitchen, and a small living room in the maids' quarters. There are also three bedrooms. One is Catherine's, one is Innis's, and the other is used to store junk. The maids' quarters smell funny. This is due to the food Catherine and Innis cook for themselves. In the maids' kitchen, it's Catherine who does most of the cooking. She likes to make curries. Some of the curries are too spicy for Dylan to even sample. But others are quite tasty. Catherine or Innis mix small portions of curry into rice and beans for Dylan. That way the curry doesn't taste so spicy. They give him a little dish of lime and mango chutney on the side to dip his fork into. Dylan likes the maids' food. This makes Catherine and Innis happy. They tell him it is because he's growing up Trinidadian.

It is time for Dylan's visit to San Fernando. Innis and Dylan climb the steps onto the bus. The bus is crowded. It smells of sour body odor and engine fumes. Innis and Dylan have to stand at first, and Innis holds Dylan tight to her soft, fat legs. Then some people get off the bus. Innis sits and picks Dylan up to sit him on her lap. She knows some of the passengers on the bus and introduces Dylan to her friends. Innis's friends don't seem particularly interested in Dylan. It's hot on the bus, even though all the windows are open.

On arrival at Innis's house, Dylan discovers that she has children. Dylan hasn't considered that Innis might be a mother. Why doesn't Innis stay at home and care for her children? Or does she have a person like Innis to do the cooking and look after her children? Another revelation: Innis has a mother. Innis's mother is the same shape as Innis, only she moves even slower. And her hair is completely white. It's long and kinky, just like Innis', but white.

Dylan is introduced to Selena. Innis calls Selena "my baby." But Selena is a big girl. Selena is seven-and-a-half. She looks wide-eyed at Dylan and approaches him to grab one of his arms. Selena inspects it. She tells her mother that Dylan is "light." She hasn't seen a white boy up close before and wants to take Dylan to the park to show him to some of her friends.

Dylan is frightened of this big girl. She has some of Innis's facial features, but she's tall and skinny. He clings to Innis's blue cotton skirt for protection. He may be about to cry. Innis tells her baby to wait a while. You've only just met him, she says. He'll go to the playground with you later. Selena isn't happy about this. She crosses her arms in front of her. She pouts. Selena was sure that Dylan would want to play with her the very moment he arrived.

Dylan asks Selena who looks after her.

"What you mean?" questions Selena, sounding indignant.

"Who cooks for you? Who gives you baths?"

Selena looks sad. "Nana do. She mean. Mammy has to care for other peoples," Selena replies resentfully.

"Why don't you come and live with us?" suggests Dylan.

"Can't," responds Selena. "Me got school to go to."

They have supper. Innis cooks the supper just like at home. Innis is making cassoulet and potato roti. Cassoulet is a spicy bean stew. After, they'll have fried plantain for dessert. These are Dylan's favorite foods that Innis makes at home. Innis puts roti onto four flat dishes and ladles cassoulet into four soup bowls. She folds up the roti and centers them on plates. She places all the dishes onto the table. The table is covered by a plastic tablecloth. When the food is put in front of him, Dylan moves his hands forward to take possession of the roti. Just before he makes contact, Nana slaps his arm. Nasty boy, she tells him. These are the first words Nana has said to him. She just shrugged when Innis introduced him to her. The slap doesn't hurt Dylan, but he's confused. Nana explains impatiently. She tells him that the food hasn't yet been blessed by the Lord. Who is the Lord? Innis exchanges cross words with Nana. Dylan struggles to understand them. Innis explains that most white people don't say their blessings. Nana informs Innis that Dylan is a devil child.

The four of them sit at the table. The table is round. Dylan sits between Nana and Selena and opposite Innis. To say grace, you're supposed to hold hands. Innis takes Nana's hand and Selena's hand. Dylan is sat between Selena and Nana, so when Selena grabs his hand, he reaches for Nana's. Nana doesn't want to hold Dylan's hand because he is a devil child. Innis says grace. She is thanking Lord God for the food they are about to eat. She also thanks Lord God for blessing them with a visit by Dylan. Dylan knows she's saying nice things about him and he smiles at her. But Innis has her eyes closed tight. So do Nana and Selena. He has heard Mommy mention God once or twice and when she's annoyed about something she says "for God's sake."

After grace is said, everyone is allowed to open their eyes. Now it's okay to eat. Dylan pastes Innis's mango chutney on his roti. It's more spicy than the chutney Innis makes at home. It burns Dylan's mouth and it's so hot, he wonders if he should swallow it. But Dylan's mom said he must be extra polite. So he eats up his roti pasted with the hot mango chutney without mentioning that it's so spicy he can't really taste it. Instead, he looks forward to the fried plantain for dessert.

Later, Dylan and Selena are having a bath. The bathtub is gray, not white. It's made out of thin galvanized steel. After getting undressed, but before getting into the tub, Selena inspects Dylan's body once again. She grabs his wrist and examines it up close. She looks at his back and pinches some skin at his shoulder blade. She can't believe that it's possible to be so white. She's looking for a bit of black skin that has not yet been covered by the white. Once again, Selena tells her mother how "light" Dylan is. She doesn't, for some reason, say white. They get into the tub.

Selena's whole body is black and she's missing a dinky. This is because she is a girl. Instead she has a little slit between her legs. "Is that where you go pee?" Dylan asks her. Selena doesn't respond. Instead she makes a funny face at her mammy, who's Innis. Selena is a girl, explains Innis. Dylan's mother is a girl, too. Dylan has seen his mother naked, but she has hairs between her legs. He's not sure whether his mommy had a slit hidden by her hairs. He's not seen any other girls naked. Selena wants to wash Dylan in the tub. Innis asks Dylan if it's alright for Selena to wash him. Dylan wanted Innis to wash him. He likes the way Innis washes him. But he remembers what his mom said about being polite. Dylan nods his head. Yes, Selena can wash him.

Selena rubs soap into a washcloth. Lots of soap. Then she scrubs him with the soapy washcloth. She begins with Dylan's back. "Gotta lose that dirt," she says, talking to herself. She scrubs so hard that Innis has to stop her and tell her to be gentle. Dylan's back has red stripes on it from the scrubbing. Dylan is pleased when Innis tells Selena not to rub his back so hard. It was hurting and he was wondering if it would be rude to tell Serena to not scrub so hard. When Selena has done with Dylan, Innis insists on washing her daughter. Innis scrubs Selena pretty hard, much harder than she scrubs Dylan when she washes him at home. But while Selena squirms and protests, she doesn't get red marks on her back.

Dylan will sleep in Selena's room. The bed he is to sleep in belongs to Selena's big brother. The big brother is fourteen and he already has a real job. The job is cutting sugar cane. Selena's brother has to travel away from home to cut sugar cane. Selena is pleased about this. She likes to have the bedroom to herself. Except, she adds, she doesn't mind sharing it with Dylan. Dylan unpacks his pajamas from his overnight bag. He puts on the pajama bottoms first, then the pajama top. Selena watches him, then unravels herself from the bath towel wrapped around her body. She puts on a pair of white underpants. The underpants appear extra white in color. This is because they are in stark contrast with Selena's black skin. This is what Selena sleeps in.

Innis is to tell Dylan and Selena a story. She lies on Selena's bed and pats the mattress, inviting Dylan to join her. Because Innis is so fat, there's not much room remaining for Dylan and Selena. But then Innis wraps an arm around Selena and Dylan on either side of her. Good thing Selena and me are so skinny, thinks Dylan, all three of us wouldn't fit on the bed otherwise. Because Innis is telling the story rather than reading it from a book, there are no pictures to look at.

Innis's story is frightening. It's about an evil medicine man who captures children and keeps them in cages until he can sell them. It's not clear who wants to buy these children. Innis has this way of making good things especially nice, but bad things especially horrible. When she tells the story, it's easy to be fooled into thinking that she really is the evil medicine man when she says his voice. However, the story has a happy ending. At least, it's happy for the one boy and girl starring in the story. They trick the evil medicine man and get free by outwitting him and pushing him into a boiling cauldron. The cauldron is full of magic potions. The good news is that the medicine man is instantly killed. But the bad news is that his spirit vaporizes from the cauldron to live on for eternity. He turns into an evil spirit. Little boys and girls have to beware this evil spirit. The medicine man's evil spirit lurks unseen and preys on children who disobey their mothers. And their nanas.

Innis pulls a sheet up around Dylan's neck. It's too hot, says Dylan. Innis pulls the sheet back again. It's there if you need, it she informs him. Innis kisses Dylan goodnight. Then Innis goes over to Selena's bed. Innis and Selena have a very long hug. Both of them are crying. They tell each other how much they love the other. This makes Dylan want to cry, too. Innis exits the bedroom and extinguishes the light.

The room is very dark and very still. After a few minutes, Dylan sees a pair of white underpants walk across the room. Selena gets into bed with Dylan without saying a word. Selena smells powerfully of the soap they were washed with in the tub. Selena wraps her arms around Dylan and they go to sleep.

In the middle of the night, Dylan is awakened by a loud bang. This is followed by a series of other random bangs that increase in frequency. At first, it sounds like popcorn popping. Then it sounds like a series of firecracker explosions. Dylan is frightened. He grabs Selena's shoulder and attempts to wake her. Selena pushes his arm away with her elbow. She tells him that the noise is just rain. How can rain be so noisy? But sure enough, Dylan is now aware that the banging noises above them are accompanied by other sounds, sounds of dripping and rushing water. The roof on the house is corrugated steel.

After breakfast the next day, Selena takes Dylan to the park. All of the other kids are black like Selena. They look at Dylan suspiciously. Dylan senses that these other kids do not like him, though he's not sure why. One boy of about his age approaches Dylan. "Hi," says Dylan, holding his hand out to shake the other boy's hand. He is being polite like his mom told him. The other boy silently stares at him. Then, without warning, the boy punches Dylan in the shoulder. The punch hurts. But he has no time to think about this. In an instant, Selena has grabbed the mean boy by his ear. She twists the boy's ear, making him squeal with pain. Selena says something to the mean boy, but Dylan cannot understand. The mean boy slinks off, rubbing his ear. Other boys join him to commiserate.

Selena and Dylan mount a teeter-totter. This is not a good plan because Selena weighs twice what Dylan does. Selena decides that they will go on the swings instead. She pushes Dylan. She pushes Dylan so hard that he fears he will go all the way around. His stomach wants to move slower than the rest of his body. There's a good chance he will upchuck. He tells Selena to stop pushing, but she pretends not to hear. When she finally tires of pushing and Dylan can get off the swing, he's giddy and nauseous. He tells Selena he wants to go back home. Selena makes fun of him. She tells him he's such a baby. She starts to talk to him in simulated baby talk. Dylan wants to cry, but manages not to. He wants his mommy. He doesn't like Selena.

Later that day, Nana, Innis, Selena, and Dylan go to market. The market is crowded and smelly. Dead animal carcasses hang on hooks in the open air. Hundreds of flies crawl over cuts of meat and dried fish. At ground level, there are plenty of live animals. These include chickens, some loose dogs, goats, and pigs of different sizes. Innis does the shopping. Before buying an item, she argues with each vendor. She complains about the prices they are charging and gets mad with them before making a purchase. Sometimes she shouts at them, but as soon as a price is agreed upon and money is handed over, it turns out that she's great friends with the vendor and they hug. This is because Innis is a good friend with every market lady. If they're not a cousin of hers, then she probably went to school with them.

After lunch, Innis and Dylan have to return. It's the end of Innis's day off. Selena is sad and grumpy after lunch. She doesn't want her mammy to leave her with Nana for a whole week again. Innis is also sad because she doesn't want to leave Selena. "Why can't we take her home with us?" suggests Dylan. "She can sleep with me." Innis shakes her head and wipes a tear from her eye. The bus stops at the sidewalk. Innis picks Dylan up and carries him onto the bus. This time, they don't have to stand and wait for seats. Innis and Dylan wave to Selena and Nana as the bus pulls away. As it does so, Nana puts an arm around Selena and they turn to head back to their home.

On the bus, Dylan is attacked by a chicken. It pecks at his toes. He's wearing sandals and his toes are exposed. Dylan attempts to move his foot out of the chicken's range, but cannot. The chicken has a string tied around its leg, but the string isn't tight enough to properly restrain it. It pecks at his toes again, this time more painfully. The chicken probably thinks that Dylan's toes are kernels of corn, says Innis. Innis kicks the chicken. The chicken doesn't like being kicked by Innis and begins to squawk at her. The owner of the chicken is sitting in the seat in front of them. He doesn't like his chicken being upset by Innis. The chicken man and Innis have an argument. Dylan cannot understand the words of this argument. Soon Innis and the chicken man are standing up shouting at each other. The bus driver stops the bus in the middle of the road. He comes back to join in the argument. He shouts the loudest. The bus driver wins the argument. He tells Innis and the chicken man that he's not planning to drive another inch until they both sit down and shut up. He tells the chicken man to keep his chicken under control. Then he tells Innis to make sure the white boy stops baiting the chicken.

Mommy wants to know about Dylan's day with Innis. Dylan thinks. He tells Mommy about the mean boy in the park. What else? Oh yes, he was attacked by a chicken on the bus. The bus driver had to stop the bus because Innis and the chicken man were having an argument. Innis only wanted the chicken man to stop his chicken from trying to eat Dylan's toes. Mommy tells Dylan that she missed him. Dylan responds that he missed her, too. Mommy tells Dylan that he's probably too young to go on overnight visits without her.

*   *   *

The Douglas and Pritchard families are going for a picnic on Maracas beach. Dylan has met the Pritchard's a couple of times. They have two girls: Melanie, who is big and ten, and Melody, who's four just like Dylan. Catherine and Innis make all the food for the picnic. They pack the food into coolers and weaved hampers. Catherine is coming with the Douglas family to help serve the food and watch over the kids. She rides in the back of the Douglas family Oldsmobile with Dylan and his brother Daniel. Daniel sits in a car seat on one side. Catherine sits on the other. She's not wearing her khaki maid's uniform and pumps. Instead, she's wearing Bermuda shorts and flip flops. Dylan is supposed to be sitting between them, but instead he's on the floor. Dylan doesn't have to sit in a car seat. He'll play on the floor between the back and front seats of the Oldsmobile. He has brought a large number of dinky and matchbox cars. It's a long drive.

They arrive at Maracas beach. It's very big and wide. No other people are there. The waves are noisy. The first thing on Dylan's mind is to run into the ocean and cool off with a swim. Dylan doesn't own a swimsuit; every time they've been to the beach before he swam naked. The adults busy themselves setting up the picnic territory under the shade of some palm trees. The palm trees are about fifty yards from the shoreline. While the adults are unpacking, Melody and Dylan meet up. They've only met a couple of times previously. Melody is wearing a one-piece swimsuit. It's pink. Dylan registers this and wonders if he's now old enough to wear a swimsuit. Melody asks Dylan if he knows how to swim.

"A little," responds Dylan. "Mommy taught me."

"I take swimming lessons," announces Melody proudly. "I can swim a little, too!"

Dylan and Melody approach the water's edge. Then they hold hands and run into the water. Dylan's mother calls over to Dylan and instructs the pair of swimmers not to go in deeper than waist high. Dylan and Melody play a game of running ten paces into the water and collapsing onto their bums to allow a wave to crash over their heads. The force of the wave sends them tumbling and rolling back toward the beach. They do this repeatedly, each time becoming a little more daring and running further out.

Melody has sand in her swimsuit. She tugs at the leg holes in the swimsuit this way and that in an attempt to remove the sand. When this fails, she removes the swimsuit entirely, peeling down the shoulder straps and stepping out of it. Passing her swimsuit for Dylan to hold, Melody runs in to the water to swish the sand out of all the places that sand gets stuck when you are rolled in the surf. Dylan observes that Melody has a little slit between her legs just like Selena. When Melody returns from the ocean, Dylan asks her if that's where she goes pee. Melody laughs. "Of course, it's my penny slot," she says. She bends over to make a brief, but closer inspection of Dylan's willy. Dylan hands Melody's swimsuit back to her. She giggles, tells Dylan to wear it, and runs back into the ocean naked. Dylan looks at the swimsuit. He decides to put it on. He steps into the legs, wriggles it over his torso, and pulls the straps over his shoulders. Then he runs into the ocean to join Melody. He's never worn a swimsuit before.

Melody and Dylan's game of running in and out of the ocean holding hands develops in sophistication. Now they stand on the water's edge observing the waves. The objective is to time their run so that they collide with the biggest wave. The big waves are more fun. A big wave can send them rolling nearly all the way back on to the dry part of the beach. Suddenly, Dylan is grabbed from behind. It's his father. With immense force, Dylan's father smacks him across the shoulders, knocking him face forward into the sand. Crying with pain and confusion, Dylan twists around. His father is shouting at him. Initially, Dylan is in shock and understands nothing. Melody is standing naked and frozen with fear, observing the scene. Her hands clutch her cheeks. Gradually, Dylan comes to understand that the reason for his father's rage is that he doesn't like him wearing Melody's swimsuit. Still seated on the sand, Dylan peels the shoulder straps of the swimsuit off his shoulders and squirms out of the swimsuit. He gets to his feet, naked, but coated with wet sand, and offers the swimsuit toward Melody. Melody has now had time to gather her wits. She's not about to get struck by an enraged man for wearing a swimsuit. She turns on her heel and runs as fast as she can back to the safety of her mother.

Dylan's father also turns heel. Still fuming, he strides back toward the family picnic. Dylan is crying. He is pasted with sand. He does not know what to do. Catherine comes to his rescue, approaching him to put an arm around his shoulder and walk him down to the water's edge. Leaving her flip flops in the dry sand, Catherine takes Dylan knee-deep into the ocean and swishes the sand off his body. She soaks Melody's swimsuit and wrings it out. Then Catherine and Dylan hold hands to return to where the family picnic has been set up. Dylan is shivering and crying. Catherine picks up a towel and begins to dry Dylan. She's interrupted by Dylan's father. Mr. Douglas orders Catherine not to mollycoddle the boy. But

Catherine, with her face rigid and expressionless, just stares Mr. Douglas down. She continues to dry off Dylan. Mr. Douglas opts for a retreat, sensing that Catherine could be formidable in battle.

Dylan's mom now notices that all's not well. As Dylan's dad backs away from the scene, Dylan's mom enters it with baby Domenic perched on her hip. Did Dylan get stung by a jellyfish, she wants to know? Catherine assures Dylan's mom that the boy is going to be just fine. He just had a little accident. Catherine holds out a pair of shorts for Dylan to step into. Then she hands Melody's swimsuit to him. She suggests he return it.

Melody is sitting naked on her mother's lap. Dylan approaches and holds out the swimsuit. On seeing Dylan, Melody twists her torso away from him to bury her face further into her mother's bosom. Mrs. Pritchard thanks Dylan. She tells him that Melody is upset now, but she'll want to play with him again later, maybe after lunch. Dylan suggests to Mrs. Pritchard that if Melody likes to play dinky cars, he just happens to have a large collection at his disposal on the floor of the Oldsmobile. But Melody doesn't want to play dinky cars. Not right now.

*   *   *

Dylan gets a pedal car. It is green. Because it's a car, it'll need fixing from time to time. After driving around the Douglas yard for three solid days, Dylan figures it's time for his car to be repaired. He's going to pull all four wheels. The axles on Dylan's car are solid steel shafts. Each wheel is held on to its axle by a cotter pin and a washer. Dylan knows how to remove a cotter pin because he's seen his dad do it. First, he lifts the car up on a pair of wooden blocks so each wheel can be spun. Then Dylan locates a pair of his dad's side cutters, and using the jaws, makes the bend in each cotter pin as straight as he can. This accomplished, he easily withdraws each cotter pin, allowing him to pull each of the four wheels off their respective axles. When he's done, he goes to find Catherine to inform her that he's fixing his car and that he already has the wheels removed.

Catherine returns with Dylan and doesn't like what she sees. Catherine and Dylan try to get the wheels put back on. Cotter pins may come out easily, but they're tough to get reinserted into their original holes. Dylan is getting worried. He needs his wheels. He's tired of fixing his car and wants to drive again. Catherine examines the cotter pins. She figures she should be able to straighten them enough using a small hammer. That works! After tapping the kinks out of each cotter pin, it can be easily reinserted into its hole in the axle shaft. Bending one leg of the cotter pin locks it into place. Dylan has his wheels again. Catherine is the best mechanic in the world!

Catherine and Dylan go to the commissary. Catherine drives the Oldsmobile. She's doing the shopping because Dylan's mommy has a headache. The commissary isn't like San Fernando market. It smells of laundry powder and concrete. The food is sold mostly in packages. There are no live animals and the dead ones are neatly sliced up and stored in coolers with glass doors. Catherine doesn't haggle over the price of anything. This is because the price of every article in the store is printed on a little sticker and pasted onto the product. Dylan is Catherine's helper. When Catherine tells Dylan to get two packets of Corn Flakes, Dylan scours the aisles to locate the cereal section where the Corn Flakes are stacked. Almost always he's told to get the extra large size. Food gets piled into the supermarket cart. The buggy is equipped with a passenger seat for young kids. Dylan used to ride in the passenger seat when he was a young kid. But now he's old enough to be a helper. The check-out clerk punches in the price of each item into a cash register as Catherine and Dylan unload it. Another clerk bags the groceries. Catherine doesn't argue about the price. She pays for everything using crisp, green paper money. This is different from Innis's money, which is mostly coins and old wrinkled notes of different faded colors.

Dylan is leaving Trinidad. Forever. Dylan has no idea what that means. In his mind, he's always lived in Trinidad. The only time the family leaves Trinidad is to go on vacation. And after a vacation, they've always returned. Vacations are spent with grandmas and grandpas. Sometimes the vacations are with Grandma and Grandpa Douglas and other times they're with Grandma and Grandpa Reardon. All the Douglas family will be leaving to go to a place called Geneva.

Dylan asks, what about Catherine and Innis? Catherine and Innis will not go, says Mommy. They'll stay in Trinidad and look after another family. Dylan wants to know why they can't take Catherine and Innis with them. He's told that it is because Catherine and Innis have to look after their own families in Trinidad. Who's going to bath me, Dylan asks. Who's going to cook our meals and do the ironing?

Mommy goes to the maids' quarters to tell Catherine and Innis that the family is leaving Trinidad forever. A frightening scream comes from the maids' quarters. This is followed by hysterical sobbing. This is Innis. At Dylan's bath time that night, only Catherine comes to wash him. Innis is too upset. Innis was trying to persuade Mommy that she should take her and Catherine with the Douglas family. Catherine's eyes too are red and sore from crying. She inserts a finger behind her glasses to rub her eyes. She tells Dylan how much she'll miss him. Yes, she'll miss Daniel and Domenic too, but Dylan has been like a son to her for over three years. She tells him she has seen him grow from being a baby into a fine young boy. Soon Dylan is crying, too. He cannot imagine life without Catherine and Innis.

Dylan's mother comes in to the bathroom. She wants to talk to Catherine in private. Outside the bathroom door. Dylan can't hear much of what they say. Something about upsetting him and this being difficult for everyone. Then he hears Catherine crying. Not loud like Innis, but crying all the same. Catherine isn't supposed to cry. She's in charge.

Dylan's Mom comes into the bathroom. She bathes Dylan. Then she dries him and puts him to bed. She reads Dylan a Pooh story he's heard several times before. But it doesn't sound the same this time. All is not well in Pooh Corner.

It's decided that Dylan's mom and the three children will leave Trinidad immediately. They will go to stay with Grandma and Grandpa Reardon. After, they'll meet up with Dylan's Dad in Geneva. Where are Grandma and Grandpa Reardon? Where's Geneva? All Dylan knows is that they're not in Trinidad.

A big black limo comes to pick up Dylan, Daniel, Domenic, and Mommy. The limo driver wears a black uniform and cap. The limo will take them to Piarco Airport, near Port of Spain. It's a long drive. Suitcases are placed in the trunk. It is a big trunk, but only just big enough to hold all the suitcases they are to take. Dylan has a carry-on bag which is not to go in the trunk. Inside the carry-on bag is *The House at Pooh Corner* and eight of his favorite dinky cars. He packed it himself.

Catherine and Innis are standing in their khaki uniforms beside the limo. They're waiting to say goodbye. Catherine is sad and subdued. She kisses and hugs each departing member of the family. Innis is quietly weeping. She hugs and kisses everyone too, but then she starts acting crazy. She stomps her feet. Suddenly, she spins around in a full circle. She grasps her face with both hands. She begins to produce a wailing noise that begins deep in her throat and finishes on a drawn out, high pitch. Dylan has never witnessed emotion expressed in this way. It's frightening.

The departing Douglases sit in the back seat of the limo. Dylan stands on the car seat to wave out the back window. Daddy is too busy trying to hold Innis still to wave. The limo pulls away. Catherine waves. Then she takes off her glasses to clean them with her apron. Now both Daddy and Catherine are standing on either side of Innis, each holding an arm as if she might collapse. Innis is making even more noise. Mommy is pulling at Dylan's shirt trying to make him sit down, to make him stop looking at what's going on behind the limo. Dylan is mesmerized. Innis, still supported on either side by Catherine and Daddy, is stomping her feet rhythmically into the ground.

"Has Innis gone mad, Mommy?" Dylan asks his mother.

"Sit down, Dylan," responds his mother, tugging at his shirt again. "She's just a little upset." Daddy, Catherine, and Innis fade into the distance as the vehicle accelerates. Dylan sits. He's unhappy for Innis. Then Dylan realizes he's also unhappy for himself. He begins to cry quietly. Mommy puts an arm around his shoulder. The anticipation and excitement of traveling on an airplane don't seem important any more. Life without Catherine and Innis begins.

2. NORAKATE

Dylan awakes before being woken. It is dawn. On the end of his bed is a pair of blue shorts, khaki socks, and a white starched shirt. Dylan is immediately alert. Today is a big day! Without a doubt, it's the most important day of his life! He's been looking forward to this day for a year and a half: his first day at school. In recent weeks, the excitement level preceding this momentous event has been ratcheted up. School uniforms were acquired. A wooden swivel pencil box was purchased.

A week prior to this day, Dylan was interviewed by the principal of the school. The principal is a smiling, kindly woman. Dylan knows her name is Margaret McKenzie because that's how she introduced herself to Mommy. Margaret informs Dylan that in school she has to be addressed as "Mrs. McKenzie" or "Principal McKenzie." During the interview, Mrs. McKenzie tells Dylan that he'll be very happy in the Kindergarten class of her school. Dylan agrees and so does Mommy.

Days before starting, Dylan goes shopping with Mommy to purchase a package of six yellow HB pencils and a set of twelve colored pencils, along with an eraser and pencil sharpener and a lined exercise book. And a satchel to put all the stuff that Mommy believes a five-year-old requires to become a successful Kindergarten student.

Mommy drives Dylan to school. She reminds Dylan that all the other children in Kindergarten started school a month earlier. Dylan doesn't think that this information is especially important until the moment he sets foot on the school property. There are more children on this playground than he's ever seen in his life! Most of these children are big kids. Mommy and Dylan enter the school property through a gate that opens into the playground. Hundreds of children, mostly big ones, are making so much noise that Dylan is frightened. All his excitement about meeting other children and making friends dissipates in an instant. He wants to cover his ears. Already he's reconsidering the wisdom of attending school. Things were pretty good at home, were they not?

Dylan grips Mommy's hand with such ferocity that she's forced to tell him to relax his hold, despite intuiting his fear. Somehow, Mommy and Dylan navigate the rowdy chaos of the playground without sustaining an injury. They enter the main school building through a big set of double doors. It is quieter indoors, although some of the noise of the playground infiltrates the thick stone walls of the building. Mommy and Dylan enter Mrs. McKenzie's office for a second time. Mrs. McKenzie tells Dylan to wait outside and have a chat with her secretary. The reason for this is that Mrs. McKenzie wants to chat with Mommy. Alone.

Dylan waits with Mrs. McKenzie's secretary. Her name is Monique and she's pretty and kind. She speaks English with an accent, but it sounds soft and soothing. Monique is very interested in the contents of Dylan's satchel. Proudly, Dylan shows her his wooden swivel pencil case. He opens the sliding wood lid and explains how the lower deck is like a secret compartment.

"You don't really know it's there until you make the box swivel," he says proudly. Monique is duly impressed. Dylan shows her the one HB pencil he has placed in the top deck of the box. It has its own eraser. This is the one he'll use for most of the writing he'll do in school. He tells her he has five others at home, all waiting to be sharpened in succession as he uses up each one doing all the writing he'll do in school.

"The top deck of my pencil box," Dylan announces importantly to Monique, "is for the HB pencil. I'll only need one at a time. My sharpener and eraser get to go in there, too. The lower swivel deck is where my twelve coloring pencils are stored."

Monique asks Dylan if he speaks any French. Dylan tells her he does not. Monique informs him that although this is an American school and all the classes are in English, most of the children speak other languages because they come from all over the world.

Just at that moment, Mrs. McKenzie's door opens. Principal McKenzie wants to have a chat with Dylan. Dylan carefully replaces his pencil case into the satchel, puts the satchel over his shoulder, and enters her office. But Mommy has disappeared. Did she climb out a window? Dylan panics. Then he notices that there is a second door to the principal's office. Mommy has abandoned him without kissing him goodbye. Tears rush to his eyes, but he manages to restrain them. Principal McKenzie is telling Dylan that he will attend some special classes three afternoons a week so that he can learn to speak French. She says that many of the other children in his class speak French. Also German and other languages. Speaking some French will make it easier to mix with other children. Dylan agrees. Speaking some French strikes him as being a good idea.

Principal McKenzie escorts Dylan down the hallway to introduce him to his Kindergarten class. The noise emanating from the playground when he arrived has abated. It's been replaced by a droning noise coming from some of the classrooms. Mrs. McKenzie and Dylan head toward the noisiest classroom in the building. As they enter, all of the children stand up and stare at them.

Mrs. McKenzie announces: "Miss Dickinson and class, it's my pleasure to introduce you to Dylan Douglas. Dylan speaks only English. This is Dylan's very first day in school, so I want you all to be especially welcoming." Dylan looks at the other children. They all continue to stare at him. They don't appear to be very welcoming. In fact, he thinks that they may be staring at him in a hostile way.

Dylan looks at Miss Dickinson. She's old and ugly and has a moustache. Miss Dickinson smiles at Dylan and takes his hand. She walks him over to a table with five small chairs. Four of the chairs are occupied by two boys and two girls. Principal McKenzie follows from behind, observing.

"This will be your seat, Dylan," Miss Dickinson says. "You are to be a member of Table Three. That," she continues, pointing at a large number three in the center of the table, "is the number three."

Dylan looks up at Miss Dickinson. Does Miss Dickinson think that he is an idiot? Even his three-year-old brother can identify a number three.

"Your table team is Pierre, Hans, Adriana, and NoraKate," Miss Dickinson gestures to each teammate as she says the names. At this point, Principal McKenzie leans over to whisper something in Dylan's ear.

"I'm going to leave you in Miss Dickinson's good hands," she informs him. "I know you're going to be very happy here." Instinctively, Dylan seeks to clutch onto Principal McKenzie, but she quickly scoots out, closing the door of Kindergarten behind her.

The instant the kindly principal exits the door, Miss Dickinson attempts to seize Dylan's satchel. Dylan snatches it away from her. Dylan's table team thinks this is hilarious. All four of them laugh. Miss Dickinson says firmly to Dylan that she must inspect his satchel because she wants to see what's inside it. Embarrassed because his table team is laughing at him, Dylan reluctantly surrenders his satchel to Miss Dickinson. Miss Dickinson opens up Dylan's satchel and removes the pencil box. She shakes her head. Then she informs Dylan that he cannot have these pencils in her class because they are dangerous. A child could be impaled on one or possibly be stabbed and lose an eye. She tells Dylan she'll take charge of his satchel until it's time to go home. Then she'll return the satchel. But he must never bring such dangerous objects back into class with him again. Not until Grade Two. In Miss Dickinson's Kindergarten, wax crayons must be used.

"What can I put my homework in?" asks Dylan meekly. Table Three collectively thinks that the notion of homework is hilarious, and once again has a laugh at Dylan's expense. Poor Dylan now stands beside Miss Dickinson, bereft of the satchel he was using as a shield. He's been trying not to cry almost since his arrival in the school.

Miss Dickinson places what might be interpreted as being a comforting hand on Dylan's shoulder. Instinctively, Dylan flinches. He does not like Miss Dickinson and doesn't want her touching him. Miss Dickinson's upper lip curls slightly and her moustache hairs quiver. She instructs Dylan to call her either "Miss Dickinson" or "Ma'am." Then she announces that she's going to sit him beside NoraKate. She tells Dylan that NoraKate's daddy also works for an oil company, just like Dylan's. NoraKate and Dylan will have lots in common. Furthermore, NoraKate also speaks only English. Three afternoons a week, Dylan will join NoraKate to attend French class.

Dylan looks at NoraKate. She has short, straight, dark brown hair. It is cut in bangs over her forehead and in a straight line above the shoulder. Her dark eyes are framed by a pair of large eyeglasses, though maybe the eyeglasses just appear large because her face is so skinny. NoraKate stands up. She takes Dylan's hand and smiles at him from behind the big glasses. Dylan does not return the smile, but he decides that he likes NoraKate better than Miss Dickinson. NoraKate sits down, still holding Dylan's hand, pulling him into the vacant seat next to her.

NoraKate tells him that they are coloring this morning. When they are done coloring, Miss Dickinson will read them a story.

"When do we do reading?" asks Dylan meekly. "When do we do writing and arithmetic?"

Miss Dickinson, who has been standing behind them, interrupts: "We don't start that until Grade One," she informs Dylan. "We do not approve of parents teaching their children to read before Grade One because they learn so many bad habits. You see, Dylan, only teachers know how to properly teach children to read. Do you know your letters yet, Dylan?"

Dylan does indeed know his letters and can read a range of simple books. He can also print letters well enough to write a short letter to his grandmas and grandpas. More excitingly, he can count to 1,000. But he doesn't know how to respond to Miss Dickinson's question. He's worried now that Mommy has taught him how to read wrong and Miss Dickinson will say more nasty things. He says nothing. He stares at Miss Dickinson, hoping the horrible woman will go away. Mrs. Dickinson returns the stare for a few moments, then shrugs, telling him she'll leave him to get to know his Table Three team. She walks off to talk with the kids at the next table.

The moment Miss Dickinson departs, NoraKate leans over to whisper in Dylan's ear. "I can read, too," she says earnestly, "but my Mom says not to tell Miss Dickinson. We call her 'Miss Dicky-bird.'" NoraKate giggles. Dylan looks over to the adjacent table to inspect Miss Dicky-bird now that she's at a safe distance.

"She doesn't look very much like a bird," he tells NoraKate. Indeed not: Miss Dickinson is a heavy, middle-aged woman who wears high heels that lend her a waddling gait as her feet click-clack around the floor. She breathes heavily, and she wears stern eyeglasses that do not quite go with her loud print dress.

NoraKate asks Dylan where he is from. Dylan has never thought about this before. Is he from Trinidad? Not any more; Mommy said they would probably not be going back. Grandma and Grandpa, with whom they were staying before they arrived in Geneva, live in a place called Chester. Maybe he is from Chester.

"I think I'm from Chester," responds Dylan, "or maybe that's West Chester?

"What state is it in?" asks NoraKate.

"State?" says Dylan, who only knew that it was not in Trinidad. "I'm not sure. You have to get there by going on an airplane."

"You have to get most anywhere by going on an airplane, silly," exasperated NoraKate informs Dylan. "I'm from Texas. We live in Houston when we're in the States. Houston is the biggest city in the world. It has the tallest buildings."

"Not taller than the Empire State building?"

NoraKate thinks about this. "Except for the Empire State building," she concedes. "But Houston is in Texas. And Texas is the biggest and most important state in the world."

After a while, Dylan needs to pee. "Where can I go pee?" Dylan asks NoraKate.

"You have to raise your hand. Then Miss comes over and you have to ask her if you can go pee. Except you have to say, 'can I be excused to go to the restroom, Ma'am?' We have our own Kindergarten restroom." NoraKate points to the back of the classroom. Dylan raises his hand. Mrs. Dickinson looks over toward Dylan. She tells him to be patient because she is occupied with Table Four. She'll get to him when she can. NoraKate informs Dylan in whispers that Miss Dickinson likes to make everybody wait to go pee. She advises him to think about something that has nothing to do with going pee and that way he should be able to hold on until Miss Dickinson arrives. Dylan looks up at the ceiling and attempts to think about the story Mommy was reading him last night.

Five minutes go by. Dylan's urge to pee is becoming overpowering. He looks over to Miss Dickinson at Table Four, but she's still busy talking to one of the kids there. Dylan sticks the hand he's not holding up in the air down the front of his shorts, and clamps his penis to help hold the pee in.

"Uh oh," says NoraKate shaking her head slowly. "I don't think Miss Dickinson will like you doing that." Dylan is desperate. He stands up. Mrs. Dickinson scowls at him and is about to tell Dylan to be patient when she notices where his hand is. A lesson in etiquette is clearly required. Her heels click-clack over to Dylan and she tells him he must not touch himself in this way.

Dylan ignores her, "I have go pee, Miss," he blurts out, "now!"

Miss Dickinson tells him that yes, he can go to the restroom, but first he must stop "touching" himself in that way; it's rude. Dylan hops from one foot to the other. Miss Dickinson grabs Dylan by the elbow and yanks his arm out of his pants.

Dylan pees.

Liquid saturates his new blue shorts. It runs down his bare legs, over his socks and shoes, and pools into a large puddle on the floor. Dylan looks down, observing the pee, wondering if all this pee can really be coming out of him. Most of the scholars in Miss Dickinson's Kindergarten class find this hilarious. Tables One through Four are laughing with abandon. In all of Kindergarten, only NoraKate doesn't think this is funny. Miss Dickinson is definitely not laughing. When his bladder has been emptied, Dylan looks up at Miss Dickinson and begins to cry. Miss Dickinson's first task is to regain control of her class, and that means stopping the laughter. She pans the room with an especially menacing "look" she has acquired from years of teaching Kindergarten. The ferocity of Miss Dickinson's special look fulfills its function of silencing the laughter. That done, she focuses on Dylan. Her look tells him she is disgusted. He will have to go to the principal's office. Dylan goes.

In her office, Principal McKenzie says: "We're not having a very good first day at school, are we Dylan?" She ruffles Dylan's hair. Dylan looks up at her. Mrs. McKenzie smiles at Dylan. "We'll get you washed up a little and find you some clean shorts. Then you can be my helper for today." After Mrs. McKenzie has helped Dylan clean himself up in the principal's private bathroom, she hands him a pair of green gym shorts. "They're a little on the large size. You may have to hold on to them at the waist to keep them up. They're the best we can do for the moment."

Dylan puts the shorts on. They're enormous on him. "I want to go home," he says. "I don't like it here. I don't like school."

Mrs. McKenzie studies Dylan. "Your mother tells me that you have been looking forward to starting school for a very long time. I think you might grow to like school, Dylan, if you give it a chance. But we'll see. Today you can help me be principal of the school. I have a very busy day and Monique and I could really do with a reliable helper. Then we can phone your mother and she can come and pick you up. How's that for a plan?"

Dylan spends most of the day with Monique. Monique finds a safety pin to trim the waist of Dylan's oversize shorts. This means that he is no longer required to hold them up with one hand to prevent them from falling around his ankles. Monique is sending letters to all of the parents who attend the American school. She gives Dylan the job of neatly folding each letter before placing it in an envelope. Then he gets to seal each envelope and lick the stamp that has to be placed on the top right corner. Monique is impressed that Dylan can read almost all of the names on each envelope.

"They don't sound like American names," comments Dylan.

"They're not," responds Monique. "In Geneva we have people from all over the world. Many of these people want their children to go to an American school – to speak English. In truth, there are not that many American children in the whole school. Maybe a couple dozen. But most of the teachers are from America. Some are from England."

✳   ✳   ✳

Dylan's second day at school is a real school day. First, he has to contend with the playground melee. He looks for NoraKate, but can't locate her before the bell goes. When the bell rings, the chaos dissipates into organized lines in front of the main entrance. Every kid seems to know which line to get into. Dylan looks for a face he recognizes from Kindergarten and quickly locates his classmates. They're easy to spot: their line consists of all the smallest kids. He spies NoraKate, who beckons to him to get behind her. Dylan obeys, but no sooner has he got in line behind NoraKate than the boy behind him punches him between the shoulder blades. Dylan is more surprised than hurt. He turns toward the boy, confused. The boy points to the back of the line and Dylan is about to head there when NoraKate grabs his shoulder and starts to shout at the boy who hit him. The boy shrugs his shoulders, evidently not wanting to tackle NoraKate.

It's NoraKate rather than Miss Dickinson who teaches Dylan about life in school. There are many rules and regulations, let alone the challenge of simple survival in a pack of so many potentially wild children. Most of the rules and regulations appear to have little grounding in the common sense or logic facilities of a five-year-old. In addition, Dylan discovers that the fallout of peeing in your shorts on your first day of school is to be reminded of the event many times over.

During the afternoon of his third day of school, Dylan raises his hand and informs Miss Dickinson that he's bored and will go to the office to see if Mrs. McKenzie and Monique require his assistance. To the amazement of Tables One through Four, Miss Dickinson just nods, albeit irritably, and says, "Go then."

Dylan walks through empty halls to Principal's office. Monique is pleased to see him. She wants to know if everything is alright. Dylan says that everything is fine, but he's bored. Monique pushes a buzzer on her phone. She tells the phone that Dylan has come for a visit. Monique then tells him that Mrs. McKenzie would like to chat with him.

Dylan discovers that Principal McKenzie likes to be read to while she works. She hands Dylan a book and asks him to read it to her. The book has a picture on every page and is easy to read. It's also boring. Nothing seems to happen. A dog jumps, then a girl jumps, followed by a boy jumping, and finally all three are jumping together. The jumping is followed by the same sequence, but now they are play-ing. What kind of book is this, thinks Dylan to himself. Could it be that Principal McKenzie truly enjoys listening to this drivel while she works?

Kindergarten recess is separate from big school recess. It's earlier. Recess in Kindergarten is only in the mornings. This is because Kindergarten has naptime after lunch. Although the Kindergarten school day begins at the same time as the big school day, it ends fifteen minutes earlier. During Kindergarten recess, the boys chase a soccer ball. The boys call the soccer ball a "fute-bal," but Dylan knows it's a soccer ball. Dylan's dad says that soccer is a game for wusses and girls. But only the boys play soccer during Kindergarten recess. Secretly, Dylan wishes he could run around chasing this soccer ball during recess like the other boys, but it's difficult to figure out what exactly they are attempting to achieve. So he has to spend recess talking to NoraKate.

Hans is big even though he is in Kindergarten. Hans doesn't like Dylan. Hans likes to punch Dylan on his shoulder on the way out to the playground for Kindergarten recess. He punches him again on the way back in when he's all puffed out from chasing the fute-bal. The punches do not bother Dylan, but Hans also taunts Dylan by calling him a baby who wets his pants. This embarrasses Dylan. It especially embarrasses Dylan when Hans taunts him like this in front of NoraKate. She tells Dylan to ignore Hans, but he can't. For the first time in his life, Dylan wants to hit and hurt another person. But Hans is so much bigger and stronger than him that he cannot retaliate. Dylan hates Hans. Things would be better in Kindergarten if Hans was to be suddenly struck dead.

Immediately after lunch, it's Kindergarten naptime. Kindergartners are not al-lowed to talk during naps. At naptime, each Kindergartner has to get a mat out of the supplies closet. The mat is unrolled and placed in front of the round tables. That means that all the table teams nap together.

Dylan and NoraKate are Table Threes. At first, Dylan and NoraKate napped be-side each other so they could spend naptime whispering. Naps are for babies – does Miss Dickinson truly expect them to go to sleep? Unfortunately, after one whisper too many, whispering is banned at naptime. To enforce the ban, Miss Dickinson tells NoraKate to move over to the other side of Hans for naps. This is NoraKate's new nap place. Now Dylan has no one to whisper to during naps. He certainly doesn't want to whisper to Hans. Or to Pierre, who's as quiet as a mouse. Pierre is so quiet because he can hardly speak a word of English. He just smiles and nods when someone says something to him.

Nap time is thirty minutes. The thirty minutes didn't seem like a long time to NoraKate and Dylan when they could spend it whispering. Now it seems like an eternity. Especially if you stare at the electric clock at the front of Kindergarten. As naptime progresses, the second hand seems to be rotating slower and slower, and sometimes Dylan is sure that it's going to shudder to a complete standstill. But it never does. The minute hand is even slower. It twitches and quivers as it progresses, moving at about one half a sector between the minute lines at each advance. Now apart, Dylan and NoraKate hate naptime even more. Naps are for babies.

Going potty is the only excuse for getting off the napping mat during naptime. For some reason, Miss Dickinson always says yes right away during naptimes. Dylan makes a habit of going potty at this time because it makes the thirty minutes go a little faster. The Kindergarten restroom consists of four mini toilets in a row. There are no stalls and no doors. The rule is you have to sit down on the mini toilet, even if you are a boy and only want to pee. Standing up to pee is forbidden. Miss Dickinson doesn't want boys peeing all over the floor.

After lunch one day, about a week after NoraKate has been moved away from Dylan for naptime, Dylan studies the second hand on the wall clock and he's sure that its movement is the slowest it's ever been. Less than five minutes into naptime, he raises his hand to ask permission for a potty break. Miss Dickinson nods and Dylan escapes to the restroom. Seconds later, he's joined by NoraKate, who sits on the toilet next to him. She grins and whispers to him. "We can spend the whole naptime here. If Dicky bird comes over and asks why we are taking so long, we can tell her our tummies are upset." NoraKate is so smart!

NoraKate and Dylan chat in whispers to their hearts' content. Naptime goes by quickly. Shortly before naptime is due to end, Miss Dickinson enters Kindergarten restroom and asks Dylan why he's taking so long. Dylan puts on a hurt face and responds, "My tummy is upset, Ma'am."

Miss Dickinson then asks NoraKate why she's taking so long and she also responds, "My tummy is upset, Miss Dickinson." Miss Dickinson says nothing, but retreats into the classroom to call an end to naptime. Simultaneously, Dylan and NoraKate rise up from their toilet seats. NoraKate points to Dylan's bum and laughs. Dylan twists around to inspect himself and sees a big red ring around his bum left by the impression of the toilet seat. NoraKate shows Dylan her bum. She also has a big red ring on the skin.

NoraKate and Dylan spend almost the entirety of three successive naptimes in the potty room whispering to each other. Miss Dickinson is suspicious. Midway through the third day of sitting as a pair in the potty room, Miss Dickinson enters.

She addresses NoraKate: "Are you quite sure your stomach is upset?"

NoraKate puts on a mournful face and whimpers, "I think I have diarrhea, Ma'am." Somehow Dylan manages to squeeze out a small, but clearly audible fart perfectly timed to punctuate the completion of NoraKate's sentence. Without a word, Miss Dickinson turns heel and click-clacks back into Kindergarten, clearly not pleased. Both Dylan and NoraKate double up with silent laughter on their perches.

At the completion of naptime, Miss Dickinson sends Dylan and NoraKate to the principal's office. When Dylan and NoraKate arrive at Principal McKenzie's office, Monique is pleased to see Dylan. She ruffles his hair and asks him who his friend is. Dylan introduces NoraKate. "She's from Texas," explains Dylan, "Texas is the biggest city in the world."

"Not city, silly," admonishes NoraKate. "Texas is a state. Houston is the biggest city in the world."

"Oh," acknowledges Dylan. Dylan and NoraKate have to sit on chairs waiting to see Principal McKenzie to explain to her about the upset tummies.

When NoraKate and Dylan get to go into Mrs. McKenzie's office, they both have to sit in front of the principal's desk. Mrs. McKenzie isn't pleased with NoraKate and Dylan. She informs the pair that they're not being good citizens. Dylan doesn't like to think of Mrs. McKenzie being unhappy with him because he likes her. Today she looks sterner than she has in the past.

"Dylan and NoraKate," says Mrs. McKenzie, sounding serious. "It's my job to determine whether you are really feeling ill. Or …" she drags this out, "or whether you are just being a little mischievous with Miss Dickinson. Now whose tummy was upset first?"

Dylan and NoraKate look at each other. Whose tummy was upset first today? NoraKate responds, "I think it was my tummy today," she says earnestly, but then adds, "But yesterday and the day before, it was Dylan's."

"Could it be," suggests Mrs. McKenzie, "that these tummy upsets are contagious? If we have to call a doctor, this information will be important."

Dylan and NoraKate look at each other, nodding in agreement, then turn to face Mrs. McKenzie, still nodding.

"Yes, that's it," volunteers NoraKate. "The tummy upsets must be contagious."

"Hmm," says Mrs. McKenzie, "This is very worrying. I cannot have children being sick in my school. Should we call a doctor to examine you both?" Simultaneously, Dylan and NoraKate shake their heads in the negative.

"We both feel perfectly fine now," Dylan assures her. "Don't we, NoraKate?"

"Yes," agrees NoraKate. "There's no sign in my tummy of it being upset."

"Strange," muses Mrs. McKenzie. "A tummy upset that begins when naptime begins and disappears the instant naptime ends. I think these tummy problems must be caused by naps." Dylan nods his head to agree, while the more astute NoraKate shakes her head, giving Dylan a discreet little kick. But the look on Mrs. McKenzie's face shows them that the game is up.

Mrs. McKenzie tells them that naptime is important. Until just two years ago, she says, Kindergarten was just half a day. Now it's all day. Naptime is important because it is 'time-out.' Time-out is very important to all people, but especially to Kindergartners. According to Principal McKenzie, more than half the Kindergartners actually sleep during naptime.

"I'm pleased that you have both found each other as companions; making special friends is part of experiencing school. But schools have to have rules. Skipping naptime isn't an option. And I don't think that sitting on a toilet for half an hour can be very good for your bodies." Both NoraKate and Dylan look down into their laps.

Mrs. McKenzie continues. "The question is, what do we do about a pair of friends who have both decided that they hate naps and who are driving their teacher to distraction?" NoraKate is more articulate than Dylan. She informs Mrs. McKenzie that she and Dylan used to spend naptime next to each other until separated by Miss Dickinson. When they whispered, they did it ever so quietly. They couldn't possibly have disturbed anyone.

Mrs. McKenzie thinks about this. "So, if I persuade Miss Dickinson to allow you to return to your previous naptime positions and not be so strict about the whispering, there'll be no more upset tummies?" Dylan and NoraKate nod their heads vigorously.

Naptimes change. After lunch, Miss Dickinson plays some recorded music. The music is sleepy time music. It's played very softly. But for those in Kindergarten who would rather whisper than nap, the whispers don't disturb the sleepers.

*   *   *

NoraKate and Dylan both have fathers that work in Saudi Arabia. American expertise is required by the Saudi oil industry, but the influence of Western personal liberties - especially as it applies to the female gender - is not welcome. For this reason, American oil companies supply the expertise by flying it in every Sunday night and duly flying it out again on Friday from countries such as Spain and Switzerland.

NoraKate complains to Dylan about how much she misses her father now that she can only see him on weekends. Dylan thinks about this. He decides that he doesn't really miss having his father around now that he's absent for five of the seven days of the week. If anything, he's inclined to think of his father as an intruder when he returns each weekend. Dylan enjoys being the number one male in the Douglas household.

On a Friday, Dylan persuades his mother he's sick. He's not sick. Dylan's mom probably knows he's not sick. She doesn't grab a thermometer and take his temperature to check for a fever. That's what Dylan's mommy usually does if she truly believes him to be sick. Dylan just needs a day off. He needs a full day of 'time-out.' He wants to catch up on reading some comics, spend some time with his mommy, and maybe even play with his little brothers. Most importantly, he needs to spend a day *not* seeing Miss Dickinson.

When Dylan's dad arrives home for the weekend, he asks Dylan how school was at the family dinner. Dylan looks inquisitively at Mommy. He wants a signal from Mommy to let him know whether it's okay to tell Daddy about the time-out day. Mommy nods at Dylan.

"My tummy was a little upset in the morning," Dylan informs his dad tentatively. "I didn't go to school today."

Dylan's dad scowls at him. "You were playing hooky?"

"What's hooky?" asks Dylan.

Dylan's dad picks up his newspaper and responds from behind it. "The first act in the life of an idle delinquent." Mommy tells Daddy not to be so silly. Mommy then informs Dylan that if he wants to invite NoraKate over to play on a Friday, she'll try to arrange it with NoraKate's mother.

On Monday morning when he returns to school, Dylan immediately seeks out NoraKate on the playground. He's excited because he wants to invite her to play hooky with him. He searches everywhere on the playground, but can't find her. When the bell goes and the lineups form, Dylan still doesn't see NoraKate. Could she be taking a time-out day?

When Dylan enters Kindergarten, Miss Dickinson cuts him off before he can sit at Table Three. She sends him to Principal McKenzie's office. Dylan says hi to Monique and, after waiting a few moments on the waiting chairs, he's sent in to see Mrs. McKenzie. Principal McKenzie looks solemn.

"Dylan," she says, "I have some news that you're probably not going to be happy with. Your friend NoraKate has returned to the States. She was due to leave after Christmas anyway, as you probably know. But her grandfather was taken ill and

NoraKate's mother decided that the family had to return immediately."

Dylan is shocked into silence. No, he didn't know that NoraKate would be leaving at the end of the term. NoraKate never mentioned this.

Principal McKenzie continues. "You do know that you are to be leaving us soon too, right Dylan? Your mother told me that your family would only be in Geneva for six months." No, Dylan didn't know that, either. What would Kindergarten be without NoraKate? He has no other friend. "NoraKate made you a card on Friday. She was very upset that you weren't in school."

The card is hand-created on school paper. A wax crayon drawing of two stick images, one female and one male, is depicted on the front. You can tell them apart because the girl has longer hair and her stick legs are half covered by a triangular skirt. The figures are holding hands. Under the stick figures, it says "best friends." Still lost for words, Dylan opens the card and reads to himself, "Best friends - write me - luv, NoraKate." In an adult hand on the back of the card, an address is printed. The address is in Houston, the biggest city in the world. Dylan is conscious that Principal McKenzie is studying him.

"You'll say a lot of goodbyes in life, Dylan. You will have to get used to it. Your father's job means that you will move around a lot."

"But ..." mumbles Dylan, protesting, "I ... she didn't say goodbye."

A couple of months later, Dylan is playing on a beach, far from Geneva. He's with his mother and brothers. His mother is sunbathing. The beach is long and straight, stretching almost out of sight in both directions. Large high-rise hotels run along its length and it's populated by crowds of people. Dylan is building a sandcastle with his two younger brothers. His mother is lying under an angled parasol propped on the sand a few yards off. The sandcastle is being formed by moist, packed sand tapped out from tapered beach buckets. Dylan's contribution to the venture is half-hearted, but his two brothers are deeply engaged in its construction.

A way down the beach, maybe fifty yards or so, Dylan spots NoraKate. He has never seen NoraKate in a swimsuit before, but he recognizes her haircut: dark, silky straight, and perfectly cut. More than the haircut, he identifies a NoraKate mannerism, the distinctive way she had of tossing her head to flick bangs away from her eyes. Dylan's heart races a couple of beats. He gets off his knees to a standing position, holding his plastic shovel by his side.

For an instant, he loses track of her. He shields his eyes and spies her again. He takes off, running toward her, taking care not to let her out of his sight. Because he focuses only on NoraKate, he inadvertently infiltrates sunbathers' territory marked by towels and parasols, provoking some indignant abuse. He ignores the shouts and continues to plough his way through the soft sand, the inconsistent nature of which prevents him from gaining any real speed. At some point, NoraKate seems to become aware that she's being chased and, without turning her head, she begins to run, too. Dylan wishes she would just turn around and see that it's him, but she doesn't. She continues to run away from him. However, Dylan can run faster. Just as Dylan is about to catch up to NoraKate, she throws herself at what is presumably her mother sunbathing on a towel, and turns in fear to face Dylan. Dylan stops, staring. It's not NoraKate, but someone who bears little resemblance to her up close. The strange girl's expression is fearful and she's in tears.

The mother, who might have been asleep before her daughter launched herself into her body, props herself onto her elbows. She begins to angrily berate her child but, quickly perceiving Dylan to be the real culprit, unleashes a tirade of anger toward the boy. The language is not English and Dylan understands none of the words, only the anger they express. "Sorry," he mumbles sadly, "I thought…"

Defeated, Dylan navigates a meandering passage between the beach towels and parasols back to the shoreline. Then he proceeds down the shoreline in quest of his brothers and the sandcastle under construction. He spies his mother first. She's standing beside the sandcastle, shielding her eyes. She's looking up and down the beach, attempting to spot Dylan. As Dylan approaches, she's relieved and drops the hand she is shielding her eyes with to her side.

"Where did you suddenly run off to, you?" she questions irritably. "I have to depend on you to help look after your brothers and I can't do that if you take to tearing off down the beach without telling me first."

3. GENEVIEVE

Dylan fancies himself as a pitcher. He's accurate and he can throw fast and he can throw slow. But at seven years old, he lacks any real game savvy, so he throws mostly strikes and wonders why they get hit hard and often. Seasoned hitters are quick to get a handle on Dylan's pitching. During all day Saturday baseball marathons, although "official" scoring is only credited to batters, Dylan keeps a private count of hits conceded and strikeouts earned. On a good day, his strikeout count exceeds hits allowed. Most days this didn't happen. As a second grader, he isn't afforded the privilege of pitching during those periods of the day when the game is at its busiest. During the course of the day, players lazily merge in and out of the game. On a typical Saturday, the game is most populated by bigger kids in the late morning and again in the late afternoon. During these times, Dylan's role in the game is relegated to a position in deep outfield and the occasional at bat.

Dylan returns home tired and thirsty, his muscles aching from an excess of baseball. It's dusk. He enters his house through the side garage door. The spring-loaded screen door bangs closed. He crosses the garage and opens the kitchen door. Once in the kitchen, he heads straight to the refrigerator, opens it, and grabs a gallon-sized bottle of ice water. He drinks directly from it, gulping the water down. The cooler of Kool-Aid on the baseball diamond had run dry hours earlier and he's dehydrated. As he chugs from the water bottle, he feels a gentle tap on the shoulder. He stops drinking and turns around. Facing him is a stranger. Actually, not quite a stranger. It's a sixth grade girl he'd noticed once or twice on the school playground during recess. He'd noticed her because she had a friendly face and thought that she may once have smiled at him, not something older girls were wont to do to kids in the lower grades at school. This face was now admonishing him with raised eyebrows.

"Bad boy. You are supposed to use a glass. You'll give everyone your germs." She tosses her head to flick her bangs out of her eyes. Dylan notices that she has a slight accent of some sort.

"Who are you?" Dylan manages to utter, a little taken aback.

"I'm babysitting your brothers and sister," the girl announces. "You should know who I am anyway, I am sure your mama told you. I'm Genevieve."

"Zhan vi ev? What kind of name is that?" asks Dylan.

"It is a Canadian name. French Canadian. And you must always say it that way. Kids in school call me 'Jean' or 'Jeanie.' I don't know why they can't say 'Genevieve' properly. The Venezuelans say Genevieve, or Genevieva. I don't like being a Jeanie. I don't feel like a Jeanie. When people call out 'Jeanie,' I always have to look around for another person called 'Jeanie' before I realize it's me they're talking to."

Yes, Genevieve. Mom had mentioned it at breakfast earlier in the day. At the time, the name had meant nothing to him. Just another Saturday night babysitter. His mother had informed him that Genevieve was a page in the library - the kid who put all the returned books back on the shelves so that the librarian could stay behind the checkout counter. His mom had gone to the library to check out some books and, while she was there, had hired another babysitter. But from Dylan's perspective, she was now a new babysitter to break in. Babysitters were a feature of Saturday nights because the Douglas family now had just one maid, who returned to her family for weekends. Hence, the succession of babysitters.

"Your supper is in the oven. I'll get it out for you." Genevieve pulls a couple of oven mitts over her hands and, with an efficiency that broadcasts familiarity around such things as stovetops and the processes of cooking, removes a covered plate from the oven and places a dish of macaroni and cheese on the kitchen table. The plate cover is removed and taken over to the kitchen sink.

"You'll have to eat by yourself," she tells him. "I'm about to read a goodnight story to your brothers. Your baby sister, she's already sleeping." With that, she tosses her head to flick away any hair that might be trespassing across her face, and exits the kitchen.

Dylan locates a couple of comic books from a magazine rack adjacent to the table, opens one of them, and begins to eat. He does this without any particular focus on either the food or the comic book he is reading. Two hours in the oven has removed whatever flavor the food may have originally possessed and the comic book is one that Dylan has read at least a couple of times previously. Thirty minutes or so pass by. The macaroni is about half consumed and is now cold as well as lacking flavor. Genevieve returns. "All settled down for the night," she announces with a sense of accomplishment. She approaches the kitchen table.

"You didn't eat very much," she says. "No wonder you are so skinny." She picks up the plate, squeezing Dylan's upper arm as she does so, making it plain that a little more muscle should be present. She's business-like in her movements around the kitchen and there is something out of the ordinary in her approach to him. Though by appearance she looks younger than most previous babysitters, she radiates an air of calm authority. Dylan observes that she even appears to enjoy what she does. Yes, she's humming and singing a song. A French song?

Dylan has plenty of experience with babysitters. His parents seldom miss an opportunity to party on a Saturday, so every weekend brings a babysitter into the Douglas household. These babysitters are an unfortunate Saturday night feature as far as Dylan is concerned. His mother tends to source babysitters from grades six through eight in the American school. The babysitters are always female, girls aged between twelve and fourteen who favor bossiness as the means to compensate for a tenuous ability to control their charges. Dylan does his best to cultivate a reputation for giving babysitters a hard time. His strategy has always been to make sure they think twice about ever returning.

Genevieve washes the dinner dish in the sink, singing softly. Dylan observes her while still sitting at the kitchen table. Having completed the task of washing dishes, she fastidiously dries her hands and turns to address Dylan, stroking hair away from her eyes.

"Your mama told me to tell you that she wants you to take a bath before going to bed."

Dylan says nothing in response.

"When you've finished, I'll read you a story if you like."

"I know how to read my own stories," Dylan informs her bluntly, "I can probably read better than you."

"Ah yes, but don't you think it is more special to have someone read a story to you? It's like you share the moment. Maybe you can read me a story, yes? Or we could take turns?"

The suggestions make Dylan warm to her slightly. "Yes, we could do that," he says, feeling more valued and now possibly interested in the proposition. Perhaps he even feels a little generous. "We can read *Treasure Island*. I am about half way through, but there are some difficult words you could help me with."

With that, he scoots out of the kitchen and heads to the bathroom. He draws a bath and, within five minutes, has completed his ablutions. After a rudimentary once over with a towel, he pulls on pajama bottoms and ties the belt cord. Arming himself with *Treasure Island* and an enthusiastic grin, Dylan heads for the living room. He jumps onto the couch in a single bound and parks himself next to Genevieve.

"That must have been the fastest bath in the whole history of the world," Genevieve observes with skepticism. But then she realizes that the boy's exposed upper body is more wet than dry, while his hair is completely dry. "Dylan, you've not washed your hair! You've been playing baseball for hours. Your hair is sweaty and I can see sand in it. You can't go to bed like that."

"But what about our story?" he pleads. "There won't be time."

"There'll be plenty of time for as much story as you want. No story until your hair is clean. Come on. I'll help you. We can wash your hair perfectly clean and it won't take two minutes."

With that, she holds his hand and guides him into the bathroom. Dylan is not sure whether to allow himself to be so easily led by the hand. Surely he isn't the hand-holding type. But there are no witnesses to the scene, nobody to tattletale that he might actually be getting along with a babysitter.

In the bathroom, Genevieve places a towel around Dylan's shoulders. She instructs him to lean over the tub. She turns the water on, balances the temperature at the faucet, then toggles the shower valve. Dylan bends over the tub. With one hand, Genevieve holds the shower flex-head, directing the stream of water through the boy's hair. With the other hand, she massages his hair to ensure it's saturated. That accomplished, she closes the water taps. Next, she squirts shampoo into one of her hands and briefly rubs it between her hands before applying it to the wet hair.

"Eyes closed tight," she instructs. She rubs the shampoo into his hair. It works up into a furious lather. Not only does Dylan have to keep his eyes closed tight, he dares not open his mouth to speak; soap is running down the side of his face and falls with splots into the tub. He'd like to inform Genevieve that she's used way too much shampoo, but can't open his mouth, for this would surely result in a mouthful of foaming lather. Genevieve's fingertips knead his scalp, beginning at the back and working toward the front. Her fingers exert a force that is surprising, but at the same time, soothing. As the oldest and most self-reliant of four siblings, it's been some time since another person has paid such attention to his cleanliness.

Genevieve maintains a running monologue of commentary while her fingers work away.

"You have the longest hair of any boy I know. It is not so often you see boys with curly hair as long as yours. Most boys here have crew cuts. I think it's kind of cute. It's funny how curly hair goes so completely straight when it is wet."

Abruptly, she stops working the shampoo and flicks the suds off her hands into the tub. "Rinse time," she announces. Dylan can do nothing but remain bent over the side of the bath with both eyes and mouth sealed shut. He hears the sounds of the water being switched on, the shower valve toggled, then adjusts to the sensation of the stream of water flowing through his hair, before a hand helps to work the remaining shampoo away. The water faucet is shut off with a clunk. Still bent over the tub with eyes squeezed closed, Dylan can finally speak. Blind, he stretches out both arms. "Towel, towel," he commands impatiently, flapping his hands like wings.

"Patience, patience, I'm getting it." Genevieve wraps the towel around Dylan's head, making a turban. Finally, the boy can get his head upright. Genevieve grabs another towel and applies it to her wet arms and those parts of her clothing that have been splashed. She uses this towel to stroke the water off the boy's shoulders and torso.

Dylan remains on his knees at the side of the tub, turban wrapped around his head. "Ooo la la, what a red little face you have," laughs Genevieve, but with a gesture of tenderness, her index finger applies a single downward stroke to Dylan's nose.

"That's because you just about drowned me," responds the boy, but with the hint of a smile on his face that said it might be okay to be just about drowned – so long as it was by the right person.

"Where is your pajama top?" asks Genevieve.

The stubbornness returns in an instant. "I don't wear pajama tops. It's too hot!"

A short while later, Dylan is seated alongside Genevieve on the living room couch. Dylan parks himself sitting very upright with a space of a foot between himself and Genevieve. He aims to impress with his reading. But playing baseball in blazing sun all day is tiring. It's not long before his eyes become blurry and there really seems to be more of those big words in this book than he thought. Maybe an eleven-year-old can read better than a seven-year-old, even if she's reading in her second language.

Genevieve takes over. Of course, she requires a little coaching to get the voices right. Long John Silver's voice has to be delivered in a ponderous, rough, but rhythmic drawl. This she manages after a fashion. The posh English accents of the Captain and the doctor prove to be more of a challenge for a French tongue. As far as Dylan is concerned, only Jim is permitted to speak in a "normal" accent. Genevieve does her best to comply with Dylan's instructions regarding tone and accent. Because Genevieve has now taken charge of the holding of the book along with the reading, Dylan is forced to insinuate himself into a cuddle position. This is so he can still see the images that appear every couple of pages. He plants his head into the crook of her shoulder. Genevieve responds by wrapping an arm around Dylan. He wonders why this feels so good. Could it be that Genevieve is his favorite sitter ever?

As the story progresses, Dylan takes it upon himself to run a dialogue of interruption to fill the reader in with all of those gaps she's missed by beginning the book half-way through. On her part, Genevieve's interest is piqued after the first few pages. "What is this *Treasure Island*?" she asks of no one in particular, flipping the book closed to examine the front cover, "I've never heard of it before."

"Duh, it's only the best book ever written," declares Dylan, "It's a movie, too."

"I don't think it could be as good as *Anne of Green Gables*," she responds skeptically. However, as she keeps reading, the interest of the reader increases as the ability of the listener to keep his eyes open diminishes. Struggling to keep awake, Dylan's head begins to slide down Genevieve's torso. It settles in her lap. Her hand remains in his hair, as if she has helped push the head downward. In a dreamy daze, Dylan inhales a familiar perfume odor of washing powder embedded in the cotton shorts of the lap that has become his pillow. The reader's voice drones forward with the story but the words cease to make sense.

When Genevieve understands that her charge is in a deep sleep, she continues reading the book to herself, becoming ever more engrossed. From time to time, she tousles the curly hair on her lap in an absent-minded way to remind herself that she has made a conquest. And that's how Dylan's astonished parents find the pair when they return two hours later. Genevieve is beaming like a Cheshire cat. Was it not perfectly obvious that no kid was too tough for her to handle? Yes sir, it might be that she happens to be the world's best babysitter.

At school the next week, Dylan glimpses Genevieve once or twice at recess. Once, from a distance, she gives him a discreet finger ripple wave when their eyes meet. And although he returns a smile, he dares not respond in kind. To do so could cost him credibility points with the second grade boys. Being friends with your babysitter was not regarded as acceptable. Dylan spends the week looking forward to Saturday night. Another Saturday night with Genevieve, the beautiful and kind Genevieve. The week passes slowly; it feels like one of the longest weeks of his life.

Saturday finally arrives; even the longest weeks eventually come to an end. Dylan's body is present for Saturday baseball, but some part of his mind is reserved for his new and exciting devotion to Genevieve. Instead of waiting until dusk before leaving the ball game, he picks up his glove and departs at a normal suppertime hour. As he enters the garage, a devastating sight beholds his eyes. The family car, a two-tone Chevrolet station wagon with a toothy mouth grill and two big head-lamp eyes, is parked in the garage. No babysitter! No Genevieve! His mom is in the kitchen. Something jolts his memory to remind him that his father is absent on a business trip. For a few moments, Dylan senses an acute pain that affects him from head to toe. It gradually dissipates when he realizes that, in compensation for being deprived of Genevieve, he will have the luxury of an exclusive on Mom's attention for some of the evening. Love would have to wait.

The line drive strikes Dylan just above his left knee. The drive was launched off the bat of Jake Tilden's Dad, with a ferocity fueled by fury. The fury resulted from the fact that, in his previous at bat, Jake Tilden's father was ignominiously struck out by a pitcher who was not yet out of Grade Two. The strikeout ball curved and bounced in the dirt an inch in front of home plate. When a Dad joined in a Saturday baseball game, the objective was usually to show the kids a thing or two.

Getting struck out by a seven-year-old chucking a junk ball was definitely not part of the game plan.

Dylan collapses on the pitcher's mound. Jake Tilden's Dad sprints to first base. While doing so, he yells instructions and waves his fists to encourage the runner on second base to attempt to make it home. Heck, surely the hit was at least worthy of a run-batted-in.

Alfredo Pineda is the school physical education teacher. Señor Pineda happens to be sitting on the bleachers observing the game with the objective of scouting any potential talent among the Americano kids playing the game. There was seldom much. The gringo kids played this game for fun. The Venezuelanos were much more skilled. The Venezuelanos played with passion. Fun didn't enter the equation when Venezuelanos played ball. When Alfredo sees the line drive strike Dylan's leg, he wonders what these Americano parents think they are achieving when they join in with their kids during the Saturday baseball games. Some of the youngest children are only five and six years old. While the Americano kids play baseball for fun, their fathers join in and play in the name of machismo. Alfredo leaves his seat in the bleachers and strolls out to the pitcher's mound. He examines the injury. The kid's leg is already swelling up pretty good. He notes that the injured party is Dylan Douglas, one of the younger regular players of Saturday baseball marathons, a kid that might have some promise as a pitcher one day. That is, provided he survived getting maimed by bozos like Señor Tilden.

"This will have to be checked out at the hospital," is his verdict. Jake Tilden's Dad has walked over. Alfredo asks him if his truck is in the vicinity. It is not. Jake Tilden's Dad came on foot to the park. Alfredo announces that he will drive the boy to the Sagrada Familia Hospital just to be sure there's no fracture or damage to the knee cap. He asks Jake Tilden's Dad to inform Dylan's folks that he's taking the boy to the hospital. He suggests that Señor Tilden do this as quickly as possible so that they can meet their son at the hospital.

Dylan's mom doesn't arrive until after Dylan has been sent to the X-ray department. She meets Señor Pineda in the emergency waiting room. Señor Alfredo assures her that the injury doesn't appear to be serious. He wanted to be on the safe side, which is why he thought it wise to take her son to the hospital. A doctor has already examined Dylan. The doctor's initial diagnosis is that there's no fracture.

"Señora, I have to tell you that your son is out pitching every Saturday. And I discover when we get to the hospital he wears no cup. A pitcher especially must wear a cup. You must understand Señora, the severity of an injury that could result from not wearing a cup."

Dylan's mom hasn't got a clue as to what Pineda is talking about. Is he insinuating that she has been somehow neglectful?

"A coop?" she asks, confused. "What is a 'coop'?" This isn't what Alfredo Pineda wants to hear. Now he's put in the position of being forced to explain.

"Señora," he says solemnly, "the 'coop' protects the manhood. In the game of baseball, the ball is very hard, like rock, and it can travel very fast." Pineda delivers this statement very slowly, emphasizing each word as if he's talking to someone whose comprehension is challenged. Dylan's mom nods her head in unison with Pineda as he speaks. She's doing her best to fathom what it is that this man is attempting to tell her. Pineda suspects that he's not getting through, so points down to his groin with his index finger. She nods to indicate that she now understands, but the only thing she really gets is that this is something to do with males and sports and that any further explanation on the subject is going to have to wait until she can discuss the issue with her husband. She assures Señor Alfredo that Dylan will soon be equipped with a "coop."

Dylan's mom sits down next to Señor Pineda, who tells her exactly how her son got injured in this way. She begins to realize that there is a culprit, someone to blame: an adult man who's irresponsibly playing in a children's ballgame. She's angry. She informs Alfredo that Señor Tilden will be getting a piece of her mind in the very near future. But before she can get too worked up about it, Dylan, seated in a wheelchair, is brought into the corridor. He's chatting animatedly with the nun pushing him. He greets his mom with a toothy grin.

"No fracture, just a bruise," he declares triumphantly. Though, he muses to himself, had there been a fracture, there would have been plenty of fuss and attention focused on him that may have compensated for it in some measure.

Dylan's mom drives him home. She asks him about a "coop." Dylan has no idea what she's talking about. His mother informs him that he can play no more baseball until a coop can be acquired. Dylan asks what a "coop" is. His mother isn't quite sure, but Señor Pineda says that he must have one. She then informs him that she and Daddy will be going out and that Genevieve will be babysitting. This news perks up Dylan immediately. His mother tells him she will give something for the pain and suggests he gets to bed early.

Later, Dylan sits with Genevieve as she reads from *Treasure Island*. Since her previous visit, the girl has checked the book from the school library and read it cover to cover. She knows the story well and has researched the voices. Dylan is prepped for bed and wearing shorts so ice packs can be held in direct contact with the swelling above his knee. Nurse Genevieve replenishes the ice pack from time to time, walking to the freezer and switching one for another.

Dylan is stoned, from both the painkiller and Genevieve's attention. This nurture seems to be out of proportion with the severity of his bruised leg and it pleases him. It seems to Dylan that Genevieve is encouraging him to act more injured and helpless than he actually is. She pulls Dylan across her body into the crook of her shoulder. She caresses his hair. Dylan has not been so pampered with this kind of physical affection for years. Best of all, the person delivering all this attention is the gorgeous Genevieve. Occasionally, Genevieve speaks unintelligible words, presumably in French. Dylan cares little for what these words might mean.

Genevieve suddenly stops reading. Out of the blue, she says, "Dylan, would you like to play a game? A make-believe game?" She pauses, then goes on. "We can pretend that I'm a mama. And you can be my baby." Dylan looks into Genevieve's eyes. Is she being serious? Dylan doesn't want to be a baby. He'd rather be a man if they're going to play make-believe. Or a boyfriend. He stares at her blankly. Events have taken a turn he hadn't planned on.

"C'mon Dylan, I want you to pretend to be my baby." With that, she unbuttons her blouse and moves Dylan's head to her breast, presenting him with a nipple no larger than those on his own chest.

"Pretend you're drinking my milk," Genevieve instructs. "But be gentle, just don't suck too hard. No milk will come, just pretend."

A part of Dylan wants to oblige. He is powerfully motivated to please Genevieve, whatever the consequences. Another part of him wants to bail. Genevieve's idea of a game has a script that defeats his comprehension. But his desire to please Genevieve trumps any doubts. He parts his lips slightly and makes a half-hearted nibbling effort at suckling her baby nipple. He looks up into Genevieve's eyes. They have a glazed, far away expression, as if he's really not there. Dylan pulls away. Genevieve speaks to him in French. She appears to be scolding him. Again, she moves Dylan's face to her nipple. As his lips contact skin, Dylan tastes its salty, sour flavor. Then in a kind of involuntary response, he sucks on the nipple with some force, drawing surrounding flesh into his mouth. He's aware of Genevieve taking a deep breath just before something, some force deep within him, makes him close his teeth and bite. Genevieve shrieks, yanking herself away from the boy's mouth.

Dylan is shocked into sitting up abruptly. He's no longer stoned. Genevieve is holding her chest, having retreated into the corner of the couch, and draws her legs up in a defensive posture. She's crying quietly.

"I'm sorry, Genevieve," Dylan splutters, confused by his action and upset by the crying. "I didn't mean to bite, it just happened. I don't know what made me do it." With that, Dylan starts to cry, too. Genevieve surveys Dylan from her sitting, fetal position in the crook of the couch. Frightened at having made a big girl cry, Dylan extends a hand to touch Genevieve's knee, a gesture intended to comfort. Instead,

Genevieve slaps his hand, turning to look away from Dylan. This has the effect of producing more pronounced sobbing from Dylan. Genevieve opens her shirt to inspect the damage. No skin is broken, but an angry impression of Dylan's teeth is displayed in the skin surrounding the nipple.

Genevieve softens. "That was mean, Dylan," she says, her tears drying. "You really hurt me. What were you thinking of? We were just playing a nice game. You ruined it."

"I couldn't help it," the boy protests through tears. "I don't know what happened. I didn't want to hurt you. I like you. Really I do."

Genevieve drops her legs off the sofa to the floor and rubs at her chest with her forearm. She buttons her blouse and, using her sleeve, wipes tears from her cheeks. Then she extends her arms, inviting a hug. "Come on," she says, now calm, "give me a hug. We're special friends. When friends fight, they should make up quickly." Despite the fact that he is unused to hugs, he joins the embrace. No one can see him here. No one can see Genevieve here. They're in their own world.

"You should go to bed," Genevieve suggests. "You need to get that knee rested up." She walks him to the upper bunk bed in his bedroom. The room is illuminated by a night light. His brothers in the bunk adjacent are fast asleep.

"You won't tell Mom and Dad that I bit you?" asks Dylan.

Genevieve shakes her head. "No Dylan," she responds slowly, "that'll be our little secret." She stands on the second rung of the bunk ladder and leans forward to kiss him on the forehead. "Sleep tight, little alligator," she says, exiting the room. In the dimness of the room, Dylan observes a hint of a smile on her face. This both comforts and mystifies him.

The week that follows flies by. Dylan is not aware of seeing Genevieve at school for the entire week. By the time another Saturday rolls around, he's forgotten about her to the extent that he may no longer be in love. Saturday and its feature of an all-day ballgame comes around. This time, he is so engrossed in baseball that dusk is in danger of turning into pitch darkness by the time he enters the kitchen through the garage door. The screen door slams. The kitchen is vacant. Dylan opens the refrigerator and chugs from the ice water bottle. He's fully aware of someone approaching from behind and his pulse increases slightly as realizes it could only be Genevieve. He gulps until his thirst is slaked. He restores the bottle to the fridge shelf and turns. He burps. Genevieve is leaning on the door frame with a hand on one hip and an exasperated expression on her face. She says nothing. Silently, she crosses the kitchen floor, opens the oven door, removes the covered plate and sets it on the table. Dylan sits himself down in front of the plate. Genevieve seats herself facing him. The desiccated food neither appears nor tastes appetizing. With his fingers, Dylan picks up a dried up sausage and takes a bite. Genevieve scowls at him. A reprimand is due even if these are the first words exchanged between them this evening.

"Dylan, you know better than to eat with your hands… and it is not good that you drink like that from the bottle. You know better. You wouldn't do that if your mama could see you. And you are way too late coming home – you should've been home an hour ago. I thought you were my friend. You could get me into trouble by coming in so late."

"You are my friend. Mom and Dad won't know. You don't have to tell them. Anyway, I'm the one that's being bad by coming home late, it's nothing to do with you."

"If we are going to be real friends, we have to help each other. You can help me by minding me when I babysit. I like to babysit with your family. You're the only problem I have when I babysit for your family. I want to be your friend as well as your babysitter. But it's important that you remember I am responsible for you." Dylan says nothing. Of course, he does like Genevieve and he wants to please her. But there's something about her motives that he can't make sense of. He picks at his food. "That food doesn't look so good any more. You want I should make you a peanut butter and jelly sandwich?"

Dylan nods his head, pushing the plate away from him.

✳   ✳   ✳

"Bath time," announces Genevieve. "I need a bath too; we can bathe together. We can be tub buddies." Tub buddies? She goes off by herself to draw the bath. Dylan listens to the sound of the water running into the tub for some moments. For the first time since the previous Saturday, he recalls the biting incident. He senses something about the scenario Genevieve is orchestrating that is both compelling and possibly frightening. He has no desire to reprise his role of Genevieve's pretend baby, but curiosity draws him to the bathroom.

The bathroom is steamy. Dylan enters. Genevieve is bent over the faucets, swishing something into the water. Is that Mom's bubble bath?

"Get in," orders Genevieve, "I'll join you when the tub's full." Dylan removes his shorts and T-shirt, depositing each item onto the floor. Naked, he momentarily feels self-conscious. This induces him to jump into the tub and immerse himself a little more quickly than would be his usual habit. The water is warmer than he'd like. Genevieve turns away and picks up each garment just thrown by Dylan onto the floor and carefully folds it.

"It's all going in the wash," Dylan assures her. "You don't have to fold anything."

Genevieve ignores him. Having folded Dylan's discarded clothing, she unbuttons her blouse and removes it. This done, she pinches the corner of each shoulder and carefully folds, placing the garment on the toilet cistern. Dylan notes that there appears to be no lingering evidence of the bite he gave her the previous week. Next, with certain elegance, Genevieve steps out of her shorts and underpants. It's in part a performance, because she is acutely aware of Dylan studying her every move. Again, each garment is carefully folded and placed on the stack on the toilet cistern. That done, she moves her hands behind her head and, with a couple of hairpins, clips her shoulder-length, brown hair above her head.

Dylan enjoys seeing her naked, though he's not sure why. At the same time, he's embarrassed to show or say anything about it. He sinks his body under the water in the tub so that only his head is not submerged. Genevieve sits on the toilet for a pee, but nothing seems to be forthcoming. Dylan watches her. She meets his gaze. "Stop staring at me! You're putting me off. I can't pee when a silly boy is gawking at me."

Dylan turns away, a little sheepishly. He thinks he's probably seen enough, anyway. Apart from the obvious difference between the legs, her body doesn't seem so different from his own. At eleven years, Genevieve's petite frame has yet made little ingress into adolescence. The toilet flushes and Genevieve steps into the bathtub, claiming the side opposing the taps by standing over Dylan and hoisting him out of her way.

"Hey, I was in first," declares Dylan with mock indignation. Genevieve lowers her body into the water and leans back, using her feet to force Dylan up against the taps. This produces a more genuine protest from Dylan. Genevieve suddenly launches her body to a sitting position. She seeks and then clasps both Dylan's hands, pulling him a little closer. Her wet body above the water line glistens under the bathroom lights.

"You like to see me naked, yes?" she asks him with a mischievous grin.

"Yes."

"And why is that, Monsieur Dylan?"

"I don't know."

"I know why. You're a boy and boys like to see girls naked. Even little boys like you. Girls like to see boys naked, too. But maybe not so much." She strokes his nose with a wet finger. "Would you like me to wash you Dylan?"

"No, I can wash myself."

"Come on, I will make you feel ever so good. Stand up."

With diminishing reluctance, Dylan stands up to face the taps. Genevieve raises herself onto her knees. She rubs a bar of soap between her hands. Beginning at the boy's neck with slippery, soapy hands, she softly massages, neck, shoulders, each arm. At regular intervals, she pauses to reapply soap to her hands to initiate each phase of the cleaning ritual. Dylan enters into a trance. When Genevieve turns him around to wash the front of his body, Dylan moves his hands to cover himself in a gesture of modesty. "Silly, don't be shy. I have brothers so I know all about wieners," she says in an abstract way, beginning a kind of monologue. "The tip on yours is naked. I asked my mother about that. You and your brothers are circumcised – when you were born, the skin around the tip of the pecker was cut off, making it a completely naked wiener like yours. The skin they cut off is called the foreskin. Mama says that Jews and rich people do this. For some reason, she doesn't like this circumcision. But I think your pecker looks kind of cute. Most boys I have seen naked have foreskins."

Dylan only has a vague idea of what she is talking about. In his previous obser-vations, limited as they might be, it has appeared to him that most males outside of his family were possessed of penises that were the visual equivalent of his. Now Genevieve is telling him that his willy had been somehow mutilated at birth. Would his mommy have allowed anyone to do this thing to him? He'd have to ask. Could it be that he was either a Jew or a rich person?

"Lie down in the water and swish the soap off," she instructs him when finished. Dylan lowers himself back into the bathwater. Genevieve helps him wash the soap off his body as he lays back. "Lean back and pass me your feet," she orders him. Genevieve is about to wash the feet of a sinner. She knows this is a good thing because the nuns have told her so in Sunday school. The forces of logic determine Dylan to be a sinner. Genevieve has never once seen him or his family in the Iglesia San Luis Obispo. That means his family either attends no church or, worse still, one of the other churches. According to the nuns, the ones who attend other churches are the real evil kind of people because they should know better. True heathens, on the other hand, do not know any better and might stand a chance of being rescued from the fires of hell. It seems likely that Dylan and his whole family are true hea-thens, so they probably don't know any better. She couldn't see them as being evil.

It was clearly a pretty good thing to wash the feet of a lost soul. For Genevieve and Dylan, there would be dual benefits. First, Jesus and Mary would be impressed by Genevieve and reserve a special place for her next to them up in heaven. Second, there's a chance she may be able to rescue Dylan from the eternal fires of hell that are surely to be his destiny. Rescue is always a possibility when heathens have their feet washed by pious virgins such as herself. Had not the heroic Jesuits saved many souls on the shores of the Orinoco using these very same techniques?

Genevieve applies soap and godly tenderness to each of Dylan's feet, paying special attention to between the toes and his soles. These parts are especially soiled, no doubt caused by going around barefoot for most of the day. She grabs a bristle nailbrush to address this problem. The nailbrush tickles Dylan's feet and makes him squirm around. When she has scrubbed both feet, she slides her body back into a lying position in the bath water to remedy the dryness she gained while sitting up. Perhaps, she muses to herself, she might ask Dylan's mother if the boy could come with her family to church next Sunday. This would be proof that the foot washing had taken. Jesus might be acquiring another soul and it would be in part due to her selfless actions.

As Genevieve reclines into the tub, Dylan is forced back into the tub faucets and into a sitting position. "I can wash you now," he suggests, reaching for the soap.

"You can wash only my back," she instructs him, sloshing and emerging from the water to a sitting position then twisting around so that her back faces him. "I am too big to be washed." Dylan wants to tell her that he is also too big to be washed, but he let her do it all the same because she insisted. He's prevented from doing so by a very distant wail, which captures the attention of both occupants of the tub. The faint cry at first seems to be coming from another world, but then the noise intrudes into the bathroom. With a sudden realization, Genevieve identifies the sound as coming from Dylan's baby sister.

"Oo la la," she purrs, athletically launching her body out of the water to a standing position. She hastily grabs a towel and passes it over her body a couple of times before stepping out of the tub whilst wrapping and pinning it under her armpits. Dylan feels deserted. He wants to say something like "she does this every night" or "let her scream for a bit," but he knows that this would be of no avail. Not to the world's best babysitter or whatever it is that Genevieve aspires to be. Genevieve exits the bathroom, feeling important and seemingly happy that her services are required.

Dylan turns in the tub and sinks his body to full immersion in the water. Genevieve will be occupied with Deidra for some time. Dylan's baby sister adores Genevieve. Within moments, the infant will have ceased her crying and want to play and be entertained for an hour before exhaustion claims her.

A short time later, Genevieve reappears in the bathroom doorway, this time cradling Deidra, whose wails have now become just sniffles.

"She's teething, Dylan. Please, Dylan, you must wash your hair. Do it properly. Do it for me, Dylan." Of course Dylan does exactly this, and does it entirely for

Genevieve. Once the job is done, he gets out of the tub and dries himself before pulling on his pajama bottoms. In the hallway, Genevieve, still wrapped in a towel, is pacing up and down with the sniffling baby, dandling it into submission.

For Dylan, the remainder of the evening passes as if in a sort of dream. Of the three, Dylan's baby sister seems to have the most energy. She's interested in playing and goo-gooing by pointing at every item in the room and inviting explanation or comment. Genevieve appears to have infinite patience for dealing with this type of infant behavior. At one point, Genevieve passes Deidra to Dylan, saying that she has to get dressed and clean up the bathroom. During this interval, Dylan actually dandles his infant sister for the first time in his life. When Genevieve returns, dressed as before in her blouse and shorts, his little brat of a sister insists on remaining seated on Dylan's lap. This is a first and Dylan is secretly flattered. Could it be that his sister is growing into a somewhat cute little brat? Genevieve laughs. "See, you're not such a tough guy. You have a heart as soft as a girl inside there." She presses her index finger into his bare chest somewhere in the vicinity of where his heart might be.

The jibe provokes the only response a seven-year-old male is capable of: "Do not so."

When Dylan awakes the next morning, he is lying by himself on the couch in the living room. Voices and noises of activity are emanating from the bedroom area of the house. His mom enters the living room with his baby sister cradled in one arm. As she crosses the living room headed toward the kitchen, she stoops and plants a perfunctory kiss on his forehead, saying nothing. Next, Genevieve enters the living room. She is wearing a pair of Dylan's pajamas, both top and bottoms. Dylan observes that the sleeves and legs are only slightly short at the arms and legs. Genevieve sits on the side of the couch. By way of explanation, she says, "Your folks got home late last night. I was sleeping with you on the sofa when they returned so they told me I should sleep over. This is my latest babysit ever! Anyway, you were dead to the world so they left you on the sofa. I slept in your bunk bed." Then she leans forward to kiss Dylan on the forehead. Dylan waits until her lips make contact before twisting away to show that he's not about to be kissed by a girl.

Unphased, Genevieve abruptly announces importantly, "I'm going to help your mama fix breakfast. It is too late for me to go to Sunday school and church." She seems pleased about this. She exits heading to the kitchen. More noises erupt from the bedrooms. With his brothers and sister on the scene, Dylan is going to cease to exist in the spectrum of Genevieve's attentions. He wanders sleepily off to his bedroom to get dressed.

*　　　　　*　　　　　*

A couple of weeks pass by. Dylan discovers that being in love with your baby-sitter when you have three younger siblings of like sentiments is a tough calling. Inevitably, he ends up feeling that he's a distant number four in the pecking order of Genevieve's attentions. To compound the difficulty, his sister and both brothers can actively compete for Genevieve's affections, whereas Dylan feels he has to pretend not to. If any of his siblings awoke after bedtime during the week, Mom would have the culprit back in bed and asleep within three minutes. Not so on babysitter nights! A wake-up was rewarded with a display of affection, perhaps an opportunity to play, followed by a tender goodnight ritual complete with a French lullaby and a special kiss. Another challenge for Dylan is that of keeping awake long enough to gain some one-on-one time with Genevieve after playing baseball for up to seven hours in 90-degree heat. Sometimes, Genevieve would no sooner start reading his story than he'd pass out, exhausted.

With the reading of *Treasure Island* complete, Genevieve is to read *Anne of Green Gables* to Dylan. This is her favorite book. Bathed and dressed in pajama bottoms, Dylan jumps onto the couch and assumes what has become his usual bedtime story position, propped into Genevieve's shoulder. The babysitter picks up the book and begins reading. She doesn't get too far into the book before the issue of adoption is introduced in its pages. This is a concept that Dylan struggles to grasp and, try as she might, Genevieve cannot find the words to explain. It becomes apparent to her that her charge is innocent of even the most rudimentary knowledge of conception and birth.

"Dylan, do you know how babies are made?" Genevieve asks, now more serious.

"Of course," responds Dylan, but as soon as he does, he wonders about the question. In a bit of a panic, he attempts to recall some of the things his mother has said on this subject. Come to think of it, his mom usually has a twinkle in her eye when speaking to him about where babies come from. Does that mean that she's not been entirely truthful with him? Genevieve just looks at him. He feels he has to say something and scratches his head. When Deidra was born, cards with storks on them arrived in the mail; the stork was usually depicted flying with a swaddled-up baby in its beak.

"Well I think a stork has to deliver the baby. Does it come down the chimney?"

Skeptical, Genevieve continues to look at Dylan. "So where's the chimney in this house?" she asks. There is something about the way she says this that suggests to Dylan that he is short of some key information. However, chimney or no chimney, Deidra somehow arrived. "Ask your mama to tell you about how babies are made," his babysitter advises. Dylan can only wonder why Genevieve doesn't tell him herself if she thinks it so important. Genevieve opens the book once again and continues reading from what, according to her, is the best book ever written. Dylan is skeptical. He's not sure that any book can be truly great without having at least one pirate in it.

*   *   *

The Douglases are weekending in Maracaibo. To Dylan's mom and dad, a trip to Maracaibo represents a return to "semi-civilization." This is what his mom calls it, anyway. They are to stay in an American hotel popular with oil company employees. The objective of the trip is shopping and fancy meals for the parents, and more modest entertainments for their children. The kids can swim all day in a swimming pool the size of a lake and consume all the hamburgers and ice cream sodas they can stuff into themselves. It's a long, hot drive to get there, but the reward is worth it. Best of all, Genevieve is coming on this trip. Genevieve has agreed to babysit so that Mom and Dad can have the evenings to themselves. The girl's parents are initially reluctant to allow their daughter to go, but finally concede when Genevieve becomes theatrical about the possible turn for the worse her whole life would take were she to be denied this opportunity.

The Douglas family books itself into a pair of conjoined rooms in the hotel. The rooms are connected by an internal door. The parents are to use one room, the five kids the other. Each room has a pair of double beds. A cot is provided for Deidra. The plan is for the cot to be placed in the children's room initially. The cot is on wheels so that it can be rolled into the parents' room if Deidra fails to settle in the kids' room.

Naturally, Dylan would prefer to share one of the beds with Genevieve, but he knows this isn't about to happen. Dylan's mother divvies up the sleeping arrangements and no arbitration is solicited. Genevieve is to share one bed with Dylan's youngest brother Domenic, while Dylan and Daniel will take the other. Daniel is incensed with rage. He'd wanted to sleep with Genevieve! Domenic, on the other hand, is quite happy about the arrangement. It seems that all the Douglas kids are besotted with their babysitter.

Getting Deidra to bed and asleep has developed into an orchestrated ritual. Each step within the ritual has to be executed with precision and to the complete satisfaction of Deidra. The consequences of any shortcomings in the routine could be cataclysmic and result in a prolonged tantrum. Unfortunately, the odds of the bedtime strategy unfolding problem-free with Deidra removed from home turf were as close to zero as you could get.

The plan is to first exhaust Deidra in the children's paddle pool during the day, skipping her customary afternoon nap. That done, at bedtime she is to be deposited in a cot in the hotel room allocated to the children. Within the cot, a large assortment of essential bedtime apparatus is to be distributed. This paraphernalia includes such items as a book, several soft toys, and a threadbare blanky approaching molecular decomposition. The latter item is deemed the most essential; she has yet to ever fall asleep without it. It was known by Deidra and thus the entire family as a "moofie."

The success of the bedtime ritual is based on Deidra's willingness to be enchanted by all of the enticements positioned around the central sleeping area of her cot. At home, she'd begin by talking to her soft toys and perhaps sing them a few songs. Next, she turns pages in the book provided, reciting the gathering of toys a story. If all goes to plan, the scene concludes when a sleepy Deidra locates the stained and disintegrating rag known as "moofie," curls up with it, and descends into sleep.

The action plan at the Maracaibo hotel is put into effect. Mrs. Douglas deposits Deidra into the cot in the kids' room. She remains with the infant, flipping pages of a picture book. The remaining children and Mr. Douglas retreat into the parents' room to wait. The kids seat themselves on the beds in the parents' room to watch television with the volume turned down. The plan appears to be working. Despite the alien surroundings, Deidra, having missed out on her usual afternoon nap, opts to fall asleep almost instantly. After a quick peek around the connecting door, Mr. and Mrs. Douglas sneak out for their evening of carousing, leaving the four awake children flickering in the reflection of the television.

Venezuelan television of this day provides the viewer with a choice of two channels. Each channel attempts to intersperse some severely edited programming between commercials to hint to the viewer that, with some perseverance, there is a remote chance of being entertained. The main reason for editing the programming is to ensure sufficient time for whatever commercials have to be run during the show. Secondary reasons are to remove any sexual or blasphemous content from imported programming. The Venezuelan television industry relies on the novelty of television itself to attract and retain viewers.

There are three categories of programming. Baseball is number one. It is shown year round, from the United States during the summer and locally-sourced for the "winterball" season. The next category is Latin romances known as "telenovelas," what North Americans might call "soap opera." These never-ending melodramas originate from all of Latin America, from the Rio Grande to Tierra del Fuego.

The final category is programming imported from North America and dubbed into Spanish by the same two persons. Such is their talent that, between them, they are able to undertake every human voice from Popeye to John Wayne, Tweety Bird to Elizabeth Taylor. Furthermore, this dubbing duo possesses the ability to enhance the dramatic tenure of any dialogue, elevating it well beyond the limitations of its original form. Words are screeched out in raucous ranting that fill every frame of film with heart-rending emotion, however mundane the onscreen action. The same two persons are also under contract to provide the vocal content of every commercial run on Venezuelan television.

To the four children sitting in front the television in their parents' hotel room, television itself is a novelty. To them, even movies are a rare treat. In his life to date, Dylan has only seen two films. For a while, the children are in awe of the grainy, flickering black and white images before them. Because of the low volume and unfamiliarity of the Spanish language outside of a school playground, they are unable to distinguish the commercials from the drama being aired. However, for a while, they're so entranced by the images before them that it doesn't really matter.

The hotel is fiercely air-conditioned. The children are unused to this adjustment in temperature and would have readily exchanged it for their more accustomed 80 degree plus ambience. Genevieve sits in the center of the one of two beds in the room, knees up and propped to a sitting position by pillows. She is wearing a housecoat over pajamas. Sitting one on either side of her are Daniel and Domenic. She has used her housecoat and a protective arm to envelope each boy. Each snuggles into her embrace and has never felt cozier.

Dylan sits by himself on the other bed in the room. Here, he has no choice but to wear his pajama top and, even with this garment on, he's shivering in the air conditioning. Like Genevieve, he is propped into a semi-sitting position, leaning into pillows, but his body is twisted away from the television. The novelty of television only held him captive for five minutes or so. Had there been a baseball game, it might have kept his attention longer. Instead, he's attempting to read a book in the flickering light and in no time has trouble keeping his eyes open.

After both the younger boys have nodded off into sleep, Genevieve suggests that they should all go to bed. It had been a long drive and they would require plenty of energy to make the most of the swimming pool the following day. They transfer to the other room on tippy-toe so as not to wake Deidra. This requires waking Daniel and Domenic. The four sleepy kids creep into the darkened room, illuminated by a thin shard of light from the doorway connecting their room with the parents'. Daniel point-blank refuses to get into his assigned sleeping place in the bed with Dylan. Why should he not continue sleeping with Genevieve and Domenic? Was there not room enough for three in the bed? Genevieve shrugs her shoulders. "It's all the same to me," she says.

However, Daniel's noisy protestations have wakened Deidra. The infant uses the cot's upright bars to leverage herself to a standing position. She stands there like a little chimp in a cage for a few moments, silently surveying the situation. She's evidently rested just enough to recharge her energy reserves. Now she has a second wind, enough to extend this day a little longer. Some socializing might be nice!

Daniel and Domenic nuzzle into bed on either side of Genevieve. A heavy load of blankets protect them from the frigid chills of the air conditioner. The air conditioner drones soothingly. What could be cozier?

Deidra's cot is located in front of the bed Dylan is occupying. Sleeping in a roomful of kids is novel to Deidra, who sleeps alone at home. She calls out Dylan's name in her usual way: "Dilla, Dilla."

Genevieve responds. "Go to sleep Deidra, it's very late and we're all in bed." "Dilla, Dilla," she calls out, beginning to whimper. Dylan ignores her. Five minutes of muted crying pass. Genevieve gets out of bed and approaches the cot. Deidra immediately retreats out of reach to the opposite side of the cot and bellows at the top of her lungs: "Dilla!" Genevieve is confused. Babies aren't supposed to do this to her. Is she not every child's favorite sitter? What's happened? Deidra evades Genevieve's outstretched arms and is working up a head of steam. Now she's close to bringing the roof down with her screaming.

Genevieve looks over to Dylan. "Dylan, help me." While Dylan would have been quite prepared to attempt sleep as Deidra bawled, a gentle plea for help from Genevieve is impossible to ignore. Pretending reluctance, he sits up in the bed and walks on his knees to its edge. As he approaches, Deidra throws out both arms toward him, still screaming his name. Genevieve observes the scene, puzzled. Dylan stands on the end of the bed and lifts his screaming sister up and out of it. The infant grasps onto her brother as if she's just been rescued from a raging sea. She immediately ceases wailing and begins hyperventilating to replace some of the air her lungs had missed out on while crying. Now Dylan is in charge.

"I'll take her into bed with me," he reassures Genevieve with a sense of importance that is new to him. Genevieve isn't so sure. Once again, she attempts to approach Deidra to get the infant into the arms of her rightful babysitter. Deidra is having none of this. She smacks out at Genevieve and turns her head away from her. Genevieve nods her head and agrees that Dylan should take his sister into bed with him.

"Sleep near the center if you're going to keep her in with you," she advises. "We don't want her to fall out of bed." Happy that she'd at least got in the last word, she climbs back into bed between Domenic and Daniel who, having been awake for the recent events, are both content to surrender to Genevieve's motherly embrace as she returns to her place between them.

Dylan, with Deidra clasped to his breast, wriggles his way into the center of the bed. He enshrouds himself and his sister with the bed covers. Deidra is already almost asleep. Although the weight of the infant feels heavy on his chest, he's reluctant to roll her off lest she awake once again. Yes, he'd have preferred to be sharing a bed with Genevieve. On the other hand, he's aware that he's notched a sort of victory with the knowledge that Genevieve would rather be in his position. You win some, you lose some, he thinks. If he can't have Genevieve, then why not settle for her envy?

An hour later, Rhianna Douglas looks into the bedroom and surmises the scene. For a moment, she considers attempting to retrieve Deidra from Dylan and getting her back into the cot. But she thinks the better of it. It might be a good thing for Dylan to begin to learn how to be a big brother.

The following morning, Dylan awakes as Genevieve lifts the covers to slide into bed with him. For a fleeting moment, Dylan thinks he might have wet the bed. Deidra is still lying on top of him in the same position she fell asleep in, dead to the world. Dylan is relieved: the wetness was caused by seepage from his sister's plastic diaper cover, which dampened his pajama top. Under the covers, Genevieve cuddles into Dylan and wraps her arm around Deidra. "Are you awake, Dylan?" she whispers in his ear.

"Yes," he responds quietly. "Deidra isn't, though. She's still sleeping. She's wet. It's leaked out."

This doesn't seem to bother Genevieve. "It's just a few drops of baby pee," she assures Dylan. Genevieve wriggles around to make sure no gaps remain between herself and her two charges, big and small. The movement stirs Deidra. She stretches out both arms then retracts them, balls her fists, and begins to rub the sleep out of both eyes. Another day is beginning.

Genevieve never did get an opportunity to save Dylan's soul. A short while after the Maracaibo trip, Dylan returns from school to discover that Genevieve visited earlier to say goodbye. His mom tells him that she and Genevieve had shared a cup of tea, after which the babysitter had said goodbye to Daniel, Domenic, and Deidra. Genevieve's family is returning to Montreal. Mom explains that Genevieve's papa is a specialty fireman and he's needed at a Montreal refinery.

Dylan is stunned by the news. After a few silent moments, he bursts into tears and sobs uncontrollably. His mother is alarmed. Is this a crush, some kind of puppy love? Who's in love at that age? He's seven years old, for goodness sake!

Panicking, she attempts to think of some way of consoling him. "Maybe we can drive to the airport and say goodbye," she suggests, hoping that she doesn't have to resort to this. "I don't think their flight actually leaves for another hour."

Dylan gulps to catch his breath. He nods in the affirmative to his mother. And while he doesn't in any way appear to be much consoled, he's no longer crying.

Dylan's two brothers are rounded up, his baby sister woken, and all are piled into the family Chevy. They drive at some velocity and the trip takes twenty minutes. Dylan's mother is not sure why she's doing this. Is it the shock of seeing Dylan burst into tears, her eldest who almost never cries for any reason these days? She thinks that she might be protecting her son's heart, but from what?

During the drive to the airport, Dylan becomes strangely subdued. He sits on the front bench seat alongside his mother, but his gaze is unfocused, directed outside the passenger side window. The local airstrip consists of a single runway and not much more than a shack for a terminal. It hosts half a dozen commuter flights to Caracas and Maracaibo per day. A twin propeller commuter aircraft is parked on the tarmac.

On arrival, Dylan lets himself out of the Chevrolet's front passenger door. While his mom attends to the business of un-harnessing kids from car seats, Dylan leaves them and, with some urgency, strides over to the terminal hut. He's familiar with the airport layout, having already passed through it himself several times previously. From the terminal gate door, he spots Genevieve and can see that she is part of a lazy procession of passengers ambling toward the boarding ramp abutting the aircraft. She's with her middle brother, the eighth grader he has seen once or twice in school, and two adults he presumes are her parents. The sight is strange; he's never envisioned Genevieve in the context of any family other than his own, even though she had routinely spoken of them. He knew there was an older brother in school back in Canada.

Genevieve is wearing a yellow dress. The dress and her hair are whipping around in the strong desert wind. She's doing her best to hold the dress down over her knees, but there's nothing she can do about her hair. Out there on the airport tarmac, Dylan no longer sees her as a big girl. She looks tiny surrounded by adults. One hand holds a carry-on bag, the other is still occupied holding her dress down against the fierce wind. Dylan observes from the terminal door, dumbstruck. He becomes aware of his mother approaching behind him with Deidra in her arms. Rhianna isn't sure why Dylan is just standing watching, but she quickly realizes there is not much time if a goodbye is to be said. She yells over the top of Dylan's head, "Genevieve!"

So loud is Dylan's mother's voice that every person on the tarmac turns to face the terminal hut. Genevieve turns, too. Her face at first looks confused, but then it lights up. Dylan's heart thumps. Genevieve deposits her carry-on bag with her mother and runs toward Dylan's family. Genevieve's brother, mother, and father remain positioned on the tarmac, watching the girl run toward the assembled Douglas family at the terminal gate.

Genevieve gushes, "How special it is for you all to have all come to say good-bye. And you too, Dylan, how precious." Now she's crying. Mrs. Douglas, Deidra perched on her hip, wanders over to introduce herself to Genevieve's parents. She's previously only spoken to the mother on the phone, and never actually met either one. Genevieve bends down to hug each of Dylan's siblings in turn, intermittently wiping tears from her eyes. While she does this, Dylan studies Genevieve's family. He tries to imagine Genevieve sitting on her mama's lap while being told the real secret of how babies are made. Papa is standing aside looking bored. So is Genevieve's big brother. He just wants to get on the plane. It looks like Dylan's mom is doing all the talking and Genevieve's folks are just being polite.

Finally, it's Dylan's turn to be hugged. His mother has rejoined them. Dylan knows that his eyes must still be red from crying earlier, but he does his best to ensure no more tears flow now. He focuses on the airplane, honing in on its every detail. Big boys don't cry, at least according to his dad, and if there's one person in this world Dylan wants to see him as a big boy, it's his beloved babysitter. Of course, it doesn't matter if she cries, because she's a girl and that's allowed. Genevieve's wet cheek touches his and her arms encircle him.

"Your plane is a Convair 440," he informs her, only half returning the hug. "It has Allison turboprop engines. It will take sixty-five minutes to get you to Caracas. There, you'll get on a big plane, probably a Boeing."

Genevieve is baffled. Her friend seems to be talking nonsense. "What is this Convair?" she asks. But there's no time to wait for a response. She hugs him a final time with all her strength. "I gave your mama our address in Montreal. Write me. I miss you already. We are friends forever." She grasps his face with both hands and whispers in his ear. "Learn to say some prayers so you can be saved. We can be saved together." Her loud sobs prevent this from being a proper whisper, however, so the blurted words are audible to anyone around. Wiping her eyes, she kisses his cheek, turns, and runs back to join her waiting mother and father. She reclaims her carry-on bag from her mother, wiping her eyes some more.

Genevieve's goodbyes on the tarmac leave the Levesque family at the end of the procession to the aircraft boarding ramp. They are the final passengers to board. Slowly, the family ascends the stepped ramp onto the aircraft. Genevieve's mama has her arm around her daughter's shoulder as they climb the steps. At the top of the ramp, Genevieve turns and blows a kiss to a world she'll probably never see again. Then she disappears into the fuselage of the aircraft. She's the last person to board it.

Dylan wants to see the plane take off. There are no tears now. He appears to his mother to be set on suppressing any outward signs of emotion, his father's influence no doubt. This has the effect of making her son appear overwhelmed. She wonders how you provide a seven-year-old with tools to deal more comfortably with the experience he had just undergone. Yes, they'll stay to watch this airplane take off and fly into the distance. Maybe it would be cathartic, like the witnessing of a corpse revealed open casket at a wake.

Dylan's mother is increasingly having difficulty understanding Dylan these days. Perhaps she should spend more time with him, but this is easier said than done. Dylan's nature is to cede attention to his younger siblings. And with three of them to care for, combined with Dylan's inclination to retreat rather than compete for attention, getting a private moment with him isn't so easy.

When the departing aircraft has diminished to a dot in the eastern sky, Dylan's mother places her free arm on her son's shoulder to guide him toward the car. Similar to the journey out to the airport, Dylan just stares out the car window. Halfway back, his mother asks him, "What about this Sunday school thing? Is this something you really want to do?" The question is put to him tentatively. She was reminded of Genevieve's Sunday school plan when she whispered to Dylan about praying. Dylan responds wordlessly by shaking his head in the negative. What would be the point if he couldn't go with Genevieve? His mother is relieved. "Well thank God for that, anyway!"

After another pause, Dylan's mom begins speaking to no one in particular. "She was such a nice girl. She loved being around the little ones, even though she seemed younger than the other sitters. I always trusted her." Pause. "And it was a bonus that you liked her. That was a first for a sitter, huh?"

Dylan nods in silent agreement.

Six weeks later, Dylan receives a postcard from Genevieve. The hurt of her departure has almost healed by this time, but the postcard jolts him with a painful aftershock. On the front of the postcard is a picture of a big church. The church is in Montreal. He studies the words on the writing side of the card. They are printed in a careful, neat script.

"Dear Dylan," it reads. *"It is not so easy for me to write in English once again, here*

we mostly speak only French. Life is swell. But it is COLD!! You would have to wear your jammy tops every nite if you moved to Montreal. School is swell and I have many new friends. My friend Gloria and me are going to the movies today. Here we get to see movies whenever. There is also TV. It is French but some English. Write me if you have time. I miss you and your folks. We had fun. Your friend, Genevieve XXX". The words on the postcard seem alien to Dylan, as if they were scripted from a voice not Genevieve's.

Dylan's mother studies her son as he carefully reads the contents of the postcard. He appears to digest each word many times over. His expression is set to betray no emotion. Finally, he puts the card down and announces that he wants to send a postcard to Genevieve. His mother grabs the postcard. There is no return address.

"Didn't Genevieve give you her address?" he asks, though there's a pointed directness to the question that turns it into more of an accusation.

"I'm not sure where I put it," his mother responds. "I'll see if I can find it."

A week later, Dylan reminds his mother about the address again. She confesses that she must have misplaced it. But this is it. Dylan never mentions Genevieve again.

4. BUNNY

Two days after Genevieve boarded a Convair 440 and flew out of Dylan's life, Bonnie and Bunny Forslund drop in to visit Mrs. Douglas. The reason for the Forslund females' visit is to solicit the Saturday babysitter position vacated by the departed Genevieve. The post is potentially lucrative for a cash-starved preteen, and although the hourly rate is pretty much standard, the Douglases are known to be regular Saturday night partiers who aren't shy about staying out well into the early hours.

Bonnie Forslund undertakes most of the talking. Rhianna Douglas is unsure about the proposition. There is something about Bunny that does not set her mind at ease. Bonnie points out that Bunny is the holder of a Girl Guides babysitter badge. As such, her daughter is a *qualified babysitter* - something that could not be said of Jeanie.

"Who's Jeanie?" asks Mrs. Douglas innocently.

Bonnie is forced to explain. "The foreign girl you were using before. I don't know to pronounce whatever it was *she* called herself." The fact that they are all foreign in this country seems to have escaped Bonnie.

She continues: "Bunny needs a little responsibility, a chance to prove herself. She has all the right tools. She has been raised a God-fearing Lutheran girl, just like her mother and father. And how she adores children! You won't be sorry! Bill and I never go out Saturday nights – if there are any problems, Bunny can phone and we'll be on the doorstep within ten minutes."

Mrs. Douglas considers this. With some measure of protest in her voice, she says, "Deidra has only just turned twelve months. She can be quite a handful. And besides Deidra, there are three other children to mind."

Bonnie intercedes again on behalf of her daughter. "Bunny is actually older than Jeanie and she has been raised right with good American values." The inference that Genevieve was not raised up right seems like a low blow, but despite suspecting that Bonny Forslund might be attempting to bully her, the better side of Mrs. Douglas's nature prevails. Perhaps Bunny did deserve a chance to prove herself. Besides, these days Deidra was getting on a lot better with Dylan. What could possibly go wrong?

Another Saturday night! When his mom informs him that Bunny would be over to babysit that night, Dylan is incredulous. He despises Bunny, who has a reputation as a playground bully. He hangs his mouth open in exaggerated disbelief.

"Everyone picks on that poor girl just because she is a little overweight and wears glasses. It's not fair," responds his mother. "I want you to be nice to her. Treat her like you did Genevieve. And keep a special eye out for Deidra and your brothers while you're at it; they don't know her yet. Deidra will be sleeping when she arrives. So probably will Daniel and Domenic." Dylan responds by scowling.

It is almost pitch dark when Dylan returns after the Saturday baseball marathon. As usual, he enters through the garage door and slips into the kitchen, making sure the screen door does not slam. He wants to delay meeting Bunny as long as possible. The house is quiet. Silently, he goes to the refrigerator and drinks from the water bottle. Next, he opens the oven door to remove a dinner plate covered by an aluminum plate warmer. This done, he sits and begins to consume an unpalatable fare of desiccated fish fingers and fries. He is halfway through eating the meal before Bunny enters the kitchen. In the context of the familiar surroundings of his kitchen, the babysitter appears even more vastly proportioned than he remembers. He acknowledges her with a nod, but no greeting. She shuffles over to the kitchen table.

"Your mother said you were to be home by six thirty and it's now gone seven fifteen," she admonishes, frowning at her wristwatch. Dylan forks a huge load of crispy fries into his mouth to avoid responding verbally.

Sitting herself down at the kitchen table, Bunny tries a new tack. "Don't worry, I am not going to tell. Dylan, I want us to be friends. You know that Jeanie was one of my best friends." This is news to Dylan and he doubts its truth. Bunny continues. "She was the one who recommended me to your mother."

Although Dylan thinks this is also unlikely to be true, he resists the temptation to refute what Bunny has told him and continues eating. Please make her go away, Dylan says to himself.

Sure enough, his baby sister Deidra comes to the rescue. The infant begins by whimpering barely audibly. Bunny looks toward the bedroom area. She says nothing. The whimpering turns into more persistent crying. Dylan fixes his gaze on Bunny, who continues to sit at the kitchen table, perhaps hoping that no intervention on her part is going to be required.

"She won't stop now," Dylan informs her. "She probably has to be changed."

With that Bunny sighs, reluctantly gets to her feet, and shuffles off to the source of the crying.

Dylan finishes the remains of his meal. The intensity of Deidra's bawling seems to have increased since Bunny's departure from the kitchen. He deposits his dinner plate in the sink, grabs a comic book, and sits back down, attempting to read. The howling continues unabated. After a quarter of an hour of listening to the ruckus, he decides he'd better check things out. He enters the living room.

Bunny is holding Deidra at an arm's length grasp. She is dandling the child up and down, perhaps hoping that this will send her back to sleep. Deidra is red-faced, screaming, and vigorously struggling to free herself from Bunny. The instant Dylan enters the room, she stretches her arms out for rescue. "Dilla, Dilla," she pleads. Bunny happily surrenders the screaming infant to Dylan's arms. This has an immediate calming effect on the youngster, who nuzzles her face into Dylan's shoulder, her wailing turning into sobs. The cause of the crying is immediately apparent to Dylan.

"She needs her diaper changed," Dylan informs Bunny. "When you change her she'll stop crying and go back to sleep."

"That baby's shit her diaper," Bunny responds with particular venom, squinting her eyes. "She can wait until your mother gets home to be changed. I'm not doing it. She stinks!"

"That's what babysitters do," responds Dylan resolutely. "They change diapers!"

"Not this one," declares Bunny with finality.

The stench from his sister's diaper all but causes Dylan to retch. Despite having witnessed diaper changing a few times, he has never actually had to do this himself. Now, it seems he has no choice. He carries Deidra into her bedroom and places her on the change table. This is going to be ugly, he tells himself. Semi-liquid excrement oozes out at the legs and the top of the plastic diaper cover. It had been seeping through Deidra's sleeper suit and has already soiled Dylan's T-shirt and forearms. The boy is breathing shallowly, fighting an inclination to throw up. He considers his options. Deidra is now subdued and shows no signs of being upset any more. In fact, his sister appears to be studying her brother, wondering how he is going to approach this challenge. This provides him with thinking time. He then has a good idea. Maybe a great idea!

"Deidra, we'll go out onto the patio. We can get you hosed off with the garden hose. That way we can get you cleaned up without making too much mess."

Deidra seems to think this is a pretty good idea, too. "Hose, hose!" she exclaims, looking up at her brother and pointing to the outdoor patio. He picks his sister up and carries her out onto the patio. He snaps on the patio lights.

"What the hell are you doing?" asks Bunny in an accusing tone. The babysitter has by now got to her feet. She follows, but keeps her distance. Dylan does not re-spond. He plants his sister standing on the patio tiles. Deidra seems to understand perfectly and buys into the plan with enthusiasm. This is an exciting new way of having a diaper changed. She assists Dylan in his efforts to remove first the sleeper suit, followed by the plastic diaper cover. Deidra even points out the location of snap buttons and pins to help her brother out. Finally, the clothing is removed. Dylan cannot imagine how it is possible for so much putrid matter to come out of a being so small and sometimes almost cute. Suppressing gags, he turns the garden hose on.

Deidra considers this to be a fun new game. She giggles with delight and stomps her feet up and down. The cleanup is executed in barely any time at all. Dylan hoses the solid contents of the diaper from the tiles into the grass. Now he can focus on the details. Excrement seems to have worked its way into every crease and crevice in Deidra's body, from her chest down to her knees. Bunny stands glaring at them from the screen door arms crossed, observing.

"Get me a towel," Dylan instructs the babysitter. He is in charge now.

Scowling, Bunny leaves and returns with a towel. "You have shit on your T-shirt," she informs him with disdain. Dylan removes his shirt, dumps it on the tiles and hoses it down along with the diaper and sleeper suit. It does cross his mind that it was perhaps strange that nobody had thought of this method of cleaning up babies before. It surely is easier than attempting the procedure on change tables and bathtubs. And there's the extra bonus of the baby involved in the procedure enjoying it, too. He shuts the hose off, takes the towel off Bunny, and swaddles his naked sister, hoisting her into the air. This elicits some squeals of pleasure from the infant.

"I can take her now," says Bunny. Dylan proffers the child toward her, but Deidra is having none of this. As Bunny approaches the toddler, Deidra's face contorts: she opens her mouth wide and delivers a scream loud enough to shatter glass. The scream, along with the general commotion of the previous half hour, has now woken both of Dylan's brothers. The pair wanders out in pajamas to investigate. Bunny orders them back to bed. She makes it her business to escort them.

Dylan tucks the towel-swaddled Deidra under his arm as if he is carrying a football and carries her to her bedroom, dumping her feet first onto the floor. Now that he has dealt with removing and cleaning one diaper, putting on a fresh one presents another challenge. How does it go? Fold the square into an isosceles triangle. Center the kid with the right angle between the legs. Fold inward to connect up the three angles. That's the easy part of the operation. He constructs the triangle and places it in on the floor. Deidra catches on to what is required. She assists by lying down and positioning herself in more or less the right location. Deidra enjoys showing Dylan that she can help, too; this, for her, is a familiar procedure. She gestures to Dylan as to what is required next, namely enclosing the diaper. That accomplished, there is now the dangerous problem of safety pins. No way is Dylan going to attempt to install these. But what to do instead? A light bulb illuminates in his mind: why not use a couple of band-aids? He enlists his sister's help in holding the folded diaper clamped in position on her tummy while he applies the band-aids. Still lying down, Deidra claps her hands to celebrate the success of this new method of fastening a diaper.

Dylan lifts his sister to deposit her onto the change table to complete the operation, but the instant she is vertical, the diaper falls to the floor. Dylan is quick to deduce that the problem is either a lack of stickiness or the short length of the band-aids. A longer section of adhesive tape is required. He's about to resort to Scotch tape when he recalls the black electrical tape his father keeps in the garage. This is about the stickiest tape he knows of. Once again, the diaper is folded into a triangle and placed on the floor. Deidra knows the routine now. For a second time, she centers herself into the triangle. "Deidra, I want you to lie here very still. Don't move until I get back. I have to go to the garage and get some tape."

Dylan runs out to the garage, locates the electrical tape, and returns. His sister has not moved, not an inch. It seems as if Deidra is just as determined as Dylan to make this new method of diaper changing a success. This time, Dylan makes a belt of the black electrical tape to ensure the diaper remains in place and winds the tape around twice. No way this diaper is going to come off by accident! Putting the plastic diaper cover and sleeper suit on after that is a cinch. All that remains is the challenge of getting his sister back into the crib without her screeching her lungs out again. But all this brotherly attention has obviously won some points. When informed that she's to be put back into her crib, Deidra's face initially contorts to unleash protest. She wants to stay up and continue having fun.

"Please, Deidra," her brother implores, "be good for me. I have to get cleaned up. I promise I'll play with you tomorrow." As he makes the promise, Dylan realizes it will have to be met in some way or another. Deidra's comprehension is spot on and her memory acute as an elephants'. The strategy works. Deidra settles immediately.

Now Dylan needs to take a bath. There is something about Bunny that makes him feel uneasy about this. There's no lock on the kids' bathroom door. Sure, he could use his parents' bathroom, but then his father would likely go ballistic if he ever found out. He looks into the living room. Bunny has obviously got his brothers back to bed and is now occupied by flipping the pages of a comic book. She's sitting on the sofa, hunched over like an orangutan. She ignores him. Dylan goes to the bathroom. He draws a bath and gets into the tub, sinking into the warm water.

A few moments later, Bunny appears at the door. She crosses her arms and looks him over. "Get out," Dylan orders her aggressively, "I don't want you in here."

Bunny continues to stare him down, propping her body into the doorframe. "Dylan, I know all about the games you and Jeanie used to get up to. She told me everything during a Guides campout. I think you are both sinful and I'm not the only one who does. You will both end up in hell. I'm thinking of telling your mother."

This announcement stuns Dylan into silence. From his sitting position, he slides his body under the water in the tub so that only his face is not submerged. He stares at the ceiling. What shocks him most about Bunny's revelation is the notion that Genevieve should have told anyone about their secret times together. And why would she have told Bunny of all people? Confusion lingers in his mind about what happened between him and Genevieve because it involved things that cannot be spoken of. Were Genevieve and he really being that bad? Probably - he would be mortified if his mother ever found out, and he cannot begin to imagine how his father would react.

Bunny speaks again. "Jeanie lied about your dinky. You have one of the tiniest dinkies I have ever seen," she declares. "I have seen babies with bigger dinkies than yours." Dylan continues to focus on the ceiling. He senses imminent danger, but he doesn't have a clue about how he should react other than to implore a higher entity not recognized in the Douglas household with a plea that she'll go away.

Movement adjacent to the tub jars his thoughts. Bunny has undressed and is standing at the side of the bathtub, completely naked other than the bulbous eyeglasses she requires to see anything further than a foot distant. To Dylan, she is a terrifying sight. Bunny's naked flesh is pasty white and variously blotched with angry red sores. She has breasts, but whether this is due to the approach of womanhood or rampant obesity is impossible to determine. Just above an otherwise bare crotch, a scattering of coarse hairs mark Bunny's progress into puberty.

After a split second of frozen mobility, Dylan thrusts himself upward onto his feet, splashing bathwater out of the tub. Simultaneously, Bunny advances one foot into the bathtub and, with an agility that defies her bulk, jams her forearm across the boy's throat, pinning him into the tiled wall behind the tub. In almost the same instant, she grabs Dylan's scrotum and deftly moves her fingers into a position that threatens to crush his balls. Dylan gags, the pressure and pain at his neck, along with fear of further grief to his testicles, causing a reaction in him that he cannot control. His entire body convulses as he retches. Whether it is solely out of revulsion for the sight before him, fear of the predicament he faces, or from his earlier exertions in suppressing the vomit reflex while changing a fouled diaper, Dylan has finally reached his limit. He retches again, the contents of his stomach surging upwards towards his throat.

The way Dylan's body spasms alarms Bunny, so she relieves pressure she is applying to his neck. It's all Dylan needs. He gasps once, sucking air deep into his lungs, and then throws up with a projectile force. Vomit splatters all over Bunny, who screams and leaps backward, her hands thrown up in an attempt to shield her naked body. Dylan draws another breath and violently retches again. Vomit pours from his mouth and nose and even attempts to exit from his eyes and ears. The puke is fluorescent green – the cooler of liquid consumed during the Saturday baseball marathon was Kool-Aid in flavor and green in color. Without doubt, green food coloring was a dominant pigment within the human digestive system.

Oblivious to the shrieking and cursing Bunny directs at him, naked Dylan, weakened by throwing up, stumbles out of the tub, lifts the toilet lid, and kneels down to puke over the bowl. By now, however, the retching is mostly without product other than tears. Meanwhile, Bunny is occupied in attempting to wipe the puke from her body using a towel. Most of the solid content of the vomit no longer adheres to her flesh. However, a deficit of pigment in her skin has made it especially vulnerable to the electric green color imparted to it by a gallon of Kool-Aid puke. The door opens. Daniel and Domenic stand in the doorway, mouths open wide. Each little boy holds a blanky in one hand. Wide-eyed, they observe the scene before them.

Bunny turns to them and screams. "Get back to bed, you little brats!" Frightened, both burst into tears and escape back to the safety of their bedroom.

On receiving a phone call from her besieged daughter, true to her word Bonnie Forslund is indeed on the scene within ten minutes. By the time her mother arrives, Bunny has managed to mostly clean herself up and squeeze back into her shorts and shirt. Poor Bunny meets Bonnie at the front door of the Douglas home in tears. Big, blubbery sobs inhibit coherent speech, and Bonnie does her best to comfort her distraught daughter. With difficulty, she attempts to piece together what has transpired; there are so many inconsistencies in Bunny's tale of agony and woe. It is, however, immediately obvious to her that Dylan is the culprit. Mrs. Forslund strides off to the bathroom to remonstrate with "the little devil."

By the time Bonnie Forslund enters the bathroom, Dylan has cleaned himself up. He stands at the bathroom sink wearing nothing but pajama bottoms and is about to brush his teeth. The boy's face is flushed from puking, his eyes reddened, and his hair damp and disheveled. He does not appear to recognize her. Bonnie is awed at the chaos in bathroom: the bathtub is filled with a putrid green liquid, there is green puke all over the floor, and it even coats the side of the toilet bowl. In addition, four or five towels, a couple stained with green, are lying on the tile floor. There is an acrid odor of fish and puke.

Mrs. Forslund is maddened with rage. She has a good idea who will be cleaning up this mess. For an instant, she considers physically punishing the horrible child, but then thinks that that this might not go down so well with Rhianna Douglas, a woman who comes equipped with a sharp tongue when pushed to use it. Instead, she lays into the boy verbally.

"You are far too old to throw up without getting to the toilet first! You disgusting child!" She glares at him, her voice filled with venom as she continues. "You should know better. What a pathetic example you are to your brothers and sister. I'm going to make sure your mother hears all about this."

Dylan is too fatigued to protest. He turns back to the sink, ignoring Mrs. Forslund, and applies some toothpaste to a toothbrush before slowly brushing his teeth.

Mrs. Forslund kicks the soiled towels into a pile. "I'm not a maid," she snaps. "There's a limit to what a babysitter can be expected to do. Or the mother of a babysitter, for that matter. Bunny has been raised as a decent Lutheran girl. She wouldn't have a clue about how to deal with situations that boys such as *you* create." Indeed, Bunny is now standing at the bathroom door, her arms folded in self-righteous indignation. A babysitter has rights, too. Her mother would now show this nasty little boy what was what!

Bonny Forslund identifies with her foot what appears to be the least soiled of the towels, picks it up with her thumb and index finger and, at arm's length, offers it to Dylan. "You made this revolting mess," she accuses the boy, "you can at least do something toward cleaning it up."

"I can clean it all up myself if you just go away and leave me alone," responds Dylan wearily.

Bonnie Forslund interprets Dylan's response as being surly. "You ungrateful brat," she snaps, "I'm called out of home in the middle of the night because chaos has broken out and you give me that kind of sass." Now she really wants to smack him. That's what she would have done with her own - they were raised right!

Suddenly, she changes her tune. What if he's actually ill? She crosses the bathroom and feels Dylan's forehead, testing his temperature. Fever or no, this boy would be communicating with his mother at some point and what he reported would be critical. It could impact on Bunny's future employability as a sitter.

"I think you have a fever. I want you to go straight to bed. Bunny and I will clean up."

Dylan is too weak to make more than a token protest. Mrs. Forslund leads Dylan off to the boys' bedroom and makes sure he mounts the bunk ladder safely to his bed. When she has left, his brother Daniel whispers, "Are you okay, Dylan?" Dylan whispers back that he is. Then both brothers creep over to Dylan's bunk, ascend the ladder and climb into bed with him on the wall side. It's a little crowded, but it's safe. Evil is afoot.

Dylan does not sleep. He hears muffled verbal exchanges between Mrs. Forslund and Bunny coming from the hallway. Time passes and he is next aware of his mother and father returning home. Is it really that late? More hushed, indecipherable conversation from the hall. Then his mother strides into the bedroom, steps on the lower rung of the bunk ladder, and feels his forehead. Dylan thinks it circumspect to feign deep sleep. Foremost in his mind is Bunny's threat to tell his mother about the "secrets" he and Genevieve share.

Rhianna, having determined that her son is not at death's door, cannot help but note that the three boys are sleeping together. She blinks, surprised. This has not happened for a while, not for at least a couple of years. It has been a long time since Dylan has been upset enough to deign to sleep with his younger brothers.

"Dylan, wake up," she whispers sharply, "I want to know what has been going on here this evening."

Groaning, Dylan responds. "Nothing, Mom. I just threw up. I wasn't feeling too good." For emphasis, he adds: "My sick was green."

"I'm coming back," responds his mother, "don't go back to sleep yet." And she's gone, the door closing quietly behind her. A minute later, Dylan hears a car engine start in the driveway. Instant relief floods into him as he concludes that the Forslund mother and daughter have departed. Rhianna returns. "Are you sure you are feeling okay, Dylan?" she asks.

Dylan can't help himself. He begins to cry, tears streaming from his eyes. His mother embraces him and this just opens the floodgates wider. But, try she might, his mother cannot get him to say anything of consequence. "I was just sick, Mom", he says, "I feel better now."

"Do you want to get up for a mug of hot chocolate and a chat, Dylan?" she asks him. "It might help you to sleep."

"No thanks, Mommy, I just want to sleep. I'll feel better in the morning."

"Did Deidra wake up?"

"Yeah, but she went right back to sleep."

Dylan says nothing more. He'll do whatever it takes to avoid Bunny's disclosure of whatever it is Genevieve and he did that was so wrong.

At the age of a little over one year, Deidra has a vocabulary sufficient to express any thought or feeling that has ever crossed her mind. She engages in long conversations embellished with compound sentences and an arsenal of gesticulations and facial expressions. Persons listening to Deidra's chatter might have interpreted it to be mere gibberish, but it all made perfect sense to Deidra.

It was also a fact that what made perfect sense to Deidra could only be deciphered by certain persons. Her brothers, Daniel and Domenic, understood around one hundred and twenty words of the Deidra vocabulary. They often had to be relied on to interpret when Deidra became infuriated at having to repeat herself for the nth time. Mrs. Douglas was cognizant of possibly fifty words in the Deidra lexicon, meaning that she functioned at about the same level of comprehension as Genevieve - that is, when Genevieve had been around. Dylan was less capable and could truly only grasp something in the region of twenty Deidra words. The infant's father, Mr. Douglas, and most of the rest of the world, were able to understand absolutely nothing that Deidra uttered. With this much reason, Deidra is thus inclined to think of her father and most persons outside of her family as morons. Especially motherly females who responded to Deidra's intelligent chit-chat with goo-gooing baby talk. These fell into the worst category of moron.

When Deidra awakes the day after the Bunny babysit debacle, Mrs. Douglas sleepily enters the nursery and goes about getting the child up. She removes the girl's sleeper suit and is confronted by a wet diaper taped up with a crude belt of black electrical tape.

"Strange," she thinks; she was sure that Bonnie Forslund had credited her daughter with changing the diaper. The use of black electrical tape suggested Dylan's handiwork. Mrs. Douglas asks Deidra who changed her diaper. Deidra then relates the entire story of how Dylan had changed her soiled diaper the night before, with masterful technique and, in addition, invented an entirely new method of cleaning her up. This all took place on the patio and involved the use of a garden hose. She further advises her mother that although her diaper is now only wet, if she wants to use Dylan's innovative method of cleaning her up then Deidra is game for the idea. Deidra is willing to show her mother exactly how to do this right now. She grabs Rhianna's hand, intending to lead her out onto the patio.

Mrs. Douglas understands enough of what Deidra is telling her to know that all had not gone smoothly the night before. It seems that there might be a different version to the story related by Bonnie Forslund. First, Mrs. Douglas informs Deidra that, as fun as Dylan's method of changing a diaper might be, the Mommy method of doing this is to prevail. Resignedly, Deidra shrugs her shoulders. What Mrs. Douglas really wants to understand are those parts of Deidra's story that defeat her comprehension. Daniel and Domenic might be able to help. Soon enough, both younger boys wander into the bedroom as she is finishing up with Deidra.

"Did you boys have fun last night?" she asks after planting a kiss onto each of their cheeks. Both boys turn and look at each other. Daniel, the elder of the two, announces, "That Bunny has a big bottom, it is the biggest bottom in the world. We saw it bare. It was enormous." He fully extends his arms horizontally so that his mom can get a measure of just how large this bottom is.

More thoughtful, Domenic pitches in. "She is mean, too. She shouts at everyone." Now Deidra elaborates in language that only Daniel and Domenic can properly understand. Mrs. Douglas is forced to interrupt.

"Whoa," she says stopping Deidra mid-sentence. Turning to Daniel she asks him, "Where was Bunny when you took a look at her bare bum?"

"In the bathroom. With Dylan. He upchucked. It was green upchuck. She was shouting at Dylan. Then she shouted at us."

Rhianna Douglas enters the boys' bedroom. Dylan is still sleeping in the upper bunk bed. There are two sets of bunk beds in the room. Dylan usually slept in the upper bunk of one of the sets, while Daniel and Domenic were nominally assigned the two lower bunk stations. The two younger boys more often elected to sleep together in one of the lower bunks. She sets about stripping back the unmade bed, knowing that this activity is likely to make Dylan stir. When this happens, she crosses over the room to the waking boy and steps on the lower rung of the bunk ladder to kiss him on the forehead.

"Up sleepy head, time to get up for breakfast." Dylan sits up. "Did you change Deidra's diaper last night?" she asks her son directly.

Dylan is occupied in rubbing the sleep out of his eyes using both hands. "I don't remember, Mom," he says. "I think it was Bunny."

This response triggers a more aggressive approach from his mother. "Now, Dylan, I want you to be honest with me. You've never changed a diaper in your life before last night and you 'don't remember' whether this momentous event took place last night or not? I want to know what happened."

There being no more sleep to rub out of his eyes, Dylan looks at his mother. "I changed the diaper, Mom. Deidra had pooed – she was crying. Bunny wanted to leave her until you got home."

"There now, that wasn't so difficult was it? And I suppose it was your idea to use that black tape?"

"I was scared to use the pins," Dylan admits.

"Then you were just using your noggin," his mother says. "Well, you certainly impressed Deidra with your diaper changing expertise. She's asking for repeat performances!" Dylan looks sheepish and turns away. "Now maybe you can tell me why Bunny was undressed with you in the bathroom?" his mother continues.

Dylan thinks fast. "I threw up on her. She had to get the sick off her."

Mrs. Douglas considers this. There is a small flaw in Dylan's story. "Dylan, when we returned home, Bunny's clothes were clean and dry. How did this happen if she had taken them off to clean them up?"

Eventually, Mrs. Douglas has to settle for a compromised version of the events of the night that she realizes cannot be close to the real truth. She believes that she has to do this for Dylan's sake. She knows that she could have eventually probed the exact truth out of her son, but the cost of doing this is likely to prove damaging.

Bunny will not be invited to babysit again, Girl Guide babysitter badge or no. Dylan is adamant in imploring his mother not to contact Bunny or Mrs. Forslund about the ordeal. But his mother truly cannot figure out why Dylan appears to want to protect Bunny from any blame.

Selecting babysitters is suddenly not such a simple task. She has gone with a mother's instinct in not exploring the real truth behind Dylan's version of the story, something not yet spoken of. She fishes. "Has anything… unpleasant… happened with other babysitters? Something you might not have told me about?"

"No, Mom, the other babysitters have been great."

"I thought you hated them all until Genevieve?"

"What I meant was that nothing bad happened."

"You liked Genevieve a lot, did you not?"

Dylan looks down and nods agreement. "Did you and Genevieve get up to anything that you might be feeling guilty about?" Has Bunny told his mom something?

"No, Mom," he responds cautiously, unsure of his ability to hide anything from his mother. "We just liked doing the same things together. We read each other stories."

"But she was a lot older than you. And girls tend to be more mature than boys."

Dylan retreats into silence. Best to let his mother just wonder.

Dylan doesn't really need a pee. But Señorita González is such a bore and "gramática español " is his least favorite class. The rule is you are supposed to wait until recess for any kind of bathroom break. Dylan stares at the classroom clock. What is it about school clocks that makes them rotate so slowly? The minute hand jerks forward in one minute graduations on the clock scale, but each jerk forward seems to take five minutes to accomplish. A change of scenery is required.

"Señorita González, quisiera ir al baño inmediatamente." A few heads turn his way, every one of them both suspicious and envious. They know exactly what Dylan is about.

"Es una emergencia, Dylan?" responds Señorita González.

"Si Señorita González, tengo que orinar con un urgencia…"

"Bueno Dylan," interrupts Señorita González, "ve y apúrate!"

Free, Dylan escapes into the hallway. The restrooms are located at the east end of the school building, the other side of Kindergarten and Grade One. From Kindergarten and Grade One, the classrooms ascend in graduated sequence toward the west of the hallway. That meant that Grades Seven and Eight are located at the extreme west of the building. Between classes, the school hallway is peacefully unpopulated. Dylan meanders down the hall to the closest water fountain, pushes the cooler button, and sucks in a little of the icy water. Just as he finishes, he observes Bunny further west in the hallway, probably also heading to the washroom. Dylan accelerates his pace. On arriving at the boys' room, he pushes the swing door open and walks inside. He is standing before the urinal, about to unzip when he is suddenly aware of a shadow behind him.

It's too late. Bunny strikes using the same method she had successfully used on Dylan a few weeks earlier. Jamming her forearm under Dylan's chin, she pins him by the neck into the porcelain tiled wall behind the urinals, choking off his ability to scream out.

"You little squirt," she accuses the boy, her eyes ablaze. "You cost me my babysitting job. I knew I'd get you sooner or later." With that, she drives her knee upward into Dylan's groin. As the pain of the strike explodes upward into his stomach, Bunny removes her forearm from Dylan's neck. He collapses downward into the base of the urinal, writhing in pain. Nausea rises through his gut, further immobilizing him. "You tell anyone about this, and next time I'll make sure you're dead meat."

Before she exits, Gianni Calderone walks in, whistling. On seeing Bunny, he stops in his tracks amazed. "What the fuck are you doing in here?" Bunny brushes him out of her way and leaves.

Gianni Calderone often plays Saturday baseball with Dylan. He's a third grader whose family hails from New Jersey. This difference of a single year usually precludes any kind of communication within the walls of the school, but Dylan is a fellow baseball player and he is sitting doubled up in pain in the base of a urinal. Gianni goes over to help. He immediately assesses the situation.

"That fat bitch bagged you?" he asks Dylan, but it is not so much a question as a statement. "Breathe deep and slow," he advises. Gianni helps Dylan hobble away from the urinal. "You have piss all over your shorts, though it's probably mostly water. You can't go back to class, though; you'll be a laughing stock. You'll have to go home and change."

Dylan nods, still unable to speak.

"You shouldn't let that cow get away with that," says Gianni. "She'll only do it again, but it'd be dumb to tell a teacher; it'd be your word against hers. But you should get revenge before she gets another shot at you. In fact, I'm going to show you how to take out a fat fuck like Bunny."

While Dylan is recovering from being kneed in the balls, Gianni instructs him in the art of fist fighting. Specifically, on how to take out a "fat fuck."

"First, you have to make the right kind of fist. Keep the knuckles uneven. Next, you have to drive a punch the right way. Aim in the middle of the triangle made by her tits and her belly button," Gianni says. "That's the solar plexus. But you wanna drive your fist through all that blubber like you're aiming at her spine. That's what you want to hit. That means you gotta get as close as possible before winding up. Get your face into hers. Then let rip. It'll only take one punch. She'll drop like a stuck pig.

"But let me tell you the most important thing. You gotta take the initiative. Don't wait until she tries to beat up on you the next time. She's smart and she's strong, I mean, she outweighs you by like, three times. Get her at recess. She always hangs out in the shade under the eaves and she's usually by herself. Walk up to her. Make sure you don't give nothing away by the expression on your face. Don't say nothin' to her, either. Walk casual. Stick your face in hers and plant that punch as deep into her gut as you can lay it. It'll only take one. Then walk away, still casual. Say nothing. If you get caught, you may take some grief from the teachers. They're going to ask you why you hit her. Say nothing more than, 'she knows why – ask her.' I guarantee you, Bunny will never come anywhere near you again.

"Now look, kiddo, you're covered in piss. You gotta go home and change. I'll stop into Grade Two and tell your teacher you threw up and had to go home."

Dylan slowly nods his head in agreement. The pain in his gut is diffusing. It's not his habit to play hooky. But he's not about to return to class soaked in urine.

Dylan doesn't sleep much that night. He goes over Gianni's words a gazillion times. He practices the motion required to drive a fist deep into a solar plexus. Dylan might admit to some occasional naughtiness, but the truth is that he has never in his life done anything truly bad or defiant. He wishes he could be Gianni for a day. Dylan knows for sure that Gianni is right on the mark as far as Bunny is concerned. By not attempting to execute Gianni's action plan, it would just be a matter of time before Bunny got him again. Gianni's words become his mantra. He resolves to put this plan into effect the next day.

At breakfast, he says almost nothing to his folks. He responds in monosyllables. In English class, he's unable to focus. All that's on his mind is "taking out Bunny." Normally eager to respond to questions by raising his hand, sometimes all but leaping out of his seat, today he gazes blankly out the window. Recess takes an eternity to arrive.

In the school yard, Dylan spots Gianni. Gianni wanders over. He's short and to the point in his conspiratorial briefing. "Okay, kiddo. Triangle between tits and belly button. Aim to make your fist come out the other side of her."

Dylan spies Bunny standing in her usual place in the shade under the eaves of the school building. She's alone. For a fleeting instant, he actually feels sorry for her. He now knows beyond doubt that his action plan is going to be successful. He breathes deeply. Then he walks in measured strides toward Bunny. He makes sure his face reveals no expression. He clenches his fist into a ball, knuckles offset, while swinging his arms in rhythm with his step. When he's about twenty paces away from her, Bunny catches sight of him. She just stares. She has no inkling of any threat. Again, Dylan feels fleetingly sorry for her. Focus. Triangle, tits, belly button. Now he is programmed. Nothing can stop him. Five paces away from Bunny, he notes that her expression changes; she's clearly confused and perhaps senses something. She starts to say, "Hi Dylan…" but does not get past the second syllable when Dylan's face is in hers, his fist rears back, and is then unloaded into her belly with a force driven by all the rage and shame that Bunny had implanted in him. Perhaps, just a split second before the fist makes contact, Bunny understands the fate that is to befall her this day. But this realization comes way too late for her to take any evasive action.

Dylan is surprised at how easily Bunny's body yields to his strike. He doesn't feel his fist contact her spine, but it must have come close. Just as Gianni had predicted, Bunny doubles up and collapses onto the ground. Every bit of air in her lungs is driven out in a muffled "hoooof." She's so winded she cannot utter any other sound. Dylan doesn't wait around. He turns away without looking at his victim. Using the same purposeful stride that he'd used to make his approach, he escapes the playground and heads to the boys' room. His eyes are full of tears.

He approaches a sink and turns the cold water on full. He splashes his face to cool it down. Gianni enters the washroom, ecstatic. "Man, you popped her good," he declares admiringly, slapping Dylan on the back. "I couldn'a done it better myself!"

He continues: "You ain't out of the woods yet. First, you can't be crying. If you are crying, the teachers will try to find out why. And you don't wanna be tellin' the world you got yourself bagged by a fat girl. Remember, when they ask you 'why' you popped her, just say, 'why don't you ask Bunny, she knows why.' And nothing more." Dylan nods in agreement.

Dylan gets himself suspended from school for three days. He is questioned extensively by Mrs. Moffit, the school principal. Mrs. Moffit concludes that Dylan probably has some valid reason for his assault on Bunny, but the fact that he's unwilling to share this with anyone is reason enough to justify a three-day suspension. Bunny's version of the event is more articulate. She was severely winded by Dylan's unprovoked assault on her solar plexus. She was a completely innocent victim. There she was, just standing on the playground, when she was subjected to a brutal attack. Following her ordeal, she's forced to take a week off school by her mother. Recovering from a vicious playground assault by a nasty little thug requires more than physical healing. More time is required to come to terms with the mental anguish occasioned by such an attack. The Forslunds' pastor has to be called upon to intervene and counsel the poor child.

Dylan's toughest time through the ordeal is in handling his mother. His mom becomes very upset with what she interprets as her son's unwillingness to confide. Sure, she knows that Bunny is not a very nice person. But hitting a girl? That is completely unacceptable. In the end, Dylan tells her that she just doesn't understand. "It's not easy being a boy sometimes. You only had a sister in your family. There are some things I just can't explain to you." His mom looks hurt and that upsets him, but how do you explain someone like Bunny to your mother? The humiliation that Bunny has subjected him to is something he wants to forget, not have investigated. As for Bunny's threat to "tell" on whatever it is that he and Genevieve might have done wrong, he hopes that his sucker punch to her gut might have neutralized it. To Dylan, along with many other kids, Bunny is a monster beyond description to an adult. Certainly, she is someone who is alien to his mother's pretty notions of the world of childhood.

Dylan spends three days at home. Three glorious days! Only kids who have grown up in large families fully appreciate the luxury of time spent alone. He reads three Hardy Boys books, every comic book in the house, and finally finishes reading *Anne of Green Gables*. Reading *Anne of Green Gables* becomes easier after he transposes a Genevieve image into Anne's role. This works pretty well on the whole. He's not prepared to revise Genevieve's role from love object to betrayer.

On the day he returns to school, Dylan notices he is the beneficiary of something that he has not experienced much of in the past - admiration and popularity. Little kids in Kindergarten and Grade One greet him enthusiastically. The Grade Twos all want to be his friend and even some of the big kids say "hi" to him.

Gianni was dead right about Bunny, too. She avoids him at all costs. It's not easy for someone as large as Bunny to slink away, but that's exactly what she does now to avoid Dylan.

5. MARIA CONSUELA

After the Bunny babysitting fiasco, the Douglas parents have no choice but to put partying on hold. This is Rhianna's doing; Mr. Douglas would have likely contracted Cruella de Vil from *101 Dalmatians* for babysitting duties if the decision had been his alone. Having concluded that young, gentle Genevieve was one in a million, Mrs. Douglas sets herself to the task of finding an older and more responsible category of babysitter for the kids. However, as all the English-speaking kids are packaged off to boarding schools at the completion of Grade Eight, the highest grade offered by the American school, this means finding a suitable local girl. A responsible high school girl. The quest begins. And it takes some time.

While Dylan dislikes babysitters invading the home every Saturday night, he soon concludes that it's preferable to having to put up with his dad. Deprived of Saturday night partying, Dylan's father feels that he's being punished. He drinks too much and is volatile around the kids, Dylan in particular.

Mr. Douglas likes rules. At least, he likes rules for us four kids, thinks Dylan, it seems that his dad doesn't have too many rules when it comes to his own behavior. Dylan discovers that he has to be home after the Saturday baseball marathon before 6:30 pm or risk being deprived of the privilege the following week. By the time a fourth Saturday passes after Bunny's departure, Dylan is hoping that a babysitter can be found, if for no other reason than to keep his father and his unpredictable moods out of the house.

At a fundraising event for local orphans, Rhianna Douglas mentions to one of her husband's co-workers, a general physician by the name of Dr. Ruiz, that she is looking for a responsible babysitter for her four children. Dr. Ruiz suggests that his daughter, María Consuela, might be interested. María Consuela is a Grade Twelve student attending the local Venezuelan convent school. The high school senior is preparing to adopt her father's occupation and will be leaving to attend the University of Caracas the following year.

It turns out that María Consuela is interested in babysitting. When she arrives for an interview, Mrs. Douglas is impressed by her, especially by her seriousness. María Consuela introduces herself as "Connie" based on her father's advice.

Connie wears her school uniform for the interview. The Venezuelan schools have a school uniform requirement and Connie's school uniform consists of a white blouse, a khaki skirt, white socks, and black shoes. The effect of the uniform is to scramble any sexual vibes that might be radiated by the wearer. The uniform is worn on a Saturday because the Venezuelan high schools have Saturday morning classes. Venezuelans are very serious about education.

Connie is clearly a studious girl who strikes Rhianna Douglas as having sound family values. Long, black hair is pulled back tight across her scalp and contained in a bun. Her features are drawn from a mix of Hispanic and Negro blood. Underneath the way she presents herself, Rhianna Douglas perceives a natural beauty. For the moment, however, it's evident that Connie has no ambition to be regarded for her looks. Hence, she dresses almost exclusively in her school uniform, even arriving for her first babysitting assignment thus attired.

The teenage girl impresses Rhianna Douglas as being trustworthy and mature, though perhaps something of a non-entity. In Rhianna's view, Connie is unlikely to strike any real positive or negative impact on the kids. She'd get the job done. The kids would neither particularly like nor dislike her. But they'd be safe and secure in her hands.

María Consuela has never in her life been called "Connie." When Rhianna addresses her as such, it takes her a second to grasp who's being referred to. On her first night of babysitting, Rhianna Douglas advises the new babysitter to give Dylan some space. He's at an age when he feels strongly that he doesn't need to be babysat.

"Don't for god's sake *tell* him to do anything," she advises Connie. "If you *ask* him, he'll do his best to make you happy and become your friend for life." This is a new notion to Connie, whose inclinations suggest to her that children of Dylan's age should be simply instructed what to do and when to do it. Venezuelan families are far stricter, she muses.

"And if you have problems with Deidra - she can be a little feisty - ask Dylan to help you. Sometimes he can be pretty good at handling her. Deidra will usually be in bed before you arrive and frankly, she's unlikely to wake up, but there's always a chance."

Connie is older and smarter than any other babysitter Dylan has experienced. Her strategy with Dylan is simple. She'll all but completely ignore the child. This appears to be what Mrs. Douglas wants. Daniel and Domenic seem like cute little boys. They're well mannered and go out of their way to please her. They are exactly the type of child she is familiar with. She bathes them, reads two stories, one chosen by each, and tucks them into bed. When she checks the boys' bedroom five minutes later, both are sound asleep. That accomplished, she opens up a bulging briefcase and pulls her homework out. She has a mound to do and she carefully arranges a stack of text and exercise books on the kitchen table.

Sweaty Dylan enters the kitchen and sits himself at the opposite end of the kitchen table, immediately tucking into his supper. Connie says hello to Dylan in English. She asks him if she prefers her to speak to him in English or Spanish.

Dylan responds that he doesn't really care; it's all the same to him.

"Fine," says Connie, "we will communicate in Spanish." That determined, she says nothing more to him and ploughs into her homework. Dylan retreats from the kitchen table and curls up with a book on the couch until sleep claims him. He awakes an hour later. Connie continues to be busy working in the kitchen. Without saying goodnight, Dylan sleepily takes himself off to bed.

Over time, Connie becomes a Saturday evening feature in the Douglas house. Every week, Mr. Douglas drives over to the Ruiz home to pick the babysitter up and, after returning from their night out, he drives the girl home again. As Mr. and Mrs. Douglas return, Connie greets the couple with, "Todo tranquilo, Señora Douglas."

That's exactly how it is. Todo tranquilo. Dylan seldom says more than a few words to Connie, and she responds with fewer, spending more time with his siblings and her homework than with him. Is Dylan a little miffed that he merits so little of Connie's attention? Perhaps. But his babysitter strikes him as being a fundamentally boring person. What normal person could possibly waste so much time on homework? So things continue "todo tranquilo," as far as Dylan is concerned.

When Dylan is granted rare permission for a Saturday sleepover, he invites Jimmy Sanders over. The two boys erect a tent in the backyard. They set about arranging it to their satisfaction. Dylan's mom has provided them with enough cold pizza and soda to make them ill if they so choose. The boys mount a telescope on a tripod. They are set for some stargazing. Moon gazing is more like it: the Sears Roebuck telescope lacks the orientation controls to focus on the few stars they can recognize with the naked eye, so the moon it has to be. When the moonscape ceases to entertain, the boys retreat into the tent to read comic books and eat cold pizza by flashlight. They are just getting to the point when exhaustion is about to claim them when they become aware of the shadow of a figure approaching the tent. The shadow taps on the flysheet as if knocking on a door. It is Connie. Connie begins by apologizing for intruding into Dylan's sleepover.

"No girls allowed," declares Jimmy aggressively. "Especially babysitters." Connie ignores him.

"Dylan," she begins, set to speak English. "Deidra is awake. She is upset and crying. She asks for you. She is not knowing me that well. I cannot convince her to sleep herself again. Please, maybe you can help me. I apologize to ask you when you are camping."

Dylan picks up a flashlight and turns to Jimmy. "I guess I better go," he says. "It shouldn't take too long."

Dylan illuminates a path back to the house for Connie and himself with his flashlight. The lights in the house seem especially bright to his eyes. Deidra's cries can be heard as soon as they pass through the back door. When Connie and Dylan enter the bedroom, Deidra is red faced from bawling and is standing up in the cot. As usual when she has been left a while unattended in the cot, she has hold of the crib bars and shakes them like a little monkey in a cage. In recent weeks, Dylan has become more comfortable in his role as big brother and sure enough, on seeing him, his kid sister immediately ceases crying and extends her arms to him for rescue. Connie has already changed her diaper, so a little comfort appears to be all that is required. Once out of the cot, Deidra's mood phases from tears, to play, finally descending into drowsiness within the space of about twenty minutes. Dylan is aware that timing is key here and he knows his baby sister's moods better than any sitter could. At the appropriate instant in time, he deposits his sister back into the cot. Within seconds, the child is in a deep sleep. Connie has stood beside Dylan as an observer through this demonstration in child minding mastery.

"Thank you," she says in English. "You are a very *amable* big brother." She pronounces the "amable" in Spanish. Dylan thinks to himself that the compliment sounds nicer said in Spanish than English. Not wanting to waste any more of her evening, Connie then returns to the kitchen to continue with her homework.

Dylan locates his flashlight and exits the back door of the house to return to the tent. He flashes the beam inside the tent. Jimmy has fallen into a deep sleep. Fully awake, Dylan returns to the telescope, still mounted on its tripod. After peeking through the viewfinder, he is surprised at just how far the moon has shifted since he and Jimmy had observed it just a little earlier in the evening. Sitting on the ground beside the telescope, he resets the orientation in accordance with the moon's new position. As he does so, headlight beams sweep across the yard and his parents' car pulls into the driveway. The car's headlamps illuminate the closed garage door which, in turn, reflects light back toward the car. The passenger side car door opens. His mother exits the automobile and enters the house.

Dylan decides that there is something appealing about being covert. Seeing, but not being seen. The car's engine continues to purr under a gentle idle. Meanwhile, his father remains in the driver's seat. He's waiting for Connie so he can drive her home. Light from the headlamps continues to reflect back toward its source, clearly illuminating his father seated in the driver's position and the interior of the car. His father rubs his chin with the palm of his hand.

Connie exits the house, carrying her heavy school briefcase. There's something about the way she carries the satchel that makes it appear lighter now. She's almost skipping. Dylan is struck by the fact that this is not her usual mode of movement. Connie rounds the automobile to approach the passenger side of the vehicle. The interior of the car lights up with greater brilliancy as a door opens. It is the rear door. Connie throws her school bag onto the back seat of the car. The rear door closes and the interior light switches off, but just for a second. Now the front door opens, switching on the interior light once again. Almost immediately, the door slams and extinguishes the interior light once again but, due to the reflected light of the headlamps, both Dylan's dad and Connie continue to be clearly illuminated. In a kind of bouncing up and down movement, Connie sidles across the bench seat of the Chevrolet. As she does, Dylan sees his dad extend an arm to meet her approach. Connie twists her body into that of Dylan's father. Now her back is almost facing the front of the car and she wraps both of her arms around the driver. Has Connie attacked his dad? Are they wrestling? No, they're kissing. Plain, quiet, boring Connie and his absentee father wrestle in an embrace that has all the histrionic passion of a Venezuelan telenovela. This drama unfolds as the car's engine continues to idle comfortably.

The kiss is brief. Dylan's dad grapples Connie away. Turning her to a sitting position next to him, he grasps the automobile's controls. The car's engine changes rhythm and the vehicle reverses. As it does so, reflected light from the garage doors ceases to illuminate the occupants of the vehicle. They become barely identifiable silhouettes tucked over close together on the driver's side of the front seat. Dylan's mom never sits like this when driving with his Dad. After reversing twenty feet back from the garage, the automobile stops, changes direction, and departs the driveway.

Dylan continues to sit by the telescope in the grass, trying to make sense of the scene he's just witnessed. Does his father love Connie? Will he divorce his mother? Initially, the thought of his father leaving doesn't distress him. In fact, he has to check himself because the notion actually has some appeal. But then reality sets in. Such a separation would turn his life upside down.

Over at the house, the patio light switches on, illuminating the backyard and breaking his train of thought. His mother has checked all the kids inside the house and is now coming to check on the boys in the tent. She has a flashlight and she whistles to scare off any snakes that may be lurking in the lawn. The beam from the flashlight locates and focuses on the tent. Dylan observes his mother as she moves toward the tent; she walks almost on tiptoe as if there is something not to be trusted in the grass, perhaps rattlesnakes or tarantulas. The boy waits until his mother is about to approach the entrance to the tent before intercepting her. He accomplishes this with a loudly whispered "Mom" and a couple of blinks from his flashlight. His mother changes direction and approaches him.

"Dylan, mi darling boy," says his mother. His mom has had a few drinks. "Connie's told me all about your heroics with Deidra this evening. You're such an angel with your sister, it does my heart good. It makes a mother feel so much more at ease going out of an evening when I know you're going to be here for your younger brothers and your sister… babysitter or no. I am going to have to think of a special treat for you. Where's your friend?"

"Jimmy. He fell asleep while I was seeing to Deidra. I didn't want to wake him when I got back so I was taking another look at the moon through the telescope. Did you have a good time, Mom?"

"Same ole," responds his mom. "We have a few drinks, tell a few tall tales. In truth, Dylan, I'd rather be staying at home, but it's your dad's only night out in a week. He'd be upset if we didn't do something."

His mom hugs him. This does not happen so often any more. For Dylan, this is the best way to get a hug: when there's no other person around to witness. The worst case would be a Grade Two observer who'd tease him about being a *mommy's boy*.

"Go on with you," says his mother. "Get to bed now and get a good night's rest." And then, with a hint of sarcasm, "As good as you can get in a sleeping bag in a tent, anyways!"

Dylan abandons the telescope, leaving it on the tripod, and makes his way toward the tent. He separates the ties and unzips the portal. As he zips the tent closed, he watches his mom retreating back to the house. He climbs into his sleeping bag. Once zipped into it, he remains sleepless for a while, disturbed by his father's behavior and how it might impact him.

6. CARRIE

Dylan is in Grade Four. He knows that being nine years old is better than being seven. He has accrued two additional years of status in his school. Perhaps more important than age or time served, he has found some success in the sporting world of his school. He owes at least part of this success to Hank, his pitching coach. Hank's credentials for coaching ball are sound: he actually played minor league ball during his college years - not that any credentials are required to coach the American school team. Any adult willing to give up a little time would have the immediate blessing of all the parents.

Hank Summers works with Dylan's father and has a wife and two daughters. He's quick to tell anyone who will listen that his wife has no desire for more children, so there's no prospect of a Hank Jr. When Hank appoints Dylan as his apprentice, Dylan doesn't realize that more will be riding on his shoulders than just the role of pitching his team to success. What Dylan does realize, however, is that an honor has been conferred on him. As a fourth grader, he's to be developed into the first-choice pitcher in a league dominated by fifth and sixth graders.

Hank's short history as a minor league pitcher convinced him that the secret to baseball success at any level is pitching. He confides in Dylan that the pitcher is the only player in the park who's actually required to have a brain. In Dylan, he observes no special talent as a pitcher, but does identify some assets that can be developed. First, he can throw accurately and understands there are different strike zones. Second, and most important to Hank, he knows how to interpret instructions from the bench.

The American school team has no choice of opponents other than the local Venezuelan school teams. This is a problem. The Venezuelan kids are not only fanatical when it comes to baseball, they also appear to develop at a faster rate physically. Games between the American school team and a local team often play out as a match-up of boys versus men. Dylan is neither fanatical nor developed. His interest in baseball is confined to playing the game. He lacks the patience to sit out a game as a spectator and, while he could recognize the names, he would not be able to say whether Sandy Koufax or Mickey Mantle was the pitcher.

Dylan actually prefers playing all-day Saturday baseball where there's no pressure, no winners and losers. In these contests, stats only matter on the day of the game. In such games, he can concede dozens of home runs without being accused of losing a game. What's a slugged home run or two? When playing for the school team, however, adding to the pressure of pitching are his at-bats, which are now of consequence. Dylan cannot hit a baseball. Whenever Dylan is required to bat in a crucial game situation, the best he can come up with is an infield ground ball. To Dylan, this is one better than striking out.

When he first took charge of his little leaguers, Hank addressed his potential pitchers about varying speed and location. The little leaguers would respectfully nod their heads as if they understood him. But the instant they got on the mound during a game, all the coach's words of wisdom were forgotten. The pitcher's imbecile of a father sitting in the bleachers would be hollering "Show 'em the high heat, Matt," and now the pitcher was pitching for Daddy and every bench instruction from Hank was ignored. Part of the reason Hank selects Dylan to be developed into a pitcher is that the boy's father never attends the games. When Dylan pitches, he dutifully looks over to Hank on the bench to pick up the signals. Then he does his best to deliver exactly the pitch that Hank has prescribed. He executes Hank's instructions without questioning them.

In baseball, coach and pitcher must be on the same page. According to Hank, he and Dylan must get to know one another. This will require coaching outside of regular practice hours. Hank undertakes to coach Dylan in his backyard on days he can get home early from work.

Until the time of his first visit to the Summers' family home, Dylan has made little connection between Hank, the baseball coach and Hank, the father of his Grade Four classmate, Karen, self-renamed as Carrie. He has never seen them together. They couldn't be more opposite. Hank is lanky and rough-edged and speaks in a drawled Louisiana accent. Carrie is poised and snooty. When he arrives at the Summers' front door for his first pitching tutorial, Carrie answers the door. Facing her is Dylan, decked out in ball gear and glove.

"What do *you* want?" she demands. Her usual air of superiority is more resolute with home advantage. Dylan is caught unaware. He wasn't expecting to be confronted by the princess of Grade Four; he was hoping Hank would answer the door. Hank's cool macho manner does not jive with his bitchy little daughter.

"I've come to p-p-p..." he stammers, the word "pitch" sticking in his throat.

Carrie interrupts. "Daddy," she hollers, turning away. She continues yelling with as much contempt as she can muster, "your friend Dylan's come to *play* with you." With that, she walks away from the entrance, leaving the boy standing at the open door. It counts to have home advantage.

Hank saunters into the hallway and beckons Dylan into the backyard. Dylan understands from the onset that the theoretical content of his pitching tutorial will exceed hands-on practice. Hank begins by instructing Dylan to look at what does not work for pitchers. Most juvenile pitchers falsely believe that good pitching is about throwing fastball strikes. Strikes located belt-high, dead center over home plate, pitches that even an idiot quickly learned to hit. Not surprisingly, Hank has different opinions on what makes a good pitcher. He believes that if a pitcher can tempt a batter to swing at a pitch in the dirt, it's not only a strike, it's the best kind of strike. Low risk! High risk strikes were those drilled into the bulls-eye of the strike zone.

For the remainder of the tutorial, Dylan pitches to Hank. He rehearses bench signals and how to respond to them. Hank's instruction for this first session is that he does not want a single pitch to land in the meat of the strike zone. Dylan pitches inside and high, outside and low. When one of Dylan's pitches does not adhere to signal and strays in over the strike zone, Hank issues no verbal reprimand, but furrows his brows and shakes his head.

From that day onward, Dylan becomes an occasional visitor to the Summers' home, as Hank makes it his business to teach Dylan the science of pitching. As a result of these visits, despite her initial hostility, Carrie and Dylan strike up a guarded friendship. It's a friendship not acknowledged within the confines of the school, because boys aren't supposed to have girlfriends in Grade Four.

In school, Dylan continues to be more likely to tease Carrie and in return, she's as snooty as ever. But their rules of engagement alter after school. Dylan discovers that he sometimes enjoys being around Carrie and will occasionally visit Carrie when no pitching school is scheduled. Carrie does likewise. She'll catch Dylan alone in a school hallway and ask him in whispered tones whether he might be planning a visit after school. Such clandestine visits are easy to justify by the fact that Dylan has a very good reason to account for his presence in the Summers' household that has nothing to do with visiting Carrie.

After catching and coaching a hundred or so pitches, a man gets hot and has to cool off with a beer or two. And maybe the pitcher could refresh himself with some ice water or a soda. At the completion of coaching sessions, Hank and Dylan sit on the patio and chat. It seems that Hank enjoys having Dylan around. After all, he's male, and none of Hank's females care much for anything he likes to talk about. Dylan enjoys Hank's company. He is impressionable and finds most of the beery anecdotes about life and baseball entertaining. Even when Hank becomes noticeably drunk - which he does with some regularity - Dylan is too deferential to do anything but politely listen; he's used to being talked at. After a while, Dylan happily claims Hank as a mentor. He never overlooks the fact that that the key to whatever success he has achieved as a pitcher is due in big part to the instructions relayed from the bench by the hands now occupied in popping the tab off a can of beer.

It is Sunday afternoon. Bored and restless, Dylan takes himself off to the Summers' household to check out what might be happening there. Such an impromptu visit could result in a swim in the pool, a chat with Carrie, or maybe throwing a few pitches to Hank. He rings the doorbell. Carrie opens the door dressed in her swimsuit, but she is so engrossed in a book, she barely takes her eye off the page while distractedly motioning Dylan to enter. Dylan follows her, out and on to the patio surrounding the swimming pool.

The heat from the sun is fierce. Carrie's father is cleaning out the barbeque. Almost immediately, Hank corrals Dylan into conversation first by offering him a beer. He checks himself: how about a soda?

"Siddown, siddown," he invites Dylan, friendly, but overbearing. Dylan duly takes a seat. They sit by the pool under a shade umbrella. Carrie has no interest in becoming part of the passive audience at one of her father's monologues about his baseball past. She has to put up with her father every day. She rounds the corner of the patio, intentionally making sure she is out of sight. There, she spreads out on a towel to bask in the sun and read.

Hank is going to recount his baseball career to Dylan. Dylan has previously heard most parts of this saga, often, but never with sufficient consistency that a listener could feel convinced that it was entirely verifiable. Certain elements of the story remained consistent: Hank had been a promising pitcher in high school and played one season of A-ball before his pitching elbow *crapped out*. Dylan wasn't sure exactly what this meant other than the fact that Hank could no longer pitch. At least, he could no longer pitch to anyone who knew how to use a bat. After recovering from elbow surgery, Hank regularly pitched in the beer leagues. He pitched with considerable success. But then the secret of being successful in that class of venue was to make sure you had consumed a few less beers than the guy you were pitching to. Being a successful beer league pitcher just didn't do it for Hank.

The reason for Hank's success as a high school pitcher and why, undoubtedly, he would have become the most successful pitcher in the history of major league baseball, was his smartness. That's the way he told it. You see, most baseball players are stupid. They have to be. Would an intelligent person be prepared to devote ten hours a day throughout childhood and adolescence to throwing and hitting a baseball around? Wasting their teenage years with no girlfriends, no booze, on a long shot that they could be the one in ten thousand who could get a professional contract? Well, maybe the odd girlfriend here and there, but only the kind that realizes your baseball career was much more important than they could ever be.

"Carrie, honey, get your pappy another beer from the fridge, sweetheart." Hank calls out, interrupting a pitch-by-pitch recounting of a game. Silence. This time he yells more assertively, "Carrie!"

Carrie responds slowly in a distracted way, "Get it yourself, Daddy, I'm reading."

"Honey," he responds with emphasis, "I'm teaching Dylan how to play the great American game. This is important guy stuff and I don't want to lose my train of thought."

"I can get you a beer, Hank," volunteers Dylan. He could do with some respite from the great baseball saga.

Hank belches. "Siddown, Dylan," he orders. Then, in confidence so that what he says cannot be heard by anyone other than the two of them, "The women around here have got to learn to be of some use to the world." He raises his voice, "Sweetheart, I'm still waiting on that beer."

After a prolonged delay and a groan from Carrie, her flip flops can be heard slowly shuffling towards the patio refrigerator. The fridge door opens. Bottles and cans jingle on wire shelves, after which the fridge emits the sucking, sighing noise produced by closing its door. Carrie's flip flops reluctantly shuffle back toward them. The can of Schlitz falling onto the patio stones makes a muted "thunk." During Carrie's protracted efforts in executing this chore, Hank has not said a word to Dylan; in fact, he's been staring down at his empty beer can. His facial expression is one of a person deep in thought, but there's something else about his appearance that telegraphs to Dylan that he is not only acutely aware of his daughter's movements, but also annoyed by them. Hank rarely gets annoyed at anything.

At the thunk of the falling beer can, he says with measured calm, "Exchange the can, honey; get another one. That one'll explode as it is opened." Hank purses his lips. Carrie emits a deep sigh of irritation, an exhalation clearly meant to be heard by her audience on the patio. Dylan senses that Hank might feel ashamed at his evident lack of authority over his daughter, but the effect of this scene is interpreted differently by Dylan. Nothing Hank has ever done outside of a ballpark has drawn more admiration from him. Initially, Dylan thought it was pretty cool that Mr. Summers insisted on being called "Hank" by a nine-year-old. Had his own father's authority been subjected to the challenge that Hank has just sustained, the result would have been an explosion of rage that would have left no one in the vicinity safe from any ensuing violence. Yes, Hank was pretty cool.

Having presumably retrieved a second beer from the fridge, Carrie's shuffling flip flops are heard again, moving ever more slowly toward the pair of baseball aficionados who remain silent, observing her while seated in wooden Adirondack deck chairs alongside the pool. The footsteps shuffle toward them, slower than slow, and, as Carrie approaches, the reason is obvious. She is walking blind, continuing to read her book and making it perfectly plain that nothing is going to interfere with this activity. Without turning her attention from the book, Carrie hands the beer can to her father. It's upside down. Hank receives it from her with a look of disdain.

Having handed over the beer can, she looks up from the book, not to her father, but to Dylan. She squints her eyes and sticks her tongue out at him. She turns, now sprite, and with her thumb marking her place in the book, skips away and out of sight, the flip flops going plippity-flop, plippity-flop across the patio stones.

Hank watches her disappear around the corner, then scowls at the beer can, which he's still holding upside down. He gets to his feet and strides barefoot over toward the refrigerator and out of Dylan's sight. Dylan hears him in muffled tones saying something about respect and tanning backsides, followed by some rather louder, indignant protestations of innocence from Carrie. Within seconds, he returns with two cans of Schlitz, and pops the opening tabs. He hands one can to Dylan and immediately guzzles at least half the contents of his beer. Dylan grasps the beer he has been handed on the arm of his chair, holding it as if it were a hand grenade.

"Dylan, have I told you before that the female gender should be handled from a distance and with great care?" He sighs with resignation, stares abstractly at the pool. "I'm surrounded by women at home," he rues, "Two daughters, mother-in-law moving in with us months on end, even the god-damned cat's a female ... that's why it's sure a hell of a good thing to have a man about the place from time to time, Dylan."

The snort of beer works its effect. Hank settles back and relaxes once again. But he doesn't progress much with his story before Carrie reappears. Unbeknownst to Hank, Carrie has crept up behind her father, on tip toe. She's achieved this with her expression serious, without conspiratorial intent, though she has been aware of attracting some casual notice from Dylan. Wanting to appear as if he's been intently listening, Dylan has done nothing to make Hank aware of what has been going on behind his back. Now directly behind her father, Carrie has placed both arms on the backrest of her father's deck chair and is making faces at Dylan. She wants to make Dylan laugh, to make him aware that, yes, her father is a silly old fool and who but Dylan would give him the time of day? Might it also be that she is a little jealous of this boy talk?

Dylan finds it increasingly difficult to concentrate on whatever Hank is talking about, but he must do this to avoid complicity with Carrie. Though he's bored with Hank's story, he immediately sides with his coach, and wishes Carrie would just go away and leave them be. Too bad if Carrie had no interest in baseball. Yes, Hank was right, this was important guy stuff and women should respect this.

Carrie sticks her tongue out at Dylan once again. Bored with her failure to distract him, she sets about ensuring she'll be noticed. She rounds her father's chair and flops her body on top of Dylan's lap, leaning her back against one arm of the chair while sprawling her bare legs over the other. This is the first time Dylan has been physically this close to Carrie. He feels some residual dampness from Carrie's swimsuit in his lap. Meanwhile, Carrie puts on a face of concentration, as if she's listening to her father's every word. Caught off guard, her father studies her suspiciously, then ignores her to address Dylan again. He laughs.

"Just as women and war do not mix, Dylan, neither do women and sports." Carrie makes a face at him.

"Drink up your beer, boy." This draws Carrie's attention to the beer can in Dylan's hand. She leans forward to sniff its contents as yet untouched.

"Daddy, you didn't?" she gasps. But realizing that he did, she snatches the beer from Dylan's hand, gets to her feet, and marches importantly off in the direction of the kitchen.

"I'm telling Mummy," she says accusingly to her father, "this is going *way* too far!"

Hank ignores his antsy daughter. He looks up at the sky, grinning as if recalling some former glory on a pitcher's mound somewhere in Louisiana. But almost immediately, Carrie returns with her mother. Carrie has her arms folded across her chest. Mrs. Summers says nothing to her husband. Instead, she addresses Dylan.

"I think you and Carrie should go and play in her room," she says firmly. Her tone indicates this is not a suggestion, but a direct order.

Hank's baseball coaching instructions do not vary a lot. "Any time you're on a pitcher's mound, tell yourself you are a king. King Dylan! Everything that unfolds on the field of play begins with what you throw over the plate; good or bad, you control the outcomes. Every person that comes up to bat is at a disadvantage; only you know what type of pitch you will throw. Outthink and outguess him. Now, judging by your school ball games, every pitcher I have seen has one pitch —throw the ball as hard as possible over the plate and hope the batter swings and misses. But that means throwing the ball exactly where the batter wants it. Good pitchers are the ones that make it their business to avoid the fat of the plate. This isn't rocket science. It's plain common sense."

Swig of beer. "So here is where we begin. Instead of throwing the ball exactly where it's easy for them to hit, you're gonna make it difficult. Confuse them. Disorient them. Make them desperate, because that's when they'll start getting careless. Your job is to create anger and frustration. Angry, frustrated batters strike out!"

The advice changes from the batter's emotional state to Dylan's. "A pitcher wins games with his head. Never show any emotion. Especially, never show anyone when you're mad. That's what your opponents want. They'll work to get a rise out of you. And even if you make a mistake and give up a home run, don't show it. Your face has to look as if you actually planned it that way. Yup, it was part of your game plan all along. Next time that guy comes up to bat, shave his ear with a ball to the head. Intimidate! And when you strike someone out, show no emotion. You struck him out, so what, that's exactly what you expected. Let him know that it means nothing to you. Show a batter that striking him out means something to you, makes it personal, you see. He'll remember you. And he'll be a tougher out next time you face him. Never gloat. A pitcher stands alone. A pitcher is a king. Hold your shoulders high and remember that, while you are playing ball, you don't need friends. So don't look for or accept the approval of your teammates. If you do, then their disapproval will start to mean something to you. They can be your friends before the game and after the game, but during the game, you are a king and you don't need any pals.

"I'll make a real pitcher out of you," Hank promises him. "But ya know what, Dylan, never forget the most important thing. While you are learning the game, you throw only what I signal from the bench. Even if you think I am signaling the dumbest call, your job is to throw what I signal. You see, I know the game and you don't. Ninety-eight times out of a hundred, I'll be right, while your instincts will be wrong."

Carrie has listened to her father's coaching conversations with Dylan more than once. She squints at her father with some incomprehension. She studies the way he interacts with Dylan. It amazes her that Dylan not only listens to her father, but at times is mesmerized by him. This intrigues her. Thank God she does not have a brother to compete with!

Dylan is to be abandoned by his family for three days. He's going to miss out on a family trip to Caracas and it's all Hank's fault. A couple of times a year, most of the families living in the desert environment of the oil refinery on the Paraguana peninsula take long weekend escapes to either Maracaibo or Caracas. The Paraguana desert is dry, hot, and ravaged by a super-heated wind that blows night and day. Most of the kids don't notice the harsh climate because they've grown up with it and know no other. While their expat parents crave air conditioning, their offspring shiver unnaturally when exposed to it. For the parents, the city environ-ment of Caracas offers a cooler climate, good shopping, restaurants, and a change of scenery. For the children, a trip to either Caracas or Maracaibo promises a change in the pace of life and hotels with large swimming pools. But Dylan is going to miss out on this family trip to Caracas. It clashes with a local three-inning baseball tournament.

Given the choice of three days in Caracas or a baseball tournament, Dylan would have no hesitation in opting for Caracas. Hank knows this. That's why Hank approaches Dylan's father and makes the request through him. Accordingly, Dylan's father has a chat with his eldest son. He speaks of the responsibility of playing on a sports team. It requires sacrifices. Team spirit is more important than a weekend of fun, hanging out around a large hotel swimming pool. Dylan's mom does not agree. She believes that Dylan should be allowed to make the choice. After all, she says, Dylan seems to do little other than play baseball these days. But what does a mother know about the world of men and sports? Dylan reluctantly agrees to forego the Caracas trip in the name of honor and team spirit.

Dylan's family drops him off at the Summers' home on a Friday afternoon. Mrs. Summers greets the Douglas family, none of whom exit the automobile other than Dylan. She picks up Dylan's overnight bag while Dylan wrestles his baseball kit bag from the trunk. Mrs. Summers and Mrs. Douglas exchange some small talk before the Chevrolet wagon drives off to the airport. Mrs. Summers deduces that Dylan is not entirely happy about this arrangement. She informs Dylan that Carrie is excited that he'll be staying for the weekend and she knows they'll have fun. Mrs. Summers then escorts Dylan to Carrie's younger sister Kelly's bedroom. This is where Dylan will sleep. Kelly is on a two-day sleepover at a friend's home. On the third day, when Kelly returns, she can bunk up with Carrie. Mrs. Summers leaves Dylan to unpack.

Dylan surveys the room. This is the bedroom of a six-year-old girl. The motif is pink and princesses. There is a bunk bed, a dresser, and small desk. Disney posters decorate the walls. On the upper tier of the bunk bed are more soft toys and dolls than Dylan has seen in his life. They cover the entire surface area of the bed. The lower tier of the bunk bed is made up for sleeping. Dylan opens his suitcase. He had packed it himself. It contains a change of clothes, swimsuit, pair of pajamas, and a toothbrush in a tube. He decides it's not worth unpacking and settles for just leaving the lid open, parked on the desk chair. A window-mounted air conditioning unit drones.

The door flies open. It's Carrie. "You're early," she says breezily. "I wanted to be home when you arrived. You are my first boy sleepover."

Dylan replies with some protest, "It's not a sleepover. I am a ... guest. I am only here because of..."

"Guests are sleepovers, silly," Carrie interrupts. "I've already planned our whole evening together. Mummy and Daddy are taking us to the drive-in movie theatre – *Lady and the Tramp* is showing. I saw it last vacation in the States; it's the best movie ever. It'll make you cry." Dylan is happy enough about the movie, but not so happy about labeling his stay with the Summers' a sleepover. The term "sleepover" implies he is staying with Carrie. This isn't true. He's staying with the Summers' only so he can play in the three-inning tournament on Saturday.

When Hank arrives home from work, he greets Dylan as if he is Sandy Koufax. This makes Dylan feel good. After dinner, the Summers parents, Carrie, and Dylan depart for the drive-in movie theatre. Dylan enjoys *Lady and the Tramp*. Carrie and Dylan sit on cushions in the backseat of the automobile, munching popcorn and drinking soda. On the return journey to the Summers' home, Carrie accuses Dylan of crying during the film.

"No way," declares Dylan adamantly.

"Did so, I was watching you because I knew you would." On the backseat of the automobile, a heated argument develops between Carrie and Dylan, the subject of which is whether Dylan cried or not during the movie. It becomes so heated that Mrs. Summers is forced to intervene. At the moment of intervention, Dylan is close to tears once again, this time due to the frustration caused by Carrie not buying his denial of tears. Star baseball pitchers don't cry when they watch a soppy Disney movie.

As the car pulls into the Summers' driveway, Carrie tries to make up. She has plans for the evening and they involve Dylan. But shame and anger linger in Dylan. He's been accused of being a crybaby. Dylan informs Carrie that he wants to go to bed. He's tired and needs to rest up for the tournament tomorrow; he is to be pitching all day. From the driver's seat, Hank agrees. Now Carrie is crying. What about her plans? This isn't supposed to happen on a sleepover. She starts throwing a tantrum. Dylan has never seen her behave like this in school. Mrs. Summers has to calm her down. Dylan is secretly pleased. That'll teach Carrie, he thinks.

Once in Kelly's room, Dylan changes into his pajamas, wearing both top and bottoms. The air conditioning has made it freezing in Kelly's room. He climbs under the covers and switches off the bedside light. A few minutes later, the door opens, allowing in a vectored shard of light. It's Hank. "Goodnight, sport," says Hank. The door closes.

The next morning, Dylan is woken by Carrie climbing into bed with him.

"Scoot your bum over," orders Carrie. She seems to be in a good mood now. Dylan slides over to the wall side of the bed. Carrie wraps her legs and arms around Dylan. She is shivering from the air conditioning. She trembles her body dramatically.

"Turn around and spoon me," she instructs Dylan, "I'm the one who is freezing, so I get to be the inside spoon." Both Dylan and Carrie roll around in the bed so that Carrie can be the inside spoon. Dylan cuddles into Carrie. He's not been so close to a girl since the days of Genevieve. Carrie feels good. She's nearly as warm as he is now.

"You can sleep in my room tonight if you want, you can be in my upstairs bunk," says Carrie, "I wanted you to sleep in my room last night. But you were being so mean to me." Dylan doesn't reply. He was under the impression that Carrie was the one being mean, but he does not want her to unload another hissy fit.

"Don't worry," she continues, "I won't tell anybody at school that you cried in *Lady and the Tramp*." After saying this, Carrie twists her head over her shoulder to observe how this announcement is received. Dylan releases Carrie from the spoon cuddle and turns onto to his back. He stares up at the ceiling. He does not want another battle with Carrie. It might ruin the concentration he needs for the baseball tournament.

Observing that her accusation has failed to elicit much of a response from Dylan, Carrie continues, "I don't know what the big deal is," she says, "even my dad cries in some movies. And when he does, he doesn't lie and pretend he hasn't." Dylan still says nothing. But he feels a little better. If Hank can cry when he watches a movie, maybe it's not so bad if he does.

Poor Hank deserves sympathy. He sincerely believes that he can build the American school baseball team into a winner. The odds are stacked against ever achieving this goal. In the American school, Hank has a selection pool of about forty possible players for his twelve-and-under team. Of the forty, only half have any actual interest in the game. The closest Venezuelan primary school boasts a total enrollment in excess of twelve hundred students, half of which are presumably male. Every other one of these males is an aspiring Mickey Mantle.

Of course, all the Venezuelan students know exactly who Mickey Mantle is and that helps. The only ball games you could catch on the local TV are Yankees games. These games guide the Venezuelan ball players and following each game, every play is dissected and analyzed as a learning opportunity. Large discussions and inevitable arguments ensue. Meanwhile, the American kids are watching Popeye. Hank is no fan of the Yankees and nothing bugs him more than someone asserting they are the best. The A-ball team with whom he experienced his brief moments of glory before the failure of his elbow was affiliated with the Cardinals.

Hank is beginning to see some results from the hours he has dedicated into developing Dylan as a pitcher. Since Dylan had become the team's first-choice pitcher, he had been able to at least keep the team in contention during ball games. Given some well-timed run support, things could sometimes come together to win the odd game or two. For the first time since assuming the coaching role with the ball team, Hank has a pitcher capable of converting his bench strategy into wins.

But the team is to meet with only partial success at this weekend, multi-school, three-inning tournament. The American school team wins its first game, but loses the second. Two first round wins out of three games are required to progress to the tournament's semi-final eliminations. In the crucial third game, Dylan pitches well enough, allowing just one run. However, the American school team couldn't score in either of its first two innings. The bottom of the final inning begins promisingly for the team and they manage to get two runners on base, but there are two outs.

Unfortunately, Dylan is up to bat. This is Dylan's worst nightmare come true. For most of the morning, he's been a star. He pitched beyond his capabilities. Now the game and the team's future in this tournament rest on what he can do with his bat. Every boy on the team is rooting for him. Hank is pumping his fist in the air. All Dylan can wonder is why they bother. How can they overlook the fact that he cannot hit when he has proven this so many times in the past? Why can't this be the major leagues, where you can pinch hit, or better still, the American League, where pitchers don't have to undergo the torment of having to bat? Dylan is almost in tears before he faces a pitch. He's thinking that he'd rather be with his family in a hotel swimming pool in Caracas. He would rather be anywhere but here.

He lasts all of one pitch, a tame pop-up fly into the infield. It's over. His teammates are silenced. Hank is silenced. The rooting and the cheers are all coming from the opposing team, which is indulging in the usual ecstasy of self-congratulation that follows a close win. Dylan hangs his head in shame. Now he has to contend with silence and phony condolences from his teammates. His creditable pitching performance means nothing now. Yes, he might have kept his team in the game. But like Hank has told him many times in the past, only the bottom line counts.

In the car on the way back to the Summers' house, Hank recounts the events of the ball games, pitch by pitch. Dylan wonders how he can possibly remember so much trivia that surely doesn't matter any more. Dylan can recall almost nothing of his own pitching performance, let alone anything else that had happened in the game beyond his last at bat. He simply hurled what Hank signaled him to throw from the bench. The one thing Hank does not mention during the drive home is Dylan's final at bat.

After a swim in the Summers' pool, Dylan feels somewhat better. Hank barbeques ribs for the evening meal. Mr. Summers, Mrs. Summers, Carrie, and Dylan sit at a picnic table to eat. Carrie informs her father that he is prohibited from talking about baseball. Mrs. Summers backs up her daughter, saying that she thinks this is a *very* good idea. Hank says nothing in response.

Toward the end of the meal, Carrie announces to her mother, "Dylan has agreed to sleep in my room tonight, Mother. We are planning to have a proper sleepover, midnight snack included. He can sleep in my upstairs bunk." Dylan looks at Carrie. He agreed to nothing of the kind.

Mrs. Summers is not so sure; the rules were surely different when a sleepover involved a boy. "You will have to ask your father about that, dear," she says, looking nervously at Hank.

Hank shrugs his shoulders. "What do you want me to say?" he says, but seeing doubt in his wife's eyes, adds: "For Chrissakes sake, Martha, they're nine years old …. What could they possibly do?"

During the course of the evening, it becomes apparent that Carrie and Dylan have little in common when it comes to amusement. By Carrie's definition of sleepover rules, she gets to choose every activity they participate in. Dylan has little tolerance for passing judgment on the photographic images in Carrie's mother's fashion magazines and even less for brushing and braiding Carrie's hair. When it comes to his own hair, he prefers it to be left alone; the sensation resulting from Carrie running a hairbrush through his scalp one hundred times is not pleasing. Dylan is not interested in any of Carrie's board games, and card games such as gin and Old Maid rapidly become boring.

Frustrated, Carrie decides to make a generous concession. "What do boys do on sleepovers?" she asks. "We can try doing something you like doing."

Dylan thinks. "We like to wrestle," he decides.

"Wrestle?" says Carrie astonished. "What for?"

Dylan is actually not much of a fan of wrestling. However, he struggles to think of something of interest that is done during a boy's sleepover that did not involve a package of firecrackers. Even if he had some firecrackers in his possession, he assumes it unlikely that Carrie would be willing to sacrifice any of her Barbie dolls to destruction.

"To see who can win," responds Dylan. Wrestling is as good an activity as any, thinks Dylan. It is unlikely that Carrie is capable of hurting him. "I'll explain the rules," he says, "No kicking, biting, pinching, or punching. To win, you have to pin shoulders, both shoulders, to the floor for a count of three – three like 'one and two and three' - or make the loser say 'uncle.'"

"Why 'uncle'?" questions Carrie, "How silly. Why not 'granddad' or 'auntie'?"

Dylan gets serious, "I am not sure why it is 'uncle' but it always is. That's what the rules say."

The wrestling does not get off to a good start. In attempting to impose a headlock on Carrie, Dylan inadvertently pulls her hair. With electric speed and vigor, Carrie swings her arm and slaps Dylan's face. Pain and surprise stun Dylan. He pauses rubbing his stinging cheek.

"I don't think slapping is allowed in the rules," he rues.

"Then you shouldn't have pulled my hair," declares Carrie, unrepentant. "Pulling hair should be banned in the rules, too."

"I didn't mean to," says Dylan. "You have so much of it. Hair, that is." Attempting to headlock someone with as much hair as Carrie is not a good idea. They wrestle some more. Carrie is surprisingly fast and agile. She turns out to be as much as Dylan can handle. Finally, Dylan maneuvers his body behind Carrie, finding some advantage. He wraps both his legs around her torso and locks his ankles in a scissor hold.

As Dylan's wiry legs clamp Carrie's stomach, all of the air in her lungs is squeezed from her. The pain is excruciating and she struggles to breathe. Behind her, Dylan is telling her she has to say "uncle." But Carrie cannot take a breath, let alone say anything. Her face turns purple, and she thinks she is in danger of passing out. She panics. Some inherent sense of self preservation helps her identify that place on a boy's body she knows is supposed to be vulnerable, and she strikes at it. The effect is instantaneous. The crushing hold on her torso is immediately relieved. Dylan's body goes limp and Carrie raises herself to a sitting position, coughing and gasping for breath.

Dylan is doubled up on the floor, gasping for breath. He is clutching the place on his body where Carrie struck him. Carrie knows what she did wasn't in the rules. Dylan appears to be crying quietly. This makes Carrie feel moderately remorseful. "I'm sorry Dylan, but you asked for that. I thought I was going to die. You must have known you were hurting me," she says.

After a pause, dazed Dylan responds. "All you had to do was say 'uncle' and I would have stopped."

"I couldn't speak," Carrie protests, "I couldn't even breathe. You'd forced all of the air out of me."

For a full five minutes, Dylan lies doubled up on the floor. Now Carrie is feeling upset for him and is close to tears.

"Is there anything I can do to help?" she asks, stroking his forehead. Dylan just shakes his head sadly. The worst of the pain has dissipated now, but the sense of defeat has not. Carrie decides that milk and a cookie might help. She informs Dylan that she will be right back with something to make him feel better.

*   *   *

It is bedtime and Carrie's bedroom is illuminated only by a night light. For a night light, it is a bright one. The room is cast in a pastel pink glow. Carrie has already installed herself in the lower bunk bed. Dylan returns from the bathroom having changed into pajamas. He places his wash bag into his overnight case and steps onto the first rung of the ladder leading to the top bunk. As he does so, Carrie tugs the fabric of his pajamas at the ankle.

"Hey, where do you think you are going?" she asks. Dylan stops and twists his neck down to look at her. "Scoot in with me," says Carrie, "I need a cuddle. That's what we do on sleepovers."

Dylan steps off the ladder and climbs into the lower bunk alongside Carrie. Carrie wraps an arm around his shoulder. Within the embrace, Dylan surrenders and adjusts to unfamiliar sensations. He inhales Carrie's gentle odor mixed with the perfume of soap.

"Are you feeling OK, down ... down there?" Carrie wants to know. Dylan nods.

"I want to touch it, Dylan"

"What?"

"Your ... thingee ... pecker or penis, whatever you call it."

"Why?"

"I don't have brothers, just a sister ... here, it's not like your family where you have boys and girls walking around naked the whole time."

"We don't walk around naked the whole time."

"You know what I mean. Come on, please. You can touch me, too."

Without waiting for a response, Carrie moves her hand under the covers to find what she wants to touch.

*   *   *

The next morning, Carrie wakes first. She hasn't slept much. While Dylan lay on his back sleeping like a log, she was unable to settle into prolonged sleep. There was always some part of Dylan's body intruding into her space. If he had been a girl, she would have kicked him out of her bed and ordered him up into the upper bunk. She'd never had any friend on a sleepover that had actually slept most of the night. Taking care not to disturb Dylan, she climbs over her sleeping partner and dresses quietly. It's daylight. She doesn't want him to see her naked. Touching is one thing, *seeing* her completely nude is another. Also, she's unsure of how the experience of the night before is going to translate into the next morning. All she knows is that they now share some secrets.

An hour later, she returns to her bedroom to wake Dylan. It's high time he got up.

"Mom wants to wash the baseball uniform you wore yesterday," she informs Dylan, without offering any other greeting. She walks over to his kit bag on the floor. After removing the uniform pants and shirt, she comes across a curious item of clothing she's never seen before. With awe, she picks it up with thumb and forefinger and displays it at arms' length.

"Yuck," she says, "what is this?"

Dylan is embarrassed. "Put it down."

But Carrie finds this hilarious, "Is this a jockstrap?" she asks. She cracks the device against the bedroom chair. It makes a clunk. Dylan is limited in his ability to intercede on behalf of his jockstrap due to his nakedness which, for some reason, he also is much more aware of in the light of the morning than he was the night before.

Curious, Carrie opens the pouch in the jockstrap and removes a pink plastic cup. She tosses her head up and laughs. Next, she pitches the cup up to the ceiling and allows it to drop to the floor. This is too much. Dylan swings his legs out of the bed, finds his shorts, and pulls them on.

"You have to wear it when you play baseball," protests Dylan, defending his jockstrap. Dylan retrieves his cup and returns it to his kit bag. "It's private," he says. Carrie dangles the jockstrap by one of its straps.

"I would sure like to see you wearing this," she says cattily. "If you put it on, can I take a photo of you? It could be quite a hit in show-and-tell." Dylan snatches at the jockstrap, but Carrie quickly yanks it from his grasp. She marches out of the bedroom with his baseball uniform tucked under one arm and the jockstrap displayed in the other. Her mother has to see this. What a good laugh they'll have! Dylan finishes dressing before following her.

Sunday morning breakfast at the Summers'. Carrie's little sister has just arrived home from her two-night sleepover. It's not usual to return for breakfast following a sleepover, but today is Sunday and that means worship for some. Not for the aggressively anti-religious Summers' family. Hank and Martha Summers don't wish to have their offspring corrupted by any ritualized Bible thumping, sleepover or no. Both girls are prohibited from attending church or Sunday school. Hank views the religious with suspicion and Southern Baptists with particular venom, convictions he makes no efforts to disguise.

Carrie's little sister, Kelly, is a first grader and a bundle of energy. Dylan hasn't really taken account of her previously. Fourth graders don't tend to notice first graders in school. The one time Kelly was present when Dylan attended a Summers family barbeque, she was occupied with a visiting playmate. Now Kelly is chattering in the kitchen to Carrie and her mother, attempting to recount every detail of her sleepover. Dylan's entry to the kitchen interrupts Kelly.

"Carrie has an apology for you, Dylan," says Mrs. Summers as the boy enters, turning to her elder daughter. Carrie puts on her most serious countenance. Dylan immediately senses this is a big fake.

"I'm sorry about making fun of your …" but before she can say "jockstrap," Carrie's ability to contain the mirth within is defeated and she explodes into histrionic laughter. She slaps her thigh.

"You should see this thing," she says turning to Kelly. "It is seriously gross!"

"Leave the room," Mrs. Summers orders Carrie as sternly as she is capable, "and don't think of returning until you are ready to apologize properly." Carrie, still suppressing laughter, exits the kitchen and stands in the doorway.

"I want to see it," enquires Kelly inquisitively, confused and not having any idea what it is that she might want to see.

"Kelly," says Mrs. Summers, "I was counting on you to know how we treat our guests in our family." Kelly looks at Dylan and smiles.

Meanwhile, Carrie has made her way back into the kitchen.

"Sorry," she says disdainfully as she passes Dylan. She grabs a cereal package and sets about pouring some of its contents into a bowl. Halfway through pouring the cereal, Carrie bursts into raucous laughter. Once again, Mrs. Summers sends Carrie out of the room. She shakes her head.

"I want to apologize, Dylan. Carrie can sometimes be a little infantile." Meanwhile, Carrie is standing giggling at the entrance to the kitchen.

"So *you're* the handsome and charming boyfriend," coos the first grader with a large grin on her face and oozing confidence, "Am I supposed to shake your hand? Or can I hug you. Do you kiss Carrie? Do you guys *smoooch?*"

Kelly provides Dylan with a welcome distraction to bypass the embarrassment caused by Carrie. He grins at Kelly. "No, we've never kissed," he says truthfully. "Are you Kelly with a C, like Carrie, or like Karen with a K?"

Kelly nods her head vigorously. "With a K. I don't think it's ever with a C. Did Carrie tell you horrible things about me?"

"Lemme see now," considers Dylan scratching his head, "Hmmm. She said you were a nosy little pest who should be … how did she put it? Yes, classified as hazardous to the environment." Carrie, who has by now snuck back into the kitchen, responds by making a face at both Dylan and Kelly. This face is mirrored by Kelly.

"Big sisters!" exclaims Kelly with phony exasperation, "She is such a witch. I'm surprised she can get any kind of boyfriend. Did you sleep in my bed last night?"

"I slept in the top bunk in Carrie's room," responds Dylan, not quite truthfully.

"And the night before?" asks Kelly.

"Yup," responds Dylan matter-of-factly, "I slept in your bed the first night. I guarded all your animals in the top bunk for you."

"They're supposed to guard you," says Kelly. "I thought so … you didn't make the bed very well."

After breakfast, it is time for a swim. Mrs. Summers coats the bodies of the three kids with sunblock, then slicks zinc barrier paste onto their noses, under their eyes, and on their shoulders. The sun here is hot. Strong swimmer Carrie dives in and quickly completes eight lengths of the pool. That done, she emerges, towels off, and extends herself, tummy down, on a lounge chair with a *Nancy Drew* book. She faces her propped up head away from the pool. She doesn't want to be disturbed by anyone.

However, she can't help but note that Dylan and Kelly are playing with each other. They are having way too much fun. They're playing in a way that she could never play with other kids. Of course, they seem to share the same mental age, she thinks. One game leads to another, to a next, and so on.

Yes, each of Dylan and Kelly's activities changes seamlessly to another by an uncanny mutual consent. They have a front crawl race. Dylan wins. They challenge each other to see who can swim furthest under water. Dylan lets Kelly win. The pair keeps on laughing, even when playing combatively, such as determining who can splash the other with the most amount of water. It seems like they never stop their silly giggling. Carrie begins to feel that her sleepover is being hijacked by her baby sister. Such a thing could never happen when she had her Grade Four girls for sleepovers. Her female cohorts were all but obliged to enthusiastically adopt whatever activities she prescribed or opinions she held. And she was inclined to have an especially low opinion of Kelly during a sleepover. This is great, thinks Carrie. My baby sister is stealing my boyfriend.

Suddenly Kelly stops playing. She scrambles out of the pool and runs off to the bathroom. "Have to go poo," she announces as she disappears.

Dylan wades over to the side of the pool closest to Carrie's lawn chair. Using a forefinger and thumb, he flicks a small amount of water so that it sprinkles across Carrie's bare back. Carrie squirms and turns to face Dylan with an annoyed frown on her face. "Why don't you come in and play with us?" he invites Carrie. Carrie stares at him.

"Maybe it's because I don't have the mind of a six-year-old." As soon as the words escape, she regrets them. Dylan stands waist high in the water and just looks at her, maybe a little sadly. Carrie suddenly feels remorse. "Sorry, Dylan," Carrie says, changing her tone, "I just prefer reading. You and Kelly play. It's kind of nice for her to have someone to play with in the pool, she's a little fish. She'll stay in with you all day if you let her. If you get tired of it, you can come on out and read with me." With that, she turns her body and attention back to her book. Dylan swims a couple of lengths of the pool vigorously.

Kelly returns running full tilt. She jumps as high as she can launch herself into the air, tucks her knees into her chest, and wraps them with her arms. Kelly prides herself on her water bombs. Who says you have to be big to make a splash? And sure enough, an unnaturally large splash results. Surfacing in the water, Kelly turns her head. She smiles with satisfaction that some of the splash from her bomb has made it as far as her big sister's sun-warmed back. Irritated, but not about to be distracted from her book, Carrie twists an arm behind her back to wipe away the offending droplets of water.

For the rest of the day, Carrie's moods run hot and cold with Dylan. This is actually okay with Dylan, who's happy to play with Kelly, practice ball with Hank, and even help Mrs. Summers make brownies. If he feels vaguely uncomfortable that Carrie is inclined to ignore him during the day, it's only because it his nature to want people to like him. For reasons Dylan can't figure out, it appears contrary to Carrie's nature to show any affection for him unless they are entirely alone. When others are around, Carrie behaves as if she disapproves of just about everything Dylan says or does.

On the Sunday evening, Carrie and Dylan are sitting up in bed reading to each other. They're in Carrie's lower bunk bed and reading a *Nancy Drew* mystery by flashlight. While the noise of the air conditioning unit makes it impossible to hear voices from outside of the door, if a light within the room was to be switched on, it could be observed outside the room under the closed door. Hence, the flashlight. Carrie informs Dylan that she reads by flashlight until she falls asleep most nights. Her official bedtime is way too early for a nine-year-old.

Dylan learns about the world of Nancy Drew, detective. Nancy does pretty much the same stuff as the Hardy boys except that she is a girl and therefore a bit of a smartass. Despite initial skepticism, Dylan becomes engrossed in the story.

Carrie ceases reading mid-sentence and switches the flashlight off. The door handle is turning slowly and sneakily. Next the door silently opens and closes very quickly, light from the corridor briefly sweeping the room. The door is open just long enough to admit an annoying little six-year-old brat. Kelly skips across the room.

"Let me in with you, guys" she whispers plaintively.

"Get out. Go back to bed -this is my sleepover," Carrie whispers furiously.

"But he's my friend, too," responds Kelly to her sister. Then to Dylan, "We played together all day, Dill, let me come in for a cuddle, too." She sounds as if she is on the verge of tears.

Carrie thinks quickly. "Get into the top bunk," she orders her sister. "We will come up and join you. I don't want you in my bed."

This plan seems to make Kelly happy. In a jiffy, she scrambles up the ladder and jumps under the covers. "Hurry up," she encourages the occupants of the bunk below.

Carrie sits up and pulls her nightdress over her head and throws Dylan's pajamas at him and gestures for him to put them on. She climbs over Dylan, and begins to mount the bunk ladder.

"Dylan, too," whispers Kelly as her big sister joins her in the upper bunk.

"I don't think the three of us will fit," responds Carrie, using her bum to force her sister toward the wall side of the bed.

By now Dylan has got into his pajamas and sits up in bed. He swings his legs out and gets to his feet.

"Why don't you both sleep in the bottom bunk," he suggests, "I'll sleep on the top. Kelly's too little to sleep on the top. She may fall out."

Now that Dylan has his pajamas on, Carrie can afford to be more aggressive with Kelly.

"Kelly, go back to your own room. These bunks are not wide enough for three. Dylan is sleeping over with me, not you. I leave you alone when you have sleepovers. You're not wanted here."

Kelly is indignant. "You guys were naked, I saw you" she accuses emphatically. "That's why you want me to go. I'm going to tell Mom if you don't let me stay." This numbs Carrie into silence. Kelly is quick to recognize that she has swung the odds in her favor and changes tack.

"Pleeeeeeze let me stay for a while, Carrie. I want a cuddle, too. We can share the sleepover. Dylan is my friend too, aren't you, Dill?" she says imploringly. Dylan looks over at Carrie and shrugs his shoulders.

A while later, when Mrs. Summers looks in on Kelly's bedroom, she's not entirely surprised to observe that her bed is vacant. Kelly had latched on to Dylan from the moment of her return that morning. She crosses the corridor to Carrie's room. Carrie is still awake reading by flashlight in the lower bunk and is unable to switch it off in time to avoid a scowl from her mother. As her mother enters the room, Carrie indicates with a finger motion pointing to the upper bunk. In the upper bunk bed, Kelly and Dylan are in a deep sleep. Both lie on their backs and each have an arm wrapped around the other. Unfortunately, Kelly is on the inside of the bunk. Mrs. Summers has to climb two rungs of the bunk ladder, lean over Dylan and scoop Kelly up. The sleeping child groans, but does not awake. Dylan doesn't even groan.

"She's such a pest," whispers Carrie grumpily. "She ruins everything for me. I hate her."

Her mother says nothing, not being exactly sure what has been ruined, and exits the room burdened with the dead weight of sleeping Kelly in her arms.

*   *   *

7. KELLY

Mr. and Mrs. Douglas and their four children fly on a jet plane to London, England. They rent a car and drive one hundred miles down to Hampshire in Southwestern England, where Elwin Park boarding school is located. They drive through majestic gates into the school grounds, which are expansive and well-groomed. Manicured cricket and rugby pitches abound. The main school building is a formidable five-story, early Victorian mansion that had been converted into a school a hundred or so years prior.

Mr. and Mrs. Douglas speak to the headmaster, bald, obese, and exquisitely dressed in a three-piece suit complete with a chain and pocket watch. He goes by the name The Reverend Cecil Rumthorpe, though Dylan will soon learn that the boys in the school call him "Dome." Rumthorpe's pompous British manner is mitigated with a grin and twinkle in his eye that occasionally displays itself when certain parents are around.

"How would you like us to address you?" asks Mrs. Douglas, apprehensively.

Dome looks over his nose. "You may refer to me as 'Headmaster,'" he responds, while displaying his captivating twinkle. He even condescends to make eye contact with the woman, a concession seldom wasted on a parent. After all, the Douglas family has two other boys well-positioned in age to be shortly joining the elder of the Douglas offspring. This fact means that Mr. and Mrs. Douglas could soon belong to a small circle of the headmaster's favorite parents.

Rhianna Douglas has her suspicions about the man. She feels unsettled in his presence. She worries about who she is about to trust her son to. She looks to her husband, hoping for some support, but none is forthcoming. And clever Dome anticipates a mother's concerns. He makes a point of informing Mr. and Mrs. Douglas that the school has achieved remarkable success with students who attended American primary schools. Indeed, at that very moment, Elwin Park boasts a dozen American students, all outstanding scholars, with one representing the school's rugby team. The headmaster chuckles. Indeed, you might even confuse them for actually being British, he chortles! Ho, ho. It all sounded great.

When Mr. and Mrs. Douglas depart from the majestic gates of Elwin Park School that day, they do so with just three of their children. They drive to Heathrow airport in their rental car. There, they board a jet plane and fly away. A very long distance away.

Dylan has been deposited to the care of Elwin Park one day before the arrival of its student population. Following the departure of the Douglas parents, Headmaster Rumthorpe informs Dylan that he will be honored by placement in Dickens House. All Elwin Park boys are placed in one of three houses. In addition to Dickens House, there is Thackery House and Hardy House. Each House has a housemaster. The headmaster himself is the housemaster of Dickens House - that is why it is an honor to be placed there. Being a housemaster and a headmaster is a lot of work, Dylan is informed. For this reason, Dickens House has an assistant housemaster to do most of the work expected of a housemaster.

Assistant Housemaster Gwilliam shows Dylan his dormitory. There are twelve beds, arranged in rows. Housemaster Gwilliam informs Dylan that he can be addressed as "Reverend Gwilliam," "Mister Gwilliam," or just plain "sir."

"What is your first name... sir?" asks Dylan. Reverend Gwilliam peers over the top of his eyeglasses to study Dylan. Sir is slightly built and balding, with a beaky face. He wears a preacher's dog collar way too large for the wrinkled, scrawny neck it attempts to enclose.

"Er, we frown on using first names here at Elwin Park, Douglas. Boys refer to each other exclusively by their surnames and it would be considered highly impertinent for an English schoolboy to refer to any adult by their first name. If that's what they do in America, you'll have to change your ways."

The school has a gloomy, desolate appearance. Beyond the oak-paneled walls and Persian carpets of the headmaster's study lies the real world of Elwin Park, one of cream green institutional paint, linoleum surfaced floors, and unconcealed ceiling plumbing. Despite the temporary absence of students, the reek of staled food, body odor, and dampness prevails.

Dylan changes into his school uniform. The uniform was purchased from the school shop in advance of his arrival. Every item of clothing is a size too large for him. The color gray dominates, and wool appears to be the fabric of choice. A red stripe around the top of Dylan's knee-high gray stockings identifies him to the Elwin population as a member of Dickens House. The stockings are worn with gray flannel shorts. Red stripes on a gray necktie fulfill the function of identifying Dickens House on Sundays, when gray flannel long pants are worn. Even the dowdy gray shirt is a wool blend. For skin unused to the sensation of all this wool, the effect is a head-to-toe itch, a feeling exacerbated by any movement.

Dylan is ushered by Assistant Housemaster Gwilliam into the school dining room for tea. There he is abandoned. It is five in the afternoon. The dining room can seat 350, but only one table is set and it is laid for two. Dylan sits. An elderly woman shuffles through swing doors from the adjacent kitchen, bearing two plates covered by galvanized plate warmers. She places one of the plates in front of Dylan and raises the plate warmer off this dish, saying something to Dylan he cannot interpret. She seems to be speaking English, but with an accent he cannot decipher. She places the other plate, still covered, in the place set opposite Dylan. It appears she expects no response and she retreats back into the kitchen. Dylan studies the contents of the plate. It contains what appears to be a brown jelly and a perfect sphere of mashed potato. He pokes at the jelly, which turns out to be some kind of ground meat in gravy, covered by a thick skin. The skin does not yield to probing with a fork and has to be peeled back intact from the more liquid contents below it. A touch of the tip of the gravy-moistened fork to his tongue is sufficient for Dylan to determine that this is not food he's about to be eating this day, if indeed it's food. He scoops some mashed potato onto his fork. Despite a creamy texture, the flavor has little resemblance to any potato product Dylan has previously sampled. Dylan places his fork on his plate to wonder what comes next.

The main dining room door opens. A gangly boy, older than Dylan, but not by much, enters. He is dressed in an identical school uniform, but the bands on this boy's socks are green in color so he's obviously not in Dickens House. Studiously averting eye contact with Dylan, the boy strides over to the table Dylan is seated at, sits, and removes the plate warmer from his own dish. Although the contents of the plate are identical to those on Dylan's, his eyes light up and he tucks into the food with apparent relish. Dylan observes him, unsure of how to initiate an approach to this boy who seems so intent on ignoring him.

"Is this your first day here?" questions Dylan. Abruptly, the boy stops eating and, with his mouth full, focuses for the first time on Dylan.

"Give me your arm," orders the boy aggressively, getting to his feet. He grabs one of Dylan's arms and drives a knuckled fist into the muscle. Had the boy not been so puny in stature, the punch may have hurt. This punishment delivered, the boy resumes his seat and proceeds to the business of gobbling his food. Dylan is confused, unsure of what has just transpired.

He waits for the boy opposite him to consume a few more mouthfuls, then asks, "Why did you hit me just now?"

Once again, the boy quits eating and raises his eyes heavenward. "Now I have to hit you again," he sighs, getting to his feet to do just this. But Dylan isn't so compliant for round two. He stands and withdraws his arm behind his back. This time the boy backs down. "Alright, for once I'll make an exception, seeing as the school term doesn't really begin until tomorrow. You're a new boy. You're not supposed to speak to me unless you are spoken to. I have seniority. I'm a second year. If you speak to a second year without being spoken to, you have to offer your arm to have it punched."

Dylan digests this information. "What's your name?" ventures Dylan. "Mine is Dylan. Dylan Douglas." The boy studies Dylan again.

"You really aren't getting it, are you? There you go speaking to me again before I've spoken to you. Already you owe me two free punches."

"Sorry," says Dylan.

"Three punches," replies the boy. By this time, the boy has gobbled the contents of his plate and looks over to Dylan's untouched food. "I say," says the boy, "aren't you going to eat your food?" Dylan pushes the plate across the table toward his adversary. "No sense in letting it go to waste," says the skinny boy, now happy.

Dylan wonders if the boy is severely malnourished to have an appetite for such unappetizing swill. In any case, he'd like to leave the table and this confusing boy, but he has no idea where to go, so he stays put.

Finally, the starving boy's appetite is sated and he addresses Dylan. "Are you American?" he asks. Dylan nods in the affirmative, not wanting his debit of punches to increase. The boy softens. "It's OK," he declares, "School doesn't really start until tomorrow so we can talk to each other. But only for today. After tomorrow, you must pretend you don't know me. My name is Friedlander. Actually, it's Moshe Friedlander, but we never use first names at Elwin. But for today, I'll call you Dylan and you can call me Moshe, my Hebrew name. I don't tell many people that, it'd just be something else to make fun of so I usually say my first name is Michael if I'm asked here. I'm fourteen and from Hampstead. It's in London." He pauses. "By the way, I hope I didn't hurt you when I punched you. You're actually the first chap I've ever hit like that!"

"No, it didn't hurt," Dylan assures Moshe, concealing the fact that it would take a lot more than his feeble punch to hurt him. "But isn't it a pretty dumb rule? What if a first year was to object? What if he decided to retaliate and punch back?"

Moshe shakes his head gravely. "All the second years would band together and beat up anyone who defied seniority rites. And it wouldn't happen just once. You've never been to boarding school before, have you?"

Dylan shakes his head.

"Then I'll do you a favor and teach you about some of the horrible things that you can look forward to at wonderful Elwin Park!"

Moshe takes Dylan on a conducted tour of the vacant school premises. Moshe Friedlander tells Dylan that he's here a day in advance because his parents have traveled to the Caribbean for a holiday.

"That sucks," says Dylan, thinking about how his own parents have done the same thing, even flying the same direction as Moshe's parents, to resume their life without him.

Moshe makes it his business to highlight all of those places on the school prem-ises where suicides have taken place. Plenty of deaths have occurred here, it seems. According to Moshe, three students have leapt from the summit of the clock tower they are now passing. As a result, access to the clock tower is now limited by a locked steel gate. It makes for a nasty mess when someone jumps from the clock tower, Moshe says. Dylan is appalled. "Why do boys want to kill themselves?"

Moshe nods gravely. "You don't know what you're in for. This school is tough. Especially for a Jew like me; they hate Jews here. In school time, even if you were a second year, you'd not dare talk to me. Mostly, I can only be friends with other Jews. There are less than twenty of us in the entire school. I'm not sure what they will think about an American. They'll probably call you a 'wog.' It stands for 'wor-thy oriental gentlemen' but to them it just means foreigner. Maybe they'll just call you a 'yank'; that's not as bad. You don't seem as foreign as the rest of them - they hate foreigners almost as much as they hate Jewish people. Anybody who's different gets persecuted in some way. I am sorry to say this, Dylan, but it's very likely there'll be times when you want to jump off a clock tower."

Dylan is numb with fear. While he suspects that his new friend Moshe may be embellishing some of the horrors of Elwin, he also senses that there is a solid core of truth behind most of what he says. It is obvious to Dylan that Moshe is deeply unhappy and the butt of a lot of bullying. "Do you tell your mother about what it is like here?"

Moshe shakes his head and answers in an irritated voice. "You are really wet be-hind the ears! You'll learn."

That night, the lone occupant of a dormitory with twelve beds, Dylan assesses his predicament. He calculates that, at this moment in time, all members of his family are sitting on an airplane returning to a life that Dylan was perfectly happy with and had no ambition to change. He feels abandoned. For the first time in many years, he recalls his feelings on his first day of Kindergarten, those few mo-ments when his mother somehow disappeared in the principal's office. Back then, as a five-year-old, the duration of even the longest day was something that could be fathomed. But how could more than three months be endured before any respite was available let alone a projected high school career of five years? He cries. He feels more alone than he has ever felt in his life. But worse than this loneliness is the fear and uncertainty of what will happen when three hundred boys arrive the next day.

When they do arrive over the course of the next day, things do indeed get worse. Nothing in Dylan's short life has prepared him for survival in a British boarding school. The culture shock is traumatic. The country is alien. The subculture of the boarding school is alien. The British schoolboy is alien. Dylan experiences some considerable difficulty understanding the language. The language spoken at the school is punctuated with a broad range of four-letter words he's never heard previously.

Almost all of the other boys in the school are institutionalized. They've been prepared for this experience since the age of seven, the age at which they first attend boarding prep schools. But not Dylan. He is completely new to this, something he's made painfully aware of thanks to his new label of "new boy." This is the label tagged to all first-year entrants, though it seems to Dylan as though most of them aren't new at all. The majority of the other new boys had attended Elwin Park's own prep school, Elfin Park, which meant that not only were they already institutionalized, but they all knew each other. These boys are quick to identify anything that falls outside their narrow spectrum of what is right and normal, and that includes Dylan.

Dylan has an accent. He's a yank. A "fucking" yank. "Fuck" is the curse word of choice, but it is just one of dozens used at Elwin. It is a versatile term that peppers every conversation. Yes, Dylan had heard the word "fuck" used before his arrival at Elwin. He understood it to be a bad word, but did not know what it actually meant. And in bonnie England, it meant so many things. He soon discovers it is the most versatile word in the English language.

Dylan is a "fag." Fagging is integral to the culture of the British boarding school. It is unpaid labor exacted from all first-year students that allows much of the unskilled labor required to operate a boarding school to be supplied, free of charge, by the offspring of parents who are paying thousands for the privilege of an Elwin education. At Elwin, there is a fag for every chore. A locker room fag is responsible for its cleanliness around the clock. There are chapel fags, dormitory fags, corridor fags, yard fags, and classroom fags. The tools of this category of fag are mop and bucket, broom and duster. There are also personal fags. These fags are assigned to prefects, and this is the type of fag Dylan has become. Not only is he the fag to a prefect, but he is to be the Dickens House captain's personal fag.

The beating Dylan receives at the hands of the newly-appointed Dickens House captain could have been a lot worse. Blatherstone is a powerfully-built eighteen-year-old rugby forward, but he neglects to fully administer the old Elwin tradition of showing a new fag who's boss, as he holds little interest in beating up a puny thirteen-year-old. But he does administer a half-hearted thrashing, understanding that tradition is more important at Elwin than any personal feelings he might possess as an individual. Tradition probably intended this ritual to act as a preemptive measure, one designed to exact the utmost degree of servitude and promote enthusiasm in the execution of fagging duties. Consequently, tradition is duly served. Blatherstone confines his assault on Dylan to kneeing a dead leg to his thigh, and a couple of half-hearted punches to the stomach. This is sufficient to wind Dylan, but inflicts little other damage. After all, Blatherstone is a practical man. Why needlessly incapacitate one's fag and deprive yourself of his ability to serve for whatever amount of time it takes the little bastard to recover?

Dylan lies doubled up on the floor, clutching his stomach. Blatherstone addresses him as if absolutely nothing has transpired between them. He informs Dylan that he has posted a schedule on the inside of his study door. This schedule must be adhered to rigidly. When no reply is forthcoming, Blatherstone turns and looks down at his fag. From the floor, Douglas is quietly observing him with a cold stare that radiates hatred. Immediately, Blatherstone regrets not having hit the boy with a lot more force. He should at least be crying, even if faking it. There is little Blatherstone can do now that the boy is doubled up on the floor; it would be cowardly to administer a couple of kicks at this stage of the proceedings.

"Douglas, get to your feet immediately," orders Blatherstone. "I want to review my expectations of your fagging duties for this term. Actually, this school year, I do not expect to retrain another fag. Although, I should say you retain the right to request alternate fagging duties after serving two terms." Still no response. Blatherstone is not pleased. He stoops, grabs Douglas by the lapels of his school blazer, and physically hauls him to a sitting position onto the bed of the study. Through this operation, Douglas continues to stare Blatherstone in the eye. Blatherstone is unsettled. He chose Douglas as his fag for what he initially interpreted as a bright, inquisitive demeanor. Now the little American brat is staring him down with a hostility that is unnerving.

Actually, Dylan is terrified. He's just been subject to an unprovoked assault by a grown man more powerfully built than his own father. He has no idea of what the outcome will be, only that physically he can do little to influence it. His years of being coached as a baseball pitcher come into play and help him respond. He's convinced that in this predicament, he must mask any outward display of emotion, just as Hank told him. Bases loaded, two out, and a full count. He remembers Hank's words. Give your opponent the cold eye. Suck in an extra deep breath. Show nothing of your real feelings. Stare the batter down. Seated on Blatherstone's bed, he realizes that he's unlikely to be struck again, but he resolutely maintains his pitcher's cold eye if for no other reason than it stops him from crying. He suspects that

Blatherstone wants nothing more than to reduce him to tears.

Blatherstone walks away from Dylan, crosses the study, and fills an electric kettle with water at the wash basin. He tries a different tack.

"How do you take your tea, Douglas?" asks Blatherstone. Dylan still says nothing, he doesn't take tea. "This is the last cup of tea I'll make for myself this school year," says Blatherstone, almost as if he is making a promise to himself. "Making tea is a fag's duty. You'll see this on the list of duties I have prepared for you. Polishing my shoes is another. When you have finished your tea, I want all my shoes shined. You should be able to see your reflection in them. In the mornings, I bathe at 7:15 on the dot. The instant morning prep finishes, you must get up here to draw my bath and then wake me. I also require a bath after rugby matches: it's your job to run down and draw a bath the instant the final whistle sounds."

Blatherstone presents Dylan with the cup of tea he has brewed. Dylan slowly takes it. It is time to cede some territory.

"Being a personal fag has responsibilities, but also advantages," continues Blatherstone. "The school population will understand that you are my fag. This means that you'll generally be left alone. The only person permitted to beat you up will be me. From now on, I'll only do that when you deserve to be thrashed. In addition, you will have access to all prefect's studies, but that means that confidentiality is required and this confidentiality must *never* be breached. What you hear in a prefect's study must never go beyond it. A personal fag is a trusted appointment; I chose you because I thought you looked like someone who could be trusted. In return, when you make tea or coffee for me or my guests, you are permitted to take a cup for yourself. I'll also bequeath to you my newspapers and magazines."

Blatherstone focuses on Dylan. Despite this more friendly approach, the house captain has never once smiled. In fact, his facial expression has remained deadpan throughout. Blatherstone speaks in an accent which Dylan supposes to be the Queen's English, in which carefully enunciated words discharge from the roof of the mouth rather than the throat, little modulated by lips. To Dylan's ear, the sound is alternately comical and grating. Blatherstone pulls a pewter hip flask from the inside breast pocket of his blazer. He unscrews the cap and pours some of the contents of the hip flask into his cup of tea. Next, he motions to Dylan to pass his cup toward him for a shot. Dylan responds with a "no thanks."

"I didn't ask you whether you wanted some or not. Pass your cup to me," orders Blatherstone. Dylan does as he's been told. Blatherstone pours in a shot of what he describes as "chipper Cognac" and says something about educating his coarse American palate.

In this way, Dylan is introduced to life as a kind of personal slave. Yes, there were some advantages – Blatherstone was dead right about his immunity to the random acts of bullying that most first-year students are subjected to at Elwin. He learns that he's off-limits to everyone – no one dares touch him, a priceless advantage in this harsh society. However, Dylan is inevitably marginalized by his duties to Blatherstone, which preclude him from unstructured free time with other first-year students. In addition to his unfamiliarity with the culture and the difference in his speech, Dylan also has to contend with some peer suspicion that comes with being the house captain's fag, a potential spy.

Dylan acclimatizes. Not quickly, but he watches and learns. He also comes to grips with the subject matter of his classes, despite it being so different from that in an American school. During the first term at the school, the underclass of new boys is not allowed off the premises. The institutional message is "this is your world, you had best get used to it." A term lasts just short of four months. Four months can seem like an eternity at thirteen years old. But end it does. He counts down every day. Finally the first term, the "Michaelmas" term, in Elwin lingo, ends.

Dylan boards a train with a bunch of other Elwin boys. The train takes him to Waterloo station in London. There he says goodbye to the Elwin boys and takes a coach to Heathrow airport. He checks in at the airline counter, where a clerk pins onto his chest a small badge with wings on it. The badge says "Junior Jet Club." This is the airline's guarantee that that they would not lose a minor in transit. Next, he boards an airplane and flies far away.

Dylan returns to a world he thinks he knows and understands. A world void of the horrors and uncertainties of the one he had left. His mom and dad and brothers and sister are waiting on the airport tarmac for him. Dylan wants so badly to appear big and grown up. But when he hugs his mother, he bursts into tears. Tears he is powerless to contain. His father turns and walks away in disgust. Dylan's tears are contagious. Within moments, his siblings are also crying and even his mother has teared up.

Does Dylan try to explain to his mother what he has gone through? A couple of times he begins to do just this, but his mom quickly does her best to change the subject. She informs her son that his experience is all about growing up. He cannot cling to childhood forever. Dylan will grow into the world at Elwin Park and, in time, come to appreciate its merits. She explains that she would like nothing better than to keep him at home with her forever. But doing so would condemn him to becoming an ignorant dolt, depriving him of the ability to make choices in this world. She loves him too much to do that.

On his second day back, Dylan visits Carrie. They had exchanged letters a number of times during his absence. Dylan has not shared with Carrie any of his true feelings about boarding school in these letters. Carrie is waiting for him at the door of her house. In just four months, she has changed in appearance so much that Dylan almost fails to recognize her. He approaches her and they hug. Kelly is standing behind her big sister. She is jumping up and down, telling Carrie to hurry up, she needs a hug too. Kelly is crying. The youngster informs Dylan that she's not going to allow him to go away again. Then Mrs. Summers hugs Dylan. Finally Hank appears. He says nothing, but gives Dylan a hug, too. Then Mrs. Summers instructs Kelly to leave Carrie and Dylan alone. It has been such a long time since they have seen each other. Kelly protests with tears, because it's been just as long since she has last seen Dylan, too. Finally, Mrs. Summers physically wrenches her younger daughter away.

Once in Carrie's room, Dylan senses that Carrie has grown distant, grown in a very different direction. He has dreamed about this moment for four months. But Carrie has fundamentally changed. It's not just that she looks different. And she does look very different! She has grown two inches in height and now has boobs; not big, but definitely noticeable. Efforts to conceal some adolescent pimples on her face are not entirely effective and there's a small pimple on her nose. Carrie informs him that she had got her first period a couple of months previously. "It's difficult to explain," she says carefully choosing her words, "It's made me not want to feel close to anyone … especially when I'm having a period … which just happens to be the truth at the moment. I feel clumsy and awkward … my breasts hurt and I get tummy cramps."

Dylan feels awkward too. Carrie seems like a stranger now. She's serious and in some ways has gotten older than him.   He wasn't counting on this. He had thought that his ordeals in boarding school would entitle him to some elevated status as the more experienced of the pair.

Carrie sits on her lower bunk bed and pats the space beside her, inviting Dylan to sit. Dylan surveys the room. In place of the cartoon movie posters she once preferred are posters of rock stars.

Carrie bluntly asks Dylan if he has experienced a wet dream yet. The question takes him by surprise because it's not the type of question a stranger asks. Has Carrie become a stranger? Then, he realizes, somewhere in the depths of this new and unfamiliar Carrie are remnants of the Carrie he once knew. Dylan blinks. Yes, he responds slowly, it had happened when he was at boarding school. He had been dreaming of her. In the dream, they were sleeping forks. The emission took him by surprise and woke him. At first, he thought he'd wet the bed, which would have been an unendurable embarrassment in a boarding school dormitory. Then he put two and two together and figured out what had happened. As for the ejaculate, it had sublimated into the atmosphere by morning. He calls it spunk. That's what the English kids call it. He omits informing Carrie that he has masturbated many times since the night of that first wet dream. Masturbation seems to Dylan like a topic he cannot discuss with Carrie. But wet dreams are okay.

While Carrie asking Dylan about the wet dream cuts the distance that has grown between them, nothing can make them feel comfortable with each other. Carrie informs Dylan that she's happy she featured in his first wet dream. But she says that's another reason they cannot do all those things they used to "back when we were kids." Her mom had warned her to be careful. Very careful. They were not kids any more.

Dylan discovers that the Summers' are "returning" to Baton Rouge. Because both Carrie and Kelly have grown up in Venezuela, they've only known the States as a place where they spend vacations. Now, they'll actually go there to live for the first time. The family is to return at the completion of the school year, says Carrie. The reason is partly Dylan. It turns out that Carrie's mom and Dylan's mom sometimes chat over coffee. One recent topic of conversation has been the necessity of sending children off to boarding schools and the effect it has on those children. Carrie's mom and dad have decided that the whole family will return to the States rather than send Carrie to boarding school.

"Are you very unhappy at school?" asks Carrie. Dylan isn't sure what to say. He doesn't know how Carrie has come to understand that he has been unhappy in boarding school. He never outright told his mother he was unhappy in letters he wrote her and he certainly didn't indicate he was unhappy in any letter he sent to Carrie. Dylan wants to be honest with Carrie, but now finds it difficult to articulate what he really feels.

"Everybody keeps telling me that I'll get used to it," he responds, "but it sure isn't easy. Everything is so different. I hate being in England. I never realized how happy I was here until I was sent away."

"Daddy thinks it was a big mistake to send you to England," says Carrie. "He says that if you had gone to a stateside school you would've had the same school courses and been able to play baseball – and it would have been a lot closer."

"Yeah, my mom wanted me to go to school in the States. My dad had this idea that schools in England have higher standards. I'm not sure that is true. The school work isn't really any harder – just different. It's not just that I don't like England or the English ... it's being so far away from everything that I know."

"Have you told your mom and dad that you are really unhappy?"

Dylan thinks. "It's not so easy. My family is bigger than yours and the littlest kids get the most attention. My dad doesn't have a lot of time for me. He'd think I was a wuss if I complained. I would never tell him how I really feel. I might try to tell Mom, but I am not sure how. It's difficult to get to talk to her about things that are personal because there is just so much other stuff going on."

"I'm scared about going back to Louisiana. It may be home to Mom and Dad, but my whole life has been here. Still, I'd rather be with my family than go to boarding school. I know I'd hate being away from home."

The Christmas vacation speeds by. Everything about "home" seems so different to Dylan. What is most scary is that his family has acquired an altered set of routines that suggest that they barely notice his absence. Yes, life had gone on in the Douglas family quite happily without him. Deidra no longer idolizes Dylan. She's a second grader now and very much her own person. She can hold her own in any squabble with Daniel or Domenic. In fact, she even has a way of getting around her father's soft side, a skill that has eluded the three boys. Deidra's second grade friends come over for visits and sleepovers. She's definitely not a baby any more. Daniel and Domenic have assumed themselves into the big brother roles that used to be Dylan's. In addition, they continue to be a twosome. Once the excitement of Dylan's return has passed, the boys seem not to notice his existence.

Dylan touches base with his former classmates. Now they are all Grade Eight kids, the kingpins in the American school. They all look up to him now. He's the one that has already experienced what they are yet to experience. Dylan is cautious about the way he answers their questions. He finds himself actually painting his boarding school experience in a way more positive light than it deserves. He does this partly because he doubts any American boarding school could replicate the hell he has experienced in England. But he also believes that it would make him appear like a wimp to complain. Not complaining means avoiding the truth. So Dylan lies to his family. And he lies to his friends.

After Christmas Day has passed, Dylan spends a full day with Carrie and the Summers' family. He and Carrie talk. They sit cross-legged on her lower bunk bed, just like in former times. Dylan lets Carrie do most of the talking. She doesn't have to lie. She seems less of a stranger now. She tells him that school has become all too serious – they have to work harder in Grade Eight. Not just work harder in school, but also at home because they are never without homework assignments.

"I miss having you in class," she informs him. "When little things happen, a teacher saying something dumb or something that I knew only you and I would find funny, we could always catch each other's eyes and share a secret chuckle between us. That was special. Gosh, the ball team misses you. I don't think they've won a game since you left, so poor Daddy spends Saturday afternoons pulling his hair out." This makes Dylan feel good.

"I miss you as a friend too, Dylan," she declares more somberly. "I have no one to talk about books, and life, and sex with now. The best thing is that I know so much about boys today because of you … I'm sure I know way more than any other girls in class, even those with brothers. We had fun being curious, didn't we?"

Dylan nods silently in agreement.

"Did you get to kiss a girl yet … an English girl?"

"You mean like with open mouth, a real kiss?"

Carrie giggles. "Let's start with *any* type of kiss?"

Dylan laughs, too. "No, no kind of kiss. Not much chance in an all-boys boarding school … unless I want to kiss another boy. And there are boys who do that." Then he adds more seriously, "I guess that's what I miss most. No girls. Never thought I'd miss having girls around. I haven't made a friend like you – one I could really trust. I mean, I know we spent a lot of time pretending to hate each other when other kids were around. But we sure got on pretty good when we were alone. We've been pretty good friends since Grade Four, I guess. My best friend. You just happened to be a girl best friend." Carrie leans forward to hug him.

"How about you? Did you get to have a *real* kiss yet?" Dylan asks.

Carrie purses her lips and nods her head in the affirmative. "Yes," she says, "It was a bit of a disaster. Alberto Rodriguez asked if he could kiss me at an eighth grade social in the school gym. I said yes; at the time I actually thought he was kind of cute. When he kissed me, he surprised me and stuck his tongue in my mouth. All the way. It was blocking my throat. He was holding the back of my head so I couldn't pull away. I was choking and coughed. After he pulled his tongue out, he got mad at me. I spat on the floor and wiped my mouth. He said I was being a baby and didn't know how to kiss. It was disgusting. His tongue tasted of onions and hamburgers."

"How come we have never kissed?" Dylan asks Carrie, wondering why this had never previously crossed his mind.

"I'm not really sure," Carrie says thinking, "I don't think it is something either of us particularly wanted, especially you. So, did you ever want to kiss me?"

"No, I guess I never really thought about it until you started talking about it just now," responds Dylan. "It was mostly you who decided what we were going to do. You made up the rules and I just followed."

Carrie laughs. "Yes, I was kind of bossy. But you didn't seem to mind too much playing along. Do you want to kiss me now?"

Dylan is wondering how to respond when they are interrupted by a series of loud thumps. Kelly is pounding her fists on the bedroom door. "I want Dylan to come swimming with me," she yells. "It's my turn to have him. You promised."

Carrie raises her eyes into her lids. "You'll have to go and play with her in the pool," Carrie advises Dylan. "She still has a terrible crush on you. Nobody else plays with her like you do. Through Christmas, she never stopped talking about your visit today."

Dylan approaches the door and opens it. Ten-year-old Kelly is standing in the doorway, togged out in a blue one-piece swimsuit. She has her hands on her hips and an admonishing scowl on her face. Then, in an instant, her facial expression changes. She smiles and twirls her body around in a circle to model the swimsuit.

"It's new," she announces proudly, "I'm on the swim team now. I do 50 and 100 meters breaststroke – I can beat all the boys. I do breast on the relay, too. I might even be able to beat you in a breast race now."

Dylan holds out a hand for Kelly. As she clasps his hand, she skips alongside him. She takes three skips to one of Dylan's strides. She is telling him all about the world of Grade Five and what she has planned for them to do that afternoon. Dylan and Kelly play. In the pool, Kelly demonstrates her newfound prowess at breaststroke. Dylan and Kelly have a breaststroke race. Kelly wins. Dylan coaches Kelly's backstroke. After, he informs her that he is quite certain she can also make the swim team competing at 50 meters backstroke. The pair practice diving. After exhausting themselves in the pool, they retreat to Kelly's bedroom to play. Kelly has somehow persuaded Dylan to play Barbie dolls with her. The truth is that, today, she could persuade Dylan to jump off a cliff if she had a mind to. When the barbeque is ready, Kelly insists on sitting next to Dylan. He doesn't mind a bit. Kelly is the only thing about home that seems not to have changed during his four month absence.

The vacation comes to an end. On the day of departure, his family, the Summers family, and most of the Grade Eight class come to the airport to see him off. Dylan's father shakes his hand, his mom hugs and kisses him with tears in her eyes. Each of his siblings kisses him in turn. Dylan turns to face the crowd that has come to see him off. Mrs. Summers steps forward to hug and kiss him on the forehead.

Hank hugs him and slips a cassette tape into Dylan's shirt pocket.

"Don't look at it now," instructs Hank in his slow drawl, "but this might help you survive boarding school."

Kelly is jumping up and down, using her father's pants pocket to leverage altitude and attention, impatiently waiting for her father to be done with Dylan. Her turn at last, Kelly throws herself airborne and locks her arms around Dylan's neck to hug him with all the force she can muster. She clings to Dylan until Hank walks over and peels her off. Hank enfolds Kelly in his arms as if he were handling a much younger child and Kelly succumbs to his embrace like a baby. Finally, Carrie cautiously approaches Dylan. She holds him by each forearm and gently guides her lips to his. It is a gentle kiss and a dry kiss. But it might count as Dylan's first real kiss, even though it is a very public one. Grade Eight spontaneously applauds. Carrie suddenly pulls away from Dylan to seek her mother's arms. She is in tears.

It is past time to exit the scene. Dylan turns, waves behind his back, and crosses the tarmac headed to the aircraft. Somehow, he manages to hold back his own tears until he has entered the fuselage.

The Convair turboprop takes off. Once the plane is airborne, Dylan removes the cassette tape Hank inserted into his shirt pocket. It is a home reproduced recording of Bob Dylan's *Blonde on Blonde*. It means nothing to Dylan at this moment. He suspects that Hank has chosen this album because he and the artist share a name, his first name and the artist's surname. But over the next couple of years, Dylan will come to memorize the lyrics on every track of the double album.

Dylan considers his kiss with Carrie on the tarmac. He's not sure whether that kiss should count as his first real kiss. It seemed that he and Carrie kissed more because it was what everyone observing the departure expected of them. Although throughout a big part of his childhood he had been closer to Carrie than any other friend, and at school they had been known for years as "boyfriend and girlfriend," Dylan wonders if this was ever really true. After a while, he concludes that, no, Carrie was a *friend*, not a proper girlfriend. He'd have to wait a little longer for his first real kiss.

At Caracas airport, Dylan has another Junior Jet Club badge pinned onto his chest by a hostess. The hostess, who must be all of nineteen years, speaks to him as if he were five years old and mentally deficient. He boards a large Boeing airliner and flies across the Atlantic. He is on his way back to Elwin Park. There is no going back. Things have changed forever.

8. HEATHER AND HAZEL

The dormitory lights snap on. Blatherstone is bellowing an order: everyone get out of bed and stand at attention. Now! It is the first night of the new school term. Having been asleep, Dylan is disoriented and blinded by the light at this inhospitable awakening. Accordingly, he is slow to respond. He's not the only one. Blatherstone struts around the dormitory and with his boot, kicks over the beds of those first-year boys not yet standing at attention in front of their beds. Dylan's bed is one of those kicked upside down. Dazed, he extricates himself from the bedding, picks himself off the floor, and stands, attempting to rub the sleep from his eyes. "Well isn't this a nice welcome back to the gulag," thinks Dylan.

It transpires that someone has been talking after lights out. Talking after lights out is a major offence in the first-year's dormitory of Dickens House. It's an offence punishable by four strokes of the cane. Once all the boys are standing at attention in front of their beds, Blatherstone asks the guilty parties to "own-up" to the offence. Silence ensues. Blatherstone struts up and down the dormitory, eyeing each boy. He is all but goose stepping. He's intent on detecting indicators of guilt in the faces of the boys. Nervously, boys look down at their feet. Not one of them utters a word. A few shuffle their feet. Silence.

Blatherstone attempts a different tack, namely that of applying some peer pressure to the guilty parties. He grandly announces that he'll leave the dormitory for three minutes. When he returns, he expects the two boys who were talking to "own up." These two boys will be duly caned. If the guilty parties are unwilling to identify themselves, then all twelve boys in the dormitory will be caned. He declares that the "honor" of the first-year Dickens House boys is at stake. Blatherstone exits the dormitory, leaving it illuminated with twelve boys standing in front of their beds.

Smythe Palmer is the self-appointed dormitory leader. Smythe Palmer is a bully. He's a year older than the other first-year boys because, somewhere along the way, his progression through primary school was stalled by having to repeat a year. His body, however, ignored the hiatus and just kept growing. The result is that, as a stocky fourteen-year-old among thirteen-year-olds, he's the current kingpin. Smythe Palmer turns on a pair of meek boys who sleep next to each other at the far corner of the dormitory. The boys go by the names of Parker and Hornby. Smythe Palmer addresses them as "fucking homos" and orders them to own up to the talking after lights out or they'll have him to contend with the following day. Parker and Hornby, who are probably just good friends and not homos, point out to Smythe Palmer that it was he who was doing the talking after lights out so "why the fuck should we take the rap for you?" Smythe Palmer makes some menacing gestures toward Parker and Hornby. Nevertheless, it appears that the two innocent boys are going to stubbornly resist becoming fall guys.

Blatherstone returns. Quietly, he asks the boys who might be guilty of the heinous crime. Silence. The consequence of this silence is that all twelve boys in the Dickens House first-year dormitory are marched to the prefect's study to receive a beating consisting of four strokes of the cane. Justice must be done. Justice is an Elwin Park tradition. Blatherstone knows this just as surely as he also knows that the ten innocent boys who are caned that evening will one day appreciate this fact. But as things turn out, only eleven of the twelve boys in the dormitory are thrashed. Smythe Palmer evades the punishment by convincing Blatherstone he has a preexisting skin condition – body acne. On no account can he be beaten. Smythe Palmer's father is the Conservative Member of Parliament for a riding in Surrey. Cunning runs in his blood.

The following morning, Dylan refuses to speak to Blatherstone. He fills Blatherstone's bath, makes his tea, and polishes his shoes. But the normally chirpy Dylan utters not a single word to the house captain. As the morning progresses, Blatherstone gets increasingly pissed off. He'll be damned if he'll tolerate this blatant "cheek" from his fag. Accordingly, he picks Douglas, the "fucking yank," up off his feet and throws him across the study. He startles at how light the boy is. Dylan is launched into the side of Blatherstone's desk, on which he cuts the back of his head. It is not a serious cut, but because it's a head wound, it bleeds dramatically. Blood runs down the back of Dylan's neck and saturates his shirt. Blatherstone instructs him to go and get cleaned up and change his shirt.

A while later, when Dylan walks into breakfast brandishing his bloody shirt, he's stopped by the duty master. Blatherstone is standing alongside the teacher.

"What happened to you?" asks the duty master.

"I tripped and hit my head on a desk," says Dylan. Blatherstone just stares blankly at Dylan. Dylan can see that he's fuming. When instructed to go and change his shirt by the duty master, Dylan explains that he's unable to do this until his school trunk is delivered from holiday storage, something not scheduled until that afternoon. Thus there is no option but to allow Dylan to continue to display his bloodied shirt to the school, a badge that gains him significant prestige. There's no doubt in the minds of the inhabitants of Dickens House first-year dorm who was responsible.

"Acne of the arse?" declares Forsythe of Dickens House first year dormitory after breakfast. "We'll see about that!" Forsythe also has a sense of justice. He's a graduate of Elfin Park Preparatory School and knows exactly what should be done. Smythe Palmer must be dealt with even if he is endowed with double the bulk of some of the smaller boys in the dormitory. His balls must be boot-polished. Furthermore, Smythe Palmer will be placed "on Coventry" for a week. Being "on Coventry" means that no first-year in the entire school will be permitted to talk to him. Forsythe selects four boys to assist him with the task of taking down Smythe Palmer. Among the first of his choices for this elite swat team is the yank with the blood-soaked shirt.

The mugging is executed after prep that evening. It takes place in the upper third form home room, seconds after the duty prefect exits the classroom. Dylan's assignment is to engage Smythe Palmer in a headlock, so he is required to make the first move. He jumps and locks his arm around Smythe Palmer's throat, and for a couple of seconds has to hang on while the older boy is neutralized by his partners in the assault. With one boy throttling him, one holding each arm, and a fourth pinning his legs, Smythe Palmer understands that the game is up and begins to blubber and plead for mercy. Forsythe, who to this point has not been physically involved in the assault, approaches the now pathetic Smythe Palmer. The smaller boy grins, then smashes his fist into Smythe Palmer's nose. He does this with such force that the impact reverberates through Dylan's body. Blood spews from Smythe Palmer's nose and sets about ruining Dylan's second shirt within the space of a day. Next, Forsythe pulls down the victim's shorts and underpants, scoops out the entire contents of a jar of black boot polish, and fastidiously pastes it onto the bared genitals before him.

Eleven boys are standing in front of their beds in Dickens House first-year dorm. This time they are dressed in day clothes, not pajamas. No boy is standing in front of Smythe Palmer's bed. This is because Smythe Palmer has been taken to Southampton Hospital to have some repairs to a broken nose. Blatherstone paces down the length of the dormitory and back up again. He pauses in front of Dylan and scrutinizes the dried blood on his shirt sleeve. Blatherstone looks grim. So do the boys. Will they be caned once again? Two nights in a row? Suddenly, Blatherstone turns heel and exits the dormitory with a departing command: "get to bed."

Dylan cannot sleep. While he despises Smythe Palmer for the bully he was, he's uncomfortable about the role he played in his toppling. Forsythe will be the new dormitory kingpin. His role in the demise of Smythe Palmer didn't begin until the bigger boy had been fully neutralized. Because Dylan was clamping the bully's neck from behind, he had a firsthand view of the pleasure Forsythe took in first injuring, then humiliating a helpless victim. God, how he hates Elwin Park.

The following morning, Dylan decides that he'll still not say a word to Blatherstone. Blatherstone is clearly peeved, but doesn't react until just before the breakfast bell is sounded. Then he grabs Dylan by the shirt collar at the throat and forces him against a wall. "I have taken all the shit I am going to take from you Douglas," he seethes. "You either shape up or I will fire you as my fag."

"Good," responds Dylan, perhaps asserting himself for the first time at Elwin, "do it right away. I don't want to be your fag." Blatherstone is lost for words.

He releases Dylan and shakes his head. "So you'd rather clean out bogs than hold the most prestigious fagging assignment in the house?"

Dylan straightens his shirt collar. He nods his head. "I'd rather clean the bogs," he affirms.

Blatherstone walks over to his desk. A silence ensues. The breakfast bell sounds and Dylan wants to be dismissed. Blatherstone speaks, but sounds different – he's not accustomed to rationalizing anything to anyone in this institution, let alone a first-year. "I did you boys a favor," he begins. "I knew who was talking the instant I entered the dormitory two nights ago. I didn't have to ask the question. I knew what I was doing when I declined to cane Smythe Palmer. I also knew what would happen to him if the boys in your dormitory had any gumption. Collectively, you did the honorable thing and dethroned a bully."

Dylan shifts his weight from one foot to the other. This was something he hadn't considered. Maybe there was activity happening under Blatherstone's thick scull, perhaps more than he'd given him credit for. Another interlude ensues. Dylan wants to escape, but can't until Blatherstone elects to dismiss him.

"Douglas," he says, "I think that you and I have an understanding. We get on well together. I wouldn't easily adjust to having to break in another fag and I don't want to replace you. As a matter of protocol, it's not your decision, it's mine. At the end of this term, you'll have been my fag for two terms, so at that point you are allowed to choose. But I want to tell you now, that it's my hope that you'll elect to be my fag for a third term."

Fat chance, thinks Dylan. Another long pause ensues, finally interrupted by Dylan. "May I please be excused to go to breakfast?"

Blatherstone shakes his head. "Get out," he says resignedly.

On the first Saturday at the beginning of the Lent term, Dylan obtains a town pass. His plan is to check out the local town of Romsey. Romsey is known as a brewery town. Naturally, that meant the town had a strong pub culture. It was said among the locals that the number of pubs in Romsey exceeded the number of shops. The town exudes a particular odor, namely the odor that results from the combustion of solid fossil fuels and coal gas, combined with the volatile discharge of brewing malt.

The town is located in a river valley about three miles east of Elwin Park. A short bus ride is all that's required for any Elwin Park student who wishes to visit on a Saturday afternoon. Few ever do; the snobby student populace of Elwin Park views anything associated with the local town with derision. In their lingo, Romsey is populated with "plebs" and "prols." In return, the agricultural townspeople of Romsey regard the Elwin Park boys with barely concealed contempt. On the part of the people of Romsey, this is a justifiable response to being looked down upon by snobbish adolescents of Elwin.

On a cold, but bright afternoon in January, Dylan steps off a bus in the Romsey town square. He is accompanied by two other third formers, also on their first town pass. His companions are interested in food. They have been dreaming of eating some greasy English-style fish and chips, and immediately take off to locate a venue that will cater to their tastes. Dylan explores alone, making a circuit of the town square, which is actually triangular in shape. On a side street, he strolls toward the Romsey abbey, the most prominent structure in the town. In doing so, he discovers the location of St. Theresa's Convent for Young Ladies. Some older girls in uniform pass him by heading toward the town square. After some more exploration, Dylan surmises that the town doesn't have much to brag about. A Woolworths store, a drugstore, a jewelry store, post office, a couple of greasy spoon style restaurants, a Smiths bookstore, and yes, many pubs. Just about everything Romsey has to offer can be checked out within twenty minutes.

Dylan enters the Smiths bookstore. He browses absent-mindedly for some moments. While doing so, he observes a girl of around his age entering the store. She's dressed in a St. Theresa Convent uniform and purposefully strides to the back of the store. She's cute, Dylan thinks, cute enough to keep his eye on. He continues to covertly observe the girl's actions. She has partially concealed herself at the end of one of the aisles and is removing her shoes. Next, she takes a peek over her shoulder, and quickly peels off the wool, gray school tights she is wearing. The tights are stuffed into her satchel, from which she then removes a pair of white panties and proceeds to wriggle into them, pulling them up under her skirt as discreetly as possible. Finally, she corrects her appearance by hitching her gray school kilt high on her waist to convert it into a miniskirt and slips her shoes back on. The entire makeover takes place in less than thirty seconds. She smoothes the kilt and advances toward the exit.

Dylan boldly approaches the now bare-legged girl to intercept her before she can exit the bookstore. "Er, can you help me find a paperback copy of Ian

Fleming's *Dr. No?*"

The girl stops, surprised, and looks at him with disdain. "Why don't you ask somebody who works here?" she suggests haughtily.

"Because I'm sure that person wouldn't have legs as cute looking as yours," Dylan responds.

This is all it takes. The girl looks at him with an even more surprised expression, but this almost instantly changes into a smile.

"Where are you from?" she asks. "You don't sound very much like an Elwin boy. Are you American?"

"Maybe I could tell you all about me over a coffee ... or do you drink just tea? And you could tell me something about yourself. Is there a place in Romsey where we could meet?"

The girl considers. "There's an espresso bar. It's above the bakery on the other side of the square. You have to walk through the bakery and go up the stairs at the back. I'm not sure if I want to meet you there, though."

"My treat," responds Dylan. "There's nothing I'd like better than to have a coffee with you. You can tell me all about Romsey. This is my first visit."

The girl considers again. "OK, but I have to go to the newsagents first. I'll meet you there in twenty minutes. Remember, you enter the bakery and go upstairs for the espresso bar."

"It's a deal," exclaims Dylan, happy at making a conquest. Picking up these English girls was not so tough! With that, the girl turns and begins to walk away. Suddenly, Dylan is aware that he doesn't know the girl's name. He runs to catch up with her and exclaims, "Wait a sec, I don't know your name. I'm Dylan."

The cute girl turns to look at Dylan, appearing flustered. "My name is ... my name is ... Heather." There's something about the way she responds that strikes Dylan as suspicious. But what? Perhaps she's just trying to get rid of him? Dylan guesses that twenty minutes from now, the odds of Heather meeting up with him in the coffee shop are not good. He stands and stares as Heather resumes her course to the newsagents and disappears into the crowd in the village square.

Twenty minutes later, Dylan enters the second floor coffee shop and is both happy and surprised to observe Heather already seated at one on the tables. She's alone and busy with what appears to be homework. Dylan walks over to the table and prepares to seat himself in a chair opposite Heather.

"Hi Heather," he announces as he drags a chair away from the table to sit, "why did you put your tights back on? I wasn't kidding when I said you had cute legs." Heather's responses are not what he expects. Her initial reaction is one of complete surprise as she looks up from her homework. She looks Dylan up and down to take measure of him.

"Can I get you a coffee?" the boy asks.

"Who exactly are you?" asks the girl. She is more composed now.

Dylan looks at her in confusion. Is this girl completely stupid?

"Dylan," he responds. "We met in the bookstore twenty minutes ago, remember? A long time ago, to be sure. Plenty of time to entirely forget a person."

Heather looks around, surveying the entire coffee shop as if she is looking for someone. Dylan wonders how he can bail from this scene. What Heather does next takes him completely by surprise. She leans over to Dylan and whispers, "You aren't going to understand this, not at first, I'll explain later, but I want you to lean over and pretend you are kissing me. Not a real kiss, I don't want that. Don't let your lips touch mine. Just pretend, but try to make it look real."

Dylan has no idea what is going on. Has he entered the twilight zone?

"Er, okay," he says nervously.

Heather leans forward over the table that separates Dylan and herself. She places one hand behind Dylan's neck and angles her head while moving her lips an inch short of Dylan's and closes her eyes. For an instant, Dylan wonders if he should close up on the one inch that separates their lips and really kiss her, but he has no time to ponder this move. From behind, two girls in Convent school uniforms burst in to the coffee shop, laughing and giggling. They skip toward the table Dylan and Heather are seated at and pull up chairs. One of the two girls is Heather without tights. Dylan feels like a bit of a chump.

After sitting, Heather without tights says to Heather with tights, "Did you really kiss? You saucy beast!"

"Of course, dahling," responds Heather with tights and a little sass. "It was love at first sight." She begins to gather up the homework she'd been working on. She places the school books into her satchel and sits back in her chair.

Heather and Hazel are identical twins. They introduce themselves, while cautioning Dylan against attempting to distinguish between them. They also introduce the third girl, whose name is Judy. No obvious physical characteristic differentiates the twins. Every facial and corporal detail of the one is replicated in the other. This is reinforced with identical haircuts. Both girls seemed to delight in their ability to create as much confusion as possible from their paternal twin status. Dylan learns that Heather and Hazel are third formers attending St. Theresa's Convent. To Dylan, this means they have to be approximately his age.

Heather, Hazel, Judy, and Dylan drink cappuccinos. Dylan can't stop talking. For the first time since he has arrived in England, he feels relaxed and unthreatened in a social situation. These girls are not about to dismiss him as a "fucking yank." Far from it, they like the way he speaks and seem to enjoy his efforts at flirting with them. Dylan asks Heather/Hazel if she/they have boyfriends. Heather and Hazel look at each other. They are wondering whether to confide in Dylan. One of them responds. "We are both madly in love with the same boy. He's an Elwin student. He's in your house – you are in Dickens right? Actually, he's the house captain."

"Blatherstone!" responds Dylan, appalled.

"Colin," both girls trill simultaneously. For a moment, Dylan is lost for words. How could anyone actually like a snobbish dolt like Blatherstone?

"How is it that you know him?" asks Dylan, still incredulous. Both Heather and Hazel look at each other again.

Hazel responds, "You don't know who we are, do you? We were hoping not to tell you." The girls switch back and forth like a tag team to inform Dylan about what he does not know.

"Daddy teaches at Elwin"

"He is the Housemaster of Thackery House."

"He teaches math."

"Just to sixth formers."

"No one else would understand him."

"He's a dreadful bore."

"You probably don't know him"

"We live in one of the staff houses at Elwin."

"It's the big one closest to the main rugby pitch."

"We take the bus to get to school in Romsey."

A pause allows Dylan to ask: "So how do you know Blatherstone?"

The tag team enlightens Dylan once again.

"We don't exactly *know* him"

"We see him playing rugby."

"We don't exactly like rugby."

"We only watch the games to spy on Colin."

"He is very sexy."

"Great legs."

"Fabulous body."

Heather and Hazel look at each other to nod agreement. "So you've never actually met Blather… Colin? Never spoken to him?" asks Dylan.

Both girls shake their heads and say together, "No, never met him. We would like to, though. Do you know him?"

Dylan feels disinclined to explain the nature of his relationship with Blatherstone. "How did you learn his first name?"

"He's in one of Daddy's sixth form math classes."

"We sneaked a look at Daddy's mark sheets."

"That's how we discovered his name. Blatherstone, Colin."

"He's not very clever."

"At least he's not very good at maths."

"Judging by his marks, he'll be lucky to pass."

"We don't love him for his brains, though."

"No, we love him for his body."

"And his face. He's ever so handsome."

"I love his eyes. They are dreamy."

Heather and Hazel are potentially the most dangerous girls Dylan could have "picked up" on the streets of Romsey. Associations with girls in Romsey are forbidden by Elwin Park. But as the daughters of an Elwin Park housemaster, Heather and Hazel could be considered as being even more out of bounds than other girls.

"You could get into serious trouble being seen with us," remarks Heather or Hazel with a certain pride in their status, "we are completely off limits. You could get caned." Dylan ignores the statement. He's looking for ways of meeting up with Heather, Hazel, and Judy in the future. This could lead to meetings with other girls. Sure Heather and Hazel are cute, but how do you handle their platonic obsession with Blatherstone? If they could actually meet the blockhead, perhaps they'd realize what a true clod he is. But such a meeting is not going to happen. He is near sure that snobbish Blatherstone would dismiss any Romsey girl with derision, even if she happened to be his schoolmaster's daughter. Blatherstone commonly uses phrases such as "town slag," "lower orders," and "country whores" to refer to any woman not qualified for write-ups on the pages of *Tatler* magazine or the Royal Box at Ascot. Dylan determines that aggression is the best approach and asks the three girls outright whether they'll meet up with him again next week in the coffee shop.

Heather and Hazel look at each other. Then they look at Judy. Simultaneously, the three nod their heads in the affirmative. Together, Heather and Hazel ask, "Can you bring a couple of …" at this moment, they break unison, and Heather, the elder sister by one full hour, continues, "other boys along with you. No Elwin boys dare speak to us on the streets of Romsey. I suppose they think we'll go running home and tell our father. But it should be safe meeting us in a coffee shop. Don't tell them who we are before they get here. After they've fallen in love with us, we can tell them." So that puts the Blatherstone obsession in perspective, thinks Dylan.

Dylan nods confidently now. "I don't think I'll have any difficulty in persuading a couple of my friends to accompany me next week. Especially when they know they are going to meet the hottest chicks in the great city of Romsey!" The girls laugh.

A week later, Dylan, accompanied by two third formers, meets up with Heather and Hazel in the Romsey coffee shop. Dylan chooses his companions carefully. It means identifying a couple of boys who are going to hold their own in female company and more important, not betray the illicit meeting. Hazel and Heather are already seated at a table, along with three other girls Dylan hasn't seen before. A table is pulled up to couple with the one the girls are seated at. Chairs are rearranged. Dylan introduces Heather and Hazel. A social thing is happening here.

A similar coming together of Elwin Park boys and St. Theresa's Convent girls repeats itself Saturday after Saturday during term time. Dylan is usually present, but his companions change from meeting to meeting. The girls usually outnumber the boys. The girls, after all, are on home territory and not hindered by being incarcerated in a gulag.

No real liaisons between male and female result from these early meetings. Much of the conversation is guarded as talk tends to be when exchanged between thirteen-year-olds. A Saturday afternoon meeting could have as few as four participants and as many as a dozen. Meetings of a dozen thirteen-year-olds required the pulling together of a minimum of three tables and elevated noise levels. But if the owners of the Romsey coffee shop had any concerns, they must have been mitigated by the spike in cappuccino sales that ensued on Saturday afternoons. Within the laughter and banter, friendships form, and contact information such as phone numbers and addresses are exchanged.

Heather and Hazel initiate Dylan to the world of English girls. From the onset, Dylan feels more at ease in this world than the harsh environment of Elwin Park. English girls, or at least those attending the Romsey Convent, didn't seem to be as alien to Dylan as their male counterparts. Thanks to this, Dylan's confident and easy manner in female company alters the way his Elwin peers perceive him. He's accorded a reputation as a bit of a stud.

Because Heather and Hazel reside in the Elwin Park grounds, they become a conduit between a number of the third formers and the outside world. As these adolescent friendships evolve, so does the need for messages to be exchanged and carried. Heather and Hazel are destined to become pivotal in their role as messengers. Dylan learns that the bus on which the twins return home from school on weekdays arrives at the main school gate just before four in the afternoon. In this way, there are days in which Dylan can contrive to be in the vicinity of the main gate at this time and walk a short distance in their company. The gulag's ability to stifle communications from the outside world has been breached.

9. BRIDGET

Things change again during Dylan's third term. This is the summer term, the final in Dylan's third form year, the final term of being a first-year. At the beginning of term, Dylan has a challenge. He must inform Blatherstone that he is to exercise his option of not fagging for him for a third successive term. While Dylan is aware that there have been some benefits to being a personal fag, he resents the notion of servitude and the fact that so much of his precious "free" time is consumed in the service of a pompous slob. Despite the fact that he has been dreading this moment throughout the Easter vacation, Dylan marches up to Blatherstone's study moments after returning to Elwin.

Blatherstone is initially dumbfounded at this unwelcome news and freezes while seated at his desk. Dylan prepares to sustain yet another physical assault. Once the news has sunk in, Blatherstone violently swipes the contents of his desk off to the floor with a single movement of his arm. He gets to his feet and rages at Dylan, defining him as an "ungrateful bastard." He cites a long list of favors he has extended to Dylan during the previous two terms. No other first year in the school has been as privileged! He informs Dylan that if that's his decision, he'll appoint him the dreaded bog fag position and he'll spend his summer cleaning out toilets. A silence ensues. Dylan hasn't yet been attacked – a positive, he thinks. Blatherstone calms a little and resorts to persuasion, not a skill he was required to practice in his position. But Dylan is resolute; he knows he has to be.

After his showdown with Blatherstone, Dylan prepares to be appointed bog fag. However, the following day, when the fagging appointments are posted, he reads with surprise that he's to be the dormitory fag, probably the least demanding of all fagging positions and a big step toward achieving a little more freedom!

Dylan first meets Bridget in the Romsey coffee shop on a Saturday afternoon town pass. By this time, clandestine Saturday afternoon meetings between Elwin boys and St. Theresa's Convent girls are now routine and no longer require arranging. Bridget is an accidental newcomer to the group, one of half a dozen Convent girls in the café that afternoon. Dylan is accompanied by three other Elwin Park third formers. He immediately notices Bridget. At first sight, she appears petite, blond, blue-eyed, and bouncy. She bubbles with a vitality that immediately attracts Dylan. He tries to guess her age. Initially, he thinks she might be younger than the mean age of the third form group, but realizes this was probably because of her slight build. Like many of the Elwin Park boys, she peppers her conversation with a colorful range of curse words, including the popular four letter ones. Some said the St. Theresa Convent girls were more inclined to coarse language than the boarding school boys, but, until he meets Bridget, Dylan has no evidence that this might be true. Although the swearing makes him feel uncomfortable, because he is as yet not fully accustomed to it among males let alone females, Bridget is sexy and flirtatious. Socially, she's a little spitfire who revels in being the center of attention. Dylan is powerfully attracted. He hasn't known her ten minutes before he begins to wonder what she looks like naked.

Bridget is supposedly "dating" another boy at Elwin Park, whatever that means when the other person is imprisoned in the gulag. For the first time in the now routine social gatherings, Dylan contributes little to the conversation. He sits back and observes. Specifically, he focuses on Bridget. The girl is a comedienne by nature. She delights in making fun of people and zones in on their frailties. She is the first to laugh at any joke she cracks and her laughter is contagious. This afternoon, the butts of her mischievousness are snobby stiffs from Elwin Park, four of whom are sitting immediately in front of her. Bridget's saucy tongue bamboozles her small audience with risqué and mocking provocations that leave Dylan's three companions stunned. The truth is that, while Bridget might have seemed to be from a slightly different mold to Dylan, she is totally alien to a pack of boys who had attended single sex boarding schools since the age of seven.

Dylan continues to remain silent and observe. He doesn't take his eyes off Bridget. He is careful to avoid displaying anything more than a gentle grin at each of the girl's wisecracks. Let everyone else in the group do the laughing, he thinks, he'll be more reserved in his appreciation. Dylan plots an approach to Bridget. It must be one that cannot fail. This is no time to make a fool of himself. For now, his reserve seems to be paying off. Bridget is clearly piqued by the fact that Dylan fails to find her antics as amusing as the remainder of her audience. Everyone else does, why not him? Dylan notes that Bridget seems to look his way after unloading each wisecrack, as if she's gauging his reaction. As time progresses, Dylan convinces himself that Bridget is putting on a show that's directed primarily at him.

It turns out that the boy Bridget is supposedly dating is named Ronald Parker. Dylan knows of him vaguely. Parker is a fifth former in Thackery House and a sub-prefect. This positions Dylan's supposed rival as at least sixteen years old. Did seniority apply to girls in England? Dylan doesn't know. It is time to make a move. He asks Bridget how old she is.

"Why do you want to know?" she asks, "are you being cheeky?" She picks up her chair and sidles up so that it abuts Dylan's chair. Then she says in a whisper, intentionally loud for everyone around the table to hear, "Is it because you fancy me?"

"Yes, it could be," Dylan deadpans, "and I reckon there's a good chance you fancy me, too." This astonishing response momentarily freezes the third form occupants of the coffee shop table. All eyes are on Bridget and Dylan. A brazen flirtation has elevated this meeting to a new level. This is a high-risk pick-up line. The statement even takes Bridget by surprise. It's simply not done to admit you fancied anyone until one hundred percent sure of the response you were likely to receive. Come-ons such as this tended to be exchanged in private so as to minimize exposure to public rejection.

"You should be so lucky," responds Bridget with indignant bravado, followed by some exaggerated laughter. Something in that laughter suggests to Dylan that he's scored a point in the jousting. Bridget's bubbling confidence is rattled. The coffee table group continues to focus exclusively on Bridget and Dylan. Something interesting could transpire.

"How about you tell me how old you are?" quizzes Bridget, "Then I might consider telling you how old I am. Actually, I'm pretty sure you're a little young for me. My boyfriend is seventeen." She looks at her Convent cohorts as if she wants to have them corroborate this information.

"I'll wager I'm older than you," ventures Dylan. "In fact, I'll bet you a cappuccino that you're younger than me." Dylan figures the bet proposition to be win-win whatever her actual age. In any case, her age couldn't be that much different from his and going by appearance, he guesses that she could be younger. Still, you could never be sure with girls. So what – win or lose the bet, it will set them on a level playing field.

Bridget turns and whispers something to the girl sitting next to her. This girl's name is Johanna. Johanna appears older, maybe sixteen, but again, with girls, you never can tell, thinks Dylan. Johanna takes charge.

She says to Dylan, "OK, you each have to write your date of birth onto a serviette. Then you have to give me the serviettes. I'll announce which of you is the older without revealing your birthdates. No other information. Bridget doesn't want anyone to know the date of her birthday. The younger is the loser and has to buy a coffee. No cheating."

Dylan nods agreement. He picks up a paper napkin and records on it his actual date of birth. For a second he does consider adding a year of longevity, but this would likely be disputed by his treacherous Elwin Park companions. He folds his napkin and presents it to Johanna. Bridget doesn't have a pen. She borrows Dylan's pen and writes, scrunching her elbow around the paper serviette to prevent peeking. She folds, then passes the paper napkin to Johanna. Johanna opens both serviettes.

With brows furrowed, she studies each serviette. She is aware that everyone's attention is focused on her and she knows how to create dramatic tension. She raises her eyebrows and looks first at Bridget, then toward Dylan. She folds, then pockets, both serviettes into her school blazer, stands, and moves between Bridget and Dylan. She grasps Bridget's wrist in one hand and Dylan's in the other in the manner of a boxing ref about to award a points decision in the ring.

"The winner is... Bridget Fairford!" she trumpets, raising Bridget's arm victoriously as she calls out her name. Bridget leaps to her feet and dances a little Celtic jig, fanning the school uniform kilt she's wearing with one hand, while raising the other to the ceiling in a twirl.

Dylan fakes indignation. He drops his jaw in exaggerated amazement. "I don't believe you," he accuses the adjudicator, "show me the napkins."

Bridget sits and spits out venomously, "Play fair, spoil sport. You agreed." She hams it up now, "I can't be dating babies. You're just an itsy bit young for a mature and debonair femme of the world, dahling!" She checks herself. The price of this victory should not be to preclude the flirtation from progressing. She adds with an American accent, "Even if you are a cutie pie baby." She chucks his chin teasingly with a finger.

"Who said anything about dating," responds Dylan cool as he can manage, "I simply bet you a cup of coffee. Anyway, I'm not convinced you are really older than me. You certainly don't look it. And I won't believe it until you show me the napkins." Then addressing to Johanna directly, he asks, "Are you sure you got the year right?"

The interest of the group is aroused. Play fair and show the napkins is the verdict of the plebiscite. It's not just a cup of coffee at stake, but perhaps the potential for romance. Surely full disclosure is required? After all, are not Bridget and Johanna best friends?

More whispering exchanges take place between Bridget and Johanna, the adjudicator of the napkin data. Finally, albeit reluctantly, Bridget agrees to the release of this oh-so-important information. She nods her head. Johanna reads and displays as evidence the birthdates recorded on the serviettes, delivering them with as much drama as she can muster. Beginning with Dylan's, she uses her tongue and voice to mimic a drum roll. The result is corroborated for all to see. According to the napkins, Bridget is three weeks Dylan's senior. Dylan says nothing, but imprints the date of her birthday in his mind. Immediately, he gets to his feet, heads for the counter, and orders a couple of cappuccinos.

Such are the clumsy rites of adolescent courtship. While Dylan might have been happier if the age advantage had favored him, it's not something that greatly concerns him. The bottom line is that he maneuvered the privilege of buying Bridget a cup of coffee and garnered a hundred percent of her attention for ten minutes. The result is that Bridget will likely remain sitting next to him, allowing him to pursue what seems to be an increasingly promising flirtation.

Sure enough, when Dylan returns with the coffees, Bridget has so many questions for Dylan, she scarcely has time for the cappuccino placed in front of her. Bridget wants to know all about life in America. It's not so often a foreigner can be found in rural Romsey. Especially a foreigner from the land of Hollywood and prime time. Now truly, Dylan knows little about life in America, though he knows plenty about life as an oil brat in expat American oil camps. But he comes equipped with the appropriate accent and he's smart enough to ride a wave in the name of romance.

Bridget is not difficult to impress, in part because she wants so much to be impressed by Dylan. Bridget is a country girl to the core. The longest journeys she has made thus far in her life have been a couple of day trips to London. Dylan is quick to realize that to Bridget, he represents something exotic, a jetsetter. Sure he travels on jet planes, and yes, he does this by himself. Does Dylan mention the Junior Jet Club badge that he has to have pinned on his lapel when he takes these flights alone? No siree, not a chance! Instead, names such as New York, Geneva, and Caracas roll off his tongue as if he had spent his entire life hopping from one location to the other. He spices up his adventures with places that Bridget can hardly pronounce. "Kuala Lum... what?" she asks. "Where in the fuck is that?"

Bridget and Dylan tune out their companions sitting around the coffee tables. For some precious moments that afternoon, Dylan and Bridget aren't aware that there are any other persons on the planet besides themselves. When the time approaches for Dylan and his cohorts to catch the bus back to Elwin, phone numbers are exchanged. The phone numbers are written onto serviettes. Dylan departs with Bridget's home phone number in his top blazer pocket, while Bridget does likewise, with the number of the public phone booth located on the ground floor corridor at Elwin Park.

Dylan's status with Elwin Park third formers rises a couple of notches on the afternoon he meets Bridget in the coffee shop. To the boys of his Elwin peer group, he has accomplished something they could only talk about. He's picked up a girl in a coffee shop. He has scored. Not only has he picked up a girl, but it appears that he might have stolen her from a fifth former. The third formers reappraise Dylan. The yank may be a little timid in the confines of Elwin Park society, but put him in a coffee shop with some girls and he somehow knows how to handle himself.

Driven by adolescent male hormones, the boys of Elwin Park have a powerful motivation to liaise with girls. Unfortunately, inexperience destines their efforts to failure. To their mindset, flirtation consists of clustering in conspicuous groups on street corners and mouthing off insults at any girl walking past. Such clumsy pick-up attempts are interpreted as what they sound like – insults – and rather than scoring any points with their targets, the Elwin boys only gain a reputation for being boorish snobs.

Dylan, on the other hand, was raised in a co-ed environment and has some familiarity with the language, behavior, and motivations of adolescent girls. In addition, his accent, rather than being held to ridicule as it was within Elwin Park, is now an asset. To the country girls of Romsey, Dylan speaks the language of pop singers and movie stars.

The public phone at Elwin Park is located outside the school dining room. The phone is primarily used for incoming calls. When Elwin Park boarders call out using this phone, it is usually to place collect calls to their parents. More often, it's the parents who call their children. Dylan's parents never phone him. They live so far away that the time zones seldom sync and the cost is perceived as being prohibitive. In addition, international calls of this era require the two parties attempting to communicate to yell at a volume so loud that an observer might wonder if the phone company had played a role in the transaction.

When the Elwin pay phone rings, the call is likely to be from one of the boarding student's parents. But not always. One evening, shortly after Dylan and Bridget's first meeting, the phone rings and a young girl's voice asks to speak to Dylan. A third former answers the phone. The message is circulated. Phone call for Douglas in Dickens. Eventually Douglas in Dickens is located and summoned to the phone. Several first-years are waiting outside the booth. They snoop around outside to see if they can catch any snippets of conversation between boyfriend and girlfriend. While the boys of Elwin would regard it as "not cricket" to snoop on a phone call between a boy and his parents, snooping on phone courtship is regarded as fair play and good meat for gossip.

Bridget is a chatterbox. Give her a phone and someone at the other end of the line and she can polish off an hour or more while barely pausing for breath. She relates to Dylan every detail of her life that has transpired since the couple met two days previously. On the other hand, Dylan does not embrace communication by telephone. His contribution to this first phone call from Bridget consists of no more than a handful of monosyllabic responses. He's content to listen to Bridget chatter because he's in love. The two or three first-year boys snooping outside the phone booth, hoping to catch tidbits of x-rated verbal canoodling between phone lovers, are condemned to disappointment. Nothing gossip-worthy can be heard from the one side of the conversation they are privy to. But, it is during the course of this protracted phone conversation that Bridget and Dylan arrange a secret meeting. It will take place within the expansive grounds of Elwin Park. Bridget provides Dylan with precise verbal instructions of how to get to the meeting place.

Bridget can navigate the grounds of Elwin Park with her eyes closed. She has done this many times on horseback, beginning when she was a small child. She knows the property better than any boy in the school. Elwin Park is set on four hundred acres of mixed forest and farmland. Trails crisscross the school grounds. The trails are mostly set in the thick forest located to the east of the school buildings. They are little used during term time. In keeping with any other English private school of its stature, Elwin Park has riding stables and a horsey set. The school's horseback riders use the Elwin trails and those on other close-by estates. On foot, an intruder onto Elwin Park property would have been immediately identified as a trespasser. But being saddled on a horse was license enough to roam the countryside at will. English horsey types stick together.

Bridget's father is a local farmer. As a well-to-do landowner of a medium-sized livestock farm, he keeps hunters for the amusement of himself and his family. He participates in local fox hunts when the occasion arises. The hunt, as it's known, gives horsey types and their packs of yelping hunting hounds license to thrash through the countryside in pursuit of foxes wherever foxes might choose to run. Often enough, pursued foxes choose to run into the forest of Elwin Park where the density of bush and trees swings the odds of evading pursuers in favor of the pursued. Unlike the rest of the participants in the hunt, the life of the fox is on the line. They are foxy enough to realize that their chances of losing a pack of hounds and half-pissed equestrians increase in dense forest, so they commonly head for the bush. And as member of the human pack on horseback that followed the hounds in pursuit of a fox, Bridget was introduced to the grounds of Elwin as a child.

In addition, Elwin Park was also integrated into the local equestrian cross-country eventing calendar. Eventing is an equestrian contest that combines speed, endurance, and jumping on horseback, activities that a pre-pubescent Bridget had commonly participated in with enthusiasm. In the horse barn, gold, red, and blue ribbons testified to a good measure of success in gymkhanas when she was a youngster. Now into her teenage years, her interest in horses and horsey types has waned. These days, she's less inclined to go riding unless she has a good reason. Dylan is a good reason.

Bridget's horse is a vast black gelding named Thor. Dylan can ride horseback, but is less familiar with the reality of horses when he's not saddled on one. A horse as enormous as Thor intimidates him. When Thor stomps his hooves, the ground shakes. When Thor exhales in irritation, he snorts like a dragon. Bridget appears tiny seated on Thor, but there's no doubt who is in control. Bridget knows and loves horses in general, Thor in particular. Witness Bridget and Thor together, and any observer would conclude that Thor felt likewise about Bridget.

On arrival at the agreed meeting place, Bridget guides Thor into the forest clearing, dismounts, and ropes the great beast to a tree. Thor is happy. He munches on forest ferns and greens. Dylan arrives at the clearing dressed in running shorts and a shirt. He's a little puffed from having run the best part of a mile. Bridget approaches Dylan and hugs him. Thor looks up from munching to take measure of Dylan and, while doing so, produces a prodigious dump while continuing to happily chomp on ferns. An acrid stench fills the air in the entire zone of the forest clearing, causing Dylan to gag. Bridget does not seem to notice.

Bridget is dressed in a pink checkered blouse, blue jeans, and sneakers. She's not about to have Dylan identify her as a horsey type. This means she is not wearing jodhpurs or a riding helmet. While Bridget has dressed in a style that allows her to feel comfortable, Dylan is dressed in the only uniform he could have worn to make this meeting possible. His running kit consists of a flimsy pair of white shorts, white T-shirt trimmed with Dickens House colors, sneakers, and a track suit top tied by the arms around his waist. To justify his absence, he has obtained permission to go for a run on the school grounds to practice for an upcoming school cross-country race. At Elwin Park, this type of healthy bodily activity is thought to be conducive to the building of moral fortitude, so obtaining permission for it was never in doubt.

After the greeting hug, Bridget goes over to Thor and from pannier bags, produces a picnic blanket and two cans of ginger beer. She rolls out the blanket on the grassy floor of the clearing. Then she sits herself in the middle of the blanket and pats the ground next to her, inviting Dylan to join her. They sit facing each other, cross-legged. Next, she pops the tabs on both cans of ginger beer, passing one to Dylan.

Face-to-face and alone for the first time, Dylan and Bridget initially struggle to find any rhythm in their conversation. Bridget chug-a-lugs from the soda can. Dylan does likewise. Bridget burps and giggles. Dylan also burps, but cannot bring himself to do it with Bridget's brazenness. His burp seems a little forced. Ginger beer burns his throat. He wants to come up with entertaining conversation, but in this forest setting, the confidence that flowed from him in the coffee shop has abandoned him. Maybe words are not the best strategy in this situation.

The cross-legged pair lean their bodies forward and closer. Eyes connect and lock into each other. Thus engaged, they lean forward into their first kiss. Lips touch. Bridget parts her lips just barely. Dylan reciprocates. Because there's not quite enough moisture to make the kiss special, Dylan tentatively moves his tongue to the parting Bridget has created between her lips. She opens her mouth wider, inviting his tongue to explore. Then, greedily, she sucks, insisting she has all of Dylan's tongue. Once the tongue is captured, she sucks at it as if it is a teat. Dylan yields his tongue to Bridget's domain, to probe and explore. But soon, sucking alone is not enough for Bridget; she wants her own tongue involved in the game. She forces her tongue to engage that of the intruder. Tongue wrestles tongue. Bridget's tongue becomes more aggressive. It wrestles Dylan's tongue into a retreat. As Dylan withdraws his tongue, Bridget's tongue advances and breaches his mouth. Now Dylan suckles. How good to yield, to be invaded and explored. Tongues advance and retreat and intertwine. Sometimes lips have to separate to enable gasps of breath, their lungs not willing to be subordinated by this game of kissing. Bridget is driven to experience every detail and intricacy of Dylan's mouth. She probes roof of mouth, under tongue. Now the mysteries and sensations between tooth and cheek and gum. Now to part lips and trace each other's lips with tongues. Saliva mixes. They suck face. So this is a real kiss, thinks Dylan. Finally! There was no comparing this with anything called a kiss he has experienced before.

A pause. Bridget wipes her mouth. She reaches for the can of ginger beer. As she goes to take a swig, she points at Dylan's groin and winks at him with a cheeky grin. The kissing has produced in Dylan an erection beyond disguise, the jock strap worn under the gym shorts inadequate to constrain its state. He feels a momentary pang of embarrassment and moves a hand to cover its source. But exiting the trance of the kiss makes him question the time and he glances at his watch. Twelve minutes before his dormitory lights out! He is a full mile away from the main school building.

Dylan is a capable rather than a skilled horseback rider. Riding behind another person on a single saddle mounted on a horse with the girth of Thor is no easy thing. Doing this attired in perfunctory gym kit with testicles inflamed by over an hour of ascending and as yet unrelieved passion is excruciatingly painful. Bridget cracks both heels into Thor's flanks and spurs the horse to a fast canter. She reins in the charging horse just enough to avoid breaking into a gallop. If Thor had galloped, both riders would have fallen, because Dylan is secured only by the arms he locks around Bridget's waist. In turn, Bridget is secured to Thor by her skinny legs, though they are skinny legs equipped with deceptively powerful muscles developed over an entire childhood of horseback riding.

Thor thunders down the trail, heading toward the main school buildings, shaking the ground as he rhythmically canters. When just short of being in sight of the school buildings, Bridget pulls up Thor abruptly. Dylan dismounts and despite the pain in his throbbing balls, runs as fast as he can to the school building, and launches himself up two flights of stairs to his dormitory. In the dormitory, he does not break stride and manages to scoot under the covers in his bed still attired in gym kit.

Dylan has the bed covers pulled up to his chin mere seconds before the prefect enters to announce lights out. Not that any lights actually get extinguished. This is June in Britain and the sun still shines brightly at nine in the evening. Geographically positioned just south of the Arctic Circle, it doesn't begin to get dark until well after ten. Dylan does his best to suppress the panting and wheezing resulting from his exertions. Wide-eyed boys stare at him in silence. Talking after lights out is prohibited, so they can only wonder: what class of daft idiot wants to practice long distance running? Especially when doing so can risk a beating?

The routine at Elwin Park is "tea" at five pm, followed by prep at six pm. Tea is supper, the evening meal, one usually not as substantial in content as lunch. Evening prep is a structured sixty minutes of what would be called "homework" had this not been a boarding school. It takes place in the student's home classroom and is supervised by a prefect. Prep is conducted in absolute silence. It begins with the sounding of a bell and its completion is sounded in the same way. At the completion of prep, Dylan runs to the Dickens House changing rooms and within seconds, is attired in gym kit. He presents himself before Blatherstone, the house captain, to once again request permission for a cross-country run on the school grounds. This time, Blatherstone raises his eyebrows in surprise. This is either an extraordinary display of house spirit… or mischief is in the air!

Dylan jogs off down the trail leading from the main school building to the bush. He disappears into the forest refraining "I Want You" from *Blonde on Blonde* in his mind over and over as he jogs. Once out of sight of the school buildings, he accelerates his pace. His mind has been focused on this second meeting with Bridget for the entire day. As he approaches the forest clearing, Dylan catches sight of the enormous dark form of Thor, already tethered to a tree and happily munching away at exotic forest greens. Bridget has spread the contents of a picnic basket over the horse blanket and is semi-reclined in the center of it. The treats she has brought to the meeting are nearly as welcome to Dylan as the potential for sex. Real food is a luxury for a boy nurtured on an Elwin Park diet. Bridget is attired in her usual jeans and buttoned blouse. They greet each other with hellos but initially shy from physical contact. In this new love, just twenty-two hours of separation has worked to create a little distance between them. Dylan gobbles the sandwich Bridget has prepared. Next, he greedily consumes some cupcakes she baked. The food is washed down with ginger beer once again. Bridget eats nothing. She remains semi-reclined, propped on an elbow, observing Dylan scoff food, bemused by his naked appetite.

His stomach sated, Dylan calms and sidles over to Bridget. He kisses her gently on the cheek. In response, Bridget fully reclines and draws Dylan to her. They kiss warmly, in an instant closing the distance created by the day of separation. Thus reconnected, they can move forward. Kissing alone can no longer satisfy their appetites. Dylan props himself onto an elbow and uses his hand to stroke hair away from Bridget's forehead. Bridget closes her eyes. Dylan tentatively moves the free hand to cup one of her breasts. As he does, he reengages his lips with hers. He becomes bolder with the pressure he applies to her breast. Bridget's response to the advance is to increase the intensity of her kiss. Dylan pauses. Braver and deliberately, he begins to unbutton Bridget's blouse. He is confronted by a soft fabric white bra. Is it a training bra?

It is the first bra Dylan has touched. The obvious next step is to bare her breasts, but he's unsure of the mechanics required to accomplish this. His understanding is that these garments fasten from behind and Bridget is lying on her back. He begins groping underneath her back, thrusting fingers into the territory between her shoulder blades. Bridget stares into Dylan's eyes. She is grinning at him, interested in observing how he'll overcome this problem. Finally, she can bear it no longer. She raises her hand and points with her finger to a pair of hook clasps at the front of the bra, connecting it between the cups. She laughs. Dylan, feeling just a little sheepish, negotiates the unhooking of the clasps in a manner clumsier than he'd like. It is a procedure that requires both hands. It's also one that he wishes he had been able to navigate without assistance.

The reward of this clumsy struggle is the sight of Bridget's breasts. Not big breasts, especially when observed reclined. But to Dylan they're beautiful. He cups one of them in his hand. He strokes the nipple. Initially almost flush with the aureole, the nipple responds to his touch. Dylan moves his head downward. He feels Bridget breathe more deeply. He sucks and nibbles. Bridget squirms underneath him and runs fingers through his hair, finally firmly clasping his head with both hands. Dylan is relieved. He must be doing this right. Bridget moves his head to her other breast. Yes, this needs attention, too. Suddenly, Dylan's hunger for these breasts is insatiable. They are not much bigger than lemons, but the pleasure they generate is immeasurable. He devotes himself first to one, pulling as much of it into his mouth as he can. Then, he does likewise to the other. Now lip on lip again. Now back to the breasts. Nipples that a combination of arousal and Dylan's nibbling have turned cherry red. Dylan notes that Bridget's squirming intensifies when he focuses on her nipples.

Once again, time has flown by. Dylan looks at his watch. He has to go if he's to avoid the close shave he had the previous night.

"Stay," suggests Bridget somberly, "just stay. What can they do to you? Expel you? You hate it there. It would be the best thing possible. You can stay with my mum and dad."

"I don't think it's as simple as that," responds Dylan. "I'm not sure how my folks would react. And if you get expelled from one school, can you ever get into another?"

Once again, Thor thunders through the woods in a rhythmic canter. Dylan's crotch is jammed behind Bridget's buttocks as he clings to the girl's waist. Once again, the taught, firm muscles of Bridget's bottom and thighs are the only force holding both riders onto the horse. Were it not for the potential jeopardy to his balls, the powerful rolling motion of Thor's canter, combined with the massaging effect of Bridget's buttocks, might have produced a pleasing effect on him.

This time, Dylan makes the dormitory curfew with a little more time to spare. Other boys have time to question his sudden enthusiasm for evening runs. The time between the ending of prep and bedtime is the only free time afforded Elwin Park boys during a school day; who but a fool would want to waste it long distance running? Dylan is smart enough to respond by saying as little as possible. He explains that he's just trying to improve his fitness. He wants to perform better in the school cross-country runs. He explains that he's not experienced at cross-country running like other boys in school who have been doing this type of activity since the age of seven.

"Is he becoming soft in the head?" wonder the other boys.

Dylan can't see Bridget the next day. It is Friday. Movies are shown on Friday nights. Attendance is compulsory. The movies are supposed to be educational. Some of them are. Any Alfred Hitchcock film is considered educational. The sex and gore that appears in some Hitchcock films is considered OK because of the director. Stabbing a sexy, naked woman to death in a shower in a Hitchcock film is OK – how much do you really see, anyway? More blood than flesh. Carry-on films are popular with the boys. They are OK, too. *Carry-on* films target a very British type of humor that other nationalities grow out of after turning eight years old. Dylan's mom would refer to them as "smut." The boys of Elwin Park love *Carry-on* films because the characters in these movies share the same confused and estranged attitudes about sex as they. There's plenty of homosexual innuendo and cross-dressing, both of which are favorite themes embedded in Elwin Park culture.

Dylan can see Bridget on Saturday, but he's worried about this meeting. He has obtained a Saturday afternoon exit pass for a visit to Romsey. He worries about Bridget showing any outward signs of affection for him in front of other boys while in the town. Dylan would like to meet up with Bridget in private in the town, but this is impossible. Other boys in his class would travel down on the bus with him, and would become immediately suspicious if Dylan attempted to go off on his own.

Dylan phones Bridget. Her dad answers. He has a stronger regional accent than Bridget. When Bridget finally gets to the phone, she sounds different. This makes Dylan stumble for words. He can't talk as he does when sitting alone with her on a picnic blanket in a forest clearing. He hears Bridget order her father to leave the room. She tells him she's having a private conversation.

After her father has presumably left the room, Bridget becomes her usual, fluent self. She's upset at Dylan's suggestion to distance themselves when they meet in the coffee shop. She has told all her girlfriends about Dylan. She wants to show him off. These girls are going to think her to be a perfect chump. No, she won't agree. "Be honest with your friends," she tells him. "I want people to know that you are my boyfriend."

Girls just don't get it, thinks Dylan. Sure, he knows Bridget is a friend who can be trusted, but he can't vouch for any of his supposed Elwin Park friends in this way. The gulag is a jungle and the requirement to survive supersedes allegiances of any sort. No one can be trusted.

Still on the phone, Dylan broaches the subject of Ronald Parker, her supposed Elwin Park boyfriend. "Boyfriend?" exclaims Bridget. "You must be bloody joking. I just said that in the coffee shop to make you jealous. He's creepy. He tried to kiss me once at a school barn dance and I slapped his face." Dylan is relieved on one level. But he informs her it is a fact that not only does Ronald Parker claim her as his girlfriend, many of the boys at Elwin Park regard Bridget as his property.

"What a bloody nerve," says Bridget, disgusted. "I'll give him a piece of my mind the next time I see him. He's a total creep as far as I'm concerned."

In the coffee shop the next day, try as he might to maintain distance between himself and Bridget, this isn't about to happen. Bridget is in an especially amorous and playful mood. She aggressively inserts her tongue into Dylan's mouth when they say hello. She wants to touch and hold hands. She wants her friends to have no doubt that she and Dylan are a thing. Seated in the coffee shop, Bridget shimmies her chair up to Dylan's. She nibbles his ear. When Dylan attempts to pretend she's not there, Bridget bites into his ear lobe. The bite is hard enough to make him yelp and squirm. Bridget isn't about to be ignored.

Dylan surrenders to the inevitable. On this day, he is accompanied by three classmates. Word would be out. The news will spread through the entire third form at Elwin within twenty-four hours. What hitherto was suspicion is now fact – Dylan and Bridget are boyfriend and girlfriend. Word will not stop with the third formers. Within a week, it would be known through the entire school that Dylan Douglas was canoodling with Bridget Fairford in the Romsey coffee shop. This had the potential to make life dangerous for Dylan in two ways. First, it was forbidden for Elwin Park boys to have liaisons with anyone in town. Town meant Romsey. Secondly, Ronald Parker was in a position of sufficient power to make Dylan's life miserable. He does not know Ronald Parker, but he doesn't have to. The way of life at Elwin Park is something that he has begun to understand. The present might be treating Dylan just fine, but future the is not looking so good.

Sunday afternoon at Elwin Park. For Dylan, one of the hardest adjustments to life in a boarding school is the near impossibility of spending time alone. Sunday lunch at Elwin begins at midday and concludes by one pm. From one to five on Sunday afternoon, there are four hours when the boys are not required to adhere to any formal structure. Some play snooker in the House common room, others participate in activities offered by chess clubs and debating societies. Until the advent of Bridget, Dylan sought and usually managed to achieve isolation on Sunday afternoons. The pleasures of solitude were seldom appreciated by other Elwin boys who were so completely institutionalized that often their greatest fear was that of having to settle for their own company. For Dylan, being alone might have been to retreat with a book to the home classroom, usually empty on Sunday afternoons. Or perhaps to wander solo in the forested acreage of the Elwin Park grounds.

Change happens. The forces within Dylan that drive him to meet up with Bridget at every possible opportunity are far too powerful for him to resist. Awake and asleep, he can focus on little other than Bridget. He daydreams about her in class. He dreams of her in sleep. In his dreams, she climbs naked into his bed, snuggles her soft body up to his, and with the sensation of her hard little breasts against his chest, Dylan awakes with damp pajamas. Thank goodness for the properties of sperm, he thinks, especially the almost miraculous speed at which it sublimates, leaving no more than a little crispiness in the texture of his pajamas. His body and his mind ache for Bridget. He can't concentrate in class. When a planned meeting with Bridget has to be cancelled due to rain, he responds by feeling nauseated.

Both Bridget and Dylan pray for sunny days. In England, dry days during the summer are precious. The rain does not have to be severe to disrupt a planned reunion. Bridget is prohibited by her parents from taking Thor out on cross-country jaunts alone when the ground is sodden. Thor is transportation. Without Thor there can be no Bridget and Dylan liaisons. There is simply no other way of closing the five mile, cross country distance between the farmhouse that is Bridget's home and the grounds of Elwin Park. By road, the distance is almost doubled.

Through Dylan, Bridget acquires a good understanding of Elwin Park routines. Bridget is better at planning and more devious than Dylan. It's also clear that she's more comfortable breaking rules, perhaps because the consequences of her doing so are tame compared to those Dylan has to contend with. For Dylan, Sunday after-noons are the preferred time to meet. Nearly four hours together.

The first time they arrange to meet on a Sunday afternoon, it rains. Bridget phones during Sunday lunch. No one is supposed to receive calls during Sunday lunch at Elwin Park. Headmaster Rumthorpe makes this perfectly plain to all parents, and it's underscored in the Elwin brochure of parental guidelines. In the middle of the meal, Dylan is informed by a prefect that his sister is on the phone. It turns out that his sister became enraged when informed she'd have to call back after lunch. What is it about the term "emergency" that prefects couldn't understand, asked the infuriated sister. Reluctantly, the prefect seeks Dylan out in the dining room and tells him he had best go and talk to his angry sister. Dylan leaves the din-ing room to answer the phone.

Bridget is steaming with rage. She's furious at not being connected immediately with Dylan. Did that idiot she was talking to not know what a *family emergency* was? She has a good mind to phone up the Elwin headmaster and lodge an official complaint. Then she informs Dylan they can't meet this day. It is pissing with rain. What woe!

When Dylan returns to his table, the prefect sitting at the head of the table isn't interested in knowing about the family emergency. "Is your sister a dame? Is she fuckable?" he asks. When Dylan fails to respond, the prefect notes, "She doesn't sound much like you. Not very American. Sounds like a Romsey tart to me." But then he loses interest and resumes eating.

Another Sunday rolls around. The sun is shining! Dylan is dressed in long pants, blazer, and tie. This attire is regulation wear on Sundays. Bridget and Thor meet up with Dylan. Bridget drops her foot from the left side stirrup and leans over to help Dylan mount the great beast. Dylan inserts his left foot into the stir-rup Bridget has freed. A combination of Bridget clutching onto his blazer and Dylan leveraging on the saddle seats him behind Bridget. She swivels on the saddle to kiss him, briefly but assertively, forcing her tongue deep into his mouth. Then, business-like, Bridget re-inserts her free foot into the stirrup and with a thump of both heels into Thor's flanks, launches him. Dylan clings to Bridget's waist. He wonders if she knows that this part of their meetings is scary for him. Probably not. Bridget fears nothing on a horse. They charge down the bridleway, Thor's hooves thumping in a rhythmic canter.

The clearing they arrive at is four miles distant and located on the Fairford property. Here, there is a better guarantee of privacy. Bridget unrolls the horse blanket onto the grass. The pair all but attacks each other. Dylan fumbles away at the buttons and clasps that attach Bridget's clothing to her upper body. He's becoming less of a klutz with navigating female clothing, or at any rate, the versions of it that adorn Bridget's body. Meanwhile, Bridget attacks Dylan's tie and, having unknotted it, chucks it over her shoulder before tackling her partner's shirt buttons. She lies on her back. Dylan moves toward her bared breasts and hungrily suckles her nipples to tumescence. He nibbles. He nibbles with a little too much tooth and receives a little tap on the side of the head. "Gentle," Bridget admonishes, "you're hurting." Dylan draws his head back. He studies her breasts, the nipples shiny and wet from his saliva. Recalled images of these breasts had prompted a continuum of wet dreams over the preceding days.

"Beautiful," he muses whimsically, stroking a nipple with the back of his index finger. What did Steinbeck call them in *Grapes of Wrath*? "Rising beauties." He always thought of this as lame until he fell in love with Bridget's tits! He studies her bared tummy. The skin on Bridget's tummy is translucent. With an index finger, Dylan picks and traces intricate patterns of veins under her ever-so-white skin. He focuses on her belly button. This is something to explore. He thrusts his tongue into the twisted little recess, producing an immediate reaction – a scream and a slap from Bridget.

"It tickles, you dummy," she admonishes, still laughing. Dylan moves his hand down the zippered fly of Bridget's jeans and cups his hand over the mound between her legs, wondering if he'll be allowed to get away with this. The reaction from Bridget catches him by surprise. She arches her back, parts her legs, and thrusts her groin into Dylan's hand with a primal force. It was as if she had been waiting for this move. Dylan kneads and explores, limited by the thick denim of Bridget's jeans. As Bridget squirms and thrusts into him, her eyes glaze. She stares at the blue sky above.

Dylan moves his hand to the seam on Bridget's fly. He wrests the fly button open, and carefully pulls the zipper downward, creating a vee opening in the jeans. He attempts to insert his hand down into the opening he has created, but is hindered by the tight jeans. He knows that to progress, he is going to have to slide the jeans down below Bridget's hips, but by now he's sensible to the fact that Bridget wants him to do just that. But just the jeans? Should he venture to remove her panties, too? Knickers, that's what they're called here. Bridget stops staring at the sky and looks at Dylan. She laughs. The laugh has a tone that suggests to Dylan that she may be making fun of him. Bridget sits, lifts her bottom, and slides out of her jeans and panties together as if they're a single unit of clothing. She executes this movement unselfconsciously, with a grin on her face and never taking her eyes off Dylan. She lies back. The only clothing she now wears is a pair of white socks. Dylan can hardly restrain himself; he wants to touch all of her so badly, he doesn't know where to begin. But he does not want ruin a good thing by appearing overeager. He moves his lips toward Bridget's and kisses her softly, before seeking the bared nub between Bridget's legs.

Dylan's initial observation is that the little slit between Bridget's legs does not appear to differ visually from his recall of that he has touched on Carrie. Bridget is so pale and fair that she as yet has little more than some blond fuzz over her vulva. But as Dylan's hand moves to cup her between the legs, Bridget responds by writhing into his touch with animal force. She gasps, parts her legs, and arches her lower body, seeking more of the hand that is exploring her. It was as if she were attempting to draw this hand, its fingers, this lover into the very quick of her being. A potent odor of ripe womanhood rises from Bridget's sex and insinuates itself into Dylan's senses. Ingested, hormones drive him toward conquest – only capitulation will suffice now. He inserts a finger. The finger navigates the mysteries in the lips and folds of this now magical orifice of Bridget's. Dylan thrusts his finger as deep into her as he can.

"Gentle," cautions Bridget, as if returning from a dream. Dylan withdraws his finger. He moves Bridget's hand to his penis, covered by his Sunday uniform gray flannel pants. Bridget strokes her hand over Dylan's erection a couple of times. A more direct approach is required. She unbuckles his belt and unbuttons his fly. It does not surprise him that Bridget has some disparaging words for his flannel trousers.

"How old-fashioned is this!" she exclaims. Who would make trousers without zips today?" In no time, she has his penis free and under scrutiny.

"Gosh, it's big. It doesn't half look funny," she declares. "I have seen a few willies before, but never one "on bonk." At least not a human one." Dylan knows what this means. The kids in school refer to a hard-on as being on bonk. He wonders where that term evolved! Bridget leans forward to span her hand to take measure of Dylan's willy. Having ascertained the length, she holds it with her spanned hand to the top of the slit between her legs to transcribe the dimensional span onto her own body. She laughs.

"Do you think all of it will fit?" she wonders. "It looks too big ... it's supposed to hurt the first time."

Bridget makes the shape of an "O" with her thumb and forefinger. She slowly runs the "O" up the shaft of Dylan's penis, sending waves of ecstasy up his spine.

"Willies look ugly," she observes philosophically, "but they feel sort of gorgeous." With that pronouncement, Bridget twists around on the blanket and grapples with the pannier bag that accompanies her when horseback riding. She fishes out a bottle.

"I am going to give you a nice wank," she announces to Dylan. Wanking was what the English called masturbation.

"My sister has told me how," Bridget declares, "not that I needed much telling." She produces a container of clear fluid. "This is baby oil," says Bridget, "I put some in my bath. It makes your skin feel soft and moist. Delia told me that it is the best thing to give a boy a wank with. It's time I wanked you, because if I don't, we'll end up going all the way. And we can't let that happen."

"I think it would be nice to go all the way," says Dylan matter-of-factly. "Have you ever done it before?"

"No, silly," responds Bridget, "I never really kissed anyone before ... at least, not like the way we kiss."

Dylan gets braver. "If we go all the way," he suggests, "I can pull out just in time."

"No, my sunshine, you cannot. Boys are unable to do that. . That means that I could end up with a bun in the oven. Not the best thing to happen to a poor country girl. Especially when darling daddy screws off back to America when he discovers the wonderful news!"

Bridget has lost Dylan. She is speaking in a language that he cannot decipher. He's too embarrassed to ask for an explanation.

Bridget holds his penis and squeezes. "Lie back and relax," she orders him. She pours some baby oil into the palm of one hand. Then she rubs both hands together to disperse the oil. Next, she cups his balls in one hand and his penis in the other. She massages the oil into Dylan's throbbing penis. Now it's his turn to squirm and writhe. Teasingly, she moves her hands away from his penis and massages the baby oil into his tummy around his hips. Bridget keeps up a running monologue while tending to the business of masturbating Dylan. "Soon we'll have a nice fuck together." She teases her hand down the shaft of the penis in her power. "Delia told me how to do this," she declares in her chatty way. "Big sisters have their uses. She said it was a bit like milking a goat. Does it feel nice?"

Dylan is in ecstasy. He does his best to nod in agreement.

"You have to tell me just before you are going to squirt," says Bridget, "Delia told me that I should stop rubbing and just squeeze when you start to squirt." At this precise moment, Dylan squirts. With consummate force. His body convulses as every muscle in his body from his toes to head goes into spasm. Sperm squirts onto Bridget's cheek and between her breasts, but it does not seem to faze her. Bridget squeezes his balls gently and his penis vigorously. It seems to Dylan like she is determined to extract every last drop of sperm from him. He can't help but wonder if Bridget thinks she is milking a goat. While Bridget's hands are at work, she never once takes her gaze off Dylan's eyes. Only after his body ceases to spasm does Bridget relinquish her grip on Dylan. Then she looks down and wipes some ejaculate from her breast. She studies it on her finger.

"So this is boy's spunk," she declares, showing little surprise. Next she wipes the shot of sperm from her cheek and studies this, too.

"It is not so different from a horse's," she surmises analytically, to herself rather than Dylan. She turns to Dylan and addresses him apocalyptically, showing him what's on her finger: "Do you know that there are gazillions of little maybe-babies in your spunk?"

She moves the finger with the spunk on it close to her nose and sniffs. "Smells different from a horse's," she notes. "The smell reminds me of something. But I can't put my finger on it." With that, Bridget inserts her spunky finger into her mouth and sucks.

"Hmm," she announces, "it actually tastes nicer than it smells. Delia tells me that boy's spunk is good for healthy skin if you swallow it."

"Wha … What about getting pregnant?" asks Dylan, knowing this is a stupid thing to say, but incredulous that his sperm had just been consumed.

Bridget nuzzles her nose into Dylan's cheeks. She grabs his ear lobes. She makes her very sternest face as she looks into his eyes. "Zat's ze ting my dahling," she says, hamming what she supposes to be a sexy Swedish film star deep throat accent. "To make ze baby, it has to go eento a different hole. Ve heff to hev a real fuck." She releases Dylan and lies on her back and stares up at the sky. "You might know a lot of big words, but you are a bit bloody innocent when it comes to sex."

Dylan says nothing. He wants Bridget to think of him as anything but a baby. But he can't find the words for a response. He leans over to Bridget to kiss her cheek. Bridget uses both hands to hold his head by his temples.

"I liked watching your eyes while I wanked you. It seemed like you were completely under my control."

Dylan considers this. "It was a nice wank," he remarks, "the best ever."

"Do you often do it to by yourself?" asks Bridget.

Dylan just nods in the affirmative. It would be embarrassing to tell Bridget just how often he indulged in this exercise. "But it doesn't feel nearly so good as when you do it to me." He rolls onto his side and studies Bridget's face. "When can we have a real fuck, do you think?" he asks. This might be the first time Dylan has ever used the word "fuck."

"Soon," replies Bridget. "We need some rubber johnnies. Rubber johnnies have to be put over your willy so that when you squirt it can't make babies. I didn't have enough pocket money to buy any this week."

"Are rubber johnnies the same thing as condoms?" asks Dylan innocently, but a little bothered by the fact that Bridget always seems to be two steps ahead of him in the language of life. Perhaps that was the advantage of having a big sister, or a big brother. To inform you about all the important stuff not taught by parents and schools.

"Hmm," affirms Bridget almost absentmindedly, her thoughts somewhere else, "condoms." She pauses. "Delia says I should wank you as much as possible. That way we are less likely to fuck. Actually, she also said that I should never have my knickers off any time your willy can be seen." With that she laughs and taps the tip of Dylan's penis. "Naughty willy," she admonishes, addressing it directly, "I was supposed to wank you before letting you inside my knickers. It's a little late for that. But I do really want to have you inside me. I had a dream about us doing it for real. It was quite heavenly." Then more seriously, "Actually, my dream was before I realized willies could get so big. It didn't feel so big when it was covered by your trousers. The first time we do it, you are not allowed to put it all inside me. Just the tip."

Dylan just wants to do it. Yes, he'll settle for just putting the tip in if he must. He immediately fantasizes about being inside Bridget's wet little cunt while she writhes around with that glazed look in her eyes. Sure, Bridget's hands were soft and nice. But what he really wants is to be inside her, sucking on her nipples, sucking on her lips as he comes. Kissing her eyelids after.

"Do you have dreams about me?" Bridget asks.

"Yes."

"Wet dreams?"

Dylan nods, "Yes."

"How often?"

"Every night. Almost every night."

"All starring me?"

"Yes."

"What happens in a wet dream? I mean, I know what happens at the end of it. What happens before it ends?"

"You just have a dream. About making out. You imagine stuff. For instance, I imagined you naked before I ever saw you naked. When you have a wet dream, you wake up just as you are coming."

"What happens to the spunk?"

"That's a problem. That's why it's not very nice to have to sleep in a dormitory with eleven other boys. There's no privacy. The spunk ends up on your tummy, in your pajamas. I keep tissues under my pillow. But it dries quickly, thank God."

"Poor baby," says Bridget, "I wish I could be there with you. I would give you delicious wanks and clean up your spunk for you."

Dylan looks at her.

"I'll get some rubber johnnies when I get my pocket money next week," Bridget tells him. "Delia will buy them for us. It is not likely a chemist shop would sell them to me, I look too young." Then she looks over at Dylan. "So do you," she says teasingly. "Actually, I think I'd stand a better chance of buying rubbers at a chemist than you."

Dylan says nothing. A pharmacy is known as a chemist in England. Walking into a chemist dressed in an Elwin Park school uniform and asking for condoms was not likely to be met with anything but derision and subsequent embarrassment. The pharmacist would most likely phone the school.

Bridget becomes very serious now. "Our first real sex has to be special," she says, talking once again to the sky above her. "We are not going to have our first screw in the woods on a horse blanket. I want it to be by candlelight."

"Is this a horse blanket?" asks Dylan. Bridget turns and looks over her nose at him, wondering whether to respond. She thinks the better of it and looks up to address the sky again.

"No," she says emphatically, "it has to be in my bed. We have to do this right. After, we have to spend the whole night together. I want us to sleep together. That way, we can be real lovers. We have to come up with a way of getting you out of that school for a weekend. Or even just a night."

Both Bridget and Dylan stare up at the sky. After a short while, Bridget grabs the container of baby oil bottle once again. "Here," she says rubbing her oily palms together, "I'll give you another wank. I want to see how far you can squirt this time. But you have to promise not to close your eyes when you start to come. I want you to look into my eyes."

It was one wank too many. Despite Thor's fleetness of foot, Dylan is late for Sunday afternoon tea. Being late for tea is a serious offence at Elwin Park. One of many serious offences. As punishment, Dylan is caned. The prefect who canes him does so with unusual violence. Unusual violence is the prerogative of a prefect. As a consequence, Dylan's buttocks are cut open where the transverse cane strokes intersect.

The next day, after evening prep, Dylan is summoned to the boy's public phone in the main hall. On the other end of the phone is what sounds like an old woman with a pompous British accent. She informs Dylan that she's his Great Auntie Josephine who lives in London. Her cat has just died. She wants Dylan to travel up to London *tout suite* to comfort her. She has tea and scones waiting for him. An even more bizarre conversation ensues.

"I don't have an Auntie Josephine in London. My name is Dylan Douglas. I don't have any relatives living in London. You have the wrong person."

"Nonsense, child," responds the old lady. "Do you have curly hair? Do you have freckles on your nose? Are you naughty and break all the rules at school? Of course you are my dear Dill. Your mummy is my niece. Your mummy and your family would be most upset to hear that you had already forgotten poor old Auntie Josephine, you selfish boy. I'm going to phone up America and let them know how ungrateful you are."

Dylan suspected something fishy from the start, but this is now confirmed, as his family is actually in Thailand. Could this be Bridget? Not likely, due to the accent and the husky old lady voice. But who else?

"Is that Bridget??" he questions tentatively.

"Bridget?" gasps the old lady shocked. "*Auntie Josephine,* you silly child. Your mummy is going to very distressed when I tell her about this conversation."

"I think you have got my name mixed up er … Auntie Josephine … I really don't know you."

"Dylan, I am beginning to lose my patience with you. I would like you to get your headmaster on the phone *immediately*. I want to give him a piece of my mind about the type of education he is providing for you boys at Elwin Park. Six months ago, you were such a sweet and polite little boy. Now you've become an insolent cad who gallivants around the countryside corrupting innocent English virgins. I'm going to suggest he has you deported imme…" At this point, there is brief evidence of a struggle at the other end of the phone and it clicks dead. Knowing the call is a prank, but confused as to its source, Dylan hangs up. As he turns to exit the phone booth, the phone rings. Dylan picks up the receiver again.

"Not bad, huh?" It's Bridget, giggling.

"That wasn't you?" asks Dylan, incredulous.

"No, silly. It was Johanna. Johanna Dempsey, you know her from the coffee shop.

She's good, no?"

"She didn't fool me for a second. I knew something was fishy. I just didn't want to be rude because I wasn't sure who it was."

"Come on, Dill. Admit that you were a little bit fooled. I was fooled. Johanna is a star in all our school plays. She's wickedly clever!" And, with her voice turned away from the phone to loudly admonish Johanna and at least a couple of other girls, adds, "When she sticks to her script."

"If you think she can pull that one off with the teachers here, you're wrong. They're not idiots. I will end up getting caned again and banished from exeats for life," responds Dylan.

Bridget becomes serious. "We can make it work, Dylan. We have to. It's just a question of planning. First, we have to provide Johanna with as much information as possible. We have to get a letter sent to your house-teacher or whatever he is called … postmarked from London or somewhere. Then Johanna can phone up and talk directly to your teacher bloke – she can be anyone you like. If Johanna has enough information, she can pull it off. Good news! Mummy and Daddy are going to a horse show in Bristol the weekend after next. That'll leave Delia and me alone. Delia has promised to help so long as we use the rubber johnnies. She's even offered to buy them for us."

Dylan is flabbergasted. He suspects this is going to have a bad ending for him. Given the choice, he'd rather have his first fuck in the woods. But at this moment in time, he has to agree. He promises to work on his part of the plan. Namely, coming up with a plausible person, a fictional relative, and subsequently, constructing a convincing information shield around this person. The good news is that it is going to be all but impossible for anyone in the school to contact his parents in Thailand to verify whatever fiction they invent.

10. BRIDGET AGAIN!

It all comes together so easily. According to Johanna, it transpired that Assistant Housemaster Dozy David sympathized with all his heart for poor Dylan, who had nearly completed his entire first year at Elwin Park and had, as yet, not one parental Sunday exeat. It was so hard on the boys whose parents lived abroad, he agreed with Johanna, who was posing as a dear old auntie in London who simply wanted a visit from her great nephew. According to the way Bridget told it, Johanna exceeded her brilliant best in navigating the phone conversation with Dozy David. "I am old and not very exciting. I can't entertain the poor boy much because of my health. But if he doesn't mind having tea with an old lady and her cats, it would be a comfort to me in my old age. If he does decide to visit, I'll send money for a train ticket to London and taxi fares." And so on.

On the Saturday immediately following the phone conversation between Dozy David and Dylan's "auntie," Johanna and Bridget are in stitches of laughter in the Romsey coffee shop. They recite the details of the phone conversation and the utter gullibility of Dozy David. Dylan is a little more skeptical, but the girls' plan unfolds perfectly. Dozy David receives a letter corroborating the phone call, complete with a ten pound note to pay for the travel. This sum greatly exceeds what is actually required to pay for the trip. Where had Bridget acquired this wealth? She stole it out of her father's wallet, she boasts. Within the typewritten letter to Dozy David, great Auntie Josephine emphatically makes the point that if this young man doesn't want to visit an elderly aunt, then she would do her best to understand. But what a comfort to her he might be if he did decide to come. On the same day, Dylan also receives a letter postmarked from an Auntie Josephine in London, inviting him for an overnight visit. Again, the point is made that should he choose not to visit, she would understand perfectly. Dylan's letter is signed by Auntie Josephine and three other names. In brackets, the other names are identified as her cats.

Dylan takes his letter to Dozy David. "I don't know her very well, sir," he informs the assistant housemaster. "I've really only met her a couple of times."

"Dylan," says Dozy David, somberly getting personal by using his first name, "duty is an important responsibility of any Elwin Park boy. It is our emphasis on adherence to duty that distinguishes the Elwin boy from the sort of riff raff produced by other schools. There are times when one has to knuckle down and consider the needs of others, even when they compromise our own. I spoke to your Auntie Josephine and she sounds like a very sweet, albeit very lonely old lady. I was left in no doubt that she would benefit enormously from a visit by her great nephew. It seems that she holds you very dear to her heart, even if you might not be aware of the fact. You'll understand these matters with greater clarity when you are older and wiser. And a bit of a break from the rigors of school routine will actually do you some good."

"Yes, sir," responds Dylan, looking down at his feet.

"Now, I've checked the train times on Saturday afternoon. You can take the 2:17 pm to Waterloo. I will drive you to Romsey station myself. When you return on Sunday afternoon, you'll have to get a taxi from the station. But your great aunt has provided you with a generous amount of money to cover your travel costs."

Dozy David drops Dylan off at the Romsey railway station. It takes some persuasion for him to assure the schoolmaster that he knows how to purchase a railway ticket. After all, he had somehow managed to get himself to Thailand and back again during the previous school vacation. After entering the station building, Dylan purchases a platform ticket, which is usually the ticket purchased by winos so they can sleep in the station waiting room, as well as by persons meeting an arriving train. Dylan produces his ticket for the ticket collector at the entrance to the platforms.

The ticket collector is South Asian. He is likely the first South Asian ever to reside in Romsey, Hampshire and may be its only immigrant. He wears his British rail uniform with pride equal to that of a military officer's love of uniform. An English ticket collector would never do that. An English ticket collector would be visibly resentful of the lowly station the British class system had assigned him. Accordingly, the uniform would have become an object of vengeance, along with any passenger who deigned to address him. The shirt would be untucked, jacket wrinkled and unbuttoned, and no more than lip service would be paid to actually performing any work for his employer, being of the belief that publicly parading himself in a demeaning British rail ticket collector's uniform should in itself warrant a weekly paycheck. Not so for the ticket collector that confronted Dylan this Saturday afternoon. The ticket collector eyes Dylan's overnight bag. He scrutinizes Dylan with suspicion.

"Ticket for platform walking only. Ticket not for train. You are having to pay more to journey on train."

"I'm just going to take some pictures of the train from the overhead walkway," explains Dylan. "I have my camera with me," he adds, waving his bag.

The ticket collector is mistrustful. "I am keeping werry watchful eye on you when train is coming in. If you are getting on London train, I am calling school authority werry fast." Pointing to the badge on Dylan's school blazer, "British Rail not tolerating delinquency."

Shit, thinks Dylan, not a great start at being as inconspicuous as possible. The movie *The Great Escape* had just been screened at school. This is a movie about a big breakout from a German prisoner of war camp during World War II. The prisoners escape en masse and get systematically recaptured over the hostile enemy countryside. Dylan feels guilty and hunted and he's only been a criminal for five minutes.

As he walks the steps to the top of the overhead crosswalk between the platforms, he senses the watchful gaze of the ticket collector. To make matters worse, there's no other person in the station. He stands on the bridge and looks to the south. He removes a camera from his overnight bag, looks back down toward the ticket collector, and smiles while waving with his camera. The rumble of the London train approaching can be heard. It arrives, squealing into the station, and Dylan times his descent from the overhead walkway to merge with passengers getting off the train. Fortunately, there are a dozen or so. Dylan exits with them and, when he surrenders his platform ticket, the ticket collector raises his eyebrows, perhaps acknowledging himself to be wrong in suspecting a delinquent. "Yolly good show," says the ticket collector.

The next step is the dangerous part of the plan. Dylan exits toward the station parking lot. He scrutinizes the area to ensure that Dozy David has departed. He must not be recognized. He looks for a military green Land Rover. In it is supposed to be Bridget's sister, Delia, who Dylan has never met. He spots a Land Rover, fortunately the only one in the parking lot, and walks quickly toward it. Yes, the girl in the driver's seat looks as if she could be Bridget's sister. He approaches the passenger side of the vehicle and through the open window asks hesitantly,

"Are you Delia?"

"Get in," says presumably Delia.

Dylan climbs in and offers his hand, but Delia isn't interested. Instead, she says, mainly to herself, "Christ, you are just a baby, too. What the hell am I doing this for?" She cranks and starts the Land Rover engine. The gears grind and the vehicle lurches forward.

Dylan doesn't know what to say to this girl, a sixth form, eighteen-year-old, practically adult girl who appears to have taken an immediate dislike to him. She's dressed in jodhpurs and leather riding boots. The boots are manure encrusted. She is actually not much bigger than Dylan. She has all of Bridget's cute features, but seemingly none of her younger sister's temperament.

"Take your school cap off ... and the tie and your blazer," orders Delia. "We don't want anyone in town identifying you as an Elwin Park boy."

Delia avoids the town square by taking a longer route. She spends the entire journey lecturing Dylan about what an evil person he very likely is, and informing him about how special a person her little sister Bridget is.

"God knows why," says Delia, "but Bridget absolutely worships you. If you do anything, and I mean *anything* to hurt her, I will very likely take your eyes out. She's at home making dinner. She's seldom boiled an egg thus far in her life and now she wants to make chicken cacciatore for you! If this meal she cooks is totally disgusting … and it probably will be… You'll just smile and tell her it is the tastiest meal you've ever eaten."

"And if you must have sex, make sure you use the rubbers. I have shown Bridget exactly how to put them on. They have to be completely on – she'll show you how. Don't even think of not wearing a rubber. A mistake could ruin both of your lives. Especially hers."

Delia does not quit laying into him the entire journey. Dylan gives up attempting to defend himself against any of the assumptions she's made about him. By the time the vehicle clunks and groans into the farmhouse laneway, he is feeling completely defeated.

As the Land Rover pulls up in the forecourt of the farmhouse, Bridget emerges from the front door. He almost doesn't recognize her. In the two months he has known Bridget, he has seen her attired in two distinct ways. Jeans, checked blouse, and sneakers or boots for horseback riding. White blouse, blazer, and kilt for school. Today, Bridget is dressed in a simple yellow summer dress and sandals. She appears skinny and awkward in the dress. She approaches Dylan slowly with a sheepish grin, as if she might be apologizing for being dressed up. She even walks differently. But once they close in, she throws her arms around Dylan's neck, pulling herself off the ground. She kisses him deeply. Dylan responds in a guarded manner, knowing that Delia is close-by and likely observing. Bridget stands back on her feet and places one arm around Dylan's waist.

"Has Delia been perfectly awful to you?" asks Bridget loud enough to ensure that Delia can hear. "She's not a real witch, though she probably wants you to think that. You wouldn't be here now if it wasn't for her. She's actually the best sister in the world." She looks over to Delia. But Delia is in no mood to acknowledge any of her younger sister's compliments. Instead, she busies herself with unloading groceries from the back of the Land Rover.

Dylan gets a tour of the farmhouse. The Fairford farm is mainly about horses and cattle, but an assortment of other animals roam at random around the mid-sized property. In addition to the horses, there are chickens, ducks, geese, and a few goats. As far as Dylan is concerned, they all stink. Bridget knows this. For this reason, she has planned that they'll confine themselves mainly to the house. That's why she is wearing a dress and sandals. There is no reason for Dylan to know that Bridget swills out stables, feeds livestock, and grooms horses as part of a daily routine. Or, for that matter, killed, feathered, and gutted the chicken they'll eat for dinner. The farmhouse is a large, brick, Victorian building. It is owned by persons who have money, but do not particularly care for it. When Dylan asks Bridget how many bedrooms there are, she doesn't know. A few, she says. Only four are really used. Mummy and Daddy have one, the biggest, Delia has one, and there is my room and a guest room. Also, there is a nursery and some bedrooms that have been assigned other functions such as her mother's sewing room, father's office, and games room. The games room has a half-sized snooker table in it.

Dylan is conducted around the rooms. Bridget is saving her domain until last. It is on the third floor. It's the only room on the third floor because it is constructed into what might have once been an attic. The walls angle inward to an apex, with the exception of one that triangulates into a large protruding bay window overlooking the forecourt. The room is full of dolls and toy horses, mostly arranged into the angular recesses of the room created by roof hips, recesses that are only two feet in height at the periphery. There is an ancient wooden rocking horse, one with arced rockers and no springs. A bureau beside Bridget's bed is covered with framed photographs. Most of these are photos of Bridget at various different ages, seated on horseback. They begin when she was about four years old. In some, she is holding up ribbons. Prizes won at gymkhanas, no doubt. Closest to her bed is a photograph of three St. Theresa Convent girls and two Elwin Park boys, taken in the Romsey coffee shop. One of the Elwin Park boys is Dylan. Next to him is Bridget. They are centered in the photograph and a red ellipse has been drawn with a marker pen around the couple's faces. Under the highlighted portion of the photo, a heart has been drawn with the same marker pen.

"I don't remember this," says Dylan, picking up the photo.

"It was taken on the day we met. Before we were a *thing*. You spent the afternoon trying to pick me up. Johanna took the photo," replies Bridget. "That's why she's not in the photo. She's coming riding with us tomorrow." Great Auntie Josephine, thinks Dylan. With a giggle, Bridget adds, "Oh yes, I forgot to tell you about the riding. We'll have to find some clothes that fit you. You can't go in your school uniform."

Dylan truly thinks that the chicken cacciatore might be the best meal he has ever eaten. Although this was the opinion of a growing youth who had been ingesting just enough of the Elwin Park meals for two months to enable survival, even skeptical Delia has to admit the meal is outstanding. The meat falls off the bone. The sauce is exquisite. The food seems to alleviate the frowning countenance Delia had worn since picking up Dylan from Romsey station.

After eating, Bridget takes Dylan for a walk to show him the woods on the Fairford farm. She describes the property as her favorite place in the whole world. In this way, Dylan is drawn into the real world of Bridget. She can identify every birdcall, tree, wild life scat, and set of animal tracks.

"Daddy comes shooting here," she informs Dylan. "If I could tell him you're my boyfriend, he'd probably ask you to come hunting with him on Sunday mornings."

Dylan looks at her wide-eyed. Almost instantly, Bridget catches on. "No, silly, not to shoot *you*!" she says, laughing. "It's just his way of being friends with blokes. Though if he knew what we have been getting up to lately, perhaps he'd want to kill you."

The sex begins terribly. Bridget ignites two candles and switches the lights out. While Dylan and Bridget undress each other without embarrassment in the outdoors, they feel bashful in the privacy of a bedroom. Once undressed, they kneel on the bed and embrace. Dylan's hard-on pushes forcefully into Bridget's tummy. They kiss deeply. This has the effect of relaxing Bridget, but inflaming Dylan's passion. He lustily grinds his penis into Bridget's abdomen, so much so that she is forced to defend herself by taking hold of it.

"I'm not ready yet," says Bridget, "I want to cuddle some more. Maybe I should give you a wank first so you're not so ... pushy."

But there is no holding Dylan back. Bridget retrieves a foil package from her bedside table. She attempts to open it. After a couple of tries, she hands it to Dylan. Eventually, he succeeds, but only when he resorts to using his teeth. He removes the rubber. It is sticky.

"Give it to me," orders Bridget, "I know what to do."

Bridget attempts to roll the condom over the tip of Dylan's penis, but it refuses to unroll. With all this attention applied to his penis, Dylan is in danger of erupting before the condom is even on. Bridget turns the rubber around. This time it unrolls. She works it down the shaft of Dylan's penis.

"I don't think much of that rubber bobble on the tip," she remarks, but then dutifully lies back on the bed. Dylan dives toward her. But the tip of his sheathed penis has just barely contacted the outer lips of Bridget's vulva, when he ejaculates. In doing so, his penis thrusts upward and over Bridget's tummy, not into her. He gasps and collapses on top of her, burying his face into her shoulder, partly to hide his embarrassment. Bridget lies patiently underneath him, stroking his hair. A few moments go by. Dylan rolls off Bridget, his face still flushed by orgasm and shame. He examines his flaccid penis under the wrinkled condom. The previously floppy capsule at the end of the condom is bursting with spunk. It looks bizarre. He is about to pull it off when Bridget tells him not to.

"Go to the bathroom," she tells him. "Wash your willy with soap and water. We can't cuddle again until you've washed."

As he gets up, Bridget gasps as Dylan twists his naked backside toward her to head for the door. His bum is displayed with a series of angry linear lesions striped across it. "What's happened to your bottom?" she asks, horrified.

"Oh that," responds Dylan matter-of-factly, relieved to divert attention from his failure as a lover. "I was caned for being late for tea after our date in the woods two weeks ago. Then last week, I was caned again by the headmaster for daydreaming in his English class. This is supposed to remind me not to daydream again."

"Daydreaming! You must be bloody joking. Those are open wounds. What were you daydreaming about?"

Dylan laughs. "Probably about having sex with you!"

"Jesus!" exclaims Bridget, indignant, "that's abuse. The skin is broken in a couple of places. When you go to the bathroom, bring back a tube of antiseptic ointment and I'll put some on for you. What a horrible place is Elwin Park. That's disgusting. Do your mother and father know about this?"

"Definitely not," responds Dylan, "but if they did, they would probably think it's good for me – who knows?"

The bathroom is on the second floor. Dylan pulls Bridget's dressing gown over his shoulders and descends the stairs. He tiptoes. He does not want to come across Delia. He is about to enter the bathroom when Bridget calls down to him. She is standing naked on the landing looking down from the top of the stairs.

"I forgot to tell you, don't try to flush it down the toilet."

"What?" asks Dylan, confused.

"It," yells Bridget, "the bloody rubber, you dimwit."

The shouting brings Delia out of her room onto the second floor landing. Dylan pulls Bridget's dressing gown tighter around his body. He doesn't want Delia looking at his willy. Especially with a wrinkled condom on it.

"Will you two shut up," says Delia, "I'm trying to do my homework." Delia pushes her way past Dylan, enters the bathroom and removes a small plastic bag from a cupboard and hands it to Dylan.

"Put it in there and throw it in the rubbish bin tomorrow," she orders him, walking out of the bathroom and adding, "And make sure you wash yourself well" as she closes the door.

Dylan is grumpy when he gets back to Bridget's bedroom. "Your sister hates me," he complains, "everything I do is wrong."

Bridget says nothing, but pats a place on the bed beside her, indicating he should lie face down. She takes the tube of antiseptic ointment from him, squeezes some onto a finger, and gently rubs some into the wounds caused by the cane. "This is awful, Dylan," she says. "I really don't know why you're so happy-go-lucky about it. Whoever did this to you is a monster."

Dylan says nothing. "Do you hate it there?" asks Bridget.

"I guess I do," the boy responds. "Until you came into my life, I was unhappier than I've ever been. Things are different now. I can take the bad stuff because I have you to look forward to."

Bridget pats his bum. "Turn over," she tells him. She lies back down beside him and softly strokes his penis. All it takes is one pass and he is ready for action. Dylan moves his hands between Bridget's legs and believes he has touched heaven once again. The feeling intoxicates his senses. It is not long before Bridget begins to respond, writhing and squirming, her eyes glazed. Her gasping breaths signal him it is time to get another rubber on. The interruption in what has up to this point flowed naturally creates a problem. The mechanics of condom usage are not easily navigated by the inexperienced. From opening the package to getting the device properly installed detracts from either romantic or lustful impetus.

Finally, however, the condom is in place. Bridget un-props herself from her elbows to lie on her back once again. She guides the condom sheathed penis to its goal. Dylan eases himself deep into Bridget. She sighs as he enters her, but Dylan can only manage two thrusts before he is betrayed once again by his adolescent body. In despair, he collapses on top of her a second time. He is sure James Bond wouldn't do this.

Bridget has technically just lost her virginity – whatever that means for a girl who has been riding horses since the age of three. But Bridget is also something of an expert on the sex act. Like any farm-raised girl, she has been witness to animals mating for her entire life. She's all too aware that a young stallion becomes so inflamed with lust at just the prospect of mating that execution of the act is usually only possible with human assistance. Evidently, this is also the case with young human stallions. Patiently, she strokes Dylan's hair, knowing he is upset.

"It's okay," she says comforting him, "you're just a little excited. We'll make it work."

Dylan lifts his face up from Bridget's shoulder to look her in the eye. It doesn't help his state of mind that she clearly comprehends what is going on so much better than he. Better go with the flow. He pulls out. This time there is less spunk contained in the sac at the end of the condom. Bridget props herself up on her elbows to observe. She gestures pointing downward toward the bathroom. Downstairs he goes on tiptoe for another wash.

At some point during the night, the two lovers get it together. They sleep little. Most of the sleep they get is post coital and conjoined. It begins to get light at four in the morning. Bridget awakes first. Dylan is asleep on top of her. She picks up the box of condoms and examines it. One condom remains of the original six. She considers the foil package. Then she inserts the condom underneath her pillow.

Bridget applies some butterfly kisses to Dylan's cheeks, then to his eyelids. Dylan awakes slowly, rubbing his eyes.

"Dill, I hate those rubbers. They smell funny. And I can't feel you properly. You feel better in my hands. I want to feel you properly. I want to do it … without the rubber. You just have to pull out. Before you squirt." With that, Bridget rolls Dylan over onto his back. She straddles him.

"Let's do it like this," she says. "You just have to tell me a couple of seconds before you squirt." She gyrates her groin into Dylan's. She grasps his penis and feeds him into her. For the first time, they fuck on equal terms. Both want it to last for an eternity. They wrestle and roll. Dylan grasps each of Bridget's buttocks as if he wants to drive himself right through them. But she wants to control the movement. She unpeels his hands from her bottom and interlocks her fingers with his. She presses forward and pins his hands to her bed. As the critical moment approaches, Dylan attempts to withdraw. But the attempt is trumped by a primal force from Bridget's small frame, generating a pelvic thrust that overpowers him, driving into his groin, ensuring that he is as deep into her as is possible. After orgasm, a series of convulsive thrusts from both participants ensures that whatever sperm yet remaining in Dylan's testicles is propelled deep into his partner. Though they have come in unison, the force and duration of Bridget's orgasm outlasts Dylan's by a margin. She collapses, quivering into Dylan's shoulder while crying convulsively. Dylan doesn't know what to make of it.

"Did I hurt you?" he asks, bewildered. Bridget, still crying into his shoulder, shakes her head. A mixture of their sex juices, mostly from Bridget, have run down Dylan's buttocks and saturated the bed sheets on which they rest. A minute passes. Bridget ceases crying and settles still, breathing deeply, each breath drawn deep down into her stomach which pumps into Dylan's beneath her. Dylan runs a finger down Bridget's spine, navigating each vertebra, and stopping when he finds her coccyx, which he explores. Both drift into sleep.

Delia scrambles eggs for breakfast. Bridget is unusually quiet. After eating, Delia approaches Bridget from behind. The older sister massages the younger sister's shoulders.

"Is everything alright?" asks Delia.

Bridget nods in the affirmative.

"Do you want to talk to me alone?" asks Delia, still worried.

Bridget shakes her head. She remains quiet through the morning, saying little to anyone. Johanna arrives mid-morning. She's on horseback. Dylan dresses in a pair of Delia's jeans and one of her father's shirts. Bridget saddles a horse for Dylan and the threesome goes riding on the trails in the woods. Most of the conversation during the ride is exchanged between Dylan and Johanna. Delia bakes a pizza for lunch, after which Johanna rides off.

Like Delia, Dylan is also concerned about Bridget's sullen mood. After they have washed and dried the lunch dishes, Dylan puts his arm around Bridget's waist. "Did I do something wrong?" he asks.

"No," responds Bridget, "I just don't want this to end. I can't see you coming like this again; it was difficult enough to arrange this time. I hate that they can be so cruel to you in that horrible school. That makes me worried, Dill. And I can't help feeling angry at you for just accepting that this is just the way things are."

"But that is how they are, Bridget," responds Dylan. "I don't know what I could do to change anything."

"What if you told your mother?"

"My mom would think I was exaggerating. She'd tell me not to worry. She would reassure me that sooner or later I would settle in and make some nice friends. She would do anything rather than admit the possibility that I might be unhappy. Especially if she thought she could be in any way to blame."

"I'll never be a mother like that," swears Bridget. "I will listen to my children. And I would never send them to a boarding school, let alone one like yours."

"I don't think mine had too much choice. There are no high school programs in the places they have to go."

"Then they should move." A silence ensues. "I want to keep you here with me. I would protect you. I could hide you in my bedroom under the bed." Bridget rides the fantasy. "We could stay up all night fucking. We could make babies. I'd like four or five." Dylan is unsure about this. Especially the bit about the four or five babies.

*   *   *

The return to school strategy is undertaken without a hitch. Dylan says good-bye to Bridget with a hug. Bridget is in a resigned and sullen mood once again. Delia drives the Land Rover to Romsey Station to drop Dylan off. Delia appears to be less resentful of Dylan during this return journey, though she's still far from friendly. Dropped off, Dylan doesn't have to enter the railway station. He walks straight up to the taxi stand and boards the only waiting vehicle. He arrives in the school grounds half an hour before curfew and surrenders his exeat voucher to the duty prefect.

Bridget does not phone the next day; a Monday. Nor does she phone on Tuesday, Wednesday, and Thursday. Dylan wonders if he should attempt to phone her. But this would risk connecting with either of Bridget's parents. Even connecting with Delia could be risky, given her apparent hostility toward Dylan. The secrecy would be blown. On the Thursday evening after prep, Dylan realizes that he had not sought permission to go on a cross-country run through the week. He does this for the sake of consistency. He navigates a five-mile course, returns, showers, and goes to bed. The run tires him and he falls into a deep sleep almost immediately.

Suddenly he is awakened. "Douglas of Dickens. Wanted in the Headmaster's study immediately," yells a prefect standing at the doorway of the dormitory. Dylan blinks his eyes. It is bright sunshine outside. For an instant, he wonders if it's the next morning, but no. He grabs his watch and it indicates that it is a quarter of an hour short of ten pm. "Wanted in the Headmaster's study" usually means a caning. Not good. The welts on his bum from the beating he received the previous week have not yet healed. The other boys in the dormitory make sympathetic faces. Dylan gets out of bed, rubbing his eyes. He locates his dressing gown and slippers and puts them on. He follows the prefect down to the Headmaster's study. While walking there, he scans his memory for misdemeanors that might have got him into trouble.

He knocks on the study door. Dozy David opens it and gestures to Dylan to enter. The scene is not what Dylan expects. It's far worse. Facing him, Dome sits behind his oversize desk. Behind Dome is a set of French doors. On Dylan's left are two adults; a man and a woman. Sitting between them is Bridget. She is wearing a white summer frock and the same sandals she wore over the weekend. Dylan notes that her eyes are reddened from crying. Dozy David sits to Dylan's right, leaving him standing in pajamas and dressing gown in the center of the room. Dome stands and moves his towering, obese frame around the desk to face Dylan.

"This is a very serious matter," says Dome with severity. But he gets no further before Bridget interrupts the solemnity of the occasion by leaping to her feet, running over to Dylan, and hugging him with a desperate fervor. She is crying in earnest now.

Dome is quick to move. He leaps from his chair, strides toward Bridget, and takes hold of her arm with authority, saying firmly, "Now then, young lady…"

At the instant Dome's hand makes contact with Bridget's shoulder, the girl turns on him, enraged, striking his arm with a vicious slap. "Keep your hands off me, you filthy pervert!" she shrieks at the top of her lungs.

Simultaneously, the man who is presumably Mr. Fairford leaps to his feet shouting, too. "Sit down, you little hussy," the man yells, "or I'll have you over my knee and take the skin off your arse with a horsewhip." His Romsey drawl is noticeably stronger than Bridget's. The flurry of emotion brings both Mrs. Fairford and Dozy David to their feet.

Mrs. Fairford physically arrests her husband's lunge on Bridget, cautioning, "Now Hubert, we agreed you were not going to behave like this."

Dozy David more gently attempts to calm Dome. "Reverend Headmaster, it behooves us to conduct this enquiry with some dignity."

Bridget stands her ground with her arms wrapped around Dylan's waist, her back to everyone else. Dylan isn't sure what to do. He settles on placing one arm around Bridget's shoulder and inserting the other in his dressing gown pocket. It's against Elwin Park rules to ever put a hand in a pocket unless in the act of retrieving an object from it. Dylan forgets that rule. There is no rule about responding to an embrace from a damsel in distress. And it is within the shroud of this embrace that Bridget moves her hand to secretly insert an envelope into Dylan's other dressing gown pocket.

Dome straightens his tie. The status quo prevails. Bridget remains in the center of the room, but has relaxed her hugging hold on Dylan. She stands up on tippy-toe to whisper to Dylan's ear, "They know pretty much everything. Don't lie. Don't say too much either."

Mr. and Mrs. Fairford return to their original seating positions, leaving the chair between them vacated by Bridget unoccupied. Dome retreats to the throne-like chair behind his desk and Dozy David sits on his other side. Dylan is at a disadvantage. Though there's little doubt he is the criminal of the occasion, only he is not aware of the level of disclosure that has already taken place. As Bridget ran toward him, he could see that she was still wearing her regulation gray school knickers, visible through the white cotton dress. Her hair is mussed and her bangs are wet. Is this sweat or tears? To show herself outside of her bedroom with this level of neglect for her appearance wasn't a Bridget trait. It was her habit to carefully scrutinize every angle of her image in a mirror, even after throwing on a pair of jeans and shirt to go riding. They must have left the Fairford farm in a hurry. So what exactly has

Bridget revealed?

Dylan has presented Dome with a dilemma. Elwin Park is struggling to maintain its optimum student numbers of 320 souls. In fact, enrollment for a couple years has been hovering at a shortfall of around 40 students. To his staff, Dome refers to students as "fee paying units" or FPUs. Of course, the acronym FPU would never be used in front of parents. It was best to let parents believe that objectives of managing a school were confined to educating students. Now some lusty little blighter sets about ravishing the local skirt in the first of a potential five-year career in the school. That said, this FPU has just been witness to an outrageous humiliation of the headmaster of Elwin Park by a fourteen-year-old strumpet of the Romsey common classes. Dome would have normally expelled the brat without an instant of hesitation. But Dylan Douglas represents the first of three potential Elwin Park FPUs, assuming the Douglas parents would enroll each of his male siblings as they became of appropriate age. The Douglas boy is clever, charismatic, and artfully deceitful – not the worst traits for a young man to have. No, the headmaster decides, the Douglas boy cannot be expelled and suspension is not an option, given that the parents reside out of country.

The great leader of Elwin Park scratches the center of his shiny, bald head. Then he strokes his cheeks. He ponders a plan of action. He considers suggesting to the Fairford parents that their daughter would benefit from a good thrashing. The thrashing would be executed with a cane within proper Elwin Park guidelines. This would spare the Fairford parents the emotional toll exacted on the executioner of a severe beating. Dome would undertake the deed himself. He would proceed to remove every bit of skin from the girl's backside. After he had finished with her, it would be years before she thought of spreading her legs before one of his FPUs a second time.

Dozy David takes over. First, he suggests that Bridget resume her original seat between her parents. Bridget adamantly shakes her head in refusal. Hence, she is permitted to remain in her protective embrace of Dylan. No one in the room wants to risk another fight with fiery Bridget.

The story of Bridget and Dylan's history of lust unfolds. Lust it is, not love; let there be no mistake on that issue. Bridget and Dylan's clandestine groping and rutting will not be dignified by elevating such lewd acts to a status of motivation by love. Love is for the mature. Mere children are not capable of such lofty emotions. The four adults nod their heads in full agreement on this matter. Yes, it's all lust and hormones.

Having defined love, each adult in the room bemoans the deceit and the betrayals. Mr. Fairford has been betrayed; years of instilling equine skills and discipline into his daughter have been abused so that she could go galloping off in to the countryside to whore with foreigners. Mrs. Fairford has been betrayed – until now, her daughter has been an open book with her. This nightmarish liaison has changed everything. It used to be that there were no secrets between mother and daughter. Dozy David has also been betrayed – after all, he swallowed the lonely auntie story hook, line, and sinker. The boy's innocent looks and faked reluctance to spend a weekend away with a counterfeit aunt is one thing. The in-your-face lies are quite another. Has there ever been a more artful conniver in the history of Elwin Park?

The time arrives for Dome to assume control over the proceedings. He's heard enough of this recounting of petty grievances. A more statesman-like approach is required. And perhaps a renewed approach might rescue three FPUs? By now, Dome has recovered from being outrageously insulted by the country girl slut.

"Elwin Park has been deceived, its honor impugned," he begins. "But is this entirely the fault of young Douglas? The Douglas boy's track record at Elwin has been exemplary up to this point. In making the transition from a backward American system of education to the lofty academics of an English school, Douglas has made admirable strides. So much so, he is now positioned to be one of the top five academic performers in the third form. All this in his first year."

He pauses for effect.

"The wile and guile of the female gender are indeed a force to be reckoned, no innocent young lad could sustain such an onslaught …"

At this point, Dozy David thinks it might be circumspect to interrupt his headmaster by standing once again and waving his hand. Dozy David observed that both Mr. Fairford's fists had become tightly clenched. Had he allowed his Headmaster to continue, one of those fists would end up implanted with considerable force into Dome's swollen nose, which was likely to burst on contact with one of Hubert Fairford's powerful farmer's fists.

Calmed once again, Dome continues. The outcomes of this discourse must be win-win. Mr. and Mrs. Fairford get what they want. What they want is that Elwin Park undertakes to ensure that lascivious cads such as Dylan remain incarcerated and never be permitted to roam the countryside, randomly corrupting the female youth of fair England. More specifically, they want the school to ensure that Dylan Douglas has no contact by phone, by mail, or in person with their daughter ever again. Dome assures the Fairford's that, should the school disciplinary process grant Dylan the privilege of remaining at Elwin, there would be no fear of him escaping the boundaries of the school.

Bridget starts to sob as the terrible verdict is delivered. The Fairford's stand in readiness to depart, but Bridget clutches her arms around Dylan's neck and kisses him feverishly with her wet, reddened face. Her father grabs her shoulder in an effort to separate his daughter from her corrupter. Bridget responds by furiously throwing his arm aside but, accepting the inevitable, untangles herself from Dylan, seeking her mother's side and protective arm. As the three exit Dome's study door, Bridget twists her shoulder away from her mother and shouts hysterically to Dylan.

"Don't let them hurt you like they did before. Phone up your mother. She will stop the bastards," and finally shouting even louder, "I love you, Dill!" The heavy oak study door closes with a deep clunk.

For a moment or two, silence reigns in the study. Dylan continues to stand in the center, looking down at the floor. Dome and Dozy David exchange glances. For a moment, Dome considers whether to ask Dylan whether he is any way ashamed of his actions and the shame he has cast upon both Elwin Park and Dickens House. He checks himself, realizing what the boy's response is likely to be. Americans had no sense of shame.

"Wait outside in the ante room, Douglas of Dickens House," orders Dome, "Mr. Gwilliam and I would like to discuss your future at Elwin in the light of this shameful incident."

Dylan waits outside in the ante room between Dome's study and the main hall. He feels for the letter in his pocket. The envelope is addressed to "Dill." A small heart is drawn in one corner. Inside the heart it says "B + D = love forever." He hears footsteps move toward the study door. Quickly, he stuffs the letter back into his pocket. Will he be expelled? He hopes so. Life at Elwin would become unbearable without being able to see Bridget.

Dome speaks. "Mr. Gwilliam and I have discussed your case in detail. We are in agreement that you are a student of enormous potential who will grow to be an outstanding asset to Elwin Park. We are not uncaring here at Elwin. Mr. Gwilliam and I both believe that your indiscretions are mitigated by your youth and the volatility of the young lady in question. In addition, you have had little time as yet to adjust to the ways of England and of Elwin Park. Consequently, we have elected to regard this incident as a youthful indiscretion. An indiscretion for which you will, nevertheless, be punished. However, we have chosen to spare your parents the shame that would result by revealing to them the details of your rebellious and deceitful actions over the past two months. First, you will be denied the privilege of exeats for one full calendar year, beginning in the September of the next Michaelmas term. More important, the same will apply to the granting of town passes. The withholding of town passes will apply indefinitely. Next, you'll be permitted no outside phone calls from any source other than your parents. This will be strictly enforced. An announcement will be made to the school population at luncheon tomorrow and a notice will be posted in the school public phone booth. In addition, all outside mail addressed to you will be routed through Mr. Gwilliam. I want to stress that no communication between Miss Fairford and yourself will be tolerated. I was required to assure Mr. and Mrs. Fairford that this condition would be strictly enforced on our part while school is in session – I will rely on your sense of responsibility to ensure this is the case during school holidays. The latter is a precondition requested by the Fairford's to ensure they would not seek to further prosecute you for the shame you brought onto their family. For the remaining three weeks of the summer term, you will cease to be responsible for fagging duties in your dormitory. You will return to your former duties as House Captain Blatherstone's personal fag – that way, he can keep an eye on you around the clock. Finally, Mr. Gwilliam will administer a beating consisting of six strokes of the cane. That portion of the punishment will take place anon."

Dylan accompanies Mr. Gwilliam to his office to receive his beating. Once there, Dozy David asks Dylan to pull down his pajama bottoms. Dylan observes the teacher grimace at the sight of the lacerations across his buttocks. After a pause, he instructs Dylan to pull his pajamas up. He then administers a caning that does not warrant the name "beating," delivering six gentle taps, well above the lacerated area of his buttocks. Dylan has received more painful physical punishment from his baby sister. The tame punishment is surely the result of Bridget's parting words. How smart is Bridget! Is it any wonder he's so crazy about her?

Dylan looks at his watch as he exits the Headmaster's study. A quarter to twelve. He has never observed the downstairs school corridors so vacated of humans. On the way back to his dormitory, he stops off at a washroom and enters a cubicle. He sits to read Bridget's letter.

Dearest, delicious, delectable, darling Dill,

I don't know where to begin. I have so much to write and so little time. If this letter is not finished when you get it, it is because I have been interrupted. Daddy is in a rage and has been phoning your school demanding an immediate appointment with your Headmaster for the past few of hours. So far he has not been able to arrange this. I am to be dragged off with Mummy and Daddy to this meeting. I am not sure whether they will get you involved. It's awful. I have been crying for hours. I should begin at the beginning.

I was sick to my tummy after you left on Sunday. When I woke up on Monday morning, I was vomiting. Mummy kept me home from school. I was sick so many times I was empty after a couple of hours. I had a fever too. When Delia got home from school, she asked me if I could be pregnant. I told Delia that I hoped I was. Delia blew a fuse. She was so angry that I thought she was going to march off tell Mummy and Daddy on the spot. I had to stay off school sick on Tuesday and Wednesday. This morning (Thursday) two things happened. First, I got my period. I know you won't understand but I was actually sad.   Second, I was not feeling sick any more so I decided to go back to school. The truth is that I was aching to see you and wanted us to get together again – I knew I couldn't do that while I was supposed to be sick. I am not sure if it is safe to fuck with a period – but I want to all the same.

As Delia and I arrived home from school this afternoon, I knew there was a problem. Both Mummy and Daddy were waiting for me. Daddy began by slapping me across the face and calling me a slut. He hit me so hard I was knocked to the ground. Mummy and Delia had to jump in to stop him from hurting me even more. It was horrible. Until now, Daddy has always been such a special friend to me. Of course, I knew this was all about you. But I couldn't figure out how they had found out. At first, I thought Delia must have ratted on us. It turned out to be actually my fault though. Remember there was one of those packets of rubbers remaining. Well, your stupid Bridget went and put it under her pillow and forgot about it. This morning Mummy decided to change the sheets on my bed after I had gone to school. The first thing she found was the rubber. Then she must have looked a little more closely at the bed sheets. Needless to say they were not exactly clean. So to make a long story short, a terrible scene erupted between the four of us. Thank god for Delia. She defended you and me… especially you. I knew in my heart she didn't really hate you. I was crying too much to join in, that was where Delia was such a big help. In the end, we had to tell them everything. I am not sure what is going to happen. Daddy wants to sue the school. He wants to kill me. He especially wants to hurt you. Delia and also Mummy have been trying to calm him down for hours. Delia is trying to tell him that he is going to make himself look ridiculous if he goes to the school ranting and raving. She says that what took place happened because both of us wanted it to and wild horses couldn't have stopped us. She told Daddy that he should know that better than anyone. Not sure what that meant.

So we are probably coming to your school tonight. I will try to find someone to pass this letter on to you so it all doesn't come as a terrible surprise when they finally involve you. Always remember Dill, I love you to pieces … I loved the sex, even the first couple of times when you were so goofy …

Here, the letter abruptly finished. Dylan tears up. He folds the letter back into his dressing gown pocket. He climbs the stairs to return to his dormitory. He navigates his way back to his bed and climbs in under the covers. Those boys in the dormitory who are still awake are only interested in knowing how many strokes of the cane he received. Dylan holds two hands up to display six fingers. That was the best thing about being caned. He was spared having to tell them anything else. He inserts Bridget's letter under his pillow.

11. BECKY, EEMO, AND TJ.

Following the drama in the headmaster's study, a mere three weeks of the Elwin Park summer term remain. The good news is that Dylan has completed a full school year at the gulag and somehow avoided the dishonor of expulsion. Is that good news? Perhaps to his father. The bad news is that he now has four more years of hell until graduation. He has no means of communicating with Bridget. Every move he makes within the school is scrutinized. For a while, he entertains a hope that either Heather or Hazel may somehow be able to smuggle a message from Bridget to him. But it turns out that Heather and Hazel have been strictly forbidden to communicate with him.

Dylan supposes that Bridget probably has more freedom than he, although her old man seems to be a bit of a terror. He knows Bridget's mail address but, given the injunction imposed on him not to communicate with her, it would be stupid to use it as doing so would likely jeopardize either his or her well-being. Could he write via big sister Delia? That would probably not work and be unfair to Delia. No, he would just have to get through the three weeks that remained of the summer term without contact. Respite would come in the form of sitting on a beach somewhere in Thailand, a world away from Elwin Park.

Somehow, the summer term at Elwin finally concludes and is followed by another long airplane ride. During this interlude, Dylan elects to withdraw into himself. He does his best to put the experiences of the previous year into some sort of perspective. Where is his life leading to? Unlike his mostly happy years in grade school, during which he felt he had some control over the events, now it seems he has none. The disconnect with his family feels greater than ever. Communications with his mother have become strained and, with his father, as always, non-existent. His siblings now regard him as an alien. His mother informs him he has puberty blues. Dylan feels insulted. His response is to turn into himself. He sails, snorkels, and goes for walks on the beach. He attempts to pick up a cute, blond tourist on the beach who appears to be around his age. But despite appearing willing, she speaks only Finnish and German, and their efforts at simple communication have to be aborted. They each shrug their shoulders, ruing what might have been. Yes, he had survived hell for a full year and in the midst of it, found a little heaven, short-lived as it was.

During this vacation, Dylan's thoughts often focus on Bridget. In some ways, she terrified him. The power of her passion overwhelmed him. Surely he did not have it in him to reciprocate on her terms? Yes, he aches for her body, yes he can think of nothing that would give him more pleasure than to just to sit on a horse blanket listening to her giggle and make fun of the world. But he suspects that he falls somewhat short of her expectations of him. Bridget possessed such fluency in expressing her emotions that it often left him feeling enfeebled. What was it that she saw in him? If Dylan added up every minute he had spent with Bridget, the total time would not exceed forty-eight hours spread over ten weeks. Two days! And half that time was accounted for by the continuous twenty-four hour period spent at Bridget's home. Yet this was all it took to launch her into the forefront of almost every thought that crossed his mind.

Another thing that confuses Dylan is why those that hold the power to control their lives are so determined to keep them apart. Forever. Why did it matter so much? Did Bridget's parents truly think that Dylan was the absolute worst boyfriend their daughter could have? Did they seriously believe that Dylan had any power within him with which he could corrupt the force that is Bridget? Why was Delia so apparently contemptuous of him, yet also willing to help when it really counted? Dylan muses over these questions. One thing is for sure – within the confines of Elwin Park, he can be neutralized by the system. The "system" controls all the obvious lines of communication, such as the phone and mail. He wonders if he did dare to breach the communication prohibition mandated by Bridget's parents, how long it would take to get back to the rulers of the gulag.

The prohibition imposed on him not to receive town passes for an indefinite period is tough. It is not just the contact with girls he would miss out on. Dylan actually looked forward to getting a half-decent cup of coffee once a week. On top of that, he isn't too likely to obtain further permissions to go on cross-country runs. The coming school year does not forbear well. He is going to be truly imprisoned in the gulag, and opportunities to come up for air are likely to be few and far between.

On returning to Elwin Park for the autumn term, Dylan does so as a "second-year" student. He's now a fourth former. If he desires, he can strut around bullying first-year boys, but this aspect of boarding school life has no appeal to him. What does appeal to him is that he is no longer assigned fagging detail. By merely surviving the gulag for a year, he has acquired status and seniority. Dylan's immediate problem is to handle the fallout from his now well-known romps with Bridget. The fallout is both good and bad. Among Elwin fourth formers, Dylan has achieved some infamy. A little notoriety is seldom a bad thing in an all-male culture. He has achieved the status of a star on the school rugby team without ever having had to risk his person on a rugby pitch. Even some of the fifth-year boys consider his Bridget adventures to be a pretty cool deal. Everyone wants details. Dylan tells them nothing. He responds to questions by grinning and shaking his head. However, things do not turn out to be so smooth with a small number of older boys and prefects.

Early in the fall term, Dylan's supposed rival for the affections of his Bridget seeks him out for the first time. This is Ronald Parker, a prefect in Hardy House. Parker is more than two years Dylan's senior, stands well over six feet in height, and weighs over 15 stone in English reckoning, or over 220 pounds by Dylan's. As befits his physical shape, Ronald Parker plays in the scrum on the school rugby team. The plus is that Parker is not the sharpest knife in the block. The minus is that rugby players on the school first fifteen tend to punch well above their position in the school pecking order. The new school year is barely a couple of days old when Dylan has a first run-in with Parker. Dylan is exiting his homeroom after evening prep when, out of nowhere, a powerful blow is delivered sideways to his shoulder. Dylan grabs his shoulder in pain and leans back against the wall. Parker stands in front of Dylan, observing him.

"I don't know what she saw in you, you little shrimp. She was a slag, Douglas," Parker strides towards him, getting in his face. "A ride, she'd been fucked by half the farm boys in Hampshire and most of the Elwin rugby team. I don't know what you saw in her." Parker hits Dylan again, this time less painfully in the chest. It becomes clear that Parker is unwilling to risk inflicting any physical damage on Dylan's person that could be evidential. A group of first- and second-year students gather around to observe the scene, while maintaining a cautious distance. Dylan does some calculations. Would his Bunny Forslund sucker-punch work on Parker? Not likely. Parker played rugby twice a week and sustained hundreds of blows to all parts of his body from savagely obsessed combatants twice Dylan's weight. No, he'd have to ride this one out. He focuses on Parker's eyes, strokes some hair away from his forehead, and says nothing. "We are watching you, Douglas, all us prefects and seniors are," continues Parker. "We believe that you should have been expelled. You betrayed the honor of the entire school by rutting with the Romsey inferior classes."

Dylan thinks some more. He could plant his foot into Parker's balls. Such a move could possibly provide him with a collateral bonus of getting himself expelled. But now something else intervenes. Gladstone, the new house captain of Dickens House, arrives by chance onto the scene. In an instant, Dylan comprehends how Gladstone is likely to interpret the scene he has happened upon. In Gladstone's mind, Dickens House honor could be at stake. A minor school prefect from another house is bullying a Dickens House boy for a crime the boy had already been punished for. Any zealous house captain is unlikely to regard Dylan's exploits with

Bridget in a bad light. Was this not a conquest by a Dickens House boy? Why not debauch the local skirt if you can get away with it? Douglas the Yank had actually succeeded in an area where dozens of Elwin boys had failed.

Gladstone stops and stares directly at Parker, saying nothing. Parker is immediately unsettled. He stammers, "I was just letting Douglas know what I thought of the shame he brought upon Elwin Park ... and Dickens House." With that, Parker slinks away, leaving Dylan to nurse his wounds. Saying nothing, Gladstone also turns heel and departs. With the two prefects out of the scene, the junior boys close in on Dylan to commiserate with him.

As the weeks go by, Dylan adjusts to his second year at Elwin. He remains guarded in his dealings with other boys and instead devotes his time to reading, working out in the gym, and wandering through the expansive grounds of Elwin Park. It is during one of these jaunts that Dylan comes across Heather and Hazel one Saturday afternoon in the woods. The girls are on bicycles on one of the trails. When the girls spy him, they pedal toward him. "We've been hoping to come across you," they announce in unison. "Where have you been hiding? Has anyone updated you on Bridget yet?"

Dylan shakes his head, "No, I've heard nothing." Both girls want to speak together. However, by exchanging a series of looks between each other, it is clear that the elder of the two, Heather, would have this privilege.

"She's been sent to prison, too," gushes Heather excitedly. "A boarding school in Somerset. It's called something like Moncton Downs ... or is that Monmouth Downs? But you probably shouldn't try to write to her; they've been told what a terrible nympho she is. And they probably know all about what a sex maniac you are. We didn't see Bridget all summer. We think she was gated by her dad; we don't ever see her out riding anymore. Her dad's a real monster. A bit like ours, I suppose. Daddy thinks you should have been expelled. And you don't want to hear about what Mother Superior at school thinks of the fact you were allowed to stay at Elwin."

Dylan distills this information and responds. "Do you know if Bridget managed to talk to Johanna? Did she maybe leave a letter for me? If I write her a letter and give it to one of you, can you try to deliver it to her over the Christmas holidays? I won't sign my name on it." So many questions.

Now Hazel speaks. "We are actually forbidden by Daddy to speak to you." She laughs. "Not that we care. Daddy says that you are an awful influence on the other boys at Elwin. But me and Heather defended you. As much as we dare. Heather even told Daddy that she wouldn't mind being corrupted by you, didn't you, Heather?" At this revelation, Heather delivers a vicious pinch into her sister's upper arm, causing her to wince. But Hazel continues all the same, "But we wouldn't betray Bridget. We all think she is terribly brave. Daddy has threatened us with a terrible fate if we try to contact you."

Heather picks up the thread. "Maybe he would send us to prison, too. I don't think we could stand life in a girl's boarding school. The good news is that they are dreadfully expensive. Not something a school teacher can afford to send twins to."

Dylan agrees to meet Heather and Hazel in secret within the Elwin grounds once a week. In this way, if there's any news of – or, better still, messages from – Bridget, he can be updated. He assures them that he doesn't want to get either of them into any trouble. He suggests that if there is any risk, to skip the arranged meeting and attempt to make it the following week.

Meetings take place. But Heather and Hazel like to gossip, and most of the information exchanged is no more than just that. Dylan delivers a letter addressed to Bridget to the girls just before the Christmas break. But despite assurances from Heather and Hazel that it was delivered to Bridget, he receives no reply. A few months later, before the Easter vacation break, he delivers another letter to Heather and Hazel to be conveyed to Bridget. As before, Dylan receives no reply. Dylan tries to come up with a reason for this and concludes that, in all probability, she has adjusted to the boarding school experience. That's the message between the lines. It would be unlike Bridget not to adjust. By this time, she probably has another boyfriend.

Two terms whiz by. Time passes more quickly now. Dylan wonders if it's because he is getting older. At Elwin Park, he's become generally popular, without making any close friends in the school. Some of this popularity is based on his reputation of expertise with "women." Ironic, thinks Dylan, who has been unable to score even a kiss from a girl since his separation from Bridget. Not for want of trying. Heather and Hazel attract him and they appear to telegraph to Dylan that they want to be more than just friends, but how to advance this attraction when the twins are never apart? If only just one of the pair could show up for one of their covert meetings. But it never happens. In addition, Dylan has been interested in some of the girls he meets on school vacations, but there never seems to be enough time to make anything of consequence happen. His parents are moving around more. In a social sense, he's forced to start from scratch each time they move. He discovers that it's tougher to breach established social networks as a teenager than as a child.

The summer term at Elwin begins in the final week of April. This particular April day is sunny and warm and Dylan is wandering through the woods by himself, enjoying the solitude of his own company. He is humming "Absolutely Sweet Marie" from *Blonde on Blonde,* while walking uphill alongside a stream. The stream is mostly a lazy trickle of water that descends into a lake on the east side of the Elwin Park grounds. This idle trickle changes into a torrid rush during a rainstorm, of which evidence can be seen in the stones that border either side of the stream. Dylan is crunching his way uphill when he spots three small children in the distance. One of them, the smallest of the three, appears to be in some distress, while the older two help.

As Dylan approaches, he identifies the three kids as the children of one of the teachers, a Mr. Rawlson, who teaches economics and politics to sixth form. Dylan could recognize Mr. Rawlson on sight, but doesn't know much else about him. There are two girls, one of around eight years of age, the other a couple of years her junior, as well as the younger boy. The boy is crying. The reason for this becomes obvious as Dylan closes in on the group. He has fallen and cut his knee, quite badly it seems, on some glass. The glass is jagged, no doubt from an aggressively discarded beer bottle tossed by an Elwin boy.

"Can I help?" suggests Dylan to the trio.

The older girl explains, "My brother tripped and fell. He has cut his knee open. I think he might need stitches." Dylan kneels to take a look at the injured boy. He's wearing shorts and rubber Wellington boots, called "wellies." The two girls also wear wellies, except they are attired in summer dresses in place of the shorts. The cut appears just as nasty close up as it did from afar.

"I have just the thing for this," Dylan says, removing a clean, white handkerchief from his pocket. Finally, a use for this accessory! All Elwin boys are required to carry handkerchiefs, preferably only used in an emergency. Failure to produce a handkerchief when asked to do so by a prefect is an offence punishable by 30 minutes' manual labor. Dylan's announcement stops the boy's crying instantly. Indeed, he turns and looks at him in wide-eyed amazement. Dylan gets to his feet and soaks the handkerchief in the stream. He returns to the injured child, who is still staring at him. "This might sting a little," Dylan informs the boy, "but we can't see how bad the cut is until we clean it up a little."

The older of the girls wraps her arms around her little brother. "Be brave, TJ," she tells him, "it will only sting for a second." As Dylan holds the knee in one hand and cleans up the wound with the other, the crying resumes with renewed vigor. But in a jiffy, the wound is cleaned and revealed to be not so bad after all. Dylan ties the wet handkerchief around the boy's knee to protect it. Once this is completed, TJ ceases crying and bends over to study the makeshift bandage. He seems pleased.

"So you're TJ," Dylan says. "How do you get to have a special name like that?"

His big sister explains in an effusive chatter, "His real name is Thomas Jonas. Thomas Jonas Rawlson. Daddy's name is also Thomas, but everyone calls him

Tom. First, we called TJ 'Tommy,' but he did not really seem to be a Tommy. Then Eemo, that's my sister here, starts to call him TJ and it just caught on. He's TJ to everyone now."

Dylan examines the three children. Cute kids. TJ has curly hair longer than that worn by most boys. The girls have similarly curly, mousy blond hair and an appealing English country rose look about them. "Well, it's a pleasure to meet you, Mr. TJ. My name is Dylan." To the child's surprise, he grabs and shakes his hand.

Instantly, the younger of the two girls bounces toward Dylan and extends her hand. "My name is Imogen. But everyone calls me Eemo now. TJ invented my nickname because he couldn't pronounce 'Imogen' when he was learning to speak. I'm six."

Big sister gets into the act. "You're not six yet, you have a whole month to go!" More cautiously than Eemo, big sister extends her hand to shake Dylan's. "I'm Rebecca, but everyone calls me 'Becky.'"

Now acquainted, Dylan gets to his feet. "It's been a pleasure to meet you, Becky, Eemo, and TJ," he tells them, "but we'd better do something about getting this injured man back to his mama and maybe a band-aid."

"What's a band-aid?" asks Eemo.

"A band-aid is what you folks might refer to as a 'plaster,' though I really don't know why," responds Dylan. With that, he picks up TJ and hoists him up onto his shoulders. TJ laughs. Eemo says she wants a shoulder ride too, but sensible Becky informs her that she is not the one who is injured. The four of them ascend the hill. Dylan clamps TJ onto his shoulders with one hand and holds Eemo's insistent hand with the other. More circumspect Becky walks alongside, but it's she that does most of the talking.

"Are you Bridget's lover?" she asks Dylan. Dylan pauses, a little taken aback by the unexpected question.

"Do you know Bridget?" Dylan asks her.

"Of course," responds Becky. "She used to visit all the time before she got sent away. She even babysat for us a few times."

Dylan has to think about this. "Yes," he says cautiously. "Bridget was my friend."

"Do you miss her?" probes Becky.

Dylan is not sure where this conversation is going. "How do you know about Bridget and me?"

"Everyone knows about you and Bridget. I thought I recognized your name and I guessed who you were when I heard your accent. You're actually a bit famous. Most people don't say nice things about you. In fact, they say you are quite horrible. You see, everybody liked Bridget. But when I asked Mummy, she said that if Bridget liked a boy, then that boy was probably a nice person. Are you a nice person?"

Eemo leaps to the rescue. "Of course he is a nice person, Becky – he rescued TJ, didn't he?" Then she turns to assure Dylan, "I think you're a nice person. And so does TJ; don't you, TJ?"

TJ nods in agreement from his perch on Dylan's shoulders. Becky says more seriously now, "I think you're nice, too. I can imagine Bridget being with you. When I have a boyfriend I think I might like him to be a bit like you."

The four approach the compound in which the schoolteachers' houses are located. When they get to the Rawlson home, Becky opens and pushes the door open just as their mother approaches. The mother is immediately flustered at seeing TJ riding Dylan's shoulders. Dylan twists around and lowers the boy to the ground.

"What happened?" the mother asks, worried.

Becky explains. "TJ fell and cut his knee. This is Dylan. Dylan found us and cleaned the cut with his hankie. Guess who Dylan is?" Mrs. Rawlson is relieved that TJ's injury is not serious. She kneels to the ground and removes the makeshift bandage. Some further repairs by a mother are required. Becky approaches her mother's ear, now at whispering height. In her loudest whisper, with as much drama as she can muster, she informs her mother: "He's Bridget's lover." At this she giggles and covers her mouth.

TJ's wound is dressed. Mrs. Rawlson, now relaxed, asks Dylan, "Would you like a cup of tea, Bridget's lover?"

"I guess you're supposed to call me by my last name – Douglas. And I'm not supposed to be here." Dylan looks at his watch.

"Nonsense," responds Mrs. Rawlson, "you have a full hour until school teatime. The least we can do for TJ's rescuer is to give him a decent cup of tea. I'm Jane, by the way."

"Thanks, Mrs. Rawlson. I'll take that cup of tea. You have cute kids; I had a nice chat with them while walking them home."

"Jane," repeats Mrs. Rawlson, "I said my name was Jane. I don't want you calling me anything but Jane when you are in our home. And I will address you as Dylan."

"Yes, ma'am," responds Dylan, confused as to how to handle this situation. Jane motions for him to sit at the kitchen table. Dylan sits. Immediately, Eemo and TJ wrestle for the privilege of sitting on Dylan's lap.

"Get off, TJ," insists Eemo, on the verge of tears, "you had the shoulder ride all the way home."

Jane intervenes. "If Dylan doesn't mind – and no one has asked him yet – I think Eemo should sit on his lap first." At this, Eemo scrambles her way up onto Dylan's lap and perches triumphantly.

Simultaneously, Dylan scoops up TJ, who is fixing to burst into tears, and plants him on his other knee. "I have two knees and plenty of room for two kids."

Jane, Dylan, Becky, Eemo, and TJ sit at the kitchen table, drinking tea. Even TJ has tea, only his cup has a little more milk in it. Everybody is addicted to tea in England and it obviously begins at a young age. This tea actually tastes pretty good compared with the concoction served at school. "Would you like a sandwich?" asks Jane.

"You know," responds Dylan, "if you have some peanut butter and some jam, there's nothing I'd like better than a peanut butter and jelly sandwich. I never used to eat them at home, but the school food … is not so great."

"Peanut butter and jelly?" exclaims Becky in horror. "That sounds disgusting."

"Coming up," says Jane. "You might have to help out with this. Peanut butter goes on first?" Dylan demonstrates to the family the technique of how to construct a perfect peanut butter and jelly sandwich. When the masterpiece is completed, TJ insists on having a bite. "Yummy," declares TJ.

Eemo grabs the sandwich and takes as large a bite as she can handle. "Delish," she announces, handing the now half-eaten sandwich back to Dylan. Before Dylan can grab a bite, Becky snatches the sandwich and takes a slightly more tentative bite than her sister.

Her verdict is the same. "It is rather scrumptious, Mummy," she says. "I think we should all have them for tea."

"We will certainly have to make Dylan another," says Jane. "You little piggies have eaten all of this starving boy's sandwich."

Jane is attractive. Her hair is a little darker than that of her children. She wears heavy-rimmed glasses that detract from her looks. She's on the tall side for a wom-an, almost exactly Dylan's height. Dylan, at fifteen years, measures five-feet-seven. She has a manner about her that suggests she is not totally sure about everything she says and does. Dylan likes this. He figures she must be around thirty years old, quite a bit younger than Mr. Rawlson. She has robust breasts, which attract Dylan. Big breasts on an attractive female are something he has little experience of, and Jane's breasts are of Penthouse magazine proportions. Jane invites Dylan to come to tea again, to visit the children. They are clearly captivated by him, she tells him.

"Mrs. Rawl …. Er Jane, I don't think I'm allowed to. I got into some trouble, as you know, about a year ago. I'm supposed to get permission to go anywhere beyond the school games fields. I shouldn't even be here now."

Rebecca chimes in. "Mummy, can't Dylan be our babysitter when you and Daddy go out? We can't stand Goofy whatever his name is. He only wants us to shut up while he does his prep when he comes. Also he smells." The boy Becky refers to is one of Mr. Rawlson's sixth form students.

"I am pretty sure I'm not allowed to do things like that," responds Dylan. "I think only sixth formers and prefects can get evening absences."

Jane leans back on her chair. She taps on the side of her teacup with a fingernail. "If I can take care of the permission for you, would you be willing to babysit once in a while? There'll be a tasty meal and a little pocket money in it for you if you agree."

"I guess so," Dylan says with some hesitation, then worries that the slowness of his response may have suggested some reluctance. He adds, "I mean, I'd love to. I think your kids are pretty neat."

With that, Becky puts her arms around the seated Dylan and says to him confidentially, "I know you'll be the best babysitter ever. We will behave ever-so-well for you."

Jane smiles at Dylan. Just at that moment, Mr. Rawlson walks through the door. All three kids run to the door to meet him. Having dragged their father into the kitchen, they hasten to introduce their new babysitter to their father. "Whoa," says Mr. Rawlson, "I don't think that's going to be possible. He's too young, for a start."

"He's the same age as Bridget," Becky informs him derisively.

"But Bridget wasn't a pupil at Elwin Park," responds her father.

Dylan thinks that it's best to split. "I have to leave to make the school tea bell," he says. "Thanks for the cup of tea and sandwich, Mrs. Rawlson. Bye, kids." Dylan leans over to hug each one in turn. TJ gives him a big, sloppy kiss. "Goodbye, sir," Dylan says, shaking Mr. Rawlson's hands, "you have a very charming family. It was a pleasure to meet them."

"Thank you, Douglas," responds Mr. Rawlson. "You seem to have made quite an impression on them."

And so Dylan is embraced by the Rawlson family. A few days after Dylan has tea with his wife and children, Mr. Rawlson approaches Dylan in the yard outside the classroom compound. "Douglas," he begins, "a word, if I may." Mr. Rawlson motions with his arm for Dylan to move to the wall adjacent to the classroom. Some privacy is evidently required. "Mrs. Rawlson was very insistent on you becoming our next babysitter," he begins. "A bit embarrassing, really; one of my most trusted sixth form lads has been doing this for a year. But the children don't warm to him. And Jane, er, Mrs. Rawlson, she dislikes him. Anyway, I spoke to Headmaster Rumthorpe and Housemaster Gwilliam about borrowing you sometimes on Saturday evenings for babysitting purposes. Housemaster Gwilliam was very opposed ... vehemently opposed, I have to say. He continues to feel you betrayed his trust on an intimate level a year ago. But, surprisingly, Headmaster Rumthorpe was for the idea. He feels you merit a higher level of trust by showing exemplary behavior since your ... unfortunate incident. More importantly, he feels that you should have some association with family life, as you are denied the opportunity of exeats what with your family being domiciled ... abroad. Rumthorpe pointed out that next year you will be joined by a sibling, which will further broaden your scope of responsibility. He always thinks of the big picture, does Rumpthorpe. That's why he's head, I suppose."

Dylan places his arms behind his back. He's listening patiently. Rawlson seems to labor over delivering the simplest message. Rawlson continues. "Anyway, if you're still willing, Mrs. Rawlson and I would like you to babysit. Starting this coming Saturday evening. We will give you a hearty meal; nothing fancy, but better than the school faire no doubt… and a little pocket money for your trouble."

Dylan replies. "I'd like that very much, sir. I hope my efforts as a babysitter will live up to your expectations."

"Right you are, right you are," responds Rawlson. "Now you have to inform your dormitory prefect, house captain, and duty master after lunch of each Saturday you are to babysit. This is essential. They must know where you are. You'll usually be out past your official bedtime, so it's your responsibility to get to bed without disrupting dormitory procedure. Mrs. Rawlson and I usually return by 11 or 11:30 pm – never will you be returning to your dorm after midnight."

When Dylan arrives at the Rawlson home the first night he is scheduled to babysit, he's greeted and hugged at the door by Becky, Eemo, and TJ. Mrs. Rawlson stands back behind the kids. "Do I get a hug, too?" she questions Dylan with a smile, knowing that this will likely embarrass him. Dylan has no choice but to give "Jane" a hug. Hugging Jane puts him on the back foot and makes him feel awkward. The awkwardness dissipates once Mr. Rawlson joins them. Dylan sits at the table with the family and hungrily attacks the food put in front of him. Jane informs her husband in no uncertain terms that he is going to be addressed as "Tom" by Dylan while the boy is a guest in their home.

"Right you are," responds Tom. He's clearly accustomed to playing second fiddle to his wife. But if Tom feels awkward about the mode of address, Dylan has become sufficiently institutionalized by the rigors of Elwin life to feel even more so. He is relieved when the couple departs. They are bound for the cinema in Romsey and will follow this with a couple of drinks in "the pub," whichever of the countless Romsey pubs that means.

Dylan relishes being in an unthreatening family setting. He gets on well with the Rawlson kids, who are open and sincere. The three children are disposed to be thoughtful and considerate of each other and of the world. They represent everything that Elwin Park is not. The savagery of a single gender boarding school has bred in Dylan an appreciation for the uncomplicated world of children. He plays with dinky cars, dresses dolls, brushes hair, reads stories, and kisses goodnights. When those chores are complete and the house silent, he curls up in front of a gas grill fire in the living room and reads. This is a luxury in itself. Life is good. Shortly after 11 pm, Tom and Jane return. Jane appears to be slightly tipsy, but Tom is sober as stone. Tom drives Dylan back to the main school building. "Thanks, Douglas," he says, "it means a lot to my wife … and, of course, me."

"It was my pleasure, sir. Goodnight," Dylan says, meaning it.

Well, it was a good night. Maybe not quite like spending an evening with Bridget, but it was six hours respite from the gulag with warm human contact, devoid of the competitiveness of institutional life. This is enough to make anyone feel good.

On the last Saturday before the summer vacation begins, Dylan informs the children he's going to Spain. "Spain?" questions Becky indignantly. "Where's that? I thought you weren't allowed off the school property. Is your punishment over?"

Dylan winks at Jane and responds to Becky. "It doesn't apply to school vacations. I have a mom and dad, too. And I have brothers and a sister. I want to see them."

"It's not fair," responds Becky, unable to hold back tears. "Who's going to look after us?" Then she realizes that girls as big as eight are not supposed to act as she just has. She wipes her eyes. "But you'll come to see us again after the holidays?"

"You bet," Dylan assures her. "I'm going to miss you guys a whole bunch, too."

12. JANE

At the beginning of his third year at Elwin Park, Dylan becomes "Douglas Major" of Dickens House. Daniel has joined him. Daniel is "Douglas Minor" of Dickens House. Dylan had thought of Daniel as being timid and perhaps overly attached to younger brother Domenic. But Daniel seems to take Elwin Park in stride. This may be in part because Dylan has acquired "seniority" and status sufficient to ensure that Daniel is not subjected to any of the random bullying entrenched in Elwin life. But, even accounting for this advantage, Dylan has to admit that Daniel adjusts to life in the gulag faster and with more aplomb than he was able during his first term. He had underestimated his little brother. Of course, having "minor" attached to your name helped. It flagged bullies planning to beat up a first-year that there was a big brother to watch out for.

Dylan is a fifth former now. This is a big deal. Important exams are scheduled to take place at the conclusion of this year. At least, these exams are regarded as important in England. Dylan's academic performance functions more or less on par with that of the median level in his fifth form class. He's come to grips with most of the differences between the American education of his primary years and the very British schooling he is now subject to. After returning from a summer vacation with his parents in Spain, Dylan bumps into Heather and Hazel during a walk in the woods. He casually enquires whether they have heard anything of Bridget. According to the twins, Bridget has spent most of the summer in Wiltshire with an aunt so they've barely seen her. Heather and Hazel mention something about continued discord between Bridget and her father. Poor Bridget.

Shortly after returning to school, Mr. Rawlson asks Dylan if he's available for babysitting once again. Yes, he is available. He's actually looking forward to seeing Mrs. Rawlson and the children. He missed them.

He arrives at the Rawlson house half an hour early. Mrs. Rawlson, Becky, Eemo, and TJ are waiting at the door. Eemo and TJ are jumping up and down with excitement. Dylan hugs each in turn, beginning with TJ. When he gets to Becky, he wipes a tear from her cheek. Jane hugs him next. He expected this. She holds him tight for just a moment too long, a moment in which Dylan thinks that the hug signals something that goes beyond mere friendship. Jane then grips him by both shoulders and beams at him. "You've grown," she declares. "Maybe an inch."

The boy responds, "I'm probably a little heavier, too."

Once again, the babysitting becomes routine. The Rawlson's invite Daniel along for dinner the second Saturday of the term. Daniel isn't especially impressed, and Dylan is irritated that his brother displays so little regard for an occasion and people he has come to regard as special. Dylan's life is changing in other ways. He has made the school rugby team. Only as a reserve, but this is good enough for Dylan. His job is to substitute for any player that becomes maimed during the game. Most importantly, he gets to ride on a coach every other Saturday to play rival schools. It's an escape from the gulag for a few hours. In most cases, the rugby games are played against other all-male gulags. Some prestige goes with the playing on any school team, especially rugby.

At no more than average height and weight, Dylan relies on speed and agility to play the game. Even so, injuries are common and Dylan minimizes his potential to be injured by ensuring that speed and a good measure of cowardice on his part trump bravado.

Saturdays also bring with them babysitting opportunities. Dylan grows closer to the Rawlson's. His fondness for the three children grows and he learns to appreciate Mr. Rawlson; Tom. In his funny, gawky, English way, Tom is a genuine person at heart and doesn't fit into the Elwin mold of schoolmaster. At around six feet and four inches, he towers over most people, but Tom is a truly gentle giant. He adores his children and they him. His manner is to respect all people and that makes him somewhat of an anomaly in the Elwin culture in the same way that makes Dozy David stand out. Dylan wishes he had a teacher such as Tom. He plans to take economics as an elective when he gets into the sixth form just so he can take one of Tom's courses.

Jane is not so straightforward. She confuses Dylan. She telegraphs messages to him that he struggles to interpret. Could there be something sexual in the way she hugs and holds him during hellos and goodbyes? Surely not! Jane is, after all, a married woman with three children. She must be having sex every night. What could she possibly see in innocent Dylan? Nevertheless, Dylan observes her staring at him in unguarded moments, moments where his focus is elsewhere. She studies him when he plays with the children. He becomes aware of being almost continually under her scrutiny. In addition, she can be verbally suggestive in ways that might be sexual. Especially when Tom isn't around.

The terms go by. Dylan turns sixteen and another summer term begins; Dylan's third summer term. One day in May, Tom approaches Dylan in the school yard and asks him if he can babysit on a Thursday. Tom is duty master on this night and this means he has to sleep in the main school building. On short notice, Jane has a commitment with a drama group she participates in. Tom would be grateful if Dylan could watch over the kids until Jane returns. She shouldn't be later than ten, he tells him. Dylan agrees. Tom has already arranged the requisite permissions. He has taken it for granted that Dylan would be OK with the idea.

When Dylan arrives at the Rawlson's, it's after prep and later than his usual time on Saturdays. It is after seven pm and only Tom is at home with the kids. Tom thanks Dylan again, picks up his overnight bag, and leaves in his car for the main school building. Dylan heads to the bedrooms. TJ is already asleep. Because it is a school night, Becky and Eemo are already in nighties, reading on one of the two beds in the girls' room. "Oh good," Eemo greets Dylan, "you're just in time to read to us – we are doing *Secret Garden*. Dylan reads. It doesn't take long before eyelids droop and heads nod. He says goodnight and retreats to the kitchen table to do some studying.

Within ten minutes, the front door unlocks and Jane enters. Dylan begins to gather his books. "No, wait a while," orders Jane. "I never get a chance to talk to you alone. I'm jealous of my own children. They have you at their beck and call, while I'm forced to sit back and watch from the sidelines." Jane walks to the kitchen larder and removes a bottle of wine. "You can open this for me," she says. Then she gets two glasses. "Have a glass of wine with me." Dylan uncorks the bottle and passes it to Jane. She pours two glasses. "Cheers," she says, raising her glass and taking a swig. Then, perhaps sensing the boy's discomfort, adds "Relax, I am not going to eat you." Dylan raises his glass and takes a small sip.

"Now," says Jane, "I want to know everything about you and Bridget. I think you would have made a very sweet couple." Dylan avoids Jane's gaze.

"It's such a shame that everyone overreacted the way they did. Tom and I were very fond of Bridget. And we have both grown to think of you as being very special – not to mention the fact that our children adore you."

If there is one subject Dylan really does not want to discuss with any adult, it is Bridget. It has seemed to him that both his and Bridget's feelings were trivialized by supposedly "adult" interpretations of their relationship from the get-go. He doesn't want to hear any more theories about "lust" and "puppy love."

"I don't really know what to say," begins Dylan. "I think it was such a shame to send Bridget to boarding school. She had so much free spirit. She lived for her horses and having fun. It isn't fair. And she really loved her family. She hated rules. It will be awful tough on her."

"I don't think you should worry about Bridget in boarding school," responds Jane. "From what I hear, she's doing just fine. There's even a rumor that she has another boyfriend." With that news, Dylan blushes deep red, but he is not sure why. He says nothing.

Jane observes him and sips from her glass. "Ooh that hurt you, didn't it? Have you met any girls since Bridget?" After a pause, she adds, "It's been nearly two years."

Dylan shakes his head sadly, still affected by the news about the possible boyfriend. "I don't get a chance really," he says. "I am no longer allowed town passes or exeats. It's like being in prison. I meet girls during the school vacations. But my folks move around a lot, so it's difficult to get to know any girl properly during a four-week vacation."

Jane gets to her feet. She walks around to stand behind the chair Dylan is sitting on. With both hands, Jane runs her fingers back through Dylan's hair. "You poor, sad boy," she says. "What can I do to make you feel better?" Quickly, Dylan gets up and turns to face Jane. His face continues to be flushed red. Something is happening here that he suspects might place him in jeopardy.

"Jane," he says, "meeting you and Tom and your children has been the best thing that has happened to me since Bridget. I don't want us to do anything to change that."

Jane stands back and responds soothingly, "Dylan, calm down, I don't want anything to change, either. Sit down and enjoy the glass of wine. To me you are a beautiful boy. I don't want to alter anything between us, either. I'm just trying to get to know you a little better." Slowly, Dylan resumes his seat. Now he takes a more serious slug of wine.

"Growing up is tough," says Jane, "and I can't even begin to imagine what it is like to be a boarder at Elwin Park. Animals would do a better job of living together. Tom tells me horrible stories. Honestly, I wish we could all leave this awful place. I'm worried about the effect it could have on our children. But I'm also worried about you. Two years is a very long time for a boy like you to get hung up over a girl. You have to move on." There is silence for a while.

Eventually, Dylan responds. "I've tried to move on. I am definitely not hung up on Bridget and I'm not surprised she has another boyfriend. I know she's probably changed; I know I have. I'm not sure how we'd get on now. One thing that puzzles me, though, is why her father seemed to hate me so much."

"You have to understand that Fairford would have probably taken an instant dislike to just about any boy Bridget took a fancy to. He's a Romsey yokel." Jane sits down and regards Dylan intently. "He actually wanted a son to inherit the family farm. Delia was always a mummy's girl, and Bridget was a second-best option to a boy, but she had to do for the old man. She became a tomboy and a daddy's girl, all in one package. She was used to getting exactly what she wanted. Her childhood was spent with horses and Daddy. However, in no time she was at an age where she wanted a boy. Her mistake was in choosing you, an Elwin Park boy – all the locals despise the Elwin boys because of what they stand for. And you, a foreigner to boot, were Fairford's worst nightmare come true. Which, incidentally, was probably why it did. What we fear the most is often what happens to us. I don't think it was anything against you personally."

There's a long pause while Jane looks at Dylan, her eyes exploring him. She shifts her position and turns to him seriously. "Were you really very in love with Bridget?"

The wine has relaxed Dylan. He has no experience of participating in an open discussion on relationships with an adult woman, but the wine warms him to the idea of making Jane a confidante. It is, after all, compelling to have someone attracted to you.

"I'm not too sure – people are always telling me you can't be in love at fourteen," Dylan responds. "But I'd say I was in love. Bridget was easy to be in love with. She was very romantic about the whole deal; everything had to be exactly right for her – the place, candlelight. She seemed to know *how* to go about everything. I just followed along. We really just had one night together. We met a few times before that night, always in the woods. I would have been quite happy to do it in woods. But not Bridget. She said that it had to be extra special the first time."

Jane laughs. "And was it special?" she asks, then immediately adds, "No, don't answer that. I know it must have been. And I'll get jealous!"

Dylan grins and looks up from his glass to stare into Jane's eyes. He's gained some confidence now. "It didn't start off so special. It took us a while to get the hang of it. I guess that was mostly my fault. But it was so nice in the end. I don't think we hardly slept and we didn't get tired."

"Yes, Bridget is a clever little thing," says Jane. "You were both lucky you didn't settle for a lay in the woods."

A long silence ensues.

"Do you love Tom?" ventures Dylan.

"Hmm, let's see. Tom is the nicest man I've ever met in my life. He was my own true love. My only love. He's the nicest … and most boring man in existence." Jane takes a sip of wine, leans back in the kitchen chair, and appears to address the ceiling rather than Dylan. "We met and married when I was eighteen. I knew a lot less about life then than Bridget did at fourteen. Tom was my first serious boyfriend. Except for the fact, he was no boy – he was already a man. He is nine years older than me. I thought he was sophisticated. At eighteen, I would have done almost anything to get away from home. Home is Cornwall. You don't get on jet planes to travel there. It's as remote as Siberia and inhabited entirely by hicks." Jane pauses, gets to her feet, and from behind some packages in a kitchen cupboard, retrieves a covert pack of smokes.

"Want one?" she offers. Dylan shakes his head. She ignites the cigarette, inhaling deeply. "Becky came less than a year later. The other kids followed. I'm twenty-seven now and wonder what life is all about. So far I have spent most of mine doing what everyone else tells me to." She draws another deep inhalation from the cigarette and stares into her wine glass. "Do you want to know something? I am going to tell you this, even though it makes me sound quite pathetic. When I heard about Bridget and you – as everybody did, because nothing ever happens around here, so we become desperate for anything to gossip about – anyway, perhaps because I'd known Bridget for a few years, seen her grow from girl to woman, I became unreasonably jealous of her. What had she done to deserve this excitement? Where were all my lovers at fourteen? Or fifteen, or sixteen? I certainly wanted them. I would have loved to be at the center of a scandal that outraged just about everybody when I was Bridget's age. I was just too timid and sheltered. This probably sounds daft – but I actually fantasized about you. I had no notion of what you even looked like, but I wanted you. I wanted you when I'd never set eyes on you. I wanted you because I never could have you when I needed you most. When I was a teenager, I had to contend with the local louts whose idea of pleasure was to get smashed into imbecility. In a small Cornish village, the sexes do not really mix – not as friends, anyway. Pretty boys with brains and who blush were eliminated from the village gene pool centuries ago. Until recently, girls like Bridget would've been burned at the stake in the village I grew up in. Not that I was any Bridget. I was never brave enough to make things happen for me. I was raised from birth to sit back and let things happen to me. The best I could hope for was that whatever happened to me was not too painful.

"Courtship in my village was a stand-up quickie outside a pub on a Saturday night. Couples were determined by how pissed each party was. The catch was that you had to get pissed to survive the monotony. If you got knocked up, the next step was wedding bells. Things are not so much different in Romsey. Bridget knew that. Her notion of romance was something you were supposed to leave behind with your childhood if you were a true Romsey lass. She defied all of Romsey and rejected it without apology. She was going to have her boy who stood for everything that Romsey was not. And then she tricked her parents and took her shining knight home to bed him in the very bosom of the family hearth, the heart of Romsey. I wasn't the only one who envied Bridget. I wanted a knight to come and rescue me, too".

Jane gets up to pour some more wine into her glass. "Want some more?" She takes a gulp from her glass. "Then lo and behold! My children go wandering around in the woods, capture you, and lead you straight to my doorstep. Somehow, they didn't have to tell me you were 'Bridget's lover,' I knew it in an instant. There was a part of me that wanted to grab you and rip all your clothes off in the front hallway. I told myself that fate was somehow plotting something to happen between us … something that went beyond mere friendship." She pauses and looks Dylan in the eye. "I know I'm embarrassing you and I don't mean to. These are just the silly ramblings of a bored housewife who has had a couple of glasses of wine. But I've reached a stage in my life where I'm no good at pretending. I want to make some things happen for me."

Dylan is actually so embarrassed he can only retreat by gulping at what remains in his wine glass. "I'm not trying to upset you," says Jane, "I'm only like this because there is no one around here for me to talk to. About anything. I am surrounded by emotionally and intellectually frigid schoolmaster's wives twice my age. I can never say anything I want so I am taking advantage and unloading on you. I'm sorry." Another silence ensues.

Then Dylan responds, "I know how you feel in a way," he says slowly. "You are in a gulag, too. You don't get to control very much in your life, and neither do I. But you have a lot of beauty in your life. You have lovely children and a husband who worships you. I think I'd rather have your life than mine. At least at the moment."

"What the hell is the 'gulag'?" says Jane, "I'm just a Cornish country bumpkin. I'm not one of your jet-set intellectual gals. And don't give me that nonsense about wanting to exchange your life for mine. You may be having a bit of a rough time at the present, but you have everything to live for. My life's bloody well over." Jane removes her glasses and wipes her eyes. Dylan stands and walks over to the seated Jane. Tenderly he puts his arm around her. Instantly, Jane responds by twisting around and turning her face into Dylan's chest. She runs her fingers deep into Dylan's back. She gets to her feet to face him. "Kiss me," she says, but even as the words come out, Dylan connects his lips with hers. For a few moments, they kiss deeply.

But then, abruptly, Dylan pulls away, sensing imminent danger. "I have to go now, Mrs. Rawlson," he blurts out hastily, turning to leave.

"Jane," commands Jane. "Don't bloody well stop calling me Jane just because we've been a little honest with each other."

"I'll see you Saturday night, huh?" says Dylan, opening the front door.

"Yes, my darling, I'll see you then. But not as I've seen you tonight. We'll pretend that nothing happened between us because we're all so proper here at Elwin Park. But something *has* happened between us. We've shared a moment that is only between us. When you come on Saturday and you play dinky cars with TJ, I will ache to be in TJ's place. Next, as Eemo unpacks her dolls and you patiently dress and undress them with her, I'll be jealous of her. Jealous of my own children! That's what my life has become. But I will take you to bed in my dreams. So don't think you can escape me." She laughs sardonically.

The front door closes and Dylan sucks in a deep breath. How much wine has he consumed? Could he be drunk? It is pitch dark outside. He could attempt to navigate back through the woods, in which case he has a walk of around fifteen minutes. But he has no flashlight. Returning by way of the meandering road would take longer, but there is less chance of getting spooked. He opts for the road. That gives him some time for reflection. There is no doubt Jane stirs him sexually. But what about Tom? To betray one of the few truly decent persons he's encountered at Elwin is not something he desires.

As Dylan enters the main school building, he almost immediately bumps into Tom. This isn't unexpected – Mr. Rawlson is the duty master that night. The duty master position rotates between the junior teachers. The duty master's room is located on the ground floor of the building. It is his job to answer the phone and patrol the corridors to ensure an uprising of plebs doesn't take place. As soon as Tom spies Dylan, he tracks toward him. "Douglas Major … er, Dylan," he begins and surprisingly, places his arm around Dylan's shoulder as they walk, "I owe you some special gratitude for the effect you have had on Mrs. Rawlson … er, Jane. It is not easy being a schoolmaster's wife at Elwin Park. It can be boring. She's younger than other Elwin wives. Jane needs more stimulation, more conversation … and I am very aware that she especially enjoys your company. Sometimes I get the impression that she derives more pleasure from the Saturday night meal we share with you than the cinema and pub that follow."

Dylan hopes that Tom does not smell the wine on his breath. "I do enjoy having those meals with your family, sir."

"I have a suggestion," Tom announces. "We are teaching Becky to play bridge and I'm aware that you're also a bridge player. If we were to have a Saturday bridge evening, perhaps you could make up the foursome. It was actually Jane's idea, but I fully endorse it."

At this point, Mr. Rawlson and Dylan have arrived at the stairway that Dylan must ascend to get to his dormitory. "Sure thing, Mr. Rawlson," responds Dylan in the only way he can. "I'd like that." Dylan is careful always to refer to Tom as "Mr. Rawlson" or "sir" while outside of the Rawlson house.

"Thank you, Dylan," replies Tom with real sincerity. "You've become a true friend of our family."

The frequency of Dylan's visits to the Rawlson family increases. Sometimes he's there as a babysitter, sometimes as a bridge player. There is inevitable tension during the visits. Jane is on edge. Dylan observes this and wonders if Tom can identify it in his wife. Maybe not – Tom seems somehow detached, removed from the interactions of the evening. From time to time, Dylan and Jane exchange covert glances below Tom's radar, but not Becky's.

Little Becky senses danger in the air and doesn't know how to respond. Which of the four of them is in danger? The uncertainty produces protective impulses in Becky. The need to protect drives her to physically cling in turns to her mother, her father, and to Dylan. This is not her nature. Eemo is the lap-sitter and the one that needs continuous cuddles. But after Eemo and TJ are in bed, leaving just the four of them playing bridge and talking, who else is there but her to create a diversion in this adult game that has nothing to do with bridge? Learning to play bridge is the easy part. The best part for Becky is just before bedtime when the deck of cards is returned to a package and her mother retreats to the kitchen to bake a late evening snack of Cornish pasties. Mum's specialty. That leaves her alone with Daddy and Dylan. Now she relaxes. With the bridge concluded and a late night achieved, now she gets to be a baby for a while. She slips out of the room, returns a few moments later with her nightie on, and curls up into Tom's lap to await the snack her mother is preparing.

Dylan grows. As the end of the Lent term in his fifth form year approaches, he clears Jane's height by two inches. He finds himself starting rugby games now, not just warming the bench. Although of average height and build, he is one of the three smallest on the team of fifteen rugby players. Physical bulk matters in the game of rugby. His play is defined by speed and kicking ability. He knows he's unlikely to become a star player on the team. Perhaps it is because he just doesn't care enough. The game of rugby is often likened to American football, but the truth is that there are few similarities between the games beyond the physical shape of the ball used. While football is coordinated with scientific precision by a coach from the sidelines, tactics are of much lesser importance in the game of rugby, which consists of random combinations of speed, brute force, and violence undertaken by participants equipped with almost no protection. Helmets and padding? That's for wusses and Americans.

Dylan looks up at a clear blue sky. He appears to be lying on his back. No sounds are apparent, but he becomes aware of being surrounded by faces staring down at him. Yes, he was playing rugby, and now he attempts to speak. But he can neither move his lips nor any other part of his body. Many arms move toward his body, under his body, and he is hoisted into the air. The arms have formed a human stretcher underneath him. He stares at the sky as he is portaged, then lowered to the ground. He attempts to speak again, but no words come out. For a moment, he wonders if he has died. People continue to surround him. This time, they are not rugby players. They are talking to each other and Dylan can hear every word they're saying. It appears that an ambulance has been summoned. He sees a pair of little knees immediately above his face. The knees rise up out of a pair of red wellies. He looks to his right. Another pair of smaller knees, and a pair of smaller red wellies than those on his left. Becky and Eemo. What are they doing? Again, Dylan attempts to speak, but his tongue, lips, and teeth won't work. Next, a blond, curly head is in his face hugging him. TJ is hugging him and appears to be crying. Perhaps he has been killed after all. He knew all along this game of rugby was not for him. The Rawlson kids must have been watching the rugby match and witnessed his death on the field of play.

Next, he shifts his eyes and spies Dome ordering everyone to stand back. "Get your children under control," Dome barks at someone, presumably Jane. But Dylan can't see Jane. An angry exchange of words is taking place, most of which is unintelligible to Dylan, but he knows Dome and Jane are involved. He hears a child crying; it must be TJ. After some time, he observes reflections of flashing lights in the faces that hover over him. Faces he cannot recognize. OK, so he is not dead, he is merely paralyzed. Possibly something worse than death, he thinks. He is aware of his body being grasped in various places. Yes, he is being lifted onto a stretcher. The stretcher rises upward and for a fleeting moment, he identifies a face he recognizes: Eemo. She appears distraught. Things must be serious. The sky disappears as he is inserted into the ambulance. Doors close with a thunk. The ambulance moves off, bumping and rolling. Someone he cannot identify is beside him inside the ambulance. A light shines brightly into first one eye then the other. Then time seems to accelerate. Dylan is vaguely aware of arriving at a hospital, having his rugby shorts and jersey removed, being transferred onto gurneys, and ending up in a hospital bed. Everything fades into a deep sleep.

When he awakes some time later, he is instantly lucid. Mr. Rawlson is standing at the doorway, talking to someone in a white coat. The face of a young woman peers down at him. It is a nurse. He also hears his brother Daniel's voice in the background. Because he has stirred, everybody in the room approaches his bedside. A guy in a white coat shines a baby flashlight into each of Dylan's eyes. Then he asks Dylan what his name is. Dylan knows his name and now is able to verbalize the answer to this and half a dozen other questions the doctor asks him. Now he twitches his toes, his fingers, clenches his buttocks. Thank god, everything seems to function as expected. Daniel says a "Hey, Dylan," as a greeting, and then Mr. Rawlson leans over.

"You took a bit of a knock, but the doctor is telling us you are going to be fine."

Now the doctor speaks. "We are going to keep you here under observation for a day, maybe two. Just as a precaution."

The next day, Dylan is picked up at Southampton hospital by Dozy David and driven back in his Ford Consul to Elwin Park. Dozy David informs Dylan that he spoke to Dylan's father in Spain the previous day. Dylan's father assured Dozy David that he knew Dylan was being provided with the best possible care. Furthermore, he would appreciate a phone call from his son. As soon as he felt well enough, that is. It's easier to make a phone call to Spain than to Thailand.

Dylan is to be admitted to the Elwin sick bay. Sick bay has six beds in it, which are usually empty – being sick at Elwin is frowned upon. He has a series of visits that last approximately two minutes apiece. These visitors include Dome, who says something about resilience and laudable Elwin team spirit, Daniel, who tells him that there are only three weeks left before they can go back home for four weeks, and Mr. Rawlson, who informs him that Becky, Eemo, and TJ all want to visit, and asks if it would it be OK.

Becky, Eemo, and TJ arrive at sick bay. Matron, the ruler of sick bay, is not happy about this plan. It's not proper. Is Dylan sick or is he not? Any person in sick bay well enough to receive visitors is probably faking. Fakers did not deserve the privilege of malingering in sick bay, making unnecessary work for Matron. Children have never once visited sick bay in the history of Elwin Park. It has never been an issue before. That's the only reason no rule prohibiting them exists. It is clear that the rules will have to be modified to preclude future intrusions by children. Children are dirty and noisy. They pick their noses. Matron will be keeping her eye on them.

Becky and Eemo are still wearing their school uniforms – they must have just arrived home from school. Becky lifts TJ up on to Dylan's bed, then she and Eemo climb onto the bed on either side of the patient. Each child has brought a homemade get well card. There is also a store-bought card signed by Tom and Jane. The three children remain with Dylan until Matron arrives at five thirty with Dylan's "tea." Matron tells the three children to go home. She informs them in no uncertain terms that she's not about to have child-minding added to her job description.

The next day, Dylan is discharged from sick bay to the care of the Rawlson's. Dozy David informs Dylan this arrangement came about due to Tom's advocacy for it. Was it not the least he and Jane could do for this upright young man who had become almost part of the Rawlson family? Dylan agrees that a few days of rest and restitution with the Rawlson's is a preferable prescription to having to contend with Matron. But he'll instead have to contend with Jane. By now, he actually experiences no ill effects from the concussion but, if everyone insists that doing nothing for a few days will benefit him, why not go for it?

Dylan is to sleep in TJ's room. TJ will bunk up with one of the girls. Tom drives Dylan from sick bay in the main school building to the Rawlson home during his Monday lunch break. Jane and TJ greet Dylan on his arrival. TJ attends school during the mornings, but spends afternoons at home. While at home, TJ wants to play dinky cars with Dylan, but Jane dissuades him. "Dylan needs rest," she cautions TJ, "that's why he is staying with us." TJ makes a face. Dylan appears to be in perfect health now. The threesome eats some lunch and TJ goes off for a nap.

Jane and Dylan talk. They spend the afternoon talking about nothing in particular. Books and films. The girls arrive home from school, TJ gets up from his nap, and the five of them drive to a local supermarket to shop. When they return, Mr. Rawlson is working at prepping classes at the kitchen table. The meal known as "tea" is consumed, then Dylan reads bedtime stories to the kids and excuses himself to Tom and Jane for an early night. Jane instructs him to sleep in the next day. Everyone will try to avoid waking him during the family breakfast and school departure circus in the morning. This routine is not too difficult to handle, thinks Dylan when alone in TJ's bed. TJ's mattress is a definite improvement on his horse-hair lair in the school dormitory.

Dylan is awakened by the sounds of breakfast the next morning, but elects against emerging from TJ's room to participate. He listens to the noises of departure. Doors thump closed, goodbyes are exchanged, and a car engine starts and departs. Then silence. He figures he is now alone with Jane. Should this be something to fear?

Dylan waits a half hour or so. He then emerges from TJ's room in his pajamas and enters the kitchen, where Jane is washing dishes. She greets him nonchalantly and instructs him to sit at the kitchen table. She will have a cup of tea and a breakfast for him just as soon as she finishes up.

Dill and Jane have tea and a talk. "I guess I have you to thank for my release from sick bay," begins Dylan. "I do appreciate you letting me stay with you."

Jane gives him a quizzical look. "Not at all," she responds, "it was all Tom. I just agreed when he came up with the idea." Dylan digests this information. Jane continues, "It isn't entirely easy for me having you around." She drinks from her teacup. "Why do you think Tom likes to have you here," she asks him, "especially at times when you and I will be alone?"

"I'm not sure," responds Dylan. "I guess I've not really thought about it too much."

"Well, I think you should think about it. Don't tell me it's because he has such a wonderful nature and a great heart. There are three hundred boys … boys and men …at Elwin Park. Why you? Is it because you have so much in common with him? Is it because you sit down and have great discussions on the state of the world economy?

"Dill, you've completed nearly three years in an all-male school, an environment in which the only sexual outlet for most is with either themselves or other boys. An environment which condones homosexuality so long as it is not brazenly expressed ... how is it that you fail to see what's perfectly obvious to people with half your intellect?" Dylan cannot look into Jane's eyes. What is she suggesting?

"Tom, a homosexual?" he ventures as a question. "But he has you. You have three children."

Jane laughs. "Tom is probably what you would call bisexual. But he definitely leans toward the male side of bisexual. A wife and the children are necessary accoutrements for bisexual teachers who choose to teach in boarding schools limited exclusively to the gender of their preference."

Dylan is shocked. He's shocked partly because he wonders why he hasn't thought this out for himself. "So why do you think Tom has encouraged me to spend time with you?"

Jane sighs. "Tom is basically good at heart. Above all, he feels guilty; he recognizes that he has betrayed me in some deep way. He's thoughtful enough to wish I was happy, rather than unhappy. When I'm happy, it makes his life easier. In his mind, you are safe. So what if you and I have a little fling? The odds are pretty good that we won't run off and abandon him to professional disgrace. On the other hand, if I was to have a fling with someone of my own age or older, that could turn out to be a real threat to him!"

Dylan shakes his head in disbelief. Jane grins at him. "It's interesting to see how the children respond to you. They do the same thing with my younger brother. I'm very sure they sense gender preference in adults. A child might not know how to define the word 'homosexual,' but by golly, they can identify one. Tom is good at nurture. He is safe. My children will retreat to Tom as a first choice when they need to feel protected. Not to me. They sense that I'm not as safe as Tom. Then, I look at the way in which they respond to you. They know darn well you are not going to protect them emotionally – there isn't much difference between a teenager and a toddler when it comes to greed for self-gratification. But guess what? Children don't always want to be protected – they're stimulated by intrigue. They sense a little danger in you and know that it can be temptingly more fun than security – so long as they can retreat back to what they see as security at a whim, you'll be a hit with them."

"You think that I'm a danger to your kids?" asks Dylan, astonished.

"No, of course not, not in a physical sense," responds Jane. "But you are from a different tribe, an attractive intruder into what they know as safe and secure. Think about it," she continues. "You speak differently, Mr. Hollywood. There are three hundred boys at Elwin, but they've only said more than half a dozen sentences to one of them, and that's you. When they first met you, you were not 'Dylan.' You were 'Bridget's lover.' To Becky and maybe Eemo too, that was important. And if you are wondering why TJ thinks you're a god – and he does – why, that's simple: he recognizes the difference between a male role model and … and one that's not quite male. Little boys like real men, even if they're just big boys. Even at four, he knows he wants to be more like you than he does his daddy."

Dylan can only wonder at all this information. It is pretty hard to take in. Jane looks at him, smiling. Is she seducing him? He wishes she would – it might be easier to handle than her conversation. Jane's conversation cuts straight to the gut. "What would you say to smoking a joint together, Dylan?" asks Jane. "Have you had marijuana before?"

"Yes," Dylan responds, "a couple of times." To be accurate, he has smoked weed twice, imbibed hash coffee once, and unwittingly consumed hash brownies on another occasion. The latter event had been the most pleasing.

"And what did you think?" asks Jane. By this time, she has set about rolling a fat joint with practiced expertise. "I'd go mad if I couldn't smoke a joint once in a while. I jolly well think you could do with some dope right now. Not to mention the entirety of the Elwin Park faculty and student body."

Dylan thinks that Jane is more stoned than he is. She inhales the toke hungrily and holds the hit until she is about to burst. But Dylan is floating through reality, too. They sit cross-legged on the living room couch, facing each other. Jane bum-walks toward Dylan until their knees contact, then proffers both hands, palms outward to Dylan. It might look like some kind of tribal gesture of peace, but Dylan gets the idea and responds, raising his palms to softly connect with Jane's. Palms kiss for some moments, their texture is explored, senses heightened by the dope. No words are exchanged, but the eyes of each lock onto the other's. Fingers feel out fingers, then interlock. The interlocked hands provide leverage to close the distance between their eyes, their lips. They kiss, gently at first, then hungrily. In the gyration that accompanies the kissing, Dylan's erection has escaped the confinement of his pajamas through the open fly. Jane observes. Without change of expression, she frees herself from the embrace, turns to drop her feet onto the floor, and begins to undress, beginning with her socks. She gets to her feet and, with a mechanical efficiency, removes first her blouse, then her bra. Next, she unzips and wriggles out of her jeans. The tightness of her jeans drags her panties half-way down her thighs. She steps out of them.

Dylan continues to sit cross-legged on the couch, in awe of the scene that unfolds before his eyes. Especially, he is in awe of Jane's breasts, the largest he has observed in the flesh. The effect of the dope has left him unconcerned that his aroused penis continues to protrude through pajama bottoms – it's as if his penis also wants to observe the striptease. With a girlish bound, breasts jiggling, Jane resumes her cross-legged position, facing Dylan on the couch. She continues to wear her thick-rimmed glasses. Dylan's hands extend to cradle Jane's breasts as she leans toward Dylan to receive his lips. While kissing, Jane's hands attack the buttons on Dylan's pajama top. She has to forcibly remove Dylan's hands from her breasts to get the pajama top wrestled from his torso. Still kissing, her hands run over Dylan's back, his chest, arms, and armpits.   She unties the cord in the pajama bottoms, and touches him where he aches to be touched. Dylan breaks from his cross-legged seating position and rises onto his knees, allowing the pajama bottoms to drop. He insinuates his penis between Jane's breasts and Jane grasps each breast to enfold his throbbing arousal. This jousting can only have one outcome. Dylan arrests Jane from her cross-legged seat, wrestles her into a lying position and penetrates her as deep as he can. Jane's fingers dig deep into his buttocks to knead his thrusting muscles.

Dylan's sexual endurance in this opening act is a thing of mastery. Could James Bond have done better? It is possible, had he been as stoned. Without the dope, Dylan reflects that he would have probably come into Jane's breasts long before he had even entered her. Two years between fucks is a long time.

After act one, Jane ignites a cigarette. This one is factory-made and filled with tobacco. She leans back against the arm on one side of the sofa. She pulls a deep draw on the smoke then hands it to Dylan. He takes a drag. Not as tasty as the joint, but hey, not bad, either. Dylan leans back against the opposite arm of the couch. Their legs intertwine. They exchange the fag back and forth until there is nothing but filter tip and an abnormally long protrusion of glowing ash.

After extinguishing the cigarette, Jane leans forward on elbows and knees and begins to lick Dylan's flaccid and sticky penis. With her tongue, she teases him into tumescence, then takes him into her mouth. Jane works long and patiently. She teases him to the point of ejaculation then pulls away, to titillate with tongue only, before accepting all of him back into her mouth, deep into her throat. Dylan eventually comes with a convulsive eruption that would have given a person of lesser build than Jane whiplash.

Jane and Dylan come up for air. But not for long. There is a time limit to these shenanigans. Little TJ will have to be picked up from nursery school at 11:45 am. They bathe together. Because this is England, the ablutions take place immersed in a tub, not standing in a shower. For the first time, Jane is forced to remove her eye glasses. They have steamed up. "I really can't see a bloody thing without these," she declares. "It probably isn't your idea of sexy, but I like to see even when in the throes of passion." Drying each other, tenderly because some parts are sore from overuse, they speak only of the pain of waiting nearly a full day before resuming their intrigue.

Jane leaves in the Ford Consul to pick up TJ. Dylan locates his pajamas and puts them on. He is sleepy from sex and dope. He goes to TJ's room and crawls up into bed. Hours later, he is awakened by Becky and Eemo shaking his shoulder. As he opens his eyes, Dylan becomes aware of TJ and TJ's comforter lying on top of him. Evidently, TJ elected to take his afternoon nap on top of Dylan. Becky and Eemo want Dylan to play with them. They've already changed out of school uniforms and want to walk in the woods. Dylan agrees, then checks himself in response to a scowl from Jane. Right –he's recovering from concussion. It might not be such a good idea to be seen in the woods.

For three glorious days that follow, Jane and Dylan fall into a routine of frenzied banging through each morning, followed by what they believe to be a pretty good act of feigned indifference to each other throughout the remainder of the day. Tom appears oblivious to anything that may be happening between his wife and Dylan. But perhaps not? In fact, he appears more relaxed than ever. Only Becky seems to sense something is different. She registers even a fleeting moment of eye contact between her mother and Dylan and regards them both with uncharacteristic suspicion. Sweet little Becky is lost; her world has suddenly become more complicated.

The Easter vacation comes and goes. Summer term brings cricket and long evenings. It also brings some considerable frustration to both Dylan and Jane. Gone is the opportunity for whole mornings spent in bed. Gone is the possibility to indulge in each other's conversation over tea and coffee or a toke for hours on end. This is history, though Tom obliges their cause by issuing invitations for Dylan to keep Jane company when he is duty master one day in ten.

But Becky is now a problem. She responds to what she cannot fathom by clinging to Dylan. She lolls around on his lap. Bedtime becomes a drawn out process. Jane has to remind her elder daughter several times that bedtime is long past. Jane has never been much of a disciplinarian; she's never had to be. Becky disappears briefly, returns with her nightie on, climbs onto Dylan's lap again, pleading for a story. Dylan accedes to the request and reads to her lying down on the couch because Eemo is already asleep in the girls' bedroom. Becky entwines her body around

Dylan. Jane is irritable. She snaps at Dylan, admonishing him for allowing a nine-year-old to manipulate him. Dylan shrugs his shoulders. He's eager to get to the part when they can have sex too, but what can he do? Becky is quick to register that Dylan is getting in trouble for her disobedience.

When Becky is deposited in her bed and kissed goodnight, Dylan and Jane finally embrace in the living room. But almost immediately, they are forced to hastily separate as they hear Becky's footsteps in the hall. The little girl returns and now wants a glass of water and yet another round of kisses. Jane lifts her daughter's nightie and swats her bare bottom. Aggressively, she orders the child off to bed. The flesh-on-flesh slap is louder than it is painful, but it nevertheless qualifies as a spanking. Becky, sobbing, retreats to her bedroom where she continues to whimper. Her mother has not spanked her since she threw a tantrum at age four. The shame! And to think that Mummy would do this awful thing in front of Dylan! She's a bridge player and the trusted older sister.

Jane retrieves her covert pack of smokes from a kitchen cabinet, sits on the couch, and lights a cigarette. She sucks in a deep drag and exhales in frustration. Becky continues to sob from her bedroom. She's in danger of waking Eemo and TJ. Dylan stares down at his feet, avoiding Jane's eyes. Jane senses Dylan's disapproval. She wants to wait out Becky's sniveling and does so while sucking furiously at her cigarette. Dylan is still saying nothing. Finally, she aggressively stubs her cigarette into a saucer, deciding she has no choice but to go to her daughter and soothe her tears with an apology. No sex is going to happen tonight!

And so the summer of frustration continues. On the couple of occasions Dylan and Jane actually manage to have sex, it has to be quick and clumsy. Their meetings become less frequent. Dylan has to study for important exams toward the end of this summer term. At the end of the school year, he learns that he is to be promoted to a junior prefect for the academic year to follow. He will be in the sixth form. This form lasts for two years. There is a lower sixth and an upper sixth. The best news is that, as a prefect, he will set his own schedules. This should afford plenty of time for extracurricular activities such as banging Jane. The summer vacation begins, taking Dylan away for four weeks of his parents and the beach.

*   *   *

Dylan arrives back in the fall for another Michaelmas term. He can hardly wait to see Jane. And Becky, Eemo, and TJ, of course. How much fun is it being adored when returning after an absence! He takes the walk up to the Rawlson house within an hour of his return onto the school premises. He has not yet unpacked his suitcase. He wants hugs, kisses, and a cup of tea. He knocks at the door using a percussive rendering of the opening to Beethoven's fifth symphony. But a strange woman answers the door. She introduces herself as "Mrs. Jameson." She and her husband have recently arrived from Cambridge and she announces that her husband, Mr. Jameson, is the new economics and political science teacher. Blinking, Dylan welcomes her to Elwin Park with an assurance that she and her husband will be favorably impressed with life at Elwin.

Stunned, Dylan returns to the main school building. There, he discovers that Tom Rawlson resigned on the last day of the previous term. It turns out he had obtained a teaching assignment in another private boarding school located somewhere in Surrey. At lunch, Dome announces the departure of Mr. Rawlson. He thanks Mr. Rawlson in absentia for seven years of dedicated service to Elwin Park and wishes him the best of luck in his new position. Dylan never hears from Jane.

More than a year later, he is informed that Tom and Jane have divorced. No other information is known. The news makes Dylan unreasonably sad. He is sad for Jane. He is sadder for TJ and Eemo, and Becky. He's sad for Tom. What will Tom do without TJ, Eemo, and Becky sitting on his lap, each wanting to be first to tell Daddy about their day at school?

13. SHARON

Dylan is in the upper sixth, beginning his final year at Elwin Park. He is seventeen and has just been appointed house captain of Dickens House. The timid new boy of four years ago has grown in stature and influence. In fact, he appears to have become a perfect Elwin Park product – could he ever have been appointed as house captain if he hadn't sold out to the system? Dylan has changed over the years: he's adapted and adhered to the strictures and constraints of Elwin life, and now even embraces many of the institution's rules and rigors that he once despised. He is no longer the frightened boy that first walked through these doors what feels like a lifetime ago.

Just as he did on his first-ever day at Elwin Park, Dylan arrives a day before the term begins. There is no Moshe to greet him now, however. But Dylan doesn't need a Moshe any more; he's the one in charge now. He is the one who is expected to administer a first beating to his personal fag, just as Blatherstone once did to him.

That day, Dylan moves into the study once occupied by Blatherstone, in which he spent most of his first year as a fag. Taking a seat behind the large desk, Dylan wonders about his new position of power and the reversal of roles that has taken place. Has he become Blatherstone? Not likely, thinks Dylan. He still remembers what he went through during his first year and has no intentions of making anybody else undergo the same. He'll use the coming school year to redefine the role of house captain. He will model his leadership style on his former coach, Hank. His first task as house captain will be to break tradition by declining to beat up his personal fag. Next, he determines to quietly resist the alpha culture of sports, bullying, beatings, and snobbery and attempt to elevate other elements of academic life onto a higher plane. He'll speak softly and govern Dickens House issues with fairness. He will lead by example.

Such were Dylan's good intentions on the first day of his tenure as house captain, though intentions can easily be overlooked when a tempting alternative arises.

Dylan seldom refers to Elwin as the "gulag" these days and his appearances in the Romsey coffee shop have become rare. He's too busy and, frankly, wonders if *women* are worth the risk to his cozy status at Elwin. Philandering will have to be put on hold – he'll cruise on reputation. While his fellow students continue to make much of this reputation, the truth is, it's mostly myth. Through four years at Elwin, the sum of his female conquests amount to nothing more than his brief fling with Bridget and his unsatisfactory affair with Jane. He dares not mention the latter, but knowledge of it runs rampant in the Elwin archives of gossip. No, women would definitely have to be put on hold through this school year. Why court disaster?

Dylan meets with Dozy David, still the Dickens House assistant housemaster. Since the days of Bridget over three years ago, Dozy David has had some good reasons to feel uncomfortable in the presence of Dylan. For his part, Dylan cannot help but feel a pang of guilt each time he bumps into the assistant housemaster. But meek Mr. Gwilliam eagerly buys into Dylan's ideas about redefining the role of a house captain.

"It will require an unusually strong leader to accomplish your goals for Dickens House," enthuses Dozy David as Dylan outlines his proposals for change. "To achieve such goals while maintaining the dignity and prestige of the house captain's office will require a special person. But by gad, Douglas, I believe you might be that person."

Dylan appoints a timid individual, new to life in a boarding school, as his personal fag. Almost immediately Dylan comes to regret the decision. Jacob Tingle is obsequious by nature and, in no time, comes to irritate Dylan by his mere presence. Tingle, the fag, is always slinking around Dylan's study and a devious side of him emerges. When the fag is instructed to dispatch the study archive of magazines to the rubbish bins, Dylan discovers he has unwittingly distributed a decade's worth of Penthouse magazines to the school population at large. The source of this booty is immediately known and there's no doubt that the newly appointed house captain of Dickens is the culprit. Dozy David upbraids Dylan for his naivety. Within a week of appointing Tingle, Dylan is left wondering whether he should have conformed with tradition when he introduced himself to the fag.

The school play for the Michaelmas term is to be *The Merchant of Venice*. The production is to be a joint one, involving Elwin Park and St. Theresa's Convent. Dylan has been invited to direct the play that will be produced by his sixth form English teacher, Roland Ebert. Does Dylan have all the skills required to direct a major play such as *The Merchant of Venice*? The answer is probably no. Sure, Dylan has a history of acting and production roles in previous Elwin theatre productions and he has acquired a certain liking for Shakespeare. But Roland Ebert will be the real mind behind the production, while Dylan will be the voice.

Unlike many other Shakespeare plays, substituting the female roles with male actors does not make for a convincing *Merchant* production. Sexual tension is a key to achieving dramatic authenticity in the *Merchant*, and hence the invitation to St. Theresa's to participate. Roland Ebert is a short, tubby little man who lives a life of the mind. He's married to a tall, domineering woman. Females, even little ones in school uniforms, tend to intimidate him. And thus, the invitation to Dylan to direct the production. In Roland's opinion, Dylan is forceful and seems to have a way with females. The challenge for Roland is to ensure that the Ebert game plan is put into play rather than allow too many of Dylan's notions to dominate.

Dylan's ideas about Shakespeare are a little too American, perhaps more avant-garde than Roland cares for; they lean toward Peter Brookish and Hollywood interpretations. The first item Roland has to suppress is Dylan's suggestion that they undertake the production in modern dress. Though Roland would have no personal objection to a modern dress performance, he suspects that Mother Superior of St. Theresa's Convent would think differently, let alone what the Reverend Cecil Rumthorpe might think!

The next item on Roland's agenda is to impress on Dylan that he's directing a play, not a movie. Dylan tends to overstate himself in debate and Roland knows that doing this with Shakespeare can make it look cheesy and amateurish. Thankfully, both Roland and Dylan understand that one key to a successful *Merchant* production is to have a convincing Shylock. Shylock in a movie can be depicted as a bad guy, plain and simple, but when this happens on stage, the effect can appear anti-Semitic. You can get away with this on film because it is comfortably remote. With the intimacy of the stage, however, a convincing Shylock is necessarily more complex. Will Dylan buy in to the concept that Shylock is not really so evil? Is it not true that Shylock cares more about *justice* than monetary gain? To paint Shylock as evil is Hollywood, but to have him represent the higher principle of justice, well now, that was the genius that is Shakespeare.

Once Roland and Dylan have settled on a general production strategy and schedule, the next challenge is casting. Most of the principal roles cast themselves. On the first night of the casting process, Dylan becomes acquainted with an old friend, a friend he once shared with Bridget. It is none other than Johanna Dempsey, the girl who voiced the role of Dylan's fake aunt over the phone three years previously. Dylan and Johanna have both changed shape with the years. While Dylan has grown upward and bulked up, Johanna has only bulked up. Although a full eight inches shorter than Dylan, she weighs as much as him. But there is a beauty and expressiveness in Johanna's face that projects itself to the world. And, as an actress, she has the intelligence and dramatic ability to capture exactly what is required to interpret a character. She is a shoo-in for the role of Portia in the *Merchant of Venice*.

Roland Ebert, Sister Mary, and Dylan collaborate on casting. There is general accord until it comes to the roles of Nerissa and Jessica. Three of the convent girls are competing for the two roles. There is no doubt that some acting talent is required for both roles, perhaps a little more to portray a convincing Jessica. In the *Merchant of Venice*, Jessica is Shylock's daughter, a daughter who sees through the shortcomings of her father. She's also madly in love, illicitly and against her father's wishes. The role is challenging and definitely requires some acting ability for its portrayal. Jessica is duplicitous and, at the same time, required to draw empathy from the audience. Nerissa is easier, but still not easy, and requires an actress who exudes maturity.

Two of the three girls auditioning are bright, capable actresses who can perfectly grasp what is required of either a Jessica or a Nerissa. Casting either one in either role would work. But a problem emerges: despite his abstemious vows regarding women made less than two weeks previously, Dylan has fallen in lust with the third girl, Sharon Fulton.

Sharon is stunning. She is blonde and svelte. She moves with grace. Her blue eyes are soft and sexy. Sharon evokes a passion in Dylan that roots itself deep in his gut. But she's only gorgeous until she opens her mouth, then two things become apparent. First, it's immediately obvious that Sharon is poorly endowed with gray matter. "Thick" is the way the English would describe her. Second, her regional Hampshire accent is a little too strong for the taste of the snooty Brits of Elwin Park.

Dylan has acquired none of the hang-ups possessed by his Elwin school chums about the strata of British regional accents and how they jive into the pecking order of the bizarre English class system. Like Bridget, Sharon speaks with a slight Romsey accent. It appears that the Romsey drawl gets homogenized by a convent education into a relaxed softening of vowels that Dylan actually finds appealing. He would have no hesitation in saying that he prefers the sonics of Sharon's speech to the grating, snobbish Oxford English that prevails within the walls of Elwin Park. No, it's not merely the sonics of Sharon's speech that is a problem. More significant to the casting crew of the *Merchant* production is that poor Sharon finds it almost impossible to articulate much beyond monosyllables in normal conversation.

Dylan wonders how someone quite as gorgeous as Sharon can be so inarticulate. Whether it's shyness, lack of confidence, or a serious deficit of intelligence, Dylan is convinced that the problem can be repaired, Henry Higgins managed it in *My Fair Lady*, did he not?

Sharon's audition goes badly. For whatever reason, Sharon recalls less than ten percent of the lines she was supposed to have memorized for the audition. She reads for both Jessica and Nerissa. Dylan prompts, hoping a miracle will transpire and lines will suddenly be spewing from her. But this isn't going to happen. Her disaster-ridden navigation through the recital should have immediately eliminated her for consideration for either role.

Dylan gets feisty with Sister Mary and Roland Ebert. His belief is that the play needs a natural beauty. Theatre thrives on star power, he informs his learned elders. Who cares if the star cannot act? Or remember lines?

Roland Ebert gently attempts to dissuade Dylan from his misguided notion that

Sharon could handle either Nerissa (doubtful) or Jessica (impossible). Sister Mary is more blunt and informs Dylan that Sharon is a complete moron. She then accuses Dylan of being shallow, sexist, and possibly perverted. Sister Mary informs him in no uncertain terms that he lacks the experience to understand that any play can be ruined by casting a klutz in a lesser role that you thought no one would notice.

Dylan digs his heels in. He's not about to allow some desiccated old bag tell him what to do just because she wears a nun's habit. He wants Sharon in the play and, after all, he is the bloody director!

Roland has to mediate. A compromise must be struck. Perhaps Sharon can become the director's personal assistant? His PA – it sounds very Hollywood, don't you agree, Sister Mary? Sister Mary looks at Ebert in horror. She flips through her *Merchant* production notes in case someone may have inserted this angle without her knowing. Why should the director require a personal assistant? Exactly what kind of personal services is Sharon to be offering the director? Would Sharon's parents approve? They are God-fearing Catholics, after all, and the director happens to be none other than the rapscallion who debauched another virtuous convent girl three years previously. How would Sister Mary find the words to explain to the Fulton parents that their innocent child, in her role of personal assistant, had been seduced by the director, an infamous rake?

With Dylan and Sister Mary locking horns, Roland knows he has to get Dylan out of the room. Once he has Sister Mary alone, Roland informs her that Dylan's status and energy is going to be required to orchestrate a successful Shakespeare production with such a large cast. Dylan Douglas understands the play and what it takes to get its actors to interpret their roles. They agree that neither one wants Sharon Fulton cast as either Jessica or Nerissa. It's simply a no-brainer to cede some ground to Dylan by providing him with an assistant. After an hour of discussion, Sister Mary reluctantly agrees to Roland Ebert's plan. If they're ever going to move on with this production, the sex maniac of a director is going to have to be appeased. But Sister Mary vows that she will make it her business to ensure that no hanky-panky takes place between the assistant director and the director. She's not going to be the one explaining to Sharon Fulton's parents that she'd allowed a notorious womanizer to become responsible for their daughter's seduction.

From the beginning, Sister Mary was not in favor of having an Elwin boy direct the play. That role should have gone to a St. Theresa girl. But the only convent girl capable of directing a complex drama is Johanna. Alas, Johanna's services are required to play the role of Portia, which is fine because Sister Mary is convinced that Johanna is going to do more than just carry the role, she'll define it.

Roland Ebert and Sister Mary confront Dylan. Roland explains that Sharon is not ready to assume a role such as Jessica or Nerissa. However, Sharon's enthusiasm to participate will make her a useful assistant to the director. Sister Mary stays silent, her lips pursed, her eyes scowling at Dylan. Dylan nods. He is secretly relieved. He knows that playing Henry Higgins to Sharon's Eliza would have likely been doomed to failure. This way, he gets to have Sharon around without being accountable to producing a measurable result.

Sharon is informed by Dylan that she is not to be selected for either the role of Jessica or Nerrissa. Sharon unabashedly bursts into tears like a six-year-old. Such is the ferocity of the initial outburst of tears that Sharon's impulse to cry supersedes her requirement to breathe. She gasps for oxygen. Dylan places a comforting arm around the distraught rejectee's shoulder and attempts to quell the tears. Dylan informs her that this wasn't his casting decision. He advocated casting her as Jessica. Sharon pauses to listen. It was a simple question of being out-voted. Sharon resumes her crying. However, Dylan informs her, he does need a personal assistant. Someone who perfectly understands the play and can act as a sort of messenger. A "gopher."

Sharon blinks away her tears. Now things are looking up. What's a gopher, she asks? Dylan explains. They "go fa" this and they "go fa" that. Sharon does not comprehend. Dylan has to elaborate. You can help me direct, he tells her. We will have fun. Sharon is happier now. So she has not been completely rejected. She'll be part of the production. Suddenly overjoyed, she throws her arms around Dylan for a hug.

During this brief physical contact, Dylan hopes that Sharon does not feel the hard-on that launches itself under his pants the instant the girl's body makes contact with his. He badly wants Sharon to see him as a loving and caring individual, not a lustful one. He is, after all, an older man. Dylan feels that having a relationship with Sharon will give him space to be himself in ways that none of his previous lovers have permitted. Sharon is no Bridget or Jane, that's for sure!

It is the first night of rehearsals. A special dispensation has been granted to the cast and company members of both genders – street clothes can be worn in place of school uniforms while in rehearsal. This indulgence had to be approved by the headmaster of Elwin and Mother Superior of the St. Theresa Convent. Street clothes mean anything that is not school uniform. To the thespians of Elwin, street clothes appear to mean jeans and sweatshirts. Alas, Dylan does not have any casual street clothes at Elwin. The best he can do is remove his tie and blazer and roll up his shirt sleeves. He regards himself in the mirror. Yes, that captures a directorial look, he thinks to himself. He sticks a New York Mets cap on his head to complete the effect. The baseball cap won't mean a thing to anyone in England, but it says something to him.

*   *   *

Dylan needs his gopher. She can help him distribute scripts and cast notes. The plan is to sit the cast in a big circle and run through a first reading. King of the castle, cock of the walk, Dylan struts across the classroom compound toward the auditorium. He heads directly for the cast changing room. A temporary sign on the changing room door says "girls only." Dylan knocks on the door. Girls in unison call out "come in" and Dylan is about to do just that but, before he can, the door flies open. Johanna is standing with one hand on the door knob and the other outstretched in the manner of female gladiator. She is wearing black knickers and a white bra.

"What, good sir!" she bellows to the world. She grabs Dylan's astonished face with a pair of powerful hands and, with an overbearing grip, pulls him toward her and forces her lips against his. Her tongue breaches first Dylan's lips, then his teeth, and finally his tonsils. Dylan could have probably stopped the intrusion of tongue into his mouth at any point, but to have done so would have made him look like a wimp in front of a group of girls he hardly knew. It would not do to be so emasculated on the night of the first rehearsal!

As abruptly as she begins the kiss, Johanna ends it. "Ah," she declares huskily, "I needed that. What can we do for you mister director?" The half dozen girls in the room, mostly in underwear, are laughing their heads off. Johanna is their queen. Yes, she knows how to handle a man. Dylan can only hope that his response to Johanna's assault on his dignity as director was interpreted by the girls as being sufficiently macho.

"I'm looking for Sharon," responds Dylan to Johanna, as if nothing had just happened. In truth, Dylan noticed Sharon the instant the door was opened. He continued to notice her through Johanna's deep throat kiss. Of the half dozen girls in underwear in the changing room, the only one embarrassed to be seen thus clad is Sharon. In addition, she is the only one of the girls not wearing a bra, meaning that Dylan got a brief glimpse of her breasts before she managed to shield them with her school blouse. And, of the six girls in the room, she's the only one wearing the despised regulation convent gray school knickers. Dylan remembers Bridget explaining that it wasn't so much that it was uncomfortable (itchy) or old-

204

maid like in appearance (granny panties), but rather the fact that it was standard that really turned the girls against it. Only the English could have a school rule which standardized underwear.

Dylan looks over to Sharon. She stands looking at him with frightened eyes, both hands holding her blouse in position to cover her breasts from Dylan's view. Dylan says to her gently, "When you're ready, can you find me in the auditorium seats? I need you to distribute scripts and production notes." Sharon just nods. Dylan turns heel and closes the changing room door behind him. Five of the six girls in the room call out flirtations such as "goodbye, gorgeous" and "come again, sweetie." It means nothing to Dylan. He takes with him only the fleeting image he captured of Sharon's breasts. Smallish but firm, the breasts of a mid-teenager. Breasts that need no bra to remind them of what position they should be in.

Dylan sits with Roland Ebert six rows back in the auditorium seats. They are going over the action plan for the first night of rehearsals. Roland is cautioning Dylan about taking on too much too soon, suggesting that the first session be more of a meet-and-greet. After all, both sets of actors attend single sex schools, so it'll take a couple of sessions before they feel comfortable with the opposite sex. Dylan reluctantly agrees. The actors are to sit in a circle onstage. Each will tell the circle group as little or as much as they want known about themselves and their lives. After, each will have an opportunity to say a little about how they envisage the role into which they have been cast.

Sharon shyly approaches Roland and Dylan from behind. Sharon's street clothes are not the jeans and sweatshirts favored by most of the remainder of the cast. Instead, she is clad in a cheap, cotton, print dress that covers her legs to mid-thigh. Although this is the age of the miniskirt, this particular dress is short in the leg, not for fashion, but because Sharon has grown out of it. Dylan observes that the waist of the dress is positioned under Sharon's ribs. It's also perfectly obvious that Sharon is still not wearing a bra. Dylan thinks this might be a good thing. Now he can stare at Sharon's breasts whenever opportunity permits. Dylan informs Sharon that there's been a slight change of plan. He explains about Mr. Ebert's circle idea.

Of course, Roland Ebert was spot-on about the need to get the actors to know one another. Dylan learns plenty about his schoolmates in the forty-five minutes it takes the students to deliver a personal pen picture. Next, the actors describe their own ideas about how their roles should be interpreted. Dylan chips in with an idea or suggestion of his own. But during this phase of the first rehearsal, it quickly becomes apparent that Johanna is going to be a dominant force in this production. She has no hesitation about shooting down Dylan's ideas. She does this in a superior, almost maternal fashion. The way she does it irks Dylan. She'll shred some suggestion of his, introduce her own counter-suggestion, then turn it around to make it appear as if it was Dylan's idea all along. Johanna establishes herself as a formidable, almost frightening presence. She captivates the entire cast with her shoot-from-the-hip wit and articulate intellect. Dylan notes that even Roland Ebert seems taken with her.

The three hours scheduled for the session speed by. Soon Sister Mary is announcing that she must get her girls back to their homes. She tells everyone that it will take her at least an hour to drop each one off and how for a couple of the younger girls, this will be a late night. Because she is not yet a sixth former, Sharon is considered one of the younger girls.

Johanna traps Dylan in the hallway as the girls are about to depart. "Dylan," she says imperiously, "I know we are both going to become very good friends over the next three months. I've always desperately wanted to play the role of Portia and I have studied the *Merchant* since I was fourteen – it ranks in the top three of my all-time Shakespeare favorites. I know I will benefit from your insights; you're so good at perceiving the depth in a character. At the same time, I hope you will seriously consider some of my suggestions as we maneuver through rehearsal and production."

Dylan is put even further onto the back foot after this diatribe. After her performance through the evening, he concludes that Johanna might be making fun of him. He responds with a diplomatic "of course Johanna," and more with the objective of changing the subject than fishing information, follows with, "By the way, have you been in touch with Bridget lately?"

Johanna responds with a breezy, "Oh yes, she's fine, she loves boarding school, does her usual gymkhanas – you know Bridget. And by the way, she got engaged. Not sure if you heard about that." After delivering her announcement, she stares hard at Dylan.

Dylan raises his eyebrows. Johanna's revelation about Bridget's engagement takes him by surprise and he feels his cheeks redden. "No, I hadn't heard," he says, doing his best to keep his cool. "But if you are in touch with her, give her my congratulations and best wishes."

Johanna chuckles. "I wondered how you'd take that piece of news. The chap she is marrying is Richard Banningham. The Banningham family owns a large dairy farm just outside of Salisbury. Good Hampshire gin and jaguar stock and money to roll around in. You can guess that Bridget's old man is ecstatic about the match – he can hardly wait for the wedding. I was told that when he heard of the engagement, he wanted to pull Bridget out of boarding school a year early to get the knot tied on the spot. He was probably scared that Bridget might run off with some bounder like you again and fuck up all his plans on expanding wealth and influence in Hampshire. You might have heard that Delia is shacked up in sin with an impoverished art student in Southampton. She dropped out of nursing school. Needless to say, Daddy's not speaking to her any more. Meanwhile, Bridget's star is flying high."

"What's this guy, Richard Banningham, like?" asks Dylan.

"It's strange," responds Johanna. "He's about the last person I can imagine Bridget with. His idea of fun is shooting grouse with the boys. Maybe Bridget can see something in him that I can't. He seems to be emotionally dead. Of course, Bridget treats him like a slave. It's rather amusing. Richard is a strapping hulk of a man, well over six feet in height, I'd say. He follows tiny Bridget around like a lapdog and meekly responds to her every whim. Of course, Bridget has changed."

"In what way?" queries Dylan.

"Difficult to say, really," continues Johanna, taking a moment to think of the words. "She's lost her sense of fun. She isn't so innocent any more, either. She can be quite the little witch now. She's still always laughing like she used to – only now, the laughing is at someone's expense. Usually poor Richard's!"

Dylan nods, taking this in, and decides it's time to wrap up the conversation. "Well anyway, if you see her, say hi from me. I'm House Captain now so no one monitors my phone calls or mail. She can safely get in touch with me if she chooses. And do pass on what I said about her engagement. I really want her to be happy." Dylan suspects that the chances of any follow-up on his message to Bridget via Johanna would be close to zero. He considers his feelings about Bridget and decides that he really is pleased that she is engaged.

The day after the night of the first rehearsal, Roland Ebert traps Dylan in one of the corridors. He is gushing about Johanna. "What a natural talent!" declares Roland. "Her grasp of the language and interpretation of character show a maturity well beyond her years. What an asset to this production she is. How lucky we are to have this marvelous Portia."

For a moment or two, Dylan doesn't respond. Of course, Roland is right; everything he's said about Johanna is true.

"Yes," Dylan agrees, "she is absolutely perfect for the role." But he says no more. Roland studies Dylan as if he were expecting a more enthusiastic confirmation of his appraisal of Johanna's qualities.

Then he says, "You know, Dylan, a clever young man such as yourself should snap up Johanna Dempsey as a companion. You can tell she's mad about you. I know Elwin Park boys are not supposed to have girlfriends, but we all know that's a rule that you have not given much credence to in the past. Johanna is so well suited to you. You'd both have horrendous rows – but have marvelous fun at the same time." Dylan can only respond by looking at Roland as if his suggestion has dropped down from another galaxy.

✳   ✳   ✳

Dylan continues to be the only member of the *Merchant* crew not to wear street clothes. At rehearsals, he removes his blazer and tie, rolls up his sleeves, and puts on his New York Mets baseball cap. This has become his concession to wearing street clothes on set.

Dylan discovers that directing a cast and crew exceeding thirty students is not an easy chore. The students range in age from thirteen to eighteen. Many egos have to be placated. Hormonal outbursts have to be diffused. His thoughts of having some quiet intimate moments with Sharon were poorly conceived. Dylan has Sharon run off her feet in her role as gopher. Fortunately, it's Sharon's nature to please. Half-way through each evening session, there is a cocoa break; this is the only time that Dylan can spend a few moments with her. On the night of the second session, Dylan takes the opportunity during the cocoa break to apologize to Sharon for barging into the changing room when she wasn't dressed at the previous rehearsal.

"Oh that's alright," responds Sharon matter-of-factly, "It wasn't your fault. The other girls made you come in. They were making fun of me for not having a bra. They wanted to embarrass me."

"That was kind of mean," says Dylan. "Is there a reason you don't wear a bra?"

Sharon looks down. "No real reason. Mummy says I don't really need one yet and we haven't got a lot of money. My dad is a builder and he's unemployed at the moment."

"I like you without the bra, you have great-looking tits," says Dylan. Sharon blushes from those great looking tits right up to the roots of her hair.

"You weren't supposed to look," she says, turning away.

Dylan thinks for a moment. "How much does a bra cost? Can I buy one for you? I don't like to think of you being teased for something as trivial as not having a bra."

Sharon stares at him in awe. "I don't know, really," she says, "I've never really looked. The only time it bothers me is when I have to change with other girls around." At that moment Johanna flounces up to the pair to interrupt with a half dozen great suggestions on how Dylan should be managing things.

Dylan cuts her off mid-sentence. "How much does a bra cost?" he asks her. Johanna stalls. Then she catches on. She stares at him stone-faced for a couple of seconds. Then she informs him of the approximate cost. She looks at Sharon. Embarrassed, Sharon looks away. As the convent girls are readying themselves to depart later that evening, Dylan slips an envelope into Sharon's jacket pocket.

"Don't open it until you get home," he whispers. Inside the envelope he has put some money and a brief note, which says:

"Dear Sharon, please accept this small gift from me. It is in appreciation for all your help so far. I know that we will become the very best of friends during this production. Dylan."

Dylan congratulates himself for speedily navigating his romancing of Sharon onto a higher plain. But what irony, he thinks ruefully, that the opportunism of the chase should present him with a clear opening that would soon result in depriving him of a valued pleasure. No longer would he capture glimpses of Sharon's firm little tits bouncing unrestrained under her cotton dress. Instead these breasts would be clamped immobile to her chest and become as sexless as the tits on a plastic store window mannequin. So be it!

The following Friday, before the rehearsal gets under way, Sharon emerges first from the changing room. Her usual apprehensive look has been replaced by a more relaxed smile. She says nothing to Dylan, but tugs his sleeve and motions him to follow her. They exit the auditorium into the foyer. Facing Dylan, she checks that no one else is around and pulls the collar of her dress away from her chest for him to take a look. Dylan peeks down the front of Sharon's dress and glimpses the top of a white bra. Sharon looks up at him and smiles. She pats the top of her dress back to her chest, then tugs his sleeve in a gesture informing him that he's done quite enough looking and it's time to return to the auditorium.

"I think I like them bare better," he informs her with a grin. Sharon gives Dylan a playful slap with her hand.

The cast gets to know one another. Friendships develop. But these friendships never develop in quite the way that you want them to. Dylan is hoping that the theatrical bond between Portia and Bassanio or Antonio might grow into a real world bond. In short, he wants Johanna off his back.

As the rehearsals continue, Dylan grows as a director. He softens his approach, replacing instruction with suggestion. He democratizes key decisions. He discovers that this approach makes him popular with both genders. Johanna Dempsey also continues to be well-regarded as a leader by both the male and female cast members. Her knowledge of all things thespian means that she must be consulted about anything of importance. Even Roland Ebert likes to bounce ideas off her. Johanna continues her theatric flirtation with Dylan, but is destined to fail in her pursuit. Everything Johanna does will be lost on him: Dylan is madly and irrationally in lust with Sharon and has eyes for no one else.

Sharon also grows. Being Dylan's gopher, she has to interact with every cast and crew member on the set. Her shyness begins to dissipate. She's the director's side-kick. She has acquired status. While Sharon is generally unpopular in the single gender environment of the convent, in the mixed sex climate of the *Merchant* production she becomes a hit. Her natural innocence and beauty might reap little regard from a group of females, but scores well with a bunch of hormonal males. Most of the boys in cast and crew are either in love or in lust with Sharon. Her naïve nature means that she's only just beginning to become aware of this fact.

Six weeks into rehearsals, Dylan, Roland, and Sharon are seated in the audience seats, observing a scene. Suddenly Dylan gets to his feet, tosses his Mets cap onto his seat, and leaps up onto the stage. It's the last time he'll wear it. He wants to show Shylock just how to merge a particular line with some appropriate body mechanics. Having imparted some small wisdom or other to Shylock, Dylan athletically jumps off the stage and returns to his seat. He wants everyone to know that he is both a director *and* a rugby player. In the meantime, Sharon has picked up his Mets cap and stuck it on her head. Dylan sits down in his seat next to her and she wrinkles her nose at him before returning her attention to the stage.

Later, as the convent girls are preparing to leave after rehearsal, Sharon is going to flirt with a male for the first time in her life. She undertakes this flirtation under the disapproving countenance of Sister Mary and her convent schoolmates. Still wearing Dylan's baseball cap, but now also her jacket, she grasps both lapels of Dylan's blazer. She leans up to whisper to him. "Please let me keep it, Dylan. It would mean so much to me. I'll only wear it for rehearsals. I'll treasure it always."

Dylan looks at Sharon. How can he deny her his Mets cap, especially when asked in this way? He pauses and then nods his head responding with a stupid, "so long as you never in your life put on a Yankees cap."

Sharon jumps with glee and plants a kiss on Dylan's cheek. Next, she skips off to Sister Mary and a scolding concerning inappropriate behavior. Never before in her school history has Sharon been able to make light of being in trouble with a teacher. Now she is blasé. Even her schoolmates are reappraising her. Could it be that Sharon is emerging from wimpdom? Will she no longer be a wet? And who the heck are the Yankees?

Of course, Sharon has no clue who the Mets or the Yankees are. In common with most people in England at this time, she's only vaguely aware of what baseball is. A game they play in America, she supposes. But from that evening thereafter, when the convent girls emerge from the changing room in their street clothes for each rehearsal, Sharon wears the Mets cap. In her mind, the cap becomes a vehicle enabling her to establish a unique identity on the *Merchant* production.

The night of the dress rehearsal approaches. Dylan is stretched every possible way. Rehearsals are now twice a week on Tuesdays and Fridays. As well as these, Dylan plays rugby every Saturday and sometimes Wednesday afternoons. These commitments increase Dylan's reliance on Roland and Sharon, but the *Merchant* has now acquired a momentum that allows it to just keep rolling along. The understanding the cast members have of each other plateaus to a level from which almost any on stage disaster can be smoothly navigated. Dylan feels that they could do without him if they had to. Perhaps this means that he's done his job properly.

Dylan knocks on the changing room door before the penultimate dress rehearsal. He has come to pick up a pair of wigs for the production that Johanna has obtained from an aunt of hers. The girls chorus a "come in" and Dylan opens the door. He is half expecting to be pounced on by Johanna for a kiss, but the leading lady simply acknowledges him with a nod and moves toward her bag to get the wigs. Sharon approaches Dylan with a peculiar grin on her face. She has already changed, though she's wearing not her usual slightly undersize dress, but what appears to be a brand new pair of jeans. The Mets cap is cocked on her head. For a brief instant, Sharon pauses in front of Dylan, still with her funny grin, a grin that perplexes him, before throwing both arms around his neck and thrusting her face toward his, inviting a kiss. Not just any kiss, but a reenactment of the Johanna kiss two months prior. Dylan is flabbergasted. As the tip of Sharon's tongue enters his mouth, her Mets cap falls to the ground. By the time Dylan has recovered his wits, Sharon is done. Wow! Four of the five spectators of the kiss cheer by clapping their hands. Sharon bends over to retrieve the cap that fell off her head.

Johanna doesn't clap. She's doing her best to suppress her rage. In an un-Portia-like loss of composure, she slams the paper bag containing the wigs into Dylan's stomach.

A short while later, with the rehearsal under way, Dylan leans over and whispers into Sharon's ear, "I like your jeans."

Sharon twists in her seat and cups a hand around Dylan's ear to whisper, "Mum bought them for me. She found out about the bra. After, she told Daddy that I needed a pair of jeans, too. We went shopping yesterday."

Later that evening, when the rehearsal is nearly done, Dylan leans over and whispers again into Sharon's ear, "That was some kiss. Not your first, I'll bet?"

Sharon giggles. "I practiced. My friend Gillian said to practice with an apple first.

That was not so hard. Then we practiced with each other."

Dylan is silent for a while.

Then he leans over to whisper "Was it as much fun kissing me as it was kissing Gillian?"

Sharon giggles again. "It was more fun. You nearly fell over backwards with surprise. And the girls couldn't believe their eyes," she announces proudly. Dylan's fear that the kiss had a lot less to do with him than with notching up status with the *Merchant* chicks seems to have been confirmed. Still, Sharon is evolving; she's a work in progress. Two months previously, she was not capable of a giggle, let alone inserting her tongue into Dylan.

The dress rehearsal is a disaster. Every possible thing that could go wrong goes wrong. Actors who had been line perfect from the night of the first rehearsal require prompts. Dylan decides to use a pair of prompters for the first night rather than just one. Each would be positioned on either side of the backstage. Sharon volunteers to be a second prompter. Dylan vetoes this. Despite Sharon's growth over the past few months, Dylan feels that she cannot be trusted to focus on the script and respond appropriately to a dropped line. He informs Sharon that she'll be more important as his gopher backstage. Sharon is miffed and shows it. She pouts like a child. Roland suggests that his wife could prompt and Dylan likes this idea. He ignores Sharon's pouting and instructs her to brew him a cup of coffee. Sharon descends into a deep sulk and says nothing for the remainder of the evening.

Unlike the dress rehearsals, the first night performance unfolds almost without a hitch. The first night audience is populated primarily by Elwin Park boys, the convent girls, and teachers from both schools. Dylan is aware that this audience, consisting primarily of teenagers and their teachers, will be the toughest to please because they will know the play. Sort of like performing opera in Milan.

In addition to the teenagers, a few of the parents of the cast that reside locally are in attendance. The parent attendees include Sharon's parents. Sharon wants to introduce Dylan as soon as they arrive, but Dylan informs her that the introduction will have to wait until after the performance, when he'll have more time to talk to them. In a way, he is apprehensive about this meeting.

Because the *Merchant* is Dylan's directorial debut, he doesn't realize that half the audience will want to talk to the director after the performance. He stands with Roland on one side of him and Sharon clad in jeans and her Mets cap on the other. Dylan attempts to diffuse some of the praise to Roland and Sharon. In Roland's case, there's no doubt the praise is justified. From a covert stance in the background, Roland toned down Dylan's excesses and provided the production with much-needed balance. Roland's put-downs were skillfully posed questions such as, "don't you think that's just a bit too Broadway, Dylan, might I suggest..." On the other hand, the praise diffused Sharon's way was probably not justified. But that depends on how important the role of a muse can be regarded.

Mr. and Mrs. Fulton are not what Dylan expects. Sharon thrusts her mother and father before him. Mr. Fulton appears to be a man of few words and what he speaks is delivered in a hesitating Irish brogue. He is a short, wiry, bronzed man with a sun-wrinkled face and longish white hair coiffed in the front with an Elvis curl and slicked back with some kind of grease. Dylan thinks his appearance and demeanor make him more like a grandfather. Mrs. Fulton is her husband's height, but heavy set, and clearly much younger. Her gait is lumbering and she appears to be even more uncomfortable than her husband immersed in the snooty climate of Elwin Park. When she opens her mouth, her speech is delivered in a thick Romsey drawl.

Dylan is surprised enough at the appearance of Mr. and Mrs. Fulton to feel lost for words in their presence. He mumbles something feeble about being grateful for lending their daughter to him ... a daughter who has been such an integral part of the *Merchant* production. He's acutely aware that what he says sounds phony and insincere.

Dylan studies Mr. and Mrs. Fulton's faces to see if he can find any evidence of Sharon's features. They seem to share no physical features with Sharon. Fortunately for Dylan, this initial meeting with Mr. and Mrs. Fulton is brief because so many other members of the first night audience want his attention. Roland comes to the rescue and engages Sharon's parents in some chit-chat. Dylan overhears typically modest Roland, praising Dylan to the Fulton's, but knows this will do nothing to close up the chasm he created between himself and Sharon's parents when introduced.

Dylan begins to seek avenues of escape. He has a hip flask of cognac in his blazer pocket. He would like to anesthetize himself from this post-performance drudgery with a slug or two.

Dylan retreats to the stage lighting control room. Inside, it is dark and empty. He sits, parks his feet up on the balustrade, and exhales. Semi-reclined, he pulls the flask from his jacket inside pocket and takes several large gulps. The fire of the cognac soothes his throat and calms his mind. He looks down on the stage. Most of the cast is still enjoying whatever accolades are forthcoming from the twenty-five percent of the audience that refuses to leave.

The door opens, briefly illuminating the small room with a shard of light. Dylan whips the cap on his flask and inserts it back into his blazer pocket. The angular shard of light recedes as the door closes.

"You aren't being very nice." It is Sharon.

She sits next to him and assumes a posture like his, feet up against the baluster.

"It's not really my thing, Sharon; I've never liked schmoozing. Why aren't you with your folks?"

"I told them I had some stuff to do before I could leave. Are you drinking?"

"Yes. I had a sip of brandy. Do you want some?"

"Not likely! You shouldn't be drinking. You will end up burning in hell."

Dylan turns to look at Sharon. Surely, she is not being serious? Yes, it does appear that she is. She is scowling at him with an indignant expression. On an impulse, Dylan takes her face in both hands and pulls her toward him. He opens her lips with his tongue, but Sharon obliges without really responding. Dylan pulls away.

"Relax," he says, "a little kiss from you was really all I needed to feel better." Dylan pulls Sharon's face toward his once again. This time she is more responsive to his kiss, but hardly swept off her feet. The kiss lasts not ten seconds before Dylan feels there is no point in continuing.

Free, Sharon wipes her mouth. "You taste of whisky. I don't like it. I wanted to kiss you again when it was just us two, nobody else around. But you ruined it." Dylan grins at Sharon. She responds by getting to her feet and exiting the lighting control room.

Dylan pulls the hip flask from his jacket pocket and takes another gentle pull. He thinks. Sharon may be gorgeous to look at, but she has almost no personality and is close to being sexually frigid. How long will it be before she takes on the appearance of either her mother or her father? The thought of either is grotesque. What about the hang-up with booze? The correlation she made with having a drink and hell was a little scary. Sharon is the first of the convent girls he has encountered who is a for-real, Bible-thumping, Catholic religious fanatic.

The day following the *Merchant* first night is a Saturday and the final day of the school term. The school empties. The Christmas vacation begins. Only the boys of the *Merchant* production will remain on the Elwin premises. They'll do a Saturday afternoon matinee, followed by a Saturday evening performance. Following the two performances, there will be a cast party in the Elwin Park gym. That is, if they have the energy. Dylan and his two brothers are scheduled to travel up to London Airport on the Sunday. Daniel and Domenic are none too happy about having to sacrifice a day of Christmas vacation for Dylan's theatre exploits, but that's just the way it's going to be.

As the Saturday unfolds, Dylan's main problem is Portia. Johanna's sweet spot for Dylan has soured and she has begun to treat him with open contempt. Dylan is conditioned enough to withstand Johanna's very potent tongue, but Sharon is not. Johanna rightly figures that she can probably hurt Dylan more by going after Sharon. But this is a risky strategy because Johanna's malice toward Sharon and Dylan is costing her status among both the male and female members of the cast. Dylan's concern is actually not with Sharon, but rather that Johanna's performances are not compromised. Thankfully, his worries are unfounded. On stage, Johanna gets stronger with each portrayal. At final curtain on the Saturday, she is triumphant. Her Portia reigns and in terms of accolades, places her on par with Shylock. The audience loves her.

Since the kiss in the lighting room, Dylan's affection toward Sharon has seasoned. Up to that point, Dylan felt he was in love with Sharon. Now he's convinced he's not in love, he just wants to bang her. He will strategize having sex with Sharon rather than work on the relationship angle.

The two Saturday performances pass in a blur for Dylan. The cast party that follows the second show is a big deal for most of the performers and crew, though not for Dylan. The actors and crew re-energize the moment the final curtain drops on *Merchant*. They change from set costumes into street clothes. They select their favorite records to pass on to one of the teachers, who will act as disc jockey for the evening.

The Beatles' "Hard Day's Night," played at an eardrum-busting volume, opens the cast party. Dylan is not really up for this occasion, but he knows what is expected of him. He immediately makes his way over to Johanna to ask her to dance. Dylan and Johanna dance. They remain on the floor for the first two discs played.

Fortunately for Dylan, the music continues to be played at a volume that precludes verbal communication. Johanna is clearly happy about being asked to dance by Dylan. She is an expert dancer, better schooled and skilled than Dylan. Despite her heavy frame, she's effortless on the dance floor and has a natural sense of rhythm. After two songs, Dylan performs a theatrical bow and Johanna responds with a regal curtsey. Dylan escapes, sneaking out the back door of the gym. The night air is cold outside. As he distances himself from the music in the gym, he becomes aware of how dark and silent the school building is, emptied out for the Christmas vacation. Dylan climbs the stairs to his study. There he makes a little hash coffee and drinks it, along with a slug or two of brandy that remains in his flask. He lies back onto the couch in the study and relaxes.

A short time later, the study door opens slowly. This is unusual in itself. Even the headmaster would knock before entering a house captain's study. Dylan is half in a dream, but focuses quickly. Amazingly, it is Sharon.

"How in hell's name did you ever find your way up here?" asks Dylan. Sharon has persuaded one of the boys in the cast to navigate her through the building. She's not pleased with Dylan.

"You are rude and hurtful," she admonishes. "I wanted to dance with you. You kept on telling me what a great team we were. But if we were really such a great team, you would have thought about not hurting my feelings."

Dylan, still reclined on the couch, props himself up on an elbow to take a closer look at Sharon. She's wearing a pink dress that he has not yet seen on her. He supposes it must be her church dress. Sharon doesn't like being stared at. She shifts from one foot to the other.

"Come over here."

Reluctantly, Sharon crosses the floor of the study to stand beside Dylan. Dylan reaches out and grasps one of Sharon's legs behind the knee. Slowly, he works his hand up her bare thigh to her buttocks, which are contained, of course, in regulation convent school knickers. Sharon twists and shifts her weight as Dylan's hand grasps and kneads her buttocks. Her face displays irritation. But even so, she does not move away. Perhaps these school knickers are not so bad, thinks Dylan, at least from a seduction perspective. They fit loose. Gently, he continues to massage her and runs his fingers down the split between her buttocks.

"Sit down," says Dylan, pulling her down beside him. In the movement that follows, Dylan somehow manages to maneuver one arm into position to cradle Sharon's shoulder, while twisting the other from her buttocks to a strategic position between her legs. Although she has not in any way resisted, Sharon retains an expression of exaggerated annoyance on her face.

"I want you to be nice to me," she says. "This is a special day for me."

"Special, like in 'thank God the *Merchant* is put to bed'?"

"Don't blaspheme," orders Sharon. "Special, like in 'it's my birthday' today."

Dylan blinks. "Why didn't you tell me? I would've got you a present!"

"I don't want a present from you," Sharon snaps. "I just want you to start being nice to me again. Like you were when we first got to know each other. Then you were the only person that was kind to me. Now everybody else is kind to me and you are always so … moody."

Dylan looks her in the eye. He doesn't really care about what she is saying to him, his mind only focused on how to get her to come around to his way of thinking. "Have you not thought about having sex with me, Sharon? I've wanted to have sex with you from almost the first moment we met. Does what I am doing to you not feel a little bit nice? It would be a perfect sixteenth birthday present." Dylan applies some movement to the hand cupping Sharon's underwear-protected vulva.

Enormous tension radiates from Sharon's cunt. So much so that Dylan feels that he cannot yet breach the boundary set by the fabric of the underwear.

"I try not to have sinful thoughts," says Sharon slowly. "I don't think it's right to have sex before getting married. We should know each other as people first. I want to cuddle with you, and I want to have a conversation with you without forty other people around."

"Oh Jasus and Mary," retorts Dylan, putting on his best Irish accent, "the holy rollers have really got to you." He pulls his hand away from between Sharon's legs. This action has the effect of checking Sharon.

"I didn't say I wanted you to stop," she says testily, then shakes her head. "I'm not ready, Dylan. I want to and I don't want to. You frighten me. Can't we just hug instead?" She is on the verge of tears.

Dylan stretches back on the couch and places his arms behind his head. He looks up at the ceiling. Sharon decides she is nevertheless going for the cuddle. She wriggles her body into Dylan's and, in doing so, moves one knee across his groin. Dylan wonders if this is intentional and decides to find out. He slips his hand up Sharon's jumper. He moves his hand to the center of Sharon's back and unhooks the bra clasps. A split second later, he has her breasts cupped and begins to work a response from her nipples. Sharon has her eyes closed and is breathing deeply, though her breaths are somewhat labored. No time to worry about that, thinks Dylan. He raises Sharon's jumper and works on a nipple with his tongue. As his hand approaches to regain the hold between her legs he released earlier, Sharon's body responds. Relaxing her hips, she cedes her groin to Dylan's groping hand. Rising lust in Dylan defeats the effect of the dope. He opens his eyes and moves to connect his lips with Sharon's without surrendering the hand cupping her between the legs. Dylan opens his eyes. He sees that Sharon is quietly crying. He freezes.

"Are you OK?"

Sharon shakes her head. "I can't do this, Dylan. Part of me wants to. I'm not trying to tease you, really, but I know that what we are doing is a sin. I am embarrassed to even think about how to confess this."

Dylan sits up on the couch, his boner cowed into recess at Sharon's disclosure. He reaches for the flask of cognac from under a cushion on the couch. He takes a gulp before looking Sharon in the eye.

"I don't know what to say, Sharon. Firstly, I certainly don't want to have sex with you if you don't want to have sex with me. It's only fun if it's something we both want. Secondly, this whole religion thing of yours is more than I can handle. What we do between us is not something to share with a celibate Father confessor who will then consider it his moral duty to tell Mother Superior who, in turn, will make it her business to inform your mother and father. Don't believe that all those fucking vows of secrecy and confidentiality mean anything. You know what? I think you should try some of my dope. Right now, I think the only way we could truly enjoy a fuck together is for you to get stoned silly."

"The Father was right about you. Along with being devilish in your ways, you also take drugs and drink liquor. He told me that boys of your type usually do. Mother Superior says that you are just a trial that God has sent to me to make me prove my faith."

Dylan shakes his head and stares at the ceiling. He suddenly feels very stoned. The room is beginning to spin and he feels nauseous. A silence ensues.

Sharon breaks the silence, her voice now remorseful. "I didn't mean what I said just now. Dylan, I think I love you and I want to save you. I want to bring you back to God if I can. If I bring you to know God then we can enjoy each other's bodies without guilt."

Dylan is pricked by a fleeting recollection of Genevieve. The memory lasts only an instant and he shakes it away. "Sharon, I think you should check out. I am tired and I am horny. If you remain here in my study, it's only a matter of time before I do something to offend you. I think you're gorgeous and there is nothing I'd like more than to fuck your brains out. But even if I could get you excited enough to willingly jump into the sack with me, I could never handle the fallout of all this Catholic guilt shit you carry around with you."

Sharon is sitting on the edge of the couch, propping her elbows on each knee, while supporting her head. Once again, she is quietly crying. She lifts the skirt of her dress to wipe her eyes. Then she gets to her feet to leave.

Dylan calls after her. "Oh, one thing Sharon: sneak out! Don't get caught inside the school building. You're not allowed to be here. Just think about how your Father confessor and Mother Superior will label you as a slut for life if you get caught. They'll have you saying fucking hail Mary's until you are a shriveled old hag who even the Holy Ghost wouldn't oblige with a fuck."

Sharon is standing at Dylan's study door. "Say what you like, Dylan. You are not hurting me. I have faith. I know you've just lost your path in the ways of evil. But I love you and I will help you find a way to righteousness." Sharon opens her purse. She removes an envelope from the purse and stoops to place it on the floor by the door.

"Have a nice Christmas, Dylan. I will pray for you every night. There is nothing you can do to stop me from doing that."

The door closes. Dylan listens to Sharon's gentle footsteps retreat down the corridor. Then he launches himself off the couch and walks over to lock the study door.

He picks up the envelope on the floor and tosses it unopened onto the study desk. Presumably, it is a Christmas card. Undressed and in bed, he recaptures the image of Sharon's eyes as they appeared during those brief seconds when she responded to his tongue and his touch. With this apparition captured, he vigorously masturbates with the very same hand that moments earlier had cupped his muse's warm little sluice.

Christmas comes and goes. The Lent term at Elwin Park begins. Dylan cannot help himself from spending some time wondering about Sharon over the four-week vacation. When he returns, he spots Sharon's as yet unopened Christmas card lying on his study desk. He opens it. The card is homemade with a crude picture of a snowman. The Merry Christmas message is signed "Sharon" and followed by Xs that fill the entire back page of the card. To pursue or not pursue? He despises himself for even considering the notion. She has gotten under his skin and it's not going to be easy for him to get rid of her. He believes that part of him has come to truly hate her. He thinks about this. He could live with the fact that she is brain dead and hung up on her primitive religious trip, but that's not the reason for his aversion. She has made him weak. She has a power over him he cannot rise above.

If he could screw her just once, perhaps he could overcome this weakness. But will it ever be possible to have sex with her? In this regard, her immaturity is a problem. Yes, she may be chronologically two years older than Bridget was during their escapades, but Sharon is emotionally still a child. If he opts to hunt and pursue, a phone call and apology will be required. He can denigrate himself as being a mean and thoughtless brute – but is it ever going to be worth it? He reflects some more. Nope. It will only result in more frustration and swollen balls and the indignity of being lambasted by religious rhetoric. The instant Dylan decides that he will never contact Sharon again, he feels as if an enormous weight has been lifted off his shoulders. He's a free man once again.

Ten days after the start of the Lent term, Dylan is summoned to the phone. Dylan's gruff hello initially produces no response. Impatiently, Dylan repeats his hello. A meek voice like that of a small child speaks. "Dylan? It's Sharon. I wanted to say I'm sorry. I know you think I was being a baby before Christmas, but you frighten me when you drink whisky and take drugs." Silence. "Are you still there, Dylan?"

"Yes, Sharon, I'm still here."

"Are you still angry with me, Dylan?"

"I was never angry with you, Sharon. I was just tired and frustrated."

"Dylan, I felt really sick after I left you on the night of the cast party. You might not believe this, but I also wanted to do all of those things you wanted. I wanted so much to make you feel happy. But I was frightened. You were so rough." The sounds of crying trickle down the line.

Jesus, thinks Dylan, wondering if he can ride this out. "I am aching to see you again, Dylan. Can't you put on another play or something? I want to be your go-pher girl again."

Left-brain Dylan responds. "We don't do plays in the Lent term, Sharon. The next school play will be in the summer term. It will be a Shaw. And no force in this world could get me to direct it." Another silence, this one longer.

"Can we meet for coffee in Romsey? I need to see you again."

Dylan sighs. "I have rugby matches on Saturday afternoons. I'd have to lie and say I had an optical or dental consultation. It isn't easy."

"Then lie, Dylan, I want to make things right between us."

"Lie! Jesus, I don't know what Father confessor, Mother Superior, let alone God would say about me telling lies to spend an afternoon with my girlfriend?" Another pause.

"Don't be nasty to me, Dylan, it doesn't suit you. I know you don't mean what you say. My faith is my business and I will do my best never to mention it around you again. Even though I have prayed for you every day since we were last together. Did you just call me your girlfriend?"

Sharon is wearing a gray duffle coat over her school uniform and is already seated at a table. When Dylan enters the coffee shop, she stands. Dylan approaches. In his determination to be free of his obsession, he has forgotten how gorgeous Sharon is. They embrace. Dylan would've kissed her, but Sharon buries her face into his shoulder. Fuck, she's crying again! He pats her back, but his heart isn't in it. They sit and drink cappuccinos. His life is being made a misery because Sharon is just too beautiful for this world. The only cure for his state of mind will be a night of unrelenting fucking with this goddess. He wants to fuck her speechless so he doesn't have to listen to her voice. He must find a way to free himself of this obsession.

"Sharon," asks Dylan, "do your folks ever go away and leave you alone for the weekend … or even a night?"

Sharon looks at Dylan with exaggerated seriousness and props her chin on the palms of both hands. "Now let me see, Dylan," she begins, taking an annoyingly long time to deliver a simple answer. Eventually, she concludes her humming and hawing and replies. "No, I don't believe they ever have yet. They are afraid a devil or a goblin – or possibly an ogre named Dylan Douglas – will emerge from the woods and carry me off to live a life of shame and sin."

Ha, ha. So Sharon is working on developing a sense of humor. They drink two more cappuccinos. Dylan has to get his bus back to the school. It's time to say goodbye.

Dylan looks at Sharon. "I'm hungry for a proper kiss." So they have a proper kiss. Dylan leans over the table. Sharon meets him in the middle. Dylan inserts a tongue deep into Sharon's coffee-flavored mouth. The kiss gets prolonged over five minutes and Dylan gets some messages that Sharon is responding to and enjoying the experience. Two middle-aged women sitting at an adjacent table eye the kissing couple with disgust. Finally, they separate.

"Wow," gasps Dylan, blinking. "How nice was that! Our best kiss ever." Sharon looks a little sheepish and smiles. She squeezes his hand. Is the woman in her beginning to emerge to the fore? Careful! It wouldn't be the first time he is fooled into thinking something had changed in Sharon.

Does this short scene in a café acquire any romantic momentum? No siree. On departing, Dylan neglects to make another date. He cannot; he plays on the school rugby team. This fact precludes most day pass visits on Saturday afternoons, and there's a limit to how many medical appointments can be used to excuse absence. Sharon phones regularly. Each time she calls, she begins the conversation sounding like she's six years old. By the time they finish talking, she gains confidence, but not much. What Dylan really wants to know is what the chances are of her parents abandoning her, leaving her home alone and open for seduction. Will they ever leave for a weekend? For a night? For an afternoon?

After a couple of weeks of pestering, Sharon has a suggestion. "My mum and dad want you to come for Sunday lunch with us."

"Sunday lunch, huh? Will Mummy and Daddy let me have you for dessert?"

"Dylan, you don't know what I had to go through to get them to agree to lunch. And all you can do is take the mickey."

"Hmm," responds Dylan, not really conceding that he has made fun of her. Sharon begins to get upset.

"You are so nice to everyone but me, Dylan. When I tell Gillian about some of the awful things you say to me, she refuses to believe me. She only knows you from the *Merchant* play and she thinks you are so gentle and thoughtful. What a joke!"

Dylan lets Sharon sob a little before making his apology. "OK, I am sorry, Sharon. It's just that I am so sex starved. You must know that I do really care for you in my own bizarre way, but I don't think we are good for each other. At the moment, all I want is to be naked with you. The fact that there is about a zero opportunity of that happening any time soon makes me a little manic."

Sharon stops crying. "Well, at least you can begin by coming to have Sunday lunch with us. We can see what happens. If nothing else, I want Mummy and Daddy to stop hating you. I know you can turn on the charm with them. It won't take an awful lot of effort on your part to win them over."

Dylan rides a bicycle over to Sharon's house. He writes the directions down over the phone. It is eight grueling miles distant. Eight miles of rolling Hampshire hills, hills that might roll by when in the comfort of an automobile, but appear mountainous from the saddle of a bicycle. The effort of cycling in this rugged terrain exhausts Dylan, despite the fact that he plays regular rugby and is at the peak of fitness. It is a sunny, but bitterly cold afternoon in the first week of February. He arrives puffing and exhaling clouds of super-heated breath.

The Fulton's live in what was once a farm laborer's abode. The tiny home is the end unit of four in a terraced row. The roof is steep and thatched. Inside, the rooms are sparsely furnished and there are just two bedrooms. The single source of heat in the home is a wood or coal burning stove called an Aga, located in the kitchen. It appears that all the family cooking takes place on top of or within the integral oven in the Aga. The temperature in the kitchen exceeds a hundred degrees. The temperature within the Fulton home descends in proportion to the distance from this stove.

When he knocks, Sharon opens the door wearing the pink dress she wore on the night of the cast party. She hugs him, keeping her mouth safely out of range of a kiss. "You poor thing," she says, "you must be frozen." Sharon clasps Dylan's hands, which are the only parts of his entire body that are actually cold; everything else is steaming from the exertions of cycling. Sharon pulls him into the living room, rubbing warmth into his hands. Dylan exchanges greetings with diffident and deferring Mr. and Mrs. Fulton. Sharon's parents are folks of few words. Mrs. Fulton suggests a cup of hot tea and Dylan accepts.

With a cup of warm tea consumed, Sharon lets her parents know that she wants to show Dylan her room.

"Don't be long, dear," advises Mrs. Fulton. "Lunch will be ready in less than a quarter of an hour." Sharon clasps one of Dylan hands and drags him off toward her room. Dylan makes a show of complying with some reluctance; he wants Mr. and Mrs. Fulton to know that he doing this just to oblige this childish whim of their daughter's.

Sharon's room is tiny. There is barely enough room for the single bed. Dylan closes the door and immediately pounces on Sharon with an ardor she probably has come to expect. With both arms, he pulls Sharon toward him in an embrace that jams their lips together. Dylan is fast. He quickly moves his hands down her back to first lift her dress above her underpants, then slips them under the elasticized waist of the knickers to grasp both bare buttocks. Although things are turning out much as Sharon had expected, she's alarmed at the speed things are progressing. She does her best to twist free of the hands clasping her bottom, while being mindful that she cannot make any noise that might alert her parents. With two fingers, she delivers a vicious pinch to Dylan's neck. Frantically, she whispers, "Behave yourself! We have not even had lunch yet."

Dylan leans his head back and pauses, but keeps his hands caressing her bottom. "Well if we have to wait until after lunch," he puffs, "then so be it!"

"I don't know what to do with you," whispers Sharon, exasperated. "It seems that the only thing you want from me is sex. I just wanted a kiss. You're a complete sex maniac." To himself, Dylan acknowledges this to be true. Sharon is right on the money this time.

Sharon shows Dylan her room. It appears that all of Sharon's worldly possessions are contained in one modest three-drawer chest and a tiny closet containing her school uniform, a couple of skirts, and the dress she wore as "street clothes" at the *Merchant* rehearsals. The room is wallpapered with a faded print. Apart from a cross above the headboard of the bed, the room is completely Spartan. So, for that matter, is the remainder of the house, other than another couple of crosses, one with a macabre bleeding Jesus hanging off it by nails. Dylan has never seen the inside of such an abode within the so-called First world. It produces a painful pang of conscience through his senses that actually draws his heart to Sharon. He has a sudden awareness of how unfair it is for him to be so hurtful to Sharon. It is just resentment, resentment that stems from her capacity to drive him into a sexual frenzy. But is that her fault? How cruel he has been for mocking her religious kick when she has nothing else. A quick examination of the house and it is obvious that her family has little in the way of material wealth. He vows to do his best to be a little gentler with Sharon.

The Sunday meal begins with grace. As a family guest, Dylan is invited to deliver the blessing. He does so in Latin in exactly the manner grace is delivered in the Elwin Park dining room before meals: "Benedicto benedicator, preasum Christum dominum nostrum." The truth is that he has no experience of saying grace in any other way. All three Fulton's closed their eyes tight to listen. Their verdict is clear. Dylan must be speaking in tongues.

All three Fulton's open their eyes to peek at each other, wondering if the grace is done. Dylan observes them because he never closed his. Mr. Fulton clears his throat. "Our Sharon," he says, "perhaps you could finish the grace and welcome our guest." Dylan learns that Sharon is often referred to by both her father and mother with the possessive "our" preceding her name. Our Sharon is clearly not familiar with the task of saying grace, either.

She squeezes her eyes tight, "Dear God, thank you for getting Daddy and Mummy to agree to have Dylan join us to share this meal. Thank you too, God, for making sure that he did not fall off his bicycle on the way here and may he also not fall off his bicycle on the way home… er, back to Elwin Park. Amen. And – oh yes! Bless this food for us. And bless Daddy and Mummy, too."

The meal is braised rabbit stew. "I don't think I've ever eaten rabbit before," observes Dylan after tasting it. "Not a bad flavor." There is a moment of silence.

Sharon leans over to Dylan and whispers in his ear, "Daddy poached it off the Elwin Park estate. Watch out for biting on buckshot. If you get some in your mouth, don't swallow, spit it out."

Mrs. Fulton administers a stern reprimand to her daughter. "Now then our Sharon, if you can tell Dylan, yous can be tellin' us all, I'm sure." It is not uncommon for Mrs. Fulton to end sentences with the suffix "I'm sure."

"I was just telling Dylan how happy I was that he could come for lunch, Mummy." It occurs to Dylan that Sharon speaks to her parents using the voice of a small child, not that of a sixteen-year-old adolescent. On the other hand, not being truthful with Mummy and Daddy has found its way into her repertoire; a good sign, thinks Dylan. Other than these few snippets of chatter, not much other conversation punctuates chewing. Sunday lunch at the Fulton's is primarily about eating.

So does Dylan have his way with reluctant Sharon after lunch? Not a chance! It is a freezing February afternoon, albeit a sunny one. Dylan and Sharon go for a brisk walk on the trails in the New Forest. Dylan is deep in thought as he attempts to figure out Sharon's parents. How is it possible that this pair of grotesque physical specimens combined to produce a beauty like Sharon? Surely Sharon was constructed from a different gene pool? She must have been adopted. Whoever heard of Catholics being content with having just one child?

"Were you adopted?" Dylan asks bluntly.

Sharon looks at him quizzically. "Don't be silly, Dylan," she responds after a pause. "I'm not sure what you are trying say. I know Mum and Dad are not comfortable with you, but it isn't their fault. They're not used to someone like you. Try to be patient with them."

Sharon holds Dylan's hand. They walk. Frustration rises in Dylan yet again. It is not as if he can have a stimulating conversation with Sharon, so his mind ends up wandering all over the place. He cannot help but compare Sharon with Johanna Dempsey. Why can he not make his life easier and become attracted to Johanna? Let me see, thinks Dylan, Johanna is funny, talented, and smart. She loves to talk and she seems to be crazy about me. Put Johanna on a dance floor and everyone's eyes are drawn to her. Dancing, she is sexy, her body ripples with the music, there's not a doubt in the world that she would be a fabulous fuck. How easy would life be if he were to fall for Johanna? Dylan looks into Sharon's face. Why does Sharon get to be so fucking gorgeous? Everything about Sharon's appearance is almost perfect – her face, her body, her hair. Whatever went wrong when her brain was being created?

Sharon and Dylan have an after lunch kiss. The spectacle must have looked like a scene out of *Wuthering Heights*. A raging wind threatens to blow the putative lovers off their feet into a clump of prickly heather. The bitter arctic gale renders hands, noses, and ears numb. It shrivels desire at its very quick. Kissing with runny noses has other ways of quelling libido. The lovers have no choice but to retreat to the Aga stove in the Fulton kitchen. It takes Dylan a full twenty minutes to thaw his hands. Mr. Fulton is sitting with a Sunday tabloid newspaper and barely glances upward as Sharon and Dylan re-enter the house.

Mrs. Fulton is knitting. Without raising her eyes from whatever it is she is knitting, she observes, "Tis a mite chilled out I'd wager. They're calling f'snow tonight, I'm sure" This is Dylan's cue to escape. He has eight miles of rugged Hampshire hills to negotiate on a bicycle before it gets dark. Or snows. It's still only mid-afternoon, but the positioning of the British Isles sees to it that night comes quickly during the winter months.

Weeks go by, and months. When Dylan returns following the Easter vacation, he begins his final term at Elwin Park. Dylan feels as if he has accomplished something as the Dickens House Captain. He may have not changed the culture dramatically, but he has at least softened it. He has established a solid profile of academic success, conquered a variety of school sports, and distinguished himself in non-sports extracurricular activities. What more could he want? The answer to that question is simple, because it is probably the only aspect of his life that he regards as being truly of consequence. A successful love life? You bet!

Sharon still phones him on a regular basis. Mostly, she is forced to leave messages, which Dylan makes a point of not returning. But it's only a matter of time before chance connects her with Dylan, voice to voice.

"Dylan," she begins in her baby voice. "You never phone. You never return my messages. You always wait for me to call you. You're not a very good boyfriend. I miss you. I never get to see you. Can't we meet in the Romsey coffee shop on Saturday?"

Dylan wants so badly for this thing to end, but just listening to Sharon arouses his passion, making him incapable of delivering the coup de grace. "I'd love to see you more often Sharon. But chats over cappuccino don't do it for me. How else would you suggest we get together? You can't really sneak up into my study for conjugal visits."

"Is this about sex again? I thought there was more to our relationship than just sex."

Dylan is lost for words because he is very sure that, for some time, he has been motivated by little other than sex in his dealings with Sharon. The prolonged silence from Dylan produces some loud sobbing on the line. Out of kindness, Dylan does a little backpedalling, but the phone conversation ends inconclusively. Dylan decides that coffee shop meetings with Sharon are something he'll never repeat. This relationship has to end. Has it ever been a relationship?

The following evening Sharon calls again. She sounds more buoyant, to the point that she is not using her baby voice. "Dylan! What are you doing on Sunday?"

"Not so much. Nothing scheduled after the school church service, as far as I know."

"Then come to visit me," insists Sharon. She sounds almost grown up now. "I want us to be close again."

"Sharon, I don't mean to sound offensive, but I don't think I can survive another Sunday lunch with your folks."

Sharon pauses, then speaks quietly with unusual resolve. "They are not going to be here, Dylan. They're going to a special church service in Cheltenham; Daddy has agreed to help the Father of our local church. It takes more than two hours to drive there. They'll be away all day."

"Why aren't you going with them?" asks Dylan.

"I'm supposed to be going," responds Sharon. "They don't know it yet, but I am going to be sick. Too sick to go with them."

Dylan pauses. "Isn't this going to result in some dreadful fallout with God and your Father confessor?"

"That's uncalled for, Dylan. I've told you before that I want you to stop making fun of my faith. I have been careful not to bring this up with you recently. But you have to play fair and not mention it to me, either."

"Are you quite sure this is something you really want to do?" asks Dylan. He mulls the consequences, but sadly, the potential delights of having Sharon to himself for a entire afternoon are destined to win.

"No, Dylan, I am not quite sure and you know I am going to feel horribly guilty," Sharon tells him. "But I also want to be with you. I know you think I have been a tease. If I have, I didn't mean it, but Gillian thinks that I have been teasing you. She says that's why you have been trying to push me away. But I know the real you. I'm not forgetting that you were the first boy to ever be really kind and thoughtful to me. I am grateful for that. When we were doing the *Merchant*, I use to ache all over between rehearsals when I couldn't see you. The pain started to go away as soon as our minibus drove through the Elwin Park main gate. Just to be in the same room as you made me happy. Now I just have the pain of never seeing you."

Sharon pauses. Dylan says nothing, taking her words in. He is surprised by her; this admission seems to have come from a depth in Sharon of which he was previously unaware. She continues. "Dylan, as soon as you started to like me, my life changed. All the other boys started to be nice to me, and then, so did the other girls. I am not good at talking like you. But what I am trying to say is that I want to spend Sunday with you. Alone with you. I know what will probably happen and I want it to. I don't want to lose you."

Dylan gets on his bike. He pauses. He realizes he has forgotten something. Rubbers. He wonders if that is being too optimistic. Nevertheless, it's best to be prepared. He goes back to his study. These rubbers have been in his possession for a while; the foil wrappers have turned crinkly. Do rubbers have a best-before date?

With the scent of sex driving him onward, the eight miles to Sharon's house fly by. It is a warm May day and, even though he is wearing gym attire, he arrives puffed and sweaty. The Fulton car is not in front of the house. Just before he arrives at the front door, it is flung open by Sharon, as if she has been waiting for his arrival. She is wearing a floral-print house coat. The skirt of a nightgown trails below it. She appears more composed and confident than Dylan has ever seen her. It is

Dylan that is lost for words.

"Put your bike around the side of the house. I don't want anybody to see it. Then you can come in and have a drink," Sharon tells him. "You must be thirsty after your ride."

"Do I get a kiss?" asks Dylan.

"Close the front door first." Perspiring, Dylan kisses Sharon, who is mildly scented with bath soap and talcum power. He does this tenderly. The prospect of imminent sex induces gentleness in him. Sharon invites his tongue into her mouth. Dylan wisely decides not to rush things. He suddenly feels embarrassed by his sweaty clothes and body.

"I don't suppose you have a shower, do you?"

Sharon shakes her head, "We have a bath. You can have a quick strip wash. You can wear my school gym kit after. I'll hang yours on the clothes line to dry out."

Dylan bathes quickly in the Fulton tub, splashing water over himself. Toweled off, he steps into a pair of Sharon's school gym shorts. There will be no hiding a boner in these, he thinks to himself, but who cares? Then he pulls on a white tennis shirt, also belonging to Sharon. Neither piece of apparel is outrageously small for him. He emerges from the bathroom holding his sweaty gym clothes and hands them to Sharon. He observes her as she takes them out to the clothes line and hangs them up. Sunlight silhouettes her body under her housecoat and night-gown. Suddenly, Dylan remembers the rubbers in the pocket of his gym shorts. Fortunately, Sharon has not discovered them. Would she be capable of identifying a rubber if she came across one? Probably not.

Sharon makes Dylan a lemon squash. Dylan drinks the contents of the glass in a single shot.

"Are you hungry?" asks Sharon.

"Only for you."

"Do you want to go into my bedroom then?" asks Sharon in a resigned way, as if she is quite prepared for the next step, but predictably lacking enthusiasm for it.

Dylan holds Sharon's hand and escorts her to her bedroom. The bed has been neatly made, the top blanket tucked in with hospital corners. Dylan pulls back the covers and sits on the bed. Sharon remains on her feet. Dylan pulls Sharon toward him and places his arms around her waist. He buries his face into the fabric of her housecoat, into her tummy and inhales her aroma. As Sharon places her hands around Dylan's neck, Dylan drops his own to behind her knees then works them upward over the back of her thigh to her buttocks, to the small of her back. She is not wearing underpants. Gently, he caresses the flesh of her bottom, exploring the cusp of her buttocks, outlining the creases that separate them from her thighs.

Dylan strokes his hands up the hollow of her back to find her shoulder blades and confirm that under the nightgown there are no encumbrances to arrest his touch. It seems to be clear that Sharon has planned to have sex with him.

Abruptly, he stops. Dylan wants Sharon to respond to his touch, not merely submit to his advances.

"Does this feel good, Sharon?" he asks. "I don't want to go on if you are just letting me do this for me. It's supposed to be fun for both of us." Sharon twists and sits on the bed beside Dylan.

"Yes, it feels nice when you touch me, Dylan. But I've told you before, it also feels like I'm being bad. I'm frightened. I've never been this naked with anyone before. I have never seen a boy undressed."

"Not even your father?" questions Dylan, incredulous.

"No, definitely not Dad," responds Sharon, "Nudity is considered sinful in my family. I've seen little boys a couple of times. Changing on a beach, and that sort of thing. I think I want to see you naked, but at the same time, I'm scared."

Dylan thinks. "Maybe we should get under the covers in your bed. Keep your nightie on if you want. I'll get undressed. The thing about sex is that it usually doesn't work out so well if do anything you don't want to." Sharon nods. She removes the housecoat and climbs into the bed, holding the nightgown to cover her knees. Once she is lying down, she pulls the bed covers up to her shoulders. Dylan leans over to kiss her on the forehead, before removing the tennis shirt he is wearing and throwing it on the floor. He is about to remove the gym shorts when Sharon interrupts him. "Fold the shirt up, Dylan, I don't want it wrinkled. I'll have to iron it again."

Dylan blinks, disbelieving. He picks the tennis shirt off the floor, holding it by the collar. He lays it flat on the bed and folds it sleeve to sleeve, carefully ensuring the back is evenly creased. That done, the collar must be first smoothed, then flattened. Sharon studies every move. He stands and places the folded tennis shirt on the dresser. Sharon continues to stare at him. He pulls the shorts down and steps out of them, but simultaneously, Sharon turns away and pulls the covers over her head.

"Fold the shorts up, too," she orders. Naked Dylan climbs in beside her. He cuddles into her body, but Sharon has pulled her nightie down to cover her buttocks and uses a protective hand to ensure that it stays there.

Dylan lies on his side, propped up by an elbow. He strokes the hair away from Sharon's cheek, but she continues to resolutely face away from him with a blank gaze fixed on the wall. Dylan attempts to gauge her mood. Perhaps she's just a little frightened. He takes her hand and slowly draws it behind her back toward his swollen penis. While Sharon does not resist, Dylan is forced to guide her hand to explore. He opens her fingers. He unpeels and wraps her fingers and thumb around his penis. Sharon breathes deeply and continues to concentrate her focus on the wall. But just as Dylan is wondering whether to give up, her hand responds, perhaps motivated by mere curiosity. First, she holds him like a cucumber that she is about to peel. Dylan frees his guiding hold on Sharon's hand to allow her some tentative exploration. Her fingers move from shaft to tip, register the different texture of the glans, travel down the shaft to pubes, then return to the tip. A finger locates the uretha in the glans. Using all her fingers once again, she runs her hand down the shaft to find his balls. Dylan flinches a little as she weighs his balls one after another, hoping that she is cognizant of the danger involved in a more aggressive exploration.

"You can turn around if you like. I kind of want to see your face," suggests Dylan. Sharon releases Dylan's penis and twists her body around in the bed to face him. There is not a lot of room to accomplish this maneuver in a narrow single bed. Sharon has a blank expression on her face. Dylan senses that during her exploration of his tumescent penis, Sharon's motives lean to being investigative rather than sexual. "Are you ready for me to touch you?" he asks gently. Sharon nods in the affirmative but, unsurprisingly, the expression on her face suggests that she's not going to be comfortable with this. Dylan moves a hand under the covers to lift the nightie. Softly, he strokes the pubic hair above her vulva, hoping that this will induce her to open her legs, which are squeezed tightly closed. Sharon closes her eyes. Using some force, Dylan works his hand down to part her legs. Sharon is barely moist, and certainly not wet. "Try to tell me what feels good," suggests Dylan. But Sharon just nods her head and says nothing.

Five minutes go by. Try as he might, Dylan cannot get Sharon wet, even though he's succeeded in getting her legs somewhat apart. Once again, he is stumped on how to elicit a genuinely sexual response from Sharon. He stops.

After a pause, Sharon opens her eyes to look at him. "Would you like me to make you a cup of tea?" Sharon asks.

Dylan laughs. "No, I don't want any tea. I'm trying to make out with you. Don't you enjoy what we are doing just a little?" Sharon stares at the ceiling. Dylan changes tack. "OK, let's try something else. I want you to lie on top of me. We are not going to have real sex, so don't get all worried. I just want to see if we can discover a way to make this fun for both of us."

Sharon raises herself onto her knees. Dylan scoots over to the center of the bed, lying on his back. He guides Sharon into an all fours, straddle position over him. Her face is immediately above his and he takes her face in his hands and kisses her deeply. Dylan's hands pass down Sharon's neck, over her back, onto her thighs. He lifts the nightie over her bottom. With a hand on each cheek of her buttocks, he guides her downward until their groins connect. The base of his penis parts the soft lips of her cunt, with the tip buried above in her pubic hair, safe for the moment from accidental penetration. He strokes her hair with one hand and guides Sharon's face into the crook of his shoulder. With his other hand, he explores the crease between her nates, locating the soft flesh between sphincter and vagina. He softly massages her here, suppressing the instinct to thrust pelvis to groin. Now some sign, some message of response is vital. Sharon breathes deeply. She twists her torso a little. Dylan wishes he had pulled her nightie up further so that her breasts were bare against his chest. Sharon adjusts her straddle position over Dylan's groin to open her legs a little wider. The movement critically adjusts the relationship between the base of penis and folds of vagina, lips which are finally beginning to moisten, suggesting that intrusion might be welcome. Dylan's mind drifts to dwell on the pair of condoms in his shorts pocket hanging on the clothesline outside. Stopping what is happening here to retrieve them would not be smart. Not at this critical juncture.

Sharon gyrates her pelvis, just fractionally, but there is no doubting the motive is pleasure. She is suddenly wet. All that going slow has paid off, reflects Dylan. Now he can begin to reciprocate. Just take it slow and easy, he cautions himself. He cups a buttock in each hand and guides her pelvis through a rhythmic, circular movement. Now she's not just a little wet; she is juiced. Sharon lifts her upper body away from Dylan's chest to prop herself on her arms. Her eyes remain closed, but her gyration becomes more strategic, her pelvic thrusting dangerously close to resulting in penetration. Dylan is about to come. He grabs Sharon's hips to pull her downward, while simultaneously thrusting his penis up into Sharon's tummy as he ejaculates. Sharon sits back on Dylan's thighs, confused that this game has concluded so suddenly, and just as it was beginning to be fun. Dylan's sperm is smeared over her midriff, extending from her pubic hair to her belly button. Quickly, Dylan moves to a half sitting position and wipes the sperm off her tummy using the skirt of the nightdress. Then he lifts the garment over Sharon's head and uses it to wipe the spunk off his own belly.

"Finally, I get to see you completely naked!" says Dylan, admiring Sharon's body as she continues to sit straddling Dylan's thighs.

Sharon still looks dazed. "Did we do it?" she asks.

"No," responds Dylan, "not properly anyway. Did you like that?"

Sharon nods. She yawns. Suddenly, she seems embarrassed by her bared breasts and crosses her arms over them. Dylan unfolds the hands shielding the breasts. "Don't cover them," he says, "I think they're beautiful. I like to see you naked."

Sharon looks down at her chest. "You don't think they're a little small?"

"They're not the biggest tits I've seen," responds Dylan, "but they are a perfect shape." He cups them in his hands. But Sharon is not interested.

"It's time for that cup of tea," she declares, twisting her body off the bed and grabbing the housecoat. She wraps herself securely in the garment and belts it around her waist. The nightie used to clean up the sperm is lying on the floor. Sharon looks at Dylan, her expression querying what to do about it.

"It dries quickly," reassures Dylan. Sharon is skeptical. She drapes the nightgown over the door handle and exits.

Dylan wants to retrieve the condoms from his shorts on the clothesline. He pulls on the pair of shorts he borrowed from Sharon and enters the kitchen. Sharon is at home in the domesticity of a kitchen. She busies herself putting cookies on a plate and tea leaves into a pot. Without saying a word, Dylan, wearing only the shorts, exits the back door.

"Where are you going? It's freezing out there."

Almost naked Dylan, walks up to the clothesline, extracts the pair of condoms from the pocket of the shorts on the line, and inserts them in the pocket of the shorts he is wearing.

"What did you go outside for?" asks Sharon. Dylan doesn't respond.

After tea and biscuits, Dylan leads Sharon back to the bedroom to resume the seduction. "Do you want to have proper sex now?" he asks.

Sharon responds with a question. "Can't we just do what we were doing before? I think I liked that."

"Proper sex is a lot more fun," Dylan assures her earnestly. Sharon nods.

Dylan figures a reenactment of the scene of an hour ago where she was on top of him might work best. This time Sharon is juiced almost immediately. Dylan can barely contain himself. He rolls Sharon off his tummy and on to her back. She obliges submissively. Dylan reaches for the shorts on the floor and removes one of the condom packages from the pocket. With his teeth, he rips the foil package open, removes the rubber, and rolls it down the shaft of his penis. Sharon stares at the procedure with glazed eyes. The rubber installed, he runs his fingers through her labia just to check that she is still juiced. He moves his penis into the outer lips of Sharon's vagina and moves against her in gently nudging thrusts, seeking invitation to penetrate. Sharon tenses. Dylan pushes in a little deeper. Sharon tenses some more. Dylan encounters considerable physical resistance from what he deduces to be hymen. But a point of no return has arrived ... instinct governs, and what initially resists Dylan's thrusts suddenly yields, allowing him to penetrate deep into Sharon. A feeling of relief possesses him as he slides in as far as he can. But as she is breached, Sharon squeals in pain and begins to cry.

At first, Dylan neither moves nor cedes any of the depth gained. Sharon sobs convulsively, like a child. As her body shakes with the crying, it reverberates into Dylan through his penis. Dylan is unsure how to react. Still without moving inside of her, he strokes Sharon's forehead. But the crying is evidently not going to stop. It continues to a point that Dylan feels he has no choice but to withdraw. He props himself on all fours, haunched over Sharon's naked body, which continues to shake with sobs. Looking down, he startles at the amount of blood in evidence. There is already a circle of blood on the bed sheet, more blood running from Sharon down the swell of her buttocks onto the sheet, and blood over his balls and upper thighs. Jesus, he thinks, what have I done?

It takes the pair over an hour to clean up the mess. Dylan's initial feelings of guilt have been staled by frustration into annoyance. He can barely suppress his irritation. He just wants to leave, but is persuaded to have yet another cup of tea. In addition to the frustration of the experience, he begins to worry about what Sharon might say in a confession booth. Did Sharon register the fact he had used a rubber, another sin? Of course she would. He snarls at her: "If you tell that goddamn padre about this, sure as fuck it will get back to your parents and bloody Mother Superior," he tells her.

Sharon is matter-of-fact. "Please don't use that horrible language, Dylan. I am not blaming you for anything. It was my fault as much as yours. I wish you had not used the rubber, though; I know that is a serious sin."

"I would have loved not to have used that fucking rubber," Dylan snaps. "The real sin would be to knock you up at sixteen years old." More tears.

Dylan changes tack and tries some tenderness. "Are you feeling better now?"

Sharon looks down. "I'm sore, but I think I'm alright. I want you to hug me." Dylan obliges and the pair engage in a prolonged embrace that Dylan truly wants no part of: all he can think of is how to leave as quickly as possible without hurting Sharon's feelings. As they separate, he tells her in a matter-of fact-way, "When we do it next time, at least it won't hurt you." Sharon looks at him blankly.

Dylan has an eight-mile bike ride to reflect on the events of the afternoon. Could all that blood be accounted for by the popping of a cherry? Had he afflicted some terrible internal damage upon Sharon? Should he have continued to fuck her until he came and ignored the blood and tears? Would that have been preferable to the sense of defeat he had taken from the experience?

After the Elwin vespers service, Dylan is called to the phone. He is expecting the worst. Yes, it is Sharon, but her mood has changed. "I just wanted to hear your voice," she begins. Mummy and Daddy haven't come back yet. They have been held up in traffic. "Do you hate me?" asks Sharon.

"Of course I don't hate you," Dylan responds, "it was just that I was trying so hard to make you feel good and all I ended up doing was hurting you."

"I don't think anything happened that was not supposed to. I'm not sure. I am a little sore, but that's all. The girls at school talk all the time about being 'deflowered.' I never made the connection between that talk and something so painful. After what we did when you first arrived, I thought it was going to feel nice, so it took me by surprise. It was the surprise as much as the pain. I felt like I was splitting apart. I wanted you to be happy too, but I was frightened."

"Well I am happy you are okay, Sharon. I guess I was scared too when I saw all that blood."

*   *   *

Weeks pass. In his mind, Dylan continues to lust after Sharon. As usual, he wonders why, but then a vision of Sharon's sultry blue eyes framed in too-perfect-to-be-true facial features intrudes and scrambles his objectivity. Certain snapshots of their afternoon together have etched themselves into his sexual audit trail. One image especially – the gentle bounce of Sharon's breasts as she straddled him and gyrated her pelvis into his groin won't leave him, it captures one of their few shared moments when she appeared to actually enjoy doing something sexual. They talk on the phone. But these stumbling exchanges are not real conversations. Dylan, the talker, now has less to say than Sharon. The pair meets once or twice over cappuccinos. A brief kiss or two is the full extent of their physical exchanges.

Dylan has his final year exams during the latter part of the summer term. These exams and the need to prepare for them temper Dylan's lust. He is disinclined to sacrifice precious hours of study for an unfulfilling canoodle over coffee. Sharon continues to be clingy, but in her usual non-physical way. Dylan becomes more and more convinced that he has nothing in common with Sharon but, try as he might, he remains captive to his obsessive lust for her body. He knows he is torturing himself.

Against his better instincts, Dylan persuades his parents to allow him to invite Sharon as a house guest to Spain. Dylan's mother thinks this would be a good idea. It would do Dylan some good to have a girl he was fond of around for the summer. There are not a lot of kids his age in Castellón, she says. His parents agree to foot the bill for Sharon's airline ticket to Spain. When Dylan asks Sharon, she's ecstatic. She informs Dylan that there is nothing in this world she wants more. But then she becomes morose and negative. She tells him that her parents will never agree. She refuses to ask them herself; Dylan must do it. If she asks, the parents are sure to refuse outright, no discussion. Sharon hopes that Dylan may intimidate them into granting permission. You are so good with words, she encourages Dylan, work some magic.

But it is not to be. Sharon was spot on. Dylan's proposal is rejected point-blank when put to Sharon's parents. "Our Sharon is brought up proper," they rationalize. She is a year-and-a-half younger than Dylan. She's a good Catholic-raised lass. She'll not be gadding about with the likes of Elwin boys in a foreign country. Not while she's living under their roof. They have never met Dylan's parents, so how could they be trusted with "our Sharon"? How were they to know what kind of people Dylan's parents might be? What if the airplane crashed on the way there? There was no telling how safe an airplane was – if the good Lord wanted people to fly, he would have equipped them with wings. Sharon begins crying even before her father launches into this diatribe. Dylan cannot believe what he hears. He hasn't got a clue how to respond to people like Sharon's parents. Part of the problem is that nearly five years of Elwin Park has rubbed off on him and taught him to regard people like them as morons. And it shows.

Dylan shrugs his shoulders. He places a comforting arm around Sharon, who sidles closer into him. This is the first time he has touched Sharon with any intimacy in full view of her parents. Mrs. Fulton bristles. "Come now, our Sharon," she says, moving toward her daughter and perhaps fighting an impulse to order Dylan to leave, "taint the end of world, lass." As the mother is about to place a hand on Sharon's shoulder, the girl lurches to avoid her touch.

Quietly, she says through her teeth, "I hate you, Mother." No tears are flowing now. Both parents are silenced. Utterly defeated, Sharon turns away from her parents.

"I hate both of you." She exits the room, headed to her bedroom, without saying goodbye to Dylan. Shrugging his shoulders, Dylan figures he should depart the scene. As he does, he hears the father muttering something barely audible about how his sweet-natured princess has been ruined by a meddling Yank who won't leave well alone. "Get thee back t'America … we dinnae wan the likes of yous here."

14. BARN DANCE

The barn dance takes place on the final Thursday night of the summer term, Dylan's penultimate day as an Elwin Park student. The barn dance outing is the brainchild of Johanna Dempsey. Dylan learned some time back that barn dances are a great Hampshire tradition, although he has yet to attend one. A farmer sponsors the event by loaning out the barn and a field to park cars in. Organizers then sell tickets to cover upfront costs such as paying a band and purchasing kegs of cider and beer. The objective is to have a large, low-cost booze fest.

The organization of this barn dance has nothing to do with either Elwin Park or the Romsey Convent. Johanna suggests attending it as a way of rewarding the cast and production crew of the combined Elwin Park and Convent theatre group. The combined group has just finished a production of *The Importance of being Ernest* and, because of the small number of cast and crew involved, a closing night party is not realistic. Instead, Johanna solicits and ultimately obtains permission for the sixth form members of this group to attend the barn dance.

The plan is that the theatre group will meet for a barbeque at the Dempsey home, following which Johanna and her father will drive the revelers to the dance four miles distant on the Salisbury road. Johanna is now in possession of a driver's license. This has vastly augmented her status. It is a stark reminder to the disenfranchised sixth form inmates of Elwin Park that they are not yet members of the free world that exists outside of the gulag: few of them have experienced the freedom that comes with an automobile and a license to drive it.

Because of final exams, Dylan's role in the *Ernest* production was limited to lighting. When invited to be part of the barn dance group, Dylan initially declines. Reluctantly, Johanna suggests that Sharon can also be invited, even though she's only a fifth former and had nothing to do with the *Ernest* production. No more bait on the hook is required to snare Dylan into accepting. He wonders if Sharon has recovered yet.

Despite the party mood at Johanna's home, Dylan cannot get into the swing of things. It is not that he is in a bad mood, but he feels somehow detached from the festivities. This has an interesting effect on Sharon. Usually, it is Dylan who has to attempt to draw Sharon out, not the other way round. Today, however, Sharon senses that Dylan is out of sorts and consequently attempts to engage him into socializing. Sharon and Dylan have experienced nothing that could be described as sex since their ill-fated afternoon together nearly two months previously. No doubt the promise of a repeat sexual encounter with Sharon would lift Dylan's spirits. But the omens suggest that achieving a mere five minutes alone with Sharon is unlikely, let alone sufficient time for a decent bang.

Food is served along with lemon squash and colas at the Dempsey barbeque. Dylan wants something a little stronger. He anticipates that the barn dance will be made bearable if he can anesthetize himself with alcohol. Sure, he'll drink a beer or two. He will avoid whatever cider is on offer. The Hampshire cider is usually tasty and refreshing, but brutal in impact, being high in alcohol and probably low on cleanliness. His previous experience of consuming the local cider left him sore in the head and weak in the gut.

At the barn, there is a loud band playing a grating mix of rehashed Brit pop rock, interspersed with American country music. This is rural Hampshire. Sharon and Dylan dance. That is, they dance to the few numbers Sharon feels she can dance to. The girl has almost no sense of rhythm. Her preferred dance numbers are those driven at the slowest tempo. During such songs, she parks her head on Dylan's shoulder, leans into his body, and shifts her weight from foot to foot while gazing vacant-eyed at other dancers. A rag doll, thinks Dylan. He drinks more to compensate for the boredom that is beginning to overcome him. He decides to ask Johanna for a dance. Not only can Johanna dance very well, but it becomes clear that she still has a bit of a thing for Dylan. They dance one number, then two and three. Throughout this, Dylan can see Sharon out of the corner of his eye. She is sitting on a bale of hay, looking miffed. Several wannabe suitors have approached her to ask her to dance, but she appears to reject each. After half an hour, Dylan and Johanna are exhausted. They return to sit on bales of hay set around a harvest table. Dylan is soaked in sweat.

On returning, Johanna and Dylan engage in conversation and ignore Sharon. For some reason, it pleases Dylan that Sharon is visibly annoyed with him. Sharon pokes Dylan in his ribs. She would like a cup of cider. As far as Dylan knows, Sharon has avoided consuming alcohol thus far in her life and now she wants to tackle the potent cider. Dylan blinks. He goes to the makeshift bar set up in a horse stall to purchase another beer and a couple ciders for Sharon and Johanna. When he returns, he resumes an animated conversation with Johanna, ignoring Sharon. Just at the moment where Dylan and Johanna might be launching a thing of their own, a pair of hands closes over Dylan's eyes from behind. Small hands. Hands a little calloused from a lifetime of holding reins. Hands that Dylan knows well. Hands that have touched Dylan in ways that no other hands have.

"Guess who?" prompts the female voice behind him. Of course, Dylan knows the voice – how could he ever forget that voice? But it would not do to identify it. Not yet, anyway. It has been four years. His eyes still blinkered, soft hair brushes against his cheek, then teeth close over an ear lobe and bite. The bite is just a tad more aggressive than one motivated solely by affection and it's delivered by a set of teeth that previously bit that same earlobe. Dylan twists and forces the hands restricting his vision aside.

Thus discovered, Bridget laughs. The laugh hasn't changed in four years. Actually, Bridget's appearance has barely changed in four years. To Dylan's six inches of growth, Bridget has grown one inch. "Dill," says Bridget, still laughing. "You still look yummy. Gosh, you've grown. Long time, no see!"

Dylan has still not gathered his wits sufficiently to make an appropriate response; he feels like a clumsy fourteen-year-old once again. He nods. Bridget turns to address Johanna and kisses her on the cheek. Johanna is a little cool with her. Bridget completely ignores Sharon.

"Dill, I want you to meet my fiancé, Richard. Richard, this is Dylan. Dill was my first boyfriend when we were just babies." Standing behind Bridget is a giant. If Bridget measures five-foot-two, then this behemoth must clear six-foot-four. Not only is the fiancé guy tall, but he is built like a Sherman tank.

"Cheers," says the behemoth in a slight Hampshire drawl, while shaking Dylan's hand, "I think I've heard your name mentioned." Bridget rolls her eyes upward, as if to inform anybody who might be watching that yes, Richard is not too well-endowed in the thinking regimen of his brain.

"Go and get us all some more drinks," Bridget orders Richard. "And get me a shandy while you're at it."

At the table shared by Sharon, Johanna, and Dylan are three bales of hay pulled around to act as benches. Each bale of hay can accommodate two adult butts with comfort. Before Bridget's arrival, Sharon was sitting by herself on one side of the table and Dylan and Johanna, freshly returned from their excursion on the dance floor, shared a bale facing Sharon. After dispatching Richard to retrieve drinks, Bridget nudges in between Johanna and Dylan and wriggles her bottom to make space between them. As a result, Johanna, being somewhat broad in the beam, is squeezed off the bale. She gets to her feet impatiently and moves to sit on the adjacent vacant bale. Bridget continues to ignore everyone but Dylan. She pecks his cheek. To his shame, Dylan reciprocates, devoting all his attention to Bridget. How can he do otherwise? Bridget may not be as beautiful as Sharon, but she oozes sex appeal.

"It's good to see you again, Bridget. It's been a very long time. I have heard about you from time to time, including your engagement. I've thought about you and hoped you were happy."

"I've heard a few stories about you, too," responds Bridget, laughing. "You randy bastard! I hope they weren't all true."

Richard returns, bearing drinks. He attempts to sit down beside Johanna, though his girth is such that he requires an entire bale, so Johanna is forced to move once again to sit beside Sharon. No conversation takes place except for that between Dylan and Bridget. And as was the case four years previously, Bridget does eighty percent of the talking to Dylan's twenty. Richard senses danger. He asks Bridget if she will dance with him. Bridget doesn't even cast a glance at him in response. Instead, she grabs both Dylan's hands pulling him toward the dance floor. "Come on," she orders him, "let's relive a memory or two."

Bridget and Dylan dance. Richard, Sharon, and Johanna look on. Dylan is quite sure Bridget is oblivious to the three scowling spectators. He also wonders why not one of the three is sufficiently proactive to suggest dancing among themselves. Bridget does not want to return to sit on a bale. She dances fast numbers and she dances the slow numbers. During the fast songs, not a dancer on the floor is more provocative. During the slow numbers, she entwines herself around Dylan in a sensual embrace. Dylan worries that Bridget's come-on may provoke the ire of the Sherman tank.

After half an hour of this courtship in dance, Bridget whispers to him. "Let's find somewhere we can be alone. There must be a loft somewhere in the stables." Dylan and Bridget do not even sneak out. They use the main barn door fronted by a bouncer. Bridget tows Dylan out, holding him by the hand. In exiting, they walk directly past the Sherman tank, Johanna, and Sharon.

Thanks to Bridget's knowledge of farm geography and outbuilding architecture, they find a horse stable, above which is a loft just perfect for wild sex. And wild sex it is. Even the horses below sense something tumultuous is happening above; they whinny and scuff the stable floor with their hooves. Dylan and Bridget almost rip the clothing off each other's bodies and fuck with wild abandon. Once is not enough. After a post-coital interval of just five minutes, Bridget is tearing with her teeth the foil package of another rubber she has retrieved from her purse. She rolls the device into position and the rutting resumes with impunity.

Not all naked bodies feel at ease lying in stable straw. Dylan, in the throes of passion, was able to congratulate himself as perhaps having overcome his aversion to straw. But after completing two rambunctious rolls in the hay, Dylan realizes this is not so. Straw, hay, and stable grit have invaded every exposed crevice and orifice of his body. Bridget is of a different cast of the die. After fuck number two, with her pale skin and blond hair blending in with floor of the loft, she lies on her back and rests her head on her palms behind her head. The fluids of sweat and sex work to adhere greater concentrations of itchy chaff in those more sensitive regions of the body under the arms and between the legs. But what irritates the sensitive skin of urban cowboy Dylan seems to have an opposite, almost soothing effect on his thoroughly rural partner.

"It's so good to be with you again, Dill. There is something about us that really seems to click. I did miss you terrible."

"Bridge … did you ever try to contact me after that Christmas letter I wrote you?"

"Oh I thought about it," responds Bridget, "But it was made very plain to me that you'd end up getting into trouble if you got found out. I didn't want to think of them hurting you again, like they did. Did you ever tell your mother about that?" Dylan shakes his head in the negative.

After a silence, he asks, "Are you really going to marry Richard? He doesn't seem to be your type."

Bridget laughs in her usual make-fun-of-the-world way. "Of course he's not my type. Who cares? He's from my world. He basically likes what I like. We have lots in common. Our families get on. He drives an E-type Jag. And he treats me like a bloody goddess. He'll just shrug his shoulders when I tell him what you and I have been up to tonight. What more could I ask for?" Dylan nods his head. Bridget stares up into the rafters.

"You might have grown a few inches taller, Dill, but you haven't really grown up very much. You and me might have been perfect for each other at fourteen. But I actually like my world here. I don't want to go flying around all over the place to different countries. I certainly don't want to go back to any kind of schooling. Even though my boarding school was no Elwin Park, I've had my bloody fill of teachers and education. University? You must be joking! I'm looking forward to being married. I want to be in charge. I don't want anybody telling me what I can or cannot do."

Bridget stands up, naked, and casually brushes hay off her buttocks and pubes before pulling on her knickers. Predictably, Dylan is more fastidious in removing the chaff clinging to his person. Bridget is dressed in a fraction of the time it takes pernickety Dylan, and she looks upon him, amused.

Bridget and Dylan arrive back in the barn, where the band continues to thump out crude rhythms. Once under the bright lights of the barn, Dylan can see that Bridget's blond hair is full of the evidence of their roll in the hay. As his eyes further adjust to the light, he sees that straw clings to most of her clothing. And to most of his clothing. Some of the local wags whistle catcalls at them as they pass by the bar. This embarrasses Dylan, but not Bridget. She curtseys to her audience with her usual swagger and ready grin.

The couple approaches the table they abandoned forty-five minutes earlier. Of the three occupants they left seated there, only Richard remains. He is nonchalant. "Ah, there you are, Bridget, I was wondering where you'd got to. People are beginning to leave. I thought that perhaps we should be on our way."

Bridget agrees, declaring that she is tired. "You must come and see us off, Dill" she insists.

Dylan says goodbye to Richard and Bridget. Richard shakes Dylan's hand a second time and tells him what a pleasure it was to meet him. "Can you attend the wedding, Dylan? No. Well you really must visit us once we've settled into the house Daddy is giving us as a wedding gift. I know Bridget would love to see you."

An E-type Jaguar is a cool two-seater sports car. Richard climbs into the driver's seat. Bridget embraces Dylan in a goodbye cuddle. She inserts her tongue deep into Dylan's mouth, but keeps it brief. She leans up to whisper in his ear, "Goodnight, gorgeous. I love you to pieces." Then she climbs over the door into the cockpit of the Jag. The engine comes to life with a growl. Bridget waves over her head without turning around as the car accelerates and roars off into the night.

It was plain to Dylan the instant he returned to the barn after his foray with Bridget that Johanna, Sharon, and the remaining drama club members had departed. He supposes that he could have asked Bridget to give him a ride back to the school grounds. But this would have been physically difficult in a two-seat convertible. More difficult still would have been asking Richard for a lift. After all, Richard had been such a good sport. The type of good sport that was so utterly English. As a matter of fact, he was so utterly Elwin Park, he was probably educated in a similar gulag. The dilemma leaves Dylan with three choices. He can return to the barn and attempt to call out a taxi, which is not an easy task past midnight in rural Hampshire. He can also go around begging for a ride from one of the remaining partiers in the barn. Or he can walk the four miles.

He elects to walk. It's time to punish himself. The cooling night air works to sober his senses, releasing him from the after-effects of booze and sex. As the throb of the music coming from the barn fades in the distance, Dylan begins to unscramble his thoughts. What surfaces into his consciousness first are thoughts of Bridget. What had happened to her? For four years, his first lover occupied a revered profile in his memory; she had become a sort of benchmark against which any prospective mate was held to for evaluation. Had Bridget changed or was his assessment of her that far off base? Has he changed that much?

Dylan realizes that his memory had elevated Bridget into something she was not. He was also sure that Bridget had evolved into something quite different from the fourteen-year-old who captured and then lived on in his heart. Well, of course she had changed! Just as Dylan understands that he has changed too. Would fourteen-year-old Bridget have ridden roughshod over people like Richard, Sharon, and her supposed friend, Johanna? Not likely. He does not blame Bridget for wanting independence and Jaguars. But he does blame her for becoming shallow and selfish. He recalls how the fourteen-year-old Bridget fretted more about the mere thought of Dylan receiving punishment than he ever worried about it himself. It seems that the eighteen-year-old version of Bridget has become callous and self-serving. Funny, thinks Dylan, she would've fit right in at Elwin Park.

The notion causes Dylan to turn his reflections on himself. Was he not also the upstanding product of Elwin, too? Cruelty and selfishness were core values at Elwin Park, two of the values that he had despised the most when he first arrived all those years ago. But what had his actions been this night if not cruel, shallow, and selfish?

A feeling of nausea comes over Dylan. A horrible realization begins to emerge. Dylan can blame Bridget all he wants, but he is the one who has done something truly awful. He has behaved thoughtlessly and spitefully to a defenseless girl who idolized him. What was it in him that had made him so horrible to poor, simple Sharon, who never harbored a malicious thought toward anyone in her life? She had given him everything she could, even though doing so conflicted with every value she held dear. How could he have been so mean to her? On what was to be their final evening together, he cruelly ditched her at a barn dance. And why had he behaved like he did with Johanna before Bridget had approached him early in the evening? He was coming on to her, though he was not attracted to her in any way. Something deep within him just wanted to wound Sharon. He shudders. Sharon deserves so much better than Dylan. Why did her first love have to be with a shit like him? He pictures Sharon sitting before her Father Confessor and Mother Superior, both elders sagely nodding their heads, repeating, "We told you so, we told you so."

Dylan figures that he should have broken up with Sharon back in the fall. Lust was not an excuse for prolonging a relationship in the way he had. He searches for another reason that he kept it on, anything to avoid the painful admission that his actions were solely driven by lust. Surely he had more in common with Sharon than with the current version of Bridget? Sadly, he is forced to dismiss this notion, knowing all too well that it's untrue. The sad truth is that he and Bridget, reunited at the barn dance, made a perfect couple who were ready to step on everyone and everything to get what they wanted. But that was Bridget – place her into the mix and he becomes a loose cannon. There was something else about Sharon. Sharon had given him the space to be himself in a way that Bridget and Jane never had. The trouble was, given some space, he displayed a side of himself that was ugly.

Despite his honorable resolutions at the beginning of the school year, Dylan has become the kind of person he despised during his earliest school days at Elwin. He has become a bully: one every bit as bad as Bunny, maybe worse, because Sharon will never get the opportunity to take him out with a sucker punch. The walk back to the school takes Dylan over an hour. He resolves that he will never treat anyone in the future in the way he has treated Sharon. He must learn how to think about the consequence of his actions in the moment, not after it. He shudders again when he momentarily recalls Jane. Did he destroy a whole family? Remorse makes him feel as if he is totally in love with Sharon once again. The chances of him seeing Sharon in the future are small. It would be impossible to make up for the cruelty he has inflicted on her. But he could at least make an effort. He will send her some flowers the next day.

Yes, flowers, backed up with a written apology to be sent in the mail. He will stay up for what remains of the night if necessary to compose some amends on paper. He wishes he could be with Sharon at that very moment. He pictures her crying in bed by herself. He wants to crawl into bed beside her and just hold her. Nothing more than a close cuddle; that was all she ever wanted anyway. Dylan knows all too well that any sex they shared was just to please him. His penis would be under strict instructions to stay out of the mix. Was that possible? He would stroke the tears from her eyes and hug her for as long as she wanted. Strolling down a dark and lonely country road past midnight somewhere in rural Hampshire, Dylan wipes a tear from his own eye. It is his very last day of five years in the gulag and he has never felt more miserable.

15. GABRIELA

Dylan is in Castellón de la Plana, a mid-sized town half way down the Mediterranean coast of Spain. The town is known for its fishing port and oranges. And now, an oil refinery! The oil refinery is being built and cranked into operation by Americans. These Americans are temporary residents, but dollar power has altered life in the town. High-end restaurants flourish, and leisure craft join the fishing boats in the port. Once the refinery is productive and Spanish workers have been trained to operate it, the Americans will abandon Castellón. Following the intrusion of Americans, Castellón will revert to its former identity as a traditional Spanish city of minor importance. But now, it will boast a shiny oil refinery, along with the by-products of the operation, namely wealth and pollution.

Castellón has an airport, but not the kind airlines fly to. Use of the airport is confined to the wealthy, who either own or can charter aircraft. There is a single runway, half a dozen hangars, and what could be called a terminal building. The terminal building is really just a place to stand should it be raining while waiting for a plane to land or take off. In the basement of the small terminal building is a bar known as Gabi's Disco. A neon sign on the approach road to the airport advertises this fact. Once dark, the Gabi's Disco sign dwarfs the one next to it, which declares to anyone who may not know that this is the "Aeropuerto Castellón de la Plana." The prices in the bar are high compared to its local competitors. After all, this bar was originally designed to cater to a clientele willing to pay a little more for a shot of brandy or even a Scotch to calm the disposition before a flight.

Gabi's Disco becomes a favored haunt among a number of American residents living in Castellón de la Plana. More accurately, it becomes a favored drinking and socializing ground among the teenaged offspring of these residents. There are two reasons for this. The first is that there is no apparent minimum age for purchasing and drinking alcohol in Spain during these times. The second is that the "disco" in the title Gabi's Disco refers to nothing grander than a juke box parked on one side of a small dance floor. But stocked inside the juke box, along with the usual Spanish language cover versions of international pop hits and smattering of flamenco recordings, is a collection of current American and English discs. This makes Gabi's Disco a rarity in this part of Spain. American teenagers consider the venue as being less hokey, a little more hip than the alternate downtown tapas bars with their televisions that show nothing other than commercials and soccer.

Dylan sits in Gabi's bar, along with his two brothers and a dozen other teenagers. He is drinking too many San Miguels and is in a contemplative mood. Perhaps he still nurses some open wounds left over from his calamitous relationship with Sharon. It seems that everyone in the bar is paired up. Both his younger brothers are latched onto girls. On this Tuesday night, the bar is populated exclusively with English-speaking customers, some of whom appear to have yet to enter their teenage years.

Dylan is bored. He surveys the tables, looking for action. There is enough booze in his blood to overlook the consequences of such action. The only possibility is a blond dimwit called Shelly Bancroft who is probably the only person in the bar besides himself not paired with anyone. Shelly is a good enough looking girl, maybe a little on the heavy side. Dylan guesses she is around his age. But there is a problem. Shelly is engaged. Dylan hasn't met Shelly's fiancé, but knows that he is the son and heir to the owner of a local supermarket that caters primarily to the American and non-Spanish European residents of Castellón. The fiancé is supposedly in his mid-twenties and the owner of a Porsche, meaning that Shelly has a taste for older men, fast cars, and Latin looks. It is probably a passing phase. He wonders how long that marriage will last once Shelly's family has returned to Maryland and abandoned her to a life as a Spanish house frau. Will she ever get to drive the Porsche? Fat chance!

Dylan asks Shelly to dance. This they do. One dance turns into three and counting. Dylan is sweating off some San Miguels and Shelly is working off a pound or two. Shelly tosses her head back and laughs. She wriggles and gyrates to the dance music, while engaging Dylan in a stream of almost non-stop chatter. Dylan is on the verge of thinking that Shelly and he might be good for a little fling and wondering how to broach a mutual departure from the bar, when a figure appears in the entrance to the bar and scowls at them. The moment Shelly catches sight of this guy in the doorway, she freezes on the dance floor and announces to Dylan that she has "gotta go." Shelly returns to the table she was sitting at, grabs a purse, and departs without further words to Dylan.

So much for that idea, muses Dylan. He goes to the bar and orders a cheap Spanish brandy. The usual barman is not working this night. Instead, a hot Spanish woman serves him the brandy. She has sultry eyes and dark, medium-length hair pulled back into a ponytail. In addition, she exudes a Latin grace and sexiness that Dylan has found enticing in the past. But Dylan's efforts to move beyond the holding hands phase with Spanish girls have always been frustrated. He suspects the padres sermonize in their pulpits to the ignorant Catholic masses about the dangers of fraternizing with "Americano'" vermin. But this bar lady is a woman, not a girl. He guesses her age to be somewhere in the mid-twenties. With attention to detail, she heats the brandy glass under running hot water and fires in the shot of brandy. She knows her way around behind a bar. When the warm wet glass is handed to him, he also gets what he likes to interpret as a special smile. A come-on? Dylan is in a mood to think so.

Returning to the table and seat he had occupied before dancing with Shelly, Dylan wonders about the sexy smile. He's all but sure it suggested invitation. At this very moment, all his companions, en masse, decide to depart. The plan is to go for a swim – skinny dipping? Dylan doesn't care. He wants to finish the brandy. In seconds, the bar empties, leaving Dylan as its lone patron. He twists his body around to catch another look at the sexy barmaid. She is busying herself cleaning and wiping behind the bar. Dylan returns his attention to his brandy glass.

Five minutes go by. From behind Dylan's back, a second brandy glass is placed on the table and alongside the glass, a bottle. It's the hot bar girl. With some elegance, she pulls away a chair from the table and sits opposite Dylan. She pours some brandy from the bottle into her glass. "Why do you drink that kerosene?" she asks Dylan in Spanish, gesturing toward his glass. "It is made for the proletariat and English tourists. Go and pour yours down the sink and come and enjoy some of this with me." Dylan is too surprised to speak.

Almost meekly, he gets to his feet and navigates to the sink behind the bar, holding his glass rigidly in front of him. He returns to the table and extends the glass, feeling like Oliver asking for more porridge. "Pour it yourself," says the bar girl. "I've poured enough drinks for one day."

Dylan is aware of being scrutinized as he glugs brandy into his glass, raises it to greet "salud!," and moves it to his lips to take a sip. The brandy is smooth and its effect soothing after the harsh firewater he was consuming moments before. Dylan continues to feel self-conscious. The hot bar girl has not changed her stance and continues to stare him down with what appears to be a disapproving expression on her face. "What?" says Dylan to break the silence, gesturing dramatically with his arms in a manner that he thinks might be considered Hispanic.

"I am called 'Gabriela,'" announces the bar girl without any warmth. "You are Dee'lan. I know because I overheard your friends using your name. I have never heard this name before. It is a strange name. You can call me 'Gabi.'" Dylan moves his hand toward Gabi for a handshake. The movement of his arm makes him aware that the beer and the brandy have been to work on his senses and he's no longer sober.

Gabriela disdainfully eyes Dylan's outstretched hand. Dylan withdraws his hand. "A man does not shake hands with a woman in Spain," Gabriela informs Dylan.

"Are you the Gabi in 'Gabi's Disco'?" asks Dylan, ignoring the put-down. Was he supposed to kiss her?

"Yes, I own the bar," replies Gabriela. "Pablo, the regular barman, has his night off on Tuesdays so I usually work in his place. I also help out on Saturdays when we have a band."

"Strange. I've never seen you in here before," says Dylan.

"I have seen you in here before," responds Gabi. "You come in with your noisy friends, who only have time for themselves, and drive my other customers out." Dylan shrugs apologetically. "Where did you learn to speak Spanish?" asks Gabi. "You seem almost fluent, but you have an accent – Colombia or Venezuela?"

"Venezuela," responds Dylan. "I attended primary school there for a few years. Half the school day was conducted in English, the other half in Spanish."

"I would like to learn English. My daughter is seven and she is already learning in school. I try to get her to speak to me in English, but she gives up. She says 'Mama, you are hopeless.'"

Dylan looks for a wedding band. "Where is your husband?" he asks.

"We are separated. My husband is in Argentina. Making his fortune, no doubt. We have been separated for five years. We were childhood novios who got married too young. Married before we realized there were other people in the world. Married when we were still children." Gabi sighs. "If you can call eighteen a child," she muses staring into her brandy glass. She looks at Dylan. "How old are you, Dee'lan?"

"Well, I'm certainly a long way past my eighteenth birthday," responds Dylan earnestly, reckoning that the event was indeed three months in the past and hoping not to be questioned to provide more details about his age. Gabi gives him a penetrating look, along with a grin to question this declaration.

"Are you sure? You don't have to lie to me; I serve drinks to anyone who has a thirst. Some of your friends look like they are twelve, no? We have no minimum drinking age here."

Dylan is indignant. The brandy makes his blood rise, even though he is attempting to conduct a flirtation here. But Gabriela is quick to detect this. She strokes a soothing finger down his face. "Tut, tut," she says flirtatiously, "you are a big boy, I'm sure. You have a baby face, no? But it is a pretty face too, even though it gets angry a little too quickly."

The same brandy that brought blood quickly to the boil cools it just as quickly in response to the sensual touch of a woman applied to an angry cheek. Dylan grins and looks slightly abashed. He knocks back the remaining brandy in his glass. Gabi pours in another two fingers worth. She is still working on her first shot.

Gabi and Dylan talk. The empty bar acquires an intimacy, despite the reality that it could be breached at any moment by an unwanted customer seeking alcohol. But this does not happen. In talking, the pair somehow evolves into a couple. At least, this is Dylan's take on the scene. In truth, Dylan is doing most of the talking and Gabi, listening. She wants to know about Dylan's life in the gulag. What is this gulag, she asks? Dylan is aware that most females enjoy hearing about the bizarre life of the English boarding school; it is a world that is so utterly alien to this age. Especially when embellished by Dylan. He is flattered that this exotic, older woman is sufficiently interested in him to listen to him babble. But it soon becomes apparent that Dylan is getting pissed. As his conversation becomes more animated, his speech becomes slurred.

At midnight, Gabi decides she is going to close up early. No customers are likely to appear after midnight on a Wednesday morning. There is a problem. Dylan is so drunk, he has difficulty getting to his feet. Gabriela is worried. Does she want to deliver a drunk, teenaged foreigner back to his mama and papa living in the rich people's houses on the sea front? Not likely. Did she get him drunk? No, he got himself drunk. But she might have helped him along a little by listening so intently. The truth is, she actually enjoyed listening to him, until the point he became smashed. Now he can barely talk or move.

Dylan awakes the next morning. Giant fingers are prying his eyelids open. Light sears his optical nerves and intrudes deeper to stir consciousness. A sensation of excruciating pain emanating from his temples, but extending through the length of his spine throbs in sync with the beat of his heart. Dylan blinks. The fingers working his eyelids open are not those of a giant, but of a small child. Dylan blinks again. He is in an entirely unfamiliar location. Evidently, he is lying on a couch. Dylan focuses on the child; a skinny girl in a nightdress. Brown-eyed, with long dark hair, she is holding a knitted stuffed toy to her breast; maybe some kind of homemade teddy bear.

"Mama, he is awake," calls out the child at the top of her lungs. She does so in Spanish. Dylan launches himself to a half-sitting position on the couch to reckon his surroundings. He twists around to focus on Mama. Memories of the previous evening download randomly into consciousness. Gabriela of Gabi's Disco. All that brandy and bravado attempting to impress a hot older woman. Hopefully, he didn't make an idiot of himself. And how did he get here? He inspects under the blanket covering him. He's dressed only in a T-shirt and boxers. Where are his pants?

"Mama," calls out the child, standing back, but still staring intently at Dylan, "is he a boy or a man?"

"That is yet to be determined," responds Gabi with a grin and a wink at Dylan. "Dee-lan, allow me to present to you my daughter, Isabela. Now Isabela, Deelan was a very naughty boy last night and that's why he comes to be inhabiting our couch."

"Should he not have been sent to his room if he was so very bad?" enquires Isabela earnestly, "and what kind of name is Dee-lan? And why did you bring him home, Mama?"

"I think I will let Dee-lan explain all that to you. He might need some coffee first, though. Dee-lan speaks English. You can talk to him in English."

Isabela stands two feet back from the couch, scrutinizing Dylan. She shifts her weight from one foot to the other. In English, she says, "how old are jyou? I am say-ven years of age."

Dylan blinks. He does not want Gabi to know his real age; not yet, anyway. "I would say I was at least three times your age." Isabela swats Dylan indignantly with the knitted teddy bear.

"Mentiroso!" she accuses, "Jyou are no twaintee one. Pia thinks you are lying, too." It appears that Pia is the name of the knitted soft toy that doubles as a weapon.

Dylan ignores her. He turns to Gabriela and asks in Spanish, "Where are my pants?"

"The pants are in the wash," responds Gabi. "You spilled my best brandy on them last night." Then turning to her daughter, "Isa, go and get this bad boy who lies about his age Micaela's housecoat."

Turning to face Dylan, she continues, "You can wear my friend Micaela's house-coat so that no one has to see your calzoncillos tontos with the smiling sun faces."

Dylan lifts the blanket. Not a thoughtful choice of boxers, he thinks. He's owned these since his fourteenth birthday. The boxer shorts were a gift from his mother, who continued to think of him as a ten-year-old until he was mid-way through his teenage years. Perhaps thoughtful on her part, to ensure he took care to whom he took his pants off in front of. He makes a mental note to remind himself that, when selecting underpants to wear for the day, to always think about who might see them if you get into a situation where you have to take them off.

"Who is Micaela?" asks Dylan.

Isa has returned with an elegant blue silk housecoat and tosses it toward Dylan. "She is Mama's friend," she responds before her mama can, nodding her head in a slow exaggerated manner. "She stays with us too often. When she stays, she sleeps in Mama's bed."

"Now, Isa," says Gabi, "we know that is because we only have two bedrooms."

The rebuke provokes Isa to roll her eyes upward. Gabi responds with authority. "Now Dee-lan, put on the housecoat … but before you do, show Isa your silly un-derpants … then come and have some breakfast."

Dylan twists around on the couch to plant his feet onto the floor. He removes the blanket and stands to slip on the housecoat, but in doing so exposes enough of the smiling sun face images on his boxer shorts to send Isa into a fit of exaggerated giggles.

"He is a boy for sure, Mama," declares Isa. "He may be awfully tall, but no real man would wear such ridiculous calzoncillos!" Dylan frowns at this impudent child, who appears so determined to reduce him to her status level rather than accord him his due merit – that of an adult and an equal to her mother. But something else intrudes on his thoughts. What could it mean if Gabi sleeps with this Micaela? The Micaela who owns the housecoat he is wearing. Could it be that Gabi is a lesbian? Do lesbians have children? Recalling his experiences with Tom and Jane, he wonders if it's possible she converted to lesbianism?

Isabela soon gives up her efforts to communicate with Dylan in English; it requires too much thought. She reverts to Spanish.

"It is my pleasure to formally introduce you to Pia," she announces to Dylan. She is holding the knitted soft toy she used to strike him a few moments earlier by each paw. Isabela, the puppeteer, dances Pia the soft toy over Dylan's thighs, accompanied by a little hum. "I think Pia may come to like you," declares Isabela, while still orchestrating the dance.

"Isa's Pia has three roles," chirps in Gabi from the kitchen. "The first is that of a weapon. Your introduction to Pia has already allowed you to experience that role." Isabela rolls her eyes heavenward to nod agreement with her mother. "The next role is that of a puppet, as Isa is demonstrating to you. And the final and most important role …. Pia is Isa's cuddle toy and confidante. She can never be without Pia."

Now, Isa shakes her head gravely from side to side. "Never at any time," declares the little girl resolutely.

Gabi is making arepas. In his drunken state the previous evening, Dylan confided that he acquired a love for the corn flour bread widely consumed in Venezuela as a breakfast dish and snack. Gabi has visited Venezuela and happens to have some of the coarse milled corn flour required to make the dish in her pantry. Over breakfast, Dylan discovers that Gabriela and Isabela in some ways function more like sisters than mother and daughter. Much of the conversation bantered by mother and daughter is a sequence of tease, joust, and cajole. Dylan's sore head to some extent restricts his participation in this exchange of chatter to that of a spectator. Isa and her mother also switch into Catalán when they don't want Dylan to understand something.

Strong coffee mitigates Dylan's hungover state. After consuming a breakfast of fruit, followed by arepas, Isa is sent off to bathe and dress. Gabi and Dylan discuss bullfighting. Gabi's opinion is that bullfighting shames Spain in the eyes of the world and should be banned. Dylan opines otherwise. He has read Hemingway on the subject of bullfighting and opts to regurgitate the famous author's opinions on bullfighting as an allegory of life itself, the inevitable conquest of "el macho" by feminine guile. This is completely contrary to Dylan's real feelings on the subject of bullfighting. He has attended all of three bullfights in his life and was secretly appalled by what he witnessed. One was so gruesome and drawn out, he was all but physically sick and he could not get it out of his thoughts for days afterward. At its most skillful execution, the debacle of life and death did not even come close to being surgical at its denouement. More often than not, closure was a prolonged and gruesome series of thrusts and stabs before a braying crowd. Observation of the crowd both fascinated and appalled Dylan – it was more frightening than the bullfight itself. Would it be any different if a human gladiator was to take the place of the bull? A crowd whooping in an ecstatic frenzy while an animal slowly choked itself to death vomiting blood was maybe a crowd you did not want to mess around with. When Gabi passionately argues that the collective hysteria of the bullfight crowd is a reason in itself to have it banned, Dylan elects to completely disagree. He does not know why. It is the macho thing to do, is it not? Hemingway would have done the same.

Gabi stops talking and studies Dylan. Slowly she says, "I sense you have little conviction in your own words. Which reflects well on you in one sense, but I wonder why you feel you have to be dishonest with me. Is it just for the sake of disagreeing?" Dylan feels sheepish. Can he really be that transparent that someone who barely knows him can catch him out telling a pointless lie? A stupid lie – whatever did he hope to achieve by telling it? Gabi shakes her head and makes him feel even smaller.

Isa rescues him. The child returns to the living room, bathed and wearing a starched white dress and armed with a hairbrush. She twirls around to display the dress. Then she approaches Dylan on the couch and taps the hairbrush on his thigh. "You can broosh my hair," she orders, speaking in English once again. In her mind, she is bestowing something of an honor on him.

Mama intervenes, not speaking in English. "Deelan does not know how to brush and fix the hair of a girl," she says. "Come to Mama and I will do for you." Isa ignores Mama – in fact, she does not turn to acknowledge her. Resolutely, Isa taps the back of the hairbrush on Dylan's thigh a second time.

Of course, Dylan knows how to brush and fix the hair of a girl. He did this for the first time when he was around Isabela's age, under the tutelage of his friend Carrie. Back then, pernickety Carrie trained him to do French braids with expertise. Dylan opens his palm to receive the hairbrush. "Come," says Dylan to Isabela, taking the hairbrush, "I will make you beautiful. I will make you a princess in French braids."

French braids are new to Isa. She sits herself on the floor, pert and cross-legged, while Dylan attends her from behind, seated on the couch. As Dylan works, she becomes increasingly impatient to see the result of whatever is going on behind her back. Dylan makes her wait until he is finished. Eventually, she gets to impose herself in front of a mirror. The small girl is ecstatic with the result. Even Gabi is impressed. "You have made a friend for life," she tells Dylan. Dylan hopes she is referring not just to her daughter. It helps him restore some of the self-esteem lost in the debate of the bullfight.

After the triumph of the French braids, Dylan figures that his hangover will require more nurturing than a couple of cups of strong, black coffee. He retreats and makes his way home, where his plan is to sleep for the remainder of the day.

Despite a number of visits to Gabi's Bar, a couple of weeks go by before Dylan encounters Gabriela behind the bar a second time. As before, it is a mid-week night in which Pablo has a night off. There is no one in the bar other than a small group of teenagers, drinking and being loud at a corner table. Dylan is acquainted with and bored with all of this crowd of kids, "home" from their schools Stateside, in Switzerland, England, or wherever. They make him feel old and out of place. He will avoid this group tonight.

Dylan seats himself at the bar and orders a beer. Gabi says nothing, but raises her eyebrows in a manner that seems to question him. Dylan's mind is made up. His prey this evening will be Gabi. He studies her as she goes about her business of dispensing alcohol and collecting cash. In serving her customers, she uses an array of seductive and flirtatious facial expressions. This makes sense, thinks Dylan. Almost all of the drinks are purchased at the bar by guys. Gabi seldom has to deal with a gal. Female customers remain seated, waiting for the guys to bring them their drinks.

Because Dylan is the only customer sitting at the bar, during those moments Gabi is not actually serving drinks, she moves over to chat with Dylan. Dylan asks her how Isa is. Then he asks her how Micaela is. "I don't believe you met Micaela?" asks Gabi, not sure.

"No. I just wore her housecoat, remember?"

Gabi laughs in recollection. "Oh yes, when you were wearing your silly underpants with the sun faces. Isabela still laughs about that – she refers to you as the 'boy with the calzoncillos tontos.' She wants know if all Americanos wear such underpants or whether 'Deelan is merely a bizarre exception'?"

Dylan makes a face at her. He is, however, comforted by the knowledge that the boxer shorts he is wearing this evening under his jeans are unlikely to provoke much hilarity if circumstance requires them to be revealed to either a lover or to the world. Using one of her flirtatious smiles, Gabi reaches up from the bar to pinch his cheek. Dylan interprets this as him being treated like a child, rather than the man he wants Gabi to see him as. Accordingly, he leans back out of her grasp.

There is movement at the table occupied by the group of gringos. In unison, they rise up to leave. They are going somewhere together to party and Dylan is asked if he wants to join. He does not. For a second time, Dylan and the beautiful Gabriela are alone in Gabi's bar. This time, Dylan resolves that he is not going to come close to being in a drunken state. The strategy now is to be invited back to Gabi's home and perhaps to her bed.

Dylan determines to take a direct approach. Immediately, he asks Gabi for a kiss. Gabi raises her eyebrows as if it is the most astonishing proposal that has ever been made to her. Dylan cajoles. Unexpectedly, Gabi changes tack. She declares to Dylan that she is owed a kiss on each cheek from him. He owes her these kisses for being so uncouth as to offer his hand rather than his lips when they were introduced two weeks earlier. Gabi leans forward over the bar toward Dylan and turns her head slightly to offer him her cheek. Dylan responds. He slowly kisses the cheek offered, then with both hands cupping Gabi's face just under the jaw, he turns her head to give the other cheek the same treatment. In doing so, he does his best to make the touch of his lips sensual and he senses that Gabi is playing along. Then he steers her lips toward his. Gabi allows him to do this, and Dylan observes that her eyes are closed. In a dry kiss, Dylan caresses her lips with his. He attempts a dry nibble. While Gabi does not respond, neither does she resist. Dylan then introduces his tongue into the game. Instantly, Gabi reacts angrily. "Tonto," she chastises wiping her mouth, "you just ruined a nice moment. That is not how we greet friends in Spain." Her rage is projected with histrionic Latin artifice that messages Dylan that, contrary to her words, Gabi actually did not too much object to the kiss.

Dylan leans back from the bar and laughs. Gabi continues to be in her fake huff. She picks up a cleaning cloth and busies herself wiping down counters behind the bar with furious aggression. She is muttering under her breath, but she is doing it in Catalán, so Dylan is unable to make much sense of her words. "Gabi, are you going to take me home with you tonight? I want to make mad, passionate love to you. I am sure there must be a full moon outside."

Gabi pauses her scrubbing of the counters to stare amazed at Dylan. "Where do you learn to speak such nonsense? You, who are barely out of short pants. In Spain, gentlemen don't speak to ladies in this way."

Dylan chuckles again. "I am no gentleman, recuerdas? Just a man passionately in love with a beautiful woman." He takes a swig from the bottle of San Miguel in front of him.

The declaration reaps another "tonto" from Gabi, but there is a hint of a smile on her face now. Still, Dylan is wondering where this could be leading, and he senses that he may be a little out of his league, recalling the embarrassment of the bullfight debate. He's on the verge of leaving the bar and making his way home when Gabi suggests, "I suppose you can accompany me home for a coffee and to entertain me with your silly talk." Dylan nods his head slowly up and down. Yes, that would be an excellent idea. If this was a sexual come-on, this time round he'd make sure he was up for the challenge. Drink no brandy tonight!

Dylan cannot figure Gabi out. Is she genuinely interested in him as a person and possible sex partner, or is she just intrigued by his not-so-ordinary social history? Dylan will go with the flow and see where it leads. It leads first to Gabi's automobile, an ancient Seat 850 that bumps and grinds its way to her apartment.

There is a brief, awkward moment when the pair arrives at Gabi's apartment. Babysitting for Isabela is an aunt of Gabi's who, at the sight of Dylan, becomes curt with Gabi and scowls with disapproval. But this brief exchange is over within a minute, as the aunt departs, and Dylan and Gabi engage each other in conversation.

Once there, Gabi wants to know more about life in an English boarding school. She wants to know about Dylan's past loves. Even the minutia, perhaps especially the minutia, of his brief sexual history. Gabi expresses disbelief. Is it not shocking that these English girls lose their virginity and their pride at fourteen years old? Who will marry such girls? And what kind of teacher's wife would seduce a boy of just fifteen years?

Dylan is disarmed by her incredulity. He laughs. "So how old were you when you had your first lover?" he asks.

"It is not something a woman would tell a boy like you," responds Gabriela with some disdain. "It was not before my wedding night." Dylan looks at her. Perhaps it is time to attempt to kiss her again, he wonders. He leans toward her lips. His initial intention is to cup her face between his palms and guide her lips to his. But this is not what Gabi wants. She grasps a hand in each of hers and guides them away from her face.

"Put your hands behind your back and remain sitting on the couch," she orders. "Do exactly that, like a good boy, and you can have your kiss." Dylan shrugs, but then obeys. Now Gabi cups Dylan's cheeks and moves her lips to his. The kiss begins dry and shallow, but quickly progresses to some in-depth probing. A point comes when Dylan unlocks his hands from behind his back but, before he can move them to assist in the seduction, Gabi breaks away from the kiss. She stands and, with exasperation approaching anger, strides out of the room. Dylan is confused. Within seconds, Gabi returns. She brandishes a set of plastic handcuffs. Dylan remembers owning a similar set of handcuffs when he was around six years old. They were an auxiliary extra in a set of Lone Ranger six shooters and holsters.

Wordlessly, Gabi motions that she is going to place the handcuffs over Dylan's wrists. She mimes that no more kissing will take place until the issue of Dylan's wandering hands has been neutralized. Dylan grins. Surely this is just some kind of kinky game? Why not play along? The toy handcuffs are unlikely to provide any real resistance to escape, should he become determined enough. He hams up a coy expression and dutifully holds his hands behind his back for cuffing. Click, click. The cuffs ratchet closed to one cog beyond wrist-tight.

Gabi unbuttons Dylan's shirt. She looks into his eyes as she loosens the belt around his jeans, then unzips the fly. She separates the fly to form a vee and frees just the tip of Dylan's penis from the top of his underwear. Dylan looks down to study his seductress's handiwork. Gabi tosses her head back and laughs. "You are in my power," she declares with exaggerated triumph. She moves her hands to Dylan's bare stomach and delicately strokes it. Suddenly, she begins to tickle. Detecting a vulnerability in Dylan to this manner of touch, she increases the intensity of the tickling. Dylan doubles up, lurches, and twists to evade the tickling fingers. He rolls to the opposite end of the couch and awkwardly gets to his feet, hindered by his jeans, which have progressed further downward over his hips. He suspects he appears somewhat ludicrous.

"OK," he says, no longer laughing, "remove the cuffs; I don't want to play any more." Gabi ignores him. She gets to her feet and, holding Dylan's shoulders, draws him toward her. She closes her lips onto his and kisses him deeply. Dylan responds for the immediate high, though in the back of his mind, he suspects that if he wants to change his predicament, this might not be so smart.

The instant Gabi senses a response from Dylan, she moves one hand from his shoulder down into the vee formed by the open fly of his jeans. She finds his penis and in moments, works him to orgasm with a seasoned woman's knowledge of how to bring a man off. Flushed and puffed, with his head resting on Gabi's shoulder, Dylan reflects on what has transpired. He has just come rather messily into a fully dressed woman's hand, shooting jism up her wrist and over her blouse. In addition, he remains cuffed.

Gabi slowly separates. Dylan resumes his seat on the couch. Gabi crosses the room and sequentially pulls a series of tissues from a box to wipe the remains of Dylan's sperm off her clothing and hand. Armed with the box of tissues, she kneels in front of Dylan. She pulls his jeans and boxers lower down his hips and carefully applies herself to wiping him clean. This procedure is executed with a detailed fastidiousness that ensures that Dylan has become fully aroused once again before she has finished. He twists his torso around to demonstrate that he remains cuffed and wants her to remove the handcuffs. Gabi shakes her head. "No, you have been a bad boy," she says authoritatively. "You must prove that you can behave yourself. Only then will I remove the handcuffs."

Dylan is miffed. With all of the might he can muster, he attempts to rip the cuffs apart. This does little more than threaten to lacerate his wrists. Gabi observes him with a grin on her face. Next, Dylan attempts to draw his underwear and pants up over his hips, but this task proves to be all but impossible with his hands cuffed behind his back.   Gabi approaches him and, with both hands, yanks both his underpants and jeans back down around his ankles. Defeated and exasperated, Dylan retreats to curl into a fetal sitting position on the couch, pondering a different tactic. Gabi seems set to subjugate, if not humiliate him.

Smug Gabi crosses to the refrigerator on the kitchen side of the room and removes a bottle of white wine. She uncorks the bottle and pours herself a glass. She takes a sip. Then, as a teasing afterthought, offers Dylan some, too. Dylan nods in the affirmative. Gabi pours the glass, crosses the room, and places it on the side table by the couch. She leans over and attempts to plant a maternal kiss on Dylan's forehead. Dylan twists away to evade the kiss. "How can I drink the wine with my hands behind my back?"

"Pobrecito!" coos Gabi. "If you desire the wine, you will find a way."

Dylan does desire the wine and, with some twisting, leans his torso over the armrest of the couch to position his lips over the glass. By extending his tongue, he manages to just dip it into the wine. The tongue draws only enough wine to titillate the palate. "If you ask me very nicely," suggests Gabi, "I may be kind and hold the glass to your lips. It is an excellent Torremolinos vintage, one of my favorites; a wine to be sipped and given time to pleasure the senses."

By now, Dylan has synthesized his situation. Gabi takes pleasure in being in control, perhaps even in humiliating him. Pleading with the woman is probably just what she wants. If he is to gain freedom from the cuffs and get his pants pulled up, nothing short of outwitting Gabi will be required. To this point in the game, the reverse has been true. He is not about to allow her to feed him a glass of wine. When Gabi raises the glass to Dylan's lips, he looks her directly in the eye and keeps his face expressionless. Gabi gently strokes the rim of the cold glass across Dylan's lower lip. His nose notes the fruit of the grape. Despite being able to almost taste the wine, Dylan knows that for the sake of his dignity, he must resist its seductive charm. Coldly, he continues to stare down Gabi. She withdraws the glass. "You are not being very much fun tonight."

An impasse ensues. Gabi takes another sip of wine. She grins provocatively at Dylan, but is interrupted from any further deeds by the creaking of an opening door. Gabi's eyes open wide to register the event. Little bare feet pitter-patter down the hallway, heading toward the living room. Isabela! Gabi leaps to her feet and has to move quickly to cut her daughter off before the scene on her couch acquires a witness. While Dylan has good reasons for not wanting anybody to witness him in his current state, Gabi has more compelling reasons for shielding her seven-year-old from a scene that would be impossible to rationalize.

Isa has had a bad dream and is crying. A cruel witch has been hiding under her bed! The little girl requires comforting and a glass of water. Comforting will require cuddles and time. The glass of water must be sourced from the kitchen. Gabi scoops tearful Isa off her feet just as she is about to exit the hallway and enter the living room. She carries the girl toward the bathroom, insisting that the first and foremost of her priorities is to have a pee. Isa vigorously protests. She insists she does not need a pee. Mama assures her daughter that no other remediation can take place until Isa has entirely emptied her bladder, even if the contents of that bladder be modest.

After depositing Isabela on the toilet, Gabi runs back into the living room and in a panic, orders Dylan to stand on his feet. This is better, thinks Dylan. Who has the upper hand now? Gabi franticly pulls up Dylan's underpants and jeans; how can it be that they are so much more difficult to wrestle over thighs and hips than to pull off? This is achieved, but before she can attend to the cosmetics of zips and buttons, the sound of the toilet flushing jolts her, and she pushes the still-cuffed Dylan back into a sitting position on the couch. Running again, Gabi intercepts her daughter by scooping her up and perching her, infant style, straddling her hip.

Dylan contemplates the sight of Gabi panicked and nervous and surmises that the balance of power has shifted to favor him now that there is another player in the room. From the onset, Isabela senses panic in her mother and ceases crying. Something is going on, and she's not about to be hastily packed off to bed again with a glass of water and a goodnight kiss. Perceptive Isabela immediately notices Dylan parked on the couch. Over her mother's shoulder, she points to him. "I want to say hello to Deelan," she informs Gabi and attempts to wriggle herself free from her mother's arms. Gabi is not pleased and overreacts. She strengthens her grip on her daughter.

"It is late Isa and this is not a social opportunity for you. You can have your water and go straight back to bed." Isa bursts into tears. Please Mama, no, no, no, she appeals. The nightmare will surely recur if she is sent back to bed without sufficient recuperation time. She will have the same dream again. And the outcome will not be a pretty one. How would Mama like having a witch living under her bed? Exasperated, Gabi lowers Isa to the floor. Isa immediately ceases the crying. She glugs some water from the glass her mother has handed her.

Isabela approaches the couch holding Pia by a paw. She climbs on to sit beside Dylan and proffers a cheek for a kiss. Dylan leans over to provide the kiss. "Your trousers are not fastened," observes Isabela, "and why are you holding your hands behind your back?"

Gabi approaches Dylan, bearing a plastic key. She winks at Dylan, hoping for complicity. "Deelan was playing a foolish game and somehow got himself locked into the handcuffs. Only silly Deelan could manage to do that to himself."

Dylan nods agreement and makes a goofy face for Isa.

"Silly boy, Deel," says Isa. Dylan leans forward and raises his wrists behind his back, leaning away from the couch to allow Gabi to unlock the cuffs. Thus freed, he stands to zip the fly and button the waist of the jeans. As he sits back down, Isa scoots over to seat herself on his lap. Holding Pia by both knitted paws, she then puppeteers the toy into a little dance to entertain Dylan. And perhaps entertain her mama, too. She hums a little tune to accompany the bear's dance. "How nice of you to visit again," says Isa. "I have decided to call you Deel – it pleases me more than Dylan. Can Deel sleep with me, Mama?"

"No," responds Mama abruptly, "Deelan can sleep on the couch."

"But Mama, he is longer than the couch. Where will he put his legs?"

Gabi thinks. "Isa," she adjudicates, "you can sleep in my bed with me. Deelan can sleep in your bed." This makes Isa happy.

"I will lend you a teddy bear to keep you warm," Isa reassures Dylan, then whispers in his ear, "but take care the witch does not get you." Then she turns to address her mama, "Mama, we are to call him Deel from now on.   It is our new name for him."

*   *   *

Later the following morning, Isa, Gabi, and Dylan go to the beach. Gabi wears a one-piece swimsuit. She is the most naked Dylan has seen her. He likes what he sees. Gabi is lying on her back, stretched out on a towel. Large sunglasses cover most of her face and her eyes are closed behind them. There is an unoccupied towel next to Gabi. This towel is Dylan's. Shortly after arriving, Dylan succumbs to a request by Isa to allow himself to be buried under sand. To oblige this request, he moves ten feet in front of Gabi to lie face down in the sand. The positioning is strategic. Dylan props his chin on crossed hands and studies Gabi's groin, nicely displayed by the fact that Gabi's legs are slightly apart.

Isa methodically flicks sand over Dylan's body with a red plastic shovel. After the first hot shovel loads, the sand is mostly cool and damp on Dylan's skin. Dylan observes Gabi. Or more accurately, he observes Gabi's groin concealed by the crotch of the navy blue swimsuit. One stray pube has escaped the confines of the garment. There is evidence of pubes removed at the top of her legs outside of the confines of the swim garment. Sleepily, Gabi inserts a finger under the elasticized boundary at the crotch of the swimsuit and slides it downward over her pubis. As a result, whether intentional or not, the previously errant pube becomes concealed. Dylan determines that he must sleep with this beautiful woman who has had sex with him without permitting him to come close to having sex with her.

Isabela dumps a shovelful of sand over Dylan's head, jolting his thoughts. As he shakes his head in an attempt to throw off some of the sand, Isa laughs. "You are all covered now. Are you going to come swimming with me yet?"

"Will your mama come, too?"

"No, Mama does not go into the ocean. She comes to the beach to sunbathe. She swims in a swimming pool sometimes. She must not get her hair wet." Dylan exaggerates the difficulty of moving under the sand to please Isabela. He groans loudly, as if fighting the weight of the sand. But then in a vigorous push-up thrust and inward tuck of his legs, he launches himself to his feet in a single movement.

"Are you as strong as Tarzan?" asks Isabela, impressed.

"Much stronger than Tarzan," boasts Dylan. "Only Superman can come close to me." He raises an arm to clench a bicep.

"Does that mean you can fly?" asks dead-serious Isa.

"Of course," responds Dylan in earnest, "so can you. Hold my hand. We can fly together."

Isa and Dylan link hands and run as fast as Isa can manage toward the sea. They continue to run until deep enough into the water that the waves cut their legs from under them and they roll into the surf, laughing. Isa sits on the sea floor, seriously impressed. "We did fly for a moment," she insists. "Just before we crashed, I'm sure we were flying. Maybe we did not run fast enough to actually take off?"

"We should try again," suggests Dylan, just as serious. This becomes a game ritual. One that Isa is unlikely to abandon in a hurry.

While playing in the surf with Isa, from the corner of an eye, Dylan observes a woman, elegantly attired in a white pants suit, leaning over and conversing with Gabi. Gabi remains lying on her back, but has propped herself into a semi-sitting position on her elbows. Isa and Dylan continue their attempts to take off, each succeeding effort seemingly outdoing the one that preceded it. In a way, Isa is indeed flying, because Dylan is launching the child off her feet at the critical moment before the wipe-out.

Back on the beach, Gabi's companion kicks off her shoes and assumes a place on the towel that was Dylan's when they first arrived at the beach. Dylan watches every movement, but Isa is unaware. He suggests to Isa that they go for a swim into deeper water. Isa grips Dylan's shoulders from behind and kicks her feet to assist, while Dylan uses a breaststroke to power them away from the shoreline. Isa advises Dylan not to swim too far out. They may attract a shark. Dylan assures Isa that Superman can take care of any old shark that is likely to swim into the Mediterranean.

Fifty meters out, Dylan pilots them around to face the shore and treads water. "Who is that with your mama on the beach, Isa?" asks Dylan.

Isa thrusts her head forward over Dylan's shoulders and squints to scrutinize the scene on the beach. She turns toward Dylan and makes a sad clown face. "It is Micaela. I do not love her much. She is bossy and has little love for children. She tells Mama that I should be sent to abuela to live. In truth, Micaela is a bruja. I will tell her you are my brother who has come to protect me. Then maybe she will not be so evil!"

The meeting with Micaela was destined. Dripping wet Isa and Dylan retreat from the water and approach Gabriela and Micaela. Shivering, teeth-chattering Isa retrieves a towel from her mother's side and wraps herself into its warmth. She hops from one foot to the other. Micaela proffers a cheek at the youngster, her gesture indicating that she is expecting a kiss. Reluctantly but dutifully, Isa pecks her on each cheek. "Deelan," says Gabi, "I want to introduce you to my dear friend Micaela."

Wet and dripping, Dylan approaches reclined Micaela, who squints up to take measure of him. As he bends over to either kiss or shake hands, he's not sure which, a flood of drips decides to release itself from his hair, wetting Micaela's pristine white pantsuit. She twists to avoid the shower, but the effort is futile. She curls her lip at Dylan in disdain. "Sorry," apologizes Dylan, "I would have dried off first, but you are lying on my towel."

With manifest distaste, Micaela offers a hand for a greeting kiss.

"Encantado," declares Dylan, "I have heard so many wonderful things about you from Isa." Isa pauses her shivering and hopping to raise her eyebrows at Dylan.

Surely Dylan is not going to betray her? Dylan winks at Isa. Isa relaxes. Gabi looks confused. What has Isa been telling Dylan about Micaela?

Dylan thinks that, in appearance, Micaela is actually quite foxy. He studies her body, her face, her expressions, her husky voice. She has a lighter complexion than Gabi's and is older by a few years; maybe she is around thirty. She radiates a certain feminine elegance and sophistication that comes with age. Dylan has previously admired, although never experienced this type of woman. In his world, women like this appear on movie screens rather than on the beach. Would he guess Micaela to be a lesbian? Not likely. Quite fuckable is his conclusion. Especially if he could engage her in a ménage a trois, along with Gabi. A tasty fantasy, indeed!

A short while later, Micaela, Gabriela, Isabela, and Dylan are lunching at the yacht club as Micaela's treat. They order a paella marinera, then settle into light conversation. Isa informs Micaela that Dylan is her new brother. Micaela looks down her nose at Dylan. From whence has this abrasive gringo appeared, she seems to ask. Just what is the nature of Gabi's attraction to this mere boy? How far has this infatuation gotten? If indeed it is an infatuation. Added to which, she doesn't need anyone around for Isabela to collude with. She will simply have to get rid of him.

Isa has climbed up onto Dylan's lap. The two have isolated themselves and are busy making a mess with crayons on a paper placemat. Good, thinks Micaela. Now she can work on Gabi. She has been trying to persuade Gabi to deposit Isabela at her grandparents' home in Valencia. This will allow Gabi and Micaela to spend some quality time in Micaela's beach house up the coast in Lloret without having a seven-year-old brat underfoot.

At the mention of Lloret, Isa is alerted to danger. This is the renewal of an ongoing dialogue. Isa has thus far managed to persuade her mother that being optioned off to abuela in Valencia will represent abandonment. Especially if such an outrage were to occur during the school summer vacation. Isa slides off Dylan's lap and insinuates herself into her mother's range of caresses, making sure she stands on the opposite side of her mother to the one on which Micaela sits.

With Isa's departure from his lap, Dylan can focus on Micaela. He asks her what she does for a living. Micaela places oversized, designer sunglasses over her face. Reluctantly, she turns to face Dylan. She tells him she owns an art gallery in the town of Castellón. The gallery only stocks the work of the finest Catalán artists. The Catalán artists exhibited in Micaela's gallery all have one thing in common – every one of them is female. "Are there no Catalán male artists worthy of exhibition?" asks Dylan, intentionally cheeky.

"They are not to my taste," Micaela says.

"Not even Miró and Dalí?" questions Dylan. "Assuming that either one would be willing to exhibit in the metropolis of Castellón de la Plana."

Micaela glares at him in response. Meantime, Isa has completely wheedled her way into her mother's caresses: could Mama possibly be so cruel as to abandon a daughter so loving? If Mama wants to spend a week on the beach with Micaela, then surely she should be accompanied by a devoted daughter. Better still, perhaps they could contrive to borrow her beach house and leave Micaela behind.

The food arrives. Considering her mother won over once again, Isa is content to return to her own chair between her mother and Dylan and dawdle over the small portion of paella her mother has served onto her plate. Isa picks out butterfly clams from the paella and eats them, and only them. First she sucks the tiny mouthful of meat from each clam. Then she works her tongue around each half shell to suck out any remaining liquor. She's a fussy eater.

"Mama, now that Micaela is to stay with us, can Deel sleep with me tonight?" asks innocent Isabela. Both Gabi and Micaela are caught off-guard by the question. For a moment, both of them stare at the little girl.

The pause gives Dylan time to formulate a response. "But Isa dearest," says Dylan with a twinkle in his eye, "your mama has already made sleeping arrangements for tonight. You are to sleep with your mama again in her bed. And Micaela and I will enjoy a night of wild passion in the comfort of your cozy little bed!"

This announcement produces an explosive reaction from Micaela. She leaps to her feet and launches an enraged verbal attack on Gabi, while pointing at Dylan. Much, but not all, of the tirade is conducted in the Catalán language, so Dylan understands little. Little Isabela is unfamiliar with persons who shout, especially ones who do so while addressing her mother. She tentatively slides off her chair and sidles into a standing position beside her seated mama once again. Her arm slides around her mother's waist to show her that she is there to protect her if required.

Gabi is surprisingly calm. She looks bemused at Micaela's fury. When Micaela appears to have finished, Gabi says, "Cálmate, Micaela, can you not see that Dylan only said that with the objective of getting you to behave in this absurd manner. He is just being a gringo." She turns her head to cast an accusing frown at Dylan. "A rather immature and attention-seeking gringo!"

Red-faced Micaela is in an unforgiving mood. "Either he goes or I do," swears Micaela.

"Please don't be so dramatic, Micaela," soothes Gabi. "Dylan is a harmless boy. For now, he amuses me. And it happens that he amuses Isabela, too."

Angry Micaela is in no mood to be consoled. She gathers her cigarettes and lighter and places each in her oversize purse. That done, the tall woman sashays her way out of the restaurant, swinging her hips with rather more inelegant roll than was her usual habit. Little Isa can barely contain her glee, but is smart enough not to show this to her mother. She raises her eyebrows to signal approval to Dylan.

Gabi places a protective arm around Isa and stares down into her plate of paella. She takes a sip from her wine glass. "Just in case you are feeling a little proud of yourself after that scene, Dylan, I want you to understand that your behavior was childish and rude. This is not how we treat friends in Spain."

Isa looks at her mother. Is Mama being unkind to Dylan? Confused, the child un-entwines herself from her mother and goes to Dylan's side. He needs protecting now. Dylan thinks it circumspect to allow Gabi to continue. Perhaps he was a little unfair to Micaela. But now Isa chirps up. "What is 'wild passion,' Deel? And why did it make Micaela so angry?"

This infuriates her mother, who snaps at her, "Shut up, Isabela. You are not so innocent in this affair. Micaela does her best to make herself agreeable to you and you repay her with contempt. I am not sure I like this tryst you have formed with Deelan." Tearful Isa twists her face to hide it in Dylan's chest.

Gabi takes a sip of wine. Dylan decides to apologize to Gabi. "I'm sorry, Gabi, I didn't think that Micaela would react like that. I was just having a little fun with her."

Gabriela rubs her eyes using her thumb and forefinger. "Ay, Dios mío."

Isa has perked up once again. "Can we go back to the beach, Mama?" asks Isa. "Deel and I want to practice our flying."

That night, after Isa has been read to by Gabi and tucked into bed, Dylan makes his move. Considering what took place during the day, he figures that it must be expected of him. Gabi is tired and stressed. Perhaps she is still perturbed at Micaela's abrupt exit from lunch earlier in the day. Dylan rubs Gabi's temples, thumb on one, forefinger on the other. It becomes instantly apparent to Dylan that this is a winning approach with Gabi. She almost purrs at the touch of his hand. Dylan extends the stroking movement to her skull, running his hand through her hair. After ten minutes, when Dylan attempts to stop, she pleads with him not to. He changes hands. Gabi purrs again. Lazily she asks him, "Which of your women taught you how to do that? I want to commend her."

"Maybe it was my mother," suggests Dylan.

Gabi sighs. "Somehow I don't think so," she replies, "but don't stop."

The massage to the temples and skull follows a predictable course, progressing to neck, shoulders, and back. And who can resist the seduction of a deep and sensuous back massage? Dylan's touch, though not a trained one, is driven by a burning desire to seduce. But this time it must be on equal terms. By the time he is ready to navigate the territory of Gabi's back, the older woman requires no persuasion to convince her that the touch of hand to bare flesh is preferable to that same touch insulated by the blouse. Step by step, clothes are removed and at some point, the contact veers from the questionably therapeutic to the undeniably sexual. Identifying the specific moment at which this deviation occurs depends on which of the pair might have been relating the scene. For Dylan, that moment occurs shortly after first contact, just as Gabi suspected it might. Her inclination is to view him as driven exclusively by an adolescent urge for sexual gratification. Was not everything he did just a step to further that objective? She was disinclined to cede him any ground when it came to innocence of motive. No, her task would be to channel his adolescent lust in ways that would pleasure her own desires. Whatever form those desires may take.

A little later, in bed, Dylan discovers Gabi to be a lover who requires a bedroom ambience of almost total darkness. A little night light glimmers in one corner of the room. Dylan greedily grabs at Gabi's breasts. "I want to see them," he declares, "turn the lights on."

Gabi slaps his hands away. "Behave yourself," snaps Gabi. "These are delicate. They are not for the rough hands of a boy. And in Spain we make love in the dark; we are not Swedish. If you cannot behave yourself in my bed, you will be sleeping on the couch. Now, lie back. Let me do the touching. In my house, we play by my rules."

Once again, Dylan feels he has no choice but to do as Gabi instructs if he wants to achieve his objective. At least he is not cuffed. He holds the palms of both hands up in a gesture of surrender, then lies back, placing his arms by his side. Gabi straddles him. Dylan's eyes begin to adjust to the dimmed lighting provided by the night light. Gabi gyrates her torso above Dylan's groin, and her thick pubic hair teases the tip of Dylan's penis. Dylan can withstand no more than a few moments before he thrusts upward in an effort to breach the barrier of the pubes. Gabi grabs his hips. "My rules," she cautions, wagging a finger.

Dylan laughs. But now Gabi lowers herself onto him. Dylan feels the wetness of her sex and, with a subtle wriggle of his hips, he penetrates deep inside her. Gabi instructs him to lie still. She is the one who will do the moving, if any is required. And not much is. In a sitting position, Gabi alternately contracts and relaxes vaginal muscles; to Dylan it feels as if she is pulling him ever deeper into her. This is a new experience for him.

Gabi remains straddled, sitting on top of Dylan, her hands on his collarbones as if she is looking for a wrestling pin. Dylan studies her in the dim light. Because they are barely moving, her large breasts shift only with her deep breathing. Her eyes are closed and her expression is blank. Dylan suspects that she might be making love to someone else. But things are coming to a closure. Gabi's breathing becomes more pronounced and Dylan is getting to the point where he can no longer hold back. He moves his hands to firmly grasp Gabi's hips and heaves his pelvis upward with a couple of thrusts, thrusts that precede the shuddering convulsion of orgasm; an orgasm all the more intense for having restrained his movement through the lovemaking that led to its climax. Gabi too is gasping and now leans over to lie on top of Dylan, nuzzling her face into his shoulder. She buries her hands deep into Dylan's hair and is crying. She releases blubbery sobs. The sobs do not appear to be sexual. Something else is going on here. Dylan holds Gabi's head in his hands. Gabi relaxes. Her breathing slows and Dylan feels the warm tears on his shoulder cool. Sleep.

At the first glint of dawn, Isa springs out of bed. She grabs Pia by an ear and steers herself directly into to the living room of the apartment. She has to check out Dylan. Did he spend the night on the couch? Will she have a playmate for another day? No one on the couch. Is he still here? Or does that mean that Micaela has returned. She peeks into Mama's bedroom. Silently, she opens the door a crack. There are two bodies in the bed. It is very dark. Surely one of them must be Dylan? Cautiously, she moves her body around the door. Yes, Dylan and Mama are sleeping together. Awed, she pauses. Might this mean that Dylan could become her papa? She wonders about this for a moment. Yes, there could be some advantages to such an arrangement – she and Dylan might practice flying a lot more often. But then, would Dylan become her papi or would he be more of a Señor to Mama? Would he send her to bed early like her friends' papas?

Isa approaches the bed. Dylan is lying on his back with one arm extended. Mama is lying on her side with her face lying in the crook of Dylan's armpit. Dylan's extended arm is her pillow. Both Mama and Dylan are naked, at least from the waist up. This probably means that they have been playing mummies and daddies. Isa shudders. Surely Mama was not going to have any more babies – the prospect of having a baby brother or sister appalls her. She's even more surprised at Dylan. Why would Dylan want to make babies? According to Mama, he was not much more than a boy himself.

Dylan is vaguely aware of some movement at the bottom of the bed. What bed is he in? He recaptures the events of the night before. Isa stands up at the bottom of the bed, straddling a foot around each of Dylan's ankles. Holding Pia by one ear, arms outstretched and body erect, she leans forward to allow gravity to topple her to a crash-landing on top of Dylan. Dylan becomes conscious just in time to break the last foot of Isa's free-fall by grabbing her shoulders with his one-and-a-half free hands. This is a good thing. It just slightly softens the impact of the girl's falling body. In an instant, both Dylan and Mama are wakened. Isa laughs histrionically. Dylan finds it in himself to deliver a sleepy chuckle, but Mama is completely disoriented as she attempts to piece together the events of the night before and connect them with this unwelcome awakening. This process is extended by the fact that she has to search for some kind of excuse for Dylan's presence in her bed.

Isa cares nothing for any of her mother's concerns. After plowing into Dylan, she opens up the bed covers and wriggles her way between Dylan and her mama. As she suspected, they are both naked. Not that she is surprised by this. Do not Micaela and Mama always sleep naked? Don't they realize it is much cozier to sleep in a nightie – how else can one keep shoulders warm?

Mama is glaring at Dylan, while speaking softly to Isa. She is saying something silly about Dylan feeling too cold to sleep on the couch. He was too cold because he forgot to bring his pajamas. Mama had to keep him warm. Isa knows that Mama is talking nonsense. Accordingly, she ignores Mama and busies herself climbing into a straddle on Dylan's stomach. Thus mounted, she begins to tickle him under his armpits. She tosses back her head to flick the hair from her eyes and laughs with glee, delighted to have identified vulnerability in Dylan.

Dylan's reaction is slightly delayed, owing to the fact that he is barely awake. But sharp little fingernails burrow deep into Dylan's armpits, suddenly producing a vigorous reaction due to a special sensitivity to tickling in this region of his body. He lurches to a sitting position and grabs the child by her skinny upper arms. Dylan's aggressive response to the tickling catches Isa by surprise. His grasp is way too rough. Isa bursts into tears. Mean Deelan has hurt her! His hands are so rough and hard. She slides off Dylan to retreat to the comfort of a cuddle into her mama's soft, warm body. Now, more awake, Dylan rolls onto his side. He attempts to apologize to Isa. Isa is not receptive. She picks up Pia and uses the stuffed toy to slap Dylan as hard as she can. It appears that Pia's role as a weapon is the predominant one.

Isa's anger at Dylan is soon mitigated. "Mama, you are so beautiful," says Isa, stroking some dark hair from her mother's face admiringly. Gabi nods and strokes her daughter's hair. "Am I beautiful, too? Am I as beautiful as you?"

"Of course, my darling," responds Gabi sleepily, "you are more beautiful than I. You have the prettiest eyes I have ever seen. And your smile is a marvel."

Isa beams with pride. Then she applies some analysis to her mother's words.

"Mama, you only think I am beautiful because I am your daughter." Isa twists around to address Dylan. "Deel, am I beautiful? Is mama also beautiful?"

Dylan props himself onto an elbow, while remaining on his side. "Now, let me consider this question," he responds with exaggerated seriousness. Isa uses Pia to strike at Dylan once again, making it clear that no hesitation in his response is to be tolerated. "Yes, now I am sure," says Dylan emphatically. "Without a doubt, I am in bed with the two most beautiful women in Spain."

Isa grimaces. "Not in the whole world?" she prompts.

Dylan sits up and gives himself a smack on the back of his head. "It is now perfectly obvious. I declare Gabi and Isa to be the most beautiful women in the entire solar system."

Isa purrs and cuddles into Mama. She whispers into Mama's ear, "Mama do you not think that Deel is the kindest and most handsome man? Think what a nice husband he could make you. He could become my papi and we all three might sleep together like this every night. How cozy that would be!"

This statement jolts Gabi out of a semi-dormant state. She sits bolt upright in the bed, forgetting that her breasts are uncovered. Impatiently, she orders Isa to stop talking nonsense. "Deel is not a man, not a husband, and certainly not a papi. He is a boy who is playing at being a man." She glares at Dylan. "And it is unfair for Deel to pretend in front of you that he can be anything but an irresponsible boy."

Tearful, Isa twists away from her mother to cuddle into Dylan once more. She does this in a desperate and clinging manner. "You must not leave, Deel. I want you to live with us and be my papa or my brother. You can protect us. Witches will not harm us when you are by our side."

But now Gabi is in a less tolerant mood. "Isa, go at once to your room and get dressed. We are wasting the day and precious time by idling in bed."

Reluctantly, Isa unravels her body from Dylan, picks up Pia by an ear, and exits, sniveling. She slams the bedroom door dramatically. The instant the door slams, Gabi covers her face with both hands. "What shame!" she cries. "What have I become? Pobrecita Isa."

Dylan is stumped for a response. Gabi is suddenly energized. She jumps out of bed, not caring that she is naked, and turns on Dylan. "You must leave and never return," she declares fervently. "We must not see each other any more."

Dylan scratches his head, still lost for words. "But," he protests, "we're only just getting to know each other. I think we have more going for us than just a single night together."

"Deel," responds Gabi more gently, "you are fun to be with. I enjoyed last night. Maybe you remind me of something I missed out on when I was your age. But I am a mother with a daughter. This is my first and most important responsibility on this earth. I cannot allow Isa to be hurt by you. Already she is bonding with you. If I allow this to continue, she will be devastated when you suddenly disappear from our lives. And disappear you will … to go to college, to go to other lovers. Worse still, Isa should not be in bed with a naked man. Or see her mama naked in bed with that man."

Dylan attempts to protest, but is interrupted. "When Isa jumped on top of you this morning, there was something about the look in her eyes that was not of a child. For just an instant, my baby was no longer a baby." Gabi pauses to wipe tears from her eyes. Then she continues with conviction, "It was not an expression I want to see on her face for at least another ten years."

Dylan attempts to interrupt again, but he is summarily shushed. "Trust me, Deel, I know more of these things than you could possibly know. If you have even a little love for me, you will do as I say and not make this difficult. It is not just my little girl's heart you are playing with, but also her morals. It scares me to think of what goes on in her mind when she frolics in bed with us after we have spent a night of lovemaking."

Silence. "Is it any worse than her being in bed with you and Micaela?"

This was the wrong thing to say. "Leave my bed," she says in a furious whisper, "You are more immature than I thought. What I do with Micaela is not your business. Get dressed. I want you to leave. Eat breakfast, say goodbye to Isa, and go. I only ask that you be kind to her. Do not suggest to her that you might not see her again – she is already upset and I don't want her to become more so today. But that said, don't even think of coming back. And please do not come to the bar. I know this has been little more than a game for you. But my heart is more vulnerable than yours. Dios mío, I should know better than to let my feelings run wild on an eighteen-year-old."

Despite the fact that this last statement is the first time Gabi has admitted any emotional connection to him, Dylan knows that Gabi is right. They must split. Dylan cannot begin to fathom Gabi's sexual motives and gets even more confused when it comes to her emotions. A shudder runs down his spine as he recalls his lust-driven behavior with Sharon and its sorry outcome. His libido must not be allowed to drive his actions once again. All said, Dylan feels a closer emotional connection with Isa than he does Gabi.

*　　　　　　　*　　　　　　　*

Gabi, Isa, and Dylan are eating breakfast on the small balcony of Gabi's apartment. It is a final breakfast for Gabi and Dylan. The breakfast is fruit followed by arepas. Arepas, cooked once again in honor of Dylan. Isa is in a terrible sulk and appears to be angry with Mama and even more so with Dylan. She picks at the fruit, but refuses to touch the arepas, declaring that they are disgusting and that Mama is favoring Dylan by making them.

Isa might be hoping that Dylan responds to her bad mood by attempting to coax her out of it. But after the conversation with Gabi in the bedroom, Dylan does not dare intercede. He simply won't be around to be a papi or a big brother. Believing that Dylan is ignoring her sours Isa's mood even more. Gabi makes some light superficial conversation with Dylan, dropping a casual platitude here and there in a conversation interspersed with gentle rebukes to Isa on the terrible things that might occur if she fails to eat a healthy breakfast.

Breakfast is soon completed. At the moment of departure, Gabi stands at the apartment door and embraces Dylan in an almost desperate hug. There is a clinging to the hug that threatens to make Dylan do some reconsidering, but he comes to realize that Gabi is still determined to bring the relationship to closure. "I will not forget you, my darling Deel," whispers Gabi into Dylan's ear. "There will always be a special little corner in my heart for you."

"I won't forget you either, Gabi," responds Dylan, "I am sorry to be saying goodbye to you in this way."

Gabi kisses him on the lips. Then she calls out to Isa who is still sulking over her food on the balcony. "Come Isa, Deel is leaving; give him a kiss."

Isa comes to the door and, still pouting, offers first one, then the other cheek for kisses from Dylan. Duly bussed, the little girl turns heel and, without a word, returns to the balcony. Dylan feels a pang of guilt, knowing that he is deceiving the child. Once cognizant that a peck on either cheek represented a final goodbye, smart little Isa will probably forever remember him as a coward, a betrayer. He shrugs, looking questioningly at Gabi. She is silently crying, tears running down her cheeks. Dylan raises a finger to stroke them away. Gabi evades the gesture by turning her head. "Go," she orders him. Dylan goes. As he leaves the apartment, he feels as if a weight has been lifted from his shoulders. After all, Gabi has done all the work in providing him with an exit path he would have had to otherwise create by himself. He just hopes that a real papi soon comes into little Isa's life to protect her from witches.

16. A BITE FROM THE PAST

The four engines on the jet plane growl and thrust the aircraft down the runway. Within moments, the jumbo has launched itself over the Mediterranean, where it will gain some altitude before banking into a 180-degree turn to leave old Europe and Dylan's childhood in the past. Dylan unbuckles his seat belt and heads to the bar, which is located on the upper deck of this oversized airliner. He thinks that it has to be kind of cool to have a drink in a bar at 35,000 feet. But as he sets forth, another thought crosses his mind. Specifically, he hopes he will not have to endure the embarrassment of being asked to produce ID when he orders beer. With trepidation, he wonders what the drinking age is on an American airliner. Eighteen years is usually more than okay to purchase alcohol in Europe, but in some states the age is nineteen and others twenty-one.

Dylan enters the bar and orders his beer. The hostess smiles at him as she pours the drink. Dylan is relieved. Maybe he is finally beginning to look his age. He glances at his watch. At two in the afternoon, Gabi and Isa could be making sandcastles on the beach in Castellón de la Plana. A painful tremor runs through him as he thinks of them. Maybe Micaela is sitting with them, trying to persuade mother and daughter to accompany her for tapas and sparkling wine, anywhere to avoid sitting on a dirty beach full of tourists. Dylan's mother is likely playing bridge. Tomorrow, his brothers will board an aircraft to return for another school year at the gulag. Yes, Dylan is free, with his whole life in front of him. He takes a swig of beer.

Dylan surveys the other passengers who have retreated to the lounge. On an early afternoon flight, the bar is not a popular place to be. There are four business suits occupied with briefcases and Manhattans. The only female passenger seated in one of a dozen fixed lounge seats arranged in a semicircle seems to be staring at him intently. Instinctively, Dylan averts his gaze and turns his body away on the swivel barstool. The woman is short, heavy-jowled, and unattractive, with very straight, blond hair cut at the mid-neck level. Her mode of dress suggests to Dylan that she is American; it is garish in color and polyester. The clothes do little to mask the fact that she is overweight. Dylan puts her age to be in the mid-twenties range, but reminds himself that guessing the age of heavy women is tricky at best. Why does she stare so intently at him? He gulps more of his beer.

The aircraft is getting into some turbulence and the "fasten seat belts sign" illuminates. The hostess behind the bar tells Dylan he'll have to move to one of the fixed lounge chairs and secure his seat belt. Dylan gets off the barstool to do as he has been instructed. The woman who was eyeballing him is now not merely staring at him, but grinning while she does so. Dylan sits himself in a lounge seat one over from the irritating woman, who continues to focus on him. He clips the seat belt closed. He elects to look the presumptuous woman in the eye. She laughs and slaps her thigh.

"You don't recognize me, do you, Dylan Douglas?" Her accent is neutral, perhaps tinged with a little mid-West. Surprised, Dylan studies her face. He scrolls through memory and finds nothing in this face that is remotely familiar to him. The woman continues, "I recognized you the instant you set foot in the lounge. You don't seem to have changed that much." She pauses to sip on a Martini. "I'll give you a little hint … Venezuela?"

A tsunami crashes through Dylan's gut as he realizes who she is. "Bunny? Bunny Forslund?"

Bunny's current appearance does not jive with the image of utter evil he has logged in memory. In fact, she looks rather dull and ordinary, not worthy of a glance. Gone are the bulbous eyeglasses; she must be wearing contacts. And while her current proportions put her in the definitely overweight category, she's no longer grotesquely obese.

Bunny laughs and slaps her thigh again. "I knew you'd get it eventually!" she screams out. The four businessmen turn from their Manhattans to grimace at Bunny. Dylan is trying to contain a complex stew of powerful emotions. For much of Dylan's life, Bunny has epitomized evil. He had nightmares about her years after she had departed his world, he hoped, forever. Fortunately, it turns out that Dylan isn't going to be required to talk much. Bunny is going to do most of that during this impromptu reunion.

"Yes," smiles Bunny, reminiscing, and doing this with fond recollection, "I used to babysit you. You had two brothers … and a sister, if I remember correctly. What a little monster you were back then! You had this angelic face and a confidence that came with knowing you could con anyone around you. But babysitters get to know the real nature of the kids they take care of. And you were the babysitter's ultimate nightmare."

All Dylan can utter in response is "No kidding?" and wait for more.

"Yes, I remember you ran me ragged. Most of the other girls refused to babysit for the Douglas family, mainly because of your terrible reputation. I don't think your brothers and sister were badly behaved. Just you. But I think I had a little more fortitude than most of the other girls. You might have met your match in me. Either that, or I was just crazy and kept coming back for more. You were certainly a tough little nut, but I believe you had a soft spot for me!"

Dylan is truly astounded at what he's hearing. Does Bunny really believe any of this gibberish she's spouting? Does she imagine he is a complete fool who is going swallow hook, line, and sinker, this perverse rewrite of the past in her favor that has no semblance of what actually took place? Dylan has to summon all his powers of restraint to avoid reacting. Bunny's sanitized version of the history they share cuts into Dylan's sense of justice. Memories of Bunny have lingered abrasively in his emotional baggage since the second grade. In fact, what Dylan most wants to do at this moment is slam another sucker punch into Bunny's solar plexus just as he did back when he was seven years old. How did that mantra go? Center of the triangle, between tits and belly button.

No, it's simply not possible that Bunny could forget that day; never in her lifetime will she do that. The hostess interrupts. She wants to know if Bunny wants another martini and Dylan another beer. They order the drinks, but Dylan thinks that what he really needs is some of Gabi's firewater brandy she feeds to drunks and English tourists.

"So what are you doing with yourself these days, Bunny?" asks Dylan. He doesn't want to talk about anything that reminds him of Bunny the Babysitter. Bunny informs Dylan that she has spent the summer traveling around England, France, Italy, and Spain. She has been suffusing herself in the culture, the history, the beauty, of old Europe. This can evidently all be observed from the windows of highway coaches and American chain hotels with the added benefit of minimal exposure to the filthy bathroom habits of Europeans. The trip was a gift from her parents for graduating college back in the spring. She is returning to the States for pre-med school and a medical career. The goal is a career in pediatrics or geriatrics – she's not sure which, but she wants to help the most helpless.

"Yeah?" Dylan raises his eyebrows. He has a bad headache and realizes that he does not want to talk about Bunny, the college graduate and future physician either. "How's Billy doing?"

"Ah, Billy," responds Bunny. "We don't hear from him much these days. He's on the West Coast – teaching metaphysics or something at Berkeley. What a brainiac! And yes, he got married and Bill Forslund the Third has made me an auntie. Can you believe that, Dylan, me an auntie?" This declaration makes Dylan wonder if Billy knows his sister well enough to never leave his son alone with his auntie.

Bunny removes a package of cigarettes from the oversized handbag in her possession. From the pack, she taps out a smoke and inserts it between her lips. As an afterthought, she gestures the pack to Dylan, offering him one. Dylan shakes his head. Bunny removes the cigarette from her mouth and taps it on the arm of her seat before reinserting it into her mouth. The cigarette is long and unnaturally slim, a cigarette selected to make a statement, though you might have had to have seen the commercial to know exactly what the message was. With the same hand that threatened to crush Dylan's balls eleven years previously, Bunny searches within the handbag once again. She withdraws a sleek butane lighter and ignites the cigarette with just the kind of poise that would befit a television commercial.

Over the consumption of two more drinks, Bunny and Dylan update their respective family histories since the time they knew each other in Venezuela. They exchange contact information. Dylan is very sure he'll never use the data Bunny provides him with, just as he is sure that he would never respond to any communication Bunny might send his way. After another beer, Dylan excuses himself by saying he wants to nap before they arrive.

Downstairs and back in his seat, Dylan's emotions are still churning. Four beers are not sufficient to numb some truly raw places in his gut. He thinks about Bunny's recall of the past. What most strikes him about the conversation is the utter conviction that Bunny seems to have in her version of past events. She can hardly be considered an ignorant person and she was a full four years older than him when their paths last crossed so, if anything, the accuracy of her recall should be superior to Dylan's. Sure, it was spin. The beauty of spin to the spinner, however, was that aberrations in the past, big or small, could be discarded and replaced with more palatable versions. Maybe spin is a survival tool required by some people so that they can live with themselves.

Dylan wonders if Bunny's real nature has undergone any change. Can a child as malicious as Bunny morph through the course of growing up into the caring type of individual you'd like to think of as your physician? During the conversation in the bar, there were fleeting moments when Dylan suspected that Bunny was fully cognizant of her corruption of truth by the way she studied Dylan to gauge his reactions. Perhaps she was just hoping that Dylan was too young to remember the events as she had.

Come to think of it, what is truth? Two persons living through the same event usually have separate versions of what took place. What did Dylan expect from Bunny anyway? An apology for her past as a violent bully? Not likely. Dylan feels that the best he can hope for is that Bunny was reminded of the pain of the sucker punch he drove into her gut eleven years ago when they were kids. What he's not sure of is whether the memory of that pain could have hurt as much as the recollection of the humiliation he had to endure.

Why could he not have had a chance encounter with Genevieve instead of Bunny? What would Genevieve remember of their "secrets"? Yeah, he would have some questions to ask, but not with any motive to condemn. The big question would be why she ever confided in Bunny. For some reason, he doesn't believe that

Genevieve could be dishonest. But who knows?

Would he even be able to recognize Genevieve today? She would be twenty-two years old, maybe married, perhaps even with some kids. Yes, he sees Genevieve surrounded by children. Maybe she is a teacher? Over the years since she left his life, Dylan has occasionally pondered on what Genevieve's recollections of their shared past might be. Is it possible she loved him anything like as much as he adored her? Or was he a mere curiosity? And what about the religion kick she was on? Whatever Genevieve's current situation, Dylan is sure he could sit down and share a glass of wine with her and chat about the secrets of their past. And who knows, this intimacy could lead to something more than just a glass of wine … perhaps a romantic dinner … and what naturally evolves from such a dinner? As the airplane continues its smooth journey through the air above the clouds, Dylan drifts off to sleep.

17. POPPY

It's past eleven on a warm, fall evening, and Dylan uses the drive-thru to avoid sitting with McDonald's late night patrons. After leaving the pick-up window, he circles back and parks in the restaurant lot to scoff a hamburger. While eating, he observes a girl togged out in a McDonald's uniform, sitting on the curb, knees tucked into chest, using a twig to scratch at the dirt. While Dylan munches, his gaze focuses on the girl, who is unaware she is being scrutinized – after all, most McDonald's patrons don't eat sitting in their vehicles in the parking lot. The girl is upset. She uses her sleeve to wipe the tears from her cheeks from time to time. There is something about the scene that attracts Dylan's curiosity … and empathy. It goes without saying, this has something to do with the fact that, at least from a distance, the girl is attractive.

Dylan finishes eating and stuffs the wrappings of the meal deal into its bag, readying it for disposal. As he opens his vehicle door, the girl becomes aware of him and wipes her eyes. Dylan opts to walk the extra distance to a garbage can close to his damsel in distress and strides toward it … as he does so, the girl turns her head away. He scrunches and trashes the garbage, then approaches the girl and sits on the curb beside her, giving her no option but to turn her head to face Dylan.

"Why are you crying?" Dylan asks.

The girl rubs her eyes on her sleeve once again. "I don't think that's any of your business. I came out here to be alone, not to have some jerk hit on me."

Dylan doesn't back off. He studies the girl, now close-up. She is way too cute to be working at a McDonald's, a fact not disguised by a blotchy face from crying. "You looked so unhappy," Dylan responds slowly. "I was watching you from my car while I was eating. I thought that maybe you could do with some comforting."

The girl looks down at her feet. Using the twig, she scribes in the curbside dirt. "There's nothing you can do to help me, so the best thing you can do is leave me alone."

Dylan persists. "Is it the job? Or a man?" The girl looks up at Dylan, shaking her head, but saying nothing.

"If I don't get back inside, I'll get fired; my break is done, and it's my first night," she says, preparing to stand up from the curb.

"Would that be such a bad thing?" asks Dylan. "I'm sure this can't be the best job you can get?" The girl looks at Dylan disdainfully. She stands and brushes dust off the backside of her uniform, leaving Dylan in his sitting position.

The girl seems to hesitate, as if she might be considering the notion. "Live on the wild side," encourages Dylan. "Allow me to drive you off into the night and pleasure you with coffee and comfort."

"You're not from Toronto, are you?" asks the girl, sitting down again beside Dylan.

Dylan shakes his head. "Just studying here. I was on my way home from a party and stopped in for a bite."

The girl raises her eyes skyward in a way that Dylan interprets as derisory. She obviously doesn't care too much for students ... or study; one or the other, probably both.

"What's your name?"

"Poppy," responds the girl. "And for the record, I quit school before I finished Grade Ten."

"For a career at McDonald's?"

"Smartass." The girl shakes her head. "No, for a career as a mother. I have a son. He's six months old."

"Geez!" asks Dylan, surprised, "How old are you?"

"Seventeen."

"Are you married?"

"No, not married. I live at home with my mother. She looks after Manny while I'm at work. I try to schedule working evenings and nights. When I have a job, that is."

"And the kid's father?"

Poppy shakes her head without responding. Dylan is looking for a way to bail the scene. It seems that a young pretty face can hide a lot of baggage. He needs an exit line, but struggles to find one. "Is there anything I can do to help?" he asks, knowing that it is the nice thing to say rather than the right thing.

Poppy looks at Dylan intently, intently enough to signal Dylan that he has connected with her. "What's your name?"

"Dylan."

"Were you hitting on me, professor Dylan? Yes, I think you were. Do you like what you see? And if you don't, at what point did you get scared off? Was it the baby, the dropping out of high school, or the living with Mom? Or did the reality of the McDonald's uniform and what goes with it just sink in?" It turns out that this Poppy possesses some verbal acuity and can be aggressive along with her good looks.

Dylan sucks in his breath. "Yeah, I was hitting on you. You're cute, and you seemed to be unhappy ... I felt sorry for you and wondered if you needed some help, that's all. The last thing I wanted to do was upset you even more."

Silence.

Dylan clears his throat and says with a grin, "So ... so, if you want to kiss your future with the McDonalds corporation goodbye forever, you could jump into my car ... and we can drive off into the night!"

Poppy looks at Dylan and smiles, a smile that telegraphs a sudden change in attitude, perhaps even spiced with come-on. She shakes her head once again, focusing on the ground as if considering the proposition.

"What the fuck!" declares the girl impulsively, jumping to her feet and dusting curb dust off her backside for a second time. She heads to the back door of the restaurant. "Wait here. I have to get my purse."

Dylan takes a reality check. What have I got myself into, he wonders as he waits outside the McDonald's.

Seated inside Dylan's aging Pontiac, Poppy stretches both arms skyward and delivers a from the gut scream directed toward the heavens. Dylan's immediate concern is that someone might have overheard and think he is murdering his passenger. "Wow, that felt good," declares Poppy, "I've never done anything like this before. I didn't say a word when I went back inside. Just grabbed my purse and left."

The car pulls out onto Bloor Street and moves with the late-night traffic. "So why were you crying?"

"I dunno. I only took that job out of desperation – in my mind it was about as low as you can sink ... to work behind the counter at a McDonald's. The reality was that it was even worse than I imagined it could be. Partly my fault, of course, I couldn't get my head into all their dumb rules and regulations. I muffed orders and every other customer was rude. The crew chief was a little dick who was on my case from the start."

"OK, so fate has determined that it's my job to cheer you up. Coffee or food?" asks Dylan. "Or should I look for a quiet alley where I can have my way with you?"

"Coffee. Then it would be nice if you can drive me home. The thought of eating anything at the moment makes me want to puke."

Poppy sniffs herself. "I stink like a Big Mac and fries. I'm trying to be a vegetarian, but the only jobs that seem to be available are in fast food restaurants serving meat, which of course I end up eating because it's free." Driving east down Bloor Street, Dylan pulls over into a coffee shop and parks.

"How many jobs have you had?"

"A couple. I've only just 'officially' returned to the workforce. I take the absolute worst type of jobs then get fired. That's what happens when you have a baby to look after. Except I never tell employers that I'm a mother; if I did, I'd never get the job in the first place. When you've got a kid, things come up. I tell them I am in school so my jobs are evening jobs – that way, Mom can babysit while I'm working."

Over coffee, Dylan and Poppy talk. Poppy turns out to be a chatterbox. The tough façade she initially presented to Dylan was a fake that quickly dissipates. She is girlish and very un-motherly. She asks Dylan how old he is and he tells her he is twenty. "My ex-boyfriend, Evan, he's the father of Manny …" she hesitates. "He's twenty … and frankly, he looked at least five years older than you."

"What is the status between you and Evan now?" asks Dylan.

"What do you mean *status*? It's over between us. I started out being crazy in love with him, but all he wanted from me was sex. He was my first real boyfriend and it took me a while before I realized how much he was dragging me down. By then I was pregnant."

Dylan says nothing for a while. "Maybe I should get you home?"

Poppy nods. They cross the parking lot and get into Dylan's car. Once in the car, Poppy slides over the bench seat and asks Dylan to hug her before he can start the engine. "Hold me," she says. Dylan cautiously extends his right arm to wrap it around Poppy. She responds by wrapping both arms around Dylan's chest in a clinging embrace. She maintains the hug for a couple of minutes, her head nuzzled into Dylan's shoulder. Dylan strokes her hair, which continues to exude odors of burgers and fries. Poppy leans her head away from Dylan's shoulder and moves to connect their lips. They kiss deeply.

Dylan awakes the next morning in bright sunshine in his single bed. Poppy has already got up. She is leaning on the window sill, wearing nothing but the shirt Dylan wore the night before, buttons undone, and is engaged in an animated conversation on Dylan's phone. Dylan blinks and takes account of his surroundings. A McDonald's uniform and female underclothing are strewn across the floor around the bed. He tunes in to the one side of the phone conversation to which he is privy.

The subject of the phone conversation has to do with Poppy's failure to return home the previous night. It appears that Poppy is having this conversation with her mother. Her initial strategy is to explain her absence by claiming that she got off work too late to return home and opted to sleep over with a girlfriend. This tack backfires when Poppy's mother informs her daughter that she has already telephoned the breakfast crew at the McDonald's restaurant where she worked, and the manager enlightens her to the fact that his records show that Poppy quit not half-way through her first shift the previous evening. Poppy is in tears. She informs her mother that she couldn't handle the losers working in a McDonald's restaurant. Her mother evidently wants to know when her loser daughter will be returning to look after her infant son. She informs Poppy that unlike her, she does have a job to get to and she is already late. Poppy explains that she is downtown and it will take her at least an hour to get back out to Scarborough.

Mother wants to know who Poppy is with – surely not with Evan? No, not Evan. With a boy? No, with a girlfriend, one called Candice. No, Mother, you have not met her. She's sorry, but she was going out of her mind and needed a break from babies and mothering … and some time for herself. Mother appears to explode at this information and it is some time before Poppy gets the opportunity to contribute any more to the conversation.

Naked Dylan has heard enough. He gets up, walks to the bathroom, and turns on the shower. As soon as the water temperature is balanced, he gets in and luxuriates in the stream of water. Within seconds, Poppy has joined him. Seen undressed and in daylight, Dylan cannot help but wonder how someone so skinny could have mothered a child. Aside from a little looseness around still-small breasts and stretch marks on the tummy, Poppy has the physical appearance of any other slightly built seventeen-year-old. She wants to fuck again. She informed Dylan the previous evening that it had been well over a year since she had sex. 'I never much liked it back then,' she explained.

After overhearing the conversation on the phone, he wonders how much credence should be given to any information coming out of Poppy's mouth. The night before, she informed him that she was on "the pill" – Dylan asked her why she was taking the pill if she was not in a current relationship. Poppy explained that her doctor put her on the pill to regulate heavy periods, which had resumed within weeks of giving birth because she could not breast feed. This seemed plausible to Dylan the night before, but now he's not so sure after the spin she served up to her mother.

Poppy and Dylan screw in the shower. Standing Dylan grasps both of feather-light Poppy's buttocks while she wraps her legs around him and locks her lips to his. Water blasts over the couple, adding a slippery erotic element to the experience and, as is his tendency, Dylan gets lost in the moment and doubts he might have about the advisability of his actions are relegated to a backburner. The bang culminates on the floor of the tub, sloshing in water under them, pounded down by the cascade from above. A nice fuck to be sure, but now reality kicks in. Dylan does not want to miss his ten-thirty class and he breaks into hurry-up mode. No way he's going to leave Poppy alone in his apartment, so he does his best to stoke her into a similar sense of urgency; not an easy task because the least of her worries is that her mother will be unable to leave for work until her return. Holding hands, the couple walks to the streetcar stop: thank God they are headed in different directions, thinks Dylan.

Seated on the streetcar, Dylan takes measure of the potential consequences. Depending on the level of deceit, in a worst case scenario, he could have acquired a dose of the clap. Or made Poppy pregnant again, even if the story about being on the pill was true, because from what he has seen of her, he doubts whether she possesses the wherewithal to remember to take one every day. And if neither of these consequences emerges, he has for sure strung something of an emotional albatross around his neck.

So why is he attracted to Poppy, he wonders? He is generally popular on campus and could choose between dozens of coeds who carry no life baggage and share the same mindset as he. Despite her efforts to deceive her mother a little earlier, Dylan decides there is a certain appealing down-to-earth aspect to Poppy, especially when contrasted with the girls on campus, with their often overbearing sense of entitlement. She reveals herself in a candid way that appeals to him, along with her unpretentious looks, not camouflaged with any obvious makeup, jewelry, or hair-effects.

Victor Lee and Dylan each rent rooms on the third floor of the Ligetti home south of the Annex area of Toronto. The Ligetti's raised four children in the large downtown house before each had married in what seemed to be quick succession and flown the nest. Sadly, their offspring dispersed themselves far and wide across the country, depriving Bruno and Gloria of the role of doting grandparents surrounded by the comforts of family. In what seemed to be no time at all, the crowded home emptied out, leaving Bruno and Gloria alone and rattling around like two peas in … an enormous pod. For a while they considered selling and retreating to the suburbs of Vaughn, where many other urban Italian immigrants headed as they accrued affluence, but Gloria decided she was comfortable right where she was in a neighborhood where she knew the grocer and fishmonger by name and never once had to enter a supermarket. Bruno too enjoyed the downtown ambience; he was a man of habit and liked to frequent a local bar where he could play dominos, discuss the Sunday Serie A soccer games, and speak in Italian when he felt so inclined.

Having made the decision not to move from the city center, Bruno fastidiously converted the third and top floor of the family home into a couple of student accommodations: it was a perfect retirement project for Bruno, who, like so many of his compatriots, was a natural craftsman. Each so-called room consisted of a small bedroom and conjoined study-living room area. The two separate living areas were connected in the center by stairway access to the lower floors in the home and a shared kitchen and bathroom. A more "private" entrance was an exterior steel fire escape, which could be accessed from the third floor kitchen window. The Ligetti's decided that the rooms were only suitable for students of the same gender.

It was Gloria's decision to limit renting the accommodations exclusively to male students. To her, it was obvious that she and her husband would get to know and feel protective of their young tenants, perhaps even become fond of them. Bruno and Gloria would interview applicants to ensure that they were serious about their studies and came from good families. Students from good families would inevitably require a proper home-cooked Italian meal and perhaps a little family support from time to time. For this reason, she didn't want her conscience to be troubled by worrying about the morals of young women living in the city, so she was firm in her mind that only male students would be accepted as tenants. What harm was there in growing young men sewing a few wild oats, so long as the young ladies they chose to do this with remained anonymous?

Dylan Douglas and Victor Lee are the first two occupants of the Ligetti student accommodations. They both seem like serious boys who declare that they require just a little more independence than that offered by a student residence. More important, Dylan and Victor are both engineering students. Until Bruno's retirement, he had a successful career as a civil engineer specializing in the construction of apartment blocks. Victor is a Chinese Canadian from British Columbia, at the University of Toronto for two years of postgraduate studies. Dylan is a second-year student with the potential to be a little wilder than Victor Lee, according to Gloria's assessment of him – but he displays a mischievous twinkle in his eye and an almost European charm during the interview conducted by Bruno and Gloria that's enough to win them over.

Victor and Dylan rapidly become friends of the Ligetti's. They allow Mrs. Ligetti to mother them once in a while, never play music at excessive volumes, and hungrily devour Sunday dinners when invited to partake. If there is one minor bone of contention, it is that the boys seem to prefer using the exterior steel fire escape and kitchen window to access their accommodations rather than use the front door of the home. Girls appear as occasional visitors, but in Gloria's mind, they are good types and are not, to her knowledge, overnight guests.

After delivering the brusque goodbye to Poppy at the streetcar stop, Dylan heads off in the opposite direction for a full day of classes. After class, he decides he will walk back to his digs, stopping on the way for a falafel. He takes his usual shortcut to his room using the fire escape – it is a short cut because it avoids getting into a protracted conversation with Mrs. Ligetti. He enters the kitchen and immediately notes that Victor is in his room – this is an unusual occurrence when Dylan is not at home. Something else is out of the ordinary, too … Victor is dandling a baby on his knee. Dylan raises his brows to enquire of Victor what is going on.

"Don't ask me," replies Victor. "Your girlfriend dropped him off. That was nearly two hours ago. She said it was an emergency and you would understand."

"My girlfriend?" exclaims Dylan, "… not Poppy."

"Yeah, I think that's what she called herself. Anyway, you can take him now; I've been babysitting for over two hours. Hey man, you didn't tell me you had a baby?"

"I don't," Dylan insists, "Are you crazy? Why did you agree to take him?"

Victor shrugs. "I thought I was doing you a favor."

Victor thrusts the baby toward Dylan, who has no option but to take the child. Dylan holds the infant awkwardly away from his body. The child is placid enough, perhaps thanks to Victor's dandling. "What the fuck is its name?" asks Dylan.

"I think she said it was Manny," responds Victor. "Anyway, I have to go, I've got a date."

Dylan now recalls Poppy saying her child was named Manny the previous evening. Manny surveys Dylan and decides that he would rather be with Victor. He begins to snuffle.

"When did Poppy say she was coming back for him?" asks Dylan.

Victor chuckles, "She told me she would be an hour max … that was two hours ago. She said she had to go to an interview. A really important interview!" With that, Victor exits Dylan's territory to return to his own room.

Manny studies Dylan. Dylan surveys Manny. What have I got myself into thinks Dylan, not for the first time? He has none of Poppy's contact information, no phone number – come to think of it, he doesn't even know her last name. Added to which, this baby has arrived without the usual baby paraphernalia consisting of something to feed it, a change of clothing, or stuff to amuse it. Where does one take an abandoned baby? To a police station?

Dylan is lost in these very thoughts when he becomes aware of a person mounting the fire escape. There is a tap on the kitchen window and he hears Victor opening it. Perhaps it's Poppy? Victor enters Dylan's room and introduces a young girl, not Poppy, dressed in Colonel Sanders pinstripes. The visitor, who looks like a twelve-year-old, announces that her name is Sandy and says that Poppy sent her. She explains that Poppy was given a Kentucky Fried Chicken associate's position on condition that she start immediately. "Fuck!" exclaims Dylan, causing Manny to startle. Sandy then says that Poppy apologizes, but says she is at Dylan's mercy – she needs the job and because Dylan got her fired the previous evening, could he please return the favor and babysit Manny for this one shift. "Fuck!" exclaims Dylan, even more loudly this time, causing Manny to start crying.

"Why can't you take him?" asks Dylan.

"Yeah, like that would go down just peachy with my mom and dad," responds Sandy. "Poppy gets off at eleven. Don't worry! Only two-and-a-half hours to go. You'll survive … maybe." She laughs.

Victor also bursts out laughing. "I'm splitting, Dill. Good luck, man!"

Sandy thrusts a shopping bag at Dylan. "Here," she says, "Poppy told me you'll need this. I gotta go, I'm already late."

The shopping bag contains the absent baby paraphernalia. Over the course of the next three hours, Dylan confirms all his suspicions regarding the repulsiveness of babies generally, and Manny in particular. Babies greedily consume at one end of their bodies and consummately produce at the other. In his mind, he likens Manny to a maggot. Dylan observes Manny drooling from his mouth and swears he's the ugliest baby he has ever seen.

When Poppy returns three hours later, wearing Colonel Sanders pinstripes and a fierce odor of fried chicken, she short-circuits Dylan's ability to express his fury by telling him that Manny will get upset if he starts shouting at her. "Don't you ever pull that one on me again," seethes Dylan in a whisper.

Poppy doesn't feel she has done anything wrong. On the contrary, she informs Dylan, it's only fair, after he got her fired from McDonald's. Dylan reminds her that she was not fired, but she walked out. Unrepentant, Poppy issues some baby talk to Manny, in which she affectionately vilifies Dylan as not caring nearly enough for either of them, while packing up the baby paraphernalia into the shopping bag. The bag, once packed, is thrust toward Dylan. It is evidently his job to carry this down the fire escape and help her pack Manny into the stroller. Poppy and Manny will return to her parents' home via subway. Dylan feels an enormous sense of guilt; he can't help but feel he should be cranking up the car and driving the pair home. But surely that would be another relationship extending move? It is just short of midnight when mother and child depart.

A couple of days pass. For two successive days, Dylan feels extreme anxiety each time he returns from school, checking the base of the fire escape for a parked stroller. On the third day after Poppy's close to midnight departure, a more serious problem emerges. Manny, the maggot's stroller is parked not at the base of the fire escape, but up on the Ligetti front porch. Dylan circumvents the porch, intending to sneak up the fire escape, but his progress is short-circuited by Signora Ligetti. He does not make the first step before his landlady raps on a window, summoning him to enter by the front door.

Two things become apparent. The first is that Poppy is not present. The second is that Mrs. Ligetti is under the impression that Dylan is the father of the maggot. Manny is happily playing in the center of a playpen that has been erected in the center of the Ligetti living room, surrounded by many more baby toys than could be carried in a stroller.

First, Dylan has to refute the notion that he is the father of Manny. Mrs. Ligetti is skeptical. She informs Dylan that Manny looks exactly like him. Dylan blinks and turns to reassess the appearance of Manny. Mrs. Ligetti says that it is time for Dylan to be truthful to her. Yes, she is upset that he was not upfront about his fatherhood when he applied for his room. But that's the past, and now she just wants him to be honest. It requires all Dylan's powers of persuasion to convince Mrs. Ligetti that not only is he not a father, but that he has not yet known Poppy four days.

"Theez Poppy, she'za loff you, no, she'za tella me so?" questions Mrs. Ligetti, now less sure. Dylan has no choice but to recite his story of rescuing a damsel in distress from the parking lot of a McDonald's restaurant. He omits the part about spending the night with her two floors up in the bosom of the Ligetti home. Finally, Mrs. Ligetti appears at least a little convinced that Dylan might be telling the truth.

Where is Poppy? It turns out that Poppy has an evening shift at Chicken Lickin' and was in need of a babysitter because her own mother was working late. Of course, she headed to Dylan's pad, hoping to find either him or Victor. Mrs. Ligetti intercepted the teenage mother just as she was about to ascend the Ligetti fire escape with a babe in arms. Close to tears, Poppy explained her desperate plight and her expectations of Dylan. One thing led to another. Poppy departed for work, Mrs. Ligetti appointed herself as child minder, and her husband was dispatched to the basement to retrieve the Ligetti children's playpen and an assortment of toys from storage.

Dylan sits down on a couch and grasps his temples with both hands. "This can't be happening," he protests to Mrs. Ligetti. But the reason it is happening soon becomes perfectly evident to Dylan. Manny, the maggot, has rekindled the instinct of primal motherhood in Gloria Ligetti. She fusses around the infant as if he were her very own. And the maggot, who Dylan has yet to see respond to any situation with much animation, is gurgling away, reveling in this opportunity to baby talk to someone who appears devoted to him.

The good news is that Gloria Ligetti is not about to entrust the care of this precious newcomer into her life to a clumsy clod such as Dylan. The bad news is that there is every indication that the situation will repeat itself, because Gloria has rediscovered in the depths of her soul a part of her being that has been dormant for three decades. As much as Dylan attempts to convince Mrs. Ligetti that a relationship that has lasted all of four days does not carry with it fathering or even babysitting obligations, the older woman fervently assures him that this is the only honorable thing to be done.

Mr. Ligetti enters the living room and noting Dylan's distress, pours him a shot of grappa. Bruno has learned through forty odd years of experience to be patient when countering any notion of Gloria's. For this reason, he opted not to protest when dispatched by his wife to the basement to retrieve the playpen and baby toys. Silently, he hopes that his partner will soon tire of this mothering when she realizes it is no job for an old lady. It would help if the baby in question was not so remarkably undemanding.

Dylan shoots a couple more shots of grappa and then asks if he can be excused to study. Gloria all but shoos him upstairs. Dylan must not worry about this bambino. The youngster could not be in better hands. Dylan retreats to a sofa in the living area of his rooms and attempts to read. However, the effect of the grappa gets the better of him and he drifts off to sleep.

A while later he is awakened by Poppy climbing through the kitchen window. It's past eleven and Poppy has snuck up the fire escape for a quick fuck before retrieving her infant from the babysitter below. Dylan quickly comes to his senses. No fucking is going to happen tonight! He attempts to dig in his heels, but Poppy seduces him into neutrality. She strokes his cheek and assures him she understands how he feels, tells him how sorry she is to impose on him in this way, and adds that she too is confused at how special he has become to her despite the fact that they have only known each other for four days. Her hand seeks his crotch through his pants and she giggles. "C'mon," she teases, "I know you want to … you're all hard and horny." While Dylan cannot find in himself the aggression required to deliver the coup de grace this relationship deserves, he is stubborn enough to resist one fuck. But in doing this, he realizes there is a side to Poppy that can enchant him. The girl settles for a quick cuddle and departs to sneak back down the fire escape.

Seconds later, Dylan hears the front doorbell ring. Some muffled conversation between Mrs. Ligetti and Poppy takes place, then footsteps mount the indoor stairs. Still on the couch, Dylan pretends to be asleep. Mrs. Ligetti and Poppy appear in the doorway and Dylan feigns being awakened. He gets to his feet, acting dopy and approaches to kiss his so-called girlfriend, a kiss in which Poppy sneaks some tongue into Dylan, ensuring that Mrs. Ligetti is fully aware of the intimacy. Gloria Ligetti shakes her head.

Poppy has struck gold. Under the guise of her supposed relationship with Dylan, she has unearthed a willing babysitting service. Gloria Ligetti latches onto Manny and, in no time, dotes on him, treating him with as much affection as she ever lavished on her own sons. She all but pleads with Poppy to drop him off for future appointments. No longer does Poppy have to put up with her own mother whining and complaining about minding Manny. Mrs. Ligetti is no mere babysitter. She proffers instructions on infant diet and management, along with lavishing the child with clothing and toys, the leftovers of raising four of her own bambinos. Should more than two days pass without a babysitting assignment, Gloria is pounding on Dylan's door, wanting to know if Manny is truly safe, and wondering if someone as young as Poppy is capable of properly caring for an infant by herself for two days in succession.

Mrs. Ligetti confronts Poppy. She tells the teenager she does not want her climbing up the fire escape to visit Dylan when it is wet outside; she could slip and break her neck, worse still, endanger the baby. Poppy puts on a guilty expression and looks at her feet. She's a convincing little actress because guilt is not foremost in her repertoire of sentiments. If Poppy must visit Dylan in this immoral way, then she will have to use the front door. Who am I, Mrs. Ligetti asks of the youngster, an out-of-touch-immigrant beginning her seventh decade, to censure the desires of the young. Certainly, she does not want the death of a young mother on her conscience. Poppy hugs Mrs. Ligetti and the older woman finds herself returning the embrace. A friendship begins.

Unfortunately for Dylan, he has become pivotal in a bizarrely parasitic relationship triangle. Without Dylan, there can be no Poppy and Gloria Ligetti ... or more to the point, no Gloria and Manny. Poppy begins to spend more time in the Ligetti household with Gloria than she does with Dylan. The seventeen-year-old and the matriarch conduct extended conversations in the kitchen, chattering over countless coffees and home-baked goodies. The aches and pains of the sexagenarian dissipate when little Manny is under her care; she strides out into Little Italy, pushing the stroller to show her charge off to her friends. Like many Italian women, she appears to have a soft spot for little blond boys.

The turn of events is a win-win one for little Manny. After being close to neglected for the first six months of life, the youngster is pampered and fussed over whenever Gloria Ligetti is around. Even the child's mother appears more attentive toward him, Gloria's influence no doubt. Little Manny hears nothing but Italian for an increasingly large percentage of his awake time and the betting is that his first words will be uttered in Italian.

A pattern emerges. Poppy stops in to the Ligetti home at around lunch time.

Dylan is typically absent, being in class at this time of day. Manny is settled into a playpen, set up in the middle of the living room floor, surrounded by toys. Sometimes Bruno will exchange a few words over the top of his newspaper with the infant – yes, he too has developed a certain fondness for the quiet little boy. Meanwhile, Poppy and Gloria form a tag team to prepare lunch. With lunch ready, the four sit at the table and eat and chat over an extended meal. When the dishes are washed and dried, Poppy departs for work and is gone for eight hours. This begins Gloria's time with Manny.

Little Manny is asleep when Poppy returns from work. She enters the Ligetti house reeking of fried chicken and kisses Gloria on both cheeks. Then she tiptoes upstairs to visit Dylan. Gloria hears the shower faucets turn on and cannot help but notice the indications that Poppy is not alone in the shower. Forty-five minutes or so after the shower shuts off, Poppy descends the two flights of stairs leading to the living room, her face a little flushed and damp hair tousled. She chats with Gloria as she wraps up Manny and his paraphernalia, collapses the stroller, packs everything into Dylan's Pontiac, and the three disappear into the night, headed back to Scarborough. Gloria's heart aches to see the pair of them off into the night. This is a situation that Gloria will only tolerate for a short while. It is clear that this confused young mother needs nurturing almost as much as does her infant child.

Bruno is assigned the task of preparing a room on the second floor of the home. The largest of the unused bedrooms on this floor is selected; it was once the bedroom of the eldest Ligetti son. Bruno paints the walls and a new mattress is purchased for the single bed in the room. The plan is yet to be discussed with Poppy herself. While she may be a mother, the girl is not yet eighteen years old, so there can be no question of her officially moving in upstairs with Dylan. Not under the Ligetti's roof.

It is Bruno that makes the proposal to Poppy. Gloria sits with Bruno, nodding her head as the proposition is outlined. Not a penny in rent will be due while Poppy is finding her feet. There is a double cohort to the proposition. Bruno has a cousin with a Tim Hortons franchise in Little Italy. The cousin is well aware of how many coffees and donuts may be sold by a pretty face and a warm smile. In consequence, he is ready to give her a job on the spot and at more money than Colonel Sanders is paying.

Poppy is overwhelmed to the point of being stunned. She makes a show of considering the offer, but in her mind, no consideration is necessary. She has wanted for some time to escape her complaining crab of a mother and was entertaining thoughts of moving in with Dylan, the challenge there being how to manipulate both Dylan and the Ligetti's into accepting the deal. This arrangement is one better and comes without the threat of being disrupted by Dylan's departure for either a summer vacation, or for some sexy, unburdened co-ed. In addition, the timing could not be better; she suspects she is on the verge of being fired for erratic time-keeping by the Colonel. Poppy sucks in a deep breath. Then she gets up from the kitchen table and embraces Mr. Ligetti. Next, she moves over to Mrs. Ligetti and hugs her for even longer. There are tears rolling down the cheeks of both females. Even Bruno is touched by the scene; could there be a tear trickling down his cheek?

By the time the arrangement is revealed to Dylan, it is fait accompli. Dylan has mixed emotions about the arrangement. But what can he do, he was effectively short-circuited out of the decision making process? For sure, it is better than Poppy moving in with him, especially were she to be accompanied by Manny, the maggot. That would be reason enough to drop out of school to escape.

The following Saturday, Dylan and Victor drive out to Scarborough and with some difficulty, locate Poppy's mother's apartment in the maze of concrete obelisks rising out of the Victoria Park and Eglinton intersection. The building has seen better times. They get buzzed in and Poppy greets them at the door, with Manny straddled on her hip.

Victor and Dylan are introduced to Poppy's mother. The mother is reclined into a Lazy Boy set before a large screen television, feet up, sucking on a cigarette. She averts her eyes from the TV screen to acknowledge the visitors with a grunt, but that's it. There is a powerful stench of stale tobacco smoke throughout the apartment.

Poppy has already packed what she plans to take with her into three beat-up suitcases. Most of her meager possessions are to do with the baby in her life, with whom she has been living in one of the two bedrooms in this diminutive apartment. It takes Victor and Dylan just two up-and-down trips to unload everything Poppy wants to remove from this world of hers and pack it into Dylan's car. Poppy, cradling Manny on her hip, exits with Victor and Dylan as they haul the second and final load of belongings down to the car. Her muted "See ya, Mom" farewell is reciprocated with a wave of the cigarette.

Driving back downtown, Victor asks all the questions. Dylan is too stunned. Does Poppy have siblings? Yes, an older sister, married now; Poppy hasn't seen her since she was ten years old. The sister and mother never got along. Does she get along with her mother? "Sort of," responds Poppy, shaking her head. She helped out with Manny and she appreciated that – she didn't like that her mom would smoke around the baby, but what could she do, her Mom didn't ask for a baby to land on her doorstep? Does her mother work? Yes, she works as an orderly in an old people's home. Money was always tight. Dylan senses the downturn in Poppy's mood. He realizes that this is the first time he has seen her upset since the evening they met around four weeks earlier and wonders how she manages to keep so upbeat most of the time, given her circumstances.

When they arrive at the Ligetti's, Poppy bathes Manny. She wants to remove the odor of tobacco smoke from him … forever, she thinks. She puts Manny down for a nap and then wants to shower with Dylan. In the shower, Dylan thinks that they are there for their usual bang, but not so; Poppy wants nothing more than to be washed. He soaps her down, massages shampoo into her hair, sleeks conditioner in, and rinses with her. After these ablutions, he tenderly towels her dry. It is the first time he has felt any real compassion for her since the evening they met.

A new routine kicks in. Poppy works days now. She gets up early for breakfast with the Ligetti's and Manny. She is out the door before seven, well before Victor and Dylan awake on the third floor. She returns from her shift at the Tim Hortons a couple of hours before the return of Dylan and Victor from class and busies herself with assisting Gloria with chores and doing baby things with both Gloria and Manny.

Poppy is a natural behind the counter of a coffee shop. Her easy manner and winning smile make her a hit with the Tim Hortons' customers, for whom a friendly environment and casual socializing is as important as the coffee and donut ingested. Her prior problems with timekeeping cease to be a factor now that she is but a ten-minute walk from her workplace. More significant, she is no longer dependent on Dylan. The Ligetti's have granted her status in the home in her own right.

Dylan and Poppy are post-coital and talkative. Dylan wants Poppy to tell him her story. She does. "My dad left home when I was three. I don't really remember him. What memories I do have of him get confused with stories my sister told me about him and a couple of photos I've seen of him. He drove a truck in the lumber industry in Northern Ontario – that meant he only worked from October through to May every year – they couldn't move the trucks in and out of the bush unless the dirt roads were frozen. He was on pogey and a hundred percent home all summer and a hundred percent away all winter. My sister, Daisy that is, we were both named after flowers, missed him a lot, but I can't say I did, because I never really knew what it was like to have him around. I was closest to Daisy through grade school … my mom was out so much, either working or with friends. She was very bitter about Dad leaving and complained all the time. She and Daisy continually argued about him, Mom saying bad things about Dad and Daisy defending him. In Mom's mind, every bad thing Daisy or I did was due to some fault of Dad's. Daisy wanted us to run away and find him, but she never knew where he was – he never once got in touch, so he couldn't really have loved us very much. But you couldn't tell Daisy that. She would cry quietly at night because she missed him so much – and I felt sort of jealous because I did not have anyone I could miss. I would climb into bed with her to comfort her and Daisy would tell me that at least we had each other.

"Daisy left home when I was ten – it was the worst day of my life. Life at home with Mom became hell after Daisy left. She was either all over me, treating me like I was four years old, or she was screaming at me as if I was Daisy. All of Mom's hatred of Dad and Daisy got focused on me and I was not good at fighting back like Daisy was.

"Daisy moved into an apartment in Mississauga with a girlfriend; she wanted to be far away from Scarborough … she phoned me and tried to persuade Mom to allow me to visit her … but Mom told her that would happen over her dead body. Then Daisy got a boyfriend … he was from Nova Scotia, which was where they soon moved to. Last count, I heard that she had four kids and was living in Dartmouth. We've spoken on the phone a couple of times, but there's not much of a connection between us any more; she's lost her fight. It's as if life has defeated her.

"I met Evan on my first day of Grade Ten. He was a laborer on the construction crew that was building an extension to our school gym – the construction crew was still cleaning up the mess they had made before the semester began. Although I had turned fifteen, I had never really had a boyfriend before, but I only had to take a glance at Evan to fall in love. He was twenty years old, tanned, and muscular … during recess he never did a stroke of work; he spent the time flirting with the girls. He was the first man I was ever really powerfully attracted to and you can bet that I made sure he noticed me. Ethan had a sort of glamorous look, like he could be on the pages of *Seventeen*. I liked that he was older and not in school and had a pick-up truck to drive me around in – I can honestly say that I was in love with him after I had known him two days. He seemed to feel the same about me and I know all my girlfriends were jealous.

"Evan shared an apartment with two other guys, just off Roncesvalles. You would not believe this place. The living room was covered with motorcycle parts, one of the guys was rebuilding a bike and the engine was in pieces on the coffee table and all over the floor. The place reeked of grease, oil, and rotting food; the kitchen was pretty disgusting. Within a week of meeting him, we had sex. This was one day later than it should have been. The sheets on Evan's bed were beyond filthy; they were stained and they stank. We had been making out, sitting on the side of the bed, but when he pulled back the covers, I knew I couldn't go on … I had totally planned to have my first sex with Evan this night … but the sight of those sheets turned me off. I told Evan he would have to take the sheets to the launderette before I was getting into that bed with him. For the first time, I saw an ugly side of Evan, something cruel in his eyes. It only lasted for a split second, but for that instant he scared me. The next night, the same sheets were on the bed, but washed … and that was my first sex. It didn't last very long and I sort of wondered what all the fuss was about. At least it didn't hurt.

"I went with Evan for not quite three months. After our first time, all he seemed to want was more fucks, the quicker the better. He said less and less to me. A date with Evan usually meant that he picked me up in Scarborough, drove me back to his place in his pick-up truck, had sex in his bed, which was ever more disgusting each time, after which he would go into the living room to drink beer and watch hockey on the television with his two buddies. I usually had to get the subway and bus home because after having sex, he had almost no interest in me. I started to hate him after knowing him for about six weeks, but I still continued to ride out to Roncesvalles in the pick-up truck, hoping he might somehow change. He didn't, it just got worse, and after every visit I took the lonely subway ride back home.

"One morning in December, I got out of bed and threw up. I thought it was because I was disgusted at how badly I would allow myself to be treated. It was at that moment I decided I never wanted to see Evan again. I made sure I was out when he called that evening for what was our usual trip across town to his filthy bed. And the next evening. The third day, he was waiting for me outside the school and I told him we were finished. He began to swear at me and I was frightened, but there were a lot of people around and he couldn't do much more than just shout. The day after, he cut me off while I was walking home from school, this time there were less people around and he punched me in the face, knocking me onto the sidewalk. Two guys, seniors from my school, were on the other side of the street… I guess they ran over the street and grabbed Evan before he could hurt me any more. They beat him up pretty good and I was happy; I thought it gave him a dose of the way he had been treating me … it was then I learned what a wuss he was; he cried like a baby. That was the last I saw of him."

"Problem was, it turned out I was pregnant. Evan used rubbers, or at least I thought he did. I never knew quite what was going on down there when we made out; he tore open packets and fiddled around with his dick before thrusting into me. Geez, I never really saw him completely naked … I mean, I touched him under the covers but never for long … he wasn't like you, walking around naked and having showers together, I guess he must have been shy, because he always covered himself up. Not sure why, because he had a nice body, from what I saw of it. Yeah, it might sound crazy, but the first male body I became completely familiar with was Manny's … it fascinated me, especially at first. I couldn't believe that this perfect little creature had somehow been made by me.

"Anyway, because my periods had always been all over the place, I was into my fourth month and showing before I realized I was pregnant … I had suspicions, I suppose, but was in denial. In my mind, I convinced myself that those rubbers that Evan appeared to use were failsafe. Nobody at school seemed to get pregnant when they used them. Once the pregnancy was confirmed, they sent me to counseling. There was no question in my mind about having an abortion; that wasn't going to happen. My big worry was how to tell my mother. But with some persuasion by my counselor, I eventually told her, and Mom surprised me by how understanding she was. She even understood that I never wanted to see Evan again, or have him know that he was to be a father. It was the first time in years I felt close to Mom. So I guess that's my story. The most important bit is Manny. Especially the first three months after he was born; they were the happiest days of my life. I named him after my dad, Emmanuel. The dad I never knew. But I've always called him 'Manny' – you can't really call a baby Emmanuel, can you?"

Despite now having her own territory, it becomes routine for Poppy to mount the stairs that connect the second and third floors of the Ligetti home. To visit with Dylan alone, to chat with Dylan and Victor together, and sometimes to join in larger groups of the university students who occasionally meet up on the third floor. Far from being intimidated by these groups of older students, Poppy establishes her own little niche within the group. They like her up-front honesty and blunt conversation. To this group of students, she's Dylan's girlfriend and because it's common knowledge that she's "living" with Dylan, it becomes all but impossible for Dylan to seek out any other female companionship.

Dylan chafes at the shackles of a steady relationship. Being "shacked up" means that his fellow students have reclassified him to a different genus, one excluded from invitations to nights out at the pub. When his monthly allowance arrives from his parents, Dylan wants to celebrate with a drink or two. And who wants to drink alone? Victor isn't in his room, so Dylan has no option but to ask Poppy if she's up for a little carousing. She's lying, belly down, on Dylan's bed, engrossed in one of her tacky women's magazines. "I'm not going, Dill," responds Poppy, adamantly not shifting her gaze from the magazine. "Manny's not feeling well and I don't want to leave him again with Mrs. Ligetti … you know how much work he is when he's feeling under the weather. Besides, I think you should save the money so we can eat out someplace nice on Saturday." Sure enough, she has barely completed the declaration when there is a crackle and some sniveling broadcast over the audio baby minder. Within two minutes, the sniveling has changed to crying and Poppy is pulling Dylan's housecoat over her shoulders to descend the flight of stairs to tend to the child.

Exasperated, Dylan sprawls over his bed and considers whether to go out by himself. Because the baby minder speaker remains switched on, he hears Poppy enter the bedroom and raise the unhappy infant out of his crib. The crying ceases almost immediately and Poppy begins her banter with Manny, which consists of platitudes and rhetorical baby talk. The noises relayed through the audio baby minder suggest that she is changing his diaper and as she does so, she chatters to the infant continuously in baby speak. "Silly Daddy wants to go out boozing. What a silly boy! If we go out drinking tonight, who's going to look after Mommy's precious little treasure? Who is going to change his diaper and give him love and cuddles?" Noises of some kisses come through the speaker. "But Mommy knows how to make little boys happy. When Mommy goes upstairs, she'll play with Daddy's pecker and then we'll see how much he wants to go out drinking. Yes, we will. Because Mommy knows how much silly little boys love to have their peckers played with. Yes, she does!" More noises of kissing are broadcast.

A short while later, Poppy climbs the stairs, enters Dylan's room, and removes his housecoat, a garment that she requisitioned as her own early on in the relationship. She flops face down onto the bed beside Dylan and retrieves the magazine she abandoned ten minutes earlier, ignoring Dylan, who is lying alongside her. Dylan waits a couple of minutes before saying anything.

"Aren't you going to play with my pecker?" Dylan deadpans. Poppy turns and looks at Dylan, confused. Dylan gestures with his index finger to the audio baby minder speaker. Poppy blushes; it is the first time Dylan has seen her do this and her face turns almost the color of scarlet. "I didn't mind the bit about playing with my pecker. But I wasn't so excited about the daddy part of the deal."

Poppy pushes the magazine aside and lowers her face into the pillow. She sucks in her breath. "Dill, it didn't mean anything, I always babble nonsense to Manny. He doesn't understand any of it and everybody knows it's important to talk to babies as much as possible. It's just my way of dealing with him." She turns back to the magazine, hoping the discussion has ended.

"I don't think you should be calling me 'daddy' in front of him because sooner or later he's going to start to understand. And in case you have any doubts, I am no daddy. Certainly not now, nor in the foreseeable future."

"Don't make a big deal about this, Dill. Like I said, it's just harmless baby talk. Maybe wishful thinking as well – it wouldn't hurt you to pay a little attention to Manny once in a while." With that, Poppy rolls onto her side to face Dylan and smiles at him, before putting into practice her method for making silly little boys happy.

Poppy and Dylan are rolling around on Dylan's bed. Manny has been settled down for the evening, evidenced by silence on the baby minder, and the Ligetti's are seated two floors below in front of a television. The couple is following a rote format of lovemaking that has made sex between them almost boring. Suddenly, Poppy breaks free of Dylan's groping and grasping and grabs him by both shoulders to stare him in the eye. "Dill, do you notice that I never have an orgasm when we have sex?"

Dylan blinks. He shrugs. Poppy continues, "I can make myself come … but when we have sex together we always do the same thing … okay, maybe two things. We make out in the shower or we make out in your bed … and you always come before I have a chance to. Sometimes I come ever so close … but you never seem to notice or care. It doesn't seem to bother you whether it's fun for me or not."

Dylan does not know what to say, so he says nothing.

"I was talking to Gloria about this …" Poppy continues, "She says that you are too uptight to be a good lover." Now Dylan is really lost for words and he is incredulous that this is something that Poppy can discuss over coffee and biscotti with Signora Ligetti.

"How … what … is it really possible??" he sputters. "How can you discuss our sex life with that old woman?"

Poppy is unapologetic. "Gloria is very passionate, she knows lots about life – you'd be surprised! She told me that it is my job to make you less uptight. She says that in terms of life experience, you are just a baby compared with me; you've never had to be responsible for anyone but yourself. I know it's my fault, too. We may have lots of sex, but we never talk about it, we just do it. She says I have to find a way of telling you what I like."

"Does that mean you don't like the way we've been doing it so far?"

"Well I did at first … sort of. I mean I never really enjoyed sex that much before Manny was born, so at the beginning I did have fun having sex with you. But now … the same old thing happens every time. It's boring for me and I want to do it in different ways. I want to come too when we make out. And I want you to care whether I come."

Dylan considers. "So what do you want me to do?" he asks. Poppy leaps off the bed and grabs Dylan's housecoat, wrapping it around herself. She exits the bedroom and heads for the kitchen. Within seconds, she returns with a glass bottle in hand.

Dylan opens his eyes wide, questioning Poppy. "Olive oil," she responds. "It has many uses in the bedroom."

"I can only guess," says Dylan, dubious, "that's according to Signora Ligetti?"

"Dill, if I suggest something we can do, maybe something a little kinky, I know you are sort of straitlaced, promise you won't make fun of me. It's something I have thought about, but never had the courage to ask … because it is something that, in my mind, is so not you."

Straitlaced? Dylan is offended; is this the way people see him? He squints, wondering what to expect. "Okay. What?"

"I want you to fuck me in the ass, Dill. It felt so good when you put your finger up my bum the first time we took a shower together. That was my all-time favorite sex,"

"Fuck you up the ass? This is Signora Ligetti's prescription for sexual satisfaction? That's where your g-spot has located itself?"

"No, I wouldn't discuss anything that personal with her, but I should be able to do so with you. It was just in talking with Mrs. Ligetti, I got to thinking about what I wanted from sex. Up to this point, it's been all about you and I was content just to make you happy. When I was giving birth to Manny, I got torn down there and had a lot of stitches. Everything got rearranged and my bum has been extra sensitive ever since."

"Are you sure it won't hurt you?" asks Dylan, who has only ever witnessed this mode of copulation in a porno movie.

"That's for me to decide. And if it does, I know that you'll stop. It is just something I have fantasized about since our first sex, even though I realize it sort of happened by accident when we were all soapy and discovering the different openings in our bodies. I don't want you to think I'm a slut."

Dylan slathers Poppy's hind quarters with President's Choice EVO. He pours more onto his penis. However, the mechanics do not quite work out as Poppy expects. She gasps. One tentative inboard thrust is all it takes for Poppy to reconsider. "OK, Dill, I've changed my mind, you're hurting me."

Dylan rolls onto his back and slithers Poppy on top of him. The lugubrious slathering of olive oil has added a dimension of its own to the coupling and Dylan sloshes his way into her cunt and simultaneously inserts his middle finger to the hilt of his palm into her anus. He works that middle finger rather than his penis and it makes a connection to something in Poppy that has thus far eluded him. While impaled on Dylan's penis, the reverberations that ripple through Poppy's central nervous system have less to do with the penis than the movement of the finger penetrated deep into her anus. For Dylan, this is an exercise in behavior observation rather than his usual thrusting and gasping for his own gratification. Orgasm convulses Poppy's delicate frame into a series of taut oscillations that reverberate through her, rhythmically clenching the cock inside her to bring her partner off seconds later.

Poppy rolls off Dylan to lie on her back. For a while, she stares at the ceiling, cupping her head with her palms. Then she stretches her arms upward and delivers a full-lung, one-ten decibel scream to the heavens, an encore of the glee expressed in a McDonald's parking lot some weeks previously. Dylan cups her mouth in a futile attempt to muffle the volume. What will the Ligetti's think? Has Dylan stabbed his lover? Immediately, Poppy bursts into hysterical laughter. Suddenly, the bedroom door flies open, startling Poppy into silence. It is Victor Lee enacting a bizarre kung fu-like stance. "Are you OK, Poppy?" asks a panicked Victor.

"What the fuck?" says naked Dylan, annoyed at the intrusion. Without making any effort to conceal her nudity, Poppy leans forward, propping herself on her elbows and belly laughs disdainfully at Victor.

"Sorry," says Victor, addressing Dylan, "I thought Poppy may have been hurt." Victor turns and exits Dylan's room.

Dylan is confused. "Why would Victor think I would hurt you?"

Poppy stops laughing. "You dummy," she says. "Dylan, you are so into yourself, you don't notice anything else that's going on in the world."

"What do you mean?" asks Dylan, nonplussed.

Poppy looks at Dylan in a way that telegraphs him that her seventeen years of existence have somehow endowed her with much more wisdom than his twenty, a theme of this evening's interaction.

"Victor is crazy about me. Everybody knows except you. All your college buddies know. Signora Ligetti told me that Victor is much more in love with me than you will ever be. She also says that he would make a much better partner for me than you. She says he has *depth*."

Dylan is hurt. He has no depth? "So why the fuck don't you go off with Victor?"

Poppy gets serious. "Depth doesn't always count, not with me anyway." She cuddles into Dylan. "You are kind of selfish … I know you don't really care about me in the way I would like … but at the same time you are cute in a way I can't quite explain … and sexy, maybe because you just so hungrily want me and that makes me feel nice."

"Poppy, I am not sure why you would accuse me of not really caring about you; that's really unfair." But even as he says this, Dylan knows the statement is something of a lie – he knows very well that Poppy cares more about him than he about her.

"Don't get uptight, Dill. I sort of like you the way you are – I just know that a year from now, we probably won't be together; there are too many differences between us. I know we have some things in common – there's a side of me that's greedy and selfish too – just not enough to keep us together"

Dylan stares at the ceiling.

"Don't worry, schmoopi, I love to just be with you, to hold your hand when we walk down a street, to listen to you talk even though I don't know what you are saying half the time … and be naked with you … I just had an orgasm with you, my very first that was not by myself. That only happened because I trust you and felt okay with telling you what I want. But you can't deny that it'll be years before you are ready to settle down with a woman. But for a real partner, someone who will look after me, protect me, remember my birthday … maybe even love Manny … well then, I will look for a Victor type."

"Well that makes me feel like shit," says Dylan, feeling sorry for himself.

"Dill, I don't know a lot about men. You're only my second lover, and the first was when I was too innocent to know any better. I know you have been with a few girls before me, but all the same, I know a lot more about the way men think than you know about the way women think. The night we met, I knew you were just a horny college boy trying to score some sex. But your timing happened to be good, because at that moment I needed to feel that I could turn someone like you on … I was in a rut and wanted something in my world to change, anything really. You hit on me and as things have turned out, I think we have been pretty good for each other. Maybe in your own way you love me, but truly, I only feel good about us as a couple when we are alone together … as soon as other people are around us, especially your university friends, I feel like a bimbo. I'm not sure if this is just me being paranoid or whether it is something you do. Maybe a bit of both. I mean … you're not about to take me home to introduce me to Mummy and Daddy, are you now?

Yeah, I can just imagine that scene – you, me, and the baby makes three?" She pauses to consider. "Victor would, though … he might even be proud to do it!"

When Dylan has time to distill these insights of Poppy's, he realizes that in the mindset of Signora Ligetti, he represents nothing more than a hindrance to Poppy attaining her true destiny with doting, reliable, older man, Victor Lee. Returning to spend the next academic year in his digs at the Ligetti's will be out of the question; sad, because issues of Poppy aside, he is so comfortable there. He will have to invent some fiction for the Ligetti's to explain the reasons he will not be returning the following school year, but he realizes whatever lies he comes up with will be acceptable from their point of view. The bottom line is that Poppy and son are more important to them than he.

Dylan is teaching Poppy to drive. Poppy actually had no compelling interest in obtaining a driver's license, but Dylan informs her that driving is critical to being independent in the world. The first lesson takes place in the nearly vacant parking lot of a commuter railway station in Rouge Hill at the east end of Toronto, the location having been identified as being usually void of cars on a Sunday. Dylan drives his teenaged Pontiac to the parking lot, steps out of the driver's door, and circles the vehicle to climb in on the passenger side. Poppy, meanwhile, slides over to the driver side of the bench seat and looks extraordinarily out of place, somehow diminished by the steering wheel in front of her. After spending some time adjusting the front bench seat, Poppy reaches into her purse and retrieves from it a pair of glasses. It is the first time she has ever worn them in the presence of Dylan and she wrinkles her nose and frowns at him to suppress any comments.

There is one parked car in this vast parking lot and Dylan has parked his vehicle as far away from it as possible. Poppy listens carefully to the verbal instructions issued by Dylan, adjusts the glasses on her nose, starts the engine, shifts the transmission into drive, releases the parking brake, and the car nudges forward. At the appropriate moment, the instructor tells the learner to depress the accelerator pedal, and somehow omits mentioning this is a modulating device, not knowing that what was obvious to him at four years of age might not have been to his student. All of the two hundred and fifty horses under the aging Pontiac's hood are unleashed into an explosive response that pins both occupants of the car into their seatbacks. Fortunately, the rookie driver recalls the location of the brake pedal and hits it with as much gusto as was applied to the accelerator a moment before, and not so fortunately, all four wheels of the car lock, sending the vehicle into a yawed skid. The car comes to a smoking standstill just inches short of the sole other vehicle in the lot. Fear for the fate that might befall his wheels, and more justified terror regarding his personal safety, causes Dylan to momentarily lose the power of speech.

Relieved that she is not dead, Poppy leans her body forward into the steering wheel, setting the horn off. Startled and feeling that the car is to blame, the girl strikes at the instrument panel, convinced that something should be punished.

Once he has recovered his wits, Dylan attempts to explain to Poppy how an accelerator functions, which prompts an enraged response. "It's a bit late to tell me that now! We nearly crashed, thanks to your stupidity. I want a real driving instructor." The instant she completes the sentence, she bursts into tears. Dylan is now lost for words for a different reason. Being blamed for this near-death incident was not the outcome he was expecting; in his mind there was no doubting where the fault lay.

Over the course of an hour, the Pontiac navigates the vacant lanes in the parking lot and for some reason, is inexplicably drawn toward the few obstructions on the vast tarmac – namely, half a dozen concrete lampposts and the single parked car. Dylan has to summon all his powers to suppress his impulses to react to the dangers to which Poppy subjects his automobile and its two occupants. The dynamics of navigating the car during the lesson are variously punctuated by Poppy angrily berating her instructor's ability to teach anybody anything, and outbursts of tears. Finally, Dylan can take this no longer and angrily responds in kind to one of Poppy's hissy fits, and the couple has its first full-fledged fight. The student is ordered out of the driver's seat and the lesson ignominiously ends.

Dylan drives back to the Ligetti's at a much faster speed than is his habit. During the ride, Poppy sits, arms crossed, glaring out of the passenger window at nothing in particular. At the moment of arrival, Poppy launches herself out of the passenger seat, slams the car door with as much force as she can summon, and disappears through the Ligetti's front door. Dylan takes a deep breath before making the short cut ascent up the fire escape to his rooms.

Two nights go by and Dylan sees nothing of Poppy. He tells himself that this is a good thing. Good riddance; it was never his idea to get into this suffocating relationship that is playing havoc with his schedule and emotions when he would rather be focusing on his studies. On the third night following the driving lesson, sleeping Dylan is awakened when his bedroom door opens quietly and Poppy enters to sit on his bed. He hears the noise of the audio baby minder being clicked on and then parked on the bedside table. Poppy slides under the covers and because she is wearing nothing more than an oversized T-shirt, which immediately rides up rib high, the result is a predictable kiss and make-up fuck with not a word exchanged.

Poppy is the first to speak. She informs Dylan that she has decided to give him another chance as a driving instructor; yes, she has forgiven him for being so perfectly horrible to her. Sure, Signor Ligetti offered to take over as driving instructor and she gave that offer some serious consideration, before declining. Teaching her to drive would be a perfect way for Dylan to prove how much he loved her: he'd just have to promise not to be such an asshole ever again in the future.

Dylan is dumbfounded. He begins to tell Poppy that he believes she was absolutely correct about his abilities as a driving instructor and that she would be much better taught by someone anonymous. "I know you don't mean that, Dylan," declares Poppy earnestly. "You are still just sore about the fact you were in the wrong. I've been big enough to forgive you so the least you can do is apologize to me. It's my belief that this fight has made us closer – Signora Ligetti said it probably would."

Dylan stares at Poppy in disbelief. Hell will freeze over before he will apologize to Poppy for his behavior three days earlier, but he avoids the inevitable confrontation that would result if he addressed the issue of her theatrics. As it turns out, Poppy doesn't seem to expect an actual apology, does she consider the fact that Dylan did not turf her out of bed a sufficient apology, or has she accurately appraised the likely reaction? Within seconds, Poppy is straddling Dylan for round two of their coupling, the round in which their recent history requires Dylan to gratify her needs over his own.

Rhianna Douglas phones her son to invite him to spend the Easter weekend at home with the family in Sarnia. A female voice answers the phone. "Who am I speaking to?" enquires Mrs. Douglas.

"Poppy," is the response. Rhianna Douglas assumes she has the wrong number and is about to hang up. "Do you want to speak to Dylan? If you do, he won't be back until after eight. I can take a message, if you like."

"Oh," responds Mrs. Douglas, puzzled. "Yes, ask him to call me when he gets in … this is his mother."

"Oh hi, Mrs. Douglas, it's nice to finally get a chance to speak to you. Has Dylan spoken of me to you yet? … I'm Poppy, his girlfriend."

"No, he hasn't," responds Rhianna, her curiosity piqued. "Dylan doesn't say a lot about what he does when he's not at home. Still, this is an opportunity for us to chat. How long have you and Dylan known each other?"

"Gosh, it must be around five months now. We've been living together for most of that time so I'm surprised Dill hasn't said something to you."

Rhianna Douglas is not surprised that Dylan hasn't mentioned this girlfriend, already a live-in. While his younger brothers Daniel and Dominic almost always have some girl or other in tow, never once has Rhianna actually met a girlfriend of Dylan's. She was made aware of an older woman he was seeing when they lived in Spain, but Dylan never spoke of this association. The girl she is talking to certainly doesn't sound like an older woman; in fact, she speaks like a fourteen-year-old. Rhianna decides this is an opportunity not to be wasted. "Five months – hard to believe! In that case, why don't you both come down and spend the Easter weekend in Sarnia."

"I'd love to, Mrs. Douglas," responds Poppy, "but it's not so simple; we don't have a car seat for Manny. Manny's my son. He's just turned eleven months."

For an instant, Rhianna is in shock, so much so that her ability to process simple math is taxed. "Is Dylan … the father?" she asks, wondering how being a grand-mother might change her life.

Poppy laughs. "Oh no, don't worry, Mrs. Douglas. But I should say that everyone who sees Manny thinks he looks just like Dylan. Everyone except Dill, that is."

"Then the three of you must come. Take the train … or better still, fly down," responds Rhianna. "That way, you'll spend more hours with us and less on the road with the Easter traffic."

"Wow, that sounds like a swell idea, Mrs. Douglas. I've never been on an airplane before."

"Tell Dylan to call me when he gets in. I'll take care of the plane tickets, just let me know what times are best. Are there any special arrangements we should know about regarding your … son?"

The conversation doesn't end here. Rhianna and Poppy get into a discussion about the trials of raising children, then get into outlining Dylan's few attributes and many shortcomings as a son, as a lover, and as a human being. At the end of the chat, Rhianna is not quite sure who she has been speaking to … certainly, Poppy is no genius, but she has an engaging freshness and sincerity. She wonders how well this naïve-sounding girlfriend will stick handle informing Dylan that he has been finessed into spending Easter with Mom, Dad, and now, no-longer secret lover and babe.

Poppy tells Dylan. Dylan is dumbstruck. When he can find words, he asks, "You spoke to my mom?"

"Yes, Dill, she sounds like a really nice person; we had a long chat. I must say, your mom and I have a lot in common – we're on the same train of thought about so many things, especially when it comes to you. And Dill, I was embarrassed. We've been together all this time and you have not mentioned a word about us to your mom."

"I had no intention of going home for the Easter weekend. I have stuff here I need to catch up on."

"What stuff? Anyway, it's too late, it's all arranged. Your mom's mailing us plane tickets for Thursday evening."

"What! We're not flying down? Without my car, we'll be stuck in the house the whole time."

"Aw schmoopie, poor thing! Spending three whole days with Mummy and Daddy, how will you survive?" she says, mimicking baby talk. Then, snapping out of it, she continues, "I want to meet your family. I never realized you had a seven-year-old sister, another sister, and two brothers. I know nothing about your folks. I found out more about you in talking with your mother for ten minutes than from you in five months. You have the coolest Mom; she's like a mother … from a television show. And I want to see for myself whether your dad is the asshole you say he is."

"Poppy, I'm not ready for this 'meet the parents' phase of the relationship. I find it difficult enough to engage in superficial chit-chat with my folks, let alone stuff that matters. And bringing your girlfriend home for the weekend is stuff that matters as far as my family is concerned."

"Dill, if this is about letting me know that we're not a permanent thing, then let me set your mind at rest by telling you, I know we're not. Right from the start, I gave us a year together at the max. I even told your mom that. There are so many ways we're not suited to each other and I don't want to get into them. I only want us to be together while it is fun. You are special to me because you helped me get my confidence back after having Manny. And though you'd be unlikely to give me any credit, I know I have made a difference in your life; I've made you less … stuck up and snobbish."

"Stuck up? Snobbish?" Dylan is appalled.

"Yeah, you know what I mean; you don't know how lucky you are to have me. You'd be like most of your university friends, uptight and neurotic if it weren't for me … people who'd rather talk about life rather than live it. Especially the girls, Dylan – can't you see how shallow they are? The right label has to be in every piece of clothing they wear, and if you ever got lucky with one of them, they'd check that the lubricant on the condom, that you'd *have* to wear, was organic."

Dylan pauses. Poppy is smart. Whoever would have thought that so much life knowledge could be gleaned from the pages of trashy women's magazines, the only education that Poppy has received since mid-way through Grade Ten. As a matter of fact, since his proactive pick-up on the first night they met, Poppy has subsequently crafted every move that has guided their relationship to this point. Dylan shakes his head. "This weekend is going to be a disaster," he rues, thinking mainly about how his father will react to his arrival with Poppy and child.

"Maybe … maybe not," says Poppy. "I realize after talking to your mother, Dylan, that you have a real family, something I've never had. Your mother loves you to pieces. I don't think anyone has ever adored me, other than Manny, that is. I wish you did sometimes. I'm curious to see how all of the pieces of the puzzle fit together … to see a real family." All Dylan can do is shake his head.

Poppy's pleasure at taking her first flight in an airplane is dampened by Manny's discomfort, not unusual in infants whose ears do not easily adapt to changes of altitude and cannot yawn to equalize pressure on the eardrums. Rhianna Douglas meets the trio at the airport. She hugs Dylan first, then warmly enshrouds Poppy and Manny. She assures Poppy that Manny is the splitting image of Dylan at the same age and she will show her the photographs to prove it. Mrs. Douglas all but ignores Dylan and focuses most of her attention on Poppy and Manny.

Thankfully, Dylan's father is not yet at home. Less thankfully, this is an opportunity for Mrs. Douglas to show off all the naked baby and other embarrassing shots taken of Dylan throughout his childhood. Each page of the aging photo album produces renewed peals of laughter from Mrs. Douglas and Poppy. Never has Dylan needed a set of wheels like he needs them now. He wants to speed off into the night and head back to Toronto … or at least to a bar.

An interesting turn of events takes place when Dylan's father returns later in the evening. Dylan would have bet on his father disdaining Poppy for no other reason than being a seventeen-year-old single mother of no social consequence. But he had overlooked the potency of a cute body and a pretty face. Contrary to Dylan's expectations, Mr. Douglas becomes embarrassingly obsequious around Poppy; he almost drools in her presence. For her part, Poppy is quick to synthesize this windfall and play up to it. To her credit, she knows how to do this and remain cool and in control; she orchestrates daddy with the same ease as she does his son. Similarly, Dylan's two sisters, Dawn, aged seven, and Deidra, aged fourteen, appear to be equally enchanted with Poppy and Manny. Dylan discovers that his best strategy is to withdraw and allow his girlfriend to assume whatever percentage of the limelight she is prepared to take.

Rhianna goes to the fridge and retrieves a nearly full bottle of white wine left over from dinner. The house is quiet; only Mrs. Douglas and her eldest son are still up. Mr. Douglas is in a scotch stupor on a recliner in the adjacent living room, while

Manny, his exhausted mother, and surrogate aunts have retreated to the bedrooms in the house. Rhianna pours wine into a pair of glasses on the kitchen table. Finally, an opportunity to chat with Dylan alone. She raises her wine glass in a silent cheers and Dylan reciprocates.

"Not the type of girl I expected you to have in tow?"

"So what do you see as being my 'type' of girl, Mom?" asks Dylan.

Rhianna looks Dylan in the eye. "I really don't know. I know so little about your taste in women. Unlike your brothers, you haven't once brought a girl home since that insidious friendship you had with that Summers girl when you were far too young to have a girlfriend. I couldn't stand that little vixen! I only allowed it to go on because you got on so well with the girl's father ... you and your own dad were never comfortable with each other ... especially back then."

"You mean Dad used to pick on me relentlessly. It bordered on cruelty ... I never understood why."

Rhianna says nothing for a few moments. It was true – in those days there had been something unnatural about the way Darren persecuted Dylan; she constantly felt that she had to either protect her oldest son or keep him out of the range of her husband's crosshairs. "You used to sleep over with Carrie so often. Sometimes, it seemed like we didn't see you for days at a time. God knows what you got up to. I shudder to imagine."

"We were kids, Mother. Other than a few isolated instances of curiosity, we basically just hung out together. I always felt that her father liked me ... I know I desperately wanted him to. The only reason I had any success as a baseball pitcher was because I wanted to please Hank ... for me, it seemed like it was impossible to do anything that would please Dad."

Mrs. Douglas takes a sip of wine. "I didn't want this to be a postmortem on the shortcomings of your childhood. I set this weekend up behind your back because I was curious about you ... and this girlfriend. You circle your wagons when it comes to talking about matters that are personal to you. Daniel and Domenic told me outrageous stories about your love life at boarding school. Did you really have an affair with a teacher's wife?"

Dylan takes a sip of wine. Daniel and Domenic still attend Elwin Park; Daniel is in his final year at the school. Should he be honest with his mother? He decides that he will. "Yes, I did. It was brief and not as simple as it may sound. The teacher was gay. For about a year, I used to babysit his kids ... and got to know his wife."

Rhianna covers her face with her hands. "How old were you?"

"I dunno ... fifteen, sixteen."

"Had I known, I would have sued the school out of existence."

"That would have been really stupid. I wanted her just as much as she wanted me. I knew what I was doing."

"At fifteen?"

Dylan laughs. "Of course. She wasn't my first lover. During my first year at Elwin, I fell for a local Romsey girl. I spent a grand total of one night with her, but it caused quite a scandal, and as a result, the girl was dispatched to a remote boarding school, a gulag for girls. At the time, I thought I was going to be expelled, but the school decided not to report the incident to you and I sure wasn't going to tell you!"

Rhianna laughs. "How ironic! The main reason your father wants to send you away to a British boarding school at the end of seventh grade, rather than wait until you'd finished eighth grade, is that nobody quite knows what you and that little witch Carrie are getting up to during your cozy little 'sleepovers.' We, meaning the collective parents, none of whom have the gumption to confront the issue, we just agree something unhealthy is happening … and somehow, you find a way of screwing everything in sight while confined in a single-sex, English boarding school in the middle of nowhere!"

"It wasn't like that, Mom. Actually, I wish that it could have been. From what I remember of Elwin Park, for the most part I was just as lonely and sex-starved as the remainder of its inmates. In addition, I found it almost impossible to strike up transient friendships during the school vacations. I always envied Daniel and Domenic for having the ability to do that."

A longer silence ensues. For a while, both Dylan and his mother focus on their wine glasses and the business of consuming their contents.

"I met your Spanish lover, your Gabi. I spoke to her, as a matter of fact, though I didn't let on who I was. She was beautiful … quite stunning. A lot older than you, of course. It was Daniel who told me you and she had a thing going. I was curious; mothers are allowed to be. I drove to the airport bar just to see her. I ordered a sherry and attempted some chit-chat … but she spoke almost no English. Still, I could see why you were attracted to her. To me, she seemed more your type than … Poppy."

Now Dylan has a chuckle. "She was divorced and had a seven-year-old kid. In addition, she was sexually confused and had a long-term lesbian lover. In total, we spent three nights together. And on the first of those nights, I was too drunk to do anything but sleep on her couch. Things are not always what they seem!"

"So what is the story behind Poppy and you?"

Dylan laughs. "She's uncomplicated. Yes, despite the baby in tow … and all of what that brings … she is what you see. Sure, we don't have a lot in common …

we certainly don't have stimulating conversations – *Seventeen* Magazine falls into the upper spectrum of her reading material. But we have fun together. She's completely unpretentious and I like that she's crazy about me. I need life to be simple at the moment and she fits the bill."

"Dylan, you sound weary, too weary for a twenty-year-old. Be careful with Poppy … you speak of her as if she is something in the short term. But I sense she is fonder of you than you may think … maybe she's not quite as simple as you believe."

"I'm not sure if this is a conversation I should be having with my mother … we have fun in bed … this has a way of compensating for other shortcomings on our mutual compatibility scorecard. Although we are not really 'living' together, Poppy is the first girlfriend I've had where routine sex has been a feature … as opposed to 'discovery' sex – its more frenzied version, that happens when bodies are in the learning-about-each-other phase. We both realize that this is not a permanent relationship – Poppy is quite blunt about the fact that she only wants us to be together while it's fun for both of us."

Rhianna chuckles and stares into her wine glass. She is pleased she is having this conversation with her son, but can't help feeling a little embarrassed. Dylan is not feeling embarrassed; the wine has worked its way into his blood. He splits what remains in the bottle into the two glasses on the kitchen table.

"So speaking of matters sexual, how are things between you and Dad," he asks, looking his mother directly in the eye.

Rhianna slowly shakes her head. "We have developed our own strategies for survival. It doesn't always make for an easy life, but we manage. I'm sure both of us have given thought to separating many times over the years. We've each had an affair or two along the way. In some ways, having Dawn brought us closer together."

Dylan looks quizzically at his mother. "Funny, I could see Dad having a fling … in fact, as a kid I accidently witnessed evidence of him being unfaithful … but not you."

Now it is his mother who feels emboldened. "I am happy you put me on a little pedestal, Dill, but I'm sorry to disappoint you. My affair was rather more serious than your father's sordid little flings. Not only was it more serious, but you knew the man … your childhood idol, your trusty baseball coach."

"Not Hank?"

"The very same. It didn't begin until after you had left for that awful school we sent you to … it began because Hank took it upon himself to advise your father and I not to send you to a British school shortly before we delivered you to the … what was it you called the place? … the gulag? Anyway, I came to realize how strongly he felt about you; the poor man desperately wanted a son … during the previous five years, he had spent far more time with you than your own father. When we returned to Venezuela, circumstance threw us into a couple of chance encounters ... after which, we arranged time together that left nothing to chance ... your father and I could have very easily split up over it. Eventually, some kind of common sense prevailed and Hank and I agreed that what we were doing didn't make sense. True to the spirit ... or lack thereof ... in our generation, we meekly retreated back into the status quo."

Dylan shakes his head. So Hank, his mentor and hero, ends up banging his mother. He can't find it in himself to condemn his mother. Never throughout childhood did he consider his father worthy of his mother's love. But having his childhood perceptions of both Hank and his mom burst within minutes makes him wish he had never got into this tête-à-tête with his mother.

Shortly after returning from the Easter weekend, Dylan learns that Victor is planning to remain in Toronto during the summer vacation. Victor explains that it is easier to find summer work in Toronto than Vancouver. There is something in the way Victor says this that leads Dylan to believe that this has more to do with not being apart from Poppy, three entire months in which he could work on the girl without her being distracted by Dylan. Dylan nods. He wants to tell Victor that everything is okay, that he believes that Poppy and Victor would make a better couple than Dylan and Poppy could ever be, that he knows Victor can provide Poppy with a level of love that he cannot. But he is unable to do this because the game is not played that way. Victor must be seen to win the damsel on merit, not by default. Dylan knows he must fade out of the picture.

18. SUMMER CAMP

Dylan's Pontiac heads north, up highways 400 and 101 and beyond, deep into the wilderness of Ontario. The highway peters out into two lane roads, then dirt roads; the towns become smaller and further apart, their names mostly French or aboriginal. Using a crude pencil-drawn map, Dylan navigates first unmade roads, followed by some even rougher gravel trails. His destination is Camp Little Wawa. He is to begin a six-week summer job as a camp counselor. The camp is managed by the parents of a classmate of his, Jeremiah Neeskins. Jeremiah is no special friend of Dylan's, just a face that appears in some of his classes, one that becomes familiar enough to warrant a nod when passed in a hallway or on the street. It's not a likeness that Dylan ever saw at a party or drinking in a pub, something that should have provoked some questions in his mind when he was propositioned for a summer job. In addition, Jeremiah is always a Jeremiah, never a Jerry.

When he finally arrives at his destination, he is confronted by a sign that drops his jaw: "Camp Little Wawa, a Christian Camp for Boys and Girls."

Dylan brakes the Pontiac to a crunching standstill on the dirt road and stares in disbelief at the sign. In his recruitment spiel, Jeremiah spoke of needing someone who could lead hiking expeditions, and teach water and boating skills. In other words, someone who could generally set a good example for a group of eight- to fifteen-year-old kids during their summer vacation. His role was to be a one of ten youth counselors. According to Jeremiah, all ten counselors were students, average age around twenty, Grade Twelve or college students, who were expected to enjoy themselves at least as much as their charges in the uncontaminated, though insect-infested, air of Northern Ontario.

Dylan considers whether to turn the car around and head back to Toronto. The downside of this option is that he has been driving for over five hours and dusk is not far away. The only condition that Dylan sought from Jeremiah Neeskins was that he travel to the camp by car, not by bus along with the other counselors and camp inmates. Thank God! Dylan well knows the importance of an automobile to maintaining independence and in this instance it would likely provide him with an escape route if required.

The car engine continues to idle. Dylan decides that he should at least confront Jeremiah Neeskins and let him know what he thinks of being deceived by him. He shifts the Pontiac into gear and navigates another mile before approaching the cluster of buildings that constitute the summer camp. The outbuildings of the camp, its "cabins," are shuttered and unpopulated, but there are two parked vehicles outside a larger central building. Dylan noses the Pontiac alongside these two vehicles and exits the vehicle to stretch.

Before he has time to approach the front door, it opens and Jeremiah strides out to greet him as if he is a long-lost friend. Framed in the doorway behind him are what appear to be Jeremiah's parents. The manner of greeting short-circuits Dylan's ability to open with a complaint about the deceit of not being informed that this is a religious camp.

Dylan is summoned into the log house and has a meal thrust in front of him; it appears as if his three hosts have already eaten. Jeremiah Neeskins and his parents are doing all of the talking; Dylan's role in the conversation is limited to monosyllables. He settles into eating his meal and decides to wait until the subject of God is raised. The issue does not come up until the outlining of schedules is discussed. Dylan braces the table with both hands and looks directly at Jeremiah rather than his parents. "Okay," he begins, "not once, when we discussed this, did you mention that this was some kind of Bible camp. I have to tell you right now that I have nothing but contempt for organized religion. I am clearly not who you might have thought I was, so if you can provide me with a place to sleep tonight, I intend to leave first thing in the morning."

Jeremiah looks toward his father, ceding the response to him. Mr. Neeskins responds, "This is not a Bible camp, it is a Christian camp. There is a difference. We uphold Christian values as our way of life, but it's not our objective to impose our views on anyone, certainly not on the youngsters we host. Participation in worship and prayer sessions is entirely voluntary ... indeed, less than half our campers choose to attend. We bear no grudge against those who choose not to embrace Jesus in their hearts. We guide rather than indoctrinate. It's a fact that I would prefer youth leaders who did attend worship and prayer, most do, because leadership by example is a feature of our philosophy here at Camp Little Wawa ... but Jeremiah assures me you have other qualities that will benefit our young guests."

Dylan is caught off-guard by this speech. It is delivered by a person who sounds rational, not a quality he generally associates with the religious. He stares at Pastor Neeskins.

"Our young guests are mostly from Toronto. About half are sponsored by Christian organizations, the remainder is funded by their parents. Some present problems of social adjustment ... frankly, they can be difficult. But never once has our ability to respond to a challenge been exceeded ... with the help of the Good Father, we do our best to ensure that every child entrusted to our care has a memorable summer experience, one they will treasure into adulthood. For Camp Little Wawa, it matters less that someone calls themselves a practicing Christian, so long as the spirit of Christianity is observed."

Dylan rubs his chin. "Should I decide to stay, I won't be attending any prayer sessions or any other kind of formal service. To be honest, I believe I've been duped into coming here and that kind of pisses me off." Dylan eyes Jeremiah with some malevolence. Jeremiah looks at his father, once again deferring a response to him.

"I don't know what my son told you about Camp Little Wawa, but I am very sure he would not have lied. I'd like you to seriously consider staying with us – my sense is that you have plenty to contribute to a summer camp environment; our greatest need is to have a leader with solid outdoor and water sport skills. Jeremiah assures me you are well qualified in these areas. Most of our youth counselors are volunteer church youth leaders from Toronto … often it takes them some time to adjust to living in the outdoors. Our campers will not arrive until tomorrow afternoon so try to make up your mind by then … it is natural for these youngsters to form friendships and indeed, bond with their counselors, who become their guiding lights. It would be unfair to them if you were to quit mid-way into what should be a special summer experience for each of them."

In the twilight, Dylan explores Camp Little Wawa; it has an unmistakably Northern Ontario ambience. Along with the clean air and natural beauty of the setting, there is no forgetting the reality of being at one with nature. Swarms of black flies consume human flesh one tiny, but painful mouthful at a time, competing for blood with deerflies and mosquitoes. On the positive side, the camp appears to be well-equipped with canoes, kayaks, rowboats, a gym, and sports facilities. Perhaps he can get in shape, get a tan, and pick up some pocket change at the same time.

Thus Dylan enters the world of Camp Little Wawa, Pastor Neeskins, Mrs. Neeskins, and head counselor Jeremiah Neeskins. Dylan's role is to be counselor Dill, leader of boy's cabin number ten. Cabin number ten houses the oldest group of male campers at Little Wawa, the Grade Seven and Eight kids known as seniors. The cabin is a rickety structure constructed of flimsy cedar boards on a rough, concrete base. The roof is panel-pressed steel that amplifies the noise of anything that falls on it, whether it be a twig from one of the surrounding trees or rain, which could be confused for machine gun fire.

A flotilla of yellow school buses arrives during the afternoon of Dylan's second day at Little Wawa. They disgorge large numbers of excitable children. To Dylan, it is immediately apparent that there is a heavy bias of children in the younger age groups versus that of the older kids. Along with the children arrives the corps of counselors, the nine other counselors. Dylan observes that there is nothing in the children attending this Christian camp that distinguishes them from a group of "normal" children, but this cannot be said for the corps of counselors that accompanies the kids. The five female and four male counselors display way over the average adornments of bad teeth, bulbous spectacles, and acne, features that mark them in Dylan's mind as oddball and indisputably Christian. There'll be no one in this group willing to sneak out for a Saturday night beer at a local bar.

Life settles into a routine. In addition to his responsibilities as a cabin chief for his group of male campers, he is assigned an activity group, which is evenly made up of senior boys and girls. Activities consist of team sports, canoeing, sailing, swimming, and hiking. Every night around dusk, a large campfire is lit, and any campers who have the fortitude sit around and are led by Jeremiah into grating renditions of hymns, Christian chants, and other popular songs with youngsters such as "Ten Green Bottles." Dylan avoids these singsongs as he does the scheduled morning and after-dinner prayer sessions.

Four days after arrival, Dylan and a second counselor are leading an expedition to climb Mount Smokey. Mount Smokey is actually a hill rather than a mountain; the expedition is more about getting ten kids there and back without sustaining casualties. The plan is to canoe across Lake Little Wawa, portage the canoes a quarter mile to the Goose River, paddle upriver to the foothills of Mount Smokey, then launch an ascent of the 300-meter summit. The hardy campers who make up the group are aged between twelve to fourteen years.

Dylan seats the troops on the sand alongside the lake to outline the action plan: his charges are adorned in swimsuits and lifejackets, and seem about as enthusiastic as can be expected of a group of kids at nine in the morning. Girls' senior counselor Rosemary is to be second in command for the expedition and she is either praying or drifting back into sleep during his briefing. Dylan has in his possession a hand-annotated map provided to him by Head Counselor Jeremiah Neeskins, a compass, and a list of names. His first duty as commander is roll call, and he attempts to make note of the names.

The day is long and tiring. Rosemary has a passive disposition, meaning that Dylan is required to both macro and micromanage every step of the all-day adventure After the ascent and lunch on top of Mount Smokey, the now-fatigued group returns to the Goose River landing and paddles with the flow to the portage point that leads back to Lake Little Wawa. After disembarking the canoes, a small problem emerges. Dylan is informed that one of the girls has twisted an ankle and is unable to walk. Dylan and Rosemary check out the injured party. One of the fourteen-year-old girls is sitting on a rock with a sneaker removed, nursing an ankle. Dylan approaches and lifts the foot to inspect the ankle. It appears to be a perfectly normal ankle and the girl is in no notable distress.

"Remove your other shoe," Dylan bosses the patient. The girl removes her other sneaker and Dylan compares the two ankles. He rotates the supposedly-injured ankle. "It doesn't look like anything is wrong with your foot. Are you sure you can't walk?"

The girl is adamant. No, this ankle got twisted as she exited the canoe and it is too painful to stand on, let alone walk. Dylan looks his patient in the eye for the first time. She is strikingly unusual, possibly mixed race, and he is surprised she didn't register in his mind before this moment. Her hair is dark and short, cut in a boyish, pixie style. Dylan looks at Rosemary, wondering if she has any ideas, but a glance is all that is required to determine that an idea has rarely passed through her mind her entire life.

"You'll have to carry me," volunteers the patient, seeming more cheerful than she should.

"What's your name?" asks Dylan.

"Megan," is the response.

"OK, Megan, I'll carry you, but first I have to portage the canoe to Lake Little Wawa – someone will have to stay with you while I do that."

"No one has to stay with me, Kommandant Dylan," responds Megan mockingly, "I'd rather wait alone – no bears will eat me; how are they to know how tasty I am?" This kid is certainly not in much pain.

Dylan shrugs. He grasps his canoe by the thwarts, positions the yoke on his shoulders, and organizes his charges into the portage trek. Once at the lakeshore, he orders the troops to wait for him until he returns with his patient.

It's Dylan's plan to piggyback the injured girl over the trail, but the mechanics of this arrangement are not going to be easy on the rough terrain. He helps the girl onto her one good foot and instructs her to remove her life jacket; this, she will have to carry. After a hundred yards, Dylan is forced to put the girl back on her foot and informs her that if he continues to transport her in this manner, it will only be a matter of time before he falls flat on his face. Can he carry her in a fireman's lift – it'll be a lot safer because her weight will be over his shoulders? "Give me a shoulder ride," suggests Megan. "My dad used to carry me on his shoulders all the time."

"Yeah, that was probably back when you were six and weighed forty pounds." Dylan kneels and thrusts his head between the girl's legs. She giggles and not for the first time conveys the impression that the injured ankle is a fake. Dylan launches himself to his feet and stabilizes his balance, holding one of Megan's hands. Playfully, she spurs him with both ankles and verbally giddy-ups him. The burden on his shoulders informs him she weighs exactly 97 pounds, a trifle for a strapping lad such as Dylan. Carried this way, Megan feels lighter and Dylan, more sure of foot. However, his passenger has determined to irritate him with attention-seeking tactics such as tickling his ears and covering his eyes with her free hand.

When they arrive at the lakeshore, Dylan discovers that his instructions to wait for his arrival have been disregarded. Four canoes, led by Rosemary, have cut out into the lake, headed for Camp Little Wawa. Annoyed, Dylan lowers his passenger into the front of his beached canoe and drags it into the water. Megan has determined that her role in the canoe will be limited to that of passenger; she has no intention of picking up a paddle.

Dylan is silent for a while. "Don't be so grumpy," says Megan, "we're obviously destined to be together. You should be happy you have me all to yourself."

"Happy?"

"Of course, happy. I'm happy."

"So your ankle no longer hurts?"

"It never hurt, I faked it. I did it because I knew you were the only one of the group who'd be able to carry me. How else was I to get time with you alone? We're the only two in Camp Wacko who are not zealots or dweebs. It's quite natural that fate should throw us together."

"Fate didn't throw us together. Your deception and my gullibility made that happen. Can you at least now help out by paddling?"

"Nope, I don't think so. It'll make us arrive more quickly and we'll have less time to share together." At this point, Dylan determines that the best strategy is not to speak to the irritating brat. Any conversation is going to be a hundred percent one-sided.

Megan is quite capable of conducting a conversation on her own. "I became very aroused while I rode your shoulders. At first, I was hoping that you wouldn't notice; I figured this would be unlikely because my swimsuit was already damp. But then I changed my mind and thought that it would add something special to the moment if you did, in fact, notice. Of course, I had to wriggle around to align myself just right with the vertebrae in your neck, which were moving so very pleasingly, more so with every step, until …"

Dylan has no choice but to hastily interrupt. "How old did you say you were?"

"I didn't. But seeing as you've asked, I'm fourteen. I am a fully formed woman, older than Shakespeare's Juliet, old enough to bear children if I so desire, old enough to be married in more parts of the world than not, old enough …"

Dylan cuts in, "Okay, this conversation has to stop. You don't sound like a fourteen-year-old, even if you look like one. You could get me into trouble talking like you do …"

"Trouble? How? Who's around to hear us? Are you going to tell? I know I'm not. In the words of Shakespeare, why jeopardize this jewel that can be ours if all it takes is a little bravery to grasp it."

"I don't think Shakespeare ever said anything so stupid."

"But he might have, Dylan, he might have, if he'd been brave enough."

Dylan does not know what to do. "You should find a boy of your age and save all your talk for him. I'm way too old to be having this kind of conversation with a kid who's not yet through puberty."

Megan laughs derisively. "So you want me to select a boyfriend from the pimpled, masturbating brethren who inhabit boy's cabin number ten. You jest?"

"Well, I'm off limits."

"No way. You're cute, maybe not the best looking guy in the world, but I can see you have other qualities. And there's no doubting that I'm the hottest female on the landscape of Camp Little Wawa. I chose you on the day we arrived and I noticed you checked me out, too."

"That's simply not true. I never noticed you until you twisted your ankle. Faked twisting your ankle."

"Your nose just grew a little longer, Pinocchio, but I'll forgive you. I've already researched you. I know your date of birth, your home address, your social security number, and exactly what they pay you here."

"And how were you able to determine that?"

"I stole ... borrowed, your keys from the boat dock yesterday, while you were giving swimming lessons ... I let myself in to the camp office and checked out your file."

"Perhaps I should report you to Kommandant Neeskins?"

"Oh, I don't think you'll be doing that, darling Dill. Already you must know there is no one else up here in the wild north you could have a half-decent conversation with."

Suddenly, Megan retrieves the canoe paddle that she previously discarded and plows the blade into water, angling it to spin the canoe into a spiral. She knows how to handle a paddle.

"What the fuck are you doing?" asks Dylan, losing his cool.

"I don't think your language is very Christian, naughty boy. I've noticed we're catching up to the others too quickly. I can see I'll need a little more time to make you fall in love with me. Who knows how long it will be before we have another opportunity to be alone like this again in Camp Sanctimony."

Dylan maneuvers the canoe back into the direction of its intended destination. He only manages a couple of paddle strokes forward before Megan deftly inserts her paddle blade into the water, causing the canoe to spin into a circle once again.

"Dill, don't fight what's perfectly obvious. You and I are destined for one another. We can be clandestine in our meetings if you prefer. During camp prayer meetings is one obvious opportunity that springs to mind, while our fellow campers get stoned on God and righteousness. After you've fallen in love with me, I'm sure both of our minds working together will be able to create many other opportunities."

Dylan realizes that attempting to paddle any further without Megan's compliance will be impossible. Resting his paddle across the gunwale, he waits for Megan to finish.

"You realize that me having any kind of association with you would be illegal. I could end up getting into some serious trouble. You, on the other hand, would be regarded as a victim."

"That, assistant chief counselor Dill, is what makes this so marvelous. If our falling in love was something approved of … or expected of us, then it would be absolutely no fun."

The canoe continues to eddy. After an impasse, Dylan says, "Are you going to allow me to get us back to the camp now you've had your say?"

Megan turns her head over her shoulder and chuckles at Dylan. Then she faces forward, and with skillful strokes, resolutely drives the canoe forward. With the two of them working together, the canoe cuts through water at some velocity and has all but caught the leading four canoes by the time the craft begin to beach. Rosemary approaches Dylan and Megan as they beach their canoe and Megan nimbly leaps out.

"So, your ankle feels better now?" asks Rosemary.

Megan chirps up. "It's all due to Dylan. If you ever need a foot massage, Rosemary, I can promise you, Dylan possesses a magic touch. He's promised to give me a shoulder rub after we've changed – it should help with the stress I've been through."

Rosemary adjusts her glasses and turns her gaze on Dylan, and asks of him a little mystified, "So you guys have got friendly?" Dylan says nothing, but shakes his head while looking at Megan.

"He is such a darling," raves Megan, but sounding phony. "Rosemary, if you're seeking a summer romance or even a little fling, look no further – Dylan's the man for you."

Dylan cannot contain himself any longer and laughs out loud.

"Look at him …he's so modest, so adorable, I think I'm going to become very fond of him," croons the youngster, stripping off her life jacket and handing it to Rosemary for hanging up as if she were her personal maid. With that, Megan wraps her towel around her shoulders and skips her way up the beach toward her cabin.

Rosemary looks at Dylan. "Funny, she's been so moody and rude. I was sure she was going to be a real troublemaker. They tell me this is her third summer here and she has a reputation for being a real bitch."

Dylan says nothing. If he is going to out Megan for the trouble she represents, doing it to Rosemary is not going to be the way.

Dylan showers, changes, and heads to the camp gym to work out. He can't get his mind off Megan and the potential for trouble she represents. He could simply leave. It's not as if he needs a summer job. He considers the tattletale option, but rejects it as a coward's exit. Megan would undoubtedly deny everything or worse still, fabricate a more damaging version of what transpired on the return from Mount Smokey. No, the best strategy will be to take the high road; he'll pay lip service to the flirtation.

In the gym, a fellow counselor and two boys are shooting hoops on the adjacent court area. Dylan begins a sequence of weight drills and is lost in the business of pumping bench presses when he is startled by Megan's voice. "Whazzup?" Dylan twists his neck to look at her, with the weight bar at the apex of its travel. The girl has changed into camp shorts and T-shirt and is sitting on an adjacent weight bench, rubbing still damp hair with a towel. He decides not to respond and continues to pump presses with an increased vigor.

"Dylan, I have such good news. I spoke to Pastor Neeskins about how gallant you were this afternoon, carrying me all that distance, then giving me such a tender foot rub to cure my ankle – well I know that didn't happen, but it would've if you were more thoughtful. I said to Pastor Neeskins, Pastor, this my third summer staying at Camp Little Wawa and never before have I felt so close to God … it was all due to Assistant Kommandant … oops, assistant head counselor, Dylan Douglas. Then, you know what, Pastor Neeskins said something interesting – he said that he didn't think you were a believer. Isn't that just dandy, I told Pastor Neeskins, here I am at Camp Little Wawa for three summers in a row surrounded by godly types and me, an atheist! … and now some unbeliever comes along, and leads me straight to God. So Pastor Neeskins tells me that perhaps I have it all wrong, it must be my calling to lead *you*, Dylan, to Jesus. Who would have thunk? I say to Pastor Neeskins, me, of all people? I told Pastor Neeskins that he must have a gift to know such things. And of course, Pastor Neeskins agreed; he declared he was not unproud of the fact he was blessed with divine insights, it was all part of his calling as a minister of the good Lord. And guess what, Dylan; this is the best bit. He suggested that he transfer me from counselor Rosemary's activity group into counselor Dylan's activity group … providing counselor Dylan will agree, the change can take place next week. Why wait until next week, I tell Pastor Neeskins, let me set about saving Dylan right away, I'll have him before your altar before the summer's done, you can bet the bank on it. Pastor Neeskins then starts rambling on about how his kind of church has no altars and the like; it's egalitarian or something stupid."

Dylan plants the dumbbell on the bar stand. He sits and stares at the diminutive fourteen-year-old. She has a presence that radiates more than mere sex appeal; there is an aura of invincibility about her.

Megan smiles sweetly, but not innocently at Dylan. "And Dill, do hurry up with your pumping iron or whatever it is you are doing. I so badly need that shoulder rub you promised me. It really has been a very stressful day for me. I'm desperately in need of your healing touch."

Dylan reminds himself that he must take the high ground and treat her like the child she actually is. He gets to his feet and towels the sweat from his head and shoulders. He approaches the girl from behind and begins to rub her shoulders – the shoulders are bony and require a gentle touch. The instant she attempts to turn her head to face him, Dylan cautions abruptly, "Turn your head around and I'll stop." He rubs shoulders and pushes aside damp hair to do the same to the neck.

"That feels so fucking good, Dill, don't ever stop."

After a pause, Dylan responds, "It probably says somewhere in my job description that I should discourage the inmates of Christian Camp Little Wawa from using language like yours."

"So you're a hypocrite too, are you, Dill? I would've never used that adjective had I not heard you use it first. No one heard me but you … just as when you said *fuck*, no one but me heard. Haha, we have only known each other for a matter of hours and already we share some secrets. They may be inconsequential, but just wait until another week has passed."

"What convinces you that I would have any interest in a scrawny fourteen-year-old?"

Megan looks at Dylan, squinting slightly. "Oh, you're interested alright," she responds. "You may not want to be interested, but I can tell that you are." She turns her head to deliver a sexy grin.

Dylan decides it's time to end the massage. He grabs his towel and wraps it around his shoulders. "Megan, you are a cute kid. I don't deny that I find you attractive, but you are way out of your league when it comes to having any kind of fling with me. Yes, I admit you scare me because you seem used to getting exactly what you want. You must know you could get me into a lot of trouble. If anything was to happen between us … you would be perceived as a victim and me as an aggressor – the fact that you might want this to happen would be irrelevant."

"Hmm ... does that little speech of yours mean that I am not actually out of your league ... just that you think I'm jailbait?"

Dylan ceases the shoulder rub, shrugs, and walks toward the exit of the gym.

Megan remains seated on the weight bench until Dylan is six strides from the exit door, then she springs to her feet, running to cut him off. She athletically leaps around Dylan, using his shoulders to pivot in front of him, and plants her feet in a karate stance. "Wanna see me be an aggressor?" she challenges. "I warn you, I'm a brown belt karate." She pronounces the word "kara-teh."

Dylan laughs out of embarrassment and moves to bypass the figure blocking the door. In less than a fraction of a second, he finds himself flat on his back as Megan simultaneously kicks out his one planted foot while effortlessly pushing him in the chest. The three hoopsters on the court pause to have a laugh at Dylan's expense. Megan is more subtle in expressing her amusement, and covers her mouth to contain it.

Dylan glares at his aggressor. He is actually enraged, but can do little more than stare her down because he is partially winded. "Sorry, Dill," says Megan, chuckling and not appearing to be in any way apologetic. "I didn't expect you to drop so easily. I guess when they teach us that move in class, our opponents know what to expect ... you obviously didn't." Almost tenderly, Megan reaches downward with both arms in an effort to offer assistance. In a flash, Dylan locks both hands around one of Megan's extended wrists and uses the full force of his body to twist the girl face down to the floor, jamming and pinning her arm behind her back. Because he is just moments away from ignominiously being slammed off his feet, Dylan uses considerably more force than is actually required to accomplish this hold, especially with an individual so diminutive, and he's aware he's likely injured her. So what, so long as nothing is broken, he tells himself. Keeping the girl's arm pinned and locked behind her back, he gets first to his knees, then to his feet. Without a word, he releases the wrist and strides out of the gym.

Outside in the cooler air, Dylan is resolutely heading back toward his cabin when Pastor Neeskins cuts him off. "Dylan," he enthuses, "I'm not sure what magic you have worked with Megan Latimer, but I have to thank you. This is Megan's third summer with us and although it sounds un-Christian, I was dreading her return. In the past, she has been a real challenge for us here at Camp Little Wawa ... but her father is an Episcopalian minister in Oakville, not really a friend, but a man of the cloth, nevertheless. It would have been embarrassing to refuse her, despite her problems."

"Yeah?" questions Dylan. "What kind of problems?"

"Anti-authority, generally antisocial – surly and plain rude to everybody – she's never had … nor seemed to want, friends here … in addition, she's been demeaning of Faith and the Faithful, which makes life difficult in a camp where our motif is Christian and social. The senior girls' counselor last summer, an exemplary youth leader, refused to return and spend another summer with us because of the Latimer girl."

Dylan is in a quandary. In some ways, Megan is exactly the kind of kid he wishes he could have been at fourteen years of age. She is rebellious, outspoken, far braver and more confident than he ever was at that age. On the other hand, she has the potential to make life impossibly difficult for him and a full five weeks of the summer camp season remain. He looks up at Pastor Neeskins.

"Dylan, Megan has requested a transfer into your activity group; I expect she has a bit of a crush on you, but this is something we can exploit. With your permission, I would like to grant the request … I'll remove one of the younger children from your group; I think your strength is working with the teenagers, in any case."

Now Dylan has to respond. "I'm not sure acceding to every request this kid makes is such a good idea … part of the problem is that she has gotten used to always getting her own way."

"Hmm … there is something else, too. Besides being placed in Rosemary's cabin, she is also in her activity group – Jeremiah and I selected you and Rosemary as being best-suited to working with the older campers, but as a result, poor Rosemary is getting a double dose of one of the most difficult characters we've ever hosted at Camp Little Wawa … she's already complaining."

At this moment, the subject of the conversation comes skipping out of the gym and bounces up to Pastor Neeskins and Dylan. She addresses Pastor Neeskins directly and wants to know whether counselor Dylan has agreed to accept her transfer into his activity group. There is a graze on Megan's cheekbone, which Dylan notices immediately and Pastor Neeskins observes while Megan is talking. The graze was no doubt caused by Dylan's roughhousing Megan onto the gym floor a few minutes earlier.

"What's happened to your face?" asks Pastor Neeskins, concerned.

"Oh, it's nothing, just a scratch," Megan responds nonchalantly, but turning to gauge the effect of her words on Dylan. "I slipped and fell on the gym floor while replacing a dumbbell."

"You should be careful of how you handle those dumbbells," admonishes Pastor Neeskins, "I think we should get Mrs. Neeskins to take a look at it for you."

Megan returns her attention to Pastor Neeskins. "That's not necessary," she says, "Dylan has a key for the first aid stations … all I need is some antiseptic and maybe a band-aid." Then she turns to Dylan, using a pleading coy smile. "Well, counselor

Dylan, what's the verdict – are you going to let me transfer into your activity team?"

"Sure," says Dylan in response, not returning Megan's smile, "it's all the same to me."

Immediately, Megan turns to Pastor Neeskins, "Thank you, thank you," she says excitably, hugging the older man. "That Rosemary was beginning to drive me frigging nuts; I've never met anyone so anal."

"Megan," replies Pastor Neeskins assertively, "I hope us agreeing to this transfer represents the turning of a page for you at Camp Little Wawa – one of the aspects of which will be to think more kindly of those who are gifted in different ways from you."

Dylan stares at his feet, wondering how Megan will respond to the gentle reprimand. "Gifted?" questions Megan, then she changes tack. "Yes, you are so right, Pastor Neeskins. It had never occurred to me that poor Rosemary might be endowed with *gifts* beyond some modesty for an absence of observable talent."

Pastor Neeskins scratches his head, confused by the response, but Megan gives him no time for thought; with both hands she grabs one of Dylan's arms. "Come," she says, dragging him away from Pastor Neeskins, "I require medical assistance before I positively bleed to death."

Dylan pours hydrogen peroxide onto a cotton swab and gently dabs the graze on Megan's cheekbone. The pair is alone, standing next to a first aid station in the boathouse. Megan closes both eyes and raises her arms to rest them on Dylan's shoulders to leverage a closing of the distance between them. It takes almost no effort on her part, because Dylan has reached a point where he surrenders to a force that he has spent most of the day attempting to suppress. The kiss that results is sensuous and probing – Megan is not lacking in skills as a kisser. As Dylan's hands massage her scalp, Megan fondles his ears.

When they break for breath, she says, "I fell in love with your ears when I was riding on your shoulders this afternoon. Do you think it's possible to have an orgasm when ears are massaged in just the right way?" asks Megan seductively.

Dylan stares at her and his lust sobers. "We must never do this again," he declares without making any move to interrupt the embrace. "We must pretend that this has never happened."

"Don't be such a wuss," replies Megan, shaking her head. "Why worry about what anybody might think when nobody knows? Or will ever likely to know. Everybody besides us is frigid in this joint, doped on Bibles and God. In any case, I'm very good with secrets; I adore them!" She moves her lips to his once again to suppress any verbal response; for the moment, Dylan is better value when his lips are occupied with something other than speech.

✳   ✳   ✳

The following morning, a Sunday, a large, black Cadillac pulls into the court-yard at Camp Little Wawa. From the driver's side, out steps a short, fat man wearing a preacher's white collar. He is old, overweight, and short. His round, bald head is supported by circular rolls of fat, coiled in tiers above the dog collar. From the passenger side of the vehicle steps a tall, slim, and fashionably-attired woman. She has Negro features and appears to be half the age of her partner. The woman ignites a cigarette with a gold lighter and exhales smoke into the clear cool air of Northern Ontario.

Pastor Neeskins exits the front door of the main building of Camp Little Wawa and approaches the short, fat man. With both of his hands, he grasps and obsequiously shakes the hand of the shorter man. The elegant black woman flicks ash off the gold cocktail dress she wears, attire that is bizarrely inappropriate for the wild north. Dylan Douglas studies the scene on the forecourt while splitting wood with an ax. Some chat is exchanged between the two men. Jeremiah Neeskins emerges from the main camp cabin and after a brief exchange of words, he heads off toward counselor Rosemary's cabin. Shortly after, Megan emerges from the cabin barefoot and in pajamas: she rubs her eyes in an effort to make sense of the scene before her. Then she hugs the short, fat man and does the same with the tall black woman in a more perfunctory manner.

Dylan rests his ax on the ground and takes in the scene before him. The visitors are obviously Megan's parents. The teenage girl, now fully awake, trots back to her cabin. More words are exchanged between Pastor Neeskins and the short, fat padre. The tall black woman exchanges words with no one; she appears to only have interest for the sky above her and the cigarette in her right hand. Megan emerges from the cabin, now dressed in a grey, pleated skirt and with an overnight case in hand. The padre and the slender black woman climb back into the front seats of Cadillac. Megan enters through the rear door and seats herself on the backseat.

The car in motion slowly crunches down the gravel driveway. From the rear window, Megan observes Dylan leaning on his ax and she twists around, blows a kiss, and waves with a sad expression on her face. The car disappears in a cloud of dust down the dirt road, presumably headed back to civilization. Dylan resumes splitting logs into firewood.

In delivering grace before Sunday breakfast, Pastor Neeskins asks all campers to hold Megan Latimer in their thoughts due to the passing of a grandfather. Of course, the grandfather has arisen to a better world. According to Pastor Neeskins, the bereavement will absent Megan from the camp for several days. Dylan is relieved that this circumstance has provided him with some breathing space; he acknowledges that Megan has gotten under his skin and he was not looking forward to the challenges this would present.

A full week goes by. Dylan enjoys life as the leader of a group of Grade Seven and Eight campers, and the schedule of hiking, swimming, canoeing, swimming, and biking suits him. Often at Rosemary's suggestion, Dylan and Rosemary's activity groups are combined, especially for ventures that take them outside the boundaries of the campground. This is largely due to Rosemary's passive nature and disinclination to lead her group: she soon realizes that any time her group merges with Dylan's for an activity, Dylan's take-charge attitude relieves her from having to do much work. Sometimes, chief counselor Jeremiah Neeskins assists because he has no assigned activity group; his function is to float from group to group on an as needed basis.

*   *   *

After a week's absence, Megan returns to Camp Little Wawa. Because the announcement of Megan's return is made during Sunday worship, Dylan is not aware of the event until after the fact. He is teaching a couple of younger children to swim, standing waist deep in the water, when Megan approaches wearing a swimsuit. "Want some help?" she enquires of Dylan.

"Oh Meg," says Dylan surprised, "Sorry to hear about your granddad. Did everything go okay at the funeral? Were you close to him?"

"Yeah, close, I suppose. I'll miss him; he was one of the few sane members of my bizarre family. Daddy said it was up to me whether I returned to camp. You should feel honored … I chose you over freedom."

Dylan says nothing and focuses on his swimmers. Fortunately, the pair demands plenty of attention and provides him with sufficient distraction to avoid having to respond directly to Megan. Megan appraises the situation and perches herself on the dock to observe. She can wait out a swim lesson.

At the conclusion of the lesson, at Megan's suggestion, Dylan and Megan swim out to an anchored pontoon raft a hundred yards off the beach. They climb onto the raft and sit. "We have a perfect excuse to hang out together. You can console me for my loss," announces Megan, moving to hold Dylan's arm. Dylan anticipates the move and quickly twists out of her reach. She puts on a hurt look.

"You can't do that kind of thing Megan … it'll end up getting me into trouble. You're going to have to start to see what anything we do together is going to look like to other people."

"But you do admit you're attracted to me?" For the first time, it appears as if Megan is seeking reassurance; the confidence of a week earlier has waned.

"You know very well how I feel about you. However, our friendship will have to be a platonic … know what that means?"

"No touching, I think. But we've already done touching, if that's what you call what we were getting up to a week ago. It goes without saying that true lovers are expected to physically express their love."

"We're not going to be lovers, we're destined to be no more than friends, and if you don't back off, not very good friends. It's just the way it has to be … and I don't want to hear any more shit about Juliet – it so happens we don't live in fifteenth century Verona; we're in the midst of a tribe of holy rollers. And for the record, the full title of that play is *The Most Lamentable Tragedy of Romeo and Juliet*."

"You're wrong, Dylan, the full title is actually *The Most Excellent and Lamentable Tragedy of Romeo and Juliet*; I know because we're studying it in school … *excellent*, Dill, remember that." But Dylan tunes out, rises to his feet, and dives off the raft, leaving it and its sole occupant rocking. Using a front crawl, he swims powerfully toward the shore; swims as if chased by demons he is determined to escape. Once on the beach, he wraps his towel around his shoulders and heads off to his cabin without looking behind him.

The conversation on the raft changes Megan's approach to Dylan. She sets about engaging his mind by conversing with him in language that is common to them and likely not so to their companions at Camp Little Wawa, a perk of an exclusive girl's school education in Oakville. Debating literature, metaphysics, and current affairs with Dylan not only automatically excludes her fellow campers from participating, it turns them off and away, with the effect of pairing her alone with Dylan.

Meanwhile, Dylan is going crazy – he is in lust with Megan and has no choice but to somehow contain himself in a state of constant denial. It does not help that the uniform at Camp Little Wawa, between breakfast and supper, is the swimsuit. Accordingly, every intimate crease and crevice of this girl's body is imprinted into his memory. When Megan emerges from a swim, her wet swimsuit details each nipple, her buttocks, her sex, images that thrive in Dylan's mind and accompany him to bed every night. While Megan's almost unrelenting presence around him during his waking hours teases him to distraction to the point he wishes she could somehow be vaporized from the face of the earth, should she actually disappear from sight for as little as ten minutes, he worries that she may be lost to him forever. He gets high on just the sound of her voice, and aches to touch, to ravish her.

When Megan asks him to massage a sore foot, Dylan understands that the foot is unlikely to be in discomfort, but by undeclared mutual accord, it is the only touch that they dare indulge that falls within the bounds of public decency at Camp Little Wawa. After affecting an appropriate degree of disinterest to the request, the foot will be lovingly caressed as no woman's foot has been fondled before – toe by toe, ankle to navicular, heel to sensuous instep. Oh, that it could be more than just this foot, how easy to include calves, the delicate inside of thighs, to progress up to the thin fabric of her swimsuit that just barely conceals her sex. Dylan is acquainted with the detail and geography of each of Megan's feet so intimately that the discovery of a new mosquito bite in the tender flesh around the ankle provokes jealousy in him.

Dylan and Rosemary's activity groups are headed for a three-day canoe trip at Lake Opeongo in Algonquin Park, which is a little over ninety minutes of a drive south. Dylan only finds out about this expedition the day before departure. The trip appears to have been conceived by floating head counselor Jeremiah Neeskins, who will accompany them. Four canoes are loaded onto the Camp Little Wawa van and a fifth onto Dylan's Pontiac. Three days worth of supplies is loaded into the vehicles. Besides the three counselors, eight campers are to go on the trip. Including Megan. The day of departure begins with Megan having a mini tantrum because she wants to ride with Dylan in his Pontiac. Head counselor Jeremiah calmly explains to Megan that none of the minors can travel in Dylan's vehicle because it is not covered under the Camp Little Wawa insurance policy. Instead, Rosemary will travel with Dylan. Reluctantly and sulking, Megan accepts this verdict and grumpily takes her place in the van.

Although it is south of Lake Little Wawa, the weather at Algonquin Park is cool and damp, and the water in Lake Opeongo is icy cold. After a brief spell of canoeing, tents are erected and Dylan organizes some of the kids into building a large fire to cook on, ward off mosquitoes, and warm hands. At dusk, both campers and counselors are ready for an early night. Dylan and Jeremiah Neeskins are to share one small tent, Rosemary another by herself, while two larger tents, one for the boys, the other for the girls, house the campers. Inside his tent, Dylan zips himself into his sleeping bag and uses a flashlight to read a book. Jeremiah Neeskins is lying on his back, quiet and evidently deep in thought. There is something about his behavior that strikes Dylan as uncharacteristic.

Half an hour passes and Jeremiah Neeskins abruptly announces that he will be spending the night in Rosemary's tent. He hopes Dylan doesn't mind. Dylan is befuddled. No, of course he doesn't mind, though inwardly, he is incredulous, because he had previously written off both Rosemary and Jeremiah as asexual. "It goes without saying that I'd rather you did not mention this to anyone back at Camp Little Wawa."

Dylan chuckles. "Why would I talk about this? Go for it, Jeremiah, have fun." Jeremiah is so serious about what he is set to do, Dylan wonders whether it might be difficult for him to actually enjoy the experience. Jeremiah stealthily exits the tent and zips it before tiptoeing over to Rosemary's tent, located on the opposite side of the campsite. Dylan snaps his flashlight off and drifts off to sleep.

It is not long before he is awakened by a bum in his face. It is a pajama-clad bottom attempting to wriggle its way into Dylan's sleeping bag. As Dylan is about to respond to the situation with a characteristic 'what the fuck?' a hand clamps his mouth into silence.

"Be quiet," is fervently whispered in his ear. Megan. "Help me get in with you."

"No," whispers back Dylan in reply, sitting up. A debate in whispers ensues.

"Dylan, listen to me! I've been planning this for a week – you've no idea what I've gone through, please don't wreck everything now. I managed to convince Rosemary that she's in love with Jeremiah Neeskins. She convinced Jeremiah to persuade his parents to okay this trip just so they could have their night of love together. I knew this would be our only chance of ever getting together."

"Jesus fucking Christ," says Dylan through his teeth. He hunts around for his flashlight, but Megan stops him before he can switch it on.

"You can't switch it on, you can see through the tent when a light is on."

Dylan covers his face with his hands.

"Dill, please let me in with you, I'm frozen. We don't have to have sex, we can just cuddle if you like."

When all is said and done, Megan cannot be allowed to feel cold when Dylan has plenty of warmth to spare. She wriggles into the sleeping bag, fully assisted by Dylan, who clamps her cold, damp feet between his and uses his hands to rub warmth into hers. "What about the other girls in your tent?" whispers Dylan. "What if Jeremiah Neeskins returns?"

"Asleep," assures Megan. "Don't be such a worrywart." In the dark, she finds his lips with hers and during the ensuing kiss, Dylan's hands find their way under her pajamas to explore those parts of her he has touched previously only in his mind.

Now hot, flustered, and needing a break in the action, Dylan props himself on an elbow, while gently caressing Megan's hair. "We can't have sex," he whispers.

"Why not? If it makes you feel any better, I'm not a virgin."

Dylan gazes down at her. There is enough radiated moonlight so that he can clearly see her features. He kisses her forehead. "I don't have a condom. I wasn't exactly preparing for a night of love in the middle of Algonquin Park."

"Poor boy," says Megan, "let's cuddle some more. I think I know how to make you feel nice."

For a couple of hours, Dylan and Megan explore different ways of making each other feel nice until an inevitable separation must take place. At the portal of the tent, Dylan asks, "What are you going to say if one of the other girls notices you've been gone rather a long time?"

"I'll say I went out for a pee and got lost. What could be easier? Goodnight, jelly bean."

"Night."

*   *   *

The next morning does not begin well. Dylan was unaware of Jeremiah returning to the tent so this likely happened after dawn, an event that occurs before five am at this latitude in the middle of summer. Dylan pulls his jeans on and exits the tent to light the campfire. The morning is cold and damp and a mist hangs over Lake Opeongo; however, the warmth of the fire draws the campers out of the two large tents for a crude breakfast of sausages and scrambled eggs cooked by Dylan over the campfire.

At the conclusion of breakfast, the campers are fully awake and eager to launch the canoes. However, three of the group are absent – Jeremiah, Rosemary and Megan. Dylan dispatches one of the girls to wake Rosemary and returns to his tent to wake Jeremiah. Jeremiah and Rosemary emerge slowly, but behave like zombies, no doubt the consequence of fucking their brains out all night. Dylan informs Rosemary that she will have to wake Megan and get her out of the girls' tent; everyone is ready to go. Dylan descends to the beach to supervise the packing of the equipment they need to take with them into the canoes.

Back at the campsite, an argument has erupted involving Rosemary, Jeremiah, and Megan. It appears that Megan is refusing to go on the canoe trip, complaining that she was unable to sleep during the night because one of the girls in the tent was snoring: her plan is to remain at the campsite and catch some shuteye. Dylan ambles back to the campsite to hurry everyone up and by the time he gets there, Megan has zipped herself back into the girls' tent.

Dylan looks at Jeremiah; he is after all, the group leader. Jeremiah realizes he is expected to take charge and orders Megan to exit the tent. Still clad in pajamas, arms crossed and grumpy, Megan exits the tent once again. "I don't care what you say, Jeremiah, I'm not going on your bloody canoe trip. I'm exhausted."

Jeremiah looks at Dylan as if looking for some kind of guidance. With his eyes, Dylan attempts to signal Jeremiah that it is time for him to assert his authority, but instead, the head counselor turns back to Megan and says, "Don't come then. Stay here and sleep, but you'll miss out on the fun."

Now Dylan is forced to intervene. Impatiently he says to Jeremiah, "You can't leave a fourteen-year-old by herself all day in the middle of Algonquin Park." Then he turns to Megan and says, "You knew what you were getting into when you volunteered for this trip. You're coming with us and that's final."

"You're not in charge – Jeremiah is, and he says I can stay, so what you say doesn't matter."

Now Jeremiah chips in, "I was wrong, Megan, you can't stay here by yourself. Dylan's right, you have to come with us."

Megan angrily turns on Dylan, "Why do you have to ruin everything?" she says, bursting into dramatic tears. "If I have to come, I'm going to sleep in the canoe; you'll wish you hadn't forced me."

Dylan gives a speech on the lakeshore. He informs his campers that although there is no wind at present, winds on larger lakes are a problem because they blow up in an instant and canoes become difficult to control. For this reason, they will hug the lakeshore, even though it is a much longer route, as they head for the mouth of the Opeongo River. Once at the river, they will head upstream a short way, have lunch, and trek a hiking trail.

The eleven canoeists, dispersed in five canoes, depart the lakeshore. Jeremiah and one of the girls are in the vanguard canoe, while Dylan's canoe takes up the rear position. Dylan pilots from the stern seat, one of the boys in the group paddles from the bow seat, while Megan, with her usual drama, settles herself into a semi-curled sleeping position in the hull, using a lifejacket as a pillow. However, any comfort she may have achieved in this posture is short-lived, because in no time, some water collects in the hull, forcing the petulant girl to sit, shoulders hunched, in the center seat.

It takes a full three hours for the group to paddle to their planned lunch destination. However, they have not been there ten minutes when one of the girls slips on the rocks and injures her forearm. A medical assessment of the injury is made collectively by Jeremiah, Rosemary, and Dylan and the verdict is a fractured wrist. The girl will have to be taken to the hospital in Huntsville and Dylan's car is the obvious means of transportation. Dylan selects one of the boys he has observed to be a strong paddler, and announces that they will shortcut across the center of the lake to return to the campground. Megan, once again, is indignant. She tells Dylan that he knows very well that she is the most experienced paddler of the campers in the group, that she should be the one going with him and the patient. Angrily, Dylan turns on Megan. "All I know is that you sat in the canoe on the way here and didn't touch a paddle for the entire trip." The girl, his love, his infatuation, walks away in a huff.

*   *   *

It is after six in the evening when Dylan and his male paddler return to the campground. Mrs. Neeskins met the threesome in the Huntsville hospital and took charge of the patient, planning to return directly to Camp Little Wawa once the required repairs to the fractured wrist have been effected. At the campground, it appears that Jeremiah and Rosemary have yet to emerge from their zombie state, because nothing has been done to organize the evening meal. In addition, it appears that several campers, Megan included, headed for the tents and sleeping bags at the completion of the canoe trip, and are sleeping.

Pissed off, Dylan sets about issuing instructions not just to the campers, but also to Jeremiah and Rosemary. A campfire is lit, sleepers are roused from their tents, and the cooking of a meal is set in motion. Because authority over the group appears to have shifted, at dusk, when ritual deems a singsong around the campfire, Dylan dispenses with the usual Christian songbook, replacing it with popular secular songs of the day. Four weeks of listening to repeated renditions of "Kumbaya" and "Michael Row" has put him off wanting to hear either song again for life.

With the campers bedded down for the night in their tents, Jeremiah interrupts Dylan's reading. He is burdened by a crisis of conscience due to his "immoral" behavior the previous night. "Immoral?" queries Dylan. "By whose definition?"

"By the standards I set myself and by my accountability to my Faith. In addition, I am not sure that I am worthy of Rosemary's love."

"Jeremiah, I'm the wrong person to have this discussion with. From my point of view, you and Rosemary did what is natural – if that was truly the first time for both of you, that in itself is something as miraculous as a virgin birth."

"It was special … but afterward, we didn't see it like that. After our … er, transgression, we spent most of last night discussing the moral implications of our weakness – both of us had previously taken vows of chastity and had committed not to break them until marriage."

Dylan cannot help but laugh; he hopes it does not sound disdainful. "Are you planning a repeat performance tonight?"

"Rosemary said that this is something I should leave for my conscience to decide.

It puts me in a rather awkward position. If I go to her again tonight, it would be an admission that my conscience does not count for very much."

Dylan doesn't know what to say to this tortured soul. He looks directly at Jeremiah. "I think, if Rosemary truly didn't not want you to spend another night with her, she would have told you so; women are usually very clear about that sort of thing. My inclination is that she would be disappointed if you didn't visit her. After all, how long will it be before you get another chance?"

Jeremiah requires no further encouragement. Full of renewed enthusiasm, he throws a jacket over his shoulders and exits the tent. Dylan hears him tiptoe across the campground and the sound of a tent unzipping.

In less than ten minutes, Dylan's tent is once again unzipped as Megan lets herself in. "Christ," she whispers furiously, "what the hell took him so long, I thought he was never going to leave."

"You were especially nasty earlier today," responds Dylan also whispering, "I really don't want you in here tonight. Besides the fact that you should never be in here, anyway."

"Hurry up and let me into the sleeping bag, Dill, I'm bloody frozen. When you've got me warmed up, I'll discuss anything you want."

All it takes is to impart a modicum of warmth into Megan's extremities, then her lips take over, and in no time, her pajama bottoms are scrunched, compressed by four writhing feet down at the bottom of the sleeping bag and Dylan's warm hands are all over her body. The odor of her sex inflames his passion and Dylan rolls her onto her back and fully penetrates her. However, just one deep thrust is enough to bring him to his senses and he rolls off her. "We can't do this. You must know how badly I want to, but it would be crazy."

"I know. It means more to you than me. I'm happy when you just touch me. It makes me feel special."

"How come you behave like a woman at night … and like a spoiled little brat at other times?"

"Hormones – what do you expect? That's my excuse, anyway. It's just me, I guess. I knew I was acting stupid this morning, but I couldn't stop myself. All the time I was thinking of you and ways to make you notice me in a good way, but I just kept putting my foot in it."

"Tell me about your first time."

"Are you jealous? Please tell me that you are."

"Maybe a little. Curious, yes."

"It happened at camp last summer. The boy's name was Nigel; he was a year older than me. We were bored and sort of kept daring each other to go all the way; it was more like a game than about sex. Finally, it happened; we did it behind the boat shed during the evening prayer meeting. It was over pretty quickly."

"Did you use any kind of protection?"

"You mean a condom? No, I was just lucky, I guess."

"Do you keep in touch with this Nigel?"

"Oh Dill, you've made me so happy, I can tell you are more than a teeny bit jealous. There is nothing I want more than to be your obsession, your femme fatale."

"The healthiest thing you could do Meg, is to link up with Nigel once again. Or someone closer to your own age, anyway."

"I don't want to. At the moment, I want you. And I've proved that I can get you, haven't I?"

At that moment, the lovers become aware of footsteps approaching the tent. Dylan rolls as much of Megan under his body as he can, enough to disguise her presence he hopes, aided by darkness, and pretends sleep. The tent door unzips and who Dylan assumes to be Jeremiah enters, and in the dark, begins to fumble around with his sleeping bag on the opposite side of the tent.

Doing his best to sound as if he has been awakened from a deep sleep, Dylan mumbles, "What's up, Jeremiah, is everything OK?"

Jeremiah sighs. "We have decided to let our prayers determine whether we should have future sex. Rosemary's opinion is that it would be better to wait until we are married before succumbing to weakness as we did last night."

At hearing this, covert Megan's body begins to silently reverberate giggles. Dylan clamps a hand over her mouth to ensure the laughter remains inside her.

"You're getting married?" asks Dylan, appalled, continuing the conversation while wondering just how awful it would be to have to stare into Rosemary's coke bottle glasses and vacant personality for a lifetime.

"It would be the honorable thing to do. Undeservingly, we have availed ourselves of God's gift reserved for those blessed by holy matrimony."

Somewhere underneath Dylan's body, Megan has located Dylan's penis and what she is doing with it makes it increasingly difficult for him to participate in this bizarre conversation. Dylan has to get Jeremiah out of the tent. "You must go back to Rosemary; this is no time to abandon her," he declares resolutely. "Can you imagine how she must feel?"

"I'm not sure what you mean?" says Jeremiah, confused, not expecting this response from Dylan.

"Jeremiah, poor Rosemary is in need of reassurance and comfort right now. In her mind, you have just deserted her in the midst of uncertainty. You must sleep with her tonight. Forego the sex if you think it appropriate. But more than ever, she needs to feel loved at this moment – show her that you can sleep with her, protect her, cradle her in your arms – while denying yourselves the pleasure of sexual gratification."

"Do you really think so, Dylan? I was truly under the impression she wanted me to leave."

"That was just a test, Jeremiah, a test of your commitment and resolve. A test you happen to be failing right now. Go to her before it's too late."

Suggestible Jeremiah unzips his sleeping bag, slips his jacket on once again, and exits the tent. As his footsteps distance themselves, Megan squeezes Dylan's penis painfully. "Dill, you are beyond evil. I thought I was bad," she whispers in his ear. "You may have changed the course of humanity. Now they will marry and the combination of bad genes and Christian self-righteousness will likely produce another Hitler."

"Get back to your tent," Dylan responds furiously, "there is no guaranteeing he'll not be back."

"No, why should I? No way he's coming back. A frump like Rosemary is lucky to get any man, let alone one like Jeremiah who comes equipped with four functional limbs and a small brain ... she'll never let him out of her sight again if she's got any sense."

"What makes you so goddamn sure about everything you say? How do you know Rosemary doesn't have qualities that have nothing to do with appearance that might appeal to men?"

"I'm a woman, Dill. Not only do I have a pretty good idea of what appeals to men, I know how to size up my competition. I don't see you chasing around after Rosemary. Meanwhile, you can't keep your hands off me, however hard you try."

It's true, thinks Dylan. I'm besotted with this girl, despite the fact that if ever found out, I could be locked up for statutory rape. "One hour," says Dylan, "then promise you'll go back to your tent. Promise too, that you won't behave like a little witch again tomorrow – I don't know how to handle you when you're like that."

"Seeing as you've asked so very nicely ... I'll go in an hour, providing you devote the hour to worshipping me." She kisses him perfunctorily, as if to punctuate her thoughts. "But I'm making no promises for tomorrow. I hate mornings, especially camping mornings with no proper washrooms or showers ... and getting into clothes I've been wearing for three days. God, how I hate camping! You should definitely feel honored that I am here with you."

The day after returning from the Algonquin trip, Pastor Neeskins summons all ten counselors, plus head counselor Jeremiah, for a meeting. Pastor Neeskins looks solemn. He begins by saying that his son Jeremiah has an announcement. "My fellow counselors," says Jeremiah, looking very uncomfortable, "during the Algonquin camping trip, I committed indiscretions which betrayed the trust placed on me as your head counselor. I failed to set the example expected of me. The nature of my indiscretions is not important, but I have confessed them to Pastor Neeskins so my conscience is now clear … but Father has suggested that I resign my position of authority for the remaining two weeks of summer camp. I apologize from my soul for betraying the trust you placed in me."

During the confession, Dylan focuses his gaze on Rosemary. She looks downward and appears impassive, but perhaps this is due to those thick-lens spectacles, which seem to block the transmission of all the usual emotions broadcast by eyes.

"Well done, son," says Pastor Neeskins, patting Jeremiah on the shoulder. Pastor Neeskins removes his own eyeglasses and cleans them by rubbing them on his shirt. "I would like to invite Dylan to assume the position of head counselor for the remaining two weeks of our camp season … Dylan has shown himself to be exemplary at Camp Little Wawa in every way over the past four weeks, and while he has yet to discover the power of the spirit, he has shown admirable leadership whenever called upon. Dylan, will you accept this position?"

Dylan is initially lost for words, but that doesn't last for long. "Whoa," he says. "No way, you've got me all wrong. Jeremiah's role at Camp Little Wawa is a pastoral one and I know he takes that responsibility very seriously. He leads the prayer groups, runs the campfire song groups, and counsels campers on spiritual matters … and he's good at all the touchy feely stuff that many of the younger campers crave. All these things count for a lot at Camp Little Wawa and I can do none of this. As for committing indiscretions, I've committed plenty, it's just that I could never be as honest as Jeremiah in confessing them. Pastor Neeskins, I think you should seriously reconsider whether having your son step down from this role makes sense. You'll not find a more honest person in this world. Whatever you do decide, I want to say that I can't replace him."

Pastor Neeskins is not expecting this response. He stares at Dylan, then turns toward Jeremiah. It's Jeremiah who speaks first. "Dylan, coming from you, these words mean a lot. You've taught us a different way of doing things this summer … I think I've learned that there are truly good people who do not adhere to any particular faith. Whether you're in name head counselor or not, the qualities you displayed during our Algonquin camping trip define you as a leader, a person who takes charge during crises."

Pastor Neeskins stumbles for words. "I'm not sure what to say." He scratches his bald head. He looks at the collective of counselors before him. "Will you give Jeremiah a vote of confidence?" The collective looks first at Dylan, who nods. Then, all raise their hands in approval. They are, after all, a flock.

Later that evening, during camp prayers, Dylan is sitting behind the boat shed with the only individual he can have a conversation with at Camp Little Wawa. He recites the details of the counselor powwow in word-for-word detail to Megan, who doubles up with laughter.

"Can they really be so fucking stupid?" asks Dylan. He takes a swig from a flask of rye he purchased in Huntsville. "Want some?" he asks Megan. The girl accepts the flask, takes a genteel sip, and ends up coughing and spluttering.

"I don't know how you can drink that stuff," declares Megan handing the bottle back, "it's seriously disgusting. Yes, Dill, they are that stupid. My dad says that accepting any formal religion requires surrendering the normal human ability to reason … it's attractive to the masses because it makes them feel protected within their comfort zones … they like to feel they'll be compensated in an afterlife for what they missed out on in this world. This allows society's leaders and the wealthy to contain 'believers,' deluded and powerless."

"Holy shit," says Dylan, "where do you come up with this crap? I thought you hadn't heard of that Plato guy?"

"Of course I have … I just wasn't sure if that 'no touching' thing you were talking about had anything to do with him. My father and I talk all the time," replies the girl. "He may be a preacher, but he understands that human endeavor shouldn't be constrained by biblical platitudes – if that were the case, evolution of mankind wouldn't be possible, according to him. But my feeling is that if most people have nothing to contribute to the world beyond their ability to procreate, why not limit their capacity for evil by giving them religion? And leave people like us to enjoy the pleasures of life."

"Doesn't your Dad feel conflicted in his role as philosopher padre?"

"I suppose he does. That's why he needs me to talk to. He tries to teach his parishioners that there is a difference between living a spiritual life and blind faith, but they insulate themselves from truth. Daddy says he hasn't lost his beliefs … but I'm not sure he has much faith in what he preaches any more."

Dylan takes another swig of whisky. Megan is making him feel stupid and he needs to change the subject. "This is where you were deflowered," he says abstractly.

"Yes," muses Megan, not particularly interested.

"Did you tell your dad about that?"

"Yes, I did. Like I said, he's not just my dad, sometimes he's my best friend.

Of course, other times I hate him. Hate him for not standing up for what he really believes."

"Will you tell him about us?"

"Maybe, but not right away."

"Will he have me arrested?"

"No, I don't think he'd want that. Actually, I'm not sure how he'd react. For the longest time, he used to think of me as innocence personified, but I'm pretty sure he's grown out of that. He'd likely be mad at me rather than you, because he believes a person draws into their lives what they want to attract."

"Where does your mom fit into the puzzle?"

"Daddy was a missionary in Kenya … that's where he and Mom met. Mom says she's always felt like a foreigner in Canada. She's not a talker like Dad … we communicate best by touch, which means that we were probably closest when I was a baby. Once when she was drunk, she confessed to me that I had become like a foreigner to her … like a Canadian. She said it like it was something bad. I wanted to reply that sometimes she felt like a stranger to me too, even though I knew what she said was just her way of asking me for a hug. But I didn't give her the hug she craved and that created a distance between us which neither of us has made the effort to close."

A silence ensues.

"Guess what I bought in Huntsville … besides whisky?"

"What?"

"Rubbers. If you want, I can corrupt you some more."

"I want."

"We might get wet bums; it's cooling down fast. There'll be a heavy dew tonight; there's already a mist on the lake."

"I still want. There's a tarp inside the shed; we can lie on that."

*   *   *

The day Megan is caught shoplifting, Dylan is on an all-day kayak trip on the Goose River, so he doesn't find out about it until he returns late in the day. It is Jeremiah Neeskins who informs Dylan. "I don't believe it," says Dylan, "there must be some mistake."

"No mistake," says Jeremiah. "After bringing her back from Huntsville, the police searched her cabin and found all kinds of other stolen goods. Clothes, cosmetics, candy. Most of it in its original packaging; she never touched the stuff. She stole it during the Tuesday girls' shopping trips to Huntsville. She admitted to stealing it … Dad said she was all but bragging about it. Two other girls were involved too, but Megan took all the blame. Not only that, she admitted shoplifting stuff the previous two summers she spent with us, stuff she didn't keep … she said she tossed most of it into campfires to get rid of it."

"Where is she now?"

"She's in the main cabin with Father and Mother. Megan's father is driving up from Oakville to take her home."

"I want to see her."

Initially, Pastor Neeskins is reluctant to allow Dylan to see Megan. Dylan insists – he tells Pastor Neeskins that he knows Megan better than anyone else at Camp Wawa and he's dumbfounded that she could have been shoplifting. "I'm not sure you could have known her that well, Dylan, because most of us that really knew her, who've known her for three summers, were not that surprised when she was returned to us in a police cruiser earlier this afternoon."

"I still want to talk to her."

"Well, she did say that she didn't want speak to anyone."

"She'll want to talk to me."

Megan is sitting cross-legged on the floor in front of an easy chair, watching television. She is dressed in a skirt and blazer, hands jammed into the blazer pockets. She appears somehow diminished, like a child. Mrs. Neeskins is sitting on an adjacent sofa and she appears wary. As Dylan enters the room, Megan briefly glances at him before fixing her gaze on the television screen. "Fuck off, Dill, I don't want to talk to you; just leave me alone."

"Please don't use that language in this house, Megan," says Mrs. Neeskins.

"Mrs. Neeskins, please let me talk to Megan alone – we became good friends over the summer, I want to find out what's happened in her own words."

"No!" shouts Megan without taking her eyes off the television screen. "Pastor Neeskins, make him go away, I don't want to talk to him; I hate him."

Dylan turns to Pastor Neeskins. "Please, allow me a few minutes alone with Megan."

"If you leave him in here with me, I'm not saying anything, so you might as well not bother."

Pastor Neeskins nods to his wife and the pair exits the living room, closing the door gently. Dylan sits in Mrs. Neeskin's vacated place on the sofa, totally confused. "Why would you talk to me like that? Have I done something wrong? Something to offend you?"

There is no verbal response from Megan; she sits red-faced, passively hostile, shoulders hunched forward, her eyes fixated on the flickering television screen.

Dylan gives up attempting to get her to talk and studies her. It's as if she has completely changed personalities. Any conversation is going to be one-sided, so he picks his words carefully. "Meg, if you are going through some kind of crisis, let me try and help. I don't know what to say to you because I don't know what's going on in your head; I wish I did. I'd like to come over and hug you and somehow make you feel better – I'd do it right now if I thought you'd let me."

Still without turning her gaze from the television, Megan responds, "Keep away from me, Dylan, or I'll scream. You don't understand what it's like to be me. This is nothing to do with you. I don't need any help, I just want you to leave me alone." As she says this, there is evidence of a tear running down her cheek. There's a gentle knock at the living room door and Mrs. Neeskins enters and speaks. "Dylan, Pastor Neeskins wants a word outside with you."

"Bye, Meg," says Dylan sadly, getting up to leave, but the goodbye is not acknowledged. In contrast to the single tear running down Megan's cheek, Dylan is completely teared up. In the hall, Pastor Neeskins places his arm around Dylan's shoulder, presumably to comfort him, but it has the opposite effect. The last thing Dylan wants to listen to are Pastor Neeskins' platitudes, especially those to the effect that Dylan never really knew the real Megan Latimer.

"Dylan, I'm aware that you feel a sense of defeat. We are a caring community at Camp Little Wawa, so we all feel betrayed. But I want you to know that for most of this summer you played a special role in that disturbed youngster's life ... and while she's obviously not of a mind to acknowledge it right now, you can be sure you made a difference. Actually, I don't know what we'd have done without you, the fact that she latched onto you relieved us all of a tremendous burden – she's one of the most cleverly manipulative young persons I've ever encountered. But I want to suggest that you seek the counsel of Jesus, ask for guidance on how to proceed with this troubled soul."

Dylan is not really listening; he is so upset by the hostility from Megan that he needs to talk, even if it is to an idiot like Pastor Neeskins. "I just don't understand why she wouldn't talk to me. For most of the summer up to this moment, I couldn't shut her up."

"Perhaps she was simply embarrassed? You were something of a shining star to her; it seems that she certainly reserved her best side for you."

"I didn't think embarrassment was in her repertoire. Until today, I thought she was so smart – she could see through everything and everyone; the accuracy of her insight was phenomenal. She was like I wished I could have been when I was her age. I don't understand how I could have been so completely fooled by her. She could see through everyone ... except herself."

"Dylan, I want you to remember something – when one of God's souls refuses to take Jesus into their hearts, it opens up a vacancy into which, sooner or later, Lucifer will take up residence. Let the fate of Megan be an example to you. I'm not sure of the state of your account with the good Lord, but you'd do well to ensure that its balance is in your favor … perhaps you should consider kneeling and joining me in prayer at this very moment … invite Jesus into your heart."

Dylan stares at Pastor Neeskins in disbelief. Was this an attempt at a sucker punch conversion?

"There is but one source of good … and one of evil in this mortal world. It is incumbent on us to choose one or the other; there is no median way. You can be saved … or you may go to the devil … there is no middle ground."

"Pastor Neeskins, please excuse me. I'm feeling nauseous and I have to be by myself."

There is a manic look in Pastor Neeskins eyes; he's all but shouting, "'Tis but the devil rising up within your soul. Cast him aside … kneel with me in prayer."

Instead, Dylan casts Pastor Neeskins aside, twisting his body out of the man's grasp. He exits the main house and heads toward the lake, knowing that he needs to clear his head. He sits on the dock and as he does, crackling gravel announces the arrival of a vehicle onto the Camp Little Wawa property. It is the black Cadillac that temporarily removed his illicit lover a few weeks earlier. This time, only the short, bald man exits the vehicle. In less than two minutes, Juliet turned Ophelia storms out of the main building, inserts herself into the rear seat of the automobile, and slams the door. The reverberations of the slamming door echo across the lake and appear to create ripples on the glassy surface of the lake. Pastor Neeskins and Reverend Latimer follow Megan out of the main cabin, walking slowly; they are engaged in conversation. Moments later, the Cadillac crunches its way through the gravel as it departs Camp Little Wawa.

Although Dylan is half-expecting a phone call from Megan during what is left of the summer camp season, the call doesn't come. On the final night of camp, during the evening prayer session, Dylan enters the camp office, locates Megan Latimer's file, and dials her home phone number.

The phone is answered by a woman with heavily accented English, presumably Megan's mother.

"I'd like to speak to Megan, please."

"May I ask who is calling?"

"Romeo. I'm a friend of hers from camp. Romeo Montague."

Megan's name is called. A couple of minutes pass before she gets to the phone. Her voice is brusque.

"Really Dylan, I would've thought you could have come up with something better than *Romeo Montague* … my mom may not make any sense of the name, but she'll remember it, and tell Daddy."

"How did you know it was me?"

"Firstly, you're the only person from camp who'd be likely to call. Secondly, who but you would be stupid enough to come up with Romeo Montague!"

"Are you okay, Meg? I was worried about you."

A short silence ensues. Megan is shifting gears. "I'm fine, Dylan. Nothing was going to happen to me over the shoplifting. I'm fourteen, remember. I could steal the Hope diamond and the worst that could happen to me is to be gated for a month – that would include the punishment and the curse."

"I did kind of miss you after you left."

"Ah, poor boy!" There is a hard mocking tone to her voice that puts Dylan on the back foot, but then she suddenly changes her tone and begins to sound more like the Megan he spent the summer with. "Really? I guess I missed you, too. Did you pine for me?"

He says nothing.

"Are you in love with me, Dill? Did I become your femme fatale?"

Dylan has now recovered. "I'm not sure what being in love means; maybe I was in love with you. Whatever it was that happened between us during the summer, I want you to know, I'll never forget you. You'll always be kind of special to me."

"Dill, we don't have to stop seeing each other. You can come to Oakville and rescue me – it's less than an hour's drive from Toronto. We can live in sin in your apartment … and eat baguettes and brie and wash it down with vin rouge …"

Dylan cuts her off, "No, Meg, that's never going to happen. I wasn't sure whether I should phone you or not, but I needed to know you were okay. Bye, mi amore." Dylan hangs up before she can respond. As he turns to exit the office, the phone rings … Dylan lifts the handset and immediately returns it to the cradle. As a precaution, he disconnects the phone at the wall jack and leaves the office. That should end it, he thinks to himself. By the next morning, he'll have slipped into some recess of Megan's memories.

19. POPPY GETS MARRIED

Another school year passes and Dylan has completed his second year when he receives the wedding invitation. It is sent via his parents' home address in Sarnia. A traditional Anglo invitation on white card and silver script informs him that Ronald and Rosemary Lee would be honored if Dylan Douglas would join them to celebrate the wedding of their son Victor Lee and his betrothed, Poppy Thompson. Dylan wonders if this is the first time he ever notes Poppy's surname. It's been over a year since he last communicated with his ex-girlfriend, and while he had bumped into Victor a couple of times at school and they had exchanged some small talk, the subject of Poppy was avoided. The wedding is to take place in Vancouver in July. After giving the matter some thought, Dylan decides to attend, even though it involves a trip to the West Coast.

The Lees are Chinese Christians, originally from Hong Kong. Dylan arrives in Vancouver the night before the wedding: because of this he opts to attend the church part of the ceremony at noon the following day, something he has tended to avoid in previous weddings to which he has been invited. He announces his name and is ushered to a pew at the back of the church. He scans the congregation, looking for someone he might recognize. Victor is standing up at the front in his groom's position at the altar and he catches his eye. Immediately, Victor walks back to where Dylan is seated and embraces him with some enthusiasm. Right behind him, Signora Ligetti, who was also somewhere up front, follows to embrace him, but the hug has to be quick; an organ is cranking up the proceedings and Victor and his ex-landlady have to resume their more exalted seating positions in the ceremony.

Dylan surveys the pews, looking for anyone else he might know. Signora Ligetti is standing in the front row, holding the hand of a larger and more grown up Manny, who is dressed in a little blue suit. He scans the church for Poppy's mother, but does not see her. Almost all of the at least one hundred people in the church appear to be Chinese.

When Poppy enters the church, she does so on the arm of Signor Ligetti. In a simple white wedding dress, she looks stunning, changed somehow during the year that has passed since Dylan last saw her. She has filled out, perhaps the result of Ligetti family nurture. Her eyes focus forward as she takes measured steps down the aisle of the church; she will notice nothing during this passage down the aisle other than Victor waiting for her at the altar. Bruno Ligetti does notice Dylan, however, and winks at him as he passes.

At the completion of the service, Dylan wants to talk to the Ligetti's, but they appear to be so integrated into the inner circle of the Lee family, something warns him it would be inappropriate. Other than the Ligetti's, all of the remaining guests are unknown to him. The taking of photographs is being orchestrated by a photographer on the steps of the church and it is during the photography session that Poppy first notices Dylan standing some way off in the crowd of guests that clusters around the church steps. She smiles and ripples her fingers in a discreet wave. Dylan acknowledges the greeting with a smile and decides to quietly leave and return to his hotel. He feels very out of place. The reception is not scheduled to begin until six in the evening.

Four hours later, at the reception, Dylan first meets Victor's parents. Mr. Lee informs Dylan in near perfect English that he is the only one of Victor's Toronto class to have made the trip to Vancouver. Dylan explains that he is not a classmate, just a friend and former roommate, and unlike Victor, who has completed his studies, he is still an undergraduate. "You must have been close friends, then?" he comments rather than asks. "We are honored to have you with us."

Navigating a reception line at a wedding is not one of Dylan's favorite tasks and it is easier with the distracting element of a girlfriend hanging on one arm. Doing this solo when you have rather separate histories with both bride and groom is grueling because the line advances at a chronically slow rate, meaning that Dylan changes his mind about what to say, and how to say it, a dozen times. Once confronted with Victor a second time, they embrace and exchange platitudes. Dylan hugs Poppy. It is the first time he has ever seen her wearing makeup and although it is lightly applied, it makes her appear almost surreal, perhaps a little like a model off the pages of *Seventeen*. Dylan is acutely aware of being scrutinized so he breaks the embrace as soon as possible, holding Poppy by both forearms at a distance he can control. "Thanks for coming Dill," she says, "it means a lot to me. We'll talk later." Poppy's eyes are loaded with tears. Tears of happiness, Dylan tells himself.

Dylan is ushered to a table shared by the Ligetti's, Manny, and two friends of Victor's from his undergraduate days at UBC. Two-year-old Manny appears to have no recollection of Dylan and is unimpressed when reintroduced. With her primary focus devoted to Manny seated next to her and in between her husband, Gloria Ligetti makes it her business to update Dylan on the events that led to the wonderful occasion that resulted in them being reunited at this table. It all unfolded pretty much as Dylan would have predicted. But where was Poppy's mom, Mrs. Thomas? "Mrs. Thompson," corrects Gloria Ligetti, "she refuse come … Mr. and Mrs. Lee, they try to persuade, they pay for airplane, but she say she no wanna come."

"Was Poppy upset?"

"I thinka no … she no really want her mama come. Itsa sad … but Poppy always have me and Bruno … and Mr. and Mrs. Lee, already, they loff Poppy lika she their own daughter."

The meal is consumed. Dylan does not speak much. He observes little Manny with Bruno and Gloria and wonders how he will fare without them as surrogate parents. Some speeches are made, all but one in English. The Lees are evidently pretty much assimilated into Canadian life. Dancing and inter-table mingling begins.

Victor and Dylan have a long chat. They catch each other up on the events of the past year. At the end of it all, Dylan tells Victor how happy he is that two of his best friends have married. "You two are so right for each other," he assures his friend, who was never a close enough friend to warrant this trip out to the West Coast without there being other factors. "I know you will be very happy."

Dylan is sitting by himself at the table and is on the point of leaving the reception when Poppy approaches. "You haven't asked me to dance," she asks him, bubbling.

"I wanted to and was debating whether I should or not. I'm not sure how many people here knew about us … and how it would go over."

"Dill, you're crazy, you really haven't changed a bit!" Poppy responds, grabbing his hand and leading him toward the dance floor. They dance. "I missed you so much. I never dared ask Victor about you because we sort of got together not long after you left … but I wanted to."

"I know you and Victor are going to be very happy," says Dylan, feeling that he is not being quite truthful, that he should have said 'I hope you and Victor are going to be very happy.'

"I think so," replies Poppy. "He adores Manny and I love that he loves me so much. In my whole life, I've never been cared for like I am now." She whispers in his ear, "Certainly not by you." The track ends and Dylan attempts to separate.

"No," says Poppy assertively, "we can dance one more number. I hardly know anyone here. Vic has danced with a dozen different women, half of them his exes for all I know. I want us to have a few moments together so I can remember what it was like to take a shower with you."

The next song begins to play – it's slow and Dylan struggles to ensure that the contact does not breach the boundaries of his definition of acceptability when danc-ing with a bride at her wedding. Poppy tosses her head to remove strands of hair from her face and looks Dylan in the eye. "Do you have another girlfriend yet?"

"No."

A silence ensues. "Do you miss me?" The question is tentative.

"Yes. I missed you. I never realized how much you had become part of my life until you were no longer around. I felt empty and had a lousy year after we split up.

I didn't fly out here to see Victor get married, we were never that close … I came to be with you as you got married. Truly, I wasn't ready for us to separate when we did. The thing is, we were … are … at different stages in our lives. I didn't think I was ready for a long-term relationship, and you were … you needed some stability in your life and I couldn't have provided any." Poppy nods her head, agreeing with Dylan, but once again there are tears in her eyes. Danger. He is conscious that he and Poppy are being closely observed by at least one person. The song ends. Dylan separates from the dance embrace and with his hand, leads Poppy away from the dance floor. He steers directly toward the head table where Victor is seated. He extends his free hand toward Victor, making a circle of three.

"This is fabulous!" exclaims Dylan with maybe too much enthusiasm, addressing both Poppy and Victor. "Sharing this beautiful day, what wonderful friends you both are. I'll treasure the memory forever." Poppy sobs and closes her arms around Dylan. It's clearly time to split. He informs the couple it is time he leaves and Victor nobly suggests that Poppy accompanies him to the exit to say goodbye. Taxis are waiting outside the reception hall.

Poppy hugs Dylan once again. She says nothing. "I really hope you are going to be happy, Poppy. You'll always be special to me. I didn't realize it at the time, but during our six months together, you helped me grow in so many different ways – you were the first real relationship I ever had with a woman, I never realized how special you were until after we split. I think you will be a good wife just like you are a great mom. I know Victor is very lucky to have you." He kisses her lightly on the lips and hastily maneuvers his body into the taxi in front of him. Poppy blinks. She turns and has already disappeared back into the reception hall by the time the taxi pulls away.

Dylan feels guilty about his role in the scene that has just transpired, but is not sure why. Maybe he does know why. In a world without constraints, he would've located a shower, pulled Poppy into it with him, and ripped the wedding dress off her. What made him surrender this woman so easily a year earlier, surrender her, before their relationship had run its natural course? Rationalizing his motives by saying he was acting in Poppy's best interests was a cop-out. Perhaps it was to do with having to fight for something he wanted – it was just so much easier to cede to what Victor, the Ligetti's, and the world, thought was right for Poppy. Part of the problem was that he failed to recognize how important Poppy had become to him until she was no longer in his life. Did he allow the love of his life to slip through his fingers? Then Dylan's left brain jumps in and reminds him of the baby in the mix. The child that Poppy declared was the most important thing in her life.

20. STONED

Dylan inexplicably finds himself at a Friday night booze fest, populated entirely by wannabe lawyers. He learns that the difference between a social gathering of student engineers and its equivalent of student lawyers is not one readily evidenced in physical appearance. However, if Dylan had possessed a more perceptive nature, the interchange of conversation would have been a dead giveaway, one he should have zoned in on within minutes of arrival. Social chat peppered with prima facies, postpriories, and compounded sentences that only end with aggressive interruption, is simply not the banter of a gathering of scientists usually intent on economy and accuracy of expression. Instead, Dylan thinks he's entered the twilight zone. He gulps at his plastic beaker of plonk and looks for an out.

The out happens sooner than planned. The partiers are quick to identify Dylan as an alien spirit, so in no time he is isolated and in need of a sink in which to dump the contents of his beaker before splitting. After locating the kitchen in the apartment, Dylan drains a nearly full plastic mug of wine down the sink.

"Ah, I detect a man of discerning taste." The voice is coming from an apparent loner sitting at the kitchen table, also drinking red wine, not from a plastic beaker, but from an actual glass. Dylan raises his eyebrows and looks at the speaker. "Grab a real glass from the cupboard and sample a little of this rather delightful Bordeaux." Dylan's interest is piqued. He nods, opens the kitchen cabinet, removes a claret glass, and holds it forth to receive wine of a different character. He pulls up a chair and sits at the kitchen table.

"Robert Grantham," the claret drinker introduces himself. Dylan studies him. He is perhaps older than the majority of the group and he wears a thick wedding band on his ring finger.

"Is this your apartment?" Dylan asks.

"Oh no, I'm an alien like yourself. Are you at Osgoode?"

"The law school? God, no."

"Well, most people here are either at Osgoode … or were, at some point. I was originally … now I'm practicing in New Brunswick … but will article here this coming year to prepare for the Ontario bar examinations." It is at this moment Dylan realizes that he has inadvertently crashed a party of lawyers; yes, in navigating to this destination, once convinced he was in the neighborhood of the address he had scrawled on a transfer, he followed the direction of the noise rather than the house numbers.

Dylan shakes his head. "Well that explains a lot," he says. "After arriving, I got into a couple of conversations and couldn't understand a fucking word anyone was saying." Robert laughs.

In this way, Rob and Dylan become friends. More important, both discover they are searching for a downtown apartment and agree to look for a place they can share – why not do so with someone who enjoys a decent wine and knows what glass to put it in? Robert Grantham is old-school Toronto, a graduate of Upper Canada College who married the daughter of a judge in New Brunswick. He has been married for eight years, a union that has produced a couple of kids. However, the wife and kids will remain in New Brunswick until Robert has passed the Ontario bar examinations, after which the family will move to Toronto. Robert is a snob, but Dylan decides he is an affable one.

Robert and Dylan move into a spacious, two-bedroom, fourth-floor apartment in an old house on Highview Avenue. The top-floor flat is equipped with a balcony that oversees a pleasant neighborhood, west of Forest Hill, but still on the hill of Toronto overlooking the downtown. Because Robert attended UCC, a gulag with some parallels to Dylan's British boarding school, the pair share common interests and hit off as friends as well as roommates. Though they might barely see each other during the week, they spend the weekends guzzling beer, quaffing wine, and barbequing illegally on the fourth-floor balcony.

Apart from an occasional party of students, there are few visitors. Dylan is in relationship withdrawal and Robert is married, so the two men live a somewhat isolated existence. They share some common protocols, the main one of which is to never speak about anything that matters in the world. Accordingly, Robert knows almost nothing of Dylan's past love life, and Dylan knows little of Robert's marriage, other than the fact that his wife is a bitch, the extent of which depends on how much alcohol has been consumed. For some reason, he's not sure why, Dylan would fully expect Robert to describe his spouse that way, it would be out of character for him to express affection for a woman.

Robert and his wife exchange a conjugal phone call every Sunday morning. However, Dylan cannot help but notice that Rob devotes the larger part of the phone call to chatting with his kids and almost none of it in conversation with his wife. September turns to October, then to November, and in no time the Christmas break arrives. Because he is articling, theoretically working, Robert is entitled to only a one-week break over the holiday in contrast to Dylan's three weeks off school. Dylan assumes that Robert will return to New Brunswick to spend Christmas with his family. For his part, he plans to spend just Christmas and Boxing days with his family in Sarnia, and enjoy the remainder of the break carousing with other students in Toronto.

*　　　　　　*　　　　　　*

Marcia, aged six, Robbie, aged four, and a suitcase arrive on Robert's doorstep on the evening of Dylan's final day of school before the Christmas break. More specifically, the pair is delivered by Robert's wife Kendra in a Volvo station wagon. Moments prior to the delivery, Robert and Dylan cleared snow off the balcony with the objective of grilling salmon and washing it down with a bottle of Sauvignon Blanc.

Kendra Grantham is a tall, bony woman of athletic appearance. She is forthright and abrupt. She has driven up from St. John, a two-day drive, with the two children to drop them off for her husband to care for over Christmas. Her plan is to have Rob drive her to Pearson Airport so she can board an aircraft and fly to Victoria to spend the three-week Christmas school break with her retired parents. She'd take the kids too, but as Rob well knew, money was tight and this would double the cost. It was high time he took some responsibility as a father, in any case. She delivers this news to her husband in a matter-of-fact manner without glancing at Dylan.

Protestations from Robert that he was given no warning and, in any case, only has a week off work over Christmas are responded to with a terse, "You'll find a way Rob – after all, I've been finding ways for the past six years, so I'm sure you can manage for three weeks."

What a bitch, thinks Dylan to himself; Robert was right, that woman is an argument against marriage if I ever saw one. Kendra gives each youngster a perfunctory hug and departs. The goodbye is not something that appears to upset the kids, both of whom seem excited about spending some time with their father.

Within less than five minutes, the serenity and structure of the bachelor world of Robert and Dylan is turned on its head. The two children set about exploring every inch of the apartment, which provides some brief thinking space for Robert. The meal is not much of a problem; a salmon divides four ways easily enough, especially when two of the persons have small appetites. The bottle of wine is consumed in its entirety, but the half Rob consumes fails to anaesthetize the reality of having a pair of kids around for a full three weeks. For his part, Dylan comforts himself with the fact that this is primarily Rob's problem, not his.

The first glitch is where the kids are going to sleep. Rob decides that they can bunk in his bed while he moves onto the couch in the living room. Next, Robert ponders whether to return to St. John with the kids … or remain in Toronto over Christmas. Dylan, anxious to safeguard his own plans for bachelor serenity over his break, attempts to convince Rob that it would be in the kids' best interest to get back to the security of hearth and home in St. John. However, while Rob is strategizing, Dylan cannot help but notice that his roommate has begun using the first person plural more often than the first person singular.

Marcia and Robbie are not only excited about spending time with Daddy, they are excited about Christmas. And where is the Christmas tree? Where are the Christmas lights and gifts to put under the tree? "We haven't got around to doing those things yet," responds Daddy. "Actually, I had thought we might spend Christmas in St. John."

"Nooo," the children chorus in unison, "we want to stay in Toronto with you, Daddy."

"Toronto, eh? Maybe. But then there is the issue of a Christmas tree. But perhaps we could skip that farce for one year, would you mind terribly? Then there's the turkey ritual, God forbid. What would you guys think of sending out for Chinese instead of doing the turkey thing?"

Toronto it is. And in the world of the apartment, what was once simple becomes difficult. Marcia and Robbie are not untidy by nature, but they are little kids and they turn the rhythm of bachelor existence upside down. Clothes are strewn on the floor in every room, dishes and cups accumulate in the kitchen at an astonishing rate, and the absence of toys has promoted the need to improvise in the kids with whatever they can discover in the world of the apartment.

On their second day, Marcia and Robbie discover a pair of high heel shoes in Dylan's closet, left by some former occupant of the apartment. The high heels are fought over, forcing Rob to schedule turns for the privilege of wearing them, regulated by the half hour. From that point on, one or the other of the kids is clack-clacking around the hardwood floors of the apartment in high heels, from breakfast to dinner, a game that continues until the enraged occupant of the apartment immediately below, a middle-aged librarian spinster, pounds at the door, begging for mercy.

When Dylan returns to Toronto after spending Christmas day with his family, the chaos that confronts him as he enters the apartment makes him wonder if he should have extended his absence. Though it is in the middle of the afternoon, the children are still in pajamas and are engaged in a tearful fight over which television show to watch. As Dylan stands at the door wrestling his jacket off, both kids turn to him and implore him to arbitrate the disagreement in their favor. "Where's your dad?" asks Dylan.

The siblings point to the couch in the living room. "He has a migraine," explains tearful Marcia.

"Have you guys had lunch?" asks Dylan. Marcia and Robbie shake their heads in unison. "How about breakfast?" Now they nod in unison. Yes, they shared a slice of pizza.

Dylan shakes Rob, who is in a deep sleep. All he can elicit are a few groans. He has never witnessed Rob or anyone else with a migraine before. Rob's face is swollen and flushed red. "Do you want me to get you to hospital?" Dylan asks him. "No" is the definite response.

"Okay Rob, I'm taking the kids out for lunch and to do some food shopping," Dylan says.

The children get dressed and the threesome holds hands to make its way to the intersection of Oakwood and St. Clair. "Are you taking us to McDonald's?" asks Marcia.

"Maybe another time," says Dylan. "You guys probably need some real food. We're going to Ennio's Trattoria, they have a lunch buffet. But no junky food is allowed. Have salad to start."

"I don't like salad," declares Robbie resolutely.

"That's the rule," says Dylan. "No salad, no other food. I'm sure you can eat a little – I bet your mom gives you salad."

"He likes carrots and tomatoes," volunteers Marcia.

"And cucumbers and beans," adds Robbie. "It's lettuce I don't like."

"No problem," says Dylan, "you get to make your own salad at Ennio's . We can fix you a carrot, tomato, cucumber, and bean salad, the best ever created."

"Are you our uncle?" asks Robbie.

"Nope. Not an uncle, just your dad's friend."

"Are you the boss of us?" asks Marcia.

"I guess I am sort of … at least, for the moment until your dad feels better."

"Daddy said that you might be babysitting us because he has to go back to work tomorrow."

"Did he now?" says Dylan, shaking his head.

On returning to the apartment, Dylan sits the children in front of the television and checks on Rob. It appears as if he has gotten worse; he is now drenched in sweat. Once again, Dylan asks him if he should take him to a hospital and Rob vigorously rejects the idea. Confused as to what to do, Dylan phones his mother.

"It sounds as if he has a fever … I think you should get him to an emergency department," is the response, "better to be safe than sorry."

"What should I do with the kids?"

"What about a neighbor?"

Dylan thinks about the spinster librarian living below them. The only words exchanged between them beyond casual greetings were those of the complaint a few days previously.

"No matter, you'll have to take them with you," says his mother.

Convincing Robert that he is in need of medical help takes some work on Dylan's part. That done, he gets the kids into snowsuits once again, loads the three Grantham's into his Pontiac, and drives to Sunnybrook Hospital. Triage processing gets Robert out of a crowded waiting room, but leaves Dylan stuck there with his two charges. After two hours in this waiting room, Marcia and Robbie are whining and generally driving everyone crazy, so Dylan elects to return to the apartment. Whatever is going to be done to Robert is not about to happen in a hurry.

Dylan prepares supper for the kids, reads them a story, and gets them to bed. He cleans up the detritus created by himself and the two youngsters in the kitchen and living room. Exhausted, he falls asleep on the living room couch.

At one in the morning he is awakened by the ringing phone. They have given Rob intravenous medication that has relieved the migraine and he is ready for discharge. "Get a taxi," says Dylan. Not so simple, the hospital will only release him into someone's care because of the medication he received.

"I'll have to get the kids up if I come to get you," says Dylan thinking aloud. "I can't leave them alone."

"I don't think it would matter for a half hour," responds Rob.

Dylan ponders this notion, thinking of worst case scenarios. "No, but I can't take the risk. Can't they wait until tomorrow before discharging you?"

"They never admitted me ... I spent the whole time on a gurney in emergency. I suppose I can sit in the emergency waiting room."

Dylan thinks again. No, this is no way to treat a friend. He'll get the kids up and drive down to pick him up ... can Rob wait by the entrance so Dylan doesn't have to park?

Dylan wakes the youngsters, pulls snowsuits over their nightclothes, then carries the pair of zombies down three flights of stairs to plant each one onto the rear seat of his Pontiac.

At Sunnybrook, Rob is sitting in a wheelchair at the entrance, accompanied by an orderly. Dylan signs a form and helps his friend into the front seat of the car. After driving back to the apartment, Rob offers to carry one of the kids upstairs. Dylan is adamant that this would be a bad idea and accompanies Rob, who is indeed wobbly on his feet, up the stairs. He makes two more round trips of the three flights of stairs, hauling each of the children up to deposit them into bed.

It's three thirty in the morning and Rob wants to talk. He informs Dylan that he has to go into work this day; this is not an elective decision on his part, it's an obligation. "Great," says Dylan sarcastically, "so what would have happened if I hadn't returned yesterday?"

"Dylan, I know it's an imposition and I can assure you I feel bad about it ... it certainly wasn't my choice to have the kids dumped on me over Christmas without warning. Do this one day and I'll check out daycare options when I'm at work to-morrow ... er, today, that is."

*   *   *

Dylan is awakened by Marcia and Robbie jumping all over him. "Wake up, Dill," they chorus, "make us breakfast."

"Where's your dad?"

"I think he's gone to work?" responds Marcia. "He must have gotten better, he's not on the couch."

"Are you going to take us skating?" asks Robbie. "Mummy said that Daddy could take us skating when we're in Toronto."

"Did you bring skates?"

"No, but we can rent them."

Three hours of skating exhausts the children. Nathan Phillips Square is crowded with kids accompanied by fathers happy to avoid the post-Christmas sales and the fervor they induce in wives. Lunch rinkside is a cinch, with street-roasted chestnuts and hot chocolate. The kids can barely keep their eyes open during the subway ride home and there is no resistance from either child when Dylan suggests they take an afternoon nap.

Later, in the afternoon, the apartment is descended on by close to a dozen of Dylan's classmates of both genders, laden with booze and pot. Marcia and Robbie are sleeping off the effects of three hours skating as this rowdy group begins to arrive and gather in the kitchen and living room. However, they soon learn that the rules of the house have changed. Twenty-four hours of babysitting have altered Dylan's mindset and seeded some paternal impulses to protect his young charges. Dylan informs the partiers that no pot can be smoked today ... not within the confines of the apartment. The choices are clear ... they can abstain, brew grass tea ... or exit the apartment to the backyard and subzero temperatures if they must puff on the weed. His companions look at Dylan, perplexed. Dylan informs them they have kids staying with them and their young lungs ... and minds ... must not be corrupted. Indeed, if they intend to brew the grass into tea, it must be referred to as "herbal tea."

No sooner is this dictate proclaimed when Marcia enters the room, rubbing sleep from her eyes. Noticing all the people in the room, she asks, "Are you guys having a party? Is there going to be dancing?" Dylan informs her that yes, it's just a small party, and yes, there may be some dancing, depending on everyone's mood.

"Wow!" says Marcia, instantly alert and awake, "I'm going to wake up Robbie. We love parties."

Self-appointed DJ, Marcia, sifts through the Robert and Dylan collection of discs to find content to her taste. With music playing, Marcia and Robbie dance with each other to begin with, but in no time, a couple of the female members of Dylan's gang join in with the youngsters. Grass tea, beer, and wine soon have everybody in the apartment gyrating to the music and Dylan has to pray that his neighbor in the apartment below is anywhere in the world but down there; perhaps libraries have extended hours after Christmas?

Sometime during the early evening, Robert gets in from work dressed in a suit, just as the party dynamic is peaking. For an instant, he fears for what his two kids might be exposed to, but then notes that this place is not the den of iniquity it usually is when Dylan's cohort gathers. Absent is the dope haze and tattletale aroma. He grabs a beer from the fridge and seeks out Marcia and Robbie. The two kids are dancing like troubadours and acknowledge the arrival of their father into the room with no more than a perfunctory finger wave. Rob studies the two youngsters while sipping on his beer: they behave with a brazen confidence within this group of young adults; not a song goes by without them pouncing on one of the students in the group, male or female, they care not which, imploring them for another dance.

Rob could do with a toke; it was after all, a long day at work. He is familiar with this group and knows there must be some action happening somewhere. He peeks out the window and standing in the snow in the backyard is a couple of smokers. He gulps down his beer and disappears down the stairs to join them.

The party gears down. Calm returns to the apartment, although the mess is yet to be picked up. At the kitchen table, Robbie climbs on to Rob's lap and Marcia does likewise onto Dylan. "Daddy, that was the best party ever," says Robbie wearily, suddenly looking like he is about to fall asleep, "can we have another party tomorrow?"

Daddy responds, "I think it's about time we got you guys into bed. It's past eleven. How about a mug of hot chocolate?"

Marcia crooks her head around to address Dylan. "Dill, instead of hot chocolate, can you make me some of your herbal tea? It was the best cup of tea I've ever had!"

Dylan blinks. Is it possible? Yes, of course it's possible; she must have helped herself from his mug. Dylan stares into Marcia's eyes. No doubt about it, she's stoned. All that effort he put into being protective and responsible and the result is a six-year-old who's high as a kite. Did Robbie have some, too? Lying is required.

"Marcia, that was a special herbal tea that one of the girls brought. We're all out of it now."

"What was it called, Dylan?" asks Rob, more fatherly than usual, no doubt due to the effects of the dope he's consumed. "We can buy some tomorrow."

"It had a funny name, something badly translated from Chinese, I think ... like 'heavenly enchantments.'"

"'Heavenly enchantments,'" repeats Marcia, dopily, "It was delish."

Over the next two weeks, Dylan would swear that he did three hours babysitting to every hour Rob puts in. No daycare is found by Rob, hardly surprising over the Christmas vacation period, thinks Dylan. He doubted that Rob ever made any effort to find a place – why would he risk the wrath of his wife when he can simply take advantage of the fact that Dylan is not in school and easy to impose upon?

On days when Rob has to go to work, Dylan's child care strategy with Marcia and Robbie relies on physically exhausting them into a neutral, generally compliant state while participating in activities that he gets at least some enjoyment from. He takes the kids skating, swimming, skiing, and snowshoeing during the mornings. By afternoon, both kids are grateful for the opportunity to slow down for an afternoon nap, even Marcia, who for a couple of years has considered herself way too old for naps.

Sedentary Rob's philosophy of handling kids is different. It relies primarily on entertainment run on a television screen between the four walls of the not particularly child-friendly living room in the apartment. The lack of activity inevitably turns the kids cranky by the middle of the day, and difficult to handle and whining for their mother, for the remainder of it. Dylan ensures that he does not hang around the apartment on those days that Rob doesn't go into work.

Dylan is not at home on the day Rob's wife Kendra picks up Marcia and Robbie. When he does return to his apartment, Rob is sitting at the kitchen table, rubbing his head. "That was the longest three weeks of my life, Dylan," he declares, feeling sorry for himself, "I don't know what I would have done without you."

Dylan laughs. "Well you'll have less than six months of freedom, then it'll be back to full-time daddyhood for you."

Robert looks at him skeptically. "Daddyhood is not an option for lawyers, thank God; children interfere with billable hours. No Dylan, Marcia and Robbie will have to put up with mummyhood from now on in their lives. I'm not going through that hell again!"

Eight months later, Dylan is still a resident in the fourth-floor apartment on Highview Crescent, but is now its sole occupant. Robert moved out three months previously and Dylan wonders whether to seek another flatmate or just accept paying a little more to maintain a solitary environment and peace of mind. Robert's hard work and bar exam results landed him employment as a corporate litigator with a prestigious law firm on Bay Street. Accordingly, he has purchased a house, no doubt with a massive mortgage, in affluent Willowdale, to which he has relocated his family from St. John. Dylan has not spoken with him since the day he moved out, no doubt because friendship, along with daddyhood, interferes with billable hours.

Late in August, a week or so before a new school year begins, Kendra Grantham phones. "Who?" asks Dylan, confused.

"I'm your ex-roommate Rob's wife. We met briefly last Christmas before I traveled out West. We're living in Willowdale now."

"Oh yes," says Dylan. His only meeting with Kendra was so brief that he struggles to picture her.

"Do you know why I'm phoning you?"

"Not a clue," says Dylan, but as he does so, a recollection of gazing into Marcia's stoned eyes intrudes into his memory.

"After picking up the kids last Christmas, Marcia and Robbie have never stopped talking about you. They constantly ask when they could go and visit 'Dill' ... that's what they call you. I'm not sure whether you are superman or a pervert."

Dylan says nothing.

"Look, I've just finished doing some back-to-school shopping downtown with the kids ... would you mind if we stopped in for a quick visit on the way home? We won't stay for long ... and it'll make the kids happy."

Dylan frantically races around cleaning the apartment, a task which involves the disposal of many empty bottles, washing dishes, and vigorous vacuuming. The prevailing odor in the apartment is akin to that of a bar, so that is countered with firing up a coffee percolator. He is in the process of stacking empty cases of beer bottles into the trunk of his car when Kendra Grantham's Volvo pulls into the driveway ... unfortunately highlighting the Pontiac full of the empties.

Yes, Marcia and Robbie are pleased to see Dylan, but they are even more excited to show off this apartment, whose geography they learned so well, and, over some months, have reminisced as a version of paradise. Only children could elevate this modest dwelling to such a lofty status. The pair literally drags their mother upstairs to show her what heaven looks like. Dylan loads the last case of empties into his car before following the threesome.

Dylan props himself in the kitchen doorway as he observes Marcia and Robbie compete for their mother's attention in revealing what they each know about this wondrous place. "Can I get you a coffee?" Dylan asks Kendra.

"That would be very nice, Dylan," Kendra responds. Kendra is close to a decade older than him and he's not sure if she is talking down to him.

Seated at the kitchen table, Dylan and Kendra engage in some light conversation. Meanwhile, Marcia has seated herself on Dylan's lap. "Dill," she asks, twisting her head in exactly the way she made the request eight months earlier, "have you got any of my favorite tea? You know the one, the 'heavenly enchantments' stuff."

Dylan lifts the kid off his lap. He opens one of the kitchen cupboards to reveal a half dozen different packages of tea. "I'm not sure which one it was, Marcia," he says, playing dumb, mostly for the benefit of the child's mother, "maybe you can help … would you recognize the package?"

Marcia shakes her head. "No, I only know that it wasn't in tea bags. It was loose leaves that floated in the mug. When you sipped the tea, you had to sieve the leaves with your teeth, like this …" She makes a hissing, sucking noise. "One guy was gross though … he said that the leaves were the tastiest bit and he ate them all! Chewed them up and swallowed them!"

Dylan looks at Kendra and shrugs. "People bring so many different types of tea when they visit … it's difficult to keep track." He returns to his chair at the kitchen table and Marcia immediately hops back onto his lap. Why can't she go and play?

Kendra looks intently at Marcia. "Now darling," she says probing, "how exactly would you describe this delightful tea?"

Marcia, pleased to have this attention from her mother focused on her, props her chin on a fist and responds, "Mummy, if you imagine the smell of the most beautiful flower … that was what this tea tasted like. I'm surprised Dylan doesn't remember it, he was drinking it all night at the party – I just helped him a little."

Timely Robbie interrupts. Quick to note that his father's former bed is unoccupied, he suggests that they all sleepover; perhaps they could have another party? Marcia agrees that this would be a wonderful idea – it has been ages since she had an opportunity to dance. Mummy has different ideas. She is quite sure they do not want to sleepover, because they live a mere thirty minutes drive away. Instead, Dylan must come for supper, it might do him some good to have something not in a liquid state for a meal, she adds sarcastically.

Dylan shakes his head. No, he has another commitment, perhaps another time. Marcia and Robbie make exaggerated sad faces. Kendra stands and empties the contents of her coffee cup down the sink, noting that it was a little strong for her taste. The four descend the stairs. At the car, Dylan warmly returns the embrace of each kid and dutifully kisses their mother on one cheek.

"Phone and let me know when you can come for a meal," says Kendra, but Dylan senses that she says this only because it is what cold courtesy requires. He stands in the driveway and waves to the departing automobile.

21. RACHEL

Marcus Rubin is a clean-cut Jewish kid and classmate of Dylan's who's most notable for the fact he sometimes wears a tie to class. Although Dylan has known Marcus since his first year in school, he was quick to dismiss him as a convergent bore and accordingly, generally ignored him. Marcus was seldom seen at the pubs and parties favored by the majority of his classmates until the beginning of his senior year, when out of the blue, he shows up at the Brunswick House pub.

When he arrives, Marcus is not by himself; in fact, had he been alone, he would have attracted little attention. After entering the pub, he almost apologetically invites himself into the group of his boozing fellow students, and introduces his girlfriend. Dylan does a double take. There is something about this girlfriend that captivates Dylan – she displays a blueprint reminiscent of his former lover Gabriela, with a similar olive complexion, long dark hair, and sultry brown eyes. Initially, Dylan fails to catch the girl's name because there is a noisy band playing in the pub. After catching his breath, he leaps to his feet, intending to ensure that in the rearranging of chairs required by the two arrivals, his chair ends up alongside that of Marcus Rubin's girlfriend.

Strategically seated, Dylan yells into the girlfriend's ear that he was unable to catch her name. This requires Marcus's girlfriend to move her lips to Dylan's ear, cup her hands, and inform him that her name is Rachel Feinstein. Following this almost intimate introduction, Dylan experiences a frustrating time sitting next to Rachel because the noisy band renders most verbal communication incomprehensible. In addition, Rachel doesn't seem much interested in Dylan. Marcus and Rachel stay for just one drink, no doubt put off by the rowdy music and prolific beer consumption of the group of mostly male students they find themselves among. However, this meeting is long enough for Dylan to resolve to get to know Marcus … and his girlfriend … a whole lot better.

In the days that follow, Marcus must have wondered at his sudden rise in popularity. He receives invitations for pub crawls and parties, and it goes without saying that these invitations include Rachel. And Rachel is always available. As a privileged Jewish princess, Rachel neither studies nor works. Indeed, it appears as if little more is required of her in this world other than to look gorgeous until the day she marries. Dylan manages to manipulate short episodes of one-on-one time with Rachel, but is disheartened to learn that she and Marcus are close to announcing their engagement. "Are your parents likely to oppose this marriage?" asks Dylan hopefully.

"Gosh no," says Rachel, "both Marcus's and my parents have wanted us married since we were like … fourteen years old. It's just that announcing our engagement will launch a fervor of preparation among our parents that will make our lives a living hell. We're probably going to wait until Marcus is done school … we'll make the announcement in April or May."

Dylan does the math. He has five months to sabotage the relationship. How could stunning Rachel hitch up with a dweeb like Marcus when she could have Dylan?

*   *   *

It is Robert Grantham who answers that question. Dylan and Robert get together for a sushi lunch on Queen Street, their first meeting since Robert departed the Highview apartment. Robert is donned in work clothing, a three-piece-suit that makes Dylan's student attire look shabby. It's the third attempt at making this lunch reunion take place, each previous one being postponed by Robert, who had a more pressing last-minute engagement.

On arrival, Robert immediately orders a bottle of the most expensive sake on the menu; he's playing the big-shot at this reunion and will insist on paying for everything. After exchanging a little chit-chat, updating their lives since Robert left Highview, Dylan can't help but mention his infatuation with Rachel, and the fact that she is "almost" engaged. He has to tell someone, a person not connected with school. "What did you say her surname was?" asks Robert, while grasping a sushi roll with chopsticks. Dylan tells him. "And his surname?"

"Feinstein and Rubin!" Robert laughs. "You're out of your league on this one, Dylan. You are nothing but a fucking goy to them. Sure, she may take the time to tease you a little, it would no doubt titillate her vanity, a Jewish princess likes to think she can attract goys. But I can promise you, you'll never get anywhere with her – trust me on this one, the legal profession and my Toronto boarding school experience have equipped me with a little more knowledge of things Semite than you."

"Doesn't love … and lust … conquer anything?"

"Not in the real world. Believe me, Feinstein and Rubin have been bred from the womb to consider everything in the non-Jewish world to be inferior … it's not their fault, blame six thousand years of inherent Semite alter ego. More important, you should thank your lucky stars that your balls are not going to win this chick. As soon as your Feinstein has popped out one baby, she'll blow up like a balloon, grow a moustache, and nag whoever she marries into an early grave so she can tramp around Europe and take cruises for the remainder of her life. And Christ … have you ever been to a Bar or Bat Mitzvah? … or any other kind of Jewish service?"

They spend hours, I mean like six hours in succession, wailing and drooling incomprehensible incantations … I'd opt for root canal surgery over being subjected to attending another Jewish religious ritual of any kind."

"Maybe she would convert?" offers Dylan meekly.

Robert bursts out laughing mid-way through swallowing a mouthful of sushi and nearly chokes. Spluttering, he says, "Dylan, you disappoint me … I used to think you were pretty smart. Convert? What a joke, convert this chick to whatever the fuck it is you believe in … atheism is it? … and I'll personally commit to a diet of kosher food for a year. That's a world cuisine you probably have no experience of, but trust me, it's a much braver proposition on my part than you might think."

"How are Kendra and the kids?" asks Dylan, changing the subject.

Robert looks at Dylan with an expression that telegraphs, why bother to ask? "Kendra is okay I suppose. She's happy *not* to be in St. John, I guess the shopping is better in Toronto. As far as I can tell, the kids have settled into their new school, kids usually adapt easily enough. I'm really too busy to notice much at home. I'll be busting my balls for a few years while I try to make partnership."

Deflated, Dylan says goodbye to Robert at Queen and Bay and heads west on Queen. He's not walked three blocks before he bumps into none other than Marcus and Rachel. He shakes Marcus's hand and moves to hug and kiss Rachel on the cheek, but an accident of awkward alignment forces his lips into the girl's ear. Dylan separates, hoping that she doesn't notice that his gauche greeting has made him blush … on her part, Rachel is clearly unsettled by the buss on the ear and wraps an arm around Marcus, as if seeking protection.

"How fortunate, meeting up with you like this, Dylan, in the middle of Queen Street!" exclaims Marcus. "I was informed that you were once a rugby player … as you know, I captain the varsity second fifteen and we are in desperate need of a fullback for our Saturday game. Would you consider joining us? You'd be doing me a big favor."

Had this request been made with any other person in the world standing in front of him other than Rachel, the response would have been outright refusal.

"Er, I haven't played in over three years, Marcus," responds Dylan, already knowing that he will accept the offer and suspecting also, that accepting it is a very bad idea, "I'm sure I'll be a little rusty … and I'm a bit out of shape."

"No matter, Dylan, this should be an easy game for us … we are playing the Balmy Beach over thirty-fives team … we'll thrash them soundly … they're nothing but a bunch of old men."

*   *   *

And this is how Dylan comes to finds himself lying on a hospital gurney. He fore-told disaster at the moment he stupidly agreed to play rugby, a game he has con-gratulated himself on being smart enough to avoid playing since leaving the gulag. He had not been on the pitch thirty minutes when he got caught in a trip tackle and in the ensuing tangle of legs, broke his left leg above the ankle. Yes, their op-ponents were old men, yes they were low on skills, but they outweighed the varsity team by a good fifty percent and made up for their lack of speed with a good mea-sure of savagery. Consequently, Dylan now awaits X-rays and the probable surgical insertion of a metal plate.

There is a small bonus, but it comes with a downside. The captain of the rugby team offered up his girlfriend to ride in the ambulance with the team's stricken fullback. The downside of this arrangement is that Rachel is visibly sickened by the sight of the injury, it is not something a Jewish princess should be required to wit-ness, and therefore she hasn't the stomach to provide any pastoral comfort. In fact, during the ambulance ride to the hospital, she requires more of the paramedic's at-tention than Dylan to prevent her from either fainting or throwing up.

On arrival at the hospital, Dylan is placed on a gurney and he and Rachel are se-questered into a curtained cubicle in the emergency department. Dylan has to pee. He sits up on the gurney and prepares to hop to a toilet. Rachel turns away to spare herself the sight of the broken leg. However, he fails to make three steps beyond the confines of his cubicle before he is intercepted by an aggressive nurse who in no un-certain terms orders the patient back to his gurney. "I have to pee," protests Dylan.

In response, the nurse grabs an oversized pair of scissors and snips Dylan out of his rugby shorts and jock strap, informing him that they are not about to pass these over the injured leg. Rachel politely looks away during this piece of surgery; the nurse obviously thinks that she is the girlfriend. She then motions to attack the rugby jersey in a similar fashion, but Dylan sits and deftly pulls it over his head. The nurse then provides her patient with a hospital gown, covers him with a sheet, and hands him a urinal bottle. When Dylan returns the now filled urinal bottle to the nurse, she informs him that the doctor has approved giving him something for pain, which she will administer momentarily.

The powerful painkiller injected into Dylan produces an interesting side effect. Within moments, Dylan experiences an erection of abnormal potency that ap-pears to have a cause, not connected to the stimuli represented by Rachel's bedside proximity. Fortunately for Dylan, the narcotic has tranquilized any inkling of em-barrassment he might have felt under ordinary circumstances. Less fortunately for Rachel, her senses are not anesthetized, and she becomes acutely embarrassed at the tent pole that launches itself under the flimsy sheet covering the lower half of his body. If only the nurse would return and *do* something. Dylan looks accusingly down at his groin as if it is somehow a separate entity from himself, and declares to Rachel with a grin, "It's all your fault … you have no right to look so gorgeous."

Rachel is not amused. Ten awkward minutes go by before the nurse re-enters the cubicle to check on Dylan. She glances down at the sheet that masks, rather than disguises the state of arousal beneath and remarks to Rachel, "It appears as if your boyfriend is in need of some comfort." She exits the cubicle, sliding the curtains closed, before Rachel has time to refute the assertion that she is "the" girlfriend.

Dylan grasps Rachel's hand. "Oh, I am so ready to be comforted by you," he tells her and as he does, becomes aware that whatever drug they have given him has provided him with some license to behave outrageously. Rachel shakes her hand free of Dylan's and jerks her chair across the floor to maneuver herself further away from the tent pole. "I'll just pretend you are touching me," he tells Rachel and as he does so, has somehow cashiered her other hand and is in the process of directing it under the sheet.

Rachel shakes this hand free and clasps both her hands together on her lap. "Dylan, I can't imagine the kind of pain you must be in, but you have to behave yourself, I am practically engaged … and we are in a public place."

"Does that mean if we were in a private place you would touch me where I want to be touched?"

"No, of course not. I don't want to touch you; in fact, what I really want is for you to stop talking like this … I know it's only the painkiller speaking."

"Wrong! I am speaking from the depths of my heart. I've been madly in love with you since the very first day I met you at the Brunswick."

"Well, I'm not in love with you and I never could be. You are a nice … boy, but not my type."

Dylan makes an exaggerated sad expression; he's coming to an awareness that this flirtation is going nowhere. "Nice enough to kiss?" he asks hopefully.

Amazingly, Rachel abruptly gets to her feet, leans over Dylan, her hair falling over his face, and kisses him on the forehead. She moves her face away and sits down before Dylan has time to react. The action even takes Dylan by surprise.

"Aw," he says, "a kiss is not a real kiss unless it's on the lips."

"Dylan," says Rachel in her best Jewish mother's voice, "I only accompanied you here as a favor to Marcus. And now you want me to betray the trust he has in me … in us … you're not treating me very nicely … I think I deserve better from you."

"Kiss me properly on the lips," says Dylan, "after, I promise to stop pestering you." Then he adds apologetically, "But I don't think I can lose my hard-on"

Again, to Dylan's surprise, Rachel sighs and with the attitude that this might be the only way she can get any peace and quiet, rises to her feet. Using her hand to hold her falling hair away from both their faces, she leans over Dylan and moves her lips to his. Dylan is alert enough to approach the critical first contact with caution, so much so, he is sure it's Rachel, not he, who allows the kiss to evolve into open mouth contact. At some point, the exchange is accompanied by heavy breathing and it's not until Dylan attempts to guide Rachel's hand under the sheet to the raging tent pole that Rachel snaps out of romantic mode.

She does this abruptly and sits, wiping her mouth. "That was very silly of us, Dylan. I'm in a relationship with a man I very much love. A man who is supposed to be your friend."

"I want more. I want to sleep with you. I don't just want you, I need you. When can we get together?"

"The answer is never, Dylan. Anyway, with that leg, it will be a while before you'll be sleeping with any woman. Marcus was right about you. He said you are the kind of person who doesn't know how to take life seriously. He also told me that you have an illegitimate son who looks exactly like you."

"Not true. I once had a *girlfriend* who had a child, but it wasn't mine. The relationship ended more than a year ago."

Rachel looks at Dylan skeptically. "Dylan, I don't deny I find you a little bit attractive, I suppose I wouldn't have kissed like that otherwise. But even when we were kissing, I was aware of how stupidly I was behaving. And because you've already experienced a long-term relationship, you likely realized that you weren't being so smart."

"How old are you Rachel? Twenty? Twenty-one? Are you ready to throw in the towel and get hitched up … spend the rest of your life with some guy just because it'll make your mommy and daddy happy?"

"If you must know Dylan, I'm twenty-one … and it's not just 'some guy,' it's a man I'm deeply in love with … anyway, how do you know that getting married won't make me happy? The thing is, I'm quite obviously a lot more mature than you are … believe it or not, I'm actually ready to settle down. I want to have children." She casts a peeved look at her watch. "Oh, I do wish Marcus would hurry up and get here. You're really upsetting me with this talk of yours. You have this way of making me feel so uncomfortable."

"That's probably because I'm talking to that side of you that suspects you'd really love nothing better than to have a little fling with me … Rachel, please, kiss me again, it makes me forget the pain in my leg … when I kiss you, I imagine we are both naked and we're the only two people in the world."

"Now you're really talking nonsense, Dylan."

"You do know the reason I agreed to play in that rugby game is you. If you hadn't been standing beside Marcus when he asked me, I would've told him to drop dead … something illogical in me suggested that you might be impressed … by a warrior going to battle for his lover."

"Men are so stupid. I've never liked Marcus playing that game and I hate watching it. And after this …" Rachel looks disdainfully toward Dylan's leg, "I'm never going to another game."

"Just think Rachel, if you become my lover, I'll never ask you to watch me play rugby because it would be a waste of an afternoon that would be better spent making mad, passionate love."

"Please stop talking like that, Dylan, you sound so juvenile." Then looking at her watch once again, she exclaims in frustration, "Oh, where has Marcus got to? The game should have ended over an hour ago."

"He'll be at least another hour … he's team captain, he'll be expected to have a minimum of one beer with the boys."

Rachel stands up and paces around the cubicle. A doctor enters and ignoring Dylan, informs Rachel that he is waiting for an orthopedic surgeon to examine the X-rays so the objective is to keep the patient comfortable … he says to let him know if she suspects her boyfriend requires more pain medication. The doctor turns and disappears before Rachel gets a chance to inform him that she is not the girl-friend. Dylan's erection subsides.

"It's obvious the whole world thinks we're made for each other," announces Dylan. Rachel shrugs. She approaches the gurney and holds Dylan's hand, then almost wistfully strokes the back of her index finger over the now flaccid penis under the sheet, saying teasingly, "Good boy." The result of this minimal contact is predictable.

"Touch me some more," pleads Dylan, "it'll help take my mind off the agony."

"I'm very sure you're not in agony – does your penis always misbehave like that or is it just the painkiller?"

"You should take pride in the fact that you are entirely to blame for my state of arousal."

Rachel paces over to the point at which the curtains meet and separates them sufficiently to peer out into the emergency department. She snaps them closed and walks back to Dylan's bedside, chastising the hospital. "I think it's disgraceful that they can leave someone so badly injured completely unattended for as long as they've left you. Everybody here is so slow. The atmosphere is the antithesis of emergency."

"Don't you fantasize about having sex with someone other than Marcus? My guess would be that he's a total bore in bed."

"You're so bloody rude, Dylan. As it happens, Marcus and I don't have … proper sex … we are saving that for our wedding day when it'll be special … and not just because our religion says it will be so. I mean … we do absolutely everything but have … intromissive sex … gosh, that sounds awful."

"Fuck is the word you are looking for."

"That sounds cheap and crude. I hate that word. What I mean is that we are mature enough to restrain ourselves."

"Mature? Don't kid yourself. And incidentally, "fuck" is one of my favorite words. I would like to fuck your brains out right now. I want to fuck you so silly that you'll never want to restrain yourself again. I want to spend all night and all day in bed with you. If we could spend a full twenty-four hours in bed with each other, I guarantee you'd be less uptight."

Rachel shakes her head. "I'm not the only person in the world that thinks that … word … debases an act which is supposed to be beautiful into something coarse and ugly." She turns her head away from Dylan as if she is thinking, but does not move away from the gurney.

Some moments pass before Rachel turns again, to look Dylan square in the eyes. Slowly, she leans over him, and holding her hair away from his face, once again kisses him. The kiss is deep and prolonged … and at some point Rachel's hand slips down Dylan's torso over the sheet. This contact is short-lived. Dylan, hoping to maximize the pleasure offered by the hand so close to his penis, contracts the muscles in his buttocks, triggering an explosion of pain from the point of fracture in his leg. He can barely suppress the inclination to scream out in agony. Rachel breaks free from Dylan. "Gosh, what have I done?" She sits back down on the chair beside the gurney, and holds one of Dylan's hands with both of hers, shaking her head. "I should know better."

Dylan is flushed and sweating. The spike of pain sobers his thinking and dowses his libido. "Rachel, you can go if you want. I don't mind waiting alone. After the bone is set, I'll call my parents … I don't want to do this until after whatever has to be done to my leg is done."

"I'm not leaving you here alone. Give me your parents' phone number … I'll call them. I think you're probably too stoned to make much sense over the phone."

Rachel exits and returns shortly afterward to inform Dylan that she was unable to get through to his parents and was reluctant to leave a message which could upset them. Dylan reflects on how her demeanor has entirely altered over the past thirty minutes. She now stands beside the gurney and strokes Dylan's forehead in a way that makes him wonder exactly what it was he did to trigger the change.

When Marcus arrives, Rachel's behavior is even more bizarre. Marcus addresses Dylan with a concerned "How are you, Dylan?"

Rachel sits back on the chair and barely registers her boyfriend's arrival. When Marcus turns and leans down to kiss her, she twists her face out of range. "Have you been drinking beer?" she asks, her voice cold.

"Just one, it's sort of expected. Rugby is a social game."

"Really! I think it's remarkably callous of you to go out drinking when one of your teammates has been so badly injured. Maybe the team captain should set a better example."

Marcus shrugs, looking at Dylan. Dylan responds, "You guys can leave now, I'll be fine. I'll be sitting around here for hours. I can take a taxi home when they're done with me."

"In that case, Dylan, we'll leave. Phone, and I'll come back and drive you to your apartment when they've finished with you."

Rachel is appalled. She says to Marcus, "You can't be serious? How would you like it if you were in Dylan's place?"

Dylan attempts to intercede; the last thing he wants is to be caught in the middle of this tiff. However, almost as he opens his mouth, Rachel aggressively turns on Dylan, "You shut up. You're so full of dope, you don't know what you're saying." Next, she turns on Marcus disdainfully, "Why don't you go back and have a few more beers with the boys?"

Dylan closes his eyes. The painkiller has fogged his thoughts and he wants to check out of the scene unfolding before him. Now the drug aids the escape; he dozes.

The events of the next few hours are muddled in Dylan's recollection. Sometime later, he finds himself on crutches with a heavy plaster cast on his leg, hobbling toward the hospital exit. Inexplicably, Rachel is walking alongside him, issuing a continuum of admonishments to Dylan, on how to avoid collisions, and to the population at large in the hospital corridors, on how to keep clear of her patient. Because, that's what Dylan appears to have become over the past few hours, Rachel's patient.

At the vehicle forecourt in front of the emergency department, a large black sedan pulls up and a well-dressed, middle-aged man exits the driver's door to open both passenger doors. It's dark and the night air is cold. Dylan is assisted into the back-seat and Rachel seats herself beside him. Dylan assumes he is being conducted back to his apartment and offers directions to the driver.

"Oh, is there a change of plan?" asks the driver, who turns out to be Rachel's father. "Rachel led me to understand that you were coming back with us ... we've already made up the bed in the ground floor guest room."

Dylan's attempt to dispel this notion is cut off mid-sentence. "Daddy, don't pay any attention to him. Dylan's apartment is on a fourth floor and he lives by himself – he cannot possibly get up all those stairs on crutches, let alone look after himself." She turns to Dylan. "You'll stay in our bubby's room. I've already arranged it with your mother. We agreed that you should not be returning to your apartment in your condition ... I told her that this was the best place for you to be while you're recovering. We live less than five minutes' walk from the subway ... so it will be easy for you to get to classes."

"Rachel, I'm grateful for all you did for me at the hospital. But I'm perfectly okay to return to my apartment ... the last thing I want to do is impose myself on your family." He turns to Rachel's father. "Please, Mr. Feinstein, take me back to my ..."

"Dylan, this is not a discussion," Rachel says emphatically, raising both arms in the air. She raises her voice a pitch to address her father. "Popsie, will you please inform Dylan there is no question of him returning to his apartment, his mother and I have already discussed the arrangements in detail ... she would be furious if there was a change in plan now ... and I would feel as if I had betrayed her."

Popsie is less sure, but obviously wary of crossing his daughter. He addresses his rear view mirror. "Dylan, try staying for a couple of days and then make your mind up. You're in no mental state to make a decision now ... you've had a traumatic experience what with the injury and surgery."

"Father, you are not being exactly helpful ... I don't want you opening the door for Dylan to start thinking he can hobble up four flights of stairs so he can fall and break his neck next time round. Like his mother said, he has the mind of a five-year-old when it comes to matters of common sense."

"My mother said that?"

"She did. She also told me that the only way to handle you was with an unequivocally firm hand." She turns to her father. "That's why I don't want you meddling into arrangements that have already been cast in stone, Popsie." Then to Dylan, "And by the way ... your mother is traveling to Toronto tomorrow to visit you. She can only stay for a couple of hours, but she wants to make sure you are okay. She's having lunch with us."

Dylan holds his head with both hands. It seems that the least agonizing outcome of breaking a leg is the physical pain.

When they arrive at the Feinstein's, Dylan discovers that it's one in the morning. Rachel disappears upstairs to speak to her mother, who has already gone to bed. Dylan crutches himself into the living room, where Mr. Feinstein offers him a brandy. "I'd rather have a beer," says Dylan.

"One cold beer coming up," says Mr. Feinstein, jovially pouring both the beer and some cognac for himself.

The two men clink their glasses and Dylan de-crutches and sits. At this moment, Rachel enters the room and her gaze zones in on Dylan's beer glass. Authoritatively, she crosses the room, grabs both the glass and the bottle, and marches out of the room, saying to her father, "You should know better, Popsie. Dylan's doctor made it perfectly clear that he was not to have any alcohol while taking painkillers."

Rachel's father smiles and shrugs his shoulders. "How were you to know what the doctor said?" asks Dylan, hoping to establish a complicit alliance with this man whose daughter has revealed herself as a controlling terror within the time frame of a few hours. Whatever happened to the mostly silent, demure beauty he fell in lust with?

"The thing you must learn about women," responds Rachel's father, "is that they expect a telepathic connection with any male in their vicinity."

Rachel marches back into the room. "Nonsense, Popsie," she says to her father, then to Dylan, "Daddy should know better because he's a physician … a heart surgeon. Come along, you're going to bed, Dylan. You've had a long day."
Dylan is introduced to his bedroom. "This is where my Bubby sleeps when she stays … she finds it difficult to climb stairs. She lives in Florida during the winters."

✳   ✳   ✳

So Dylan enters a period of virtual incarceration at the Feinstein's. The pain he experienced at the time of the fracture to his leg is nothing to what he undergoes in the days that follow. In her adopted pastoral role, Rachel smothers Dylan with attentiveness, which she never allows to become sexual. Although Dylan rises in the morning feeling all but pain-free, after a school day consisting of a subway ride and several hours of classes, his leg is throbbing and in dire need of rest. Furthermore, the painkillers in capsule form prescribed on his discharge from hospital fail to function like their intravenous counterparts; they make him feel dozy and accomplish little in the way of meaningful pain relief. After classes, he attempts to remain on campus for as long as possible to avoid a return to the Feinstein's, but pain and exhaustion soon drive him back to Rachel and her ministrations.

Pain and an awareness of this new Rachel combine to suppress Dylan's libido for the first week. During this period, Rachel's attentions to Dylan are so bossy and business-like that a repeat of the kisses they shared in the emergency department is never a threat. However, a week after Dylan's accident, Saturday for Dylan, the Sabbath for the Feinstein's, Dylan has no school. He sleeps until awakened by Rachel wearing a housecoat.

"I'm going to help give you a strip wash, Dylan," announces Rachel merrily, "you're beginning to smell not so good." For the first time in a week, a tingle of arousal runs up Dylan's spine.

"Are we both going to be naked?" he asks, perking up.

Rachel says nothing. Dylan grabs his crutches and the pair makes its way to the ground floor bathroom. "Where are your mother and father?" asks Dylan.

"They're at the synagogue."

"I thought you guys weren't orthodox?"

"We're not. We still go to the synagogue several times a year. Don't you ever go to church?"

"No, never. Churches give me the creeps. It has always amazed me how a religious service can turn apparently normal persons into irrational zombies. In my opinion, people that consider the Bible to be spiritually motivated are likely to have a far greater capacity for evil than those that don't."

Rachel ponders this. "Maybe it's best we don't talk about religion."

"No, we should talk about it. Your tribe is about as bad as it gets when it comes to zealotry."

This talk of religion has made Dylan's blood rise in all the wrong places. They arrive in the bathroom. "Dylan, I didn't go to the synagogue because I wanted us to be alone. Don't ruin it by getting all wound up about our religious differences."

Dylan pauses. "Just differences. I don't have religious differences. Let's have sex. Not sure if it's allowed on your Sabbath, but I want to fuck your brains out."

Rachel raises her hands, gesturing Dylan to stop. "Dylan, I won't deny that I've become very fond of you over the past week. I've risked a lot for you. But if we are going to get anywhere with each other, I want you to humor me and stop saying the word 'fuck,' I've already told you how much I hate it. Can't you be like most normal people and say 'make love' or 'have sex'?"

"Okay, how's this? … I want to inseminate you until your brain explodes."

"You have a remarkable knack for vulgarity. I think I liked you better last week when you were all dopey and in agony. Anyway, we can't have real sex because I have my period."

Dylan looks quizzically at Rachel. "With the few women I've known, I don't pretend to be an expert, their sexual sensitivities heighten during menstruation … you have to figure that when both the Bible and the Torah rail against something, it is likely something pretty damn good they want women to miss out on."

"I'd be embarrassed … especially the first time for real."

Dylan shrugs. "I just happen to enjoy the odors and mess of sex. But I guess you shouldn't do anything that makes you feel uncomfortable. Still, an added bonus of having sex during menstruation is that it's a relatively safe time to have unprotected sex … if your periods are regular, you're not going to be ovulating. Which, if we are going to fu ... make love … is a good thing because I don't have anything with me."

Dylan is sitting on the edge of the bathtub and a silence falls over the room. Rachel, leaning against the sink, looks at her feet as if considering what to do. She looks Dylan in the eye and finding his gaze already focused on her, looks away again. She shrugs and with apparent reluctance, crosses the bathroom to sit beside him on the edge of the tub. She moves her lips to Dylan's and they kiss.

As the kiss becomes deeper, Rachel's hand finds Dylan's penis and she begins to fondle him. Dylan doesn't allow her more than a couple of strokes before he moves his hand down to remove hers. "I don't want to be jacked off," says Dylan, breaking away from the kiss, "that's probably how you avoided having sex with Marcus for the God knows how many years you've known him. I want to make love to you properly."

Rachel's shoulders slump. "I'm bleeding heavily," she says despairingly.

"That doesn't matter to me … I'll make you feel nice … but, with the small problem of my leg, you'll have to help a little. To begin with, what we need is a large, dark-colored towel …"

With enthusiasm, Dylan speedily crutches his way back to Bubby's room with a brown bath sheet clamped between his teeth to await his lover. And it is on the Sabbath, straddled over a goy lying on her bubby's bed that Rachel learns at the grand age of twenty-one, the meaning of the word *fuck*. After the third time, spread over Dylan, she dreamily whispers into his ear, "Guess what?"

"What?"

"I love to fuck."

✳   ✳   ✳

The dynamics within the Feinstein residence change. While Dr. and Mrs. Feinstein might have had some questions about the nature of the relationship between their daughter and the goy occupant of their bubby's room during the first week, they harbor no doubts about what is going on after this point. This is Rachel's fault. She refuses to keep her hands off Dylan. During the evening meal, a semi-formal occasion at the Feinstein's, Rachel leaps up between courses to canoodle with Dylan, kissing him on the cheek and whispering endearments into his ear. Mrs. Feinstein glowers at her daughter in repressed fury, while Dr. Feinstein does his best to make casual conversation and pretends not to notice.

During five years in the gulag, Dylan had the value of discretion driven into him daily, so he is embarrassed by Rachel's affections, but he hasn't got a clue as to how to rebuff them without creating other indiscretions, perhaps more obnoxious. Rachel, on the other hand, raised as a Jewish princess, was encouraged to act out her emotions, something that she tended to do with reluctance until the arrival of Dylan. For most of her life, the Feinstein parents worried that their quiet, compliant little girl failed to realize her rightful calling as a princess, so little noise did she make in the world. A natural beauty she was, but can looks alone carry a girl … and later the woman … through the trials of life, especially when those looks were destined to fade? Perhaps motherhood would change her, or so they hoped.

Two days after being debauched, an ugly mother and daughter confrontation takes place. Fortunately, it happens when Dylan is in class. Rachel has just returned from a shopping trip. During this venture, she consulted the family doctor to obtain a prescription for birth control pills. This was followed by a visit to a pharmacy, where she converted the prescription and then purchased several types of condom to take care of the interim. She was surprised at the variety of size and range of stimuli claimed on the packaging. Still, there must be no impediment to interfere with this wonderful fucking.

Unfortunately, the family doctor who attends the same synagogue as the Feinstein's, in breach of his professional oaths, picked up the phone and informed Mrs. Feinstein that, with great reluctance, he was forced to accede to her daughter's request for birth control pills. Yes, he had attempted to advise the girl to the contrary, but she was of age, and his duty as a physician required him to write the prescription.

Mrs. Feinstein confronts her daughter, demanding that she reveal the contents of her Shoppers Drug Mart package, neatly stapled closed. Rachel is defiant. "It's really none of your business, Mother. But, if you really must know, it contains a six-month supply of birth control pills and two dozen condoms."

Mrs. Feinstein grasps her forehead in horror. "You are a … a whore … for that goy. What have I done to deserve a daughter such as you?" Rachel brushes past her mother and heads upstairs to her room. Mrs. Feinstein retreats to her room with a migraine.

Later, catching his daughter alone, Dr. Feinstein ventures to ask some tentative questions about the status of Marcus.

"Marcus and I are through, Popsie. You, more than anyone, should know that Marcus and I are ill suited to one another. I'm actually disappointed that you did not sit me down and persuade me to break up with him years ago. He stifled me.

He treated me like some kind of trophy doll."

"You are in love with this Dylan?"

"I don't know for sure, Popsie. What I do know is that he lets me be myself. He's right for me … at least for the moment."

"We have to look beyond the moment to survive in this world." Then, sadly, he says "You know your mother wants him out of the house."

"Fine! Typical that she would get you to tell me that rather than do the dirty work herself. So you can tell dearest Mumsie that when Dylan leaves, I'm leaving with him."

"Let's not be hasty, Rachel. There has never been a daughter more treasured in the eye of her parents than you. And I don't think I'm being presumptuous in saying that you and I have always been especially close. If this boy is what you want, I will accept him. So too, will your mother … in time."

Rachel hugs her father. She tears up. "Popsie, I know this will sound strange to you, but I don't think Dylan will turn out to be my life partner. He is just right for me … in this moment. He brought me to my senses and rescued me from a dead relationship … he gave me the energy to fight to be myself. I haven't felt like that since my Bat Mitzvah. Before my Bat Mitzvah, I felt like a princess. After, I've felt like a slave. A big part of the problem was Marcus – everybody was pushing us together and I was too weak to do anything about it. The frightening thing is that I could have ended up being married to him."

Popsie shakes his head. "There are too many things that I don't understand about your world. I can only speak from my perspective. I can't speak for your mother, but I don't want you to leave home. I want you to stay even if it means I have to share you with this new boy of yours."

"Popsie, I love you very much. Sooner or later, I will have to leave home. I think it may be sooner, because I suspect I may have to leave with Dylan to flush him out of my system. I only know that right now, I want to be with him all the time – it pains me when he is out of sight, and anything that gets in the way of us being together drives me crazy."

"I'll talk to your mother. She loves you just as much as I. It's just that the spectrum of her aspirations for you is a little narrower than mine."

Rachel relates the details of her conversations with Mumsie and Popsie to Dylan in bed. She has taken to descending the stairs to Dylan's lair in Bubby's bed every night, and is no longer concerned at getting caught in the act by her parents, sometimes remaining until summoned for breakfast. Dylan is more pragmatic. "I think I should leave."

"Don't be absurd. When your cast is removed, we can move then … it would be ludicrous to do so beforehand." A little shiver runs down Dylan's spine. Rachel's use of "we" brings home the consequences of a successful seduction … yes, he triumphed against the odds, but in doing so he has placed his independence at risk.

"Your mother never comes out of her room. I feel like an intruder … like I'm hated here."

"Nonsense, don't be melodramatic. Don't worry about Mother. Her migraines are just her way of demanding attention … she's doing this hoping that she'll get her own way. She'll get over it. Daddy is fine with you … he would never admit it, but I know he likes you better than he liked Marcus."

"But it must matter to him that I'm not Jewish."

"Maybe it does a little. But who cares? It doesn't matter to me."

A silence ensues. Rachel breaks it. "Dylan, give me the keys to your apartment, I want to go there tomorrow while you're at school. I want to see it for myself … maybe make a few alterations so I can set it up for both of us to live in. Perhaps give it a woman's touch."

The request doesn't surprise Dylan; he'd come to expect it.

"Yeah, sure. But I don't want you throwing away any of my stuff."

Over the next three weeks, Rachel is seldom home before Dylan returns from school because she has set about the task of "redecorating" Dylan's Highview apartment. Things change at the Feinsteins once again.

Miraculously, Dylan has managed to strike up something of a friendship with Mrs. Feinstein. The change is sudden. Call me 'Mumsie,' Mrs. Feinstein tells Dylan. This, Dylan finds almost impossible to put into practice. Now migraine free, Mumsie takes to having a cup of tea ready for Dylan as he returns from class. Then she sits and talks his head off. At first, Dylan is expected to do no more than listen and nod. Much of her early conversations with Dylan focus on what a "wonderful man" Marcus is and how she'll never understand why Rachel ditched him. Shaking her head, she rues, "That girl will live to regret the day she said goodbye to that noble boy. I will tell her, 'I told you so, I told you so.'"

Astonishingly, she gradually comes to accept Dylan. For his part, Dylan aids this transition, taking on Mumsie in gently mocking overtures, combined with a little flattery and flirtation. Once Mumsie is won over, she takes to airing her daughter's shortcomings, even going so far as to contrast them with Dylan's attributes. She rebukes her daughter for never taking the trouble to sit and talk to her any more; surely an alien has occupied her body. "She is too high and mighty to call me

'Mumsie' now? No, I am 'Mother' now. What am I, a goy like the boyfriend?"

Occasionally, she even goes so far as to brag up Dylan's virtues, "That boy can talk, if a boy could ever talk, that Dylan can. He knows how to make even an old woman feel special with his words."

"So who's the old woman, Mother?"

Mumsie blinks and responds accusingly, "It's daughters like you that turn mothers into old women, mark my words."

When Rachel returns from long days of "fixing up" the Highview apartment, more often than not, she is accompanied by a couple of girlfriends or cousins. They wear baggy men's shirts, ball caps, and jeans splattered with paint. Dylan can but only wonder what is happening to his beloved bachelor pad; based on the evidence of the paint spattered on the girls' clothing, at least one of the rooms has succumbed to becoming an electric pink. Rachel refuses to discuss her interior decorating ambitions for the pad because she wants to surprise Dylan. Poor Dylan can hardly wait to get the cast removed – he needs to escape the Feinstein's and reestablish a territorial identity within which he can have some beers with the boys, barbeque on his balcony, and be free to sow a few wild oats.

The day before his cast is to be removed, Dylan asks Rachel to return his keys. She refuses outright. She wants to be there with him when he first sees the renovated apartment, so she can witness firsthand his wonder at the changes she's made. "Where are my car keys?"

"Oh, I forgot to mention … Popsie doesn't like the idea of me riding around with you in that old jalopy of yours … he says it's a fuel-guzzling death trap. Popsie says you should borrow one of our cars … or he'll get you another car."

"No fucking way. I like my car. If you don't want to ride around in it, drive yours or take a taxi."

"He was just trying to be nice, Dylan. Don't be so chippy."

Dylan discovers that once his cast has been removed, his left leg remains severely weakened and he is unable to dispense with the crutches. However, in anticipation of this day, he has packed his few belongings and said his goodbyes to Popsie and Mumsie. After arriving at his apartment, the enormity of ascending four flights of steep and narrow stairs with an impaired leg sets in. He is aided by a fussing Rachel, who latches onto his torso to assist his ascent. At the door, Rachel insists on covering his eyes. Eyes closed, he hops into the corridor and is guided into the living room.

Dylan is horrified. Not a single item of his furniture remains other than his stereo system. Floral prints in grotesquely gilded frames decorate the walls and there is a garish Persian carpet on the floor. Rachel jumps up and down in excitement like a four-year-old. She assumes that Dylan is so in awe at her decorating prowess, he's lost for words. "Come, I want to show you the bedroom," she sings out.

So this is where the pink paint was applied. Gone is Dylan's rudimentary futon and in its place is a four-poster double bed. On the bed is a floral quilt and the base of the bed is complemented with a lace bed skirt. Half a dozen of Rachel's favorite stuffed animals are arranged sitting in front of pillow shams. "I know it's a little girly, Dylan, I guess I got carried away. Do you forgive me? Come, let me show you your study."

Sure enough, the spare bedroom has been converted into an office area. Dylan's books, previously housed in orderly rows on the floor, are arranged in a jumbled sequence within a pair of matching bookcases. There is a new desk and a real office chair.

Dylan still cannot speak. He hops on his one good foot to the kitchen. Gone is his collection of thrift store utensils, plates, and glassware. In its place are matching eights of crockery, crystal stemware, and cutlery. He pulls a chair up to the kitchen table and sits resting his head in his hands. The respite is short. A moving van has arrived. A pair of muscular movers begins to unload Rachel possessions and it requires all of her attention to organize these movers into positioning each unloaded item in its exact correct location. It's clear that she intends to shack up with her man in plenty of style.

What to do? Rachel's knockout looks no longer seem to mean much. The problem with Rachel is that she has led an existence of getting pretty much whatever she wants … while being surrounded by persons who adore her. It will not be easy for Dylan to assert himself in his cave now that it has been commandeered by Rachel. A more pressing problem is that Dylan wants immediate sex with Rachel. He has been dreaming of this day for eight weeks, the day in which his cast is removed and he can finally fuck Rachel … with him on top. Hindered by the cast, all of their previous sex has been with Rachel straddling him. Time to change that!

It seems to take Rachel and two movers an age to unload and arrange her possessions. Does Dylan rebuke Rachel for turning his world upside down? Does he complain about the pink walls in the bedroom, the tacky paintings on the walls, and gaudy furniture? No way. Puffed out, Rachel joins Dylan at the kitchen table. "Want a cup of tea?" she asks.

Dylan shakes his head. "Why don't we try out the bed first?"

"Wash your hands first."

Rachel and Dylan fall onto the canopy bed, pulling clothing off each other. This will be their first ever fuck where they don't have to be concerned about how much noise they make … in no time they are naked and Dylan is attending to the business of going down on Rachel … when the door bell rings. Dylan comes up for air … "ignore it," he splutters, and gets back on task.

But Rachel is not about to ignore a doorbell. With both hands, she grabs Dylan's hair to yank him out of her crotch, leaps to her feet, and peeks down out of the bedroom window. All it takes is a split-second glance, and she's in a panic. "It's Popsie and Mumsie," she gasps, hopping around on the floor and pulling on clothing. "Get dressed, Dylan. I should've mentioned that they might be coming over."

Not about to be rushed, Dylan allows Rachel to run down the four flights of stairs to open the door for her parents. Listening to the greetings exchanged between Rachel, Popsie, and Mumsie, an observer would assume they had been separated for months, not a matter of hours. Dylan hears the threesome tromp up the narrow wooden stairs, and he slowly begins to get dressed. Disheveled and deflated, Dylan exits the bedroom five minutes after the Feinstein's have seated themselves around the kitchen table, and hops into the kitchen. "Dylan was just having a little nap," lies Rachel, "the stress of having his cast removed tired him, didn't it, dear?"

Dylan nods and exchanges the requisite embraces with Popsie and Mumsie … what else can a man do after being denigrated by his partner calling him "dear" for the first time? A bottle of chilled champagne sits on the table. Popsie gestures to the bottle, "We were waiting for you to open it … just a little something to warm the new apartment." Dylan chooses to overlook the fact that he'd been living in this apartment for a year-and-a-half, prior to its recent overhaul. He twists the cork out of the bottle with a snap of his wrist and pours the overflowing froth into one of the four crystal flutes Rachel has placed in front of him. Mumsie is disappointed. She wanted the cork fired up into the kitchen ceiling. Rachel furrows her eyes. "But it could have scratched the new paint, Mumsie."

Mumsie begins to marvel at her daughter's eye for interior decorating, predictably crediting herself. "This girl has taste, it all comes from her mother's side … the Feinstein half of the family never had an eye for class … I'm going to say it again, that girl has class, it's in her genes."

The fourth night back at his apartment is a Monday, specifically, Monday night football. Six of Dylan's classmates arrive laden with beer. While surprised at the changes that have taken place in Dylan's pad, they politely say nothing and set to making themselves comfortable, first occupying the spanking new living room suite, followed by the floor.

Rachel is unsettled by this intrusion of ruffians. She issues admonitions regarding the tossing of beer bottle caps onto the new carpet, placing feet on coffee tables, and the consequences of failing to use coasters on "my" furniture. Miffed, she picks up Dylan's open beer bottle, marches to the kitchen, and pours the contents into a crystal tumbler before returning it; the least Dylan can do is not to behave like a slob.

Before the first quarter has ended, Rachel has cloistered herself into the bedroom claiming the onset of a migraine. The only concession Dylan makes to Rachel's renovation of his lifestyle is to prohibit the smoking of a large toke rolled by one of the football spectators in the living room. "Out on the balcony? It's like minus ten out there."

"New rules," responds Dylan.

The following day, Rachel shifts into litigation mode. She defines Dylan's football guests as a bunch of oafish, beer-swilling, high school throwbacks. "They're such … simians! One guy never stopped staring at my ass … I felt like he was undressing me in his mind the whole time I was in the room. Why do they have to come to our place to watch football … why don't they go to a bar where they can consort with other louts of like intellect? I find it hard to believe that you find them to be stimulating company, Dylan."

Dylan is in a battle. At stake is what little remains of his independence. He settles on pursuing a course of expedience, submitting to Rachel nine tenths of the time, but aggressively defending that small ten percent that means most to him. He bites his tongue rather than pass comment on the cutesy-poo furniture that has invaded his pad. Yes, his friends will continue to come over for Monday night football, just as he will tolerate Rachel's giggling hens that occupy the apartment most other nights of the week. No, he will not accompany Rachel shopping in supermarkets for bargains with her snipped coupons; it had been his preference to shop from the grocers, fishmongers, and vendors on St. Clair Street – who cares if you pay a few cents more? Yes, he will attend once-weekly dinners at the Feinstein's, but he will drive there in his Pontiac, and Rachel can either drive with him, leaving her Corolla idle in the Highview driveway or travel by herself separately. No, he will not attend the Bar Mitzvah of one of Rachel's innumerable favorite cousins.

Rachel too feels she is in a battle. Her objective is to somehow civilize the Neanderthal inclinations she observes in Dylan, a coarseness that grates the very core of her soul, while somehow managing to retain the playful, sexy side of him that won her heart. Why can't Dylan behave like Dylan when in bed, and conduct himself a lot more like Marcus when not in the sack? Her task will be to change Dylan in ways that will improve his personality and suit her taste, just as her mother succeeded with her father a couple of decades earlier. It is an oft recounted mother to daughter tale, dating back to when Rachel was a six-year-old.

Dylan's reluctance to stand his ground in an effort to avoid confrontation sets him at a disadvantage and makes him vulnerable to Rachel's superior tactics. Although he was the beneficiary of Rachel's sexual awakening, almost everything Rachel does when she is wearing clothes grates on him to the point that he can no longer disguise it. Dylan knows that regular sex calms his disposition and actually helps to sharpen his academic focus, so his intention is to bite the bullet with Rachel, set in the knowledge that at the end of the school year he can abandon both her and the apartment, along with her garish furniture.

*   *   *

Rachel's tactical maneuvering catches Dylan by surprise during the first week of December. To this point in their relationship, it had been Rachel's tendency to allow Dylan to take the first step in initiating sex. Since returning to Highview, it had been Dylan's preference to indulge in sex accompanied by pounding music on the stereo, usually Beethoven piano sonatas. While Rachel doesn't object to the music, it's clear she doesn't see the point of it, a fact made obvious by her requests to turn the volume down lest the neighbors complain and interrupt the lovemaking. So when Dylan gets home from school and Rachel puts Beethoven's 15th piano sonata on the stereo and sets about seduction, he's immediately suspicious. However, his suspicions are not of sufficient potency to overcome his appetite for sex, so it is not until the couple is post-coital, and he is dozy and discombobulated, that he's enlightened.

"Dill, I have to tell you about my Christmas present early … like right now. It's not the kind of thing that can be left until the last minute."

"I thought your tribe didn't celebrate Christmas? I was hoping for a little sanity to prevail over the Christmas break."

"We have Hanukkah; it's the same thing really. Anyway, my present to you is very special … and I have to tell you about it right now. Close your eyes tight!"

Dylan sits up against the pillows and closes his eyes. Rachel jumps off the bed, but within seconds is kneeling on it once again, facing Dylan. "Put your hands out." Dylan does so and feels Rachel place a sheet of paper in them.

"Okay, you can look now." Dylan opens his eyes. Rachel is naked and kneeling on the bed in front of him. Dylan can see that she can barely contain her excitement. He focuses on the paper. It is an itinerary of some sort.

"What is it?" he asks, not really registering the contents of the itinerary.

Rachel claps her hands and squeals, "It's a cruise, Dill, we're going on a Caribbean cruise."

For some moments, Dylan is dumbstruck. "A cruise? Over Christmas?"

Rachel shifts on the bed to position herself beside Dylan, to better guide him through the outline of the itinerary.

Finally, Dylan recovers his senses. "No way. I'm not going on any cruise. Why the fuck didn't you ask me first? I've been looking forward to my Christmas break and I've no intention of spending it imprisoned with a boatload of geriatrics."

Rachel is on the verge of tears. "It's not like that Dill, my family goes every year. The food is to die for and there are spas … and shopping … and gyms … you'll love it, I promise."

"Rachel, I won't love it, it's not my thing, and I've no intention of going. Take one of your cousins."

"You don't know whether you'll hate it until you've tried it. You've no idea what I had to go through to arrange this. First, I had to deal with Mumsie and Popsie; their preference was for me to go alone with them … as I have every year since I was about four, sleeping on a cot in their stateroom. After I finally got them to agree, I phoned your mother to ask if it was okay for you to miss spending Christmas with your family … she told me that she was certain you'd love to go on a cruise … that's what made me book it without asking you." By this time, Rachel is blubbering through tears.

"Why would you involve my mother? It would appeal to her sense of mischief to tell you I'd love to go on a cruise, knowing perfectly well that I would hate it."

"I had to get your passport number to make the booking," says Rachel sniveling, "and I knew it would involve you spending Christmas away from your family so I had to ask her permission."

"Jesus," says Dylan, exasperated. Rachel puts her arm around Dylan's shoulder, but this has the effect of making him more resolute.

"I'm not going, Rachel. Find a cousin to go with."

Sobbing, Rachel gets off the bed and starts pulling her clothes on. She exits the bedroom and Dylan hears her grab her purse and run down the stairs. Almost immediately, she's forced to return to ask Dylan to move his car out of the driveway so she can get her Corolla out … Rachel refuses to drive Dylan's Pontiac, not even to back it out of a driveway. Silently, Dylan descends the stairs to do as he is bid. He wonders if Rachel's exit will be permanent.

Three hours pass by. Three hours in which Dylan cranks up the stereo to levels that well exceed Rachel's level of approval and consumes the first meal he has prepared by himself for months. For some reason, it tastes abnormally good.

At eight in the evening, the doorbell rings and Dylan descends the stairs. Dr. Feinstein is at the door and asks, with his usual reticence, if he can come in. Dylan motions him upstairs. Dr. Feinstein has a bottle of single malt whiskey tucked under his arm. Dylan goes to the kitchen cupboard and removes a couple of Rachel's crystal tumblers. He throws a couple of ice cubes into each. Dr. Feinstein pours three fingers of liquor into each tumbler.

"I know I shouldn't be here, Dylan, whatever transpired between you and Rachel earlier today is your business and something that the pair of you should resolve … but there are two women in my life and my duty is to do what I can to keep them both happy, not an easy task, I may say … and the pair of them have sent me on this mission. Rachel is not practiced when it comes to relationships … in high school, she was chased by boys … I know she enjoyed the experience of being sought after … but sadly, the only person who came close to being called a boyfriend was the Rubin boy. From the beginning, I could see there was not a true emotional attachment on Rachel's part, but I never said anything. Had you not come along, Marcus and Rachel may have gone as far as getting married … and in retrospect, I can see this would have been disastrous … for Rachel anyway. Then you came along … and Rachel changed overnight. As parents, this change took us by surprise."

Dr. Feinstein pauses to take a sip of whisky. Dylan twists uneasily on his chair. "Dr. Feinstein, I'm not sure where this is going …"

"Call me Leo," interrupts Dr. Feinstein. "Let me finish, Dylan, then I will give you plenty of time to say your piece. In our family, the women plan and organize everything … my role is usually a minor one in the scheme of family life … it is confined to earning our living. Last week, my wife wanted to know if we would be taking our usual cruise during the December holidays … at first, she assumed that Rachel would not want to accompany us this year. I suggested we invite both Rachel and you … and provide you with a private stateroom. Lottie was unsure of this proposition at first … after all, we travel as a family group when we cruise … my sister's family, you've already met my nieces … join us … and a sleeping arrangement that included a boyfriend sharing a cabin with our daughter was destined to be controversial in the family and its old-fashioned notions. But as so often is the case with Lotte, she grew to embrace the idea, and from the moment we informed Rachel … it goes without saying that she was ecstatic … wheels were set in motion, without any of us taking the trouble to consider how you would react to the news."

Dylan shakes his head and sighs. He takes a gulp of whisky; it's now clear where this conversation is headed.

Leo continues, "For that I apologize, I know the two women in my life well enough that I should have cautioned them about proceeding without involving you … it is not every man in this world that can sit back and allow his life to be arranged by his family. Sadly, you were not brought into the discussion … and as a consequence, I've just spent two very difficult hours with my daughter, who's been in a hysterical state.

"So that's how it's fallen upon me to attempt to persuade you to join us on this cruise. Rachel has made it plain that she's not going if you don't come. I'm not sure what your specific objections are to going on a cruise, but if you need time to study, you will have all the privacy and time you need … your stateroom will be spacious and has a private balcony. You can be as social as you wish … for my part, I hope that you will be occasionally social because it will be nice to have another male around … it's not easy cruising with a wife, a daughter, a sister, and two nieces. When we are in port, you can take excursions … or not, it will be as you wish. For her part, I think Rachel has begun to see that she was remiss in not discussing this with you … and I believe she will give whatever latitude you wish to claim, should you agree to come."

"May I ask why Rachel didn't come back and attempt to have this conversation with me?"

Leo chuckles. "It's simple … you frighten her. You see, the only male she has had to confront thus far in her world, is me … we can't really count Marcus because she never cared that much … and as you can see, I have always been a pushover as far as she is concerned."

Dylan goes to bed half-cut, but fully aware that he has been railroaded. For sure, Leo Feinstein accomplishes what his daughter never could have. The next morning, he is awakened by the sounds of Rachel fixing breakfast in the kitchen. She must have slept at her parent's house and just driven over. He stumbles into the kitchen … Rachel greets him with a peck on the cheek and a perfunctory caution that he had better hurry lest he be late for class. She doesn't mention the events of the previous evening or the upcoming cruise.

Dylan somehow survives an awkward introduction to Ellen and Agnes' mother, Dottie Weinburg, at the airport in Toronto. Rachel had previously enlightened Dylan to the fact that Auntie Dottie Weinburg was vehemently opposed to Dylan accompanying the family on their seasonal cruise and even more outrageously, to Rachel sharing a bed with her goy partner. Had not Ellen, Agnes, and Rachel vowed abstinence until their respective wedding days? Just because one of the cousins has broken her vow, should she flaunt this man she was living in sin with by taking him on what had become an annual Feinstein-Weinburg tradition? What kind of message would that send to her daughters, one of whom was already engaged? And who will want Rachel once this goy has tired of her? What can Leo and Lotte be thinking of in endorsing this illicit union?

Thus prepared by Rachel, at the moment of introduction, Dylan grabs an astonished Dottie Weinburg by both shoulders, busses her on each cheek, and marvels, "This confirms that Weinburg genes produce truly gorgeous women."

A glance at Rachel's aunt identifies this as an outrageous lie, but try as she might, Dottie Weinburg cannot help but feel flattered and, worse still, betray it with a hint of a smile. At the same time, Rachel raises her eyes to the heavens, and Leo Feinstein turns away with a wry grin, wise to Dylan's fraud and flattery. Dylan doesn't need an introduction to Ellen and Agnes, as he had met them some weeks earlier when they were recruited as members of Rachel's Highview renovation team. There was nothing special about this pair that would make them register in anybody's memory, least of all Dylan's.

Rachel and Dylan sit next to each other on the flight from Toronto to San Juan, Ellen sits on the other side of Rachel, and the two females jabber with each other from takeoff to touchdown. The group embarks on the cruise ship *Behemoth*, and the vast ship departs from the port of San Juan at ten in the evening, shortly after Rachel and Dylan check into their stateroom. Before they've had time to unpack, Ellen and Agnes join them. Because the cousins share a suite with their mother, the stateroom shared by Rachel and Dylan becomes designated as the "youngsters" stateroom by the two female elders of the family. Dylan soon realizes that he is going to be seeing a lot of Ellen and Agnes during this trip.

On this first night of the cruise, Rachel, perhaps sensing discord in Dylan, shoos her cousins out of the stateroom shortly after departure, and orders a bottle of champagne from room service. The bottle of champagne is quickly guzzled and it has its intended effect of bedding the couple. However, no sooner is coitus initiated than it is interrupted by the phone. Dylan freezes, knowing Rachel's difficulty in resisting the allure of a ringing phone, casting the phone a disdainful look.

"I have to answer it," declares Rachel, twisting from underneath Dylan, "it's probably Mumsie calling to say goodnight. Or it might be Ellen."

"Couldn't you, for once, just let it ring?"

"They'd guess we were having sex."

"So what ... what do they think we're doing here?"

"It would embarrass me, Dylan ... something you wouldn't understand ... not everyone is as ... shamelessly amoral as you."

Rachel has by now squirmed over to the side of the bed and picked up the phone. It's Mumsie calling to make sure that that her daughter understands the importance of closing the sliding doors between the stateroom and balcony to ensure the couple is not molested by mosquitoes when they arrive in port the following morning. And to make sure she gets a good night's sleep, because the shopping in St. Thomas is to die for.

✳   ✳   ✳

Steaming away from some island or other, Dylan sits alone on the balcony outside his stateroom, attempting to read a novel illuminated by an exterior light. Inside the stateroom, Rachel, Ellen, and Agnes are sitting cross-legged on the bed, chattering; every now and then, they burst into bouts of giggling. Ellen and Agnes have all but moved into Rachel and Dylan's cabin. Dylan is in a thoughtful mood and reflecting on the recent events that have got him to this point in his life. He somehow survived a day's shopping in St. Thomas, where he was dragged through more jewelry stores in one day than he had previously visited in his life. Rachel, Ellen, Agnes, Dottie, and Mumsie admired much but purchased nothing; each time a purchase was on the brink of execution, the co-shoppers reminded each other of greater bargains forthcoming on islands yet to be visited. To Dylan, the jewelry and watches appeared identical in every store they entered. After several hours, Leo, sensing Dylan's agitation, suggested a visit to a bar. Dylan could have spent the afternoon sousing himself on mojitos, but Leo was strictly a one drink guy, and that consumed, there was no option but to rejoin and trail after the women.

Dylan decides that it's probable he hates Rachel; the more time he spends with her, the more he can't stand to be with her. How can it be that the two women in his life with whom he has cohabited both orchestrated the arrangement without any upfront discussion with him? What kind of wuss had he become? These thoughts make him recall Poppy, and he does so with a surge of affection. Despite their many differences, Poppy was fun to be with, and what great sex they had – there was something so earthy and natural about Poppy in bed! And the last thing Poppy would want to shop for was jewelry, no, she would have been game to go on the white water kayaking option. How shortsighted he'd been walking away from her!

More to the point, how had he been so stupid to allow Rachel to manipulate her way into shacking up with him? All he had really wanted was a quick fuck, but once that was achieved, did it give Rachel license to take over his life, commandeer his apartment, and manipulate him into going on this awful cruise? Of course, he rues, he did sabotage her relationship with Marcus, but wasn't he doing her a favor? How blind he was to ignore Robert Grantham's advice. Now, he had to endure another six days stuck on this ship, followed by four more months of cohabitation. Yes, he was gutless. Nothing scared him more than the thought of undergoing a messy breakup. He would prioritize graduate school options based on their geographical distance from Toronto.

Observing movement inside the cabin, he sees Ellen and Agnes depart. Dylan gets to his feet and heads for the shower. He passes by Rachel, who is now leaning back on the pillows watching the television: she focuses on the flickering image and says nothing to Dylan as he passes the front of the bed, still peeved that he didn't embrace the all-day shopping excursion with more enthusiasm.

Dylan showers. After toweling off, he exits the bathroom naked and strides half-way across the stateroom before realizing the two cousins have returned and sit cross-legged on the bed, now dressed in pajamas. Ellen and Agnes drop their jaws and Rachel raises her eyes to the heavens. Dylan decides that his best option is to ignore his audience, so he calmly walks over to the dresser and rummages in one of the drawers, looking for a pair of underpants.

Boxers on, he jumps onto the bed, mimics the girls' cross-legged stance, and says, "Whazzup?"

Ellen and Agnes have no idea how to respond so they look to Rachel. "Don't mind Dylan, ladies," says Rachel, using her peeved-with-Dylan tone of voice, "he may have the body of a grown man, but he has the mind of a little boy, that's why he's inclined to go around exposing himself like a pervert."

Dylan looks directly at Agnes. "Agnes, do you ever walk around naked in your own bedroom? And assuming that you do, would you consider this act of nudity one of exposing yourself?" Dylan grabs one of the pillows and tucks it onto his lap. "Now, I would like to suggest that we all jump under the covers and expose our-selves; the four of us can enjoy a merry little orgy." With the sentence completed, Dylan swats Rachel over the head with the pillow with just a little more vigor than affection alone permits.

Ellen and Agnes see nothing humorous in Dylan's antics. Faces taut in a display of disapproval, the cousins simultaneously swing their legs off the bed, truss their housecoats more protectively around their waists, announcing, "Right, we're leav-ing," adding a "G'night Rachel" as they close the stateroom door.

"I wish you weren't so bloody brazen about everything, Dylan, you embarrass me."

"How was I supposed to know they'd come back while I was in the shower? They're practically living with us."

"You could have easily gone back into the bathroom and grabbed a towel. But no,

Dylan has to make a big show of himself. Then saying that stuff about an orgy ... why don't you think of how your words might hurt me for once?"

Dylan scratches his head. "Rachel, this works both ways. If I have to go through another day like this one, I'll be forced to jump overboard before the seven days are through. You are going to have to start to make some accommodation for what I want. For the record, one thing I don't want is to ever see another jewelry store in my life."

Rachel is tearful. "All you have to tell me is what you like to do and I'll be happy to do it with you. It wasn't exactly easy for me today having to put up with you being so grumpy."

"I want to propose a deal, Rachel. You spend the daytime with your family shopping. I'll either stay on the boat or go on an excursion, whatever. But after dinner in the evenings, I would rather spend time with you ... without Ellen and Agnes hanging around."

"They're my cousins, Dylan, their feelings would be hurt. They probably already are, after you threw them out of our room."

"I didn't throw them out. They could have stayed for an orgy. It might have been fun. And on the subject of wild sex, let's have some."

"Ellen and Agnes are not like me. They've lived a more protected life. Please don't talk like that in front of them again – as it is, I'd be mortified if they told Auntie Dottie, who'd then tell Mumsie." Even as she is saying this, Dylan can't help but think that Ellen and Agnes are exactly like Rachel in personality, only with plain Jane looks.

Some silence ensues. Dylan breaks it, "Rachel, why don't we go down to a bar for a couple of drinks to make you less uptight, I like you best when you are a bit tipsy. Then we can go and check out the disco. This is what lovers are supposed to do on vacation, not gossip all day with their frumpy cousins. We can cap off the evening with a nice fuck."

"Sometimes I think that sex is all you ever think about. Is that all I am to you? Some sort of sex toy."

Dylan takes a deep breath. "I don't deny that the sex we have is important to me. It is to you, too, or it used to be. At first, you appeared to really enjoy it ... but now, you start talking in the middle of sex about what items you have to add to your shopping list ... or answer the goddamn phone, in case Mumsie suspects we are actually *doing it*, god forbid! If I'm doing something wrong in bed, you should tell me. Maybe we're not compatible."

Rachel buries her face into a pillow and sobs. Dylan rolls onto his side to read, hoping she'll get over it, but after five minutes go by, he feels obligated to offer some comfort by stroking her shoulder. Rachel immediately turns into Dylan, replacing the abandoned pillow by nuzzling into his chest.

The emotional outburst by Rachel cuts short any further meaningful discussion between the pair, not that Dylan could consider breaking up with her twenty-four hours into a cruise. When Dylan suggests that they go to one of the bars for a drink, Rachel informs him that she can't go out because her eyes are red from crying. They settle for a room service delivery of a bottle of wine.

Sitting on the balcony, not half-way through the first glass, the phone rings. Dylan looks intently at Rachel, gauging how she might respond. He can see that every fiber in Rachel's body wants to dive back into the stateroom and answer the ringing phone, but somehow she manages to suppress this almost overwhelming urge by gulping glugs of wine. Whoever is calling allows the phone to ring a dozen times. When it finally quits, Dylan raises his glass in a salute, which draws a sheepish grin from his lover, whose eyes are no longer red, but pleasantly … and yes, sexily … fogged by alcohol.

At breakfast the next morning, Rachel announces to her family that Dylan will not accompany them shopping, but rather, will take a Top of the Jungle excursion in Grenada. This news is greeted with disbelief by Mumsie and Dottie. What is a Top of the Jungle excursion, asks Mumsie. Rachel explains that it involves being harnessed by pulley to interconnecting cables and hurtling through the treetops to observe flora and monkeys. Dottie wants to know if such an activity could possibly be safe on a primitive island such as Grenada – would the rope be of sufficient strength and what about the mosquitoes? Dylan explains that the only qualifications for embarking on this terrifying adventure are to be older than six years and to weigh less than 300 pounds, so it's unlikely he'll encounter anything that could be considered dangerous.

After a pause, Leo tentatively, maybe even timidly, suggests this might be an activity he might enjoy. Mumsie turns on him horrified. For the remainder of breakfast, Mumsie doesn't quit laying into her husband for being so inconsiderate as to consider risking his life and the possibility of leaving his loved ones destitute. Poor Leo has no choice but to back down and resign himself to accompanying the women shopping.

The final day of the cruise is a "sea day." It is also a storm day – the vast ship rocks, groans, and rolls through the Caribbean, confining all but a small percentage of passengers to their cabins with seasickness. The Feinstein family are among the afflicted, Rachel, especially so. She retreats to Mumsie and Popsie, where she can benefit from a level of pastoral nurture that exceeds Dylan's capacity.

Dylan is in heaven. Cruise ship *Behemoth* is a lot more fun when most of its passengers are confined to quarters. He heads up to the gym, works out without having to compete for the equipment, swims in the pool, and relaxes in the spa with a soothing massage. After taking a prolonged afternoon nap in the stateroom, of which he is now the sole occupant, he consumes a large meal, and heads up to an observation gallery located high over the ship's bridge.

The sea is wild that night. The bow of the great ship routinely dips into waves, sending a gush of spray back over the upper decks that in no time, soaks Dylan. At some point, Dylan becomes aware of a Filipino sailor shouting at him; evidently he wants to close off the observation deck, believing it to be too dangerous for passengers. Reluctantly, Dylan heads off and somehow winds up in the disco. Normally populated by hundreds of gyrating, mostly drunken, twenty-something's, there are no more than a dozen occupants on this evening. After ordering a beer at the bar, he sits to better check out the scene before him.

Within five minutes, he is approached by a woman. "Mind if I join you?" she asks, seating herself facing Dylan, and plants a glass of wine on the table as if staking a claim on it. "Dylan is your name, is it not? Mine's Pandora."

Dylan looks quizzically at the woman – maybe she's around his age, but he's almost sure he has never met her. "Yes, the name is right. Do I know you?"

"As a matter of fact, you do. We've met within the last … let's say four months or so."

Dylan studies the face in front of him. There is something vaguely familiar about her. Did he meet her at a party? Is she some acquaintance of Rachel's?

Dylan shakes his head, conceding that he requires more of a clue than he has thus far been offered.

"I'll give you a hint … Sunnybrook Hospital … back in September."

"OK, you were my doctor? … my radiologist? … a nurse? …Rumpelstiltskin?"

"Wrong, wrong, and wrong. I took blood from you … twice! I was your charming phlebotomist."

"So how come you remember my name?"

"Good question; I wouldn't normally. I take blood from hundreds of patients a month. But I remember you and your name … you had a particularly nasty leg fracture … not that that's unusual. What was out of the ordinary is that when I entered your ER cubicle, you and your girlfriend had obviously been making out, because you had a full erection, not very well concealed by a hospital gown. It struck me as odd for someone with a severe injury. You didn't seem to be even slightly embarrassed; no, I'd say you were quite proud of your hard-on, like a thirteen-year-old. It didn't go away the whole time I was drawing blood. I'm not surprised you don't remember me, your mind was elsewhere."

"Oh great! The funny thing is, the girl you're talking about wasn't my girlfriend back then. I mean, I was trying to make her my girlfriend, but she was actually going with someone else. I guess you could say I was … wooing her."

"So you wooed successfully. She's definitely your girlfriend now; I've seen you guys together a dozen times on this trip, you don't just look like a couple, you're more like a married couple. You have that weary, shacked-up look about you"

"Yeah, that's life. I was crazy about her back in September … but now, just about everything she does drives me nuts. She may be beautiful, but our personalities just don't connect … outside of bed."

"Wanna dance?"

"Sure."

They dance. "Are you here with a boyfriend?"

"No, there's a boyfriend back in Toronto, but I'm actually here with three girls, we all work in the lab at Sunnybrook Hospital … we're sharing an inside cabin, not the best way to cruise the Caribbean … just the most cost-effective, especially when you purchase the tickets three days before departure."

Pandora and Dylan dance and talk the night away and at some point, approaching dawn, the great ship *SS Behemoth* ceases shuddering and groaning as it quits the Atlantic for the shelter of the Port of San Juan. This jolts the now sole occupants of the disco out of their reverie and into a realization that they would soon be docking and required to do such things as pack suitcases and prepare to disembark. Together the couple, for that's what they have become, head back to their staterooms. "Can I kiss you goodnight?" asks hopeful Dylan.

Pandora shakes her head. "I don't think so. We're both in committed relationships … and even if yours doesn't sound like it will last much longer, mine is generally pretty okay. I've enjoyed talking to you, though. We can exchange phone numbers if you like … things might turn out differently when you are … unencumbered."

Dylan nods. Affectionately, he stokes a strand of hair away from Pandora's eyes, a gesture of affection that should have presaged more than just an exchange of phone numbers. Separated, the pair heads off to their separate lives and cabins. Pandora may not possess Rachel's drop-dead gorgeous looks, but there is something about her that seems to click with Dylan. It reinforces his notion that he has to end the relationship with Rachel.

Rob and Dylan meet for lunch. Rob chooses a trattoria close to his Bay and

Queen Street offices. For their past couple of meetings, the assumption has been that because he is working and evidently prosperous, Rob will pick up the tab. A good thing, too, given his taste for high end wine and feast-sized lunches. Both have been factors in noticeably increasing his girth in the eight months he has been practicing law in Toronto.

On hearing of Dylan's predicament, Rob strokes his chin, takes a sip of wine, and muses, "Am I allowed to tell you I told you so?"

Dylan shakes his head. Rob continues, "I am truly amazed that she dumped the reliable Jewish fiancé. It might make sense though … I have a theory that the strictures the Jewish impose on their teenagers, especially those of the female gender, deprives them of a natural phase of rebellion that should take place around puberty … and postpones it into adulthood. Your timing must have coincided with her need for a shiksa rebellious phase. The odds are that this'll be brief. You can either wait it out, hoping that she'll soon see the error of her ways … or you can consult Paul Simon."

"Paul Simon?"

"Fifty ways."

"Yeah, I get you now. Sneak out the back, Jack."

"Not recommended, in my opinion. Especially as the apartment lease is probably in your name alone."

"True. However, in terms of the contents, she cleaned out all of my …our … furniture … except for my books and the stereo … and replaced it with brand new … and especially cheesy, furniture. This so-called relationship is interfering with school … heck, I've got final exams coming up in just over three months!"

Robert swirls more red wine onto his palate and says ponderously, "I think you should confront her directly. Tell her that you don't think the relationship is working and mention that it's affecting your studies. Give her a choice … either she moves out … or you do."

"What if she won't move out? Where could I find another place for just over three months?"

"I suppose you could stay with Kendra and I … we have a granny flat above the garage. It's a little shabby … but it should clean up. Kendra wants to eventually convert it into a studio … but for now, it's just a sort of storage room. As for … Rachel, is that her name? … being willing to move out, from the sound of it, that's not likely. You might find that the apartment and all that furniture are more important to her than you are."

"Rob, I don't think Kendra likes me. Somehow she scares me … it's like she's always trying to see through me, looking for sinister ulterior motives. She thinks

I'm an alcoholic. I'm not sure she would like the idea of me moving into your garage studio."

"I don't think Kendra dislikes you, fuck, she scares everybody, me included. If anything, she's a little put out by the fact that you've never responded to her invitation to have dinner with us. She does suspect that you got Marcia high by allowing her to drink grass tea. Underscored by Marcia reminding her mother from time to time that she doesn't know how to make a cup of tea half as well as Dylan." He chuckles.

"You know, it wasn't really my fault … I guess I wasn't paying attention to what she was doing because I was talking to everyone sitting around the table … along with being a little stoned myself."

"Still, I don't think you have to worry about Kendra … while she probably doesn't want Marcia stoned again for a few years yet, she's not adverse to a toke now and then herself. Let me ask her anyway … if she says yes, it'll provide you with an escape if you need it."

Dylan nods. "Thanks, Rob, I appreciate that. Let me know what Kendra says … it'll make me feel more comfortable having a back-up plan."

22. KENDRA

All the worldly possessions that Dylan requires to exit his life with Rachel at Highview Avenue are loaded into Dylan's Pontiac. When Dylan arrives at the Grantham's house, Rob is at work and the kids are at school, so he has to face the feared Kendra alone. Dylan is not sure what it is about Kendra that unsettles him. She is tall for a woman, almost Dylan's height, but it's nothing to do with her physical presence. No, Kendra's tongue is like a loose cannon; you could never be quite sure of what it might target from one moment to the next ... and what she says is usually disparaging, though not directly so. Her mind ran at a couple of ticks of the clock ahead of most other peoples'. Dylan got the feeling that she was constantly talking down to him, mocking him, though she did this with Rob, too, and had a way of talking about people in general as if they were lesser mortals than herself. As he pulls into the driveway, Kendra exits the house, arms crossed in front of her, as if she had been waiting for his arrival. She walks around the Pontiac inspecting it. Grinning, she approaches the driver's door.

"Hopefully, the neighborhood does not launch a petition against this rusty old boat. It doesn't quite jive with the manicured lawns and beamers of Willowdale suburbia." Sheepishly, Dylan returns the grin; it is important to get off to a good start with Rob's wife. "Do you want me to hide it somewhere?"

"No, don't be silly. It would deprive Willowdale of one more thing to gossip over." Kendra helps Dylan unload the Pontiac and when this is done, she invites him in to the main house for coffee.

"Marcia and Robbie are excited about you coming; it was actually difficult for me to get them off to school this morning. They are counting on you devoting some time to them."

Dylan shrugs. "I'll do my best to be the fun kind of guy they think I am ... but I have my finals coming up in three months and I won't have a lot of time on my hands."

"I did tell them that. Incidentally, Marcia is going to ask you for a repeat performance on the cup of tea you made her last summer ... I know that was an accident, but I want to stress ... no drugs during the hours the kids might be awake. If you must partake ... stay out in your granny flat. As for making a cup of tea that can compete with the one you gave her last summer, there's some loose peppermint tea in the cupboard ... try it and see if that does the trick with my wannabe stoner."

"Kendra, please understand, I didn't 'give' Marcia that cup of tea ... she was taking sips out of my cup and I didn't realize until she had obviously had a few. Even so, I don't think she was very stoned."

"Whatever. I know the kids were at an adult party and that what happened was more Rob's fault than yours. I don't expect a twenty-something bachelor to look out for someone else's children. But here things will be different. You have to realize that in our home we attempt to behave as if we are a family and not on campus. No wild parties either … unless you invite Rob and me … no, I'm kidding, no wild parties period … welcome to the 'burbs.'"

"I'll be on best behavior, promise. I'm actually very grateful to you and Rob for taking me in – I'm not sure what I would have done otherwise. It would've been nearly impossible to get an apartment for just three months."

"Well, you might have just had to sleep in the bed you made for yourself. I hope you weren't too cruel to that girl."

"I'm not certain that she ever had much real feeling for me. In retrospect, I think I was little more than an exit route from a stale relationship that was propelling its way into what would have been a disastrous marriage for her. She was so hot to look at, I was incredibly attracted to her from the first … maybe especially so because I had been out of a relationship for a year. We got together just after my leg fracture. It started off with her having some kind of power over me … and after, it seemed like I was never able to regain the territory I'd ceded. I realized over our Christmas cruise, after being confined in a stateroom with her for seven days, she was suffocating me. I had to escape to retain my own sanity. When I finally worked up the guts to tell her we were through, I don't think she was that upset once she discovered that she could keep the apartment and her precious furniture."

Kendra sets a coffee cup in front of Dylan. There is something feline about Kendra, she's sensual and sexual for sure, but her femininity is laced with a suggestion of danger. Yes, Dylan thinks, she reminds me of the cat that purrs when her belly is stroked, only to pounce without warning and embed her claws into the hand stroking her. But for the first time, he sees her as a woman rather than an authority figure.

Rob's birthday falls on a Friday and there will be a celebration dinner. Dylan is invited, but there will be no other guests at Rob's request. Kendra buys lobsters, chills a couple of bottles of Rob's favorite Sancerre in the fridge, and makes vichyssoise. Marcia and Robbie prepare a packaged cake mix, a chore that has to be micromanaged by Kendra for the sake of the children's personal security and the cleanliness of the entire house.

Dylan is studying when some frenzied banging on his granny flat door interrupts him. Marcia is wide-eyed and in a panic. A lobster has somehow broken free of the elastic bands clamping its claws, and is now rampaging around the kitchen floor, terrorizing the threesome of chefs. Marcia is so excited her words trip over each other, so desperate is she to impart their meaning to Dylan, who appears altogether too calm. She grabs one of Dylan's hands with both of hers and drags him into following her down the staircase. Not a moment must be lost; Mummy and Robbie could be in mortal danger.

Dylan registers the scene in the kitchen. Robbie is standing on a kitchen chair, wailing, and Kendra is wielding a pair of kitchen tongs at a cornered lobster. The lobster is defiantly defending his turf and when Kendra advances too close, lunging tongs, he menacingly raises his claws. Dylan chuckles.

Kendra looks daggers at Dylan and thrusts the tongs toward him. "See if you can do any better, smartass," she tells him, backing away from the lobster.

Yes, Dylan thinks the situation is comical, but now that he has the tongs in hand, he wonders how he can tackle the crustacean without sustaining an injury. There is no doubt this lobster is capable of inflicting damage with either claw. What's worse, his trouser prestige is now at stake with Kendra, Marcia, and Robbie expecting an act of heroism. As Dylan approaches, the lobster fixes little black eyes on him, evaluating the threat of every movement. Dylan thrusts the tongs toward the larger of the two claws. Instantly, the claw clamps the tongs with surprising force. The maneuver allows Dylan to twist the creature sideways and grab its torso from behind, a position just out of reach of the ferocious claws. However, this does not stop the creature from attempting to effect a strike from behind the instant it understands that the tongs are no more than a decoy.

Round one to Dylan. Robbie quits crying and Marcia claps her hands in applause. With the lobster in hand, Dylan strides over to the open pot and is about to return the creature to its two properly restrained companions when Kendra shrieks, "Don't do that. It'll just climb out again. You have to do something with its claws … it uses them to climb out of the pot."

Dylan looks at Kendra, holding the lobster at arms' length. "Well what do you want me to do with it?"

"You'll just have to hold it until … we're ready to eat."

"Jesus," exclaims Dylan, "how long is that going to be? Where is Rob, anyway?"

"God knows. He was due home half an hour ago. Don't worry, we'll just advance the schedule a little."

Kendra switches the gas range on. "Let's open the wine … it'll make the time pass quicker. We both need a drink."

Kendra removes a bottle of wine from the refrigerator, wrestles the cork from the bottle, and pours two glasses of wine. She puts a glass into Dylan's free hand, clinks her own against it, and chugs down a few gulps. Still holding the lobster at arms' length, Dylan sits at the kitchen table. But Marcia and Robbie aren't coming anywhere near the table, not with a lobster in the vicinity.

Revitalized by the swig of wine, Kendra phones her husband's office, but there is no answer. "That means he's on his way home," says Dylan hopefully.

Kendra emits a sardonic guffaw, "You don't know Rob. He is just as likely to be in the boardroom. We're starting without him."

"But Mummy, it's Daddy's birthday. We can't have it without him," says Marcia.

"If Daddy dearest was as concerned about his birthday as are his darling children, then he would have made sure he was home by now," responds Kendra. "We'll pretend it's Dylan's birthday instead."

Dylan's arm is tiring. "Have you given any thought as to how you are going to ... execute the lobsters?" he asks Kendra.

Kendra laughs. "Yes, Dylan, I may be a vegetarian, but I'm also a New Brunswick lass. I may not be able to capture a freaked out, unshackled lobster, but I do know what is required to *execute* one."

"What does execute mean, Mummy?" asks Marcia.

"It's just another way of saying cook, my cherub," responds Kendra to her wine glass rather than her daughter.

During the course of the evening, Dylan decides he has less appetite for lobster now that he comprehends the procedure required to execute them. This is an act so horrendous that Marcia and Robbie are dispatched to their rooms to tidy them in honor of Daddy's birthday. "But Daddy never cares if our rooms are in a mess," protests Robbie, "only you care about that, Mummy."

Kendra announces that they will be eating in the kitchen, not the dining room. Eating lobster is a messy business, especially when children are involved, so why not confine the activity to a location easy to clean up afterwards? Will Daddy get any lobster? Of course, my darlings, he's right on schedule for a lobster omelet for breakfast tomorrow, prepared from whatever is not consumed by the birthday celebrants.

Kendra, Marcia, Robbie, and Dylan eat the vichyssoise. The starter is followed by the lobster, shed of its armor to enable small fingers to dip into butter liquor and suck on. The dish is almost entirely consumed before any connection is made by the kids between the meal on their plates and the very alive creature that was terrorizing them not much over an hour before. "I wonder who's eating the ferocious one?" asks Robbie.

Marcia stares at her brother. Of course, the meals on their plates came from those rather nasty … but nevertheless, extremely animate creatures. She puts down her cutlery. Although she was absent from the kitchen during the critical event that somehow converted live animals into dinner, she has completely lost her appetite. It's time for birthday cake.

Marcia determines that if this is to be a cake for Dylan, because it is a full two months away from his birthday, eight of the candles will have to be removed; no way will he be credited with eight years he has yet to live. She counts out and extracts the requisite candles from the chocolate goo crudely pasted onto the cake, and with her finger, pats and patches the holes that remain in the icing. Meanwhile, Kendra uncorks the second bottle of Sancerre and refills the two glasses on the kitchen table.

Ten in the evening arrives and there is still no sign of the absent birthday boy. Both kids are complaining of sore stomachs, the effect of the volume of garlic butter and chocolate frosting consumed. In addition, Robbie is having trouble keeping his eyes open and both kids make only a token protest when their mother suggests they go to bed. They appear unperturbed that their father has yet to appear, evidently he is a regular no show during their waking hours, and they do not think it extraordinary that this should occur on his birthday. Kendra marches the kids upstairs and to bed.

There is something about the events of the evening that has already caused Dylan to feel guilty and he's not sure why. Perhaps this has something to do with the fact that he has been a party to consuming a birthday dinner in the absence of its guest of honor. Not just a lobster feast, but one that included two bottles of upscale wine that would have truly only been appreciated by the palate of the absent birthday boy. Dylan takes a final sip from his glass of wine and realizes he is slightly drunk and that it is probably time to retreat to his granny flat.

If Kendra is annoyed by her husband failing to show for a birthday dinner she took considerable pains to prepare, she doesn't express it outwardly. She returns from tucking the children into bed, plunks herself on the sofa beside Dylan, and drains the contents of her wine glass. She exhales deeply and looks at the ceiling. A hint of a smile appears on her expression. Then, in a movement that seems to flow from the ingested wine, she rotates her torso, moves her lips to Dylan's, and kisses him. Her kiss is closed mouth and dry, she merely teases her lips over Dylan's. Dylan is too surprised, and perhaps too drunk, by the action to know what kind of response is expected of him. It doesn't surprise him when Kendra breaks the kiss, tosses back her head and laughs, maybe a little disdainfully. Was she making fun of him; did he fail some sort of test by responding inappropriately? She stretches each of her arms over the back of the sofa and studies Dylan, perhaps satisfied that she has intimidated him. This is Dylan's cue to beat a hasty departure. He all but leaps to his feet and pulls on his boots and jacket for the trek across the snow-covered yard.

A pounding on the door wakes Dylan. For some reason, he has been sleeping on his stomach, face buried into his pillow. Then he recalls the reason; he went to bed somewhat drunk and this often ends up with him sleeping in this infantile posture. He raises his head out of the pillow and mumbles an instruction to enter. It is Rob, dressed in pajamas, housecoat, and snow boots. Actually, Rob must have been entering ahead of the invitation because he is already rolling Dylan's desk chair toward the bed. Dylan rolls onto his side. Rob straddles the desk chair in reverse, leaning over the back. He means to initiate a discussion.

"Did I ever mention to you, Douglas," he begins looking not at Dylan but out the window, shaking his head, "that marriage is hell?"

Dylan levers himself into a semi-sitting position and attempts to shake the sleep out of his head. Fortunately, he understands that Rob's opening statement requires no response. "Fuck," declares Rob, "if there was a single reason I married Kendra it was that she was the daughter of a lawyer, and trained as a lawyer herself. If anyone could understand what I have to go through, it should be her. The bitch hasn't stopped ragging at me all night!" He sips a coffee.

Dylan doesn't know what to say. When Rob and he can get drunk together on equal terms, they do share some commonalities. But when Rob has problems of a wifely nature, Dylan is in alien territory. The notion of matrimony is alien to Dylan, and the thought of matrimony with a woman like Kendra especially intimidates him because she scares the shit out of him.

Fortunately, they are interrupted. Robbie junior enters. He doesn't knock. The youngster throws the door open, immediately sits on the floor to pull his snow boots off, then runs over to Dylan's bed and jumps under the covers. Shivering, he snuggles up to Dylan to steal some warmth off him. The legs of Robbie's pajamas are saturated by the snow he has picked up while crossing the yard to the garage steps. Rob senior is uncertain as to how to act.

"Robbie, you're supposed to knock. You shouldn't be going outside in your pajamas in this weather, it's below zero." Robbie doesn't acknowledge any of this admonition by doing anything but shivering. Rob runs his fingers through his hair. Lost is the opportunity for a tête-à-tête with a sympathetic ear.

Only seconds pass before more footsteps are heard on the metal staircase leading up to Dylan's granny flat and the door flies open. This time it is Marcia. Like her father and brother before her, Marcia is also dressed in nightclothes and snow boots. Standing, she wrestles the snow boots off her feet and then scoots across the room to jump into Dylan's bed alongside Robbie. Robbie punches his sister with a violence called for only when fending off a big sister. "Get out," complains Robbie, "you're wet … and freezing."

"Jesus," exclaims Rob senior, disgusted, "do they do this every weekend?"

"They're just kids," excuses Dylan, beginning to wake up, "I don't mind, really."

"Dylan plays street hockey with us on Saturdays," announces Robbie. "You can play, too, Daddy, if you don't have to go to work."

"But I want to be on Dylan's team," declares Marcia resolutely. It's true, among a group of five- to ten-year-olds on Burgess Street, twenty-one-year-old Dylan is the undisputed star player famed as such from East to West. Along with being the game's ref and coach for both sides.

"I have to pee," declares Robbie junior, climbing over his sister and sustaining a couple of punches in the process. Robbie runs to the bathroom, and leaving the door wide open, pulls his pajamas down to his ankles and begins to pee.

"I can see your bum," chants Marcia, commenting on a bum she sees daily in a bathtub.

"Who cares?" retorts her brother, twisting around to return the jibe, "at least it's not a fat bum like yours." In the act of turning his torso to exchange barbs with his sister, the stream of urine is directed away from the toilet bowl onto the floor.

"Robbie!" snaps his father, leaping off the desk chair and striding toward the bathroom, "concentrate on what you're doing."

Marcia cuddles into Dylan. "My bum isn't fat," she says, seeking assurance that it really isn't.

Dylan is now fully awake. Rob is mopping up pee off the bathroom floor and Robbie and Marcia are in the bed, fighting over which of them should be next to Dylan, the warmer of the threesome.

Having cleaned up the pee, Rob decides to take action. "Alright kids, up to your rooms and get dressed. Breakfast will be in fifteen minutes." Both Robbie and Marcia pause in their exchange of punches. Propping themselves onto their elbows they look at their father, surprised. They don't move.

"If I have to ask you again, you'll both be getting spankings." Surprised, Robbie and Marcia look at each other.

Marcia protests, "But Daddy, Dylan needs us for his Saturday morning workout."

Menacingly, Rob moves toward his children. Simultaneously, both Marcia and Robbie realize that their father might mean business. They leap out of the bed and run to the door to wrestle their snow boots on. They clatter down the metal steps back to the main house.

Rob sits back down on Dylan's desk chair. "I'm sorry about the kids; I didn't realize what an imposition they must be. I'll tell them they are not allowed to come over here any more."

"It really isn't a problem, Rob," says Dylan. "It's only at weekends, Kendra doesn't let them on weekdays, and frankly they're usually pretty well-behaved."

"I wish I could say the same about my dearly beloved," says Rob, mournfully looking at the floor.

A silence ensues. Dylan does not know how to respond to his friend. Surely he must have some notion that he was to blame for not showing up to his birthday dinner. To have not even phoned? Dylan's sympathies are with Kendra and because of this, he cannot say much.

Rob shakes his head. "Jeezus, I work eighty hours plus a week so we can live this lifestyle and I get precious thanks for it."

Another prolonged silence ensues. The silence is long enough that Dylan senses that Rob may have acquired some awareness that he may be at fault.

"We waited for hours for you last night. I know Kendra was hoping you'd phone. The kids didn't expect you to show … but Kendra did. I understand why she's a little upset. Your vegetarian wife … against her better instincts … goes out and purchases live lobsters for your birthday dinner … and you're a no-show. I think she'd be abnormal if she wasn't pissed off."

Rob shakes his head again. "Yeah, I guess you're right. Although I know you wouldn't understand … but Kendra should … that's why I married a lawyer … the most important thing at this moment is for me to make partnership. That means accruing billable hours … and billable hours don't always come at convenient times, they come when clients are accessible. In the world of corporate litigation, clients are often only accessible outside of what are considered normal business hours."

Dylan has so little empathy with Rob's thinking, he doesn't know what to say. To change the subject he says, "Perhaps you should play street hockey with us this morning. It's become a Burgess Street Saturday morning tradition."

"I can't," says Rob, "I have to get back into work this morning. I'm going to be late as it is, but obviously, I can't afford to rile Kendra any more than I have. Speaking of hockey, I have a pair of the firm's box seats for the Leafs game tonight against the Bruins … do you want to go with me?"

Dylan is nonplussed. Again, he's lost for words. "Don't you want to go with Kendra? … I'll babysit."

"Jesus, no. Kendra hates hockey … anyway, I have no intention of telling her I'm going to the game, please keep this quiet. God no, I'll just tell her I'm working late."

"You could take one of the kids?" suggest Dylan. He really has no real desire to go to a hockey game.

Rob shakes his head, "No, they fall asleep five minutes into the first period. Come to the game, it'll be fun."

Dylan nods. He's not quite sure why he has agreed to go the Leafs game, but he thinks it might be some latent guilt stemming from the manner of his goodnight to Kendra the night before. Not only has he agreed to keep Rob company during the hockey game, but by doing so he's become complicit in the lie to Kendra.

Dylan's Saturday morning no-equipment workout:

1.   Perform 25 high speed push-ups. Encourage Marcia and Robbie to do likewise, urging them to keep their backs straight while doing so.

2.   Perform medium intensity Robbie presses – requires the cooperation of a 40 lb kid. Assume bench press position on bed … urge child to remain rigid as a statue, advise that giggling is prohibited, and bench press 25 times.

3.   Perform high intensity Marcia presses – requires the cooperation of a 50 lb kid. Another set of 25 bench presses using the heavier kid as a dumbbell.

4.   Perform medium intensity Robbie leg squats. Hoist 40 lb kid over head and perform 12 leg squats as rapidly as possible.

5.   Perform high intensity Marcia leg squats. Hoist 50 lb kid over head and perform another set of 12 leg squats as rapidly as possible.

6.   Lateral plank. Begin with the kids and threaten them that failure to hold plank for a count of 30 seconds will endanger Dylan's willingness to participate in after-breakfast street hockey. When the children have completed the plank count, Dylan must do likewise and hold the plank posture for 60 seconds, counted out in unison by Marcia and Robbie, who count increasingly slowly as the number 60 approaches, ultimately forcing Dylan to plead for mercy … to the glee of the two kids.

Dylan is in Maple Leaf Gardens watching the Leafs game by himself. It is mid-way through the second period and the Leafs are down by four goals. Rob is yet to show and it's looking unlikely that he will. Dylan wants to leave and he is on the verge of doing just that when Rob arrives. He is holding a pair of beers in wax cups, raising them high above the heads of those sitting below. While Rob is not drunk, neither is he sober; he stumbles as he navigates the seats. He jovially greets Dylan and thrusts a cup of beer at him. "How are we doing?"

"Not so great, Rob, not so great. Four down and counting!"

At Kendra's suggestion, Dylan's birthday is celebrated two days after the event. This is to enable Marcia and Robbie to be part of the celebration when it can take place on a non-school night. Rob has promised to attend, but Kendra, Marcia, and Robbie are skeptical. Has it not been months since Daddy sat down for any meal other than a weekend breakfast with them? Noting to himself that the Leafs have a Friday night home game, Dylan thinks that it is unlikely that Rob would make it home for something as trivial as a friend's birthday celebration when he wouldn't show up to his own.

Kendra has cooked Moroccan chickpea stew. Chickpeas don't flee the pot, menace cooks, or complain about dying, Kendra explains to Dylan. The kids think it's tasty and it has never once made them throw up, plus the leftovers put out in the trash do not attract every raccoon within a five-mile radius. Washed down with a couple of bottles of Pinot Grigiot, it is a dish that will do any birthday proud. Marcia has baked a Duncan Hines chocolate cake, a feat that provided her mother with two hours of clean-up labor in the kitchen. The cake was subsequently thickly pasted with pre-mixed chocolate frosting by Marcia and Robbie, who somehow got as much applied to each other as on the cake, requiring an earlier than scheduled session in the tub with admonishments from their mother not to dare to exit the bathroom until both it, and they, are clean and in pajamas.

The meal is consumed, the wine flows, and the birthday cake is proudly exhibited by its creators. Twenty-two candles spell "Dill" on the surface of the cake, though an observer would have had to have been informed of this fact before being able to identify it. Dylan extinguishes all twenty-two in a single puff, provoking admiration and clapping from Marcia and Robbie – how little one has to do to impress the innocent! They grant him a wish, so what is it he wishes? Dylan tells them he wishes to have friends such as Kendra, Marcia, and Robbie for all his life. Not Daddy, too, asks Robbie? Of course, how could he forget, and Daddy, too! Kendra winks at Dylan.

On the couch, stories are read to the children, one by Kendra, one by Dylan, and more wine flows into the adults. In no time the youngsters are yawning and prepped for bed. Kendra and the two kids climb the stairs and sounds of running water and goodnights broadcast the bedtime routine.

Dylan knows what will happen when Kendra descends the stairs after bedding the kids; it's a premonition that entered his mind at the uncorking of the first bottle of Pinot Grigiot. Of course, these thoughts were seeded by the hesitant kiss exchanged a couple of months previously, but what intimidated Dylan back then has fermented into rising lust, along with a reasonable expectation that it will be sated.

On the floor of the living room, Kendra and Dylan engage in an almost frantic embrace that lasts less than two minutes before they set about tearing each others' clothes off. The first coupling is too frenzied for either party to be satisfied, so it is only natural that a second follows.

With the fervor of lust spent, one of the lovers sobers sufficiently to take account of risk and consequences. There are after all, two children sleeping upstairs and a husband who was scheduled to return three hours previously. Dylan asks Kendra whether they should consider an emergency action plan. Kendra, lying on her back, responds absentmindedly to the ceiling, "Both kids are exhausted, that's why I let them stay up late. And let's not kid ourselves, both you and I know that Rob's at the hockey game, he'll be at least another hour. Eight years of marriage have taught me how to interpret his claims of working late just by the tone of his voice. Of all the lawyers in his firm, he populates the corporate box seats at the Gardens most often. You think I don't know where he was for his own birthday?"

Dylan says nothing. And when he does say something, he says the most stupid thing he could possibly say. "What kind of protection do you use? ... er, birth control?"

Kendra props herself on her elbows and twists around to look at Dylan in disbelief. Her mouth all but hangs open. The she bursts out laughing. She laughs hysterically and Dylan is left in no doubt that he is being laughed at.

"Oh Dylan, you are such a goof, I thought there was more between your ears. Did it not occur to you, that's the type of question you are supposed to ask before you get your rocks off ... twice?" She punctuates the end of the question by laughing some more. Affectionately, she strokes some hair away from his eyes.

Feeling belittled, Dylan cannot help but press the issue, "Are you on the pill?"

Kendra puts on a straight face. "Not on the pill," she answers, but focuses on his eyes to gauge his response.

Dylan struggles for a follow-up. He is aware of, although not experienced with diaphragms, but isn't their use, accompanied by spermicides messily dispensed like shaving cream, surely something he would have noticed during his pre-coital explorations? "A diaphragm?"

Kendra continues to stare down Dylan. "No diaphragm," she says with exaggerated seriousness.

Dylan synthesizes this information. Kendra is older, maybe she's had her tubes tied … or had some kind of hysterectomy. He decides not to risk more ridicule and surrenders to lie on his back and stare at the ceiling.

Kendra chuckles. "No, Dylan, I am completely 'unprotected' as you might put it, my ovaries are at your mercy. Also, I just happen to be ovulating at the moment. "

"Isn't that going to prove rather awkward if you should happen to conceive?"

"Not really. I've being trying to get pregnant for over a year. The only time Rob wants to have sex with me these days is when he's drunk and then he can't get it up half the time. He's probably porking some young secretary at the office. It's been months since we last made love."

"Jeez," says Dylan contemplating the prospect of fatherhood and all that might entail, along with messy divorces and a platter of unwanted responsibilities.

"Don't worry," Kendra reassures Dylan, "whatever happens isn't going to affect your life in any way … so long as you're smart enough to keep your mouth shut."

"Isn't Rob likely to notice? Especially if you both haven't had sex in a while?"

"Why should he notice? If I was to conceive by you, the baby isn't going to turn out to be black. You don't look dissimilar to Rob … you're not unintelligent … I considered all of this ahead of time. As for remembering the timing of a fuck, these days Rob remembers nothing unless it is a billable event."

"You planned for this to happen?"

"Sort of! In the absence of a penis, my brain is in charge of my body for all but a couple of days a month. Don't get me wrong … I didn't do this just to conceive, it was sort of nice to have sex with someone who wanted it so badly, he disregarded every consequence … at least, until after it had taken place! Twice!" Another chuckle. "That hasn't happened to me since the days before Marcia was born."

Dylan doesn't know what to think. "What am I supposed to do?"

"Do? Nothing, you'll graduate. You'll have abandoned our garage before you'll have any awareness of whether I'm pregnant. You'll work somewhere, hopefully not in Toronto. It's highly unlikely you and Rob will maintain any kind of contact. You may have shared some common interests when he was studying for the Ontario bar, but not now. Perhaps you guys look a little alike, but other than that, you are opposites. Are you going to be politically or professionally useful to him? That's all the word 'friend' means to him now."

Dylan furrows his brow. "I don't think I've ever met anyone as hard-nosed as you before."

"Don't talk nonsense, Dylan. At my age, you cease to see the world through rose-colored glasses. I'm practical and realistic, along with being a loving and caring mother to two ... and potentially more ... children. The children are all that matters to me. Sure, I'm happy that you were sufficiently attracted to me to make this evening a possibility ... but let's not pretend that either of us was driven by romantic impulses. We were responding to our instinctive programming ... yours, to sow seeds ... mine to procreate worthy genes."

Dylan scratches his head. Emerging is a side of Kendra's personality that he would not have deemed possible a few hours ago. "Why did you and Rob get together?"

"Things weren't always like they are now between us. There was a time when all I had to do was walk into a room and Rob would get a hard-on. We were happy most of the time we lived in St. John ... always broke, but happy all the same. After Marcia was born, Rob doted on her ... when she awoke during the night, I usually brought her into bed with us to breast feed her ... after, Rob would insist on keeping her in bed with us, he'd cradle her in his arms and that's how the two of them would sleep. I'd watch them and wonder if there could ever be a better father."

"So what changed?"

"We had to leave St. John. Although I graduated from law school, this was something I did just to please my father. I never had any interest in working as a lawyer. When Rob and I got together, we always planned for me to be a stay-at-home mother. But with just Rob working, money was always tight when we lived in St. John ... the plan was for us to resettle in Toronto when my father retired from the bench ... and my parents moved to Victoria. So when that happened, Rob returned to Ontario to article and prepare for the Ontario bar exams. I know Rob worked very hard because his objective was to get a position with one of the top legal firms. Well, he's achieved that goal ... but in doing so, he's changed to the core. I was never aware of him being dishonest before we moved to Toronto, but now he's all spin – there something iniquitous about the way he treats the truth – his lies are cleverly crafted, there's always some element of truth woven into them. Lawyer's lies, I guess. And he has no time for the kids any more, he just tunes out when they try to talk to him. I feel bad for them; they try so hard to impress him."

Dylan is thoroughly depressed.

Kendra looks at her wrist watch and then casually strokes Dylan's balls. "Wanna see if there's anything left to harvest? ... we have time."

Dylan looks Kendra square in the eyes. Procreate genes ... sow seeds ... is that really all it amounts to? He shrugs. "What the heck!"

*　　　　　　　*　　　　　　　*

The highlight of the Burgess Hill Elementary School April Olympics is the Parent and Child triathlon. This is a father-daughter, mother-son triathlon for each grade, consisting of three-legged, wheelbarrow, and piggyback races, in three sections totaling 75 meters. Although Marcia elicited a promise from her father two months earlier to make sure he was available for this premier event, the Wednesday before, Rob informs Kendra that he has to be in Ottawa for a pre-court hearing. He shares this information with Kendra at breakfast the morning he is to depart. Kendra glowers with hostility, "I don't suppose you are going to wait around until she gets up so you can tell her yourself."

Rob shrugs a response. "As a junior litigator, this is something that's beyond my control. I feel bad, but there's nothing I can do about it."

Kendra elects not to inform Marcia at breakfast. Instead, she collars Dylan as he is leaving for school a couple of hours after her two have departed. Dylan agrees to surrogate if he is allowed. "I'm going to tell the school you're her uncle … that way they won't accuse us of having parachuted in a gladiator for the event."

When Dylan arrives home from class, Marcia visits Dylan's granny pad, something Kendra does not normally allow the children to do on school days. "Mummy said I should thank you for agreeing to race the triathlon with me."

"Are they going to let me sub for your dad?"

"I guess so. Mum called the school this morning. I'm supposed to say you're my uncle from New Brunswick."

"Well, I guess we had better practice then."

"Practice?"

"You want to win, don't you?"

"Yeah, I guess so," responds Marcia, but now getting more enthusiastic, "Yes, we'll practice, we can go to the park, what do you want to start with?

"We only have to practice the three-legged and wheelbarrow portions … a piggyback is just a piggyback, I do the work for that … you don't have to do anything other than pretend you're a knapsack."

Marcia and Dylan go to the ballpark and truss a pair of their legs together. In this way, they learn what makes them fall, and more important, learn what they have to do to avoid falling. They develop a step timing routine that they call out numerically using a one-two count rather than calling out left and right … which would always be contradictory for one of them. The wheelbarrow portion is a cinch; Dylan tells Marcia it should be easy for her after mastering the plank exercise during their Saturday morning workouts. A wheelbarrow race is just being a plank while using your arms to walk as fast they'll move.

On the Saturday of the event, Kendra and Robbie don't do so well in the Grade

One mother-son triathlon; according to Kendra, there are just too many ultra-fit yoga mums to compete with. But later, in the Grade Three triathlon, Dylan and Marcia leave their competition in the dust. By the time they come to the final piggyback leg, they are so far ahead that Dylan scoops Marcia onto his back and strolls the final 25 meters. At the finish line, Dylan turns and crosses it walking backwards. He lowers Marcia and they exchange a victory high-five.

Because this is Willowdale and not conducive to gracious defeat, there are murmurings from the non-victorious parents, both mummies and daddies. Should an uncle, especially one so young, be allowed to compete in the April Olympics? The event is, after all, called the mother-son, father-daughter triathlon.

Kendra approaches Dylan, the first moment she can get at him without Marcia being at his side. "Thanks a ton for doing that, you've made her so happy. I worry about Marcia because outside of home, she has a soft core, not like her little brother who's as tough as nails. She's going through a phase where she feels she has to be perfect, the best at everything. I'm not sure how to change that in her, though I wish I could. She hasn't really made any close friends since we moved; the other kids make fun of her for being so perfect. Poor Marcia, who wants to be loved by everyone, is regarded with suspicion and avoided, while Robbie, who doesn't give a darn about anybody but himself, is the most popular kid in his class."

"No problem. I'm pleased it made Marcia happy."

At the completion of the Olympics, trophies are awarded. When Marcia's name is called to receive the third grade triathlon cup, she self-consciously goes to retrieve her award and as she holds the small trophy over her head, a lone voice, a male, adult voice chants out, "cheat."

Kendra hopes that Marcia didn't hear, but it is obvious she did. Marcia blinks and lowers the trophy. Her eyes suggest she is about to burst into tears. She collects the cup into her chest and retreats to search out her mother.

On the drive home, Marcia quietly asks Kendra, "Mummy, why did that man say I cheated?"

"I think he was just joking, darling. Everyone was a little jealous of the way you and Dylan ran off, leaving everybody else gaping."

Still troubled, Marcia turns to Dylan, sitting in the passenger seat of the Volvo, "We shouldn't have practiced, Dylan. We would have still won even if we hadn't. Just not by so much."

Kendra changes her tone with Marcia. "If you want to be the best at anything Marcia, you'll have to get used to the fact it'll upset some people. It's part of being successful. If you don't want people to be envious of you, don't get straight A's and don't try to win races. Be more like Robbie and everyone will love you."

Robbie punches his sister's shoulder and chimes in, "Yeah, be more like me."

Marcia is more philosophical. "But I was cheating, wasn't I? Dylan isn't my daddy and he's not a real uncle, either. If I'd been in the triathlon with Daddy, we wouldn't have won, he's too fat. He wouldn't have practiced with me before the race and we'd have fallen over with all the others."

Kendra decides to be more assertive, "Marcia, Daddy had a work obligation that he had to fulfill. I know it came up at the last minute, but that's the nature of his job, it's not his fault. It was either do the triathlon with Dylan … or not do it at all. Maybe next year they'll have a mothers and daughters triathlon."

Marcia is tearful. "He promised, he promised … before the 'obligation.' All the other daddies were there."

Dylan decides to add his two cents worth. "Marcia, did you have fun doing the triathlon? If you had to do it again, would you want us to lose?"

Marcia shakes her head.

"Think of it this way. In the three-legged race, we both had an equal amount of work to do and we won that section because we practiced … everybody else was falling over … like we were the first time we practiced. In the wheelbarrow section, you did all the work, I was just carrying the weight of your legs … you didn't fall once, whereas the others kept collapsing because most of the other girls couldn't support the weight of their bodies for more than three steps at a time. And when it came to the piggyback section where I had to do all the work, we were so far ahead by that time, I could walk the final 25 meters. We won because you were the best. If anyone says you cheated, they're just jealous. And the most important thing is that I had fun winning with you … and I think you enjoyed winning with me."

"I guess," says Marcia, not sounding convinced.

Robbie gets into the act, yelling, "I want to win, too. It was Mummy's fault we lost! She kept falling down."

"No Robbie, you and Mummy could have won if you'd practiced like Marcia and I. Next year, you and Mummy will have to go to the park and practice – then maybe you can be as good as Marcia and I, champions of the Grade Three triathlon."

"Thanks a bloody lot, Dylan," says Kendra with faked indignation, "is there anything else you'd like to have me commit to while you're at it?"

23. IN VINO VERITAS

Although Dylan had been an occupant of the Grantham granny flat for more than two months and doing occasional babysitting was part of the agreed deal, this was the first time he'd actually been asked. For Rob and Kendra, the occasion was a Saturday night social at Rob's firm, pretty much the only type of leisure-based activity Rob would entertain these days … if indeed, it could be truly classified as a "leisure" occasion. Kendra ensured that the meal Dylan was to prepare for Marcia and Robbie fell within the limits of his competency, so she prepared a salad herself and informed Dylan that it should be followed by two boxes of Kraft dinner, which he would have to prepare "from scratch."

"I'm not completely lacking in culinary skills," protests Dylan, miffed that he had not been asked to prepare something more challenging, such as fried eggs and oven fries.

"They both love Kraft dinner. You can allow them to sprinkle a little extra parmesan on top. Get Robbie to eat as much of his salad as you can … it's not going to be popular with him … but sometimes if he's hungry enough, he'll pick at a salad. Don't allow him to con you into giving him potato chips; he consumed two packages for lunch … tell him there are none." Dylan nods.

Rob and Kendra climb into the family Volvo and with a wave, drive off into the night.

Marcia asks Dylan if they can play Monopoly. Dylan thinks this is a good idea, a nice quiet game to make the kids sleepy before bedtime. Robbie is not so enthusiastic and he murmurs, "Mummy says we're not allowed to play Monopoly."

Dylan looks at Marcia. The youngster raises her eyebrows and circles a finger around her ear to signal Dylan that her little brother is crazy. Dylan shrugs. "Do you want to play Monopoly?" he asks Robbie.

The little boy is sullen, but he nods his head. With enthusiasm, Marcia runs upstairs to retrieve the game, and within moments, she has the board set up on the living room floor with each competitor's money allocated. She appoints Dylan to be the banker and magnanimously suggests that Robbie be credited with an extra $1,000 dollars on account of his age. Banker Dylan agrees that this is an excellent idea and counts out five extra $200 bills.

An hour into the game, it becomes clear to Dylan why the game of Monopoly is a prohibited activity in the Grantham household. Marcia is a ruthless capitalist. Having acquired every property on the final millionaire's quadrant of the board, she proceeds to pauperize Dylan and Robbie, dispensing the occasional financial straw for either to survive, simply for no other reason than to prolong the game.

Robbie is in a rage. Dylan attempts to suggest that they should abandon this game, proclaim Marcia queen, and tackle something more fun, meaning anything. Robbie resists. He is under the misconception that this is a game of luck and surely his luck must turn. This makes it all but impossible for Dylan to forcibly end the game, with both the kids wanting to continue. Finally, Robbie can take the humiliation no longer. He picks up the board with both hands and dumps its contents of hotels, houses, dice, and cards onto the carpet. Marcia bursts into tears while Robbie screams that the outcome of the game is a tie.

In vain, Dylan attempts to restore order. Until the events of the preceding hour, he had always thought of Robbie and Marcia as being generally well-behaved, polite children. Now Robbie is in a sullen rage and Marcia, deprived of an actual proclamation of victory, is curled up on the couch, crying. Dylan hasn't got a clue what he should do. He sets about retrieving and reorganizing the spoiled game and getting it packaged up into the box. It takes a full twenty minutes, after which Marcia has ceased crying, but Robbie continues to sulk. Suppertime!

Dylan locates three bowls and retrieves the salad Kendra prepared from the refrigerator. Marcia, at least, is back onboard, and helps Dylan set the table and prep the Kraft dinner. From a container of orange-colored French dressing, he pours equal amounts over each of the three salads, then announces to Robbie that it's time to eat. Some time goes by before Robbie enters the kitchen, still in a dark mood. He sits at the table and props his forehead using his hands, elbows on table. Dylan and Marcia join him sitting at the table.

Dylan and Marcia begin to eat the salad. Marcia announces that the salad is more delicious than ever, but there is something about the way she says this that Dylan senses is designed to provoke Robbie. Sure enough, as if on cue, Robbie says, "I don't like salad."

Dylan suggests he just try a few bites of it, it just may taste nicer than it looks. Robbie looks up at Dylan and screams, "I told you, I hate salad." And to demonstrate that this really is the case, he uses his forearm to swipe the salad bowl off the kitchen table. The bowl crashes onto the floor and explodes into tiny pieces. A mixture of china shards, salad greens, and orange dressing decorates much of the kitchen floor. Dylan looks at Robbie, then he looks at Marcia as if seeking some kind of guidance as to how to deal with this turn of events.

"You have to spank him," announces Marcia officiously to Dylan, as if giving him a direct order, "he's in one of his moods. After you spank him, he'll be alright again. Mummy says that the only way to snap him out of his tantrums is to spank him and send him to his room."

Dylan contemplates the ceiling, wondering what to do. Robbie continues to sit at the table, forehead propped into his palms, probably also wondering what Dylan is planning to do. First things first! There are shards of china all over the floor, so the two barefoot kids must be told not to move from their chairs. With Marcia relaying instructions on where to locate brooms, dustpans, and a mop, Dylan cleans up the mess, a feat that takes at least fifteen minutes.

When the floor is finally clean, Dylan sets about preparing the main course, Kraft dinner. Marcia wants to help, informing Dylan that if he pulls up a chair in front of the stove, she can stir the contents of the pot. Dylan does this and Marcia advises him that he can finally administer the spanking Robbie deserves and send him to his room. As she delivers the instruction, Dylan cannot help but think how similar the youngster is to her mother, something he has not been aware of until this evening. Robbie reacts to the comment by screaming at the top of his lungs to Marcia, "I hate you!"

Once again, Dylan attempts to reassert some authority. "Nobody's getting spankings, Robbie, I want you to settle down. I don't care if you eat anything ... or not. But you're being a pain in the ass, and I want you to stop."

This statement produces a squeal of giggles from Marcia and even a grin from Robbie. Marcia turns around on the chair on which she is standing. Covering her mouth, she says, "You said 'ass.' That's rude. Mummy would send you to your room!"

Still chuckling, Marcia pivots around on the chair to return her focus to the pot of Kraft dinner, but in doing so, slightly loses her footing, and has to grasp at the surface of the stove to steady herself. A piercing scream sends Dylan's pulse racing. Panicked, he rushes toward Marcia to assess the damage. Marcia is clutching her palm, reddened by the burn. Dylan hoists the youngster off her feet, and with an arm wrapped around her waist, takes her to the sink and holds her hand under running cold water.

After a few minutes, Marcia's tears have dissipated, but Dylan is hyperventilating. Under the running water, he inspects the burn. With a sigh of relief, he diagnoses it not as bad as it could have been. But next, a popping and crackling noise coming from the stove alerts his attention, just ahead of the piercing electronic squeal of the smoke alarm. He turns and tucks simpering Marcia onto his hip with one arm and walks over to the stove top, where smoke, a burning odor, and contiguous lump of scorched pasta leave him in no doubt that he has destroyed supper. The squealing smoke alarm has both kids covering their ears. Dylan deposits Marcia on a chair, opens the kitchen window, and vigorously fans smoke away from the smoke detector.

Pasting Marcia's burned palm with some Ozonal that Robbie locates in the bathroom soothes what remains of her tears, but she now decides that she is sufficiently impaired to merit the level of nurture required for an infant. Can she feed herself the substitute meal of baked beans on toast Dylan has prepared? Not with her left hand; Dylan will have to feed her. Is she able to clean her teeth without assistance? Not when someone as gullible as Dylan is around to do it for her. While Dylan knows he is being manipulated, he obliges because he feels that he has somehow been responsible for the succession of disasters that punctuated the evening.

By the time he finally gets both kids in bed and the lights snapped off, he is exhausted. He looks at his watch. It is a full two hours later than the bedtime prescribed by Kendra. He retreats to the living room couch, lays himself full-length across it, and attempts to study. Within ten minutes he is just beginning to doze when Robbie arrives downstairs equipped with a blankie. He can't sleep; he needs to first get into a sleepy mood by lying on the couch with Dylan. Lacking the energy to embroil himself in another battle, Dylan shrugs as Robbie settles onto the couch beside him. Within five minutes, Marcia arrives downstairs, dragging her housecoat behind her and announcing that she can't be expected to sleep upstairs by herself. She climbs over Robbie, who lashes out with a punch as she does so, wriggles over the top of Dylan, and wedges herself between Dylan and the back of the sofa. Sitting, she fastidiously arranges her housecoat over the three of them, and cozies herself in for a night's sleep.

Dylan is the last of the three sleepers to awake when Rob and Kendra return sometime after midnight. Marcia and Robbie are facing Kendra, enthusiastically reciting all of the disasters that had transpired during the evening. The prize revelation of the many, proudly related by Robbie himself, is the fact that Dylan defined him as a "pain in the ass." Dylan rubs his eyes and rolls his feet from the sofa to the floor. Kendra says to the kids, "I think we can declare Dylan to be the most incompetent babysitter we've ever had." She turns to Dylan with a grin, "Dylan, I'm going to have to ask you to enroll in a babysitter's course before we can invite you back." Then she snaps her fingers at the kids, pointing upstairs. They run up the stairs.

Rob approaches the couch with a pair of brandy snifters half-full of cognac. He hands one of them to Dylan. "It looks as if you could do with some of this," he says, sitting himself down. What Dylan really wants is not a significant slug of brandy, but to retreat to his lair above the garage. He takes a sip and it wakes his senses. "Thanks for watching the kids," says Rob, "they can be quite a handful."

"I've always thought of them as being so well-behaved before. They were never like this when they stayed with us at Highview."

"It's all a matter of territorial imperative. Back then, they were on your patch. Tonight, you experienced them on home turf."

At this point, Kendra returns downstairs from tucking the kids in. Dylan feels he should apologize. "Sorry about the succession of disasters … it just seemed that whatever I did was the wrong thing to do."

Kendra laughs. "Well, the children are still alive. I suppose I should have warned you about the Monopoly, the game is now banned in the Grantham household, we have a couple too many nasty capitalists," she says, looking at Rob, "… as for the other stuff, you have to realize that no kids are as innocent as they appear … they can sense weakness in an instant and delight in exploiting it. They knew you to be a pushover from your past with them so they were ready for you the moment you stepped through the door."

"Thanks!" says Dylan, taking a gulp of brandy.

"No problem," responds Kendra. "As a consequence, you have been proclaimed as their favorite babysitter ever … that's what happens when you make yourself easier to bully than the tough little eighth graders they are more accustomed to. Now, no offence at your ability to clean up, Dylan, but I am going to check the kitchen floor for pieces of the broken dish you might have missed."

Dylan chugs on the brandy. He wants to go to bed. He is emptying the glass and preparing to leave when Kendra emerges from the kitchen, proudly displaying half a dozen shards of china dish retrieved from the kitchen floor, somehow missed by Dylan. A couple of them are unbelievably large. He shrugs, but inwardly he is confused as to how he could have missed these pieces after his meticulous clean-up of the kitchen floor. Rob catches his eye and shrugs sympathetically, but then responds provocatively, "you can't expect a man to do woman's work." Kendra gives her husband an evil eye that signals Dylan it is time to leave.

Dylan seats himself in the outdoor patio of a popular Mexican restaurant and orders a beer and burrito lunch. It's a warm spring day and the sun provides just enough warmth to make sitting outside a possibility. Just as his beer is delivered, he catches sight of Kendra seated at a table in the far corner of the patio. She is engaged in a tête-à-tête with a girlfriend. They are sucking on straws protruding from bowl-sized margaritas. They are jabbering like a couple of schoolgirls, giggling intermittently. Dylan covertly observes them from his table and when his burrito arrives, he picks up the dish and his beer and walks over to join them.

"Mind if I join you, ladies," he announces, dragging out a chair and joining them anyway. Dylan senses that Kendra is unsettled by his arrival. She lowers her sunglasses down her nose and leans forward to make the required introduction, which she does almost stammering,

"Liz, this is Dylan, our ... *tenant* ... Dylan, Liz."

"Well, well, well, speak of the devil," says Liz, leaning forward to shake Dylan's hand, "Kendra was just telling me about some of the advantages of having a live-in babysitter."

Kendra grimaces.

Dylan swigs some beer to better examine Liz. There is something in Liz's eyes and Kendra's awkwardness that suggests to Dylan that Kendra has said something about their recent liaison.

"Babysitter?" queries Dylan, looking directly at Liz. "Not one of my services that she has often taken advantage of, she seldom goes out ... but Robert and Kendra have been truly wonderful, caring friends. They have been special to me in ways that are difficult to describe. As for the babysitting, Kendra has described me as their most incompetent babysitter ever."

Kendra recovers somewhat. "Nonsense, Dylan, don't sell yourself short, you are perfectly wonderful with the children, I think it's something to do with being so close to them in age... they are going to miss you terribly when you graduate and abandon our garage." She slurps margarita froth and turns to snap her fingers to catch the attention of the waitress for replenishment.

Liz's curiosity is piqued. "Now, Dylan, I want you to tell me all about yourself. Kendra informs me you've had an interesting childhood ... that you've lived in all kinds of exotic places. I want to know everything, tell me about your family history."

Yes, now he is certain Kendra has said something, the question is how much; could this woman be checking out his genes? Dylan runs his index finger around the rim of his beer glass. "What's to tell?" he says, turning to look at Kendra rather than Liz. "I hail from a long line of Irish ruffians and recidivists who have struggled to remain on the right side of the law ... and not always succeeded."

Kendra raises her eyes skyward and says to Liz. "Now you can see why he gets on so famously with Marcia and Robbie ... the ability to talk like a ninth grader may be tiresome for adults, but is much admired by second graders." Fresh margaritas arrive and Kendra immediately tucks into hers while, in between sips, launching into a more brazen attack. "Dylan has a bit of the inverted snob in his nature ... he likes to con everyone into thinking he's vaguely loutish and coarse ... but the fact is, if anyone tried to yank that silver spoon out of his mouth, he'd bite their fingers off ... he does so enjoy everyone else's struggles to grasp at what he takes for granted."

"Ouch! That was nasty." Dylan laughs, but the reality is that the last thing he wants to be doing is jousting with Kendra and her seasoned tongue. In addition, he's not really sure why she's being such a bitch. Should he leave?

"Yes, I probably overlooked mentioning to you before, Dylan, but us frustrated housewives can be meaner than jackals once a couple of margaritas have got our blood up. Liz, you should know that Dylan's father is an oil company executive, one who I doubt has to worry about having his electricity cut off for the lack of a couple of nickels to pay the bill. Now, to Dylan's credit, he does drive an ancient Pontiac jalopy … a vehicle that, since it has become resident in our driveway, has outraged neighbors who claim that it is not only a blight on the community, but is contributing to declining property values."

"Kendra is only jealous because it has claimed the neighborly ire that was hitherto reserved for her decade-old Volvo wagon. She has ceded some notoriety, a distinction she values in snooty suburbia."

Liz is not taking the bait from Kendra. She turns to Dylan. "How did you and Rob meet up? If you don't mind me saying, you are not the type I envision Rob associating with?"

"I bumped into him at a lawyers' party I inadvertently crashed. We started talking and discovered we were both looking for a downtown apartment. We decided that we could tolerate each others' company – and together, look for a two bedroom place. After Rob passed his bar examinations, I decided to keep the apartment anyway … and Rob and I stayed in touch."

"Okay … but now you're living in Rob and Kendra's granny flat?"

"Well yes … Rob and Kendra kindly rescued me when my girlfriend threw me out of the apart…"

Dylan is interrupted by a raucous laugh from Kendra. "Oh, Dylan, you are a prize fraudster …" she turns to Liz. "Don't believe a word of what he says, Liz. Let me tell you what really happened. Randy Dylan here falls in lust with a happily engaged girl, a classic JAP … engaged to her fairytale childhood sweetheart, a well brought up Willowdale Jew … he sets about sabotaging their relationship, shacks up with the poor girl, then discovers that he bit off more than he can chew. The very thought of finishing up the school year living with this woman is more than he can contemplate." Teasing, Kendra pushes her face so close to Dylan that if he moved his face forward two inches, he'd kiss her. As if suddenly realizing this herself, Kendra pulls back a little. She inhales deeply and continues, "Like all cowards, Dylan looks for an escape."

Sensing acute sexual tension, Liz has heard enough. Abruptly, she announces, "I'm off." Although she has barely started her second bowl of margarita, she gathers her purse and prepares to leave. "Excuse me, but I feel like surplus in your little tiff … you both need a little time alone. Call me, Kendra … nice to meet you, Dylan."

As soon as she is out of sight, Kendra props her elbows on the table and shrouds her face in her hands. "I think I made a fool of myself. Liz is my best friend." Then she aggressively turns on Dylan. "What are you doing here?"

"Well, I could have just stayed at my original table and observed the pair of you from afar. But I thought that might have been dishonest. Believe me, I wish I hadn't intruded … you weren't very nice."

"I'm sorry. I've just been a little emotional lately."

"You're not pregnant, are you? You didn't say anything about our little encounter to Liz?"

"No. Almost certainly not pregnant. With Marcia and Robbie I knew almost immediately … with Robbie, I was certain the next morning. As for telling Liz … about us … I didn't tell her in so many words. I just bounced some hypothetical situations off her. That's why I was so pissed off when you intruded. I'm a woman, Dylan; I need to talk to other women sometimes."

"I've never seen you behave like that before. You're usually so composed."

"Dylan, you don't know me that well. I hide a lot of myself. And right now I just happen to be an eensy little bit drunk."

"Did you drive down?"

"Yes. But first, I'll kill time shopping before driving back."

"I can drive you. It won't hurt to skip one afternoon of classes."

Dylan drives Kendra home in the Volvo. Kendra, sitting beside him, is remote and apparently more drunk than a person should be after a couple of margaritas. Dylan wonders if she might have been drinking before the lunch date with Liz. From the moment Kendra agrees to allow Dylan to drive her home, Dylan senses that another sexual encounter could be in the offing, while not being sure how this is going to come about, because for sure he isn't going to initiate it.

As it turns out, Kendra aggressively sets about making sure that the sex happens. But from the moment she has Dylan at the point of no return, she switches off. In fact, she dissociates herself to such an extent that Dylan is left wondering why she initiated it; she seems to tune him out from the moment they become conjoined. After coming and culminating a profoundly dissatisfying experience, Dylan rolls off Kendra and asks, "Are you feeling okay?"

"Sorry, Dylan, it's not you, I think I'm getting a migraine?"

After a prolonged silence, Kendra provides Dylan with an escape route. "Do you think you could pick the kids up from school? I'll call Rob's office and get him to come home to mind the kids this evening."

"Yeah, I guess so; I've got no intention of returning to school myself today."

"I'll have to phone first … they won't release the kids to you unless I do."

"Release them?"

*   *   *

Burgess Hill Primary School is a preparatory gulag. The uniform is identical for the children of both genders, with the exception of gray flannel pants worn by boys and pleated flannel skirts worn by girls. At the end of the school day, most of the children wear defeated expressions, there is little evidence of the chaotic gaiety that marks the end of the teaching day in a public school; these are definitively "well-behaved" kids. Marcia and Robbie are happy enough to see Dylan, and after a brief explanation as to their mother's absence, they each grab a hand and want to haul him out of the school yard and head home. However, an officious middle-aged woman approaches the threesome and challenges Dylan to identify himself. Before he can do so, he is cut short by the woman, who orders him to report to the office. She tells him that all children being picked up from school by a person other than a parent must first be cleared by the principal's office. It takes a full twenty minutes to track Kendra's phone message to verify that Dylan is neither kidnapper nor pervert, with Marcia whining at his side that they're going to be late.

"Late for what?" asks Dylan when they finally escape the principal's office.

"Gymnastics for me, soccer for Robbie," Marcia explains. "We have to go home and change, then we drop Robbie at soccer, and go to gymnastics. You stay for the gymnastics class, then after, we pick up Robbie. Then we go home again."

"I don't want to go to soccer," whines Robbie, petulant after being bossed at school for nearly seven hours.

"You do this every day after school?"

"No, only on Wednesdays," says Marcia, who is well versed in the routine, "It's different every day. Tomorrow, Robbie has hockey practice and I have swimming lessons."

"Can't we play street hockey instead?" asks Robbie.

"Jesus. No wonder your mom has a migraine!"

"Mummy never gets migraines," says Marcia, "only Daddy gets migraines."

"Okay, so let me get a measure of this. First we go home to change. Then Robbie gets dropped off at soccer, then you get dropped off at the gym?"

"No. You stay and watch me at gymnastics. It lasts for an hour, after that, we go and pick up Robbie from soccer ... it finishes later." Marcia is delighted, she has been pestering Dylan to come and watch her gymnastics expertise for some weeks. "Finally," she declares triumphantly, "you get to see my gymnastics class."

When they get home, Robbie and Marcia run upstairs and into their mother's bedroom. Dylan stands at the door while the kids chat with their mother who, propped up in bed, is dopily responsive. She asks why they are so late and Dylan leaves it to the kids to explain how their departure from the school grounds was policed.

Robbie immediately begins negotiating a respite from soccer practice, for which he will be late. Kendra snaps out of her dopey state to brusquely inform Robbie that if he forgoes the soccer, he must go to the gymnastics class with Marcia and Dylan and promise to behave.

Marcia works herself into a panic because she can't find her leotard and finally Kendra has to be intruded upon once again so she can suggest that they look in the laundry. By the time the two kids are bundled into the car, Marcia has worked herself into a frenzy, supposing she will be late. She implores Dylan to drive as fast as he can. Marcia doesn't like to be late for anything.

The gymnastics class takes place in a converted warehouse. The class is just beginning as they arrive and Marcia peels herself out of her track pants and jacket in a combination of hop and run, throwing the discarded garments at Dylan. The gym is equipped with a double row of bleachers and Dylan sits in the middle. For some reason, Robbie sits at the far end of the gymnasium, away from Dylan.

Marcia is in her element in this environment and is intent on putting on a show for Dylan. She constantly catches his eye and smiles at him, confident that she is a queen among this small group of performers. Dylan does his part by focusing entirely on Marcia and silently applauding at appropriate moments.

However, not five minutes into the class, the senior of the two instructors approaches Dylan and curtly asks him to control Robbie, who is evidently teasing one of the younger gymnasts who happens to be in his class at school. Dylan gets to his feet and ambles toward Robbie. He grabs him by the shoulders and steers him to the central bleachers, attempting to sit him down. But Robbie is antsy and rebellious. He twists and turns out of Dylan's reach. It seems that Robbie is once again on the cusp of creating a scene, so Dylan elects to steer him out of the gymnasium.

Outside in the parking lot, Dylan locates a soccer ball in the rear of the Volvo and after creating a makeshift goal using Marcia's track pants and jacket, Robbie is quite happy to take shots at goalkeeper Dylan. While shooting the soccer ball, Robbie runs a commentary on his goal-scoring prowess and Dylan's goalkeeping shortcomings. In fact, Dylan's goalkeeping is sharper than it would normally be because each time he misses a shot, the ball pounds against the outside wall of the gymnasium. However, Robbie's shooting is not that accurate, and there is little Dylan can do about the majority of shots that miss the goal by a wide margin, thudding against the gym wall.

After fifteen minutes, the older of the instructors appears at the gym door and motions Dylan toward the entrance. Dylan assumes that the summons has something to do with the noise of the soccer ball pounding against the wall, so he scoops up the ball and Marcia's clothing and uses his head to motion Robbie toward the door. However, the instructor does not move out of the doorway and when Dylan arrives, she explains that Marcia took a fall from a beam onto her back. "I think she's okay, just winded and a little tearful. She's asking for you."

Dylan approaches Marcia, who is sitting on the floor with one leg extended, the other bent clamped with her arms, chin on knee. She is silent and pointedly avoids eye contact. Dylan asks her if she's okay, but other than to blink a tear from her eye, she does not respond. "Marcia, would you like me to carry you over to the bleachers?" This elicits a nod.

Dylan bends, scoops the girl up, lifting her first under her arms, then cradling her under her buttocks. The instant she is face-to-face with Dylan, Marcia leans back, raises both arms, and thumps her fists into Dylan's chest. She bursts into tears. Dylan is surprised rather than injured, not to say embarrassed, with the entire gymnastics class as witnesses. "You were supposed to be watching me. You promised. It's not fair. You're always playing with Robbie. When do I get a turn?"

Not replying, Dylan carries Marcia over to the bleachers, sits and positions her on his lap. Marcia continues to cry. "I'm sorry, Marcia … I really did want to see you doing gymnastics. But Robbie was being a pest and I thought it was best to get him out of here."

This produces a couple more spasms of blubbering. "What would you like me to do? Do you want to go home? Or stay? I'll watch the remainder of the class if you choose to stay."

"You've ruined it now. It's your fault that I fell. I stopped concentrating; I was looking at the door wondering if you were coming back." More sobbing.

Dylan starts to wonder who's to blame for this mess. Was he not acting with the best intentions? Is it really his fault that these kids have appointed him to this quasi father role he is so ill-equipped for? Sure, he is screwing their mother, but that would never have happened if Rob was around a little more. He supposes it is mostly guilt that has drawn him into playing daddy to this pair of kids who are so opposite in nature that keeping one happy inevitably upsets the other. What would a real father do?

"I play street hockey with you almost every weekend, Marcia. I don't just play with Robbie."

Marcia wipes her face with her wrist and becomes more aggressive. "I hate street hockey. I only play because you're playing and I don't have a game to play with you."

Fortunately, at this point, the gym instructors decide to end the show and summon their charges back onto the gym floor to proceed with the class.

"Tell me what to do, Marcia. Go home? Or stay? I'm really sorry. Whatever you choose, I promise to come to another class with you." But Dylan knows that the damage is already done and this is inadequate compensation for his thoughtlessness. In his mind are recollections of his own father, who always seemed so absent during his childhood. Soon, Marcia and Robbie will have to search out other random father figures to fill in voids here and there in their lives.

A knock at the door of his granny flat jolts Dylan's thoughts away from his studies. Rob enters, a bottle of wine tucked under his arm and a pair of claret glasses pinched between his fingers.

"Douglas, I'm inviting you to share an experience more precious than sex can ever be," announces Rob, placing the bottle of wine onto the table as if it were a trophy. Dylan looks at Rob, unsure if any worldly experience can be more precious than good sex. "The wine?" he asks, confused.

"Observe the label, my friend. It's a vintage Chateau Margaux – men have gone to the guillotine, fought duels, and abandoned women for wines such as this. One of the partners bought a case of the stuff and offered me this bottle. Where's your corkscrew?"

Dylan locates the only corkscrew in his possession, a crude tool imprinted with a chain hotel logo that came into his possession via a thrift store. Rob studies it with distaste, wondering whether a trek back to his kitchen to retrieve an instrument more worthy of this noble bottle is warranted. Having succeeded in getting the kids in bed and sneaking out of the house without awaking Kendra, he decides against this. He resolutely plunges the corkscrew into the bottle, eyeballing its progress to ensure that it doesn't fully penetrate the cork and thus contaminate the precious wine. He snaps the cork out of the bottle. Immediately, he whiffs the neck of the bottle under his nose so as not to needlessly waste any of what evaporates from the liquid within as it combines with air for the first time in a decade. He pours a small quantity of wine into each glass, then picks them up together to swirl the contents within. Next, he studies the evidence of lubricity adhered to the bowl of each glass after swirling. "No tasting until fifteen minutes have gone by – it must properly air. Sniffing is allowed, though. Patience is required to properly experience any good Bordeaux." Rob begins sniffing.

Dylan sniffs. He struggles to steer the conversation into a realm that falls within his level of comprehension. This means talking about something other than wine. "How's Kendra's headache?"

Rob is still busy studying the appearance of the swirled wine on the walls of one of the wine glasses and snorting its aroma. Absentmindedly, he responds, "Kendra? I think she's OK. I looked in on her shortly after getting home. By the way, thanks for minding the kids this afternoon."

Rob pulls a package of supermarket brie from his jacket pocket and busies himself with chopping it into bite-sized pieces.

"Is Marcia still mad at me?"

"Marcia, mad at you? No, I don't think so. Does Marcia get mad at anybody? Actually, she wanted to come over to say goodnight – I told her she couldn't because it was a school night, that's Kendra's rule. I don't know what came over Kendra – it's not like her to get a migraine. Damn inconvenient time for it to happen, I was with a client."

The moment for tasting arrives. Rob and Dylan clink glasses. Dylan takes a small sip and swallows. Rob takes a cautious sip and holds what he draws within his mouth, rolling his tongue to distribute the liquid into every recess. He sucks in air, making a gurgling noise before swallowing. Observing, Dylan finds it believable that Rob has a preference for an oenological experience over sex. On the other hand, in his analysis of the Margaux on his own uncultured palate, he struggles to differentiate the flavor from that of a run-of-the-mill California Cabernet Sauvignon. It'll be a long time before he'll be exchanging sex for a glass of wine, he thinks.

After finishing the first glass of claret, the conversation between the pair changes. It's Rob that turns the subject matter onto the topic of women, beginning with Kendra, specifically on how she has changed over the years. "It might be hard to believe now, but she wasn't always this ball-busting Amazon of a figure. She's fast becoming a real bitch. How times have changed! We used to be such a perfect couple."

"Do you consider that you might have changed over the years?" ventures Dylan. "Maybe she's changed in response to changes in you?"

"No, I don't think I've changed much over the years," declares Rob.

"Bullshit," says Dylan, "you've changed plenty in the short time I've known you. Especially since you started working as a litigator. Changed in ways that are not good."

Rob studies Dylan as if he's not sure about this. "What do you mean?"

"The only thing you care about now is work … making partnership. In my opinion, your priorities are twisted. You have two great kids … who you ignore most of the time. And you surely must see that Kendra wants more out of life than to be a wealthy housefrau – she's smart and funny. Yeah, I know she's a lawyer by training, but she's going to need more stimuli around her than the other legal types she gets to associate with connected with your work. If you don't recognize that, you guys aren't going to be together for much longer … and if you want to put that statement into a legal career perspective, I'll bet a happily married litigator is likely to make partner well ahead of one going through a messy and costly divorce."

Rob takes a gulp of wine and gargles it. He shakes his head. "Have you and Kendra been talking?" he asks suspiciously.

Dylan laughs. "No, that's something Kendra and I don't do except at the most superficial level. No, these are just the observations of your lowly student tenant – who spends a max of six hours a week total with your family – but then, that's probably as much as you do."

"Perhaps I have changed," Rob reflects. "I've never been aggressive by nature, but a corporate litigator is sometimes required to be ruthless … and behave in ways that are contrary to my core values. I guess this exacts a toll. You're right about Kendra … she's an asset I undervalue." He pauses. "In vino veritas!"

Not quite, thinks Dylan reflecting on his own past, in fact, hardly ever. Rob raises his glass. Dylan reciprocates, while wondering how Kendra would respond to being valued only as an *asset*.

Two years later, Dylan is living in Ann Arbor, Michigan, some three hundred miles west of Toronto. He is applying for a job and he requires references from an upstanding member of the community. Despite the jokes and good evidence of their truth, lawyers are always considered as community stalwarts. He phones Rob's office and speaks to a secretary, who takes his number and promises a call back. Hanging up, he curses, thinking it unlikely that Rob will return the call.

Within seconds, the phone rings and it's Rob. He sounds jovial and friendly. Of course he will act as a reference. They do some catching up. First, Dylan has to listen to an account of two dismal Leaf seasons. Then, Rob shares the information that he is to be offered a partnership in the summer, the reward of all those billable hours and accompanying clients to Maple Leaf Gardens. "Of course, it will mean some sacrifices," he informs Dylan, "financial for sure, perhaps longer hours at first." So what's new!

"How is Kendra?" ventures Dylan. "How are Marcia and Robbie?"

"Oh, same ole," says Rob, immediately bored. "Of course, Robbie has had to get used to the fact that he's no longer the baby of the family."

"You had another kid?"

"Yeah, I forgot to say, I guess it's been a while since we last spoke. Yes, Emily was born … when was it? She had her first birthday a couple of months ago."

Dylan's heart stops for two full beats. He sucks in his breath. "Congratulations."

"My role was limited, believe me. It was Kendra who wanted it, God knows why? And maybe I'm getting older, but this one seems twice as demanding as the other two. Oh well, she wanted another one."

"Say hi to Kendra from me. And Marcia and Robbie."

"Sure thing. Are you married yet? About to be?"

"Nope. Neither one."

"Take some advice from a voice of experience. Don't!"

*   *   *

ABOUT THE AUTHOR

Jonathan Bennett had a childhood that somewhat resembled that of his protagonist in the novel Oil Brat. Like his character Dylan, he attended American schools until the age of twelve when he was sent to boarding school in the U.K.

Bennett is a full time technical author who has published over thirty books in the U.S. under an altered rendering of his name. His work as an author requires extensive travel and when at home, he splits his time between downtown Toronto and a residence in the Kawarthas area of Ontario. Oil Brat is his first work of fiction.

www.ingramcontent.com/pod-product-compliance
Lightning Source LLC
Chambersburg PA
CBHW030030030726
47500CB00001B/35